Modern Greek Writing

Modern Greek Writing

AN ANTHOLOGY IN ENGLISH TRANSLATION

Edited by David Ricks

HELLENIC MINISTRY
OF CULTURE

THE CENTRE FOR THE
GREEK LANGUAGE

PETER OWEN PUBLISHERS
London & Chester Springs

PETER OWEN PUBLISHERS
73 Kenway Road, London SW5 0RE

Peter Owen books are distributed in the USA by
Dufour Editions Inc., Chester Springs, PA 19425-0007

First published in Great Britain 2003
Editor's preface and introductions to pieces © David Ricks 2003

With the subsidy of the Hellenic Ministry of Culture

ISBN 0 7206 1086 9

A catalogue record for this book is available from the British Library

Printed and bound in India by
Thomson Press (India) Ltd

Acknowledgements

This volume has been surprisingly long in the making, produced as it has been in those tiny interstices of time not intruded on by government agencies in the era of what, when we awake from our narcosis, may prove to have been nothing less than the Dissolution of the Universities. My main debt of gratitude is, of course, to the Centre for the Greek Language in Thessaloniki – this anthology is the product of a research project carried out with the authorization of the Centre's board of directors, which, through a grant from the Hellenic Ministry of Culture, also generously subsidized the costs of production – and to that doyen of Greek poet-critics Professor Nasos Vayenas, who extended the initial invitation to conduct the work. I am also most grateful to Peter Owen and Antonia Owen of Peter Owen Publishers for their patience in awaiting a considerably delayed manuscript. Without the tangible practical help given me by, in turn, Dr George Vassiadis and Dr Liana Giannakopoulou this project could not have reached completion. Nor could the materials have been found without the excellent facilities of the following libraries: the Burrows Library, King's College London; the British Library; the Bodleian Library and Taylor Institution, University of Oxford; Widener Library of Harvard College; Firestone Library, Princeton University; Olin Library, Cornell University; and the Saison Poetry Library, South Bank Centre, London. The editor hopes that the task of promoting modern Greek literature with discernment and imagination will continue in the years to come: the Hellenic Foundation for Culture Award for Greek Translation, first awarded in 2002, is a good augury.

It is to be noted that, except for the correction of obvious typographical errors, I have generally preserved the spelling and punctuation of the texts reproduced, sometimes at the expense of consistency. It is also to be noted, I hope not in a churlish spirit, that the inclusion of a translation here is not an endorsement of its complete fidelity and felicity.

Sources of of all the translations in this anthology are listed below. Grateful acknowledgement is made to the copyright holders for permission to reprint the works in this volume.

Anon. 'The Night Journey', Charles Brinsley Sheridan (tr.), *The Songs of Greece, from the Romaic Text*, M.C. Fauriel (ed.), London: Longman, 1825
Aris Alexandrou 'Promotion', 'The First Anatomist', Peter Mackridge (tr.), *Aegean Review*, 1986, Vol. 1, pp. 17–18; 'No Man's Land', 'In Camp',

'Chaerophon to Pindar', David Ricks (tr.), *Grand Street*, 1989, Vol. 8, No. 2 (Winter), pp. 122–7; 'Meditations of Flavius Marcus', David Ricks (tr.), in David Ricks, *The Shade of Homer*, Cambridge: Cambridge University Press, 1989; *The Strongbox*, Kay Cicellis (tr.), *Aegean Review*, 1989, Vol. 6, pp. 57–62

Manolis Anagnostakis 'Haris 1944', 'Poetics', 'The New Song', 'Epilogue [I]', 'You Came When I . . .', 'There . . .', 'Thessaloniki, Days of AD 1969', 'If', 'Epilogue [II]', David Ricks (tr.), *Journal of Modern Hellenism*, 1995/6, Vol. 12, pp. 1–25; 'Instead of Clamouring', David Ricks (tr.), *The Spoon River Poetry Review*, 1996, Vol. 21, No. 1 (Winter/Spring), p. 74

Katerina Anghelaki-Rooke 'In This House Settling Time's Account', *From Purple into Night*, Katerina Anghelaki-Rooke and Jackie Willcox (trs), Beeston, Nottinghamshire: Shoestring Press, 1997

Nikos Bakolas *Crossroads*, Caroline Harbouri (tr.), Athens: Kedros, 1997

Dimitrios Bikelas (= Vikelas) *Loukis Laras. Reminiscences of a Chiote Merchant During the War of Independence*, J. Gennadius (tr.), London: Macmillan, 1881

Nicolas Calas 'Cavafy', 'Santorini VII', 'The Dream', Avi Sharon (tr.), *Modern Poetry in Translation*, (n.s.) 1998, Vol. 13, pp. 21–2

C.P. Cavafy 'An Old Man', Robert Pinsky (tr.), *The Figured Wheel: New and Collected Poems*, New York: Farrar, Strauss and Giroux, 1996; 'Waiting for the Barbarians', 'Philhellene', 'Come Back', 'Tomb of Evrion', 'One of their Gods', 'Days of 1903', 'Young Men of Sidon (AD 400)', 'Dareios', 'From the School of the Renowned Philosopher', 'John Kantakuzinos Triumphs', 'In a Township of Asia Minor', 'To Have Taken the Trouble', Edmund Keeley and Philip Sherrard (trs), *C.P. Cavafy, Collected Poems*, Princeton: Princeton University Press, revised edition 1992; 'Cavafy's Desires', adapted by Michael Longley, *The Ghost Orchid*, London: Jonathan Cape, 1995; 'Bacchus and His Crew', 'The Battle of Magnesia', 'In the Month of Athyr', 'The Tomb of Ignatios', 'To Remain', 'A Byzantine Nobleman in Exile Writing Verses', 'Favour of Alexander Balas', 'In Alexandria, 31 BC', 'In a Great Greek Colony', 200 BC', 'Myris: Alexandria 340 AD', 'In This Very Space', 'From Recipes of Ancient Greco-Syrian Magi', John Mavrogordato (tr.), *The Poems of C.P. Cavafy*, London: Hogarth Press, 1951; 'Sculptor from Tyana', 'For Ammones, Who Died at the Age of 29 in 610', 'Caesarion', 'Simeon', David Ricks (tr.), *Modern Poetry in Translation*, (n.s.) 1998, Vol. 13, pp. 9–12; 'Alexandrian Kings', 'An Evening', Memas Kolaitis (tr.), *The Greek Poems of C.P. Cavafy*, New Rochelle, New York: Aristide Caratzas, 1989; 'On an Italian Shore', James Merrill (tr.), *Grand Street*, 1987, Vol. 6, No. 2 (Winter), p. 125

Kyriakos Charalambides: 'At His Daughter's Wedding', 'The Apple', Dino

Siotis (tr.), *Aegean Review*, 1990, Vol. 9 (Fall/Winter), pp. 31–3; 'Missing Person', Kimon Friar (tr.), *Contemporary Greek Poetry*, Athens: Greek Ministry of Culture, 1985

Stratis Doukas *A Prisoner of War's Story*, Petro Alexiou (tr.), Birmingham: Centre for Byzantine, Ottoman and Modern Greek Studies, 1999

Odysseus Elytis 'Helen', 'Form of Boeotia', 'Genesis', from *The Axion Esti*, Edmund Keeley and Philip Sherrard (trs), *Odysseus Elytis, Selected Poetry*, Edmund Keeley and Philip Sherrard (eds), London: Anvil Press, 1981; 'The Fresco', 'Death and Resurrection of Constantine Palaiologos', John Stathatos (tr.), ibid.; *Heroic and Elegiac Song for the Lost Second Lieutenant of Albania*, Paul Merchant (tr.), *Modern Poetry in Translation*, 1968, Vol. 4, unpaginated; 'The Monogram', Avi Sharon (tr.), *International Quarterly*, 1997, Vol. 3, No. 1, pp. 56–60; 'With Light and Death', *The Little Mariner*, Olga Broumas (tr.), Port Townsend, Washington: Copper Canyon Press, 1988; 'Solomos: Submission and Awe', David Connolly (tr.), *The Oxopetra Elegies*, Amsterdam: Harwood Academic Press, 1996

Andreas Embiricos 'Orion', 'Insight of Morning Hours', Paul Merchant (tr.), *Modern Poetry in Translation*, 1968, Vol. 4, unpaginated; 'The Texts', 'Aphrodite', Alan Ross and Nanos Valaoritis (trs), *Amour Amour*, London: Alan Ross, 1966; 'In Philhellenes Street', David Ricks (tr.), *Modern Poetry in Translation*, 1998, Vol. 13, pp. 19–20; 'King Kong', Roderick Beaton (tr.), *The Dedalus Book of Surrealism: The Identity of Things*, Michael Richardson (ed.), Sawtry, Cambridgeshire: Dedalus 1993

Nikos Engonopoulos *Bolivar*, David Connolly (tr.), *Oraios san Ellinas*, Yoryis Yatromanolakis (ed.), Athens: Idryma Goulandri-Horn, 1996

Rhea Galanaki *The Life of Ismail Ferik Pasha: Spina nel Cuore*, Kay Cicellis (tr.), London: Peter Owen, 1996

Michalis Ganas 'My Homeland Brimming', 'Period', David Ricks (tr.), *London Magazine*, 1996, Vol. 36, Nos 1–2 (April/May), pp. 47–9; 'Shipwreck', 'George M., Florina 1949', 'Persistence', 'Concerning the Ascension', John Stathatos (tr.), *Aegean Review*, 1987, Vol. 2, pp. 66–8; 'I Want To Be Buried in Chafteia', 'Drowned All These Years', 'In Memory of K.G. Karyotakis', David Ricks (tr.), *Modern Poetry in Translation*, (n.s.) 1998, Vol. 13, pp. 43–5

Nikos Gatsos *Amorgos*, Edmund Keeley and Philip Sherrard (trs), *The Dark Crystal*, Athens: Denise Harvey, 1981

Dimitris Hatzis 'Sioulas the Tanner', *The End of Our Small Town*, David Vere (tr.), Birmingham: Centre for Byzantine, Ottoman and Modern Greek Studies, 1996

Yorgos Heimonas *The Builders*, Robert Crist (tr.), Athens: Kedros, 1991

Yorgos Ioannou '"Voungari"', Roderick Beaton (tr.), *Shenandoah*, 1975, Vol. 27, No. 1 (Fall), pp. 104–17

Andreas Kalvos 'Elegy on the Sacred Battalion', Florence McPherson (tr.), *Poetry of Modern Greece: Specimens and Extracts*, London: Macmillan, 1884

Ioannis Karasoutsas 'To a Star', 'The Last Dryad', E.M. Edmonds (tr.), *Greek Lays, Idylls, Legends, &c.*, London: Trübner and Co., 1886

Andreas Karkavitsas *The Beggar*, William F. Wyatt Jr (tr.), New Rochelle, New York: Caratzas Brothers, 1982

K.G. Karyotakis 'I am the Garden', 'Posthumous Fame', Rachel Hadas (tr.), *Other Worlds than This*, New Brunswick, New Jersey: Rutgers University Press, 1994; 'Marche Funèbre et Perpendiculaire', adapted by David Ricks, *Modern Poetry in Translation* (n.s) 1998, Vol. 13, p. 16

Nikos Kazantzakis *Zorba the Greek* [sic], Carl Wildman (tr.), London: Faber and Faber, 1961

Alexandros Kotzias *Jaguar*, H.E. Criton (tr.), Athens: Kedros, 1991

Yannis Makriyannis *Makriyannis: The Memoirs of General Makriyannis 1797–1864*, H.A. Lidderdale (tr.), London: Oxford University Press, 1960

Jenny Mastoraki: '[The Wooden Horse . . .]', Roderick Beaton (tr.), *An Introduction to Modern Greek Literature*, Oxford: Clarendon Press, revised edition 1999; 'The Battle Fought and Won', 'They Sang a Song All Their Own', John Stathatos (tr.), *Translation*, 1985, Vol. 14 (Spring), pp. 23, 27; 'The Death of a Warrior', Kimon Friar (tr.), *Contemporary Greek Poetry*, Athens: Greek Ministry of Culture, 1985; 'Note', 'The Match', David Ricks (tr.), *London Magazine*, 1996, Vol. 36, Nos 1–2 (April/May), pp. 51–2; 'The Underground', 'Of the Underworld', 'Of the Sufferings of Love', Karen Van Dyck (tr.), *The Rehearsal of Misunderstanding: Three Collections by Contemporary Greek Women Poets*, Middletown, Connecticut: Wesleyan University Press, 1998

Michail Mitsakis 'By His Own Hand', David Ricks (tr.), *Dialogos: Hellenic Studies Review*, 1999, Vol. 6, pp. 83–97

Stratis Myrivilis *Life in the Tomb*, Peter Bien (tr.), Hanover, New Hampshire: University of New England Press, 1977

Kostis Palamas 'The Death of the Gods', from *The Twelve Words of the Gypsy*, Theodore Ph. Stephanides and George C. Katsimbalis (trs), Athens: privately printed, 1974

Alexandros Papadiamantis 'Homesick', Leo Marshall (tr.), *Dialogos: Hellenic Studies Review*, 1996, Vol. 3, pp. 51–71

Titos Patrikios 'Memory of Villages on the Spercheios', 'Athenian Summer in 1956', 'At the Cinema', 'Idyll', 'Rehabilitation of Laszlo Rajk', 'Like Grave-Robbers', 'Verses 2', 'Indebtedness', 'Words', 'Eight Years',

'Half-Forgotten Poem', 'Epitaph', David Ricks (tr.), *Kampos: Cambridge Papers in Modern Greek*, 1996, Vol. 4, pp. 90–101; 'A Town in Southern Greece', 'Loves', 'My Language', Peter Mackridge (tr.), *Modern Poetry in Translation* (n.s.) 1998, Vol. 13, pp. 33–4

Yorgis Pavlopoulos 'Written on a Wall', 'The Cellar', Peter Levi (tr.), *The Cellar*, London: Anvil Press Poetry, 1977; 'It Could Nowhere Be Found', 'Details from a Poem', Kimon Friar (tr.), *Contemporary Greek Poetry*, Athens: Greek Ministry of Culture, 1985; 'A Child's Drawing', George Thaniel (tr.), *The Amaranth*, 1983, Vol. 5, p. 16; 'The Heifer', Peter Levi (tr.), *London Magazine*, 1996, Vol. 36, Nos 1–2 (April/May), p. 127

Nikos Gabriel Pentzikis 'Mother Thessaloniki', *Mother Thessaloniki*, Leo Marshall (tr.), Athens: Kedros, 1998

Kosmas Politis *Eroica*, Robert Liddell and Andreas Cambas (trs), *Atlantic Monthly*, Vol. 195, No. 6, June 1955, pp. 139–41

Lefteris Poulios 'Roads', David Ricks (tr.), *London Magazine*, 1996, Vol. 26, Nos 1–2 (April/May), pp. 54–5; 'American Bar in Athens', Katerina Anghelaki-Rooke and Philip Ramp (trs), *Boundary 2* (Special Issue on Contemporary Greek Writing), N.C. Germanacos and William V. Spanos (eds), 1973, Vol. 1, No.2 (Winter), pp. 517–18: 'To Karyotakis', Chris Williams (tr.), *A Greek Anthology: Poetry from the Seventies Generation*, Peterborough, Northamptonshire: Spectacular Diseases, 1991

Pantelis Prevelakis *The Tale of a Town*, Kenneth Johnstone (tr.), Athens: Doric Publications, 1976

Yannis Ritsos *Romiosini*, Avi Sharon (tr.), *Arion* (3rd series), Vol. 4, No. 2 (Fall), pp. 115–27; 'The Meaning of Simplicity', Edmund Keeley (tr.), *Ritsos in Parentheses*, Princeton: Princeton University Press, 1979; 'Misunderstandings' from *Twelve Poems for Cavafy*, Paul Merchant (tr.), *Modern Poetry in Translation*, 1968, Vol. 4, unpaginated; 'Non-Hero', David Ricks (tr.), in David Ricks, *The Shade of Homer*, Cambridge: Cambridge University Press 1989; 'Trivial Details', 'Niobe', 'The Tombs of Our Ancestors', 'Penelope's Despair', 'The Usual', 'Afternoon in the Old Neighbourhood', 'Sources', 'The Same Course', Edmund Keeley (tr.), *Exile and Return. Selected Poems 1967–1974*, New York: Ecco, 1989; 'Tokens', 'Pilgrimage', 'Two in the Afternoon', 'On Silence', 'Ticks of the Clock, 13', Martin McKinsey (tr.), *Late into the Night*, Oberlin, Ohio: Oberlin College Press, 1995

E.D. Roïdis *Pope Joan: A Historical Romance*, J.H. Freese (tr.), London: H.J. Cook, 1900

Miltos Sachtouris 'The Dead Man in Our Life, John Benjamin d'Arkozi', 'He Is Not Oedipus', 'The Scene', 'Nostalgia Returns', 'My Brothers', Kimon Friar (tr.), *Miltos Sachtouris, Selected Poems*, Old Chatham, New York:

Sachem Press, 1982; 'The Dove', John Stathatos (tr.), *Strange Sunday: Miltos Sachtouris: Selected Poems 1952–1971*, Frome, Somerset: Bran's Head Books, 1984; 'The Inspector', 'The Watch', John Stathatos (tr.), *Translation*, 1985, Vol. 14 (Spring), pp. 63–5; 'The Visit', Dino Siotis (tr.), *Aegean Review*, 1986, Vol. 1 (Fall/Winter), p. 59

George Seferis 'Upon a Foreign Verse', 'The King of Asine', David Ricks (tr.), in David Ricks, *The Shade of Homer*, Cambridge: Cambridge University Press, 1989; *Mythistorema*, 'An Old Man on the River Bank', 'Last Stop', 'The Light' from *Thrush*, 'Memory I', Edmund Keeley and Philip Sherrard (trs), *George Seferis: Complete Poems*, London: Anvil Press Poetry, 1995; 'Memory II', Rex Warner (tr.), *George Seferis, Poems*, London: Bodley Head, 1960; 'On Stage IV', David Ricks (tr.), *Greek Modernism and Beyond*, Dimitris Tziovas (ed.), Lanham, Maryland: Rowman and Littlefield, 1997

Angelos Sikelianos 'The First Rain', Philip Sherrard and Edmund Keeley (trs), *The Charioteer*, 1960, Vol. 1, pp. 69–70; 'Yannis Keats', David Ricks (tr.), in David Ricks, *The Shade of Homer*, Cambridge: Cambridge University Press 1989; 'The Sacred Road', 'Agraphon', Edmund Keeley and Philip Sherrard (trs), *The Dark Crystal*, Athens: Denise Harvey, 1981

Takis Sinopoulos 'Philip', 'Doanna', 'The Mother Interprets the Land', 'The Window', 'Above the Seasons', 'Deathfeast', 'The Train', 'The Grey Light', John Stathatos (tr.), *Takis Sinopoulos, Selected Poems*, San Francisco: Wire Press, 1981; 'Sophia Etc', 'Magda', Edmund Keeley (tr.), *Poetry*, 1964, Vol. 105, No. 1 (October), pp. 36–41

Dionysios Solomos 'Hymn to Liberty', Rudyard Kipling (tr.), *A Choice of Kipling's Verse*, T.S. Eliot (ed.), London: Faber and Faber, 1941; 'The Destruction of Psara', G.M. Edmonds (tr.), *Greek Lays, Idylls, Legends, &c.*, London: Trübner and Co., 1886; 'The Cretan', Roderick Beaton (tr.), *Dionysios Solomos, The Free Besieged and Other Poems*, Peter Mackridge (ed.), Beeston, Nottinghamshire: Shoestring Press, 2000; 'The Shark', David Ricks (tr.), *Greek Letters*, 1993/4, Vol. 8, p. 73; *The Woman of Zakythos* Peter Colaclides and Michael Green (trs), *Modern Greek Studies Yearbook*, 1985, Vol. 1, pp. 158–70

Kostas Taktsis (= Tachtsis) *The Third Wedding*, Leslie Finer (tr.), London: Alan Ross, 1967

Konstantinos Theotokis 'Face Down!', Theodore Sampson (tr.), revised Dorothy Trollope, *Modern Greek Short Stories, Vol. 1*, ?? (ed.), Athens: Kathimerini Publications, 1981

Stratis Tsirkas *Ariagne*, *Drifting Cities*, Kay Cicellis (tr.), Athens: Kedros, 1995

Thanasis Valtinos 'Panayotis: A Biographical Note', John Taylor (tr.), *Aegean Review*, 1987, Vol. 2 (Spring/Summer), pp. 49–51

Nasos Vayenas 'Death in Exarchia', John Stathatos (tr.), *Biography and Other Poems*, London: Oxus Press, 1979; 'A Game of Chess', Kimon Friar (tr.), *Contemporary Greek Poetry*, Athens: Greek Ministry of Culture, 1985; 'National Garden', 'Beautiful Summer Morning', 'Calvos in Geneva', Chris Williams (tr.), *A Greek Anthology: Poetry from the Seventies Generation*, Peterborough, Northamptonshire: Spectacular Diseases, 1991; 'Jorge Luis Borges on Panepistimiou Street', Edward S. Phinney (tr.), *The Amaranth*, 1987, Vol. 10, pp. 47–8; 'Flyer's Fall', 'Après le Déluge', 'Barbarous Odes XVI', David Ricks (tr.), *London Magazine*, 1996, Vol. 36, Nos 1–2 (April/May), p.58; 'Dialectic', David Ricks (tr.), *Modern Poetry in Translation*, 1998, Vol. 13, pp. 46–7
Dimitrios Vikelas *see* **Bikelas**
G.M. Vizyenos (= Vizyinos) 'My Mother's Sin', *My Mother's Sin and Other Stories*, William F. Wyatt Jr (tr.), Hanover, New Hampshire: University Press of New England, 1988
Yorgi Yatromanolakis *History of a Vendetta*, Helen Cavanagh (tr.), Sawtry, Cambridgeshire: Dedalus, 1991

Efforts have been made to contact all copyright holders prior to publication. If notified, the editor and publisher undertake to rectify any errors or omissions in any future editions.

Editor's Preface

The aim of this volume is to give the English-speaking reader a taste of the writing of independent Greece in some of its diversity. Modern Greek writing has attained its greatest prominence through two winners of the Nobel Prize for Literature, George Seferis (1963) and Odysseus Elytis (1979), and through Nikos Kazantzakis, a novelist who combines a disputed reputation with a huge world readership. But at least one other poet, C.P. Cavafy, is a towering international presence, and a steady stream of English translations of Greek poetry and fiction has in recent years appeared through periodicals and small presses. The result is that the picture which the Greekless reader now possesses of modern Greek literature is very much wider and richer than it appeared to be in the only previous anthology of this type thirty-odd years ago.[1]

The aim of the present anthology is simply to whet the reader's appetite for more: though it is based on twenty years' reading in the field, it is not in its nature a work of scholarship. The hope is that, struck by a particular selection, the interested reader will go on to track down the volumes of poetry, the short stories and the novels from which the present selection comes and thus enlarge his or her sense of what modern Greece has contributed to the republic of letters – even seen in a glass darkly, through translation. In deepening his knowledge by identifying further works in translation, alternative translations of the same works and discussion of the literary and historical contexts, the reader will want also to turn to invaluable works of reference by Dia M.L. Philippides and Roderick Beaton and follow leads which appear there.[2] Best of all would be to embark on a study of the modern Greek language itself, as more and more foreigners do: more and more summer schools make such courses available. In this sense, too, the resources which are there for a close encounter with Greek writing of the modern period dwarf those that were available even a few years ago.

Which is not to say that in producing this anthology its editor has had an entirely free hand. He has on some occasions been inhibited from including a particular version because the permissions fee appeared to him exorbitant or because permission was not granted at all. Inevitably, it has also proved impossible to include any versions which were not at least in press by 1998, when the initial selection of texts was completed. Above all, the editor has faithfully abided by the conditions set by the funding bodies, the Centre for the Greek Language and the Hellenic Ministry of Culture, in presenting, not specially commissioned versions, but an anthology of existing versions. As a consequence, he has been at the mercy of what translations existed in the public domain. In some cases this has meant that writers appearing here are not represented ~~by their best or most~~ characteristic work; in others it has meant that a writer of real merit has gone unrepresented altogether, either because existing translations are quite inadequate or because none exists.

That said, the editor does not regard his choice of a half-century of names from approaching two centuries of years as particularly likely to raise eyebrows or ruffle feathers – that is, beyond the fraternity of translators and the living writers they translate. Inevitably, anyone familiar with Greek literature in the original will find personal favourites missing or the occasional *bête noire* granted admission. (There has also, for good or ill, been no attempt to impose 'gender quotas'.) It would be tiresome to mention many specific cases, but it should be noted that the two great founding writers of modern Greece, Dionysios Solomos and Andreas Kalvos, have become available in English only since the present selection was completed.[3] Two great poets of the twentieth century, moreover, Angelos Sikelianos and K.G. Karyotakis, await bolder translators to do them justice in the future – their virtual absence is the greatest distortion in the present volume – and three variously experimental prose writers of the mid twentieth century, each with his own genius, Fotis Kontoglou, Yannis Skarimbas and Yannis Beratis, will, I hope, tempt resourceful translators, too. Their absence from this volume is the cause of particular regret. Despite these grievous lacunae, the editor has attempted, through the shape of the selection and through the concise headnotes which accompany the entries, to present a picture of Greek writing since Independence as a continuing story with its own dynamic, a story in which valuable pages continue to be written.

What gets translated, and how, is often – too often – a matter of fashion or luck or straightforward puffing. But sometimes, when the contours of the translated literature greatly diverge from the lineaments of that literature itself, one may ask what wider causes lie behind this and what breaching of cultural barriers needs still to be performed by the translator who is willing to be creative. One of our foremost poet-translators makes the point fairly and squarely: 'an anthology consisting of translations is not the same sort of thing as an anthology of originals. Its limits are, to a degree, the limits of translatability.'[4] Here such a work as the opening section of Sikelianos' *Mitir Theou* (*Mater Dei*) presents the greatest possible challenge. A sensibility forged by Hopkins will go some way to adumbrating the Greek poet's insight that 'There lives the dearest freshness deep down things' and that the Blessed Virgin may be 'compared to the air we breathe' – yet sub-Hopkins is ghastly. An ear forged by *The Prelude* and, behind it, *Paradise Lost* may be able to create a blank verse equivalent for the rhyming couplet Sikelianos has taken from Solomos in the Romantic period and ultimately from Kornaros' *Erotokritos* in the Cretan Renaissance – yet sub-Milton or sub-Wordsworth is about as grim as it gets. But how can an English translation hope either to evoke the Eastern Orthodox imagery and tradition latent in every verse of this devout but unorthodox poem or to catch its most elusive device for creating a synaes-thetic *poésie pure* – the repeated suppression of the caesura? Only a more drastic creativity than is on view in most of the present volume can hope to succeed.[5]

There is always a danger that the foreign work which finds a translator will be one which is already culturally familiar – in which case, the boundaries of understanding are never enlarged. In fact, some of the most vexed problems in translating modern Greek literature concern the very terms in which Greek iden-tity has been defined *vis-à-vis* the West, as a famous phrase from a poem by George Seferis shows. In 'Neophytos the Cloisterer Speaks' (1955), Seferis has a medieval Cypriot saint speak of '*ton kaïmó tis romiosínis*'. The phrase has become almost as much a part of public discourse in Greek as Cavafy's 'Waiting for the Barbarians' – but, unlike the latter, it is in its nature inward-looking and not readily translated. Coming from one of Greece's most notable translators (of, *inter alia*, *The Waste Land*), this can be no coincidence. The poem's setting and outlook confirm this: at the time of the EOKA rising against British rule, in which the poet played a behind-the-scenes role, Seferis adopts the persona of a saint who symbolizes Orthodox resistance to the medieval West; indeed, he ends with the (only too translatable) words from *Othello*: 'You are welcome, sir, to Cyprus. Goats and monkeys!' The less translatable phrase cited earlier may by contrast be glossed as 'the sense of yearning or unfulfilment which is part of the condition of being an Orthodox Greek after 1453'. Before Independence Greeks referred to themselves (and in certain contexts they still can) not as *Ellines* ('Hellenes') but as *Romioi* (from *Rhomaios*, Roman, by which the Byzantines identified themselves). *Romiosini* is a late-nineteenth-century neologism, appar-ently coined by the poet Kostis Palamas, to give a name to an idea of Greece based less on the ancient heritage than on Eastern Christendom, its medieval past and its modern irredentist aspirations.[6] Clearly, a rendering such as 'Romanhood' would never pass muster, and the difficulty of the case (beyond the fact that Seferis' poem is in rhyme) is perhaps most graphically shown by the fact that Edmund Keeley and Philip Sherrard omit the poem from their standard translation of Seferis' collected poems.

If such difficulties attend the rendering of a Nobel Prize winner heavily influ-enced by Anglo-American Modernism, it is not surprising that coverage of Modern Greek literature in English, let alone in book form, is patchy. But their compiler hopes that even so the English-speaking reader will be able to find in these pages (to adopt Pound's evergreen formulation) 'news that STAYS news'.

Notes

1. Mary P. Gianos (ed.), *Introduction to Modern Greek Literature. An Anthology of Fiction, Drama, and Poetry* (New York: Twayne, 1969). This large volume includes no writer born before 1850 (my selection has eight) or after 1914 (not surprisingly, in a selection made

at the end of the twentieth century there are no fewer than twenty-one writers born after the First World War). Of Gianos' forty writers, only seventeen appear in the present volume, indicating not just a radical difference of personal and, indeed, generational taste (the self-proclaimed Generation of the Thirties so extensively represented in Gianos' anthology is now widely felt rather to have punched above its weight) but an entirely different picture of what Greek writing has contributed to the literature of the world. It should be noted, moreover, that my own selection does not include either drama, which would be ill served in this context, or the essay. Distinguished examples of the latter genre, which shed considerable light on the selections in the present volume, are George Seferis, *On the Greek Style*, translated by Rex Warner and Th.D. Frangopoulos (Boston: Little, Brown, 1966; reprinted Limni, Evia: Denise Harvey, 1982) and Zissimos Lorenzatos, *The Lost Center*, translated by Kay Cicellis (Princeton: Princeton University Press, 1980) and *The Drama of Quality* translated by Liadain Sherrard (Limni, Evia: Denise Harvey, 2000).

2. Dia M.L. Philippides, *CENSUS of Modern Greek Literature* (New Haven: Modern Greek Studies Association, second edition, 2002) of English translations of Greek writers and writings in English about them). Roderick Beaton, *An Introduction to Modern Greek Literature* (Oxford: Clarendon Press, second, revised, edition, 1999) is a detailed scholarly account of the literary history of modern Greece, in which all but a handful of the writers represented in the present volume are the subject of critical discussion.

3. Dionysios Solomos, *The Free Besieged and Other Poems*, translated by Peter Thompson, Roderick Beaton, Peter Colaclides, Michael Green and David Ricks (Beeston, Nottinghamshire: Shoestring Press, 2000) has the great virtue of being a bilingual edition, a form one would wish to see restored to its former prominence. A cooler welcome must be accorded to Andreas Kalvos, *Odes*, translated by George Dandoulakis (Beeston, Nottinghamshire: Shoestring Press, 1998): it is hard to imagine this volume's being picked up and read as one might read an English translation of Kalvos' contemporary Leopardi or his estranged master Foscolo.

4. Christopher Middleton (ed.), *German Writing Today* (Harmondsworth: Penguin, 1969), 13.

5. I discuss some comparable difficulties in two rather more tractable poets in my articles, 'Translating Palamas', *Journal of Modern Greek Studies 8*, pp. 275–90 (1990), and 'Cavafy translated', *Kampos: Cambridge Papers in Modern Greek 1*, pp. 85–110 (1993).

6. For the general issue, the reader may consult David Ricks and Paul Magdalino (eds), *Byzantium and the Modern Greek Identity* (Aldershot, Hampshire: Ashgate, 1998). I readily concede that the present anthology is somewhat thin when it comes to that dimension of modern Greek literature which has a distinctly Eastern and Orthodox cast. An English selection from Fotis Kontoglou's multifarious works would go some way towards correcting this.

Contents

Anon.

This anthology begins with a folk ballad, 'The Night Journey', the first item of Modern Greek poetry that might have reached the eyes of an English reader. It appeared in the almost instant English translation (1825) of the first volume of Claude Fauriel's great *Chants populaires de la Grèce moderne* – itself part of the Philhellenic effort in the West on the outbreak of the Greek Revolution in 1821 – made by Charles Brinsley Sheridan, son of the playwright. None of the ballads would have been so likely to strike a chord with the English reader in the Romantic period – the same theme had been the subject of Gottfried Bürger's 'Ellenore' as so influentially translated by Sir Walter Scott – and no ballad has had so pervasive an influence on later Greek literature as this one, best known as the 'Ballad of the Dead Brother'. The reader will find sharp echoes of the ballad in the troubled 1940s generation of Takis Sinopoulos and Miltos Sachtouris (qq.v.), and Michalis Ganas, the poet with whom this anthology concludes, has shown himself to be haunted by the song.

The Night Journey

'Oh, Mother! thou who still dost choose
    'Some pool retired and wild,
'In which to bathe our Aretè,
    'Thy fair and only child;

'Thou who dost braid her silky locks,
    'And bind her slender waist,
'Only when darkness shrouds our home,
    'With mystery's trembling haste;

'Fearing the Pasha's gloating eye,
    'And unrelenting hand!
'Oh! send for her, mother! as a bride,
    'To Europe's happier land.

'Then if I leave this wretched Greece.
    'To feed my soul with lore;
'I shall enjoy a home and friends
    'On some far distant shore!'

'Oh, Constantine! thou dost not know
    'What bitter schemes are here!
'For who will bring my child to pour
    'Her sorrows in my ear?'

He call'd on Heaven, and all the saints,
    To witness what he swore;
That *he* would bring his sister back
    To tell the woes she bore.

Two years roll'd on, in which he fed
    Consumption's sad complaint;
The third beheld upon his corse
    His frantic mother faint!

'I ne'er shall see my daughter more!
    'Oh! Constantine, awake!
'By Heaven, and all the saints, whom thou
    'For witnesses didst take!'

The corse at midnight slowly rose,
    And thro' the watchers past;
Tho' rough the night, the steed he rode
    Went faster than the blast.

Ere dawn he met his sister's gaze
    That sadly watch'd the moon:
'Sister, thy mother ask'd for *thee*, –
    'I did her bidding *soon!*' –

'Brother! Great God! what brought thee here?
    'Is this an hour to start?
'Say, didst thou leave our father's home
    'In sad or joyous heart?

'If glad, my robes should all be white;
    'If mournful, these are black!' –
'Nor sad, nor joyous, Aretè!
    'We must be riding back.'

While still they journey'd on their way,
　　As Dawn began to peep,
The birds pour'd forth not thrilling notes,
　　But accents strange and deep!

'Oh! dost thou hear, my Constantine!
　　'What birds around us say?' –
'They *are* but birds, – so let them sing,
　　'While we pursue our way.' –

'Brother! I tremble every limb!
　　'They say, 'Behold the *dead!*'
'I smell the incense; incense breathes
　　'From all thy robes and head.'

'But yester-eve these sacred drops
　　'Were thrown with liberal hand! –
'Open! I bring thee back thy child
　　'From Europe's distant land!' –

'Stranger, away! nor basely mock
　　'A widow's anguish'd ear;
'My Aretè is far away,
　　'And cannot now be here!' –

'Open! I am the Constantine
　　'Thou didst reproach before;
'Because I call'd the saints and Heaven
　　'To witness what I swore!'

She opened and beheld what earth
　　Had never seen before;
And in that instant sank a corse
　　Before her husband's door!

Translated by Charles Brinsley Sheridan

Dionysios Solomos (1798–1857)

Solomos has for Greeks much the same place that Pushkin has for Russians, and the open-ing stanzas of his 'Hymn to Liberty' (1823–4) were adopted for the national anthem in 1864. But Solomos' position in the national literature is much odder than this would make it sound. In the first place, born in Zante (Zakynthos) and spending his life there and in Corfu, Solomos never visited the newborn Greek state. And like Coleridge, and for some of the same reasons, he was a great projector of poetic schemes without being able to complete them. Of his Greek poems only a handful appeared in print in his lifetime, his reputation being based on a posthumous (and far from complete) edition of his literary remains in 1859. Solomos worked towards ever denser expression, and the chaos of his manuscripts, written in a mixture of Greek and Italian – the latter the language of his education – is the greatest treasure-house of poetic craft in the modern Greek language and one of the most illuminating poetic documents of the Romantic period in any European country. Yet the complexity of Solomos' poetic forms has been the despair of translators as well as of himself, and the selections given here are but the *disjecta membra* of a work of the highest ambition.

This selection begins with the opening verses of the 'Hymn to Liberty'. Rudyard Kipling's translation of those verses which form the lyric of the Greek national anthem (wisely turn-ing the original's trochaics into anapaests) was, as the date included in the text attests, by way of tribute to Greece's contribution to the Allied cause in the First World War: a divided country eventually entered the war under the great Prime Minister Eleftherios Venizelos in 1917 and was briefly the beneficiary of Western favour. The tide of fortune soon turned (a course of events obliquely alluded to in Cavafy's poems 'Dareios' and 'A Byzantine Nobleman in Exile Writing Verses', qq.v.), and in 1923, just over a century after Greece's declaration of independence, all Greeks except for those in Istanbul were forced to leave Turkey under the Treaty of Lausanne's provisions for the exchange of populations. It had all looked very different to Solomos, whose fervent but uneven long poem had first been printed as an appendix to Fauriel's *Chants populaires de la Grèce moderne* (q.v.). Yet destruc-tion was memorably encapsulated by Solomos in 'The Destruction of Psara'. This poem, learnt by every Greek schoolchild, was written in commemoration of the destruction of the small island off the coast of Chios in 1822.

Solomos spent much of his career working on his *magnum opus*, *The Free Besieged*, epic in scope but compressed in expression, in which he planned to narrate and reflect on the heroic tale of the inhabitants of Missolonghi. Byron had died there in the Greek cause on 19 April 1824, inspiring in Solomos a long and turgid poem which he never published but which survives in his manuscripts with some unprintable second thoughts. A year or so later (Palm Sunday 1826) the besieged and starving population of the town tried to make a break for it (now known as the Exodus) and was largely wiped out; those survivors left in the town blew up what they could at the loss of their own lives. Solomos could hear the cannon from Zante over the water and dedicated himself to commemorating these events in two parallel artistic channels. One is *The Free Besieged*, of which a reliable translation appeared only after the present selection was completed. The other is the prose work *The Woman of Zakythos* [sic] (q.v.).

Solomos' great poem 'The Cretan' is a striking literary-historical case. In the same year, 1833, two great poets at opposite ends of the European continent, Tennyson and Solomos, reinvented the dormant form of the dramatic monologue. The results were 'St Simeon Stylites' (later engaged with by Cavafy in 'Simeon', q.v.) and 'The Cretan'. The poem begins *in medias res*, and its turbulent, ecstatic narrative reflects the state of the mind of a Cretan insurgent of 1823–4, now reduced to beggary, as he tells of love and death. (Much ink has been spilt, in much the same way as it has over the Real Presence, on the question of just who the 'moon-clad girl' is: the answer is that we must hold in balance the soul of the expiring fiancée, the kindly presence of the Motherland and a recollection of our Lady.) The poem may illuminatingly be compared with *The Rime of the Ancient Mariner*, and also with a very different cast of poem about an exile in revolutionary Europe, Browning's 'The Italian in England' (1845): What no translation could succeed in conveying is the richness of the couplets in which the Cretan (and Solomos' own ancestors had moved from Crete after 1669) not only professes but embodies his cultural allegiances to his native island.

After the *annus mirabilis* of 1833–4 (compare Keats' 'living year') Solomos seemed a spent force and indeed fell away from the use of Greek as a poetic medium. But 'The Shark', a late poem (1849), shows a last rallying of his powers. In this poem a young English soldier of the Corfu garrison (the Ionian islands were ruled by Britain between 1815 and Union with Greece in 1864) communes with nature before a shark arrives on the scene to devour him – a true story which appeared in the Corfu papers in 1847. The reconstruction of the poem from the manuscripts (here, following the edition of Stylianos Alexiou) is controversial, and the plot summary may sound bathetic, evoking as it does that great comic creation Fotherington-Thomas ('Hullo clouds hullo sky') or the scenario of *Jaws*, but the concentrated power of the original provokes awe.

Finally, this selection presents that strange unfinished prose work *The Woman of Zakythos* in its entirety. Written at the height of Solomos' powers, in it the stark contrast between the peaceful Ionian islands and the suffering Greeks of the mainland during the War of Independence is drawn with the ire of an Old Testament prophet and in a form echoing biblical verses. This work, which remained unpublished until 1927, has, like that of Solomos' very different contemporary, the man of action General Makriyannis, become a model for later writers as diverse as Stratis Doukas and Yorgi Yatromanolakis (qq.v.). Though his greatest effect has been on poets (see, for example, Elytis' poem, 'Solomos: Submission and Awe', q.v.), Solomos is not important as a poet only.

Hymn to Liberty (*extract*)
(Published as 'The Greek National Anthem' in 1918)

We knew thee of old,
    Oh, divinely restored,
By the light of thine eyes
    And the light of thy Sword.

From the graves of our slain
    Shall thy valour prevail
As we greet thee again –
    Hail, Liberty! Hail!

Long time didst thou dwell
    Mid the peoples that mourn,
Awaiting some voice
    That should bid thee return.

Ah, slow broke the day
    And no man dared call,
For the shadow of tyranny
    Lay over all:

And we saw thee sad-eyed,
    The tears on thy cheeks
While thy raiment was dyed
    In the blood of the Greeks.

Yet, behold now thy sons
    With impetuous breath
Go forth to the fight
    Seeking Freedom or Death.

From the graves of our slain
    Shall thy valour prevail
As we greet thee again –
    Hail, Liberty! Hail!

Translated by Rudyard Kipling

The Destruction of Psara

> Alone – on Psara's blackened height
> Walks Glory – musing o'er the site
> Of many valiant – daring deeds.
> A crown upon her brow she wears –
> Made of the scant and withered weeds
> The desolate earth in silence bears.

Translated by E.M. Edmonds

The Cretan

I

I gazed, and still far distant was the shore.
'Blest thunderbolt, give light, I pray, once more!'
Three thunderbolts fell, one behind the other,
close by the girl, and made a fearful din.
From sea and sky the lightning struck an echo,
mountains and shores gave tongue with many voices.

II

What I shall tell, believe me, is pure truth.
I swear this by my body's many wounds,
by those who fought with me and fell in Crete,
by her who grieved me sore, this world forsaking.
(Sound, Trumpet; shaking off the shroud, I forge
a path among the pallid resurrected,
cry: 'Who has seen the one whose beauty hallows
the Vale? Speak now and see all that is good.
No shred remains of earth; and heaven's made new.
I love her still and with her will be judged.'
'On high we saw her first, her garland trembling
at Heaven's gate where singing she came forth.
Her voice was joy and sang the Resurrection,
all eagerness to live again as flesh;
the whole of Heaven heard and was amazed;
the conflagration of the world was lulled;
she was but now before us, making haste;

33

this way and that she looks and someone seeks.')

III

On rolled the thunder . . .
And then the sea, that raged like boiling broth,
was quieted, all calm and polished clean,
a fragrant garden, filled with all the stars;
Nature, by some deep mystery constrained,
shone forth in beauty and forgot her wrath.
No breath of wind touched sea or sky, not even
such as a passing bee makes on a flower,
but close by the girl, who gladly clung to me,
the full moon quivered limpid on the water;
something at once unravelled there and lo,
before me was a woman clothed in moonlight.

IV

The cool light trembled in her godlike visage,
in her deep jet-black eyes and golden hair.
She gazed upon the stars, and they exulted,
and shed their beams and did not dim the sight,
and from the unruffled surface of the sea,
a cypress-tree, ethereal, she rose,
reached out a lover's arms, but humbly too,
all radiant with beauty and with goodness.
Then noonday brilliance washed away the night,
creation, filled with light, became a temple.
At last, to me, who faced her in the currents,
the way a lodestone turns towards the North,
to me, not to the girl, she bent her head;
wretched, I gazed at her, and she at me.
I thought: could I have seen her long ago,
painted in church with awesome splendour,
or had my lovesick mind created her,
or dreamed her, even, with my mother's milk?
Sweet memory of old, and long forgotten,
it came before me then in all its power,
as when from mountain depths a spring bursts forth
and all at once is gilded by the sun!

A spring then did my eyes become; for long
that godlike face was hidden from my sight,
while deep within me I could feel her gaze
that made me tremble so, I could not speak.
But these are gods, that look from whence they dwell
down into the abyss where is the heart
of man: I felt her read my mind more clearly
than ever could my tongue have told my grief:
. . .

. . .
'My brothers in their prime the Turks snatched from me,
defiled my sister, slew her in hot blood,
at nightfall burnt to death my aged father
and next day threw my mother in the well.
In Crete . . .
two fistfuls of her earth I brought away.
O Goddess, help, keep safe this tender shoot,
my only hold against the precipice.'

V

Sweetly she smiled upon my spirit's pain,
tears filled her eyes, and they were like my girl's.
Alas, she vanished, but I felt her teardrop
touch my uplifted hand that reached towards her. –
From then till now this hand has not been mine,
that once was quick to draw upon the infidel.
It takes no joy in war: a beggar's hand,
for bread it reaches out to tearful strangers.
And when, at night, my eye from so much grief
grows weary, harsh dreams drag me back again,
and thunder crashes once more on the sea,
whose waves once more seek out my girl to drown her,
I wake near frantic and my mind gives way,
until the touch of this same hand brings calm. –
With this I cleft the waves, that smelled so sweet,
and knew a strength I had not known before,
not even when we fought with naked swords,
a handful of brave men against so many,
or when I struck down Yusuf and two more
close by the Labyrinth where we were pressed.

So strong my stroke, the louder beat my heart
because it beat against my loved one's side.
But then my stroke grew weary, when a sound,
sweetest of sounds, came forth across the waters.
This was no young girl's voice in budding woods
(hour of the evening star when waters darken)
who to the wellhead sings her secret love,
to trees and flowers that, opening, bend to hear.
This was no song of Cretan nightingale,
whose voice pours from its nest on high, wild crags
and sweetly strikes an echo all night long
from seas far distant and the distant plains,
until the stars dissolve before the Dawn
who, hearing, drops the roses from her fingers.
This was no shepherd's pipe on Psiloritis
such as I used to hear, alone and grieving,
when high in heaven blazed the noonday sun,
and mountains, seas and plains in light exulted,
and, seized by hope of liberty, aloud
I'd cry: 'My hallowed country bathed in blood!'
and weeping then, would lay my hands with pride
upon her blackened stones and shrivelled weeds.
Pipe, bird, voice: none of these could match that sound,
whose like perhaps has vanished from the earth:
not words, but sound so light . . .
too soft to echo even from close by.
Whether close by or distant I knew not,
like scent of May there wafted on the air
the sweetest, inexplicable . . .
Such power as this have Love and Death alone.
The sound seized all my soul and quite shut out
the sky, the sea, the shore, even the girl;
it seized my soul and often made me yearn
to leave behind my body and to follow.
It ceased, drained nature empty and my soul
that sighed and at once filled with my beloved.
And now at last the shore: I laid her head
upon the strand with joy, but she was dead.

Translated by Roderick Beaton

The Shark

'Here comes the golden-winged bird, even now
Leaving its bough to seek the rocky shore;
And feeling there the sea's and heavens' beauty,
There it draws forth its sound with all its magic,
Binding in sweet bonds sea and lonely rock.
(Before its hour the star will venture out.
Send stars in thousands, night, to bathe with me!)
Bird, little bird, singing with all your magic,
If bliss is not your miracle of voice,
No good has flowered on earth, in heaven, none.
I had not hoped that life could be so good.
But oh! if I could only speed like lightning,
With you, foam, holding firm till I were back,
Twice kissed by mother, fists full of home earth!'

And all of nature laughed and was his own.
Hope, you embraced him, speaking secret words,
Bound in tight bonds his mind with all your magic.
New world and lovely, all of joy and goodness.

But his eyes meet the great beast of the deep,
And far, alas! is sword and far is musket.
Hard by the youth, the tiger of the deep.
But as it cut with ease the fathoms, rising

Towards the white throat gleaming like a swan's,
Towards the broad chest and the head so blond,
Just so, the young man, freed with all his might
From nature's lovely, mightiest embrace
– She who so sweetly bound him, sweetly spoken –
Unites in naked body flashing white
The swimmer's art and all the surge of battle.
Expiring, the great soul was filled with joy:
In a lightning flash the young man knew himself.

Wonderful remnant of a fallen greatness,
Dear lovely stranger in the flower of youth,
Come and receive ashore the strong man's tears.

Translated by David Ricks

The Woman of Zakythos

CHAPTER ONE
THE ANCHORET IS GRIEVED

1. I, Dionysios the anchoret, of the chapel of St Lypios, I say, being resolved to set forth what is in my mind:

2. I was just returning from the monastery of St Dionysios, whither I had gone to speak with a monk of certain spiritual matters,

3. And it was summer, and it was the time when the waters grow turbid, and I had come to the place called Three Wells, and the earth around the wells was covered in water, for the women go there often and do their washing.

4. I stopped at one of the three wells, and placing my hands on the rim of the well I leaned forward to see if there was much water.

5. And I saw that it was filled to the middle, and I said: 'Praise be to God,

6. Sweet is the freshness that He sends to man's vitals in summertime, great are His works, and great is man's thanklessness.

7. But the just, according to the Holy Scriptures, how many are they?' And as I pondered this my eyes fell on my hands, which were placed on the rim.

8. And wishing to count the just on my fingers, I raised my left hand from the rim, and looking at the fingers of the right one, I said: 'Would they be too many?'

9. And I started to compare the number of the just I knew with these five fingers, and seeing that they were too many, I made one less by hiding my little finger between the rim and the palm of my hand.

10. And I stood looking at my four fingers for a long time, and I felt great agony of spirit, for I knew that I would be constrained to diminish their number, and next to my little finger I put its neighbour, in the same position.

11. So there remained under my eyes three fingers only, and I drummed them restlessly on the rim to help my mind discover at least three just men.

12. But since my innards began to tremble like the sea, which is never stilled,

13. I raised my poor three fingers and I crossed myself.

14. Then, wishing to count the unjust, I thrust one hand in the pocket of my cassock and the other in my girdle, for I understood, alas, that my fingers would be of no use at all.

15. And my mind was confused by the great number, but I was comforted by seeing that each had something good about him. And I heard a terrible laughter from the well, and I saw two horns sticking up.

16. And more than all of these there came to my mind the Woman of Zakythos, who strives to harm others by word and by deed and was a mortal enemy of the nation.

17. And as I sought to discover if ever into this soul, in which the malignity of Satan seethes, there had ever fallen the desire of the smallest good,

18. I paused in order to consider well, and I lifted my head and my hands to the heavens and I cried: 'My God, I seek a grain of salt in hot water.'

19. And I saw that all the stars were shining above me, and I discerned Orion, which gives me great delight.

20. And I hastened to be on my way to the chapel of St Lypios, for I saw that I had wasted time, and I wanted to get there that I might describe the Woman of Zakythos.

21. And all at once there appeared a dozen mangy curs which tried to bar my way,

22. And since I had no desire to kick them lest I touch their mangy hides and the blood that was on them, they took it into their heads that I was afraid of them,

23. And they came toward me, barking. And I made as if to bend down and pick up a stone,

24. And they all ran off; and the mangy wretches vented their rage by biting each other.

25. But someone who was protecting certain of these mangy curs, he also picked up a stone,

26. Which he aimed, the godless one, at my head, at the head of Dionysios the anchoret; but he missed. For in the great haste in which he threw the stone he slipped and fell.

27. Thus I came to my cell at the chapel of St Lypios, comforted by the scents of the plain, by the sweet running waters, by the starry sky, which seemed a resurrection above my head.

Chapter Two
The Anchoret Seeks Comfort

1. Now the Woman's body was small and misshapen.

2. And her breast was almost always marked by the leeches that she would apply to suck the consumption and there hung down two dugs like tobacco pouches.

3. And this small body moved very quickly, and its joints seemed loose.

4. Her face was shaped like a shoemaker's last, and you saw a thing of great length if you looked at it from the point of the chin to the crown of the head.

5. About which was coiled a braid, surmounted by an enormous comb.

6. And if anyone had spanned the Woman with his hand to measure her, he would have found a quarter of the body to be head.

7. And her cheek, festered with sores, was sometimes flushed with life, sometimes flaccid and withered.

8. And every now and then she would open her large mouth to mock others, showing her lower front teeth, small and decayed, which met the upper ones, very white and long.

9. And although she was young, her temples and her forehead and her eyebrows and the slope of her nose were those of an old woman,

10. Especially when she leant her head on her right fist, thinking malicious thoughts.

11. And this old woman's look was enlivened by two eyes, bright and of the deepest black, one of which had a slight cast in it;

12. And they darted hither and thither seeking evil, and they would find it even where it was not.

13. And there was a certain gleam in her eyes that made you fancy either that madness had just left her or that it was about to burst forth.

14. Such was the dwelling place of her cunning and sinful soul.

15. And she revealed her malice both when she spoke and when she was silent.

16. And when she spoke secretly to harm a man's good name, her voice was like the whisper of straw matting trodden by the foot of a thief.

17. And when she spoke loudly, her voice was like that which men use to mock others.

18. And yet when she was alone, she would go to the mirror, and looking into it she would laugh and cry,

19. Thinking herself the most beautiful of all the women in the Ionian Islands.

20. And she was skilful as Death in dividing husband from wife and brother from brother.

21. And when she dreamed of her sister's lovely body, she would wake up in terror.

22. Envy, hatred, suspicion, untruth tore at her vitals,

23. As when you see the neighbourhood urchins, bedraggled and filthy, ringing church bells at a fair and driving everyone mad.

24. And when she talked of the misdeeds of other women, her mind would falter and become frenzied,

25. And she would feel a certain delight in turning these misdeeds over in her mind when she was alone.

26. And yet she held back from wrongdoing.

27. But, hearing that she was called ugly, she was wounded in her pride and she sinned.

28. And at last she lost all self-restraint etc.

CHAPTER THREE
THE WOMEN FROM MISSOLONGHI

1. And it happened in these days that the Turks were laying siege to Missolonghi, and often the whole day and sometimes the whole night long Zakythos trembled from the heavy cannon fire.

2. And certain women from Missolonghi went around begging alms for their husbands, their children and their brothers who were fighting.

3. At first they were ashamed to go out, and they would wait until darkness to reach out their hands, for they were not accustomed to it.

4. They had servants and they had much land with many goats and sheep and cattle.

5. Then they would become restless and would keep gazing from the window, waiting for the sun to set so that they might go out.

6. But when their need overcame them, they lost all shame and would run about all day long.

7. And when they grew tired, they would sit by the seashore and listen, for they feared that Missolonghi would fall.

8. And everyone could see them running from one place to another – crossroads, houses, lower floors, upper floors, churches, wayside chapels – begging alms.

9. And they were given money and rags to bundle the wounded.

10. And no one refused them, for the women's pleas were often accompanied by cannon fire from Missolonghi, and the earth trembled beneath our feet.

11. And even the poorest took out their mite and gave it, crossing themselves and weeping as they looked toward Missolonghi.

CHAPTER FOUR
THE WOMEN FROM MISSOLONGHI BEG
AND THE WOMAN OF ZAKYTHOS IS KEPT BUSY

1. Meanwhile the Woman of Zakythos had her daughter on her knees and was trying to cosset her.

2. Then the crazy Woman pushed the hair dishevelled by her restlessness back behind her ears and said, kissing her daughter's eyes:

3. 'My darling, my pretty, be a good girl, get married and we'll go out and come back together, look at people and sit together at the window and read the Bible and the Thousand and One Nights.'

4. And when she had caressed and kissed her eyes and lips, she put her on the chair, telling her: 'There, take the little mirror and see how pretty you are, and how much you look like me.'

5. And the daughter, who was not used to kindness, became quiet, and tears of joy came to her eyes.

6. And all at once there was a clatter of feet, growing louder and louder.

7. And she stood still, staring at the door and flaring her nostrils.

8. And there appeared before her the women from Missolonghi. They put their right hands on their breasts and bowed their heads. And they remained silent and motionless.

9. 'So that's it then? What would you like us to do? Is this a game? What are your orders, ladies? You made such a noise with your clogs coming up, that I think you came to give me orders.'

10. And they all remained silent and motionless; but one said: 'You are right. You are in your own country, in your own house, and we are strangers. We need a helping hand.'

11. And the Woman of Zakythos interrupted her and answered: 'My lady schoolmistress, you have lost everything, but from what I hear, you have kept your tongue.

12. 'I am in my own country and my own house, and wasn't your ladyship in your own country and in your own house?

13. 'And what were you lacking? And what harm did the Turk do you? Didn't he leave you food, servants, gardens, riches? And you had more than I, God be thanked.

14. 'Did I ask you to fight the Turks, that you come now to beg from me and insult me?

15. 'Yes indeed, you came out of doors to do brave deeds. You, the women, were fighting (a fine sight you'd have made with guns and skirts; or did you put on breeches?), and at first you fared well, as the unfortunate Turkish lads were taken by surprise.

16. 'And how could the Turk have suspected such treachery? Was it God's will? Did you not mingle with the Turk day and night?

17. 'It would be the same if I thrust a knife at dawn into my husband's throat (devil take him).

18. 'And now that things are going badly you want the burden to fall on me.

19. 'That's a good one, to be sure. Tomorrow Missolonghi falls, the kings, on whom I rest all my hopes, will put mad Greece in order,

20. 'And those who survive the slaughter come to Zakythos to be fed by us, and with full bellies they insult us.'

21. She fell silent for a moment and looked at the women from Missolonghi straight in the eye.

22. 'I can talk too. Yes or no? What are you waiting for? Perhaps you found some pleasure in listening to me?

23. 'You have nothing better to do than to go begging. And I think, to tell the truth, that it's a pleasure for those who have no shame.

24. 'I have work to do, do you hear? I have work.' And as she shouted such things, she no longer seemed a coffee-pot no more than three spans tall, but a normal woman.

25. For in her great anger she stood on tiptoe, barely touching the floor; and her eyes popped out of their sockets and her sound eye appeared to squint and her squinting eye appeared sound. And she became like a plaster mask that painters cast from the faces of the dead in order to . . .

26. And anyone who had seen her reassume her former shape would have said that the devil had seized her, but had changed his mind and let her be because of the hatred she bore mankind.

27. And her daughter screamed, looking at her; and the servants forgot their hunger, and the women of Missolonghi went downstairs without a sound.

28. And the Woman of Zakythos, laying her hand on her heart and sighing deeply, said:

29. 'My God, how my heart, that you did create good, is beating!

30. 'Those whores put me in a rage. All the women in the world are whores.

31. 'But you, my daughter, you will not be a whore like my sister and like all the other women of my land.

32. 'Better to die. And were you scared, my darling? There, stand still – if you move from this chair, I'll call those witches back at once, and they'll eat you up.'

33. And the servants had gone to the kitchen without waiting for the Woman's leave, and there they began to speak of their hunger.

34. And the Woman went to her bedroom.

35. And then there was great silence, and I heard the bed creaking, faintly first, and then loudly. And between the creakings came heavy breathing and sobs,

36. Like those of porters when the poor wretches carry an unbearable weight on their backs.

37. And I, Dionysios the anchoret, departed from this stumbling block, and as I was leaving the house, I met the Woman's husband, who was coming up.

CHAPTER FIVE
PROPHECY CONCERNING THE FALL OF MISSOLONGHI

1. And I followed the women of Missolonghi, who sat down on the strand, and I was behind a fence and I was looking.

2. And each took out whatever she had gathered, and they made a pile.

3. And one of them, reaching out her hand and touching the shore, cried: 'Sisters,

4. 'Listen, did you ever hear such a rumbling from Missolonghi; are they winning or is the town falling?'

5. And I was about to leave, when I saw behind the church (I forget its name) a little old woman, who had placed candles amid the grass and was burning incense; and the candles lit up the green, and the incense was rising.

6. And she was lifting up her withered hands, scattering the incense and weeping, and, moving her toothless mouth, she was praying.

7. And I heard within me a great commotion, *and the spirit bore me away to Missolonghi*. And I could see neither the fortress nor the city, nor the camp, nor the houses, nor the lake; and everything was covered by thick smoke filled with lightning, thunder and thunderbolts.

8. And I raised my eyes and my hands to heaven to offer up a prayer with all the fervour of my soul, and I saw amid the smoke, lit by an endless shower of sparks, a woman holding a lyre, who halted above me in the smoke.

9. And I hardly had time to wonder at her raiment, which was black as the blood of hares, or her eyes etc., when the woman halted in the smoke and gazed at the battle, and the myriad sparks that shot up would touch her raiment and be extinguished.

10. She laid her fingers on the lyre, and I heard her sing these words:

> At dawn I took the way of the sun,
> Slinging my lyre, my righteous lyre, behind me,
> And from where it rises to where it sets etc.

11. And the Goddess had hardly finished speaking when our men gave a terrible shout for the victory they had won. And our men and everything disappeared from sight, and my vitals were again terribly shaken, and it seemed that I lost hearing and sight.

12. And in a little while I saw in front of me the little old woman, who said to me: 'Thank God, anchoret, I thought that some ill had befallen you. I was calling you, I was shaking you, and you could hear nothing, and your eyes were staring up into the air, while a moment ago the earth was trembling like the seething of boiling water. It has just stopped now that the candles and incense are finished. Would you say that our men have won?'

13. And I was about to leave with Death in my heart. And then the little old woman bent to kiss my hand and said: 'How cold your hand is!'

CHAPTER SIX
THE FUTURE BECOMES THE PRESENT
EVIL IS THE END

1. And I looked around and I saw nothing, and I said:

2. 'The Lord does not wish me to see anything more.' And I faced about and set out for St Lypios.

3. And I heard the earth trembling beneath my feet, and a multitude of lightnings filled the air, increasing in swiftness and brightness. And fear overcame me because the dread hour of midnight was at hand.

4. So great was my fear that I stretched my arms before me as does a sightless man.

5. And I found myself behind a mirror, between the mirror and the wall. And the mirror was as high as the room.

6. And a voice, strong and rapid of speech, fell on my ears:

7. 'O Dionysios, anchoret, the future will now become present for you. Wait and you shall see the vengeance of God.'

8. And another voice stammered out the same words to me indistinctly.

9. And this second voice was that of an old man I had known, who had died. And I was astonished, for it was the first time that I had heard a man's soul stammer. And I heard a third voice, a murmur like the wind blowing through the reeds, but I heard no words.

10. And I looked up to see where the voices were coming from, and I saw only two long, thick nails sticking out of the wall, on which the mirror rested, strung at the middle.

11. And sighing deeply, like a man who finds himself deceived, I smelled the odour of a corpse.

12. And I came out, and I looked about me, and I saw.

13. I saw facing the mirror in the corner of the room a bed, and near the bed a light. And it seemed that there was nothing in the bed, but it was swarming with flies.

14. And on the pillow I thought I saw a motionless head, faint as those which seamen make with a needle on their arms and chests.

15. And I said to myself: 'The Lord has sent me this vision as a dark symbol of His will.'

16. Therefore, fervently imploring God that He should deign to help me understand this symbol, I approached the bed.

17. And something moved under the dirty, ragged, bloodstained sheets.

18. And looking more closely at the image on the pillow, I was shaken to the core, for by a movement that she made with her mouth I recognized the Woman of Zakythos, who was sleeping covered to the neck with a sheet, all ravaged with consumption.

CHAPTER SEVEN
I WON'T GIVE YOU A SINGLE CRUMB

1. But I looked hard at this sleep, and I understood that it would last just a little while before it yielded to the other one that is without dreams.

2. And since within there was no friend, no kin, no physician, no confessor, I,

Dionysios the anchoret, bent over her and urgently bade her confess.

3. And she half-opened her mouth, baring her teeth, and went on sleeping.

4. And the first voice, the unknown one, said in my right ear: 'The wretched Woman's mind is full of gallows, prisons, and Turks who win and Greeks who are slaughtered.

5. At this moment she sees in her sleep the thing she always desired – her sister a beggar, and that's why you saw her smile.'

6. And the second voice, the one I knew, repeated the same words in a stammer, with many oaths, as had been its habit when it was that of a living creature:

7. 'In truth, b-y-y-y the Holy Virgin, hearken, in truth, b-y-y St Nicholas, hearken, in t-t-truth, by St Spy-ri-don, in truth, by the imma-acu-u-ulate mysteries of God.' And then came the murmur like the wind blowing through the reeds.

8. And suddenly the Woman thrust her hands out from under the sheet and clapped, and the flies rose up.

9. And through the noise they made I heard the voice of the Woman crying: 'Get out of here, you whore. I won't give you a single crumb.'

10. And she shook her fist from the bed, as if to drive away her sister, who she imagined had come to beg.

11. And the dirty sheet had slipped down, leaving her almost naked, a dead cat that a whirlwind blows out of a pile of manure.

12. And she struck her hand against a coffin, which was suddenly there, and the sinful Woman's dream was broken.

13. And she opened her eyes, and seeing the coffin, she shuddered, in the fear that they would put her in it, thinking her dead.

14. And she was about to cry out to show that she was not dead, but there rose out of the coffin the head of a woman also ravaged by consumption, who, although older, looked very much like her.

15. She threw herself to the left side of the bed and she hit her face against another coffin, and out of it came the face of an old man – the old man I knew.

16. And thus I understood that before she gave up the ghost the Woman was to find herself with her father, her mother, and her daughter.

17. And I was stricken with horror, and I turned my face the other way and my eye fell with relief on the mirror, which showed only the Woman alone, and me, and finally the light.

18. For the bodies of the other three are resting in their graves, whence they will leap at the last trump,

19. Together with me, Dionysios the anchoret, with the Woman of Zakythos, with all the children of Adam in the great valley of Jehosaphat.

20. And I fell to thinking on God's justice, which will be revealed on that day, and my eye (fixed on the mirror) was distracted by my thoughts,

21. And my thoughts were distracted by my eye,

22. For as I turned my eyes here and there like one pondering a difficult thing that he strives to understand,

23. I saw through the keyhole something that was blocking the light; and this lasted for some time, and then it reappeared.

24. And then in the other room I heard a murmur, and I understood nothing, and I gazed in the direction of the *vision*.

25. And there was a great silence, and you could not hear a single fly buzzing out of all that great swarm, for they were all clustered on the mirror,

26. Much of which was the colour of the veil that is draped over mirrors when someone leaves the family for ever.

CHAPTER EIGHT
THE BELT

1. But her mother, without looking at the door, without looking at her daughter, without looking at anybody, began:

2. 'At this moment the eye and the ear of your child are fixed on you through the keyhole, and she is keeping away from you because she is afraid of the evil you bring. And that's what you did to me too.

3. 'For this, in the bitterness of my soul, I put my curse on you, kneeling and with my hair unbound, when all the church bells were ringing on Easter Day.

4. 'I cursed you one hour before dying, and now again I curse you, evil and perverse woman.

5. 'And the threefold curse will be sure and potent in your body and your soul as are sure and potent in the visible and invisible worlds the three persons of the Holy Trinity.'

6. Having spoken thus, she took off a belt that had belonged to her husband, blew on it three times and flung it in the Woman's face.

7. And the old man mumbled these last words, and the little girl stirred on the red pillow like a wounded bird.

CHAPTER NINE
THE WOMAN OF ZAKYTHOS RECEIVES
HER LAST SATISFACTION

1. And they disappeared with their coffins. And only then did the Woman feel strong enough to jump up.

2. And she threw herself forward with a bound like a star in summer shoots through the air leaving a trail ten fathoms long.

3. And she hit against the mirror, and the flies rose up and buzzed in clusters about her face.

4. And thinking that they were her parents, she darted back and forth,

5. Groping about to find something to protect herself, she found the belt and began to lash out with it.

6. And the more she lashed, the more the flies buzzed and the more terrified she became until at last she went completely out of her wits. And her wits left her, but not her passions, suspicion, harshness, malice, mockery, etc.

7. And as she was running in her shift, which she had made too short out of her miserliness, her eye darted to the mirror,

8. She stopped, not recognizing herself, and she pointed a finger and laughed:

9. 'O body, O body! What a shift! Now I see it all. And who is the cunning one who can hide his cunning from me? That shift makes me see that the creature is feigning madness to have an excuse for sinning.

10. 'But who can it be? I swear this creature looks a bit like her. Ah, it's you! Depraved creature, filthy whore, hospital fly-shit, dirt in a sow's eye, heap of manure, you shameless hussy, you foul-mouth.

11. 'There, you see what I foretold, what they are, those beloved friends of yours. Not even a begging bowl is left for you to beg with.

12. 'You are in my hands. What do you want? Do you want me to do you a favour? Now I'm going to do it. Let me see if you have a voice left to say that I'm crazy.'

13. Having spoken thus, she made a circle and then she began dancing with great fury, and her short shift was about her face. And her hair, black and greasy, was snakes writhing in the dust.

14. And in the heat of the dance she made a noose with the belt, and the dance lasted until she had made the noose.

15. And she said: 'Come behind the mirror with me so that I can do you this favour.

16. 'The doctor, who will look after you too, comes from time to time, the silly ass. He's got it into his head that I'm ill.'

17. And she went behind the mirror, and I heard her making a great noise.

18. And there came a burst of laughter, and the room echoed with her shouts: 'There's the favour, my dear.'

19. Then I fell to my knees to pray that the Lord would take her madness from her, even for the little time she had to live, so that her wickedness would cease.

20. And having prayed, I looked down behind the mirror, thinking that she had swooned, but she was not there.

21. And I felt my blood drain from my cheeks.

22. And my head fell forward on my chest, and I said to myself:

23. 'God knows where the wretched woman disappeared while I was praying for her with all the fervour of my soul.'

24. And I moved forward, my head bowed, and deep in thought, in order to go find her.

25. And I felt something hit me on the forehead, and I fell on my back in amazement.

26. And I saw the Woman of Zakythos, who was hanging and swaying.

CHAPTER TEN
UNTITLED

1. And I got up in terror, shouting: 'Lord have mercy, Lord have mercy,' and I heard the clatter of people mounting the stairs.

2. And there were about fifteen people, and most of them were wearing masks, except for five whom I knew very well.

3. One of them (describe all five of them).

4. Although they had no love for the Woman, they frequented her house, and they all began to weep.

5. So I turned to them and said: 'Out of here, out of here! Your sins dragged you here. This place is doomed to destruction, for God hates it.'

6. And they were somewhat frightened, but they did not leave.

7. And I remained silent, seeking words that would make them leave.

8. And I said to them: 'Listen, my children, to the words of Dionysios the anchoret. As for me, I am going now to pray and I shall leave you here.

9. 'Look into your consciences, you M., you G., you K., you P., you T. (I don't know the rest of you), and see what the outcome will be if you stay. The authorities know you, and finding you here, they will say that you have hanged her.'

10. Then I saw them all turn their backs, shoving each other to be the first to escape, and they tumbled down the stairs in such confusion that it seemed to me that most of them fell headlong.

Translated by Peter Colaclides and Michael Green

Andreas Kalvos (1792–1869)

Kalvos, born in Zante, first came to England as the amanuensis of his compatriot Ugo Foscolo and spent some time in London, where he married the first of his two English wives. Turning from Italian to Greek poetry on the outbreak of the War of Independence, he published two collections of patriotic and classical odes (Paris, 1824, and Geneva, 1826: Nasos Vayenas' poem, 'Calvos in Geneva', q.v., evokes this phase of Kalvos' life), totalling twenty poems, before lapsing into poetic silence. He eventually returned to England, where he ran a girls' school and died in Tennyson country: Louth, Lincolnshire. Kalvos' poetry did not go wholly unrecognized in his lifetime, but it was only with the discussion of his work by Palamas and later Seferis that it began to exert its central influence on later poets, an example of which is Elytis' 'With Light and Death' (q.v.). The following rendering – though a number of stanzas have been omitted – gives some idea of Kalvos' curious archaizing idiom, even if the metrical mastery of the original is lost. The original ode's title is simply 'On the Sacred Band'. It commemorates the wiping out in 1821 of the young troops who first raised the flag of Liberty against the Ottomans in the Trans-Danubian Principalities. Behind this, however, there was in the mind of some of the fighters, and certainly of the poet, the original Sacred Band of Thebans, which had been defeated by Philip II of Macedon at Chaeronea in 338 BC. 'Fatal to liberty' Milton had called that battle, and his Greek successor, who knew something of Milton, concurred in the then conventional view that Hellas had simply ceased to exist between 338 BC and the raising of the standard in AD 1821.

Elegy on the Sacred Battalion

> Never may storm-clouds
> Here pour down heavy showers,
> Nor the harsh lightning blast
> Scatter the blessèd
> Soil that enshrouds you.
>
> But with her silvery tears
> May the rose-robéd Maid
> Ever bedew it;
> Here everlastingly
> Forth blossom flowers.

Fortune that reft from you
Laurels of victory
Wove of the myrtle
And sorrowful cypress
For you other crowns.

But, when for Fatherland
Fighting man finds his death,
Myrtles are priceless,
Fair is the foliage
Of the dark cypress.

Hellenes, of your birthland,
Your forefathers worthy,
Hellenes, was there one of you all
Who rather had chosen
A grave void of glory?

Time, envious greybeard,
Foe of the works of men,
Foe of all memories,
Creeps o'er the wide earth,
Roams over ocean

From his urn pouring forth
Waters of Lethe.
All he effaces,
Cities are vanished,
Nations and kingdoms;

But, soon as the soil
He approaches that holds you,
Time's self will turn aside
And that illustrious
Ground will revere.

Then, when to Hellas
We have given as of old
Sceptre and purple,
Thither will mothers come
Leading their children;

And, as with flowing tears
Kiss they the hallowed dust,
Say: 'Sons of that glorious
Legion be followers,
The Legion of Heroes.'

Translated by Florence McPherson

Yannis Makriyannis (1798–1864)

Many veterans of the War of Independence published their memoirs, usually with the assistance of men of letters who smoothed away the raw and lively idiom of action. Makriyannis' memoirs fall into a rather special category: illiterate until the age of thirty-two, he learnt enough of the art of writing during a lull in the Independence campaign to set about writing his memoirs in a painfully rough-hewn and not easily deciphered hand. A controversial figure in peacetime, the old general's opposition to King Otho led him to hide his writings in a tin box in the garden, and the memoirs were published only in 1907. (Because almost all of the manuscript was lost in the Second World War, some conspiracy theorists have alleged that the whole work is a forgery by the hand of its first editor.) Palamas immediately saw their value, as Seferis later did, and few would disagree that Makriyannis is, along with Alexander Papadiamantis (q.v.), the greatest prose writer in the modern language. It is hard to imagine that Stratis Doukas or, today, Rhea Galanaki (qq.v.) could have gone about their ambitious task of getting inside the history of the Greeks without Makriyannis' example. The passage that follows is one of the *Memoirs*' most memorable.

Memoirs (*extract*)

The wound in my arm was going badly: my arm swelled up and the skin was tight as a drum. The doctors who had been put to tend me at Nauplion wanted to cut it off at the shoulder. For thirty-eight days and nights I never closed my eyes. They got me ready for my death: the doctor brought in all his instruments to cut off my arm. I got hold of my scimitar and he threw himself down the stairs and escaped; otherwise I'd have cut him to pieces. I went off to Athens to a doctor who gave me treatment. But I had been crippled because of those doctors in Nauplion: bones had to be taken out through their mistakes. And if I had not gone to Athens I should have lost my life.

While I was still in Athens under treatment, Ibrahim threatened to sail for Hydra with all his fleet and destroy it. The Hydriots demanded a military force from the Government and told them, 'You must assign us a force, but don't let us be without Makriyannis and we'll see to his treatment here.' For when I had to go to Athens I had first passed through Hydra, and everyone had come out to welcome me, and two of my friends had cast lots who should receive me in his house; I had been received by Dimitris Lazarinos. He spent a fair sum of money on my friends, with whom the house was filled day and night. The Hydriots would not let me go. They brought me a doctor and all my needs; it was much against my will that I had to leave for Athens. Later, the Hydriots sent a special messenger to Athens with a letter from the leading householders requesting a permit from the Government for a caique for me to return in. I sailed off with my troop, and they gave me many proofs of their esteem.

There arrived Karatassios with his troop, the Grivas brothers, Katzikoyannis, and others; we stayed there for some time. The people gave us our fodder and rations. The troops wanted us to plunder the houses of the leading citizens and hold them by force and strip them of their wealth. I would not assent to this and drew from my own resources to give them their pay. And I told them they should tell the other troops to lay hands on their own Kapetans and get them to pay from their own purses, for the Hydriots owed us nothing. These men were going in their ships to die for the country, and ourselves – we had been sent by the Government to keep guard over the island and were being provided with pure bread and all our rations; we should get our pay from the Government. If we were to rob the leading citizens why were we there to guard them? This would be a fine Turkish thing to do to them – and put ourselves in danger of death.

So they laid hold of all their commanders, who paid them from their own purses as I had done. All of these last threatened to kill me for this. But those who hear threats live longer than those who do not.

We stayed some time in Hydra. I was given a fine acknowledgement of my services and another for the money due to me, and I took another for all the soldiers who had drawn pay from my own purse. Then I left and went to the Government and told them I would disband my troop and go into the regulars as a simple private; I had been made a general. I said, 'The country will not go forward without a regular army and I'm going to enlist in it.' They tried hard but could not hold me back. I abandoned my rank and disbanded my troop: I took some officers with me on my way to Athens, where Fabvier was, to train as a simple private. Gouras learns of this, wants to enlist in the regulars himself – but first must be paid all his pay and the former sums due to him, eight hundred thousand groschen. They promised him this and he enlisted. However, he did this to get hold of the money and then – back to business. I got to Athens and they made me a wooden musket as the wound in my arm was still raw, and I was trained along with the privates: I was also given an instructor to myself. Then Gouras enlisted and he too underwent training: and many others enlisted at our side. And the troop grew to more than five thousand. The commander of the troop was the brave French Philhellene Fabvier and there were many other brave officers with him, both French and of our own race. The country owes a debt of thanks to all those humane benefactors of ours from every nation, and especially those brave Frenchmen who made a sacrifice of toil and hardship and battle to shape us into good order and concord. All the patriotic Athenians, the sons of the great houses, enlisted in the regulars and fought as common soldiers.

Now Gouras had enlisted in the regulars, and he had his marriage kinsman Yannakos Vlachos and other friends in the Government. All of these made an agreement to send a committee of their own, formed of their friends, into Athens to sell up the national lands and have them taken over by Gouras and his allies: fields, olive groves, houses, workshops, and so forth. They sent a committee consisting of John Koundoumas, Thanasis Lidorikis, and Georgakis Mostras. When they arrived they made an announcement about this sale. One day I was out riding with Gouras; he was out to flatter me as he wanted to give me one of his nieces in marriage. Says he, 'I'm going to take the estate of Haseki, the olive-groves, the enclosure and all the ground there about, in payment of the debt the nation owes me.'

Say I, 'You have taken ample treasuries from this wretched nation in your campaigns in Athens and the Peloponnese; what was the muster under your command? It never came up to three hundred men, and all eastern Greece and the Government is paying for them! And you are robbing everybody. You and your creature Mamouris tear people's teeth out and chop them to pieces for their money. You murdered Sarris: the fifty thousand groschen that he had on him in cash and jewellery was taken by Mamouris and you shared it between you. To cap all this you are still trying to get eight hundred thousand groschen more from the Government; and through the committee, to which all of your friends have been appointed, you'll get hold of property that's worth fifty for every ten you pay: that's the price that this committee is going to set on it. Your friends and your kinsmen of the Government will confirm this and, to cap that, you and Mamouris between you will be Mahomet Ali and Ibrahim and have us as your helots. I shit on such a freedom where I have to make a pasha of you!' 'What are you chattering about?' says he. 'Chattering about!' say I. 'When you and your friends get hold of these things you can spit on me!' I left him and went back to my quarters.

The next day the committee posted up the announcement; we went and smeared it with dung. And as often as it was posted up it suffered the same fate. All these people and their committee spoke to me and promised that whatever was owing to me from the nation – they'd let me have what I asked for. 'I'm asking for nothing,' I told them. So all the plans of Gouras and the committee were killed stone dead. Gouras quit the regulars. And he and his allies in Athens and in the Government made one plot after another to get the regular troops disbanded.

Poor Fabvier ran to our progressive Government to get the wherewithal. In Athens there was clothing for the regulars and other requirements, and the fine patriots were trying to fight over them for plunder. Fabvier made me a member of a committee formed from all the regulars to keep guard over these things and stop the others making off with them. The committee included Skarvelis, Stavris

Vlachos, other officers, and myself. And we guarded these stores till the leader of the troop should return. So Gouras, Zacharitsas, Varelas, Sourmelis, and others of their allies among the Athenians and their friends from the Government, including Yannakos Vlachos, Gouras' kinsman, whom he used as his agent in the Government, made a thousand plots to bring the regular force to ruin and cut it off from every supply, and above all to get it disbanded, for regular discipline had no place for robbery and violence towards citizens. The poor Athenians would have snatched their last morsel from their own lips to give to the regulars. They were raising subscriptions all day to provision the force. For they had been able to call their homes their own from the time that Fabvier had arrived in Athens with his troop.

When the Athenians saw that the regular force was in danger and that, on its disbandment, they would be the first to enjoy the benefits of Commander Gouras' justice, they all gathered together and held an assembly and formed a force of a thousand Athenians: all sons of great houses, with myself as their commander, to maintain good order in the city and, if need should arise, to march them out against the enemy. The assembly met and made every necessary provision. Then Gouras learns of this and it is agreeable neither to him nor his friends, nor to the Government, nor to the august committee that was sitting in Athens. They write the news to the Government and the Government sends an order to this pretty little committee, and I'm summoned by this pretty little committee and told that I'm an officer in the Government employ, and that I must have nothing to do with this command to which the Athenians had appointed me. I answered them, 'I shall not abandon of my own free will what my fellow-countrymen have granted me. I shall do so only if these same people do not want me. As an officer I do not recognize the Government, as I have resigned: I was a general and now I'm a simple private in the regulars. I have Fabvier as my commander. If I have done wrong he will punish me. It was to him I swore loyalty as a simple private. The Government has nothing to do with me from now on, nor has the pretty little committee it appointed.'

We learnt that Kioutachis was preparing to move on Athens. Poor Fabvier suggested to the Athenians that he should be in sole control and put all the regulars on to turning Phaleron into an island so the Athenians would not have to run off to the island but stay upon home ground: and Athens would not be put up for sale again. When Gouras heard this he felt the chill of death on him, for this would indeed be the death of the trading house of this gentleman and all his alliance, the citadel of Athens, the milch-cow of Gouras and his alliance. This was what ate up the money and all the produce, the treasury of eastern Greece. To prevent this disaster, of having Piraeus cut off like an island, they all fought against Fabvier and he took off the regular force here over to Methana, to a bare and unhealthy place where he built a fort and houses. And as the place was unhealthy the men were ravaged by sickness and suffered grievous losses. And of all those weapons, cannon, clothing, and other warlike supplies which the regulars had in double supply, not one item was left. And had all that not been lost the Turks would never have become masters of Athens once more and made us buy it back with our blood, nor would men who had fought no battle and made no sacrifice have bought up the land, both fallow and tillage, at a penny an acre and set us to work upon it as their serfs: nor could the bones of our brothers and our kinsmen have been thrown up by the ploughshare. And we have freed ourselves from the Turks to become the slaves of men of an evil seed, the very scum of Europe.

Kioutachis approached with a large force with cavalry, artillery, and all the supplies of war. He occupied Patisia. Most of the villages round Athens paid homage to him, for he had found many of the countryfolk used as pack-mules for carrying stone under our order of justice, and had freed them from their burdens: and others whom we had punished to get hold of their money he released from prison. When the Athenians learned that Kioutachis was coming they asked Fabvier for me, for I was under his command, and I was granted leave to stay while he went off to Methana with his force. And I was given a command with two other Athenians, Symeon Zacharitsas and Neroutsos Metselos, and we were stationed with our men at the walls: and we fought night and day for thirty-four days. Kioutachis destroyed the walls with his cannon and we built them up again. And we had heavy losses in killed and wounded.

One morning, an hour before light, when the city walls had been knocked down at many points and the unceasing cannonade prevented us from repairing the walls, the Turks forced an entry. They had been made drunk with rum first and came on at three points. We move back towards the citadel in a mêlée with the Turks. At the outer and longer walls which faced Patisia, we men of Athens were on guard with that fine brave patriot Eumorphopoulos from Boubounistra; as far as the foot of the citadel there was Mamouris with men from Gouras' troop and villagers. From the pillars by St George's as far as the foot of the citadel there was Stathis Katzikoyannis. Everyone fought like a brave patriot. The country owes them a debt of thanks. Gouras was up on the citadel: whenever there was need, and where the fight was thickest, there he would appear. All in all, everybody fought like a patriot and a brave man. The Turks had gun emplacements and strong-points all round the place and kept up a fire with cannons, mortars, grenade-throwers, and small arms. They were in great number and we were few, up to five hundred men, less rather than more, and our posts were too far spread out.

We went to the command post. There was utter confusion there: women, children, baggage beasts; Serpentzé was full of people. Divine Providence, my brother readers, is great and righteous. The Turks – with every post captured round about in the plain and the citadel: and men, women, and children, all crying, going with such a train of baggage beasts – yet the Turks never got wind of them at all: and the whole lot were saved without a bloody nose amongst them and went off to Ambelaki and Salamis.

We held the low ground for thirty-four days. We went up into the citadel on 3 August 1826. When we entered the citadel there were a lot of cattle in it. Gouras, a man unschooled in blockades, had the lot of them led out and set free outside, where they were taken by the Turks. I said, 'What are you doing, brother? This is a siege!' 'We shan't do this for long,' says he. That was what he had been told by the Europeans who had visited the citadel, and he believed them. When we had no longer even bread, he beat his head with his hands. The cattle were eaten by the Turks, who blessed Gouras' folly. I had had my lesson burnt into me from the citadel of Arta, where I had starved, and from Neokastron where we didn't even have water. I put in the wine and all the supplies of my wife's kinfolk, and bought six hundred okes of rice and pulse and every necessity. And I salted down many oxen and pigs. And this supplied whatever men I had under me, not counting the wounded and the others, till the time that Kriezotis arrived with the regulars: when butter and other necessities had gone up to a hundred groschen the oke and could no more be found.

When we had gone up into the citadel each one of us took the post that had fallen to his share. Papakostas, Eumorphopoulos and myself were at Chryssospeliotissa, where there is a cave and two pillars above. We suffered grievously in killed and wounded, for we were facing Setsos and Kolonaki, where the Turkish cannons were employed. Within Serpentzé there were the Athenians, Symeon, Neroutsos, Petro Litsos and Davaris, as far as the outside of the citadel: from Odysseus' former strong-point and beyond were Gouras' men. By the strong point at Leondari the Athenians were at a point of much danger; the wretched men were without clothing and in poor condition, for Gouras' men had robbed them. And poor Anagnostis Davaris came with so many of his countrymen and his old father Litsos to face death alongside the men of their village, and they brought all their cattle and the clothing from their houses and clothed and fed their wretched fellow-countrymen of Athens, who had been from the very beginning amidst our country's danger. Then they shared out all they had like brothers. Gouras' men, having plundered Athens and having prevented the Athenians from taking out anything with them, were now selling this self-same property back to the Athenians, and it was from their supply that food and clothing came to those who were for the most part serving night and day in the trenches and mines. The Athenians had with them both myself and 'Sapper' Kostas, and had we not fought side by side, the citadel would have been in danger and would have made an untimely surrender. Above on Serpentzé, by the theatre, Katzikoyannis was on guard. Then all those under siege appointed me commandant for the citadel to patrol all round the citadel to maintain order, and to run out to every post where firing started and nip any Turkish attack in the bud. I had men on guard at Odysseus' strong-point and the other one: and I portioned out the water for everyone in the citadel.

Outside Serpentzé, facing Setsos, there was stationed a marriage kinsman of Gouras, Dedoussis, an honest patriot and a brave man: dangerous ground, on which he was killed. I had orders to take my men from Chryssospeliotissa and we went to hold this ground ourselves. The Turks had dug in four strides away or less, deep trenches with baskets of earth on the parapets. I also had two strong-points dug and we made loopholes up on the citadel and took up station there. By night we made up the strong-points and by day the guns on Setsos knocked them down for us. For it faced us and was close at hand. We were losing heavily in killed. They suffered as much and more on the citadel, for it was stony ground. The men were slaughtered by the shells and mortar bombs; the graves up on the citadel became full and we buried the dead at Serpentzé.

The citadel was now ready to devour those who had fed upon it for so many years and had been nourished like prize stock; and every day the slaughter went on. Gouras had prepared himself a famous temple, which he had heaped over with earth to stop bombs from breaking in, and he installed his family within and stayed there himself. He brought into the citadel his marriage kinsman Stavris Vlachos, Karoris, Varelas Zacharitsas, all his party, all his alliance; and provided them with a fine cellar. And he made of them a council of elders and appointed as their secretary Dionysios Sourmelis, who had written such flattering things about him when he and all this alliance had control of the plain. He brought them into the citadel, put them in the cellar, where they ate and drank without one of them ever setting his foot outside the cellar door. For outside there were bombs and grenades and cannon-shell, and every man went in danger, but in the cellar there was a snug safety. Except for Nikolakis Zacharitsas. This poor fellow came out and fought like the rest of the patriots and shared danger with us. All the others were in the cellar: and Gouras stayed with his family. We went and fought to the death with the Turks outside the citadel: the council of elders and Sourmelis would write to the Government and to the Kapetans and to the press, 'Today the commander Gouras made a sally against the Turks and won such-and-such a victory.' Every so often those in the cellar would sing the praises of those in the temple. We saw this written in the papers, for they were sent from outside to Anastassis Lidorikis and Vlachos, the brother-in-law and marriage kinsman of Gouras.

Then we fell to quarrelling and reproaches, and I told them, 'Unless we see every letter and all of us sign them we won't send another messenger on foot out of the camp.' And we followed this rule from then on. Then I told Gouras, 'You should hold some post outside the citadel, and then you can have dispatches written according to your exploits.' He was a brave gallant, quick on a point of honour. We went out and there some days after he was killed, and it was said that I had killed him. May I not render my soul to God at the latter day if I had any such plan or if this idea passed through my mind. Later that famous temple was destroyed by bombardment, and Gouras' family was lost with so many other souls. From all these there escaped alive but one innocent boy; all the others were killed.

We had dug out a mine running out from Odysseus' strong-point to the strong-point of Leondari: we had put in the gunpowder and the fuse ran from there to the mid-point of the trench. The fuse of the mine was of cotton. The post at Leondari was guarded by the ragged Athenians. At their head was Danilis, a brave man and an honest patriot. He was later taken prisoner along with Mitros Lekas, and these good patriots were impaled by the Turks at Euripus. The men had made water in the trench as there was nowhere else to go, for the Turks were firing on them from Karassoui and other places: and they were losing men every day. The Turks decided to make a charge through this place and a good number of them had formed up at the strong-point under which our mine had been dug. We brought our men into line and some of us went forward and stood our ground with our knives in our hands. We set light to the fuse but it was damp and did not catch – the flame went some way and then died out.

Then I saw an example of the spirit of patriotism. An Athenian took the burning tinder in his hand and went and threw it on the fuse: for his country's sake he treated fire like water, but still it did not catch. The Turks rushed on us – we gave them a hammering and went hunting after them among the houses to the edge of their line: but we failed with the mine which was to have wiped them out. We killed a few of them, among them a man of importance. His death was a great grief to Kioutachis, for he was a very brave man. While we still held the place I had one day gone beyond the walls into the plain with about ten men, when the cavalry rode down on us, and we faced death. We stood our ground and killed their commander and another soldier, which cooled the Turks' ardour, and we found time to save ourselves. Kioutachis mourned for this man too as he was dearly loved by him.

When we moved up into the citadel we still held the quarter of the Plaka as far as the Albanian gate. Below the citadel among the houses there was a church, and a mine had been run under it by the famous immortal 'Sapper' Kostas, a brave and honest patriot who fought like a lion for his country with his skill and with his musket. This brave man had wrought miracles at Missolonghi and everywhere. We were together and fought side by side like brothers night and day. And we were working with the men, the good Athenians, digging the mines: and we were all bound together in love without cease. My country, you owe much to this fighter Kostas. Kioutachis offered him a fortune to win him over: for your sake, my country, he spurned all.

He had a mine under the church. A crowd of Turks came up: we joined battle, and pretended to be routed (we wanted to abandon the quarter, as we were few and our line too long). So the Turks came to grips with us. We were holding Chryssospeliotissa and the foot of the citadel where we had redoubts, and there we took post. When the church was full of the enemy, inside and in the galleries, there stood up two brave gallants, Michalis Kounelis of Athens and Thomas, either of Argyrokastro or Hormova; these two brave immortals went and fired the fuse: happily they saved themselves, but the church and all the Turks went up into the air. Then the other Turks near by where routed and we shot at them point blank, from below and above from the citadel, and destroyed them. And there was a great slaughter of the Turks.

From outside Serpentzé, where we were on guard, the Turks were driving their mines towards us. They were making also for the citadel and were working from the three pit-heads. The Turks were close to us, and there had come up a young pasha with a fine troop. And they came very close to us there in their trenches and hurled insults at us and called us cowards, Jews. At Missolonghi too they had been gallants and we good-for-nothings: and in a day or two, so they said, they would hem us in with their trenches and take us prisoners and have us pass under their swords. 'Sapper' Kostas and I were tired out, for we had been digging mines night and day to destroy those of the Turks. It was always myself who rallied the Athenians (I loved them as they did me) and guided them to the mine pits where we worked together. I had all the sons of the great houses with me and I protected them from the cannibals who even within the citadel wanted to rob those to whom so little property remained: to strip them even of that. As we were tired from working day and night, I told them to slaughter an ox I had kept alive for the men to have a little meat. And they cooked a meal for us. So I invited the 'Sapper' and the priest who was Kriezotis' brother, who was with Stathis Katzikoyannis on the same stretch of the Serpentzé wall, keeping watch from inside with ourselves on the outside. I had also invited Papakostas, a brave gallant and good patriot and a kinsman of Gouras; I had been at odds with Gouras but I was close friends with Papakostas, because he knew who was to blame and who was in the right. Just as we were beginning our meal, the Turks began to hurl insults at us through the night. I had my posse with me as we were all eating together with our guests; say I, 'Brothers, I've brought you the supplies you are eating, the wine, the raki and all your provisions. Everybody else on the citadel is eating dry bread. Right then! It's not to be borne that we should eat while the Turks are shaming us. I want some Turkish baskets from their trenches!' I was answered by these brave men – all sons of great Athenian houses and a few Thebans whom I always had at my side. When I had made them this speech they felt jealous for their good name and inspired with patriotism. We had not made a sally into the Turkish trenches before; this was the first time, and they answered

'Let us drink one cup more from your hands.' I gave them this. They said. 'And give us your blessing.' I told them 'You have first the blessing of God, who's the commander of all things, and the blessing of the country.'

They all rose up and went against the Turks in their trenches and routed them: and they killed half a dozen Turks and took a few baskets. The Turks returned to the charge. This was an ugly moment for it was their first move, and if any of them found their courage they would keep it for all time. The cry comes, 'Come out yourself, captain.' I'm a man who loves his life but I was stung by my respect for my good name, for I was to blame for having proposed this plan to them. So we all went forward together and gave the Turks a beating. But after a little they went for us with their knives and went hunting after us as far as our post. About two of us were wounded. We gave them another beating. They returned to the charge. While we were beating them back we took some booty and among it a long coat. I had with me Katzikoyannis' secretary, a man called Alexandris, the son of a great house, a youth with a good name to maintain, and a person of sharp wits and quality. I told him, 'You must back me up in what I'm going to do: I'm going to play a trick.' 'I'll do whatever you tell me,' says the youth. I fill the Turkish coat with earth and the pair of us pick it up and I bring it to our post whither our comrades had fled from the Turks, and I call for the 'Sapper' and Kriezotis' brother, the priest, and Papakostas – to shout so that the Greeks will hear me: I call for the three of them by name, 'Come up and I'll give the three of you this treasure hoard of the Turks we have taken, and you three can guard it while I go over and fetch the other that's over there. Stay back till I've sealed it first to stop you stealing from me! I unwound a garter from my leg and tied the bundle up and got out my seal to seal it and Alexandris pretended to hunt for wax. When the Greeks heard the words 'money' and 'seals' they drew their knives and fell upon the Turks like lions. And in truth they took a heap of treasure: they took muskets, they took swords and they killed many Turks: and we took possession of the three mines they were driving against us to wipe out ourselves and the citadel. We took some two dozen prisoners, their sappers and others; their coffee stores which they had there and all their supplies: wine and raki by the barrel-full. We went hunting after them as far as Karassoui: there was a large force of Turks there and their redoubts, and we called a halt. We destroyed all their entrenchments from Karassoui up to our post and took more than two thousand baskets from them.

So this ground was held by us with Papakostas, Gouras, and that good, brave patriot Thomas of Argyrokastro. We all held our ground fighting against the Turks – and the 'Sapper' joined up the three Turkish mines into one and ran it into our own: and, as we held the whole length of it, we ran a mine under a Turkish post where there was a kind of square upon which the Turks would gather to talk and drink coffee, and there below we piled up gunpowder without the

Turks knowing a thing about it. We gathered all the baskets together and built up the post, my two strong-points, and wherever else there was need. It was then that I lost one of the rarest of young gallants, Theodore Stamas, the son of Peter, an Athenian: I had him as my ensign: a very honourable, brave, good man. When we had routed the Turks he had rushed on to Karassoui and been killed together with Prapas, the brother of Pagonas. They were mourned for by all the citadel, and I was bitterly grieved as I had had him at my side for so many years.

The Turks began to dig their trenches and drove them as far as that post of theirs where we had secretly set the gunpowder. Then the troops gathered at my post and we started a friendly talk with the Turks to bring many of them to the place, so we would have the lot of them in our power when we set fire to the mine. Our men deployed into line: I gave out a bottle of rum to every ten men: there was one man to whom I gave rum, the leader of my posse, who did not let his comrades have a drink but drank the lot himself and got drunk. We were all prepared, but the Turks – the place was full of them and we would have wiped them out when we touched off the fuse – they knocked some holes in this mine to weaken the blast. As bad luck would have it, some gunpowder had spilt into this hole. The flame reaching this place, this gunpowder caught fire. We knew nothing about mines, we supposed this fire was the mine going off. That drunken man drew his knife and started shouting. The Turks got wind of the plan. We moved forward in disorder; the Turks withdrew, so we rushed upon them and risked suffering ourselves what we wished to visit on the Turks. By God's grace the flame caught before we got close and sent a shower of bedrock into the air. And not a man was hurt, either of ourselves or the Turks. Then the Turks fell upon is with their knives and drove us back. And there began a storm of small-arms fire from the Turks, along with mortar bombs, shells and grenades. Some of us were wounded and there was killed a young Athenian, the son of a great house, called Nestor Kopidis, the friend of my ensign, a very brave lad. Then we fared badly. The Turks pushed us back into our posts outside and they might have forced us into the citadel. Then God gives me inspiration and I take a lighted torch in my hand and shout, 'Fire off the other mine now the Turks have come close and we'll wipe them out.'

The Turks hear this, see the light, and fly back, and the immortal Greeks come to grips with them: and they get a fine taste of the sword's edge. Once more we destroyed their trenches, and took many heads and a pile of booty, muskets, swords, and clothes. We hadn't a mine left nor a fuse to set one off with. But from then on the Turks had learnt much wisdom: they neither hurled insults at us nor came near us. We had got the measure of them. Five or ten could go out and give them a beating. I had one young gallant called Hadjis Meletis, an Athenian. Every time he went out he'd bring back one or two heads to the post: a brave, honest gallant. The Turks were driving a mine underneath the citadel;

we promised him ten thousand groschen and sent him down from the citadel by himself at the end of a rope, and he spied out this mine; so the citadel was saved. We uncovered the sap from above, and he escaped by the skin of his teeth with all Turkey at his heels. And we didn't give him ten farthings. (Later I presented him before Agostino and Viaro Capodistrias. 'No money in the treasury!' But there was plenty for the spies to pay them well to find out what every house-holder was doing in his own house.)

While I was sharing out the rum among the men before making our charge for the mine, there was with us one of Gouras' officers, a favourite of his. He had been put in the way of much profit by Gouras and was called John Balomenos – the devil has him now, sewn up and sealed, this disgrace to his country. This shame-less man, while we were in the thick of the fight and trading gashes with the Turks, led off his comrades and fled to Salamis: and there they fought a battle with the loose women: they had left their post, staring in the Turks' faces, above my own post, empty. Then poor Gouras – I had fallen out with him badly by reason of these deceitful men who surrounded him, they and his friends from Athens who gave him corrupt counsel, and ruined this brave fighter, and it was for this reason that I would not speak with him – then he came to my post in grief and my soul burned with sorrow to see him thus. He had grievous complaints to tell me of. I told him, 'Brother, from today consider me like the friend I once was, and even closer. I'm in the fight', say I, 'night and day, as you see, and while we're here I'm your brother, but when this fight finishes I do not desire your friendship.' (He had held our crowns at my wedding.) He said, 'I have had you as a brother for so many years: I made you my kinsman, why do you not desire my friendship?' 'Because when you came to Athens I warned you not to have an eye for your own enrichment, as you would bring disgrace on yourself and Athens would lie in danger because of you. For you are no small personage, to do the city but slight harm. What can I hope for now? You have grown rich on the pillage and plunder of Athens. Those shameless people whom you had at your side – it was August when we moved up into the garrison and in the self-same month they tried to desert you and made off as you have seen them do. We have been fighting to the death with the Turks, and Balomenos and the rest made off. And they have set you against the Athenians and aroused their enmity against you because these people have robbed them. They are cowards, dogs that hang around the slaughter-house. What need have you for riches, which you have gained already, with so many coffers full of treasure buried away? You have paid men – have you not? – to maintain your command to win glory for yourself and benefit for the country, not for them to be pressing you to let them quit after one month. The tricksters have put the suspicion in your mind that I shall murder you by treachery because of Odysseus, whom you murdered. Brother, your benefactor should never have met with such an end, nor was it for you to have compassed it. Now it has happened. Remember what I told you at Agoriani, that they would set us on to kill one another. Then you listened to me and held your hand: now, it is happening. Now, however, you must know who are your friends and who the tricksters. A man is enriched not only by money, but by his good deeds.'

The poor man's eyes filled with tears: his conscience was touched because of the deed he had done to Odysseus. He said, 'If I live and come out of here I don't want to know those scoundrels any more. As for money,' he said, 'I'm about making my will and I will leave money to found schools and other benefits to the country. And I'll leave the half of everything to you.' I said, 'May you live to enjoy your wealth, brother, and perform good deeds for the country and wipe out this stain which is upon you, for everyone who holds you as his friend has been saddened. For my part I want nothing. From now on if you listen to me and hearken to whatever comes into my head for me to tell you, we shall be brothers and friends as we once were: otherwise, each of us can mind his own business. As for those friends of yours, I want no friendship with them, as I know them for what they have done to you and to the country. And those whom you keep inside here as a council of elders, together with the others, liars, they are digging a mine to blow you up.' He answered, 'I know just how all these people have entangled me, but there's nothing I can do for the moment.' We kissed and swore from then on we would be better friends than ever before.

When we had made this agreement, his wife and his kinsmen come to hear of it and rejoiced. I went and saw them in the temple. We agreed that he should come to dine with me at my post that evening with Papakostas and Katzikoyannis, for I had fresh supplies, meat and other things. Poor Katzikoyannis was very sad. So many of his kinsmen had been killed and a nephew of his that day. He was a fine patriot and a good man. And all his kinsmen had been slaughtered in the citadel. When we had got ready the meal, all his allies told Gouras that they would leave as Balomenos had left. Then poor Gouras was bitterly grieved. I told him, 'Waste no time in bitterness. Make an understanding with them for eight days, in which we must write of this to the Government so that they may send fresh men, and in the days left to us let them help us dig the mines round Serpentzé and all the gates of the citadel and wherever there is need, for we are at work digging mines everywhere and getting all these places ready, and this needs much work. So let us hold the men here for that purpose. And at the same time write to the Government to send us a fresh garrison. And tell those who want to quit to make out a report for us to send to the Government and in eight days a reply will come, either the Government is sending us fresh men or not: if not, let these people quit. If fresh men come, we shall not need the mines: or else if they don't come there will be very few of us left and we shall shorten our line by withdrawing from Serpentzé. And when the Turks come on and we cannot stand our ground we'll touch off the fuses and blow Serpentzé into the air with the Turks who'll be there, and in this way we'll go back fighting into the temple [the Parthenon] itself. And there we'll lay a mine all round and send ourselves and the Turks and the temple into the air. For if the Government does not send us fresh men – or if they refuse to come – shall we abandon the citadel without a fight and quit after doing battle for a month and a half? And where shall we live to hide from the shame of the world, you above all, who have told all the foreign travellers and the people of this town that you could fight on in the citadel for two or three years?' He liked my views and we spoke about all these matters with his men: and we proposed that all of us should work to dig the mines.

He composed the letters for the Government as agreed, and waited for the moon to go down for me to send the messenger to the Government, for messengers used to leave from my post. Poor Gouras was very sad about his wretched comrades who had become greedy for their lives in that hour of danger for their country and their leader. Faced with the fine provisions stored in the citadel, they had behaved like fearless heroes. And they had devoured the poor Athenians. When I beheld his grief I spoke with some Athenians of high place and they went and told him, 'Do not take it too hard that those men want to quit. This citadel will be guarded by us who won it from the Turks. And we shall not give it them back now unless they kill us.'

So Gouras and the others sat down and we took our meal. We sang and made merry. Gouras and Papakostas asked me to sing, for we had gone so long without singing, so long since the self-seekers set us to quarrelling so they might accomplish their evil plans. I sang well, and I gave them this song:

> The Sun had set (ah, men of Greece, a Sunset for you!)
> And the Moon was no more to be seen,
> No more to be seen the clear Morning Star,
> Nor the Star of Eve that shines in its place,
> For these four held council, and spoke in secret,
> The Sun spins round and tells them, spins round and says
> 'Last night when I set I hid myself behind a little rock,
> And I heard the weeping of women, and the mourning of men
> For those slain heroes lying in the field,
> And all the earth soaked in their blood –
> Poor souls all gone below in their country's cause.'

Gouras groaned in his misery and said, 'Brother Makriyannis, may God grant a good end to this: you have never sung with such feeling before. May this song bode well for us.' 'I was in the mood,' I said, 'for we have not sung for so long.'

For formerly in our camps we were always making merry.

The fighting started and a fierce firing flared up. I took my men and went to our appointed post. I stayed there some time while we fought. I made a tour round the posts outside. I went to my quarters to send out the messenger to the Government, as the moon had begun to set. Men came up and said, 'Come quick, Gouras has been killed at his post. He fired at the Turks, they shot back at the flash and hit him in the temple, and he never spoke a word.' I went, and we took him on our shoulders and put him inside a dungeon; his family laid him out and we buried him.

We all gathered together and I made a speech to the ungrateful soldiers and told them it was their fault he had been killed because they had left their posts and he had gone on alone. 'And every minute you were pressing him to let you quit.' The besieged appointed a committee of Gouras' widow, Papakostas, Katzikoyannis, Eumorphopoulos and myself to keep order until the Government should send fresh men. We wrote to them of the death of Gouras and sent other letters. Gouras was killed at the beginning of October outside the citadel by the upper gate.

A good Christian came and told us secretly that the Turks were about to move in great force and would seize the arches below Serpentzé which were facing my post and would make their way to the citadel. For in that part lay both the pitheads of the Turkish mines and our own. We too had made ready a mine against them but had not yet put powder in it. So when we learned of the Turkish move we urged the 'Sapper' to go and lay the fuse and put in the powder. Says he, 'The mine runs underneath the Turks and I'll make a noise when I'm laying the fuse and the Turks will hear me: and I'll be in danger. If you keep watch for me I'll go, otherwise I won't.' 'Get in and do your work,' I said, 'and I'll keep watch for you.' The 'Sapper' went into the mine. I had been without sleep for so many nights, as we had been working night and day to make some sort of entrenchment and I had been building my strong-points, that I dropped off to sleep. Hearing the noise the 'Sapper' was making, the Turks gathered in force, made a charge and got into my outer strong-point (for I had divided it into two, and had a vaulted way by which I moved between the posts). Then my men fought hand to hand with the Turks.

I start up suddenly from where I have been resting, and climb up to the strong-point. The Turks shoot at me and I shoot into the mass of them. I'm hit and wounded in the neck. So I take a step to get down from the strong-point and fall. It was a narrow space; my men were routed from the other strong-point. I was trampled on as they passed, and in such a narrow space was almost knocked to pieces. They saw the blood and supposed I was dead. When all these had passed and but few stayed outside, these too were making ready to get inside the citadel, and then the Turks would enter at the same moment as they. Katzikoyannis was inside: he had left his post and run off to the inner gate of the citadel by the dome: and not one person was fighting the Turks. Then I got to my feet, half dizzy, and kept some ten of our men out at the point of the knife. I refused to let them in. I closed the door which we had left open and we joined battle again. And we fought it with our pistols; neither the Turks nor we could fire our muskets. We fought for more than three hours there. The Turks made a rush, wounded me again in the head, on the top. My body was covered with blood. The men tried to carry me inside, so I say, 'Brothers, go we inside or stay we out we are lost if we do not hold the Turks and set the 'Sapper' free.' For the Turks had the pitheads of the mines and the 'Sapper' at their mercy. Say I, 'If we do not hold and the 'Sapper' is taken, the citadel is lost and we with it. But hold we must and hold we will.'

Then the brave Greeks held their ground like lions. There came to us a brave gallant from Katzikoyannis called Dalamangas, with his Egyptian servant and some ten others of my own, and we went into battle and fought. As the sun became lower I handed the men out more cartridges and yet more of our comrades came up. A fresh reinforcement came for the Turks. They came on us with a rush, got into the archways, seized hold of the lot, opened up loopholes, and fired into the citadel. They came on at a rush to take both us and our strong-point. Dalamangas and some half dozen others were killed there. I was wounded again, an ugly cut on the back of my head: the shreds of my cap went into the bone to the skin over my brain. I fell down like one dead. The men pulled me in; then I came to myself. I told them, 'Leave me to be killed here, so that I'll never live to see my post under a Turkish foot.' Then the poor Greeks were very grieved for me. They fought bravely, threw the Turks out of our strong-point and sent them back to the archway: from there they shot into the citadel. Then the 'Sapper' came out and joined us. He said he would stay there himself, to let me climb back to the citadel and be bandaged by the doctor. I told him, 'Be off with you inside: if I die the citadel is not lost: if you die, it is.' Our own men climbed down Serpentzé and threw lighted rags and straw into the archway. The Turks were stifled by the smoke: the whole troop had their muskets at the ready. Towards evening they made a bid to escape; our men fired into the brown and a fair number of the Turks were killed.

On no other day was there such a battle or such slaughter on our side. We lost many officers and that good patriot Neroutsos Mertzelos. Shells, mortar bombs, grenades and small-arms fire rained down on us. The battle began at dawn and ended in the evening. I was carried up into the citadel. Kourtali, the doctor, did not wish to operate on me for I was gravely wounded and had lost almost all my blood. Then those who were within the citadel put it in writing to him that he was free from all suspicion (for he feared I would die, and they would say he had murdered me). Then he operated on me, and I came near to dying from the pains in my head and the trampling I had suffered upon my body, on my belly. Something was broken inside me through this trampling and I suffer bleeding to this day. The doctor left the bones where they were in my head, for if he had disturbed them if would have broken the skin over my brain, and that would surely have been the end of me.

The battle took place in the month of October, six days after the death of Gouras. When this battle was over the besieged sent word to the Government and Karaiskakis, who was in command outside, in the Peloponnese, and Kriezotis and Mamouris were sent with troops into the citadel. Then Mamouris strove to be made garrison commander – so that if the citadel were relieved he should once more have the Athenians as his slaves. It was Mamouris' brother-in-law, Yannakos Vlachos, who had been installed by him as a member of the Government, that gave advice to Mamouris; he also counselled him to confer with his brother Stouris Vlachos to give effect to this purpose. When we saw Mamouris' intent and his desire to be made garrison commander, so that this fabrica di cogion could suck the blood from the wretched Athenians, to rescue them from such crime against God I conferred with Kriezotis, the Lekas family, the Phokas family, Eumorphopoulos, and with whatever Athenian officers were in the camp, made a count and found ourselves to be twenty in all: those who were in alliance with Mamouris were four. I proposed that in the posts outside the citadel we should assign men according to the numbers under each commander, who was to guard their posts with as many men as the position demanded. In the watchtower of the citadel and in the store-houses which are the key-point of the citadel – and if you hold these places you have the citadel in your hands – in these two places each commander from the highest to the lowest should send one man apiece, so that to each place they would go in measure twenty of ours and four of theirs. We made a point of holding these two places with the majority of our own men so that if a quarrel sprang up we should have these places in our hands and suffer no hurt. The citadel was in my hands, as I had been appointed town commandant. And if the citadel were to be liberated, the Athenians were to take it over. This secret union of ours was put in writing. Having bound ourselves to these terms I brought Mamouris with his friends and the others to my quarters for them to dine, for I was not eating myself as I was wounded and still sick. When they had eaten I made them this proposal. It came as a bitter shock to them. We told them that each one of us had put his hand to this and there could be no other way of carrying on. I said, 'This must be agreed to, and there must be a committee to govern the citadel till the siege should be raised, and then it is up to the Government to re-appoint you.' They refused outright. Many of them begged me to stand aside. Gouras' widow begged me. I told them, 'This is the right course to take: if you accept it, well and good, otherwise we shall all quit, and you can stay here to fight. Or else you can quit and we'll fight.' We had a long quarrel before they agreed to the plan we wanted – the right one. But ill-luck dogs the country and the Athenians; the citadel fell to the Turks.

Translated by H.A. Lidderdale

Ioannis Karasoutsas (1822–1873)

Neglected today, Karasoutsas is perhaps the most delicate craftsman among the Athenian poets of the mid nineteenth century who wrote in the archaizing *katharevousa*, and as such he had the respect of Seferis. A strong liberal, Karasoutsas also produced an early translation of *Uncle Tom's Cabin*. The frail and wistful *Weltschmerz* that brought the poet to eventual suicide is tangible in the two poems selected here, both taken from his volume of collected poems, *The Lyre* (1860).

To a Star

O Thou who in yon ether's boundless vast
   Dost show so doubting and uncertain light,
As glittering shells from depths of ocean cast,
   Now lost to view, now back, with gleaming bright:

Should that amass of diamonds which gem
   The heav'ns be God's mantle over all,
Thou art a little brilliant on the hem
   Of those thick folds which round the Maker fall;

But if no garment, but an altar high,
   Where thousand thousand lights in worship burn,
Thou a small lamp, a spark from the northern sky,
   One holy ray wilt yet unceasing turn.

Yet if this firmament, if this great dome,
   With all its emerald and sapphire host,
Nor altar is, nor raiment, but outcome
   Of worlds on worlds in long extension lost –

Parent of Beauty art thou then – and Light!
   A sun with planets moving in thy train,
While every planet hath attendants bright,
   Like birds their mother following o'er the plain:

Then, like a giant upon shoulders broad,
   Thou bearest earths, and seas, and hills, and vales;
Myriads of towns, where strifes have long abode.
   Tell now one page of thy historic tales.

Is it with thee, O world, as it is here?
   Are thousands born, do thousands daily die?
Do thousands laugh, while thousands shed the tear?
   Are funeral, bridal lamps still passing by?

What laws doth Justice to thy children lend?
   Doth a pure freedom in thy councils speak?
Or before tyrants do thy people bend
   The knee, and do the strong oppress the weak?

O Star! whilst now to thee my eye upstrains,
   Maybe with thee are fleets in war array,
The crash of battles echoing o'er thy plains,
   And armies falling on the blood-stained way!

And yet thy children with their noise and strife
   Within one little point are closed and held,
With all thy silent dead passed out of life
   In that one glittering speck by us beheld –

That spark which glints in highest heav'n! yet this
   Nor place nor hour changeth, but holds good,
Though if Night came, and 'twere not, who would miss
   A grain i' the sands, a leaf from out the wood!

O Star! who setting, rising evermore,
   We 'mong the hosts of other stars neglect,
That faithfully thy path still goest o'er,
   Yet what thou art by us so little reckt:

When Night ariseth, thou like timid maid
   Com'st forth, the last of all the stars in space;
Scarce twinkling, when behind the hills in shade
   Thou hastest first 'mong all to hide thy face.

Unnamed the Argive left thee. From afar –
   Now – beautiful thou comest as of yore,
Through the blue ether flashing; yet, O Star,
   A Night will come when *thou* shalt shine no more.

The Last Dryad

A thousand winters have despoiled my lustrous verdant hair,
But when spring smiles, and fresh leaves to the bare boughs bring repair,
  I bloom again.

So far agone yet seem to me my first years until now,
That if some other, or the same old self I dare not know –
  If I remain.

What sweet sound that! was it some old companion's voice that spoke?
No; the north wind hath fiercely blown, and 'twas my own lov'd oak
  That whispered low:

Ah, sad one! thou forgettest too that thou hast lived beyond
The law of Fate. With thine old age the breezes make no bond,
  But scorn thee now.

Man's race once flourished here: in years past hither came
The hunters, and the rustics brought their toils to snare the game
  These woods among.

When the wild beast went slowly forth from out his thicket lair,
The Sun God, as those hunters, was not so swift, so fair,
  So brave, or strong.

With booty safe, when came the dextrous youth, he little knew
What other secret wounds had made those arrows which he threw,
  Unknowing where.

The nymph who, breathless and unseen, for him had waited long,
Found all her kinship with the gods, 'gainst love to make her strong,
  Unavailing there.

When to my shade he wearied came, with what fond zeal and care
For his refreshing, out from my dark leaves I shook the air,
  Bade the zephyrs haste.

For he to me was much more dear, yea, dearer far than they –
Those dusky Satyrs who once came, my ears polluting aye
  With lyres unchaste.

Translated by E.M. Edmonds

E.D. Roïdis (1822–1900)

Roïdis is, along with Nikos Kazantzakis (q.v.), the only writer in this volume to have had an English-language film made out of the book represented here: *Pope Joan*, a costume romp with Liv Ullmann in the title role, came out in 1972. It isn't easy to know what the bitter scepticism of the author would have made of this, especially when Lawrence Durrell has, in the general perception, got the credit with his English version of *Pope Joan*. In an Enlightenment spirit more mordant yet than that of Gibbon, Roïdis set out in 1866 to retell the story of the allegedly female ninth-century pope in such a way as to combine a mock-scholarly apparatus of preface, introduction, footnotes and endnotes with biting and rhetorically artful darts at the Christian religion, its Eastern Orthodox form not excepted. He was prosecuted for his pains and excommunicated, which only earned his work further notoriety. Kazantzakis, excommunicated for *The Last Temptation*, inherited Roïdis' misogyny and his wish to shock but not his irony or the high finish of his classicizing Greek. And if Roïdis' work has a true successor, it would probably be in Cavafy's much more ambivalent poems about Christianity. In the passage quoted below, the devout young nun Joan is falling in love with the monk Frumentius in a delicious parody of Canto V of Dante's *Inferno*.

Pope Joan (*extract*)

Ennui and idleness, are, I think, the most powerful incentives to piety. Anyhow, Joan, who formerly considered her theological knowledge merely as a means of livelihood, reciting passages from the Scriptures and the Fathers, like Ristori the verses of Alfieri, when she found herself within the four walls of her cell, finding her existence no existence at all, began to consider her future, a strange occupation for a maiden of seventeen years. But monasteries have ever been the palaces of curious fancies. The Egyptian monks watered staves until they bore fruit: the holy women of Hungary ate lice and the Quietists remained for years with their eyes fixed upon their bodies expecting to see the light of truth come forth. But Joan, given up to metaphysical studies, spent the day at one time poring over the writings of St Augustine, who described as an eye-witness the delights of the blessed and the flames of Hell, while at another time, burying her fingers in her fair hair, she put questions to herself concerning our present and future existence, questions which all the inhabitants of this vale of tears address despairingly to themselves, and to which confessors and theologians reply with subterfuges and 'common places', in the same manner as ministers answer troublesome place-hunters. Strange dreams disturbed the poor maiden's rest: the good St Liobba no longer promised her inexhaustible pleasures, but evil spirits shook their frightful horns and angels brandished two-edged swords. At one time she hoped for the joys of Paradise; at another she dreaded the claws of the Evil One. One day she believed in the truths of Christianity from the Gospel to the miracles of St Martin, and for three days doubted everything. At one time she bowed her head beneath the divine sentence which weighs heavily upon us all: at another, if she had any stones she would have thrown them against the firmament, to try to break it. In a word, she had been attacked by that monomania into which everyone falls who attempts in all sincerity to solve the mysterious problem of our existence. What we are, whence came we, what shall be our future destiny? Such questions, insoluble in the brain of man, like wax in water, she attempted to solve. During that time poor Joan's hair remained unkempt and her teeth idle: her eyes were red from want of sleep, her face pale, and her nails black. Such, according to the illustrious Pascal, should be the natural state of the true Christian upon earth: he ought to live perpetually between the fear of punishment and the hope of salvation, and to seek, with sighs and groans, the road to Paradise in the darkness. But however aristocratic and suitable to lofty spirits this condition may be, I do not desire it for you, dear reader. I myself prefer the cheerful and happy piety of those good Christians, who, singing anthems in honour of the saints and eating lobsters on Friday, await with tranquillity the delights of Paradise. Many, wishing to make a show of their superiority, affect compassion for these unhappy mortals; but I myself envy the calm repose of their soul and their double chins.

Diseases, the plague, the small-pox, love and its attendant evils, have this advantage, that we are only subject to them once. Such also was the nature of Joan's metaphysical complaint. After having scratched her head for three months, in search of the solution of the insoluble riddle, she at last shut her books, and, opening the window of her cell, smelt the fragrance of spring. April was nearly over; nature, clotted with verdure, smiling and exhaling perfumes, resembled a maiden decked out by a skilful lady's-maid. The scents of spring intoxicated the youthful recluse, who, for three months buried in the darkness of her cell and of metaphysics, contemplated and breathed, with increasing avidity, the scent of the grass in the meadows and the perfumes of violets. According to poets and physicians, there exists between springtime and the heart, when we are twenty years of age, a relation as mysterious and inexplicable as that between Socrates and Alcibiades. The sight of the green trees, of the soft grass and shady grottoes makes us feel the want of a companion in this Paradise. Joan, who felt her bosom heave like the waves of the sea, remembered her dream and the hopes with which she had been inspired when she entered the monastery in which she had found nothing but ennui, old books, and troublesome thoughts. 'Liobba! Liobba! when wilt thou fulfil thy promises?' she cried, shaking the bars of her prison in despair.

But the bars were iron, and the young nun's hands, from want of use, had become as white and tender as the wax of candles; she therefore let them go, and, having in her cell neither a dog to beat nor crockery to smash, she hid her face between her hands and began to weep. There is nothing sweeter than tears, when another's hand or lips are ready to wipe away or quench this 'rain of the heart', to use the language of the Indians. But when we weep alone, our tears are then as real and bitter as any truth in the world; and still more bitter when we weep, not for the loss of some earthly blessing, but because we cannot enjoy that upon which we have fixed our eyes.

The noise of footsteps in the corridor soon distracted Joan's attention from her gloomy reflections. The door opened, and the Abbess entered, holding by the hand a beardless youth wearing the robe of St Benedict, whose eyes were modestly fixed upon his shoes.

'Joan,' said the Lady Superior, presenting the young monk to our astonished heroine. 'The Superior of Fulda, the holy Raban Maur, being about to send missionaries into Thuringia, has asked me for a copy of the Epistles of St Paul, written in letters of gold on a valuable parchment, that with the brightness of the gold he may dazzle the eyes of the unbelievers and inspire them with greater respect for the truths of the Gospel. This young Benedictine is Father Frumentius, distinguished, like yourself, for piety and beautiful writing. Work in company with him until you have finished the commission of our brother Raban. Here is the golden ink: you already have pens: your food I will send from my own table. Farewell, my children!'

With these words St Blidtrude went out, shutting the door behind her, like the Moldavian peasants when the ruler of the village pays a visit to their wives. But St Blidtrude was one of those excellent women, whose mind is unable to imagine evil. If she had seen a monk embracing one of the nuns she would have believed that he was bestowing a blessing upon her. Having been disfigured by the small-pox during her childhood, she had never known anything but the kisses of innocence and could not believe that there were any others in the world. Besides, at that time, the followers of St Benedict, both men and women, all lived together without distinction in monasteries.

Once left to themselves, the youthful pair, knowing how valuable time was, turned up the wristbands of their frocks, and immediately began the task of copying the Epistles of St Paul. For fifteen days the young monk entered Joan's cell every morning, and worked together with her until the evening. This young man of eighteen years, who had been since his boyhood engaged in copying books of ritual, and had never read the Bible, the Confessions of St Augustine, or any other sacred volume, was as pure and chaste as snow; so that the copying of St Paul's Epistles proceeded rapidly.

As time went on, they began to look forward with dread to the time when their task would be finished and they would have to part. The copying was nearly over: there only remained the Epistle to the Hebrews, after which was to come the bitter and inevitable separation. Joan, like a second Penelope, frequently erased during the night what she had written the day before. Her companion perceived the device, guessed its object, and blushed or uttered sighs powerful enough to turn the sails of a windmill, but this was all: the day passed like the rest. But neither you nor I, dear reader, have so many days to lose. Besides, as I am writing a true history, I cannot imitate those poets or authors who, heaping together emotions, tears, blushes or other Platonic furniture, couple their honeyed verses in pairs, as husbandmen yoke oxen, or turn out periods as round as the bosom of Aphrodite. The great Dante called such people 'panderers', but I myself like neither the name nor the profession. Abandoning, therefore, such fashions to Plato, Ovid and Petrarch, and the whining disciples of their school, I shall always exhibit the truth, naked and unadorned, just as it has left the well.

The two lovers had finished copying the last of St Paul's Epistles, and the sun, which Galileo had not yet condemned to immobility, was finishing its daily revolution. It was the hour when the oxen return to the stall and when Christians salute the Virgin with the *Ave Maria*. The bell had summoned the nuns to evening prayer, and no noise broke the silence in the corridor of the monastery. Joan was sitting near the window, turning over the leaves of a volume of the Scriptures, while Frumentius was gazing in ecstasy upon his companion, whom the rays of the setting sun, passing through the red glass of the cell-windows, crowned with a fiery nimbus such as the Russian painters put round the heads of their saints.

Frumentius continued silent, while Joan turned over the leaves of the Sacred Book, at one time murmuring between her teeth, at another reading a verse aloud. Often, at the hour of Vespers, seated near the open window, while the bells tolled mournfully, as if they were lamenting the expiring day, they too wept, and, like Joshua, said to the sun, 'Stand still'; but that luminary went on his course to give light to the Antipodes, and our lovers separated, to wait for the morning.

They spent ten days longer in the narrow cell, writing and eating, finding no fault with the weather, which was fine, except that the days passed too quickly. But at last the dreaded day of separation arrived. The copy of the Epistles had been finished some time, and the Superior sent Frumentius a mule and special instructions to return to the fold. The unhappy youth, cursing his vows, his Superior and all the Saints, went to take leave of his beloved, holding in his hand his traveller's staff, but unable to restrain his tears. Joan did not weep, for some of her companions were present; and women, however sensitive, never weep except for proper and necessary occasions. Take for instance those English ladies, who, when they go to the Opera, mark in the margin of the libretto the places where they ought to weep.

When Joan was again left by herself, she felt within her that sensation of heaviness which attacks us after too good a dinner, the loss of a mother, a mistress or some property. According to the ancient Plutarch, women are ignorant even of the shadow of true love: I, however, for my part think that it is with them an accidental complaint, which has its origin in ennui and solitude. Women of the world, who every evening pass from the arms of one man to those of another – I mean in the dance – have no time to sigh or feel affection for anything else but their fans. They resemble the ass which remained fasting in the midst of four heaps of clover, not knowing which to choose. I may be mistaken, but all the females whom I have known attacked by the tender passion were either young girls shut up and guarded by watchful parents like the apples of the Hesperides by the dragons, or well-seasoned matrons who reckoned more years than admirers. The despair of the unhappy Joan, confined in her solitude between those four walls, which but yesterday re-echoed the sound of vows of love and of kisses, increased every day. St Augustine, whenever he was attacked by melancholy, used to roll in the mud, as if it were a sweet-scented bath: St Francis embraced statues covered with snow: St Libania tore her flesh with an iron comb: and St Luitbirge strangled rats. Our heroine, wiser than all these, reclining in the corner of her cell, endeavoured to scare the flies and troublesome thoughts with a fan made of doves' wings, the only ones allowed in monasteries. The heat of June made her grief still more poignant, and the days seemed to her longer than the life of an aged uncle to his heirs. In her paroxysms of despair, in order to drive away the troublesome phantoms that surrounded her, she sometimes had recourse to the pious recipes of legendary writers, flogging herself with her girdle or endeavouring to drown her sorrow in wine. But all these miracle-working remedies, even *agnus castus* itself, the smell of which, according to the hagiographers, is enough to drive away love, were of no avail against the bitterness of separation.

Time is said to heal all wounds; but I make an exception of love and hunger. The longer one remains chaste or without food, the greater the appetite grows, until one ends by eating one's shoes, like Napoleon's soldiers in Russia. Such was almost the condition of our heroine when, one evening, while she was sitting on the edge of the fish-pond, dividing her supper amongst the carp, the gardener of the convent approached her mysteriously, and, after having looked around uneasily, with an equally mysterious air put into her hand a letter written in purple ink on the fine skin of a still-born lamb. Joan, having unrolled it, covered with garlands of flowers, wounded hearts, doves billing and cooing, blazing torches and other tender symbols, with which the lovers of that age used to decorate their letters, in the same way as soldiers tattoo their arms and legs, read the following:

'Frumentius to his sister Joan:

'Lamentation hath seized upon me, and my eyelids run with water. Tears are my food by day and sleep by night. As the hungry man dreams of bread, so I dreamed of thee, O Joan: but when I awoke, I found thee not beside me. Then I mounted my ass and came to thy holy dwelling-place. I await thee at the tomb of St Bomma. Come, my dove fair as the sun, come, eclipse the moon with the brightness of thy rays.'

Such was the letter. At the present day, when we write to a woman, we borrow from Foscolo and Sand; but the lovers of those times copied the Psalms and the Prophets, so that their letters were as burning as the sand of the desert.

About five o'clock, when the bell summoned the maidens to the early service, Joan, holding her shoes in her right hand and her heart in her left, to silence its palpitations, descended the convent stairs, gliding noiselessly like a snake over the grass. The moon, that faithful lamp of smugglers and adulteresses, whom the poets call 'chaste' by euphemism, as they call the Erinnyes 'holy', rising just at this moment behind the walls of the convent, lighted up the path of our runaway heroine, who hastened to the rendezvous, treading under foot without mercy the parsley and leeks of the kitchen garden. Having walked in this manner for about half-an-hour, she at length reached the cemetery, so thickly shaded by yews and cypresses that neither the rays of the sun nor a breath of wind could penetrate this gloomy refectory of the worms. Frumentius had fastened his animal to the branch of a tree which overhung the tomb of St Bomma, upon which he was sitting, holding up on the end of this staff a lantern of horn to serve as a beacon for his beloved. As soon as he saw Joan advancing timidly among the tombs, he rushed towards her like a Capuchin towards a knuckle of ham at the end of Lent. The place, however, was unsuitable for such displays of affection; accordingly, hanging the lantern round the ass's neck, he got upon its back together with Joan, and made haste to leave the shady abode of the dead. The wretched animal, bending under a double burden, and encouraged by two pairs of heels, laid back its long ears and began to run, sending forth by way of protest such resounding brayings that, according to a trustworthy chronicler, several of the maidens who were asleep, thinking that the trumpet of the Judgment Day had sounded, came out of the tombs with their heads bare.

Joan, making a girdle of Frumentius' arms and a support of his breast, breathed, with indescribable delight, the air of the country. The youthful pair, having crossed the forest, hastened over an open plain, planted with barley and beans. The sun rose soon afterwards, and the young monk, in order to protect his companion from the heat of its summer rays, by a miraculous invocation compelled a large eagle to spread its wings above their heads, following in its flight the track of the ass. Such miracles were easy for the Christians of those times, whose hearts were simple, their faith vigorous, and their prayers all-powerful, whereas the learned but sceptical wise men of this generation, who carry the microscope and compass instead of the cross and the rosary, can tell you how many feathers there are in each bird's tail and how many seeds in the ovary of a flower, but are utterly incapable of taming eagles by a single nod or changing thorns into lilies by a single tear. Besides, they are insulted by the most reverend Abbé Guérin – who calls them idolaters, because they keep Mercury and Venus in the Christian heaven, and atheists, because they change the names of plants – and, like a second Jeremiah, cries out, 'Anathema! anathema! and again anathema! on progress and science.'

After four hours' journey the runaways halted to rest themselves near a small lake, on the edge of which had formerly stood a gigantic statue of Erminsul. St Boniface had overthrown this image by a single breath and blown it into the lake: but its ancient worshippers, although they had turned Christians, cherished at the bottom of their hearts some remains of devotion to their drowned patron, to whom they continued to offer presents, throwing every year into the lake candles, cakes, honeycombs, and cheeses, to the exceeding delight of the fishes, who, thanks to those offerings, grew as fat as the priests of Rhea. Frumentius, who was descended on the mother's side from the heroic companions of Witikind, was, in superstition, a genuine child of Saxony, while Joan, although a clever theologian, shared, like Socrates, the prejudices of her contemporaries. Most Christians during those times, still hesitating between Christ and idols, resembled that devout old woman of Chios, who every day lighted a candle in front of the image of St George, and another in front of that of the Devil, saying that it was good to have friends everywhere.

The two lovers, kneeling down by the lake, offered to Erminsul the remains of their breakfast, some hairs out of their heads and some drops of blood mingled together, rendering their union, by means of this libation, eternal and indissoluble, like that of the Doge of Venice with the sea. After this ceremony Frumentius took out of his bag the dress of a monk, which he begged Joan to put on, that she might be received as a novice into the Convent of Fulda. 'By this means', added the young man, 'we shall be able to inhabit the same cell without being disturbed, to eat off the same plate and to dip our pens in the same inkstand: while, if they think that you are a woman, the Superiors will shut you up with the rest of the catechumens, in the women's quarters, where they alone possess the right of entry, and I shall die of despair on the threshold.'

Joan refused the disguise as an impious thing, opposing her lover's entreaties with the words of Scripture: a woman shall not put upon her the dress of a man, nor a man the robes of a woman. Frumentius insisted and to the verse of Deuteronomy opposed the opinion of Origen, according to whom women will be changed into men at the Day of Judgment. When Joan replied that Origen was a heretic and eunuch besides, the young man reminded her of the examples of St Thecla, sister of the Apostle Paul, of St Margaret, St Eugenia, St Matrona, and others who, having hidden their persons under a monk's frock, acquired holiness by living amongst men, in the same manner as the Turks reach paradise by living in the midst of women. Youth, beauty and passion were arguments that rendered the eloquence of the youthful catechist invincible, so that Joan, soon trampling under her tiny feet the commands of Moses and her female attire, put on the frock and shoes which, some years later, she was destined to offer to the salutations of the great ones of the earth, kneeling before her throne. When the change was complete, Frumentius led her to the edge of the lake that she might look at herself in the water. Never had a girdle encircled the waist of a prettier monk, and our heroine's face shone beneath the cowl like a pearl in its shell.

Translated by J.H. Freese

Dimitrios Vikelas (1835–1908)

While Solomos (q.v.) commemorated the massacres at Chios and Makriyannis (q.v.) related deeds of heroism as well of internecine strife, Vikelas set out to pay tribute – not without ironic distance – to the fact that Greek commercial genius was to thrive in the less heroic modern world ushered in by Independence. A long-time resident of London, where many of the leading Chiot families settled and remain – their cemetery in South Norwood is a wonderful sign of how Victorian these Greeks became while losing nothing of their Greekness – Vikelas was in a good position to observe the phenomenon, as was his translator Johannes Gennadius, for many years Ambassador to the Court of St James.

Loukis Laras. Reminiscences of a Chiote Merchant During the War of Independence (*extract*)

Those who from childhood have been accustomed to traverse sea and land by steam have no conception of what travelling was in those days. It is only in our own Aegean Sea that even now, if we cannot wait for the fortnightly steamboat, we may yet find ourselves exposed to peregrinations not unlike those of Ulysses and his companions. But after all, the inhabitant of the very remotest of our islands is no longer the perpetual slave of the winds. If he be only patient enough, the steamer will call for him. In those days steamboats were unknown. Our skies had not yet smelt the smoke of coal, and our waves were still virgin to the flapping of paddle and screw.

The wind blew fair when we started from Mykonos; but it soon fell, and we found ourselves in a dead calm. For hours and hours together we saw immovable in front of us the rock of Syra, and the use of two ponderous oars did little to move our heavy lugger. At length the wind freshened again towards sunset, and the sails began to fill. But it blew from the south, and pushed us on to Andros. All night through we were on the tack, trying to get under shelter behind Cape Sunium, and after much trouble we succeeded next day in reaching the Piraeus, there to take in fresh water.

When years later I again visited the port of Piraeus, it appeared to me to have shrunk in size. Then it seemed enormous, for it was desolate. Our ship and two small fishing boats were the only craft floating on the expanse of its undisturbed waters. There, on the space now covered by its marble quays, the waves, slowly advancing, rolled on bare rock. Farther on, where a flourishing town now spreads out, and where large manufactories with their tall chimneys have sprung up, nothing was to be seen but a barren plain, the very picture of desolation. A solitary house by the beach, tottering into ruins, contributed to make the absence of animation and movement all the more apparent.

Athens was then besieged by the Greek troops, and a small detachment of armed men occupied that half-ruined house. But we did not hear any firing at that distance, nor did we see any other sign of hostilities, save that military occupation of the Piraeus.

War is a savage business! It certainly does not tend to the improvement of human nature. Those soldiers we saw did us no harm; they placed no difficulties in our way. But I was glad when our ship moved off again. Their appearance had something harsh about it; their very greetings were terrifying.

On the third day of our departure from Mykonos we reached Spetzae, the wind having prevented our sailing into the Gulf of Nauplia. The captain landed, and, wearied with the confinement on board ship, we followed his example, and had the satisfaction of again setting foot on dry land.

We sat on the rocks by the outskirts of the town, and we all kept silent, my father appearing very downcast. I had never seen him look so depressed. He seemed ailing, but he did not complain. He only held his head between his hands, and his eyes were heavy and dim.

We were alone there, but farther on we could see the bustle and movement of the townsfolk on the beach. The harbour was full of shipping, and our boat lay moored on the rocks, awaiting the return of the captain.

My eyes were fixed on the little craft. I was thinking what would become of us if my father were taken ill; and I remembered our tower and his comfortable quarters in it, when I saw a young Spetziote approach.

'Welcome, Christian brethren,' said he. 'Do you come from Chio?'

'From Chio!' replied my father, lifting up his head with an effort.

'And why sit out here? why do you not come into the town?'

'We are going to Argos.'

'Argos! Argos is not the place for women and children. You had better stop here.'

My father explained that we were going there in the hope of finding some means of livelihood. But the Spetziote went on to say that Argos was but a camp, and Nauplia was still besieged. He represented to us the inconvenience of the presence of women in the midst of such warlike scenes, and urged us to put off our departure.

While he was still speaking the captain returned, and corroborating the words of the young Spetziote, he recommended us to remain at Spetzae.

There was no difficulty in prevailing upon us to remain. But where could we put up? Where lay our heads in this new station of our exile? The good Spetziote understood, apparently, the cause of our hesitation.

'Come to my house,' he said. 'My father was killed fighting; my mother died soon after him; and my house is now deserted. Stay in it as long as you please. Come.'

We accepted with emotion the offer of that good and generous man. From that moment he became the staunchest of friends for me. We have since been like brothers to one another, and our friendship remained undisturbed to the hour of his death, a few years ago. He died full of honours, having proved himself a most worthy and upright servant of his country, both in war and in time of peace.

We now moved to the house of our new friend, and took possession of its spacious and comfortable rooms. My father soon began to feel his strength fail him. Perhaps he foresaw his end approach, and he did not wish to die without securing to his widow and his orphans their daily bread. He did not give expression to such forebodings; but that same day he urged me to proceed to Argos without delay, and making use of the letter of recommendation, solicit from Negris some employment.

Two days later I landed at the Mills of Nauplia, and thence I proceeded on foot to Argos.

Our Spetziote friend and the captain were perfectly right. Their words and my first impressions at the Piraeus had already prepared me for what I was about to witness; but at the Piraeus I had seen only in miniature what I now beheld. I found myself in a world quite new to me. The thousands of warriors in fustanellas, their haughty demeanour, their rude expressions, the contemptuous looks with which they measured every inch of me, their abrupt replies to my timid inquiries, the noise and the movement, and the confusion of the camp, all this troubled me. Certainly this was no place for women and children. I myself felt that I was not in a congenial atmosphere; I was not in my element.

When at last, Mavroyenis' letter in hand, I succeeded in penetrating into the minister's presence, and saw before me, standing in front of a high desk, an ugly little man, I was taken aback, and I hesitated to believe that this was the principal Secretary of State, the great and renowned Theodore Negris. He was busy writing, and while waiting with the letter in my hand, I examined the scene around me. The little room was full of books – books on the table, books on the chairs, books on the strong box, books everywhere; and in their midst rose the high desk, and Negris stood by it writing. He was even shorter than I. I am convinced no feeling of self-love misled me into this estimate.

I looked at him, and I thought to myself, now, there he is; a puny, ugly, defence-less-looking man; and yet they all obey him – those savage warriors, and he governs them. Why? Because he is their superior in intellect and education. Intellect cannot be called into existence; but one may become learned. Good sense is the gift of God; but knowledge may be acquired. Thus I reasoned then, forgetting that human intelligence is of many degrees and of various tendencies;

that the power of regulating one's own will according to circumstances has not been given to all; nor yet the ability of imposing that will on one's fellow creatures. I overlooked such considerations; but while I gazed upon Negris I formed the resolution to add to my stock of knowledge; and, in fact, ever after that time I applied myself to reading and studying. Naturally I have not been able to do much. But whatever I learnt in after life, whatever thirst for knowledge there is in me, it dates from that hour – when I waited till Negris had done writing. That was the starting point of my intellectual regeneration, though its extent may have remained necessarily restricted.

Negris at length laid down his pen, and asked me what I wanted. I silently held out my hand and presented to him the letter. Having read it he bade me sit on the only vacant chair near him, and began questioning me what I knew, and what he could do for me. I felt I blushed as I attempted to enumerate my accomplishments, and to express the desire to obtain a clerkship under him.

'Very well,' said he, when I had done; 'very well. I have need of young men such as you, and I shall give you a suitable post. But we must first settle down a little. Wait until we take Nauplia, and then look in again.'

Wait till Nauplia is taken! I left utterly dispirited. Why, for the last three weeks they had considered the capitulation of the fortress as certain, and the plenipotentiaries of the besiegers were already inside Nauplia negotiating the terms, while armed men gathered from every part of the surrounding country, in the hope of celebrating, each in his own fashion, this fresh triumph of the Greek arms. Yet the Turks had not surrendered, and Dram-Ali was on his way from Northern Greece at the head of a powerful army. The rumour of his progress southward spread, and had already began to shake the confidence of many on our side. Such, at least, were the news I heard during my two days' sojourn at Argos. The tide of events seemed to be turning against us; and being still swayed by my impressions of Chio, I became a ready victim to fear. How was I to foresee then or hope that Colocotronis would annihilate Dram-Ali at Dervenaki?

On the second night, while tossing sleeplessly over the hard boards which served as a bed, I made up my mind as to what I should do. I was not destined for the life of camps. Commerce was my vocation.

Next morning I repaired to the Mills, where I was lucky enough to find a ship ready to start for Spetzae, and I took my passage accordingly.

I have never since visited Nauplia, but the stern rock of Fort Palamidi remains imprinted on my mind, as it overshadowed the valley, where thickets of reeds fence in the course of a little stream, with the town spreading below, on the walls of which I could see from afar the crescent wave.

At Spetzae I found both my parents and my sisters laid up with sickness. How much we then again felt the absence of poor Adriana! How often we all thought of her! It was I who had now to undertake, of necessity, the care of all the family.

I became at one and the same time chambermaid, sick-nurse, and cook. The good housewives of our neighbourhood were amazed to see a man – contrary to all the usages of the island – stoop to such feminine work, and their thoughts were betrayed by the contemptuous smiles with which they accompanied their oblig-ing offers of assistance.

Fortunately, the illness of my mother and sisters was but the temporary result of moral and physical prostration, and in a few days they one after the other left their beds. But my father was not destined to recover. I cannot say what was his illness. The so-called doctor whom we had recourse to, as soon as we began to be seriously alarmed, declared he was suffering from heart disease, and promised to cure him.

But evidently he did not know what he was about, and I doubt if he had ever set foot in a medical school of any kind. He was an old Maltese, who for many years past had exercised, not for humanity's sake alone, the calling of itinerant physician in many a Levantine city. At that time any Frank easily passed muster as a 'doctor', and God only knows in what circumstances his Excellency was improvised into a physician. But gradually he must have persuaded himself that he was proficient in the science, while beneficent nature aided his efforts some-times, and at others he himself conscientiously hurried on the end of his unfortunate patients.

Still my father remained prostrate. Fever undermined his already exhausted system, and agonizing pains deprived him of rest. He felt death approach, and he awaited his end bravely. And we, forgetting our manifold privations of the time being, and our past comforts, thought only how to relieve his sufferings and how to save him, if possible. But our hopes disappeared day by day, as the cold hand of decay seemed to spread over his body.

One night I remained alone by his pillow, having with much difficulty prevailed upon my mother to take some rest in the adjoining room. My father had sunk into a torpor, which seemed like sleep. I sat near him, with my hands crossed, and while watching him my mind strayed away into sad thoughts. The sick-room was lit up only by the candle burning before the sacred icons, and the night was perfectly still. Suddenly I fancied I heard an unusual noise outside, and talking in the street. I crept to the window, and half opening the shutter, I distin-guished the moving shadows of men. I dare not throw open the window for fear of awaking my father, who seemed reposing. But I tried to listen to what they were saying. I did hear, but I could not understand, for they spoke in Albanian. The word *Armàta*, however, which was often repeated, aroused my suspicions. Presently the doors were shut, and the shadows disappeared, bearing, as they seemed to me, cases and sacks on their shoulders. Silence again reigned supreme, but the word *Armàta* resounded in my ears. I knew enough to understand it meant a fleet. But to which fleet did they refer? I waited impatiently for the day, not knowing what to think of it all, dreading fresh complications. I was involuntarily reminded of that first night at Smyrna, when the war-cries of the Turks had awakened me.

Towards dawn my mother returned to her post by the bedside of our patient, and sent me to rest. But instead of going to sleep, I quickly left the house. We were its only occupants, for our kind-hearted host lived on board his ship. From the extremity of the town, where our house lay, I descended towards the port, and, as I approached, I met with increasing animation and movement. I inquired what it was all about, and I was informed that on the island of Hydra they had lit up beacon-fires at nightfall.

'And what do the beacons signify?' I asked.

'That a Turkish fleet is descending towards us.'

The Spetziotes had already transported on board their ships all their valuables, and were making ready, in case the Turks did in fact approach, to embark their women and children. They knew the enemy's fleet was powerful and numerous, and they were anxious about their homes, but they had every confidence in their floating fortresses.

In the port I met some of my compatriots who had taken refuge at Spetzae. They also were making ready for escape. A vessel from Mytilene, under Russian flag, was anchored on the other side of the island, and they had sent to negotiate for a passage to Ancona. They offered to take us with them. But how could we leave? How move my father, who was on the point of death? And yet, how remain on the island if the Turks came to land?

I returned home in trouble and dismay. I beckoned my mother to come out. I explained to her briefly how matters stood, and I asked her if she thought we might move my father. She led me by the hand to his bedside, and pointed towards him. He was still unconscious, his eyes were shut, his mouth half open, and he breathed heavily. Then for the first time I saw before me the agony of death, and the dying man was my beloved father.

My mother held my hand tight, and did not say a word in her efforts to subdue her anguish. Thus we stood by the bed, speechless and motionless, listening to the last agony of the dying man. I bent my head and kissed my mother's hand; she did not stoop to embrace me, but she only put her other hand on my head, and told me in a subdued voice, 'Go, fetch a priest.' I rushed out at once. I did not wish to give vent to my grief in her presence. At the door-steps I met the doctor, who was coming in.

'We have escaped it, my friend!' he cried cheerfully as soon as he saw me. But his expression was at once changed on seeing the trouble I was in, and lowering his voice, he inquired, 'How is he getting on upstairs?'

I did not reply, but shook my head.

'I suppose it is all his fright at the Turks. But they have beaten a retreat, and we are safe.'

I left him going up the steps, and went my way with a lighter heart. At least, I thought to myself, he will die in peace, and the Turks will allow us to mourn him undisturbed.

The doctor's words brought back to my mind the horrors of Turkish invasion, and all the consequences which would have resulted from their presence on the island; and while I hurried on, I prayed God it might be true indeed that we were spared from the terrors of their appearance.

When I returned with the priest my father still breathed heavily. Only once did he open his eyes, and his look betokened recognition of us; but he could not utter a word, and he again shut his eyes. His respiration grew more difficult, and he seemed to suffer for want of breath. The doctor lifted him on the bed, and my mother propped him up with pillows, while I cut his shirt open with a pair of scissors, that we might give some relief to his wearied lungs.

What was the sentiment which then moved my father in his last agony? Why did he frown and move his hand, as if wishing to prevent his shirt being torn? That incident remained indelibly impressed on my mind, and I revert to it involuntarily whenever I think of the vanity of the things of this world. Such is man! Death had already spread its black wings, and the last hour, eternal rest, darkness itself, was approaching. Yet the dying man, that good, loving old man, instinctively waved his hand, that he might save the bit of linen which covered his bosom!

His death agony continued all day. Meanwhile the Turkish fleet moved away to the south. The danger passed away from over Spetzae, and the islanders were again quiet.

Towards nightfall my father breathed his last. Next day I sold my mother's ring, and we buried our beloved dead in a humble and tombless grave.

It was 5 July 1822. Such dates are never forgotten.

Translated by J. Gennadius

G.M. Vizyinos (1849–1896)

Born to a poor family under Ottoman rule in Vizyi, Eastern Thrace, Vizyinos, like Vikelas, spent some time in London, where he wrote some of his six major short stories, now considered to be among the finest in the language. His career was cut short by the onset at an early age of acute mania, culminating in an infatuation with a ten-year-old girl, and he died in the Dromokaïteion asylum in Athens years after his last story seems to have been written. While many of his contemporaries confined themselves to rather dutiful folkloric recreations of Greek rural life for a readership now losing touch with its rural roots and wishing to be served up with a sentimentalized picture of them, Vizyinos combined an Ottoman peasant background and a traditional priestly education with an early doctorate in child psychology from Göttingen, and his stories contain a subtle and original mixture of oriental wonder-tale and modern speculation. 'My Mother's Sin' is perhaps the best loved, and – on the face of it – the simplest.

My Mother's Sin

We had no other sister, only Annio. She was the darling of our small family and we all loved her. But our mother loved her most of all. She always sat beside her at table and gave her the best of whatever we had. And while she dressed us in our deceased father's clothes, she usually bought new ones for Annio. She did not rush her into school, either. If she wanted, she went to school; if she didn't, she stayed home. Something we'd never have been allowed to do for any reason.

Naturally such special exceptions had to cause harmful jealousies among children, especially children as little as my two other brothers and I were at the time that these events took place. But we knew deep down inside that our mother's affection continued impartial and equal towards all her children. We were sure that those exceptions were only external demonstrations of a certain natural favour towards our household's only girl. And not only did we put up with these attentions without a complaint, we even contributed to increasing them as best we could, because Annio, besides being our only sister, had unfortunately always been weak and sickly. And even the youngest in the house who was justified more than any other in claiming his mother's attentions because his father had died before he was born, ceded his rights to his sister, and the more gladly since Annio did not become bossy or conceited on account of this.

On the contrary, she was very sweet to us and loved us all deeply. And – strange to say – the girl's affection for us increased instead of diminishing as her illness progressed. I remember her large black eyes and her eyebrows that met over her nose and appeared all the darker the paler her face became. A face by nature dreamy and sad on to which a certain sweet gaiety spread only when she saw us all gathered together near her. She would frequently hide under her pillow those fruits that neighbourhood women brought her as a 'tonic', and she'd parcel them out to us when we came back from school. But she always did this in secret because it enraged our mother, who did not like us wolfing down anything that she wanted her sick daughter even just to have tasted.

Nonetheless, Annio's illness grew steadily worse, and our mother's concerns centred more and more on her.

Mother hadn't left the house since the day our father died: she had been widowed very young, and was too modest to make use of the freedom of movement that, even in Turkey itself, belongs to every mother of many children. But the day that Annio fell seriously ill she cast modesty aside.

Someone had once had a similar illness – she ran to ask how he had been cured. Somewhere an old woman harbours plants of miraculous medicinal power – she hurried to buy them. Some queer-looking stranger had come from somewhere, or one renowned for his knowledge – she did not hesitate to beg his assistance. The 'learned', according to folk wisdom, are omniscient. And sometimes behind the disguise of a travelling beggar there lurk mysterious beings of supernatural power.

The neighbourhood's fat barber came to visit us, unsummoned and as a matter of right. He was the only official doctor in our district. As soon as I saw him I had to run to the grocer because he never went near the invalid before gulping down at least fifty drams of *raki*.

'I'm old, my girl,' he would say to the impatient mother. 'I'm old, and if I don't have a nip, my eyes don't see well.'

And it seems he wasn't lying. The more he drank, the more easily he was able to pick out the fattest hen in our courtyard to take with him when he left.

Although my mother had already stopped using his medicines, she nonetheless paid him regularly and without complaint. She did this in the first place so as not to displease him, and also because he often maintained by way of assurance that the course of the disease was good, and exactly what science had the right to expect from his prescriptions. This last was unfortunately all too true. Annio's condition went slowly and imperceptibly, but constantly, from bad to worse. And this prolongation of the unseen malady drove our mother wild.

According to folk wisdom, if an unknown disease is to be viewed as a natural affliction, it must either yield to the elementary medical knowledge of the area, or bring death within a short time. As soon as it becomes prolonged and chronic, it is attributed to supernatural causes and is characterized as 'due to an evil spirit'. The invalid had sat on an evil spot. He had crossed the river at night at the very instant the Neraides, unseen, were celebrating their rites. He had stepped over a black cat which was in reality the Devil in disguise.

Our mother was more devout than superstitious. At first she viewed such diagnoses with horror, and refused to put the suggested spells into effect for fear of committing a sin. Besides, the priest had already read the exorcisms of evil over the invalid, just in case. But she changed her mind after a while.

The invalid's condition was growing worse, and motherly love conquered fear of sin – religion had to come to terms with superstition. Next to the cross on Annio's chest she hung a charm with mysterious Arabic words on it. Magic took the place of blessings and after the priest's prayer-books came the witches' 'spells'.

But all went for naught. The child grew worse and worse, and our mother became more and more distraught. You'd think she'd forgotten she had other children, too. She didn't even care to know who fed us boys, who bathed us, who mended our clothes. An old woman from the neighbouring village of Sofides who had been living with us for many years now took care of us as far as her Methuselah-like age allowed. There were times when we didn't see our mother for days on end.

Sometimes she took a ribbon from Annio's dress and tied it at some wonder-working location in the hope that the disease, too, would be tied up far from the patient. Sometimes she went to churches in neighbouring villages who happened to be celebrating a saint's day carrying a candle of yellow wax that she had dipped with her own hands and that was exactly the sick girl's height. But all these things proved useless. Our poor sister's illness was incurable.

Finally when all means had been exhausted and all cures had been attempted, we reached the final refuge in such cases.

Our mother took the wasted girl up in her arms and carried her to the church. My older brother and I loaded ourselves with the bedding and followed along behind. And there, on the damp, chill pavement, in front of the icon of the Virgin, we made the bed and placed down in it the sweetest object of our concerns, our one and only sister. Everybody said she had an 'evil spirit'. Our mother no longer had any doubt about this, and even the patient herself began to recognize it. So she had to stay in the church forty days and forty nights in front of the sanctuary and facing the Mother of our Saviour, trusting only that their mercy and compassion would rescue her from that satanic affliction that lurked within and was so mercilessly grinding down the delicate tree of her life.

Forty days and forty nights. That is how long the demons with their frightful perseverance can hold out in their invisible battle with divine grace. After this period of time the evil is defeated and retreats in disgrace. And accounts are not lacking in which patients feel within their body the awful writhings of the final battle and see their enemy fleeing in a strange shape, especially at the moment when they bring out the sacred vessels or the 'In Fear' is pronounced. Lucky are they if they have sufficient strength at that time to withstand the shocks of the struggle. The weak are shattered by the immensity of the miracle taking place within them. But they have no regrets on this account. If they lose their life, at least they gain the most valuable thing. They save their soul.

Nevertheless some such eventuality plunged our mother into deep distress, and as soon as we set Annio down, she began with great concern to ask her how she felt. The sanctity of the place, the sight of the icons, the aroma of the incense had, it seems, a beneficial effect on her melancholy spirit, for, after the first few moments, she brightened up and began to banter with us. 'Which of the two do you want to play with?' my mother asked her tenderly – 'Hristakis or Yoryis?'

The invalid cast her a sidelong but expressive glance and, as if reproaching her for her indifference towards us, answered slowly and deliberately: 'Which of the two do I want? I don't want either without the other. I want all my brothers, all the brothers I have.'

My mother drew back and fell silent.

A short while later she also brought our littlest brother to the church, but only for that first day. In the evening she sent the other two away and kept me alone at her side. I still remember what an impression that first night in the church made on my childish imagination. The faint light of the lamps in front of the iconostasion, barely able to illumine it and the steps in front of it, rendered the darkness around us even more dubious and frightening than if we had been completely in the dark. Whenever the flame of a candle flickered, it seemed to me that the Saint on the icon facing it had begun to come to life and was stirring, trying to wrench free of the wood and come down on to the pavement, dressed in his broad, red robes, with the halo around his head, and with those staring eyes on his pale and impassive face.

Or again, when the chill wind whistled through the high windows, noisily rattling their small windowpanes, I thought that the dead buried about the church were clambering up the walls and trying to get in. And, shaking from fright, I sometimes saw a skeleton across from me reaching out to warm its fleshless hands over the brazier that burned in front of us. And yet I did not dare show even the slightest anxiety because I loved my sister and thought it a great honour to be constantly near her side and near my mother, who would surely have sent me home as soon as she suspected I was afraid.

So during the following nights as well I suffered these terrors with a forced stoicism, and I eagerly discharged my duties, trying to prove as agreeable as possible. On weekdays I lighted the fire, I fetched water, I swept the church. Feast-days and Sundays during matins I would lead my sister by the hand and stand her below the Gospels from which the priest was reading at the Beautiful Gate. During the service I spread out the woollen blanket on to which the invalid would fall – flat on her face – so that the Host could pass over her. But during the recessional I brought her pillow over to face the left door of the Sanctuary so she could kneel on it until 'the priest draped his stole over her' and made the sign of the cross over her face with the Spear, mumbling the 'Through thy crucifixion, Oh Christ, the tyranny has been destroyed, the power of the Enemy has been crushed,' etc.

And in all this my poor sister followed me, her face pale and mournful, her step slow and uncertain, attracting the pity of the church-goers and calling forth their prayers for her recovery, a recovery that, unfortunately, was slow in coming. On the contrary, the dampness, the chill, the strangeness and yes, the ghastliness of those nights in the church were not slow to have a harmful effect on the invalid whose condition by now had begun to inspire the worst fears. My mother realized this, and began, even in the church itself, to show a sorrowful indifference to anything other than the invalid. She did not open her mouth to anyone anymore except to Annio and the saints when she prayed. One day I came up to her unobserved while she was on her knees weeping in front of the icon of the Saviour. 'Take from me whatever you want,' she was saying, 'and leave me the girl. I see that it has to happen. You recalled my sin and are determined to take the child from me to punish me. I thank you, Lord!'

After several moments of deep silence during which her tears could be heard as they dropped on to the stones, she sighed from the bottom of her heart, hesitated a little, and then added: 'I've brought two of my children to your feet . . . let me have the girl!'

When I heard these words, an icy shudder coursed through my nerves and my ears began to roar. I could hear nothing more. And when I saw that my mother, overcome by her frightful anguish, was falling limply on to the marble slabs, instead of running to her assistance I took the opportunity to dash out of the church, running in a frenzy, and crying out as if Death itself incarnate were threatening to seize me. My teeth chattered from fright, and I ran and kept on running. And without realizing it I suddenly found myself far, far away from the church. Then I stopped to catch my breath and dared to turn to look behind me. No one was chasing me.

So I began to come to my senses little by little and to reflect. I recollected all my acts of tenderness and affection toward my mother. I tried to remember whether I had ever been at fault toward her, had ever wronged her, but could not. On the contrary I began to see that from the day that this sister of ours had been born, I not only was not loved as I should have wished, but in fact was being shunted aside more and more. Then I remembered, and it seemed to me that I understood, why my father had been in the habit of calling me his 'wronged one'. And my outrage got the better of me and I began to cry. 'Oh,' I said, 'my mother doesn't love me and doesn't want me! I am never going to church again – never!' And I turned toward home, gloomily and in despair.

My mother was not long in following me home with the sick girl. For the priest, alarmed by my cries, had come into the church, and, when he saw her, had advised my mother to remove her. 'God is great, daughter,' he told her, 'and His grace extends over all the world. If He's going to heal your child, He'll heal her in your house as well.' Unhappy the mother who heard him! for those are the formal words with which priests usually send away those about to die so they don't expire in the church and defile the sanctity of the place.

When I saw my mother again, she was more melancholy than ever. But she behaved toward me especially with great sweetness and gentleness. She took me in her arms, she fondled me, she kissed me tenderly and repeatedly. You'd think she was trying to mollify me. I, however, could neither eat nor sleep that night. I lay on my bed with my eyes closed, but I strained my ears attentively to catch my mother's every move. She, as always, was keeping watch at the sick girl's pillow.

It must have been about midnight when she began moving about the room. I thought she was laying out the bed to go to sleep, but I was wrong because after a short while she sat down and began to chant a lament in a low voice.

It was the lament for our father. She used to chant it frequently before Annio fell ill, but I was hearing it now for the first time since then. This lament had been composed for our father's death, at her orders, by a sunburnt, ragged Gypsy who was well known in the area for his skill in composing verses extemporaneously. I can still see his black, greasy hair, his small, fiery eyes and his exposed, hairy chest. He sat inside our courtyard gate surrounded by the bronze pots and pans that he had collected for tin-plating. And, with his head tilted to the side, he accompanied his mournful air with the plaintive sounds of his three-stringed viol. My mother stood before him with Annio in her arms and listened attentively and tearfully. I was holding tightly on to her dress and hiding my face in its folds because, sweet as those sounds were, the face of their fierce singer terrified me.

When my mother had memorized her mournful lesson, she took two *rubiédes* from the corner of her kerchief and gave them to the Gypsy – we still had enough at that time. Then she placed bread and wine in front of him and whatever other food was handy. And while he ate down below, my mother went upstairs and repeated his lament to herself so as to fix it in her memory. And it seems she found it very beautiful, for as the Gypsy was about to leave, she ran after him and made him the gift of a pair of my father's good trousers.

'May God forgive your husband's soul, daughter,' the singer called out in surprise as he went out of our courtyard loaded down with his copper pots and pans.

That was the lament my mother was chanting that night. I listened and let my tears flow in silence, but I didn't dare move. Suddenly I picked up the smell of incense! 'Oh,' I thought, 'our poor Annio has died!' And I jumped from my bed.

I found a strange scene before me. The sick girl was breathing heavily, as always. Near her lay a man's suit, arranged as a man would wear it. To its right was a stool covered with black cloth on which rested a pan full of water flanked by two lighted candles. My mother was on her knees swinging a censer over these objects and staring at the surface of the water.

It seems I turned pale from fright, because when she saw me, she hastened to calm me. 'Don't be afraid, my child,' she said mysteriously. 'They're your father's clothes. Come, you also ask him to come and heal our Annio.' And she made me kneel beside her. 'Come, Father – please take me – let Annio get well!' I cried out between my sobs. And I cast a reproachful glance at my mother to show her that I knew that she was asking for me to die instead of my sister. Fool that I was, I didn't see that I was heightening her despair by doing this! I believe she forgave me. I was very young then and couldn't understand her heart.

After a few moments of profound silence, she again swung the censer over the objects in front of us and directed all her attention to the water in the large pan on the stool. Suddenly a small moth circled over it, touched the surface with its wings, disturbing it slightly.

My mother bowed piously and made the sign of the cross, as she did when they parade the Host in church. 'Cross yourself, my child!' she whispered, deeply moved and not daring to raise her eyes. I obeyed mechanically.

When that small moth disappeared at the other end of the room, my mother took a deep breath, got up happily, and said with satisfaction, 'Your father's soul has visited us!' as she continued to follow the flight of the little moth with looks of affection and devotion. Then she drank from the water and gave it to me to drink as well. I recalled then that occasionally in the past she used to have us drink from that same pan as soon as we woke up. And I remembered that every time she did this, she was lively and cheerful all that day, as if she had enjoyed some great but secret happiness.

After she had had me drink, she went over to Annio's bed with the pan in her hands. The sick girl was not sleeping, but she was not entirely awake, either. Her eyelids were half closed; and her eyes, in so far as they were visible, emitted a kind of strange brilliance through her thick, black lashes. My mother carefully lifted up the girl's thin body. And while she supported her back with one hand, she offered the pan to her wasted lips with the other.

'Come, my love,' she said to her, 'drink some of this water to get well.' The sick girl didn't open her eyes, but apparently she heard the voice and understood the words. Her lips spread in a lovely, sweet smile. Then she sipped a few drops of the water that was in fact about to cure her. As soon as she had drunk it she opened her eyes and tried to draw a breath. A light sigh escaped her lips, and she fell back heavily against my mother's forearm.

Our poor Annio! She had escaped her torments!

Many had reproached my mother, saying that while unrelated women had wailed loudly over my father's corpse, she alone shed bounteous, but silent, tears. The poor woman did this from fear that she might be misunderstood, that she might overstep the bounds of decorum appropriate to young women, because, as I said, my mother was widowed very young. She wasn't much older when our sister died. But now she didn't even give a thought to what people would say about her heart-rending lamentations. The entire neighbourhood got up and came to console her. But her sorrow was frightful, it was inconsolable.

'She'll go out of her mind,' whispered those who saw her bent over and wailing between our father's and our sister's graves. 'She'll abandon them to the four winds,' said those who met us in the street, forsaken and uncared for. And time was needed, time and the admonitions and reproaches of the church, for her to come to her senses, remember her surviving children and take up her household responsibilities again.

But then she discovered the state in which our sister's long illness had left us. All our money had gone for doctors and medicines. She had sold many woollen coverlets and rugs, works of her own hands, for trifling sums, or she had given them as barter to charlatans and sorceresses. Others they and their ilk had stolen from us, taking advantage of the lack of attention that prevailed in our house. In addition, our supplies of food had also been exhausted, and we no longer had anything to live on.

Instead of daunting my mother, however, this fact gave her twice the energy she had had before Annio fell ill. She moderated or, more accurately, concealed, her grief; she overcame the timidity of her age and sex and, taking mattock in hand, she hired herself out as a 'hired hand', just as if she had never known a life of ease and independence. For a long time she supported us by the sweat of her brow. Her wages were small and our needs great, yet she refused to allow any of us to work with her and lighten her load.

Plans for our future were formed and reviewed in the evening by the hearth. My older brother was to learn our father's trade so as to take his place in the family. I was destined, or rather wanted, to leave home, and so forth. But prior to this all of us had to learn our letters, to finish school because, as our mother used to say, 'illiterate person, unhewn log'.

Our money problems reached a peak when a drought hit the area and food prices went up. But our mother, instead of despairing about supporting just us, increased our number by one, an unrelated girl whom she managed to adopt after protracted attempts. That event transformed the monotony and austerity of our family life and introduced some new liveliness.

Even the adoption ceremony was festive. For the first time my mother wore her 'Sunday best' and led us to the church clean and combed, as if we were about to take communion. After the service ended we all stood in front of the icon of

Christ, and there, in the midst of the surrounding throng, in the presence of its natural parents, my mother received her adopted daughter from the hands of the priest, after first having promised in the hearing of all that she would love and raise it as if it were flesh of her flesh and bone of her bone.

The child's entry into our house was no less impressive and in a way triumphant. The village elder and my mother led the procession with the girl; then we came. Our relatives and our new sister's relatives followed up to our courtyard gate. Outside the gate the elder took the girl in his hands and raised her high above his head, displaying her for a few moments to all present. Then he asked in a loud voice, 'Which of you is more relative or family or parent of this child than Michael's wife Despinio and her relatives?'

The girl's father was pale, and, grief-stricken, stared straight ahead. His wife was leaning on his shoulder and weeping. My mother was trembling from fear that some voice might be heard 'I!' and would thwart her happiness. But no one answered. Then the child's parents embraced it for the last time and left with their relatives. Our relatives and the elder came in and enjoyed our hospitality.

From that moment our mother began to lavish on our adopted sister attentions such as we had not had the good fortune to obtain at her age and in far happier times. And while I shortly thereafter began my homesick wanderings in foreign lands, and my other brothers endured a wretched existence living as apprentices in artisans' workshops, the unrelated girl lorded it in our house as if it were her own.

My brothers' meagre wages would have been enough to relieve my mother, and they gave her the money for this reason. But she, instead of spending the money to lighten her load, acquired a dowry with it for her adopted daughter and continued working to support her. I was far, far away, and for many years did not know what was going on in our house. And before I could manage to return, the unrelated girl had grown up, been educated, provided with a dowry, and married, as if she had really been a member of our family.

Her marriage, which it seems was purposely hurried on, was a real 'ball' for my brothers. The poor fellows, freed of the added burden, breathed a sigh of relief. And they were right because that girl, aside from the fact that she never felt any sisterly affection for them, in the end proved herself ungrateful to the woman who had looked after her with an affection few legitimate children have known. So my brothers had reasons to be pleased, and they also had reasons to believe their mother had learned her lesson sufficiently from that bad experience. But imagine their consternation when a few days after the wedding they saw her coming into the house tenderly cradling a second girl in her arms, this time in swaddling clothes!

'The poor thing!' our mother exclaimed, bending lovingly over the baby's face. 'It's not enough that it was orphaned in the womb, but its mother died, too, and left it in the street!' And, in a way pleased at this unfortunate event, she triumphantly showed off her prize to my brothers, who were speechless in amazement. Filial respect was strong, and my mother's authority great, but my brothers were so disappointed that they didn't hesitate to indicate to their mother, decorously to be sure, that it would be a good idea to give up her plan. But they found her obstinate. Then they openly revealed their displeasure and denied her the use of their purse. All in vain.

'Don't bring me anything,' my mother said. 'I'll work and I'll take care of her just as I took care of you. And when my Yoryis comes back from abroad, he'll give her a dowry and he'll marry her off. What, you don't believe me? My child promised me that himself. "Mother, I'll provide for you, both you and your adopted child." Yes! That's what he said, and may he have my blessing!'

Yoryis was me. And I had actually made that promise, but much earlier. It was during the time that our mother was working to take care of our first adopted sister as well as ourselves. I used to go with her during school vacations, playing by her side while she dug or weeded. On day we stopped work early and were coming back from the fields to get away from the unbearable heat that had nearly caused my mother to faint. Along the way we were caught in one of those violent rainstorms that in our region usually occurs after a preceding intense hot spell – or 'scorcher', as the natives call it. We weren't very far from the village now, but we had to cross a river bed that had become a violently rushing torrent. My mother wanted to lift me on to her shoulders, but I refused.

'You're weak from the fainting spell,' I told her. 'You'll drop me in the river.' And I hitched up my clothes and ran into the stream before she had a chance to grab me. I had trusted in my strength more than I should have because before I could think to go back, I lost my footing and was bowled over and dragged along by the torrent like a walnut shell. A heart-rending cry of terror is all I remember after that. It was the voice of my mother as she threw herself into the stream to save me.

It's a wonder that I wasn't responsible for her drowning as well as my own. That river bed has a bad reputation in those parts, and when they say of someone that 'the river got him', they mean that he drowned in that very spot. And yet my mother, faint as she was, exhausted, and weighed down by the native costume that was enough to drown even the most skilful swimmer, did not hesitate to expose her own life to danger. She had to save me, even though I was the child she once offered to God in exchange for her daughter.

When she got me home and set me down from her shoulder, I was still very dazed. For this reason, instead of blaming my own lack of foresight for what had happened, I attributed it to my mother's labours.

'Don't work any more, *Mana*,' I told her while she was putting dry clothes on me.

'Well, my child, who'll take care of us if I don't work?' she asked with a sigh.

'I will, *Mana!* I will!' I answered with childish self-importance.

'And our adopted daughter?'

'Her, too!'

My mother smiled in spite of herself at the impressive pose I assumed in pronouncing this assurance. Then she put an end to the subject by adding, 'Well, take care of yourself first, and then we'll see.'

Not much later I left home.

I didn't think my mother would even notice that promise. I, however, always remembered that her selflessness had for a second time granted me the life that I owed to her in the first place. For this reason I kept that promise in my heart, and the older I got, the more seriously I thought myself obliged to fulfil it. 'Don't cry, Mother,' I said to her as I left. 'I'm on my way to make money now. You'll see! From now on I'll take care of both you and your adopted daughter. But – do you hear? –I don't want you to work any more!'

I did not yet know that a ten-year-old child, far from being able to take care of his mother, can't even take care of himself. And I didn't imagine what frightful adventures awaited me, and how many bitter draughts I was yet to force my mother to drink during that absence from home by which I had hoped to ease her burden. For many years not only did I not manage to send her any assistance, I didn't even send a single letter. For many years she prowled the streets asking passers-by if they had seen me anywhere.

Once they told her I had run into money problems in Constantinople and had turned Turk. 'May those who spread that rumour eat their tongue!' my mother said in reply. 'The one they're talking about, he can't have been my child!' But after a short while she shut herself up all atremble in front of our iconostasion and with tears running down her face prayed God to enlighten me so I would come back to the faith of my fathers.

Once they told her I had shipwrecked on the shores of Cyprus and was dressed in rags and begging in the streets. 'May fire burn them!' she answered. 'They're saying that out of jealousy. My child must have made his fortune and is going on a pilgrimage to the Holy Sepulchre in Jerusalem.' But after a little while she went out into the streets, questioning the travelling beggars, and she went wherever she heard of a shipwrecked person in the forlorn hope that she would discover in him her own child, with the intent of giving him her last coins in the same way that I found them abroad from the hands of others.

And yet, whenever it was a question of her adopted daughter, she forgot all of this and threatened my brothers, saying that when I came back from abroad, I would put them to shame with my generosity, and I would dower and marry off her daughter with pomp and ceremony. 'What? You don't believe me? My child promised me this himself! May he have my blessing!'

Fortunately those dire reports were not true. And when, after a long absence,

I returned to our house, I was in a position to fulfil my promise, at least as far as my mother was concerned because she was so frugal. As for her adopted daughter, however, she did not find me so eager as she had hoped. On the contrary, as soon as I arrived, I spoke out against keeping her, to my mother's great surprise.

It's true I was not really opposed to my mother's obsession. I found that her partiality for girls conformed to my own feelings and desires. There was nothing I desired more upon my return than to find in our house a sister whose cheerful face and loving concerns would banish the lonely sadness from my heart, who would erase from memory all the hardships I had suffered abroad. In return I would have been eager to tell her the wonders of foreign lands, my wanderings and my accomplishments, and I would have been eager to buy her whatever she wanted; to take her to dances and festivals, to dower her and, finally, to dance at her wedding.

But I imagined that sister pretty and likeable, educated and bright, knowing how to read and embroider – in short with all the accomplishments possessed by the girls of the lands in which I had lived up till then. And instead of all this what did I find? Exactly the opposite. My adopted sister was still young, an emaciated, ill-formed, ill-willed and above all hostile little girl, so hostile that right from the start she prompted my dislike. 'Give Katerinio back,' I said to my mother one day. 'Give her back, if you love me. I mean it this time! I'll bring you another sister from the City, a pretty girl, a bright one who'll be an ornament to our house one day.' Then I described in the most lively colours what the orphan I would bring her would be like, and how much I would love it.

When I raised my eyes to look at her, I saw to my astonishment that large tears were flowing silently down over her pale cheeks, while her downcast eyes expressed an indescribable sorrow! 'Oh!' she said in a despairing tone of voice. 'I thought you would love Katerinio more than the others, but I was wrong! They don't want a sister at all, and you want a different one! And how is the poor thing at fault if she was born as God made her? If you had a stupid, ugly sister, would you throw her into the street for that reason, to get another one who was beautiful and intelligent?'

'No, Mother, surely not,' I answered. 'But she would be your child, just as I am. But this one isn't anything to you. She's a complete stranger to us.'

'No,' my mother cried out with a sob, 'no! The child isn't a stranger! She's mine! I took her from her mother's dead body when she was three months old; and whenever she cried, I stuck my breast into her mouth to fool her; and I wrapped her in your swaddling clothes, and I put her to bed in your cradle. She's my child and she's your sister!'

After these words which she uttered forcefully and impressively, she raised her head and fixed her eyes on me. She awaited my answer belligerently. But I did not say a word. Then she lowered her eyes again and continued in a weak and mournful tone: 'Eh! What can be done? I wanted her better, too, but . . . my sin, you see, hasn't been lifted yet. And God has made her like this to test my endurance and to forgive me. I thank you, oh Lord.' And with this she placed her right hand on her breast, raised her tear-filled eyes to heaven, and remained silent in this position for several moments.

'You must have something weighing on your heart, Mother,' I said somewhat timidly. 'Don't be angry.'

I took her cold hand in mine and kissed it to appease her.

'Yes!' she said decisively. 'I do have something heavy inside me, something very heavy, my child! Up till now only God and my confessor has known about it. You've read a lot and sometimes talk like my confessor himself, even better. Get up, close the door, and sit while I tell you. Perhaps you'll provide me a little consolation, perhaps you'll feel sorry for me and come to love Katerinio as if she were your sister.'

These words, and the manner in which she pronounced them, threw my heart into great confusion. What had my mother to entrust to me and not to my brothers? She had told me all she'd suffered while I was away. All her life before that I knew as if it were a fairy tale. So what was it she had been keeping from us up till now? What had she not dared to reveal to anyone except God and her confessor? When I came over and sat down next to her, my legs were shaking from a vague but powerful fear.

My mother hung her head as a condemned person does when facing his judge in the consciousness of some awful crime.

'Do you remember our Annio?' she asked after a few moments of oppressive silence.

'Yes, Mother, of course I remember her! She was our only sister, and she died before my very eyes.'

'Yes,' she said with a deep sigh, 'but she wasn't my only girl! You're four years younger than Hristakis. A year after he was born I had my first daughter.

'It was about the time Fotis Mylonas was wanting to get married. Your late father delayed their wedding until I had completed my forty days after delivery so we could give them away together. He also wanted to take me out in public so I could have the good time as a married woman that your grandmother hadn't allowed me as a girl.

'The wedding took place in the morning, and in the evening everybody was invited to their house. There was violin music, and everybody ate in the court-yard, and the wine jug passed from hand to hand. And your late father was in a good mood, fun-loving man that he was, and he threw me his handkerchief to get up and dance with him. When I saw him dancing, my heart opened up to him and, being a young woman, I, too, loved to dance. So we danced, and the others danced on our heels. But we danced both better and more.

'When it got close to midnight I took your father aside and said to him: "Husband, I have a baby in the cradle and can't stay any longer. The baby's hungry; I'm full of milk. How can I feed it in public and in my good clothes? You stay if you want and have a good time. I'll take the baby and go home." "Eh, very well, wife!" he said, God bless his soul, and he patted me on the shoulder. "Come, dance this dance with me, and then we'll go home. The wine's begun to go to my head and I'm looking for a reason to leave, too."

'When we had danced that dance, we set out. The groom sent the players, and they escorted us half-way. But we had a long way to go to the house because the wedding took place in Karsimahalá on the other side of town. The servant went ahead with the lantern. Your father carried the baby, and also supported me on his arm.

'"You're tired, I see, wife."

'"Yes, Mihalio, I'm tired."

'"Come on, just a little more strength until we get home. I'll lay out the beds myself. I'm sorry I made you dance so much."

'"No matter, husband," I told him. "I did it to please you. Tomorrow I'll be rested again."

'So we arrived home. I swaddled and fed the child while he laid out the beds. Hristakis was sleeping with Venetia, whom I had left to watch him. In a little while we went to bed, too. There, in my sleep, I thought I heard the baby begin to cry. The poor thing, I thought; it hasn't had enough to eat today. And I leaned over its crib to suckle it. But I was too tired and couldn't hold myself up. So I took it out and laid it on the mattress beside me and put the nipple in its mouth. Then sleep took hold of me again.

'I don't know how long it was till morning, but when I felt that day was breaking – "Better put the baby back again," I said. But when I went to pick it up, what did I see? The baby didn't move! I woke your father up. We unswaddled it, we warmed it, we rubbed its little nose – nothing! It was dead!

'"You smothered my baby, woman!" said your father and he burst into tears. Then I began to cry and wail, too. But your father put his hand on my mouth and said, "Shush! Why are you bellowing like that, you ox?" That's what he said to me, God forgive him. We'd been married three years, and he'd never said a harsh word to me. But he said one then. "Eh? Why are you bellowing like this? Do you want to rouse the neighbourhood so that everybody can say you got drunk and smothered your baby?"

'And he was right, God bless the dust that covers him! Because if people found out, I would have had to split the earth and enter it out of shame. But what can you do? A sin is a sin. When we had buried the child and come back from the church, then the formal mourning began. Then at last I did not cry in secret. "You're young," they told me, "and you'll have others." But time passed and

God didn't give us one. "There!" I said to myself. "God is punishing me because I wasn't worthy to take care of the child he gave me." And I felt ashamed in the company of others and was afraid of your father because all that year he pretended not to be sad, and tried to comfort me so as to give me courage. Later, however, he began to fall silent and thoughtful.

'Three years passed – without eating bread that could go to my heart. But after these three years you were born. You can imagine the thank-offerings I made. When you were born my heart settled down but did not find peace. Your father wanted you a girl and one day he told me so: "This one is welcome, too, Despinio, but I wanted it to be a girl."

'When your grandmother went to the Holy Sepulchre, I sent twelve shirts and three *konstantináta* with her to get me a pardon. And just look! The month your grandmother came back from Jerusalem with the pardon, that very month I began to be pregnant with Annio.

'I called the midwife frequently. "Come here, lady, and let's have a look. Is it a girl?" "Yes, daughter," said the midwife. "A girl. Don't you see? Your clothes aren't big enough for you!" What joy I felt when I heard this! When the baby was born and turned out actually to be a girl, then my heart returned to its proper place. We named it Annio, the same name the dead girl had, so it wouldn't seem that anybody was missing from our house. "Thank you, Lord," I said night and day. "This sinner thanks you because you have lifted my shame and blotted out my sin."

'And we loved Annio more than life itself. And you were jealous, and could have died from your jealousy. Your father called you "his wronged one" because I weaned you so soon, and he yelled at me every once in a while for neglecting you. My heart was torn apart when I saw you wasting away. But, you see, I couldn't let Annio out of my hands! I was afraid that at any moment something might happen to her. And your father, God rest his soul, no matter how often he yelled at me, he, too, was very protective of her.

'But the poor child, the more attention she got, the worse her health became. You'd think God had regretted giving her to us. You all were ruddy and lively and active. She was quiet and silent and sickly. When I saw her so pale, so very pale, the dead girl came to my mind, and the thought that I had killed her began to take over within me again. Until one day the second one died, too!

'Whoever hasn't experienced it himself, my child, doesn't know what a bitter draught that was. There was no hope I would have another girl. Your father had died. If there hadn't been some parent to give me his girl, I'd have taken to the hills and run away. It's true she didn't turn out good-natured. But as long as I had her and took care of her and cherished her, I thought I had my own, and I forgot the one I'd lost, and I calmed my conscience. As the saying goes, another's child is a torture. But for me this torture is a consolation and relief because the more I'm tormented and torn apart, the less God will punish me for the child I smothered.

'And so – and may you have my blessing – don't ask me now to get rid of Katerinio and get another good-natured and industrious child.'

'No, no, Mother!' I cried out, interrupting her impetuously. 'I don't ask for anything. After what you've told me I beg your pardon for my heartlessness. I promise you I'll love Katerinio as my sister and will never say anything harsh to her again.'

'May you have the blessings of Christ and the Virgin!' my mother said with a sigh, 'because, you see, my heart is filled with pity for the poor child, and I don't want them to say bad things about her. I don't know, you see. Was it fate? Was it God's doing? No matter how bad and slow she is, I'm responsible,' she concluded.

This revelation made a profound impression on me. Now my eyes were opened, and now I understood many of my mother's actions that had at some times seemed like superstition, at others purely the results of obsession. That frightful accident had had all the greater influence on my mother's entire life because she was unsophisticated and virtuous and God-fearing. The conscious-ness of her sin, the moral necessity of expiation and the impossibility of expiation – what a horrible and implacable Hell! The poor woman had been tormented for twenty-eight years now without being able to put to rest the reproaches of her conscience either in good times or in bad.

From the moment I learned her sad story I directed all my attention to light-ening her heart by trying to represent to her on the one hand the unpremeditated and involuntary nature of her sin, and on the other God's extreme compassion and His justice, which does not requite like with like, but judges us according to our thoughts and intentions. And there was a time when I believed my attempts were not without success.

Nonetheless, when, after a new absence of two years, my mother came to see me in Constantinople, I thought it a good idea to do something still more impres-sive on her behalf. At that time I was a guest in the most distinguished house in Constantinople, in which I had occasion to become acquainted with the Patriarch Ioakim II. While we were walking alone one day under the spreading shade of the trees in the garden, I laid out the story to him and asked his assistance. His high office, the remarkable authority in which his every religious pronouncement was clad, would surely inspire the conviction in my mother that her sin had been pardoned. That old man of blessed memory praised my zeal in religious matters and promised me his eager cooperation.

So after a little while I took my mother to the Patriarchate to confess to his Holiness. The confession lasted a long time, and from the Patriarch's gestures and words I saw that he was being compelled to use all the force of his plain,

clear eloquence in order to bring about the desired result. My joy was indescribable. My mother bade the venerable Patriarch farewell with sincere gratitude,
and came out of the Patriarchate as happy and as buoyant as if a large millstone
had been removed from her heart.

When we reached her lodging, she took a cross out of her bosom, a gift from
His Holiness, kissed it, and began to examine it carefully, little by little sinking
deeper into thought.

'A good man, the Patriarch, don't you think?' I said. 'Now at last, I imagine,
your heart has returned to its proper place.'

My mother didn't answer.

'Haven't you anything to say, Mother?' I asked with some hesitation.

'What can I tell you, my child?' she answered, still deep in thought. 'The
Patriarch is a wise and holy man. He knows all God's plans and wishes, and he
pardons everybody's sins. But what can I tell you? He's a monk. He never had
children, so he can't know what a thing it is to kill one's own child!'

Her eyes filled with tears, and I said nothing.

Translated by William F. Wyatt Jr

Alexandros Papadiamantis (1851–1910)

Papadiamantis was, like his contemporary Vizyinos (q.v.), the son of a peasant family (in his case, a clerical one) who came to know the benefits – and the costs – of a modern education. Papadiamantis spent most of his life in Athens, longing for his native island of Skiathos – in its pristine post-Byzantine form, before modern life had eroded its religious foundations – but acutely attentive to the life of the big city in all its manifestations. In between back-breaking labours as a professional translator, punctuated by frequent visits to church and tavern, Papadiamantis produced an important short novel, *The Murderess*, and a body of short stories which bears comparison with Chekhov's. The subtleties of Papadiamantis' style – which reaches into all corners of the Greek language from ancient literature and the liturgy to dialect and song – has done much to deter translators; and conveying his gifts as that rare thing in modern Greece, a great comic writer, is no easy task. Here we include a seemingly light-hearted and insubstantial tale, 'Homesick' (1896), which shows him at the height of his powers.

Homesick

The moon appeared, just waning now three nights past its utmost fullness, at the summit of the mountain, and she, all in white, after many a sigh and many a melancholy song, cried out:

'Oh! If I could just get in a boat . . . right now . . . that's what I'd like . . . so we could go over there!'

And with her hand she was pointing beyond the harbour.

Mathios had not perhaps noted that in her speech she had shifted to the plural – at the close of her wish. But instinctively, without thinking about it, he replied:

'I could push out that boat on the beach . . . How about it? Shall we give it a try?'

And he too used the plural at the end of his speech. Without moreover pausing to think, as though he wanted to see if his muscles were strong, he started to push the boat.

The lad was standing near the water's edge, where, time after time, whispering softly as they arrived, the waves were swallowed by the sand – without their becoming tired ever of this their eternal monotonous diversion, without its becoming sated ever with this its everlasting salty irrigation. The woman was on the balcony of the house, which her husband, an elderly 53-year-old, had rented to receive her in; a house situated on the shore, now in and now out of the waves: in with the flood-tide brought by the south wind, or out with the ebb-tide induced by the north. The boat was resting on the land and rocking on the sea, its bow stuck in the sand, its stern swayed by the waves, a light skiff, grace-ful, with a pointed prow and space for four or five.

A large local schooner with its cargo had put in at the harbour three days before and was waiting for a favourable wind before setting off on the final leg of its voyage; the captain for the third night now had reposed at home, made much of in the proximity of spouse and offspring; his ship-mates, all of them locals, were making the round of the bars, compensating in three nights for the enforced abstinence of weeks and months; the ship's boy, not himself a local, was left sole guard of the ship with its tackle and its freight; and the sole guard of the ship's boy was the ship's dog. But that evening, the ship's boy, a lanky eighteen-year-old who had all the expectations of a sailor but not the wage, had lingered at a bar which was somewhat out of the way, being on the inner road of the coastal market, and had found his own consolation there, as a stranger among strangers. He had left the dinghy half dragged up on the beach, with its bow stuck in the sand and its stern swaying on the waves, with its two oars rest-ing on the stern, two light oars which a youth would handle with indescribable joy, glorying, as he did so, in a strength multiplied by the fleeting softness of the waves, as yielding as a mother in her weakness for a pampered child, which carries her where it wills with its whimpers, with its wants; oars that, resembling a gull's two wings, which carry the downy white body of the bird to the surface of the sea, would guide the boat towards the sand and the outstretched arms of the land, as its wings guide the gull to its cave in the sea-washed rock.

Mathios placed his two hands on the bow, braced his two legs behind him, pushed with all his strength, and the small dinghy gave ground and fell with a splash into the sea. It nearly got away, acting under the powerful impetus; for he had neglected to hang on to the bowfast, the line attached to the bow. But at that, he threw off his flimsy sandals, he did not have time to roll up his trousers, he went up to his knees in the water, and he caught the boat by its bow. He dragged it toward a small and makeshift mole.

She meanwhile had vanished from the balcony, and a few moments later she appeared, with her white smock shining in the light of the moon, at the north-ern corner of the house, stepping down on to the sand.

The youth saw her and felt both joy and fear. He was acting almost uncon-sciously. He had not dared to hope her capable of doing it.

She, not caring to disclose her innermost reflections, said:

'Yes . . . Why not? Yes. Let's go once round the harbour, now in the moonlight.'

And then, shortly after, came:

'So that I can see how I'll like it, when I take ship to go over there . . .'

She said *over there* each time, and she meant home. Behind the first, green mountain, that above which the moon had risen, a mountain black at night, but ashen now and umbrous in the light of the moon, there rose the peak of a high, a white, a sometimes snow-covered and sometimes bare and rocky mountain. That was her home, the place where she was born. And she sighed after it as if separated from it by an entire ocean, when, in fact, there was but scarcely twelve miles between and in daylight the green mountain's low ridge did not suffice to conceal the tall summit of the white mountain. And she yearned after it as much as if she had been parted from it many years since, when but scarcely a few weeks had she been on the neighbouring island.

At all events, she placed her hand, white and so light, innocently on the shoulder of the young man, who trembled at the touch from head to toe, and she stepped into the little boat.

He followed after her and, taking an oar, began clumsily to push off. But instead of pushing against the pier, he pushed on the left against the bottom, and in consequence the boat swung round, and it bumped slightly against one of the stones in the pier.

'Watch out! We'll damage their boat.'

This made her reflect more soberly on things, and afterwards came:

'Won't the boat be missed? Won't they want it? . . . Whose can it be?'

Disconcerted, the youth replied:

'Seeing we're just going once round the harbour and coming back . . . I shouldn't think it'll be missed that soon, whoever it belongs to.'

*

He sat at the oars and started rowing. She was seated in the stern, and the moon's pale light was shining on her, seeming to dust the fine features of her handsome face with silver. The lad was gazing timidly at her.

He was not a sailor, but having been reared near the sea, he could row. He had come home half-way through the year, having left the school in the region's capital, at which he had been a pupil, after declining the punishment prescribed for him following an argument with a schoolmaster of his, one seeming to him to be possessed of a greater than his due degree of ignorance. He was just eighteen, but with the already dense first growth of his chestnut beard and moustache, he looked nineteen or twenty.

The young woman, once she had sat down, by way of afterword to her expression of anxiety of shortly before as to the possibility of the boat's being sought by its owner, facetiously voiced this thought of hers too:

'The boat's owner will be looking for his boat, and Uncle-Monachakis will be looking for his Lialio.'

The young man grinned. Uncle-Monachakis was the name of her husband. Lialio was her own.

*

At that moment a dog could be heard barking loudly on the deck of a ship. It was the ship's dog on the same laden schooner to which the dinghy belonged, and it had jumped on to the fo'c'sle, next to the *Macedonian Girl*, the crude crested figurehead in the bows. At first, recognizing the boat, the dog whined and wagged its tail, but when the boat got closer, and the dog recognized in the two passengers neither the ship's boy nor any other member of the crew, it started frantically to yelp and howl.

The young student went a little wide of the schooner, but the further away the dog saw the boat go, the more frantically it howled.

'What's got into it? Why doesn't it stop?' Lialio asked anxiously.

'It must have recognized the boat.'

'Is this little boat that schooner's?'

'So it seems.'

The youth voiced this conjecture with regret, foreseeing that this circum-stance would of necessity cut short this for him dream-like excursion; but, instead, like an ill-behaved child that gets most pleasure from doing what others forbid it, Lialio clapped her hands.

'Then, I'm glad,' she said. 'Let the dog howl for his boat, and let them hunt for me at home . . .'

The youth found the courage to ask:

'Where was Kir-Monachakis when you came down from the house?'

'He's always at the café . . . He never budges from there before midnight . . . I'm always left on my own.'

And she seemed on the point of tears. But with an effort she held herself in check, and no tears came.

The youth went on rowing. Soon they were not far from the eastern entrance to the harbour, from which was visible, breaking the horizon opposite, the long island on which stood the white, sometimes snowy, sometimes bare and rocky mountain. When they were nearing the cape that shut off there on one side the harbour mouth, which further to the south-east was shut off by two or three small islands, the young woman gazed steadily beyond, towards the horizon, as though she wished to see further and more, or as much at least as the pale gleam of the moon allowed.

'Let me see over there, and then we can go back,' she said.

And she sighed.

The youth found the courage to make a request:

'How does that song go that you sing sometimes?'

'Which song?'

'The song . . . about sails, and the wheel . . . and about the far mountains,' stammered the youth.

'Ah!'

And with that, in a low contralto, on a passionate murmured note, she started to sing:

> When will we make sail, that I might take the wheel,
> Might see the far mountains, my pains to heal

She repeated this couplet a second time, then a third, to an old tune long known to her.

'Here, you can see them now, the far mountains,' said Mathios, 'only instead of sails we have oars; and we're missing the wheel too.'

Once again the young woman sighed.

'Is it time we went back now?' asked the youth.

He said this with sadness; the words seemed to shrivel on his tongue.

'A bit further, just a bit further,' said Lialio. 'The shadow cast by those islands stops you seeing right over there . . . All I can see is Derfi.'

'Derfi's down there,' said the youth, pointing towards Euboea in the south.

'We call the tall mountain at home Derfi,' responded Lialio, pointing to the east.

And once again she sang her song, but with one phrase changed:

> When will we make sail, that I might take the wheel,
> Might see Mount Derfi, my pains to heal

The youth let out a deep breath, exactly like a sigh.

'Oh, I wasn't thinking. This much rowing must be back-breaking for you,' said Lialio. 'I must be out of my mind . . . Your dainty hands aren't meant for rowing, Master Mathios.'

The youth protested:

'No, no, I'm not tired . . . The oars are quite light . . . How could little oars like these tire me?'

Lialio insisted she have one of the oars, and bending forward a little, she started to pull with her white hands at one of the rowlocks: wanting to move it further towards her in the stern. But the youth resisted, and their hands came together in warm contact.

'And you say that my hands are soft,' he said, restrained reproach in his voice.

'Well then, what about putting up a sail like it says in the song?' proposed the young woman playfully.

'What with?'

And he was looking involuntarily at her pure white smock.

Lialio laughed and leant back again against the stern.

*

Already they had reached the mouth of the harbour and had on one side of them the cliffs of the cape, which seemed, breaking as they did the verdant harmony of the mountain, to be the result of an earthquake or a landslide, and, on the other, two or three islands, those closing the harbour to the south east. The moon was rising constantly higher in the firmament, darkening the last of the stars, which, though invisible now, still shone meekly in the depths of the sky. The sea was trembling a little in the slight breeze – all that was left of the wind which had furrowed it in the morning. It was a warm May night and the slight breeze was cooler there, blowing as it did across the open sea at the mouth of the harbour. Two dark masses, faintly silvered and polished by the melancholy light of the moon, one to the east and one to the west, stood out without its being possible through the alternations of light and shadow to distinguish the features of the land. These were the two neighbouring islands. Mysterious enchantment filled the moonlit night. The boat was floating past the first small island, and emerging there in turn were patches of light and darkness, rocks glowing lambently in the moonlight, shadowy foliage rustling gently in the eddies of the evening breeze, and caverns washed by swirling waves, where one sensed the presence of sea birds and heard the anxious wing beat of wild doves put up by the soft plash of the oars and the small boat's proximity. Beyond, to the north-east, on a declivity of the mountain, were some flickering lights, marking the point at which, visible during the day, were the small white dwellings of a village high above the sea. Next to the island was a rock, hollowed and holed, and the waves falling on it boomed and roared, and it seemed as if, sonorous within the general harmony of the moonlit sea, there were a separate orchestra there that on its own produced more sound than was generated by every beach, by every bay and gulf, by every reef and every shore, that was washed by the waves. Unthinkingly, Mathios raised the oars and rested them on the gunwale, and lapsing into stillness, he became like that white bird of the sea dropping gracefully towards the waves, one wing down, the other up, motionless a few moments, before swooping to catch the swimming fish and lift it gasping and writhing through the air. He was experiencing indescribable rapture. Lialio too was feeling mysterious entrancement, and their gazes met.

'Shall we make sail?' repeated the young woman.

It seems she had not ceased to think about this since she had first said it; and she was saying it now in a manner so simple and natural it was as if she were merely formulating a thought common to them both.

'Let's,' Mathios responded innocently.

And as he no longer knew what he was saying, this time he didn't ask *what with*.

But Lialio spared him the trouble of seeking the means. She stood up and, bending down gracefully, with a few dextrous movements took off her white, finely pleated smock, and proffered it to Mathios.

'You get the mast ready,' she said.

Surprised, but spellbound and smiling, the youngster took one oar, raised it perpendicular to the cross-beam, took one end of the bowfast, and tied the oar to the beam with it. Next, having freed the other end of the bowfast from the ring on the bow, he took the other oar and tied it to the first, cross-wise, like a yard to the mast. And then he took hold, warm still from its contact with her skin, of the young woman's white smock, and he fastened it to the second oar, as a sail.

Lialio was left with her shift, stopping at the calf and white as her smock, and with her white stockings, through which, whiter still, might be divined her shapely rounded calves. She was left with the lily-white of her neck imperfectly concealed by her silken, purple kerchief, and she sat constrainedly, near the stern, seeming shorter than she was, given her medium and handsome build.

And the breeze had strengthened, and the improvised sail was filling, and the small boat was gathering speed.

*

Nothing more was said about returning to the harbour. What for? It was evident henceforth that they were sailing 'to the far mountains'.

Shyly, Mathios sat down not very near her, on the other side of the stern, and, so as not to look too long at his companion and embarrass her, he was looking at the sea.

At that moment, that verse by a poet of the Ionian Islands was coming into his mind that figured so largely in all the love affairs of that time, 'Awake, my sweet love . . .' and he was thinking of the couplet, 'The misty moon alone . . .' and of this one also:

> Farewell you gorges, springs, and icy waters
> Sweet dawns, small birds, farewell for ever!

He was thinking of these lines, but he didn't want to sing them. They seemed to him now to be out of place. Instead, the song that he judged best fitted that night was the song best loved by Lialio.

> When will we make sail, that I might take the wheel,
> Might see the far mountains, my pains to heal

*

He had sat down not very far from her, close enough to her for it to be impossible for him to look at her without an effort, far enough from her for him not to sense her warm flesh's and her breath's proximity. All the same he kept wanting to look at her, and, in the end, became dizzy from looking at the waves.

The youth took off his thin, short jacket and was pleading with her to cover herself with it to keep herself from getting cold – for, as the night advanced, the off-shore winds started coming off the mountains. She was refusing to take the garment, saying she did not feel in the least cold; no, she was rather hot.

Mathios insisted no further, but started to reflect on matters concerning her, on whatever of her life and lot was known to him. For among those with whom he was intimate there were people that the young woman had come into contact with during her brief time on the island. Lialio was not in her first youth, albeit she retained almost all her girlish freshness. Nor in respect of her marriage to Kir-Monachakis was she still newly wed. She was twenty-five, and she had married five years before. Kir-Monachakis had taken her as his second wife, having buried his first and married off his daughter, who was Lialio's senior by one year. It had appeared to him that in marrying this twenty-year-old girl, he would become younger by twenty years himself. Still, as long as he'd been kept far from his birth-place, working for the revenue service wherever the government chose to send him, Lialio had not suffered greatly. She had stayed by her parents' side, unable to follow Kir-Monachakis on his gipsy-like wanderings round Greece, in which he went wherever he was required, like, as he said himself, 'an old boat yawing this way and that'.

Ah! No air was there fit for tender blooms, and she would have wilted there in a month had irreverent hands dared transplant her. The pot was of alabaster, the plant was delicate, and the bloom exuded a perfume too fine for vulgar nostrils. But, recently, when, after long efforts, Kir-Monachakis had had himself transferred to the neighbouring island, he persuaded his father-in-law, who esteemed him above all others of their generation, to send Lialio to him at his posting, that he might live with her under one roof. Weeping, Lialio, who bore toward her a sisterly affection, said good-bye to her step-daughter – just become a mother and ceasing now to fear that she might have a little step-brother there, an uncle to her new-born child – and having boarded ship, she came, or rather removed, to the neighbouring island.

On the day of her arrival, Kir-Monachakis entertained his friends liberally, but on the morrow he ceased to receive at home. And in this, there was nothing strange, since, in fact, he was never there. He was either at his office or at the café. He would light his yard-long hubble-bubble, which would burn without let almost along the whole length of his sky-blue breeches, and he would become jovial, a garrulous ever and noisy boaster, his cheeks as red almost as his tall, scarlet fez, which was given a slight tilt towards his right ear by a crease it had in one side, and which had too, covering his shoulder with its strands, a heavy, corded tassel.

From the second week on, Lialio never failed, if she was awake as he returned homeward during the early hours, to moan and to demand he send her back to her parents. It was impossible, so she said, for her to live far from them. And, in truth, from the first days of her removal her heart began to hurt, her appetite to leave her, and her face to grow constantly paler. But Uncle-Monachakis sternly gave her to understand that it would not be fitting for her, having once come, to leave him so soon. He expounded a lengthy theory according to which it is the duty of a woman to be wherever her husband is; for to do otherwise is to frustrate the purpose of Christian marriage, which according to the most orthodox sources is not to multiply the species, but is rather to instil restraint in man and woman; for were it otherwise, he said, childlessness would naturally be sufficient grounds for divorce, and, besides, all that is required for the multiplying of the species is common-law marriage, which is altogether different from religious and civil marriage; and he ranged against her numerous quotations from the two Testaments, such as 'This is now bone of my bones, and flesh of my flesh' and 'Those whom God hath joined together let no man put asunder' and 'The head of the woman is the man', and so forth. She stifled her sobs in the two palms of her hands and in her two plaits, and with the two ends of her white head-scarf she sponged the traces of her tears.

*

The youth, as a neighbour, had heard how things stood, and fell secretly in love with her. The grace of her lithe figure was not concealed by the waistless frock she wore. And the curls adorning her lovely forehead were natural and not factitious. The light in her dark, deep-set eyes burned darkly below her vaulted brows, and her crimson lips showed, rose-like, against the translucent pallor of her cheeks, which easily, with the slightest effort or the least emotion, became faintly flushed. Yet the fine, calm fire in her eyes was what burned the youngster's heart.

In fine, he loved her. She, when she came out on to the balcony, as she often did, would look, pensive and abstracted, towards him for a moment. Then, her gaze straying, she would look towards a point on the eastern horizon, towards the *far mountains*; till, that is, that night, when, with the moon rising, her husband missing, she saw the lad, out after supper for a breath of sea air, standing on the shore. Mathios, seeing her on the balcony, wished her good evening, exchanged a few words with her, and then, quite by chance, without its being in her mind either, made the altogether unexpected proposal of a brief boat trip from which this curious voyage ensued. The young woman seemed to live a life of dreams, a dream existence. From time to time, waking suddenly from her long trance, she seemed to become aware again of the real world, but no more than a few minutes would go by before she dropped once more into her torpid slumber and sank deeper still into her treasured dream.

It was already midnight, and either because of the current or because of the off-shore wind, and because they had no rudder, they had been carried little by little northwards: to a point opposite the high village's flickering lights, which now looked closer, and next to the isolated, small and rocky island off the north-eastern shore, which to a few coneys put there by the islanders was their prison, and to every kind of gull and other sea bird was their palace; it was called White Isle.

Not till then did Mathios take one of the oars (he had been obliged to take down the makeshift sail to give Lialio her smock; for although she wouldn't admit it, she had got cold, and he had had to abolish mast and sail) and use it as a rudder to try to turn the bow to the right, towards the easternmost point on the opposite shore, that known as Trachili. But he saw that he was achieving nothing, it being impossible with this surrogate rudder to turn the current to advantage, and he was forced to take his seat again at the oars.

But it seems either the nymphs of the night breezes, which were starting to blow off the land, or those of the ocean currents, furrowing the sound between the two islands, wished Lialio well. For they were but a few metres beyond the White Isle when, close to the three south-eastern islands, coming from the harbour, there appeared a large launch, which, moving at great speed, its bows pointing toward Cape Trachili, its six oars striking the water, dashed over the sea's back as a mare bolting from the race-track dashes over the meadow.

Lialio gave a start. The youth turned and looked. Automatically, he stopped rowing and sat undecided.

'Quick, quick,' said Lialio in a whisper, as though the sound of her voice might be heard. 'Get behind the White Isle, quick! . . .'

The youth started backing the oars rapidly. Already, they lay just within the shadow of the land, which screened the moon from view. They rounded a rocky point and hid behind the island.

'What do you think it is?' asked Lialio uneasily.

'It must have come after us,' replied the youth.

'They've come out to catch us?'

'It's us they're after. No question.'

'And what's that big boat?'

'It's a launch, with lots of oars, very fast.'

'So if we were out there, they'd catch us?'

'They're making for Trachili. They'd soon have caught up with us if we'd headed that way.'

'So, we were right to come this way, were we?'

'We didn't do it intentionally; we were carried here by the current.'

'The currents know what they are about!' said Lialio in a tone so exalted that she seemed like certain people who, whilst having premonitory dreams, extemporize apophthegms in their trance. And, at that moment, as she spoke, she believed that inanimate things were possessed of understanding, and that for each thing there was a god under whose custodianship it fell.

In truth, she wanted that it should seem as if the Nereid of ocean currents, or the Nymph of off-shore winds, had brought the little boat and its comely freight there deliberately and by design.

'And what shall we do now?' asked Mathios, feeling inwardly that he was helpless without the support of that benevolent nymph. And he understood then why the world had never, not since the Creation, ceased to be ruled by women.

'Now,' Lialio said, so lucidly and articulately that it was as if she had foreseen the whole situation. 'We'll wait half an hour, and if they don't suspect something and come and look over here, we'll go and land over at St Nicholas while they're still heading for Trachili. From there, in half an hour on foot, we can get up to Platana, the high village, and when God brings the dawn, in three hours we can walk from there to the big village, my village. Oh! if I might only set foot on that sacred soil again just once! If, though, they should suspect something and come this way, then off we go to your Xanemo, or whatever you call it, your Kefala; there, we dump the boat on the beach and go back over land to your village. "Where were you, Lialio?" . . . "I gave myself a bit of an outing, Uncle-Monachakis, and here I am again, back".'

She laughed to herself as she said this. Then, as the youth still looked anxious:

'The main thing is for them not to catch us, she added. I don't care what people will say! Not one jot! I couldn't care less! As long as we're really innocent, let the fools say what they like.'

The youth leant forward passionately and kissed the tips of her fingers, thinking that, yes, he was innocent, like many of those who, as History relates, were unjustly condemned to slow death by fire. She reacted sternly:

'If I wanted to fool around, the safest thing would be for me to stick with Uncle-Monachakis. Proof that I don't want to is that I set out to go back to my parents. My parents couldn't cover for me if I played around: Uncle-Monachakis could, and would very well, what's more.'

A sharp knife clove the young man's heart. He imagined that doubtless the young woman had another lover at home. It was towards him then that she was running, towards him that she was charting this singular course. And his own role then was what? What was he in that event? A bridge on which two beings in love trod that they might meet, a Charon in the service of infernal passions! . . .

Oh! what fire flamed within him! And how he felt roaring and raging inside him at that moment all the instincts of a tragic hero! (And, did the artistic conscience of the writer but allow it, how easy for the present idyll to be transformed into a melodrama! Imagine the launch giving chase to the two fugitives on the light skiff, Mathios by a miraculous feat of oarsmanship giving their pursuers the slip, and then, having discovered at the last moment that the homesick girl had a lover, plunging his dagger into her breast or sinking the boat and drowning the woman before abandoning himself too to the waves! Finally, under the light of the moon, the launch searching for the two bodies in the depths of the sea! What prodigies of romance, what sensitive shedding of tears! . . .)

And so, with a great effort, he restrained himself, and gazing at the young woman, he asked her simply:

'And before Kir-Monachakis wed you, was there no-one over there that loved you?'

'Well, I like that! Of course there was. Lots of them, what's more!' Lialio declared gaily. 'But the thing is, they only love poor girls the way they love flowers; they sniff at them once, then let them wither, or they pluck their petals; and, you see, I wasn't some heiress for them to fall in love with me and marry me formally with a fine ceremony, or even for them to elope with me and get a priest to marry us in secret, knowing all the while that my parents would get so desperate they'd hand over the dowry in the end . . . That's why nobody but Uncle-Monachakis could be found to take me. Lucky he did!'

Then in a whisper she pronounced this popular rhyme:

> My parents gave me away
> But me they gave no say . . .

'Then why are you leaving Kir-Monachakis?' asked the youth, referring back to the exclamation at the close of her speech.

'I'm not leaving him, I'm going home, back to my parents . . . Should Uncle-Monachakis come to look for me, he'll be welcome! He knows very well I wouldn't dishonour him. But he knows this too: I can't live away from home.'

The youth had not calmed down. He suspected the woman was deceitful, and he imagined himself to be a victim. Abruptly he asked her.

'Can it be that apart from the others there was no-one special that loved you? . . . that you wanted too . . . before you were married . . . or later, after you were married?'

Lialio sighed deeply and said:

'Ah! yes . . . to tell you the truth . . . The one they wanted for me . . . and I wanted too . . . It's six years now since the Black Sea took him . . . The boat went down with all hands . . . But if you've any heart, don't make me talk about it . . .'

*

Meanwhile, the launch, which the two fugitives had not ceased to observe, had gone quite some way with its bow pointing eastwards, when, suddenly, as it reached the furthermost side of the third and easternmost islet, it stopped for a few moments. Mathios pointed this out to his fellow-traveller.

'I know what's going on,' she said.

'What?'

'You'll see in a moment.'

The youth looked her in the eyes.

'Be patient, and I'll let you into the secret. Now you'll see it making for Trachili.'

'How can you tell? You must be a witch.'

'Yes, I am . . . I'm a witch!' she said with conviction.

Mathios sensed an indefinite apprehension in her flashing gaze.

That same moment, the launch finally turned to the east and continued rapidly on its way.

Mathios gave a gasp of wonder.

'Here's what's been going on,' repeated Lialio. 'I bet, in fact, I'm ninety-five per cent sure, that Uncle-Monachakis is in the launch.'

'And so?'

'The others, the oarsmen, partly because they want to get out of breaking their backs on the long crossing, and partly because it strikes them as more sensible, will have suggested looking round the islands, hoping that maybe they'll find us holed up there somewhere. Uncle-Monachakis, who well knows I'd have no business on the island and that all I would want to do is go home, is certain that I've headed straight over there for Trachili; and he hopes that if he catches up with me before I set foot in Agnonda, our island's little port, he'll get me to go back with him to your village. That's why he won't have wanted to lose time looking round the islands – so I won't have time to get over there and get away from him. And so he's persuaded the ones who are rowing to keep on going; and if that's got them cursing him under their breath, too bad!'

'So?'

'Now, once they've gone on some way, we'll cross over. Give me one of the oars.'

The youth did not resist; he shifted an oar towards the stern.

A short time elapsed, and the launch had gone so far that it was just visible in the depths of the immense horizon as a dark dot in motion and as a black speck on the silver-plate surface of the sea.

'Now let's row for it!' Lialio called out with engaging high spirits.

*

Kir-Monachakis was indeed on the launch, and the homesick young woman had not been mistaken. Half an hour after the two fugitives had embarked, he learned to his displeasure that 'his Lialio' was no longer at home. At the café, where he sat engaged in lively political discussion, with the smoke rising unremittingly from the long hubble-bubble beyond his wide breeches, a ten-year-old boy came in, without shoes, with a shirt with stripes and trousers the same, and said:

'Please, Mister, yer missus's gone.'

'Gone? Gone where?' said the worthy fellow, startled.

'I dunno.'

'You don't know? Who told you?'

'Markina's Vasilis. 'Ee were down on the beach an' 'ee seen 'er.'

'And who's he, this Markina's Vasilis?'

Turning towards the door the boy said:

'There. 'Im standing outside the door.'

Kir-Monachakis and the others, his fellow-disputants of a moment before, whose curiosity was greatly whetted, all turned towards the door.

A second boy, an eight-year-old, bare-footed, capless, with one leg of his trousers rolled up to just below the knee and his feet still wet from the sea, was standing outside the door, one half of his face hidden behind the door-post and one half of his body behind the wall, looking into the café with one eye.

'You there! Did you see my wife leaving?' shouted Kir-Monachakis.

'I seen 'er, mister,' replied the youngster.

'And where's she going?'

'I dunno.'

Kir-Monachakis jumped up in great distress, and with an angry gesture made as if to dash his hubble-bubble to the ground.

The first boy, who stood five paces from him, trembling lest he be hit with the hubble-bubble, took fright and made to run off.

The second boy, outside the door, vanished behind the wall.

'Don't be afraid,' said Kir-Monachakis, 'nobody'll hurt you if you're telling the truth, but, come here . . . tell me what you know . . . because . . .'

This was to be the only word that he would utter to express his grief, his rage and shame.

'Well, mister,' said the lad, feeling reassured and stopping near the door, 'Vasilis, ee saw the boat as your missus got into with Kalior's son, an' them go rowing around near the school-house. An' ee called me an' all, an' ee showed me the boat in the distance, but I never seen no people. An' we thought as how they were going to come back, an' they didn't come back.'

'And how long is it since you saw them?'

'Well, a couple o' hours per'aps, bit more maybe . . . only a while ago.'

'And why didn't you come and tell me sooner?'

'But it weren't very long . . . an hour or so, per'aps, no more'n an hour . . .and a bit maybe . . . a short while ago really.'

Kir-Monachakis made a second enraged gesture, as if to hurl his hubble-bubble into the corner. The boy hastened to make his escape.

*

Meanwhile Markina's Vasilis, who was some three hundred paces further on, was running with the eagerness that children display when bearing good news or bad, hoping as they do, in the first case, to secure for themselves thereby a reward, and, in the second, to enjoy the spectacle provided by the discomfiture of those involved. Panting, he reached the home of the schooner's master, and, seeing the door to the balcony was open and the chamber beyond well-lit, he stood underneath and started shouting with the full force of his lungs.

'Hey, Mister! They've taken yer boat.'

Vasilis had not earlier had the courage to go into the café and tell Kir-Monachakis the news. But now, seeing that his companion had communicated the news without getting a hiding, and knowing also that it would be impossible for the captain's stout stick to reach him from the balcony, he had became bolder and hastened to anticipate his companion in order that this time he might himself savour the pleasure.

Captain Kiriakos, who was still seated at his table, never wearying of another nibble or another sip, like many another sailor come home for a few days to his fireside, endlessly prolonging and ruminating on a pleasure for him so rare, stood up and came out on to the balcony.

'Well, what is it, then?'

'They've taken yer boat, 'aven't they.'

'Who has?'

'Malamo's Mathios.'

'What Malamo's Mathios?'

'You know, 'im what's the son of Ma Kaliori, what's 'is name?'

'And where's he taken it?'

'Out o' the 'arbour!'

'On his own?'

'He were with a woman.'

'With a woman,' repeated Captain Kiriakos astonished. 'What woman?'

The lad's answer remained unheard; for, just to be on the safe side, he sought the protection of the balcony.

'And why on earth didn't you come and tell me while they were taking it!' shouted Captain Kiriakos.

But the boy had disappeared round the corner of the wall, and only his footsteps were heard as he raced headlong over the cobblestones.

'That damned fool of a ship's boy must have gone and got himself pie-eyed somewhere,' the captain started muttering to himself, and left the dinghy to take its chances.

Right away, he sent out in search of the ship's boy, whom, after many fruitless inquiries made in the bars in the port, they finally found in an out-of-the-way bar on the inner road.

*

The captain gave orders for two of his comrades, then taking their ease at home, to procure themselves the use of a boat, so they could row over to the schooner and lower the big six-oared launch from the deck. He was concerned not so much about the woman who had, so it seemed, been abducted, or the young man fortunate enough to be her companion, as about his newly built, sound and shapely skiff. He further instructed that two or three boatmen be recruited on the quay to man the oars, and that they set off in pursuit of the little boat.

In the meantime, Kir-Monachakis, having learnt to whom the stolen boat belonged, appeared at the captain's house, looking wretched.

'You can go along in the launch yourself,' Captain Kiriakos said, having learnt at last whose wife the abducted woman (according, that is, to the interpretation that people naturally put on the incident) was.

Kir-Monachakis wanted precisely that, to go with the launch. He was afraid of staying waiting in the town in anguished anticipation, and it seemed to him that if he took part in the pursuit, he might through this distraction feel his pain less keenly. He had complete trust in Lialio, holding her incapable, as she herself said, of betraying his honour. But there again, who can tell? To whom is it given to penetrate the mysteries of the female mind? He recognized in her a dreamy tendency, a tendency toward languidness, and he was aware of her great, her profound homesickness. But how could he get others to understand? Let water be never so clean, woe to him that stumbles into a pit full of it. Though they may well decide to proffer a helping hand, people will never thereafter cease to mock you. But he was sure himself, though, of his Lialio, as sure as a man ever can be of a woman. From the time when, a close friend of the family, he, then a thirty-year-old, had kissed and dandled her, then a three-year-old, on his knee; from the time when in her fifth year, with no ulterior motive, with no prophetic eye to the future, he had treated her to sweets; from the years when, still lisping, she had called him 'Uncou-Monachakis', till now, when, though now his wife, she addressed him as 'Uncle-Monachakis', he had observed her, child, girl, and woman, and he had studied her well, and he knew that more than any other woman, she was ruled by her nerve and her head.

Half an hour passed before Captain Kiriakos' sailors could be persuaded to turn out of their homes. Another half hour before they found a boat, reached the schooner, and lowered the launch into the sea. A further half hour on the quay till some boatmen or fishermen had been enlisted to man the launch – their own boats, being heavy and only two or four-oared, were pronounced unsuitable for the chase – and until everyone had come to an understanding and agreed to put to sea. Finally, they boarded the launch. Kir-Monachakis, as seventh man, sat at the rudder, and they set off.

Concerted rowing brought them out of the harbour. But where could they find the little boat? The sea, while garrulous as a woman, is no less secretive, and never yields its secrets. As easy as it is for someone to discover the traces of another's kisses on a woman's lips, so easy is it to discover on that limitless blue expanse a trace of the little boat. Who could say! Kir-Monachakis was thinking;

after all, she was a woman. Love is a cheat and youth is easily led astray. Who could say whether she had not sinned already? Ah! how right he had been when he had told her that at his side she would be safe; for among other things an older husband is like a parent to his young wife. How right she had been, too, when she had said that at his side she would be safe even if she chose to do wrong. Now, innocent though she might be a thousand times over, the world would condemn her. But at his side, even had she actually sinned a thousand times over, still would she have remained *virtuous* in the eyes of the world.

Alas! like the princess of the fairy tale, were she to be shot at with arrows, and were it to be a sign of God's judgement that she be hit, then would an arrow but barely touch the tips of the pale fingers of one hand.

*

On the ocean, in the sound between the two islands, the boat was sailing on. The kindly naiad of the ocean currents bore a favourable current beneath its keel, and the gentle nymph of off-shore winds set a soft breeze at its stern. The cool wind brought new strength to the arms and shoulders of the youth and tempered the young woman's slender muscles. They were rowing like two skilled oarsmen; the light oars did not tire them; and already they had travelled more than half their watery course.

It was when the launch, moving at the pace of a mare set loose, was nearing Cape Trachili, not till then, that the sailors on board it sighted the small boat.

'What's that?'

'The boat!'

Kir-Monachakis turned his head to the left.

'Yes! It is!'

'Hard to say. I shouldn't think so, though,' said a sailor, who, so as to be spared further, additional, extremely wearisome efforts, wished that there might be some way of its not being it.

'Yes, it is. It must be,' said another, who desired that it should in every possible way be it; for he was greatly excited at the thought of the curious sea-borne drama that would ensue, if they did succeed in apprehending the boat and with it the woman and her lover.

'Yes, it is!' declared Kir-Monachakis. 'Turn that way, lads, and I'll bring her round.'

'What's it doing over there?' asked one sailor.

'It's heading for St Nicholas; they've gone the quickest way, see; and all this time we've been breaking our backs for nothing.'

'Let's put about, lads!' called out Kir-Monachakis. 'Quickly, for God's sake, put about; one of you back, so I can bring her round!'

The six oarsmen had laid down their oars, and the launch was still being carried onwards by its 'acquired momentum'. Kir-Monachakis, however, begrudging the time being lost, shouted:

'Back them, lads, back. Turn that way! . . . Round with the launch!'

But no-one was listening to him. A conference was being held in mid-ocean. Some favoured keeping on the way they were going, others turning north in the direction of the small boat. Those finally to prevail were the latter, who were electrified at the entrancing spectacle envisaged.

They turned the bows leftwards and took up the oars with the new zest engendered in them by the prospect of their exotic prey and by the exaltation natural in sight of victory. But the launch was still three times more distant than the boat was from the bay to which they were headed. And if the first had three times the man-power, it also had, however, five times the volume and three times the draught.

Mathios was quick to see the turn suddenly being executed by the launch, and he pointed it out to his companion.

'Look,' he said. 'They're coming after us.'

'Let them catch us now, if they can!' cried Lialio gaily. 'They've further to go than us, haven't they?'

'Oh! yes. Much further. But they've got a lot of oars.'

'And we've got a lot of strength.'

And she redoubled the vigour of her rowing.

For a full hour and more, while the sallow moon went slowly down in the west, and the cockerel was heard to crow, sending out its second call over fields sown in hollow and on crest, was the game played out, along the whole length of that coast, of the terrible and mighty-tentacled octopus hunting down the baby fry and of the submerged and game-loving dolphin coursing after the horn-fish. The launch moved with the rhythmic knock of the oars in the oar-locks' iron forks, with the dire power of the shark, imposing and insistent. The little boat was carried on the waves like a cork, its small toy-like oars, with a soft as the sound of a kiss swish, pushing away the waves, which, attending it and accompanying it, ran with it, like an escort of honour preceding and succeeding a royal carriage; and one would have thought it had been raised by unseen Tritons to the surface of the waves so that its speed might not be checked by the depth of its keel.

*

Even so, the launch was visibly gaining on the little boat. They rowed on, they rowed hard, and all the while the launch kept gaining, and all the while it seemed to get closer – until the distance separating the boat from the beach was already small, very small, and fast though the launch was going, Mathios still had time to drive the boat hard on to the sand beneath the shallows.

'We've done it!' Lialio called out happily.

She turned; seeing the white wall of the chapel of St Nicholas shining brightly in the moonlight, she crossed herself; and she jumped off first on to the sand on the shore, wetting her heels in the water

Mathios jumped after her and tried to drag up the boat.

The launch was already no more than forty yards from the bay.

The youth was struggling to drag the boat up on to the beach, hurrying to accompany Lialio up to the village. He suspected that those on the launch would pursue them on shore, and, without knowing why, he was glad of it. Lialio's last revelation, regarding her fiancé drowned in the Black Sea, had not sufficed to soothe his fears, and temptation was prompting in him now the thought that a woman who could so far forget that first hapless wretch as to marry an old man might well forsake this second for a third, if this last lived where she came from. But if, though, he and she should be pursued together on shore, and, there, she should entrust herself once more to him, and, at her village, they should arrive together, oh! why, his love would have been sanctified then both at sea and on shore.

Suddenly, the voice of Kir-Monachakis, who could be seen upright in the moonlight, near the launch's stern, was heard in the silence of the night.

'Lialio! Hey! Lialio!'

Lialio stood, thoughtful, her head bowed, and then cried out in answer:

'Yes, Uncle-Monachakis!'

'Is it your parents you want to go to, my sweet? Quite right! Wait, I'll come too. I'll go along with you till you get there – so no harm can come to you, my love, *all alone* on the road.'

'And welcome, Uncle-Monachakis,' answered Lialio unhesitatingly.

The youth was standing shyly beside her, looking at her, apprehensive and uncomprehending.

'Go back with the launch. Goodbye Mathios. Good luck, my lamb,' Lialio said to him, a note of undisguised emotion in her voice. 'Too bad that I'm older by years than you are; if Uncle-Monachakis died, I'd want you.'

Translated by Leo Marshall

Michail Mitsakis (*c.* 1868–1916)

Mitsakis is one of the more intriguing nineteenth-century Greek writers whose work has in recent years been resurfacing after decades of neglect. Active in the lively world of the Athenian periodical press in the 1880s and the first half of the 1890s, he succumbed to acute mania in 1896 and was, like poor Vizyinos (q.v.) before him, placed in the Dromokaïteion asylum, where he died two decades later. Mitsakis' best-known work falls into the thematic categories of 'Athenian Pages' and 'Travel Impressions': such texts, often barely if at all fictionalized, tend to depict unsavoury or even horrific aspects of everyday life. A scene in which a horse is ill-treated, for example, forms a vivid coincidence with the episode which is said to have driven Nietzsche mad; and other incidents narrated elsewhere range from graphic cruelty, on the one hand, to barely suppressed quotidian hatreds and lusts on the other. In perhaps his most celebrated story, 'By His Own Hand', first published in 1895, we can see that the story, while taking as its point of departure Poe's 'The Man of the Crowd', develops its own obsessive spatial, temporal and narrative logic, and the banked paragraphs of repetition which are the story's backbone reveal a mind at the very limits of sanity.

By His Own Hand

That day, I found myself, just as I do now, why or wherefore I no longer know, in Patras. I had arrived that morning, left my bag as usual in a room in the Grande Bretagne, up on the third floor, right at the top, with a view of Mount Varasova and of all the harbour below, and set off into town. In town, my first errand was to look in at the Prefecture and see Christakis Palamas, a friend of mine and in those days Secretary there – for it seemed ordained from on high that the man would spend his life in the Prefecture of Patras as Secretary, as Secretary-General, as Prefect – and then shortly leave him to his papers and documents and make my way to the Castle district and set to wandering in its old streets and thorough-fares, its picturesque alleys and curious quarters. As I stood there at some point of vantage gazing at the extraordinary panorama which the emerald Gulf of Corinth extends before the eye, as too the mountains on the other side with their rosy, sunned heights, and, beyond, the open sea, the heat of the day caught up with me and forced me to make my way down to the Market and take refuge in a grocer's, and there – with the distinctive sight of the square before me: narrow and rectangular, with the little fountain in the middle from which a grocer's boy was getting water, tin in hand; filled with the cries of the stall-holders, with the to-ing and fro-ing of customers, with villagers' capes and shoes – sit down and eat. I then rambled at my leisure off to King George's Square and went up to the club, there to sink into a prolonged perusal of the *Débats* and the *Revue*, the favourite cultural indulgences of the good merchants of Patras. It seems that this intellectual feast was of no short duration, for when I re-emerged it was already almost dusk, and so, on meeting shortly thereafter my friend Leonidas Kanellopoulos, councillor of the Turkish consulate in the city and writer of articles in his spare time, I took him by the arm and set off in his company for the mole, the favoured Patras promenade. At the mole, four or five groups of people were strolling up and down; bound by their thick cables to the cannons planted on their ends to either side, a dozen or a score of ships shifted slowly, their masts' lances pointed at the clear skies above; a steamship, hugely tall, broad, long, towered, a dark black mass, at one end; a cool breeze blew from land, the sea stretched peacefully into the distance, and the only sound to be heard was the sweet dying away at the rocks' edge of the waves' unending song. And when we too had gone up and down a few times, now that the pointed beacon that like a minaret guards the end of the esplanade had come to cast there its beam of white light, we parted and went our separate ways, one to home sweet home, and one, that is myself, to his hotel. The large room which functions as the restaurant of that huge hotel the Bretagne was empty when I went in; no-one had come along to eat yet, and there all alone were – on his feet and leaning against the counter under the dim glimmer of the gas-light, round of figure and contemplative – that good fellow Kosmas, and, seated at one of the nearer tables, finishing their supper, it seemed, my friend Mr Panayotis Chrysanthakis, the proprietor, his tall, stout Hungarian wife Mme Jovana, and a younger man, of thirty or so, with a narrow, black beard. I bade them good evening, then, and at my friend Panayotis' invitation joined them at their table, in the empty fourth place, and, when he came bustling along for my order, sent the good Kosmas to get me a chop.

'Well then, where have you been? Have you had a walk?' Mme Jovana asked me once I had taken my seat.

'Yes, quite a bit of a walk,' I replied.

'Did you go as far as the Old People's Home?'

'No, just to the mole,' I replied, unable to suppress a little smile, knowing as I did the harmless weakness of the estimable people of Patras for inquiring, as their very first and indeed indispensable question to anyone from out of town who sets foot in their city, whether he has been to the indeed pleasant rural location of the Old People's Home.

'And what do you think of our city, Mr Mitsakis?' The cue was taken by the third person seated, the younger man with the black beard.

'The gentleman is a policeman and a friend of ours,' Mme Jovana interrupted by way of introduction.

'Well, I knew the town, I've been here before, it's not my first visit, I rather like it,' I said.

'Oh well . . . commercial town . . . outsiders don't usually think much of it . . . there's nothing to see . . .'

'Oh, I don't know . . . I invariably find plenty to interest me . . .'

'And will we have the pleasure for a few days yet . . . ?'

'Oh, a few yet . . .'

'We had a suicide today . . . you must have heard about it of course . . .'

'No . . . good heavens! Who?'

'Why . . . someone from out of town . . . it was yesterday he arrived . . . and he stayed in one of those hotels down by the front . . . he said he'd come from Athens . . . but he wasn't from those parts . . . I think he must have been from Smyrna . . . but, as a matter of fact, at the hotel they didn't even know his name . . .'

'And did nothing come to light about his reasons?'

'Well . . . they say he was suffering from a chronic illness . . . how should I know . . . he arrived last night, left his bag and went out, came back late, slept, ordered his coffee in the morning, a quiet sort, nothing in his outward appearance to give anything away, went out again, took a walk to the Willows, ate luncheon at another hotel, came back about two, greeted the chap at the door, went up to his room, locked the door, and then shortly afterwards they heard the pistol-shot . . . They got a message to me, I smashed down the door, found him fully dressed on the bed . . . with a wound here . . .' – and the policeman pointed to his heart – '. . . instantly . . . he can't have lived for a second . . . He also left a piece of paper, as a matter of fact . . .'

And the young policeman took out his wallet, opened it, pulled out a small piece of paper folded in two, reached across the dishes, and gave it me to read. It was a half sheet of that paper you get at the post office, which they customarily use in the provinces, lined paper with green horizontal lines; pretty wrinkled, crumpled even, with finger marks clearly visible, as if it had passed through various hands; completely blank, except that indeed on one line, the top line, there could be made out, written out ever so carefully, in the tiniest letters, these words: *I'm killing myself. Don't let it bother anyone.* And below, the name of the city, the date and year, and the suicide's signature. That was it. And all this in the neatest writing, written with a steady hand, easy to read, free of misspellings, not an accent or comma out of place, the work of a man of some education evidently, without a trace of fear, emotion, unease even, perfectly simple, perfectly natural, perfectly ordinary. I perused for a while the hideous bit of paper, that wrinkled, crumpled thing which contained the last manifestation of a life, then re-folded it and gave it back to the policeman. And after some further desultory conversation, and on finishing my meal, I summoned my good friend Kosmas once again, paid, said my good nights, and directed my steps to my room. The hotel staircase, high and partly in darkness, wound its way to its summit step by step; the deserted corridors extended into the distance; the lights were not yet properly lit; peace reigned. It was only that, from the top floor, a bell was echoing away, protracted and insistent, shrill and violent in its tinkling, as if someone had been ringing for some time and was finally waxing impatient; and from the murky depths of the stairwell, down at the entrance, a voice could be heard rising in a shout of rage, evidently the doorman calling to some other servant:

'Oi-i-i, Di-imi-itra-akis, can't you hear, then? Are you deaf as a post? That one on the third floor's been ringing for three hours. Bloody well get up there, you sod!'

And shortly after, as I was on my way up from the second floor, a shadow flitted by me, jostling me as it sped on and disappeared up ahead of me. The boards creaked under its feet, its tread thudded, a puff of wind in the deserted corridor slammed a window shut, the ringing died away to a distant, enfeebled 'ding ding'. And when I reached the next floor I saw the servant's shadow standing outside the door of the room next to mine, and through the half-open door some woman in nothing but her stockings and slip, leaning forward with her uncovered bosom and bare arms, passed him a basin. I put the key in my door, opened it, fumbled for my matches, lit my candle, and went to the window, which looked straight out on the darkness. In the night now descending, the broad sea's waveless surface stretched out in its dark smoothness; motionless, the mountains on the far side reared their shadowy outlines; the roofs of the surrounding houses were starting to fuse into a single dark plane; the sky had now been sown with its first stars; and in the street below trembled the first gas burners. And as I leant out, breathing in with my five senses the sea's deep exhalation, and the gentle breeze conveyed downward from the mountains opposite, and the vague rustle of life emanating from the houses round about, and the distant star's ray, and the diverse bustle rising from the street below, the phrase on the bit of paper I had just been looking at came as a sudden blow to my spirits, returning with its full gravity, like a hammer on an anvil, making its sudden and unexpected return by an irresistible incursion violent in its laconic paradox and harshness.

Don't let it bother anyone! As if anyone on earth ever was bothered about those on whom death's hand has set its black seal! As if anyone on earth ever was bothered about those whom the grip of Passion, Disease or Want scatters to the ends of the earth, a herd of wretched victims! As if anyone on earth ever was bothered about the unhappy or the unwise, who, oppressed by their Fate and ridden by their Hag, had never while there was yet time reflected that they would die! Who then was going to be bothered on his account, that unknown man from out of town, who had come for one night, only to sleep his final sleep in a hotel? Who then was going to be bothered on his account, that odd traveller who was on his way from Athens, but was probably from Smyrna, perhaps even from Çeşme, but who might quite possibly have been from Bucharest? Who then was going to be bothered on his account, that man whose very name was unknown to the waiters that served him? Was it really going to be bothered, that boundless sea which, tired from its incessant struggle to undermine the dry land and devour the shipping, was now asleep down below, breathing dully and deeply, like a sated beast? Were they really going to be bothered, those peaceful mountains which looked out on the open sea, standing comfortably on their sturdy feet, and resting in the full enjoyment of existence, motionless and tranquil? Were they really going to be bothered, those distant stars which sent one to another, by some secret understanding, in what you might think looks of love, their frolic twinkling? Were they really going to be bothered, those gloomy houses from which vaguely wafted the diverse rustle of life? Were they really going to be bothered, Mme Jovana and Mr Panayotis, who, worn out by the day's work, exhausted by their honest toil, were now eating with relish at that table with the policeman? Was he really going to be bothered, that doorman cursing his colleague, or that servant running upstairs to see who was ringing? Was she really going to be bothered, that woman who had passed the basin through her doorway, in nothing but her stockings and slip, leaning forward with her uncovered bosom and bare arms, and who was now at her toilet? Or, for that matter, was I really going to be bothered myself, I who had been staring out in the full enjoyment of the cool morning up on the heights of the Castle? And with a chuckle, half-exasperated by the intense stupidity of a doomed man's last thought, I shut the window, took my hat, and went down into the street. St Andrew's Street was thronging with the bustle of people, noisily heading for the part with the grocer's shops in particular, near the little club. The shops shone under the flickering line of gas lamps in front of them, with the row of barrels laid out in a line in front of their doors or windows; buzzing with the ceaseless din of scales rattling or coins being counted or glasses clinking, with the sound of footsteps or the hum of talk; while a strong smell of sardines and cheese rose from every quarter, and the grocer's boys standing there as the upstanding guardians of the barrels, in their sopping aprons, let out shrill cries in advertisement of their wares. A varied throng of passers-by, men young and old, civilians and soldiers, middle and working class, sailors and locals, in village or town dress, would stop in large groups in front of the shops or in the middle of the street, conversing, strolling, going in to buy something, looking, shoving, buying one another drinks. Throughout this whole block the crowd was extremely lively, forming here and there a compact mass, dispersing in the streets around, and then renewed once again. And in this continually and multifariously crowding throng there would come and go other tradesmen also crying their wares, each carrying his portable shop and announcing, this man his fish, another his eggs, and a third his greens. By the gutter, there on a corner, one of them would sit and, with a crate before him which had a dark look to its inside, would screech hoarsely: 'Fivepence for two sea urchins! Fivepence for two sea urchins!'; while two others, each holding to one side a huge basket, lit up from inside by a small oil lamp placed in the bottom, would pass by shouting: 'Shri-i-imps! Fre-e-esh shri-i-imps!'

Further along, the little club was now open, brightly lit, its tall windows allowing free passage to the pandemonium of the gathered throng within, and the hiss of chatter, and the clatter of backgammon, and the scraping of chairs, and the sputtering sound of dominoes being shuffled, and the bubbling gurgle of the hubble-bubble, and the dry crack as the billiard balls hit into each other and went into the pocket. And in front, the little square lay empty, dotted only with a few empty tables and chairs. And down below, at the mole, towards which I headed, the pointed beacon cast its white beam as before, the dozen or score of ships tied up on either side shifted slowly, the dark steamship reared its mass at one end, and the groups of people had once again, after eating, it seemed, resumed their strolling. Pointing straight ahead, the thin strip of land, starting from the little square in front of the club, went on into the sea, went on further still, and ended at the lighthouse, which marked the final point with its two little lights pointing inland, a little above ground level, next to its retaining wall, and with its great round light high above. The land was at that point free, overlaid by nothing but a few logs, rounded and thick, laid to one side. The cannons, stuck on end in the earth and projecting half the length of their upright trunks in a dark, paradoxical and massive configuration, once proud engines of war, now humble attendants of peace, stood in long lines on both sides, face to face in the mute discharge of their passive duties. And beyond them, the gas lamps too stood tall, themselves in lines and face to face, thin, perpendicular, with the delicate diadem of glass atop them. Two tugs, to one side, close in, stretched towards the land their derricks, pointed, thick, stiff and threatening. Beyond, the green-painted wooden shack by the sea's edge to the side of the lighthouse clung to the larger building's sides, taking on in the darkness the odd shape of a colossal natural outgrowth like an oyster covered in weed. And among the ships by the jetties a few small boats, also at their moorings, shifted like the larger vessels, while one of them continued to wander over the waters, bearing at its prow a large light that cast on them a deep red flame, whose light the boatman fished by. And on this narrow strip of dry land, setting out from the nearer end, and then reaching the turning-point at the lighthouse wall, the promenaders walked up and down in the regular and prescribed fashion, lengthways, turning back when necessary. Among them this time were two or three ladies, and a short, plump one could be heard tittering in amusement. A fat man with a double chin, who walked with tiny quick steps and panted like an asthmatic, was saying to his companion: 'A man of capital, sir, cannot entrust his capital like that. He has to have guarantees.'

The gangplanks which led to the moored vessels would creak from time to time; a ship's dog, on its front legs at the bow, would start barking wildly at those who walked by. Further in, the Port Authority on the one side, and the Customs House on the other, stood silent at the edge of the mainland. And beyond, dimly lit by its few lamps, the front stretched into the distance. The steelyards from which the currant-weighing scales hang cast over the front their skittish shadows, and at intervals, the crates, laden with the currant, dark queen of Patras, and gathered into broad stacks, stood ready for loading, their sides showing white as they spent the night in the open. The warehouses were shut, mute, the other buildings sunk in torpor. Barrels, buckets, sacks, hand-carts left casually ready for the work of the coming dawn, covered the pavements in places. Two or three carts, unyoked, were also there to one side, leaning their shafts face down on the earth. One or two small cafés drowsily let out from dirty windows a little light which could not disperse the darkness, any more than could the street-lights' anaemic gleam. No bustle, no noise of life down at the front. Busy all day long, it appeared impatient to get a bit of extra sleep. Only rarely did some straggler make his way along the front, and in the water, from one end to the other, along the front's entire length, at their moorings and at peace, the little boats were sunk in dreams. The only sign of life, in a tavern at the far end, was a group of Italians singing as they tippled, and the harsh roll of their 'r's was audible in the still air. And a lone pair of urchins, with a taste, it seemed, for a solitary vein of *flânerie*, their bare feet dragging doggedly in the dust, yelled into the void:

> Why on earth does your mother need
> Why on earth does your mother need
> Why on earth does your mother need
> A lamp at night, oh,
> A lamp at night, oh.

> When she has in her own home
> When she has in her own home
> When she has in her own home
> A star and moon, oh,
> A star and moon, oh!

I stopped two or three who came my way and asked where the suicide had taken place; for I was curious to see even the outward appearance of the hotel in question; but no-one could say. In the end, someone sitting outside a little café showed me the building, one of the end ones over there, behind and just this side of the Customs House. And I went up and looked it over carefully, getting a careful view of the whole. Tall, unlit, silent, it reared as if empty of life in the shadows.

No-one stood in front of it, no-one inside appeared to be up and about. Still and mute and dark, it stood to attention in its place, casting a dispassionate gaze on the street. Only the lights at the entrance burned with a weak light, and only at one window high up on the third floor did a pane reveal a candle's trembling light. It was in there, of course, that the corpse must have been lying, an unlovely mass, motionless on its mournful bed, the bed embracing the outsider for whom none would weep tomorrow. And this time saddened, I knew not why, my heart in the grip of a vague anxiety at the sight of the utter stillness of that building, I turned my steps away from that corner and set off once again away from the front. And after a dozen or so paces I came out through a side street into St Andrew's Street. In the shops the crowds had noticeably dwindled, most of the townsfolk had gone home some while before with their purchases, and only a few dawdlers now wound their way through the surrounding streets. But, just as before, groups of people would stop or pass on, the hurly burly in the shops was still intense, the grocer's boys continued to cry their wares without respite, the gas lamps to shine, the shrimp sellers to make their rounds, and the sea-urchin-master to yell at the top of his voice. A carriage slowly made its way, almost inaudible in the thick dust, displacing those in its path. And behind it a little chap was trundling a hand-cart, clapping his hands and bellowing in a stentorian voice: 'Mi-ind o-out!', as if his vehicle were ten times the size of the carriage in front. Two soldiers emerged from a wine-shop, jostling one another, after a quick drink clearly, and wiping their wet lips with the back of the hand. And where the road makes a turning, by the club, four or five men were standing in a group talking vehemently; and one of them, tall and broad of back, was saying with violent gestures to the rest: 'So, my friend, it's the other fellow's respect and affection you want? Then you should do him all the harm you can! . . .'

In King George's Square, which I soon reached, most of the shops round about were shut, a few cabs waited for fares, and in the silence the two fountains endowed by the late George Roufos, with their weird gryphons, poured their streams into the basins with a pleasant splashing. Silent too, the arcades of the city streets blocked the view here and there with their massive columns and semi-circular arches, under which the mass of varied shops which nestle there had now settled down to roost. Making my way through these streets, I headed for the upper part of town and ascended the three high ramps of marble stairway which lead there, while a man in villager's dress, of middle age, pretty drunk, made his own way up, holding on to the balustrade with some difficulty and murmuring some slurred soliloquy, and I set about wandering in its old lanes. The same peace reigned here too, the same deserted air, and only from some wine-shop whose little red awning fluttered in the night breeze could one hear talk carrying, the clink of glasses, or the mournful sound of some Turkish love song. Overhung by the heavy shadow of the venerable castle, like sparrows, you might say, seeking protection under an eagle's broad wings, the neighbourhood's little houses went with their ups and downs, jostling, spreading over the slopes, and between them wound the little lanes, stairs, paths of every variety and charm. Their little doors bolted, their little windows barred, the poor had laid their heads to rest under the benign roof of a humble home. By this route, I reached the High Threshing-Floors, emerging from a narrow alley into that open space. The lovely plain was wrapped in its usual tranquillity; the moon hung above it dimly; the herbage rustled faintly in the light breeze that came from afar and ever so gently and tenderly caressed your legs, as if with the loving touch of a tender hand; the trees stirred, dim and full of mystery. And approaching the square's far edge, where its stone balustrade lends it the aspect of some vast natural balcony overhanging the low-lying terrain below, I leant over and looked down. And faced with the formless mass of the city now half-asleep, with the dead calm of the sea, with the utter motionlessness and unbroken silence of the mountains opposite, my mind flitted once again to the wretch down below who lay alone on the lifeless bed in that dark hotel. Well, yes indeed, even if life had played him false, he had at least determined to carry out to the letter his last wish! Not that she was bothered by him, that short, plump lady now in fits of laughter down at the mole. Not that he was bothered by him, that fat, pot-bellied man walking with tiny, quick steps and panting like an asthmatic and speaking to his companion of capital and guarantees. Not that they were bothered by him, those grocer's boys standing to attention in their sopping aprons, like upstanding guardians of the barrels, beneath the flickering line of gas lamps, and crying their wares. Not that they were bothered by him, the men in conversation in the little club, the men rattling the backgammon dice, the men shuffling the dominoes, the men playing a short-tempered game of billiards on the far side of the room. Not that they were bothered by him, those steelyards waiting, as they cast on the front their skittish shadow, for work to begin again the following day, or those crates spending the night in the open, gathered in broad stacks, as they waited patiently, their sides showing white, for the hour to come when they would embark for unknown lands. Not that they were bothered by him, those small ships which, moored peacefully from one end of the front to the other, along its entire length, were dreaming, still a-tremble, of sea winds and the wave's force. Not that they were bothered by him, those Italian fishermen tippling in the tavern and rolling their harsh 'r's in the still air. Not that they were bothered about him, those soldiers emerging from the wine-shop merry and wiping down their lips with the back of the hand. Not that he was bothered by him, that philosopher on the street corner, the man tall and broad of back, gesticulating and instructing his associates that, for someone to have respect and affection for you, you should do him all the harm you can! And meanwhile the city was sinking ever deeper into sleep, night was coming on in all her grandeur, the stars were twinkling brightly, the dew was falling, sharp, penetrating to the marrow. In no hurry, I ambled down the road on the far side, which leads by a short country lane to the road for the Willows, and emerged into the countryside. The fields, freshly dug, gave off a strong scent of earth and grass; the hedges were green; the sleepless little world of the insects was astir, full of life and seemingly full of joy; a nightingale, intoxicated with night's beauty, conveyed to her its sweet salutations from a poplar's top; a company of frogs croaked in their jolly way. Beneath the unclouded stillness of the heavens, beside the unruffled lethargy of the sea, the earth too, feeling a sense of security, was now beginning to relax. The gardens, with their sturdy trees, their perpendicular cypresses, their rich plots of flowers, were swimming in dew and scent. And the vineyards outlined on the earth's surface their straight, regular furrows, extending here and there in all directions. And in the midst of vines and furrows could be seen cottages and wine-presses, in white or shady masses, dumb, as if themselves the progeny of mother earth. Here and there a glow-worm fluttered as it flew low and in its swift passage traced a thin bright line, let a brief but dazzling little flash of lightning escape its tiny posterior. Leaves stirred in secret discourse, reeds whispered in hushed tones. Somewhere, a stream was flowing, but so softly that you thought it was out of a wish not to disturb the tranquillity. Mount Panachaïkos, wide and high, presided over the plain imposingly. Further down, and coming in the other direction from me, a group of people were making their way on foot, a young couple at their head and, a little way behind, two ladies and two gentlemen, all of them employees of the Old People's Home. The young man was playing with his little cane, inclining towards the young woman, and saying, as I went by:

'Why, how can you say that to me, miss?'

'I can say it to you, sir, because you have been making a nuisance of yourself,' replied the young woman with the cooing of a dove, tossing her head back with a teasing air.

The couple went by smelling of violets. The girl had a bunch of them in her bosom. I went on to the coast road which goes towards Ities and then turned off for town. Soon I was back in St Andrew's Street, passing the church which stands at its head and from which it takes its name. And I stood and looked at it, at its white walls, at its arched door, at the cross on its roof, at the huge bell-tower next to it, the splendid work of Gravaris. The church too, shut and still and calm, was asleep, impassive. I went on. The same quiet, the same silence, deeper, denser. Now, sure enough, the houses, everything, were overcome by sleep, the city now snoring. But from a large, tall building over there somewhere, to one side, a roar was coming nonetheless. A steam mill, livid of aspect, was groaning through the night. People were at work preparing the bread which feeds the world. And a little further on, from another building, the din of musical instruments could be heard: violin notes, the wail of a clarinet, a song tearing a passage through the darkness. A *café-chantant* was staying open through the night, an establishment of good cheer, and here a rather different set of people were paying the debt to pleasure. I went up the narrow staircase, ordered a beer, and sat down. On that humble stage, under the dark smokiness produced by the gas burners stood a woman in motley dress extending only to the knee and revealing thick legs barely fitting into her black stockings, *décolleté*, with her white arms roughly powdered, her bosom half-exposed, ruddy of cheek, singing. Mouth agape, she stuck out her leg, put her hand to her left eye, pulled down the lower lid and opened it wide, and shrieked hoarsely: 'Regardez-moi dans l'œil, dans l'œil, dans l'œil. / Regardez-moi dans l'œil, dans l'œil, dans l'œil . . .'

On closer inspection, I recognized the woman who had passed the basin to the servant, in just her stockings and slip, in the doorway of the room next to mine. She was succeeded by another woman, and she by another, as the violins and clarinets went on with their moan. And as each finished her song she would take a little tray or bag and descend the two or three steps from the stage and start to make the rounds of the men at the rows of tables. And the dead man's stupidity once again presented itself before me, colossal in its laconic brevity. Who then was going to be bothered by him: the sot in villager's dress clambering up the stairway to the upper town and reeling and grasping hold of the balustrade to steady himself? Who then was going to be bothered by him: that nightingale intoxicated with the beauty of the night and the sweetness of its own voice, happily aswim in the cool of the breeze and the light of the moon? Who then was going to be bothered by him: that young man flirting with the girl, that girl who had set the violets in her bosom and, with the cooing of a dove, tossed her head back with a teasing laugh? Were they really going to be bothered, the church's shut doors, white walls and sleeping Cross? Were they really going to be bothered, the workers in the steam mill as it groaned through the night and they prepared in the sweat of their brow the bread that feeds the world? Were they really going to be bothered, those merrymakers in the *café-chantant*, agape at those females' sturdy calves and swooning eyes? Gradually the room emptied out, the lights went down, the violins fell silent; the *café-chantant* was closing. I was the last to go back down the stairs, and I took a little turn at the mole. Over it, the pointed beacon in its perpetual revolution continued to cast its white beam, the moored ships shifted as one, the sea spread out peacefully, a cool breeze blew from land, and the only sound that could be heard was the sweet dying away at the rocks' edge of the waves' unending song. Not a soul was to be seen, not a whisper heard. Dark of visage, the cannons stood to attention, protruding the half of their length that was above ground, on this side and that, facing one another in the discharge of their peaceable duties; the gas lamps, thin and perpendicular, watched over them. The tug boats to one side stretched out their thick arms towards the land, stiff and threatening. The pile of buckets blocked the way on one side, their bellies idiotically swollen under the intermittent beam from the lamp. The boat with the fishing lamp had been eclipsed; it was evidently lying quiet, at its mooring somewhere. The silence was intense, and even the gang-planks to the ships had ceased to creak. The ship's dog too must have fallen asleep at his prow, bored with barking. The moon was moving in its course, the dark-ness thickening. A light shone far away at sea. A steam-boat was on its way from the open seas, approaching at some speed; its breathing audible, its horn now heard, protracted and abrupt. I set off back to get some sleep and once again went by the hotel where the corpse lay. The lights at the entrance now extin-guished, pitch dark, shut, it rose tall in the shadows. Only up there on the third floor, as if in fear, the candle trembled, pale and exhausted. I reached my place of lodging, banged on the door; the doorman woke, with a snort, in his under-wear, and opened up for me. The entire hotel, void of light and sound alike, was sunk in sleep. Only up on the second floor, seeming louder for the surrounding deep silence, some sleeper's snoring could be heard, audible through doors and windows and all but shaking the walls.

And from the room next to mine, where I had had a passing sight of the half-naked *chanteuse*, came improper sounds, strange noises carrying, the rustle of bedclothes and a hiss of sheets; the bed started to move back and forth, banging again and again into the wall, tempest-tossed like a ship in a storm. Oh, in very truth, that man had been, when all was said and done, an utter fool! Was he really going to be bothered, that boy who this evening, his bare feet dragging in the dust, had been singing the song of the lamp? Were they really going to be both-ered, those nocturnal sailors on their way from the deep seas, eyes fixed to the compass, with no concern but for the journey's destination, and seeking its furrow in the salty plain? Was he really going to be bothered, that snorer, glutting himself on sleep, absorbing it in his every pore and shaking the walls, or would they, the debauchees on their bed of lust? And I tossed and turned in bed, uneasy. It was that thick undersheet making me itch and not letting me sleep. Two or three hours went by, and I had slept not a wink. Night was galloping away; dawn had made giant strides. And despairing of sleep I got up, drew the curtains and opened the window. The sea stretched out below, calm and waveless, ever waveless, and ever calm; motionless, the outlines of the mountains on the far side rose tall; and from the direction of Mount Panachaïkos the sun was rising, wonderfully unvary-ing and matchlessly unchanged . . .

Translated by David Ricks

Kostis Palamas (1859–1943)

Palamas bestrode the world of Greek poetry from the 1880s to the 1930s with a large, hugely varied and admittedly very uneven *œuvre*: his funeral, under the Axis Occupation, was the occasion for a rousing verse tribute by Angelos Sikelianos (q.v.). Palamas' two epic-scale works, *The Twelve Words of the Gypsy* (1907) and *The King's Flute* (1910), have few volunteer readers today, and they have been assimilated by the Greek educational system to a naive nationalism of which the poet cannot be accused. But his shorter poems contain many fine things, though often in complex and muscular forms resistant to translation. Palamas also merits comparison with his contemporary Thomas Hardy as his language's most versatile creator of stanza forms – and for a forthright godlessness deeply engaged with the language of Christianity. And even those who find his poetry dated acknowledge Palamas' contribution as perhaps modern Greece's largest-minded critic: without his interventions Solomos, Kalvos and Makriyannis (qq.v) would be neglected or misunderstood, and his comments on his younger contemporaries, Cavafy, Seferis and Ritsos (qq.v.), are also remarkably open-minded and penetrating.

Palamas' finest achievement, *The Palm-Tree* (1900), the purest poem of Greek Symbolism, and as dense as Valéry, little lends itself to translation: the results are Swinburnian. I have thought it best here to represent Palamas by the most famous section of *The Twelve Words of the Gypsy*, in which a fervent – if not especially discerning – Nietzschean streak is on show. This is not to be confused with nationalism: indeed, the poem adapts and subverts the stanza form of the 'Hymn to Liberty' by Palamas' most revered predecessor Solomos.

The Twelve Words of the Gypsy

WORD IV
THE DEATH OF THE GODS

'Divine worship is dying.' – Sophocles, *Oedipus the King*

'Land, sea, gods are destined to perish.' – Indian Song

'Those visions of a day, it is you who created them.' – Leconte de Lisle, *La Paix des Dieux*

> In every land through which I travelled,
> In front of temples I would pitch my tent;
> I visited a host of churches,

To mosques and monasteries I went.
With all the faiths I had sharp argument,
With Christian and with Levite;
I entered a basilica at dawning,
A cloister or a hermitage at night;
And everywhere, from old Hellenic ruins
To pagodas in their eastern ostentation,
I sampled, unabashed, and bruised the petals
Of every sacred rose of adoration.
Yet I remained a stranger and unslaved
By reverence for prayer, vow or ritual;
In me behold the prophet of the godless,
With my own life for miracle!
Once only – it was in the City –
Have I been shaken by a sacred awe;
And it was you who stirred it in me,
O dishevelled Gipsy woman,
Running, crazed, through street and alley,
With a pack of yelping curs before,
And, behind, a swarm of brats to stone you,
And a mob's pursuing roar.
What accursèd hour begot you?
From what womb accursèd were you born?
Gipsy witch, of all earth the outcast,
Faithless Sibyl, prey to every scorn!
As you ran, I heard you screaming hoarsely –
I never can forget that yell:
'Bring me fire to burn down Heaven!
Water to extinguish Hell!'

*

Stately pageant of the gods,
Of the gods whom I deny;
More majestic here I stand,
Calmly watching you pass by.

As I ride through forest glade,
Or along a wooded track,
Or past hedgerow, copse and grove,
On my rapid mule, bareback,

All the holm-oaks and the elms,
Right and left, the firs and pines,
All the trees, too, seem to race
Like swift horses in long lines.

They slip past like flying birds,
They appear and then they all
Vanish like wind-footed deer
Startled by a sudden squall.

Puzzle, if you wish, the mind,
Play a trick upon the eye;
There are no wind-footed deer,
Racing horses, birds that fly!

It is I who race, not you;
You are all deep-rooted, bound;
Each time I rein in my mule,
You are all chained to the ground!

Of the everlasting gods
Pomps and arrogant parades,
Where and how and if you be,
You are but the shades of shades!

O you phantoms of deceit,
Gods, you? – You no longer count!
From the moment that a man
Dares before you to dismount

And behold you standing still
Like an oak or pine may stand,
He perceives he holds you now
In the hollow of his hand;

Should he see then that you hide
From his eyes the world around
And the vision of the skies,
He will fell you to the ground;

Should he see, too, that you mask
From his gaze the morning sun,
He will bear you to his hearth
And burn you, one by one!

*

No beginning and no end
Ever fenced my thought around;
And of Nothingness I am
The announcer, free, unbound.

I am he who quells the Why,
To the Cause I give no heed –
Ever like a riderless,
Wind-devouring desert steed!

Never from my eyes or lips
Has a bolt of blasphemy
Been towards you hurled, O god
Whosoever you may be!

At no moment have I felt
For you anger, love, dismay –
Who attacks that which is not,
Fears what he cannot portray?

I can no more nail on you
Any thought of mine, O god,
Than attempt to cross the sea
On my own two feet, dry-shod.

Never have I said a prayer,
By your shadow's might oppressed;
Nor, in terror, bound myself
To any heaven of the blessed.

In the tongue inherited
– Where? when? how? – by me of old,
Valued like a relic wrapped
In a tattered purple fold,

And in that new tongue which I
Have rewoven from the best
Of the countless golden words
Garnered from both East and West,

One deceptive word alone
– Prayer – never once appears!
O seers, temples, idols,
O idols, temples, seers!

Distant from you, where I trod,
From my footprints there was born
The enchanted Herb of Fate,
Blossom of a future dawn.

From my footprints it arose,
Herb that ransoms and redeems,
In the wilderness it bloomed
From my life-blood and my dreams,

Bloomed, the Resurrection Tree!
When will come the hour, the hour,
When from deserts it will spread
Into peopled lands to tower?

That the whole world may rejoice,
Plucking each victorious flower,
Breathing in its vital balm –
When will come the hour, the hour?

O the deep ecstatic breath,
O the cry of victory,
After aeons of constraint,
After chains of slavery!

On that day when Man will draw,
Corals first brought up to view,
Things of beauty from the deep,
Virgin, roseate and new.

And the sky, no longer poised
Like a nightmare of the soul,
Looms once more, an unconcerned,
Boundless void from pole to pole!

But, if destiny doomed Man
To await for long your day,
O sweet legendary Flower,
And, meanwhile, to make his way

Wasting all his frankincense
On the gods' phantasmal crowd,
And his powers worshipping,
At the feet of idols bowed;

And if prophets still extol
All those gods and their decrees,
And if artists labour still
On their carven effigies,

I am now the prophet, I,
Who has come here to forecast
Nothingness as god and king
For all time to be and past.

I am the artist who has come,
Without love and without hate,
In the temple shrine, O Man,
Of your false dreams to create

A monstrous effigy of Nothing,
With the faiths of all earth,
A monster to excite your fear
And, with it all, your mirth!

Translated by Theodore Ph. Stephanides and George C. Katsimbalis

C.P. Cavafy (1863–1933)

C.P. Cavafy (K.P. Kavafis in Greek) is *the* modern Greek poet for English readers and a poet's poet almost without equal in contemporary world literature. Cavafy's collected poems have been translated into English no fewer than five times since 1951 and have exerted a considerable influence on Anglo-American poets as prominent – and different – as W.H. Auden, James Merrill and Derek Mahon, not to mention the Nobel laureates Eugenio Montale, Joseph Brodsky and Czesław Miłosz, who have all expressed a debt to Cavafy's work. It is true that Cavafy's poems of sensuality have been less successfully brought over into English than those of moral or historical content, but the following, drastically limited selection by various hands aims to show the variety of the *œuvre* in its subject-matter and forms, as well as the evolution of English-speaking poets' encounters with Cavafy's work. (For tributes by Greek poets, see Nicolas Calas' 'Cavafy' and Yannis Ritsos' 'Twelve Poems for Cavafy' included in this anthology.) Cavafy, who never allowed a collection of his work into a publisher's hands, preferring to publish in periodicals and, increasingly, in home-made folders, had no mock-modesty: he was playing a long game, and he would be the last to be surprised that a recent anthology containing poems written under his influence takes up well over three hundred pages. Why else would he have taken the trouble, inveterate hoarder as he was, to ensure that the number of canonical poems he left behind him was none other than the number of Shakespeare's sonnets?

An Old Man

Back in a corner, alone in the clatter and babble
An old man sits with his head bent over a table
And his newspaper in front of him, in the café.

Sour with old age, he ponders a dreary truth –
How little he enjoyed the years when he had youth,
Good looks and strength and clever things to say.

He knows he's quite old now: he feels it, he sees it,
And yet the time when he was young seems – was it?
Yesterday. How quickly, how quickly it slipped away.

Now he sees how Discretion has betrayed him,
And how stupidly he let the liar persuade him
With phrases: *Tomorrow. There's plenty of time. Some day.*

He recalls the pull of impulses he suppressed,
The joy he sacrificed. Every chance he lost
Ridicules his brainless prudence another way.

But all these thoughts and memories have made
The old man dizzy. He falls asleep, his head
Resting on the table in the noisy café.

Translated by Robert Pinsky

Waiting for the Barbarians

What are we waiting for, assembled in the forum?

The barbarians are due here today.

Why isn't anything happening in the senate?
Why do the senators sit there without legislating?

Because the barbarians are coming today.
What laws can the senators make now?
Once the barbarians are here, they'll do the legislating.

Why did our emperor get up so early,
and why is he sitting at the city's main gate
on his throne, in state, wearing the crown?

Because the barbarians are coming today
and the emperor is waiting to receive their leader.
He has even prepared a scroll to give him,
replete with titles, with imposing names.

Why have our two consuls and praetors come out today
wearing their embroidered, their scarlet togas?
Why have they put on bracelets with so many amethysts,
and rings sparkling with magnificent emeralds?

Why are they carrying elegant canes
beautifully worked in silver and gold?

    Because the barbarians are coming today
    and things like that dazzle the barbarians.

Why don't our distinguished orators come forward as usual
to make their speeches, say what they have to say?

    Because the barbarians are coming today
    and they're bored by rhetoric and public speaking.

Why this sudden restlessness, this confusion?
(How serious people's faces have become.)
Why are the streets and squares emptying so rapidly,
everyone going home so lost in thought?

    Because night has fallen and the barbarians have not come.
    And some who have just returned from the border say
    there are no barbarians any longer.

And now, what's going to happen to us without barbarians?
They were, those people, a kind of solution.

Translated by Edmund Keeley and Philip Sherrard

Cavafy's Desires

Like corpses that the undertaker makes beautiful
And shuts, with tears, inside a mausoleum
– Roses at the fore head, jasmine at the feet – so
Desires look after they have passed away
Unconsummated, without one night of passion
Or a morning when the moon stays in the sky.

Adapted by Michael Longley

Bacchus and His Crew

Damon (and of craftsmen he's
Best in all Peloponnese)
In Parian marble carves the crew
Of Bacchus. First with glory due
The god, with power in his stride.
Licence next; and at his side
Drunkenness pours the Satyrs wine
From a jar that ivies twine.
Near them languid Winesweet lies
Bringing sleep, with half-closed eyes.
Two singers, Tune and Sweetsong, stand
Below, while Revelry at hand
Never lets plenty's lamp go out;
And strict Ceremony devout. –
    These Damon makes; and making these
Once and again things on the fees
From Syracuse's king to come,
Three talents, quite a proper sum.
Add this to what he's got, he can
Live like a rich and serious man,
In politics – what joy to grace
The Council, and the market-place!

Translated by John Mavrogordato

Sculptor from Tyana

You'll have heard I'm no tyro.
I see my share of stone.
Back home, in Tyana, I'm quite well known.
And here too I've had a good many statues
commissioned by senators.
                    And let me show you
a few without further ado. Notice that Rhea:
august, primordial, austere.
Notice that Pompey. Marius,
Aemilius Paulus, Scipio Africanus.
To the best of my abilities, true copies.

Patroclus (I shall be touching him up a little later on).
There, by those bits of yellow
marble, is Caesarion.

And lately I've been taken up for quite some time
with the making of a Neptune. My concern
is above all his horses, how to shape them.
They must be light as if
their bodies and their feet are visibly
not treading earth but racing over the sea.

But here's the piece dearest of all to me,
on which I worked with feeling and with the greatest care;
this one here, on a hot summer's day,
my mind ascending to the realm of the ideal,
this one here in my dreams, young Mercury.

Translated by David Ricks

Philhellene

Make sure the engraving is done skilfully.
The expression serious, majestic.
The diadem preferably somewhat narrow:
I don't like that broad kind the Parthians wear.
The inscription, as usual, in Greek:
nothing excessive, nothing pompous –
we don't want the proconsul to take it the wrong way:
he's always nosing things out and reporting back to Rome –
but of course giving me due honour.
Something very special on the other side:
some discus-thrower, young, good-looking.
Above all I urge you to see to it
(Sithaspis, for God's sake don't let them forget)
that after 'King' and 'Saviour',
they engrave 'Philhellene' in elegant characters.
Now don't try to be clever
with your 'where are the Greeks?' and 'what things Greek
here behind Zagros, out beyond Phraata?'
Since so many others more barbarian than ourselves

choose to inscribe it, we will inscribe it too.
And besides, don't forget that sometimes
sophists do come to us from Syria,
and versifiers, and other triflers of that kind.
So we are not, I think, un-Greek.

Translated by Edmund Keeley and Philip Sherrard

Alexandrian Kings

The Alexandrians came out in throngs
to have a sight of Cleopatra's sons,
Caesarion, and his two brothers, too
young Alexander, and the little Ptolemy,
who for the first time were brought out to the Gymnasium,
to be proclaimed kings there,
before a splendid soldiery array.

First Alexander – they now named him king
of all Armenia, Media, and the Parthians.
Then Ptolemy – they made him king
of all Cicilia, Syria, and Phoenicia.
Caesarion was standing slightly to the fore,
decked out in silk of madder pink,
a bunch of hyacinths upon his breast,
his girdle double-studded with sapphires and amethysts,
his shoes held on by long
white thongs encrusted with rose pearls.
Him they now called much greater than the younger ones;
him they now named King of Kings.

The Alexandrians sensed well of course
that this was naught but patter and theatricals.

But then the day was balmy and was lyrical,
the sky a clear cerulean blue,
the Alexandrian Gymnasium
a most triumphal feat of art,
the sumptuousness of the courtiers extraordinary,
Caesarion in all his charm and beauty

(and he was Cleopatra's son, a Lagid by his blood);
and crowds of Alexandrians ran to the feast,
and all rejoiced, and all now cheered
in Greek, and in Egyptian, and some in Hebrew too,
enchanted by the gracious spectacle –
although of course they knew how little it was worth,
what empty words these kingships really were.

Translated by Memas Kolaitis

Come Back

Come back and take hold of me,
sensation that I love come back and take hold of me –
when the body's memory awakens
and an old longing again moves into the blood,
when lips and skin remember
and hands feel as though they touch again.

Come back often, take hold of me in the night
when lips and skin remember . . .

Tomb of Evrion

In this tomb – ornately designed,
the whole of syenite stone,
covered by so many violets, so many lilies –
lies handsome Evrion,
an Alexandrian, twenty-five years old.
On his father's side, he was of old Macedonian stock,
on his mother's side, descended from a line of magistrates.
He studied philosophy with Aristokleitos,
rhetoric with Paros, and at Thebes
the sacred scriptures. He wrote a history
of the province of the Arsinoites. That at least will survive.
But we've lost what was really precious: his form –
like a vision of Apollo.

Translated by Edmund Keeley and Philip Sherrard

The Battle of Magnesia

All his old vigour, all his courage lost,
His body now tired out and ill almost

Must be his only care. Through what remains
Of life he'll bear no burdens. So maintains

Philip at least; tonight he's playing dice
And wants amusement. 'Roses would be nice,

'Lots, on the table! Antiochus may
Be smashed. So what? Magnesia, they say,

'Annihilated his grand host. They do
Exaggerate. It cannot all be true –

We hope! No friend, he's still our kin. For such
One hope is quite enough – perhaps too much.'

Philip of course will not put off the feast.
However hard his life has been, at least

One quality remains; a mind well kept
Remembers just how long the Syrians wept

When mother Macedonia went down fighting.
'To dinner! Slaves! The music and the lighting!'

Translated by John Mavrogordato

For Ammones, Who Died at the Age of 29 in 610

Raphael, they want you to compose a few
verses for the poet Ammones' epitaph.
Something in the best taste and polished. You'll be able,
you're the right one, to write just as befits
the poet Ammones, one of us.

You will of course speak of his poems –
but speak of his beauty too,
that delicate beauty we so loved.

Your Greek is always fine and musical.
But now we need all of your virtuosity.
Into a foreign tongue our grief and love will pass.
Pour your Egyptian feeling into the foreign tongue.

Raphael, let your verses so be written
that they have, you know, something of our life in them,
so that the rhythm and each phrase may show
that an Alexandrian writes of an Alexandrian.

Translated by David Ricks

One of Their Gods

When one of them moved through the marketplace of Selefkia
just as it was getting dark –
moved like a young man, tall, extremely handsome,
with the joy of being immortal in his eyes,
with his black and perfumed hair –
the people going by would gaze at him,
and one would ask the other if he knew him,
if he was a Greek from Syria, or a stranger.
But some who looked more carefully
would understand and step aside;
and as he disappeared under the arcades,
among the shadows and the evening lights,
going toward the quarter that lives
only at night, with orgies and debauchery,
with every kind of intoxication and desire,
they would wonder which of Them it could be,
and for what suspicious pleasure
he had come down into the streets of Selefkia
from the August Celestial Mansions.

Translated by Edmund Keeley and Philip Sherrard

An Evening

It would not, anyway, have lasted long. Experience
of years has made me know it well. Somehow a hurried
Fate had intervened and put an end to it.
The lovely life was far too short.
But yet, how musky were the fragrances,
how splendid was the bed we lay upon,
and what voluptuous pleasures to our bodies we allowed!

An echo of those days of pleasuring,
an echo of those days has come to me,
a reminiscence of the ardour of us both.
I took a letter up again,
and read it through and through until the light was gone.

And then, in sadness, I walked over to the balcony –
I stepped out there to clear my brain, by gazing out upon
a little of a city dearly loved,
a little bustle of the streets and of the shops.

Translated by Memas Kolaitis

In the Month of Athyr

I read with difficulty
        upon the ancient stone
'O LO(RD) JESUS CHRIST'.
        I can make out a 'SO(U)L'.
'IN THE MO(NTH) OF ATHYR'
        'LEVKI(OS) FELL AS(LEE)P.'
At the mention of his age
        'HE LI(VE)D' so many 'YEARS'
The Kappa Zeta means
        quite young he fell asleep.
In the damaged part I see
        'HI(M) . . . ALEXANDRIAN'.
Then there are three more lines
        very much mutilated;
But I make out some words

> like 'OVR T(E)ARS', and 'SORROW',
> Afterwards 'TEARS' again,
> and 'OF H(IS) GRIEVING (FR)IENDS'.
> I see that Levkios
> had friends whose love was deep.
> In the month of Athyr
> Levkios fell asleep.

Translated by John Mavrogordato

The Tomb of Ignatios

> Here I am not that Kleon who was talked about
> In Alexandria (where it is difficult to impress them)
> For my splendid houses, for my gardens,
> And for my horses and my carriages,
> For the diamonds and the silks I used to wear.
> Nay: here am I not that Kleon;
> Let his eight and twenty years be blotted out.
> I am Ignatios, a lay-reader, who very late
> Came to myself; even so ten happy months I lived
> In the tranquillity and in the safety of Christ.

Translated by John Mavrogordato

Days of 1903

> I never found them again – all lost so quickly . . .
> the poetic eyes, the pale face . . .
> in the darkening street . . .
>
> I never found them again – mine entirely by chance,
> and so easily given up,
> then longed for so painfully.
> The poetic eyes, the pale face,
> those lips – I never found them again.

Translated by Edmund Keeley and Philip Sherrard

Caesarion

In part to check a date,
in part to pass the time,
last night, late, I took down a collection
of Ptolemaic inscriptions for my reading.
The boundless praise and flattery
are much alike for all the monarchs. All are illustrious,
glorious, mighty, beneficent;
each of their enterprises most wise.
As for the women of that line, they too,
every Berenice and Cleopatra, worthy of our awe.

On managing to check the date,
I'd have set the book aside had a reference, brief
and insignificant enough, to King Caesarion,
not drawn my attention to it instantly.

Ha! and there you were with your indefinable
charm. In history but few
lines are to be found about you,
and so I shaped you the more freely in my mind.
I shaped you handsome and sensitive.
My art endows your face
with a dreamy, appealing beauty.
And so completely did I imagine you
that late last night, as my lamp
was starting to go out – I meant it to –
I fancied you had come into my room;
it seemed to me that there you were before me; just as you will have been
in conquered Alexandria;
pale and weary, ideal in your sorrow,
still hoping they would show some tenderness,
the base – who were a-whispering of 'too many Caesars'.

Translated by David Ricks

To Remain

It must have been one o'clock at night,
Or half past one.
                     In a corner of the wine shop;
Behind the wooden partition.
Except the two of us the shop quite empty.
A paraffin lamp hardly lighted it.
The waiter who had to sit up was asleep at the door.

No one would have seen us. But anyhow
We had become so excited
We were incapable of precautions.

Our clothes had been half opened – they were not many
For a divine month of July was blazing.

Enjoyment of the flesh in the middle
Of our half-opened clothes;
Quick baring of the flesh – and the vision of it
Has passed over twenty-six years; and now has come
Here in these verses to remain.

Translated by John Mavrogordato

Simeon

I've seen his latest poems, yes;
Beirut is wild about them.
I'll have a proper look at them some other day.
I can't today: I'm in a bit of a state.

He is indeed a better Grecian than Libanius.
But is he one step up from Meleager? I think not.

Oh Mebes, what of Libanius! and what of books!
and what of petty matters! . . . Mebes, yesterday I found myself
– as luck would have it – at the foot of Simeon's pillar.

I squeezed in with the Christians
at their silent prayer and worship
and devotions; except that, being no Christian,
I lacked their spiritual tranquillity –
and I started trembling all over and feeling awful;
and I started to shudder and shake and find it all too much.

I can see you smiling! Think of it, though: thirty-five years,
winter, summer, night, day, thirty-five
years on top of a pillar, bearing living witness.
Before we were even born – I'm twenty-nine,
and you, I take it, younger –
before we were even born, imagine it,
Simeon made the ascent to the top of his pillar
and ever since has stayed there face to face with God.

I don't feel up to work today.
But Mebes, I won't object to its being said
that, whatever the other sophists say,
Yes, I acknowledge Lamon
is Syria's leading poet.

Translated by David Ricks

Young Men of Sidon (AD 400)

The actor they had brought in to entertain them
also recited a few choice epigrams.

The room opened out on to the garden,
and a delicate odour of flowers
mingled with the scent
of the five perfumed young Sidonians.

There were readings from Meleager, Krinagoras, Rhianos.
But when the actor recited
'Here lies Aeschylus, the Athenian, son of Euphorion'
(stressing maybe more than he should have
'his renowned valour' and 'sacred Marathonian grove'),
a vivacious young man, mad about literature,

suddenly jumped up and said:

'I don't like that quatrain at all.
Sentiments of that kind seem somehow weak.
Give, I say, all your strength to your work,
make it your total concern. And don't forget your work
even in times of trial or when you near your end.
This is what I expect, what I demand of you –
and not that you completely dismiss from your mind
the magnificent art of your tragedies –
your *Agamemnon,* your marvellous *Prometheus,*
your representations of Orestes and Cassandra,
your *Seven Against Thebes* – to set down for your memorial
merely that as an ordinary soldier, one of the herd,
you too fought against Datis and Artaphernis.'

Dareios

Phernazis the poet is at work
on the crucial part of his epic:
how Dareios, son of Hystaspis,
took over the Persian kingdom.
(It's from him, Dareios, that our glorious king,
Mithridatis, Dionysos and Evpator, descends.)
But this calls for serious thought; Phernazis has to analyse
the feelings Dareios must have had:
arrogance, maybe, and intoxication? No – more likely
a certain insight into the vanities of greatness.
The poet thinks deeply about the question.

But his servant, rushing in, cuts him short
to announce very serious news:
the war with the Romans has begun;
most of our army has crossed the borders.

The poet is dumbfounded. What a disaster!
How can our glorious king,
Mithridatis, Dionysos and Evpator,
bother about Greek poems now?
In the middle of a war – just think, Greek poems!

Phernazis gets all worked up. What bad luck!
Just when he was sure to distinguish himself
with his *Dareios,* sure to silence
his envious critics once and for all.
What a setback, terrible setback to his plans.

And if it's only a setback, that wouldn't be too bad.
But can we really consider ourselves safe in Amisos?
The town isn't very well fortified,
and the Romans are the most awful enemies.

Are we, Cappadocians, really a match for them?
Is it conceivable?
Are we now to pit ourselves against the legions?
Great gods, protectors of Asia, help us.

But through all his distress, all the turmoil,
the poetic idea comes and goes insistently:
arrogance and intoxication – that's the most likely, of course:
arrogance and intoxication are what Dareios must have felt.

Translated by Edmund Keeley and Philip Sherrard

A Byzantine Nobleman in Exile Writing Verses

Those who are frivolous themselves may call me
Frivolous. In serious matters I was always most
Attentive. I am ready to insist
That no one is more familiar than I am
With Fathers or Scriptures or Conciliar Canons.
Whenever he was in doubt, Botaneiates,
In any ecclesiastical difficulty,
Used to consult me, and me first of all.
But banished here, (let her look to it, the malicious
Eirene Doukaina), where afflictions gall me,
It is not strange if I amuse myself
Making my six or eight verses – or if it enthral me
To make mythological stories
Of Hermes, and of Dionysos, and of Apollo,
Of Thessalian and Peloponnesian heroes; and I follow

The strictest rules composing my iambics,
Such as – allow me to say – the literary men
Of Constantinople don't know how to write.
Probably my very correctness provokes their censure.

Translated by John Mavrogordato

Favour of Alexander Balas

O, I don't mind that my chariot broke a wheel,
And I lost a ridiculous race. With some good wine,
And lots of lovely roses I will steal
The hours of night. All Antioch is mine,
Giving to none more glory than to me.
I am Balas' weakness, his idolatry.
Tomorrow they'll say that the race was unfair, you'll see.
(But if I had told them privately – if I had the bad taste –
Even my one wheeled car would have been first-placed).

Translated by John Mavrogordato

From the School of the Renowned Philosopher

For two years he studied with Ammonios Sakkas,
but he was bored by both philosophy and Sakkas.

Then he went into politics.
But he gave that up. That Prefect was an idiot,
and those around him, sombre-faced officious nitwits:
their Greek – poor fools – absolutely barbaric.

After that he became
vaguely curious about the church: to be baptized
and pass as a Christian. But he soon
changed his mind: it would certainly have caused a row
with his parents, ostentatious pagans,
and – horrible thought –
they would have cut off at once
their extremely generous allowance.

But he had to do something. He began to haunt
the corrupt houses of Alexandria,
every secret den of debauchery.

In this fortune favoured him:
he'd been given an extremely handsome figure.
And he enjoyed the divine gift.

His looks would last
at least another ten years. And after that?
Maybe he'll go back to Sakkas.
Or if the old man has died meanwhile,
he'll go to another philosopher or sophist:
there's always someone suitable around.

Or in the end he might possibly return
even to politics – commendably remembering
the traditions of his family,
duty towards the country,
and other resonant banalities of that kind.

Translated by Edmund Keeley and Philip Sherrard

In Alexandria, 31 BC

Coming from his little village, that lies just
Near the suburbs, still covered with the journey's dust,

The trader arrives. 'Frankincense' and 'Gum', his wares,
And 'Best Olive Oil' and 'Perfume for the Hair'

He cried along the streets. But in the noisy herd,
The music, the processions, how can he be heard?

The moving crowd around him jostles, hustles, thunders.
At last bewildered, What's the madness here? he wonders.

And someone tosses him too the gigantic piece
Of palace fiction – Antony's victory in Greece.

Translated by John Mavrogordato

John Kantakuzinos Triumphs

He sees the fields that still belong to him:
the wheat, the animals, the trees laden with fruit;
and beyond them his ancestral home
full of clothes, costly furniture, silverware.

They'll take it away from him – O God – they'll take it all away from him now.

Would Kantakuzinos show pity for him
if he went and fell at his feet? They say he's merciful,
very merciful. But those around him? And the army? –
Or should he fall down and plead before Lady Irini?

Fool that he was to get mixed up in Anna's party!
If only Lord Andronikos had never married her!
Has she ever done anything good, shown any humanity?
Even the Franks don't respect her any longer.
Her plans were ridiculous, all her plotting farcical.
While they were threatening everyone from Constantinople,
Kantakuzinos demolished them, Lord John demolished them.

And to think he'd planned to join Lord John's party!
And he would have done it, and would have been happy now,
a great nobleman still, his position secure,
if the bishop hadn't dissuaded him at the last moment
with his imposing hieratic presence,
his information bogus from beginning to end,
his promises, and all his drivel.

Translated by Edmund Keeley and Philip Sherrard

On an Italian Shore

The son of Menedoros,
    Kimos, a Greek-Italian,
fritters his life away
    in the pursuit of pleasure,
according to the common
    practice in Magna Graecia

among the rich, unruly
    young men of today.

Today, however, wholly
    counter to his nature,
he's lost in thought, dejected.
    There on the shore he sees
with bitter melancholy
    ship upon ship that slowly
disgorges crates of booty
    from the Peloponnese.

Greek booty. Spoils of Corinth.

Today don't be surprised
    if it's unsuitable,
indeed impossible,
    for the Italicized
young man to dream of giving
    himself to pleasure fully.

Translated by James Merrill

In a Township of Asia Minor

The news about the outcome of the sea-battle at Actium
was of course unexpected.
But there's no need for us to draft a new proclamation.
The name's the only thing that has to be changed.
There, in the concluding lines, instead of: 'Having freed the Romans
from Octavius, that disaster,
that parody of a Caesar,'
we'll substitute: 'Having freed the Romans
from Antony, that disaster, . . .'
The whole text fits very nicely.

'To the most glorious victor,
matchless in his military ventures,
prodigious in his political operations,
on whose behalf the township ardently wished

for Antony's triumph, . . .'
here, as we said, the substitution: 'for Octavius Caesar's triumph,
regarding it as Zeus' finest gift –
to this mighty protector of the Greeks,
who graciously honours Greek customs,
who is beloved in every Greek domain,
who clearly deserves exalted praise,
and whose exploits should be recorded at length
in the Greek language, in both verse and prose,
in the *Greek language,* the vehicle of fame,'
et cetera, et cetera. It all fits brilliantly.

Translated by Edmund Keeley and Philip Sherrard

In a Great Greek Colony, 200 BC

That the things in the Colony are not going to perfection
Not the least doubt bears inspection,
And although somehow or other we do get along,
Perhaps it is time, as a good many think, to bring in a strong
Man to Reform the Constitution.

But the great difficulty and the objection
Is that they make a business erection
Of everything they talk about redressing,
These Reformers. (It would be a blessing
If nobody ever wanted them.) For the solution
Of the smallest detail they have questions and examinations,
And at once get into their heads the most radical alterations,
Insisting that they must be carried out without delay.

They also have a great liking for sacrifices.
    'You must give up that profit, don't be sentimental:
    Your enjoyment of it is precarious: in the Colonies today
    It is just such increments which exact their prices.
    This income of yours – some restitution;
    Of this connection again some diminution;
    And thirdly, something less: only the natural prosecution
    Of a system; what else can you do? They seem fundamental;
    But create a responsibility which is detrimental.'

And as they go ahead with their inquisition,
They keep on finding superfluities, for abolition;
Things however that it is very hard for a man to put away.

And when, with luck, they have finished their work of direction,
And, after arranging and trimming everything little and long,
They depart, not without the proper collection
Of their salary, let us just see what the surgeons have left,
After so much expert execution. –

Perhaps it is not yet the moment, perhaps we were wrong.
We must not hurry; hurry is dangerous without circumspection.
Premature measures only bring repentance.
Undoubtedly and unfortunately the Colony has many irregularities for
    correction.
Imperfect? Does anything human escape that sentence?
And after all, you see, we are getting along.

Translated by John Mavrogordato

Myris: Alexandria, AD 340

When I heard the terrible news, that Myris was dead,
I went to his house, although I avoid
going to the houses of Christians,
especially during times of mourning or festivity.

I stood in the corridor. I didn't want
to go further inside because I noticed
that the relatives of the deceased looked at me
with obvious surprise and displeasure.
They had him in a large room,
and from the corner where I stood
I could catch a glimpse of it: all precious carpets,
and vessels in silver and gold.

I stood and wept in a corner of the corridor.
And I thought how our parties and excursions
would no longer be worthwhile without Myris;
and I thought how I'd no longer see him

at our wonderfully indecent night-long sessions
enjoying himself, laughing, and reciting verses
with his perfect feel for Greek rhythm;
and I thought how I'd lost forever
his beauty, lost forever
the young man I'd worshipped so passionately.

Some old women close to me were talking with lowered voices
about the last day he lived:
the name of Christ constantly on his lips,
his hand holding a cross.

Then four Christian priests
came into the room, and said prayers
fervently, and orisons to Jesus,
or to Mary (I'm not very familiar with their religion).
We'd known, of course, that Myris was a Christian,
known it from the very start,
when he first joined our group the year before last.
But he lived exactly as we did.
More devoted to pleasure than all of us,
he scattered his money lavishly on amusements.
Not caring what anyone thought of him,
he threw himself eagerly into night-time scuffles
when our group happened to clash
with some rival group in the street.
He never spoke about his religion.
And once we even told him
that we'd take him with us to the Serapeion.
But – I remember now –
he didn't seem to like this joke of ours.
And yes, now I recall two other incidents.
When we made libations to Poseidon,
he drew himself back from our circle and looked elsewhere.
And when one of us in his fervour said:
'May all of us be favoured and protected
by the great, the sublime Apollo' –
Myris, unheard by the others, whispered: 'not counting me'.

The Christian priests were praying loudly
for the young man's soul.

I noticed with how much diligence,
how much intense concern
for the forms of their religion, they were preparing
everything for the Christian funeral.
And suddenly an odd sensation
took hold of me. Indefinably I felt
as if Myris were going from me;
I felt that he, a Christian, was united
with his own people and that I was becoming
a stranger, a total stranger. I even felt
a doubt come over me: that I'd also been deceived by my passion
and had always been a stranger to him.
I rushed out of their horrible house,
rushed away before my memory of Myris
could be captured, could be perverted by their Christianity.

Translated by Edmund Keeley and Philip Sherrard

In This Very Space

Environment of house, of place, of neighbourhood,
which I must see and where I walk, year in, year out.

In joy and sorrow I created you,
with many happenings, with many things.

And now you have become all sentiment for me.

From Recipes of Ancient Greco-Syrian Magi

'What extract can one find from herbs
of witchery', an aesthete asked,
'what extract that, from recipes
of ancient Greco-Syrian magi made,
could for a single day (unless much longer still
its potency can last), or even for a while,
my three and twenty years bring back to me
again; my friend of two and twenty years
bring back to me again – his beauty and his love?

'What extract can one find that from the recipes
of ancient Greco-Syrian magi made,
can also, by the precept of recurrence, bring
our little room back once again?'

Translated by Memas Kolaitis

To Have Taken the Trouble

I'm broke and practically homeless.
This fatal city, Antioch,
has devoured all my money:
this fatal city with its extravagant life.

But I'm young and in excellent health.
Prodigious master of things Greek,
I know Aristotle and Plato through and through,
poets, orators, or anyone else you could mention.
I have some idea about military matters
and friends among the senior mercenaries.
I also have a foot in the administrative world;
I spent six months in Alexandria last year:
I know (and this is useful) something about what goes on there –
the scheming of Kakergetis, his dirty deals, and the rest of it.

So I consider myself completely qualified
to serve this country,
my beloved fatherland, Syria.

Whatever job they give me,
I'll try to be useful to the country. That's my intention.
But if they frustrate me with their manoeuvres –
we know them, those smart operators: no need to say more here –
if they frustrate me, it's not my fault.

I'll approach Zabinas first,
and if that idiot doesn't appreciate me,
I'll go to his rival, Grypos.
And if that imbecile doesn't take me on,
I'll go straight to Hyrkanos.

One of the three will want me anyway.

And my conscience is quiet
about my not caring which one I choose:
the three of them are equally bad for Syria.

But, a ruined man, it's not my fault.
I'm only trying, poor devil, to make ends meet.
The almighty gods ought to have taken the trouble
to create a fourth, an honest man.
I would gladly have gone along with him.

Translated by Edmund Keeley and Philip Sherrard

Andreas Karkavitsas (1866–1922)

A ship's doctor by profession, Karkavitsas studied Greek traditional life as closely as Vizyinos or Papadiamantis (qq.v), but in giving artistic form to what he found he clove relentlessly, in the most successful of his novels, to Zola's naturalism and its preoccupation with the *bête humaine*. *The Beggar* (1896) tells of how Tziritokostas, a resourceful beggar from the Kravara area in central Greece (whose poverty had traditionally driven many of its people to this profession), deceives some of the oppressed and guileless Karagounides community in Thessaly, a province only recently annexed to the Greek state. In the passage that follows we witness the confrontation between a representative of that state, the bullying Valachas, and the satanic beggar Tziritokostas.

The Beggar (*extract*)

If that painful beating which the customs guard was giving the beggar moved the peasants to any feeling at all, it was neither sympathy nor indignation on behalf of the victim. Karagounedes do not feel such things. One thing alone – astonishment – overwhelmed them. They could not understand why the beggar was rolling around on the ground without saying a word or putting up any resistance and without showing any sign of anger on his face. What the hell! Even endurance has its limits! . . .

But the peasants did not understand what the beggar really meant. Tziritokostas was in fact twice the size of the customs guard. Beneath his filthy rags were arms of iron and steely muscles and strong shoulders, the neck of an ox and the strength of a bull. In his own country, where they knew him well, everybody was terrified of him. His exploits were recounted like the deeds of giants in fairy tales. Once, in order to help a friend of his who was a candidate in the mayoral elections, alone and unaided he prevented the inhabitants of Hagios Vlases – who supported the other candidate – from going to the polls. And that evening, when they were counting the ballots and he realized that his friend was going to lose, again alone and unaided he burst into the church with his revolver, drove out the guard and overturned the polls, ballot-boxes and all.

But Tziritokostas had accomplished not a little on his journeys as well. Up till now he had secretly dispatched three souls to Hades. He never said a word. He endured everything they did to him with the patience of Job. But in his mind he engraved those responsible in black letters, and woe to them if they ever happened to fall into his hands.

Kostas Tzirites – also known as Tziritokostas in accordance with the custom they have in Roumeli of joining first and last names – was from an area that contains within its narrow boundaries the entire unbridled history of Greek beggary. It had been the custom in his day, when the able-bodied men were away on their journeys and the women were outside in the surrounding hills breaking up the sod around their consumptive corn, for the old people to gather the children together in the dancing-place and to drill them in the tricks of beggary. Before those foreheads crowned with white hair which a long life of humiliation had debased; before those deformed faces which incessant fraudulent expressions had hardened; before those crippled bodies which had been altered, not by the swift passage of the years, not by the hidden activity of disease, not by the sudden impact of the weather, but by deliberate attempt; the young, the village's hope and joy, drilled in order to be worthy of their fathers, if not better. The lame-maimed-blind dance was the chief exercise during those days. The children, each holding a beggar's staff, circled hand in hand and each pretended a bodily defect. One played lame, and he raised and lowered his body at each step like the piston inside the metal sides of a pump. Another played totally blind: he stepped gingerly, placing his staff in front of him and feeling the ground with its tip lest he come upon a mound or a hole, a cliff or a bank, a rock or a tree stump, and fall and break and break his bones, poor fellow! And his face showed graphically the uncertainty and terror of the blind. A third played the paralytic: he placed both hands on the ground, and springing like a swift-footed hare, managed to lift his stiff dead legs, at the same time raising his clear and guileless eyes and imbuing his perspiring face with an expression of gentle sorrow and resigned endurance in the will of God, the just and all-powerful Judge! Another, supposedly bewitched by the Neraids, pulled himself erect and shook all over as he walked, taking one step forward, two backward, three right, four left; he wanted to go one place and went another; he tried to turn right and turned left; he attempted to bring his arms together and they spread apart; he wanted to fold his arms and they stretched out like stiff sticks; and he walked with all his limbs shaking, as if all his joints had become loosened. Another said that from envy the Neraids had taken away his voice at the ravine of Kavale, and he stretched his neck and with great effort formed his lips for speech. He wanted to speak, but managed to produce only a hair-raising howling from within his constricted larynx. Another pretended to have but one leg and balanced his body on crutches like a filthy rag flapping in the breeze. And another ten or twenty feigned ten or twenty other bodily infirmities, many known to man, but many as yet unheard of in this world.

While the children were drilling in this way in order to deceive the generous feelings of their fellow man later on, one of the elders, a famed musician and sweet of voice, placed a three-stringed lyre upright on his knees. With his song he endeavoured to lighten their daily labours and to show them how enviably and blessedly happy their future life would be. With wheedling, constricted, monotonous tone; with a brief allegro at the beginning; then with a sudden rise and fall in pitch; then with a continuous low drone stretching endlessly on and on, he sang an abject song, as native as the wild mustard of the dry hills, and like it, insipid, mean, louse-infested. He accompanied his song with a monotonous, constricted, wheedling whine of his lyre. And with his song he showed the children the sere and dispiriting mountains of their country, the land, their harsh and completely barren stepmother. He likened its birth to God's curse and triple damnation, as, wafted on the wings of an angel, he moved backwards in time to the creation of the Universe when the All was Chaos and Nothing. God, he said, wanted to form the world at that time. He took a large sieve and hung it like a cloud in the abyss. Then he took dirt in his hand and threw it into the sieve and shook it up and down. The good and fertile dirt naturally fell down and filled the abyss, and suddenly the Earth appeared, fruitful and very beautiful. Finally there remained in the sieve only rocks and rubble. Angered because he had not thought beforehand to make a fair apportionment of these things also, The Creator kicked the sieve, and all that remained in it poured out together into one place. And God named that place Krakoura, which means 'cursed like Sarah's womb'.

But the singer did not recite these things in order to cause his listeners to despair. Quite the contrary. Like an inspired cantor of olden times he derived grandeur from debasement and valour from fear, and his voice suddenly became golden and sweet. While he cursed the land, he pronounced its children blessed. When the demons, he said, wanted to divide the earth into kingdoms, no one of them was willing to take Krakoura under his sway, and they left it unassigned, and all were declared its rulers and protectors.

But, added the old man, a place which has such protectors is happy and blessed in every way. Its inhabitant will never experience hunger, nor will he ever thirst. His hands will never know the rough handle of plough and axe; his golden youth will not be blasted by prying rocks from the earth; his forehead will not be furrowed by thought. He will not fear that the south-west wind will sear the crops in the field, or that drought will waste the grapes, or that rain will ruin the melon fields. Others will attend to these matters and others will plant the grape – he will drink the wine. Others will sow and others will reap the grain – he will eat the bread. Others will gather the olives, others will press out the oil. He will have but one goal: to circle the Globe from East to West, and inspired by his all-powerful guide to deceive the foolish herd of men and then return home laden down with wealth.

Thus the old man spoke to them, and thus he advised them. And at each break in the song, at each rest of his lyre, that weird chorus approached with its lame-

maimed-blind motion and sang in a wheedling and constricted and monotonous
voice:

> May God forgive your mother's soul –
> Give me a little flour
> for me to make some porridge.
> One, Two, Three . . .
>
> May God forgive your father's soul –
> Give me a little oil
> for me to put in my porridge.
> One, Two, Three . . .
>
> May God forgive your grandmother's soul –
> Give me a little onion
> for me to cook with the oil,
> for me to put in the porridge,
> for me to eat in the evening.
> One, Two, Three . . .

In this singular school Tziritokostas quickly excelled and gained recognition.
He was not yet ten when he began to enrich the lame-maimed-blind dance with
strange and unnatural new steps; to add to the beggars' songs new measures and
unheard of themes. The revered countenance of the elders who formed The
Twelve of the village council shuddered in wonder and joy at this new star that
was rising brilliantly to illumine their fatherland. The bones of Pelalomoutres,
Kalligospilles, Pastrogonias, which were buried deep in slumber in the courtyard
of the Church of the Virgin, wearied with the weight of their many journeyings
and their immense reputation, stirred, coffin and all, when they heard the new
beggar who was coming to eclipse their memory. And even the beggars' staffs
which were hung on the walls of the houses shook with an almost religious excite-
ment, wondering which of them might be honoured to accompany the new prince
of rogues on his first journey. And Tziritogiorgas, his father, lifted up his hands
in all sincerity for perhaps the first time in his life and thanked God from the
bottom of his heart for having sent him such a son to continue his calling and
bring honour to his house. But before deciding to send the boy on his first journey the lucky father summoned him to an out of the way room of the house as
if to tell him secrets. Then he sat the boy down on the floor and told him to look
around. And when the young man turned his eyes, for the first time he saw clearly
the ancient source and standing of his family.

The room was not really lavishly furnished. A single termite-eaten table covered with a coloured wool tablecloth was set against one wall with a yellow, pimply gourd resting on it. A wooden bench covered with a spread took up a second wall. Two large wooden chests carved with strange, coarse designs took up a third. And from the unceilinged roof hung five or ten braids of dried quinces with their leaves and fuzz still on them, and two plum branches with dust resting like foam on their blue-black skin. Yet behind the blackened door and all around the walls the boy saw hanging from their nails all shapes and sizes of beggars' staffs ordered by rank and age. Some were moulded straight from top to bottom; others were twisted, others forked; some had a thick root at their tip; this one had knots; that one was crooked; this one had had its bark stripped off; another still bore the marks of dogs' teeth; still another had the lines on its back which its late master had carved as he counted whatever it was that he considered worth remembering in his life or calling; this one was half broken, that one bent. All were enveloped in dust as if in the shroud of time, and all were sunk in silence and sleep like the weapons of an illustrious warrior, hanging there as his deathless memorial and an example worthy of emulation by his descendants.

In fact the staffs had been hung there as an example worthy of emulation by his descendants, and Tziritogiorgas had brought his son there to see them and get instruction before he set out on his journey. Each one of them had its own story equal to and better than that of Achilles' spear. Each had accompanied his father, his grandfather, his great-grandfather in all the bitterness and misfortune of the beggar's life – in rain and cold in winter, in sun and heat in summer. Each had supported him as he crossed frozen streams; had helped him detach clothes from clotheslines, curtains from windows, rolls from ovens; to shake fruit from trees during the painful days of hunger. Stronger than Ajax's seven-oxhide shield, it kept its master's body safe from every hound's sharp tooth and from every wolf's fierce attack. Blind, it guided him on marble stairs; crippled, it enabled him to pass through crowded markets; maimed, it propped him up; paralytic, it put him to bed; frightened, it protected him; bold, it armed him with super-human strength. And for years on end it had witnessed all his fraudulent expressions, all his disguises. It had heard all his lies, all his 'God forgives'. And who knows whether the staff did not itself bring to his mind his most skilfully contrived deformity and to his lips his most clever prayer?

Lost to the world, Tziritogiorgas looked from one to the other of the trophies hanging there. Immense awe flooded his heart, and his chest grew heavy as a millstone at that ancestral glory. Like an unsaddled colt which races in the plain the old beggar's mind darted back to the past, and he saw his ancestors one after another ravaged by hardship and unrecognizable from deceit. What those unfortunates had endured in order to bring their family to its present eminence! They suffered beatings, put up with bites from sheep dogs, kicks from horses, shoves and punches from drunks. They heard the whistles of street urchins; they saw maids smash entire plates over their heads; they put up with piss being poured over them and being smeared with excrement. Unwearied they crossed seas and rivers; they strode over plains and mountains and hills. They rested in towns and villages and hamlets. They accepted the wealthy man's generosity and the widow's mite. They ate scraps left by master and slave; they drank the dregs of healthy and sick. They slept in stables and hay-lofts; on the thresholds of houses and in the forecourts of churches; on the saddles of mountains and below in the hollowed plains. Truly, what those unfortunates had endured, what they had endured!

And in his melancholy mental flashback the old beggar suddenly encountered his own journeys. Filled with emotion, he turned to the wall opposite and fixed his gaze motionless on it. There they hung, twenty staffs representing twenty journeys, each one lasting two or three years. And now in the appearance and posture of each he found the story of his travels clearly written out. The first one, at the right end of the wall, a small, thin staff, broken in two – snivelling, worthless and foolish – spoke of the time when, young and ignorant, he made his first journey under his father's watchful surveillance. That time he lost his sack and his money, and the old man split the staff on his back and made him hang it on the wall as a reminder. Right after that one, though, the staff from his second journey rose up large and stout and mighty and fierce, as if urging him to take it in his hands again, and the two of them – ancient combatants of life – to run swiftly to new gains and new triumphs. Then one after another came other staffs in turn, each one with a different posture and expression and life, each one reminding him of many sufferings and misfortunes, but also of many gains and joys. And with a mournful shake of his head Tziritogiorgas lowered his eyes to his son and, with a regal gesture of his right hand, suddenly said in a loud and vibrant voice:

'You see these, hey? See you don't shame 'em!' Those pegs down there are yours. Fill 'em!'

And he pointed to another ten or twenty pegs which continued the series of staffs to the far end of the wall and were waiting, impatient to support the family's new trophies. Tziritokostas raised his eyes, took a careless look at the pegs, and in a steady and serious voice replied:

'Yeah, I'll fill 'em, and I'll drive others besides.'

'That's my boy!' cried Tziritogiorgas ecstatically.

In spite of all his promises, though, and in spite of the elders' confidence in him, Tziritokostas proved no luckier on his first journey than his father had. While he was making the circuit of the Morea, he met up with a blind Kloutsiniote who suggested they should form a team and split the profits. Kloutsines is in the Morea, but it is in all respects the rival of Krakoura. The Kloutsiniote would contribute his blindness and the Kravarite his wiles, two things completely antithetical and yet so conformable and helpful to their craft. Tziritokostas was easily persuaded to join up with the blind man, and after two or three months of travel they had made a considerable amount of money. The novice beggar could not conceal his pride. He reflected on the great joy his relatives would feel and what sorrow he would cause others when they saw the amount of money he had made which was unexpectedly large for a beggar making his first journey. One night, however, while they were sleeping in a hay-loft in Souleimanaga, the blind man suddenly regained his sight and took off with the money. In his despair Tziritokostas wanted to go back to his village. But he had barely reached the outskirts when his fellow citizens greeted him with hoots of derision. And his father shouted to him from a distance brandishing a fearsome club in his hand:

'You bastard, you've disgraced my house! Get out of here – you're no child of mine!'

The young beggar quickly realized that his misfortune had become known in the village well before he arrived. He even suspected that it was his father's doing – perhaps the Kloutsiniote was a local, purposely disguised in order to test his credulity – and that his misfortune was intended to serve as an unforgettable lesson. Thoroughly disgraced, he turned back again, and in his pride he swore not to come back unless he had accomplished something for all to marvel at.

He said it and he did it. Two years later he returned, in August, on the day the village holds its festival celebrating the Dormition of the Virgin. And he returned with many spoils. But that was not much of an accomplishment: all who return from a journey come back with money. Tziritokostas accomplished something else. In his own village, while all the men – their bodily defects put aside and impeccably dressed – were dancing in the dancing-place with their richly decked-out wives, he, wretched and deformed, circulated in their midst for three days and accepted their alms. Three times his own father gave to him, and would have given a fourth, if Tziritokostas had not been overcome with emotion and revealed himself.

The fame of this event spread to all the neighbouring villages. People ran to see him from all over, and those who had given him money were angry, wondering how arch-deceivers could have been deceived. They all quickly agreed that they had found their teacher. And that same day old Lykogiannos – another veteran of that illustrious army – Lykogiannos, who had a lot of money and an only daughter, and who was frequently in despair because he could not find among the young beggars anyone worthy of himself as a son-in-law; Lykogiannos ran to the house, embraced him warmly, and addressed him thus:

'I have one daughter, she's yours and my money too! Many have asked me for her before now, but you're the best and worthiest. You'll honour us all!'

Tziritokostas did in fact honour them all. Eight days after his wedding he began his second journey. Little by little he advanced to areas outside of Greece. He hired the children of impoverished parents – lame, maimed, blind, dumb children – whom he instructed for a while in the rites of beggary, and then took them as a migratory crane does the swallows, to Smyrna, Constantinople, Bulgaria, up even into Roumania! When he had his leather belt well filled with money and had decided to return, he hired the children out again to other beggars who took them to the depths of Russia and Asia Minor until they lost even the memory of their homeland. And he collected other children and began another journey.

But now Tziritokostas no longer travelled abroad. He had sent his two sons there, sons who – God bless them! – were like him in all respects. By means of regular exchange of letters he learned of their doings and sent them the replacements they needed with people he could trust. He contented himself with the proceeds of the Morea and Roumeli. Now he had only two months to go before he completed this year's journey. But in two months what couldn't a man like Tziritokostas accomplish! With his apprentice Mountzoures he had already crossed Archontopelio and the plain of Larisa and gone up to the villages of Kissavos and down to the river-basin. From there he intended to make the rounds of the villages of lower Olympus up to Tyrnavo, and then to drop down to the plain of Pharsala and head straight on home from there. In this historic course of his he gathered in whatever the Christians gave him and what they did not give. Into his sacks he jammed chunks of bread and table scraps, large handfuls of wheat and bundles of still green oats, unripe beans and chick-peas and old clothes, old shoes and scrap iron and every manner of coin. If he saw anything discarded when he entered a house, he asked for it. If they gave it to him, he chucked it into the sack. If they did not, and he was able, he took it then and there, or later, sending his apprentice. When he arrived at some market town he sold the table scraps and the bread crumbs at the cheap eateries; the wheat and oats, the beans and chick-peas at the grocery stores; the old shoes and scrap iron to the blacksmiths for whatever he could get. In this way even the smallest and most ordinary finds in his hands changed their nature and became pure gold.

The day before, though, he had all but paid the price for his successes and then some. They had come down to Kiserle at daybreak and were going from house to house, and the Turks were being most generous. About midday they found themselves at the gate of Galip Aga's courtyard. The Aga was seated on a carpet in the men's quarters and was eating with his children. When he saw them, he asked them in and generously gave them something to eat. Then he asked them a few questions about one thing and another and withdrew to the women's quarters, telling them to rest there to avoid being baked by the midday sun.

In front of the Aga's house there was a large orchard enclosed by high walls. The orchard contained various fruit trees and many almonds, the village's principal source of wealth. Tziritokostas glanced in that direction and could find no peace. In fact the almonds were not yet ripe, and yet the other fruits were still worse. If he stuffed his shirt with almonds, he could sell them to some fool on the road. And, if he couldn't sell them, he could throw them away. What did he have to lose? He wasn't a tailor who'd lose both his material and his wages. The beggar let a little time pass. Then he roused his apprentice and they went into the orchard. They approached the almond trees cautiously; he himself climbed the most heavily loaded and began to beat the plaint branches with a stick while the apprentice gathered the nuts in his apron.

The aga had not fallen asleep yet, however. He heard the sound of the beating, snatched up his broad, curved sword and ran out and grabbed the apprentice by the neck. When the beggar saw him, he summoned all his strength and leapt up on to the wall. From there he dropped to the road and disappeared. The aga beat the apprentice with the flat of his sword until he was exhausted. Then he threw him out the gate, all covered with blood. When Mountzoures was sure he was alone, he managed to get up and staggered out of the village more dead than alive. The beggar was hiding nearby in a ruined mosque. He found a donkey grazing with its saddle on, tied his apprentice on its back in a ball, and left as quickly as he could.

But the beggars had left one beating and had fallen on another. It seems it was their unlucky week. Valachas was beating him with his fists and his feet whenever he could find an opening, like a madman, and was not yet willing to let Tziritokostas go. And even he by now had begun to lose patience. Ah, he thought, but the customs guard has gone too far! His face caught fire, his eyes shot sparks. Just a little longer and he would stretch out his hands – those fingers which, although they had learned to stretch out and gather in like the tentacles of an octopus if the situation demanded, had nevertheless not forgotten how to squeeze, to crush bones and flesh together, to beat the arrogant bastard to a pulp. But, wise and experienced as he was, he held back. Two or three times he turned his eyes to the giapi to ask for help from the peasants. But he saw that they were looking on with amazing indifference.

The Karagounedes had now stopped their conversation. The paredros and Birbiles had put off to another time their attempts to persuade one another by blows which political figure in the area was the best. They watched the beating which the customs guard was giving the beggar as coolly as if they were watching a cock-fight. They looked on, and each expressed with different words, gestures and facial expression his great astonishment at why the beggar rolled around on the ground so long without saying a word, without offering resistance, without showing a sign of anger in his face. What the hell! Even endurance has its limits!

'What do you think?' said Chadoules blinking his eyes rapidly as if dazzled because unused to the light of day. 'He looks strong, but he's chicken: what good's strength without courage?'

'My horse's got strength, too,' said Tzoumas, 'but when I grab the whip he pisses blood.'

Paparrizos, still scratching his chest and grimacing in sympathy said: 'Can't he have courage and still not like to fight? Why risk my soul, he says.'

'I'll risk my soul, he says' interrupted Krapas angrily and looking at the priest: 'If I lose my body, the hell with my soul!'

'Spit quick, you damned fool! Spit quick!' shouted the priest, as he made the sign of the cross. 'The Accursed put those words in your mouth. Spit, I say.'

All the peasants spat right away at Paparrizos' command. Even Krapas spat over his shoulder three times, guffawing.

'I wish he'd belt him one!' said Chadoules. 'I'd eat a fatted lamb!'

'Me too!' added the paredros. 'You don't know how I hate the arrogant bastard!'

'What about me? Let me find him in even a drop of water and I'll drown him!' said Birbiles with hatred in his voice. 'He thinks we're nothings! I'd like to know what kind of place he's from and who he thinks he is.'

'He's from a big city, idiot,' said Magoulas. 'As he'll tell you, it's the birth-place of the vizier Tricoupes – think about it! And he's from an old distinguished family. His roots go back to Zontanos, and that's seventeen belts!'

'No kidding!'

And they turned as one to admire Valachas with an expression of reverence in their eyes. Now they saw that the young man was right – more than right – since his noble family extended back seventeen generations. Such a gentleman surely has the right to do what he wants. And he did well and more than well not to talk to them. Why should he speak, and what could he say, since they don't even count one belt? . . . And dazzled by the brilliance of Valachas' family, the Karagounedes now scarcely dared to raise their eyes to look at him. But at that very instant the wheedling voice of the beggar was heard:

'Help me, you guys! I'm a Christian, too. Pity me!'

The man had now become fed up at the peasants' insensitivity and Valachas' rage and had finally decided to ask for help. And if this didn't bring them to his rescue, he would now leave off pretending and would free himself at a single bound. But as if just awakened from a deep sleep by his cry, the peasants all got up and ran to separate them. The customs guard, however, would not let his victim go. Paparrizos, because he was an object of respect, went to grab his arm, but Valachas, blind with rage, raised his fist and struck him a blow on the fore-head which caused his hat to fly sixty feet away and left his unkempt grey hair free to the breeze.

That blow was the beggar's salvation.

Translated by William F. Wyatt Jr

Konstantinos Theotokis (1872–1923)

A Corfiot nobleman and scholar and a life-long socialist, Theotokis denounced injustice in a number of powerful novels and stories. He also translated Lucretius, and a text like the one that follows, which really requires no comment, shows all the dispassion of the natural historian.

Face Down!

After civil order had finally been restored and general amnesty granted following a period of rampant lawlessness which had encouraged criminals throughout the country to commit every kind of skulduggery or crime imaginable, all the outlaws were allowed to return home from their mountain hideouts. Among those who came back was Antonis Magouliaditis, better known as Koukouliotis.

At the time he must have been about forty years old, a man short in stature, with a dark complexion, black wavy hair, and a very fine, bushy beard. He had a kind face, and the expression of his eyes, except for the green specks in them, was gentle; his mouth, however, was very small and thin-lipped.

Before all this anarchy had broken loose, Koukouliotis had married, and when he became an outlaw and took to the mountains in fear of the law, he left his wife behind alone to fend for herself. She then became unfaithful to him (whom she presumed killed or dead) by loving another man, and soon afterwards gave birth to a very beautiful child, which she came to love dearly.

And so, one day, the renegade husband returned home, in the early evening, bursting into the house unexpectedly, like death. The unfortunate woman was so frightened that, seizing and holding her fair-haired child to her bosom, she stood in terror, unable to utter a word and looking as if she were about to faint. But Koukouliotis smiled wryly and said to her: 'Don't be afraid, woman; I am not about to do you any harm, although you deserve to be punished. This may be your child, but it is not mine, by any means. Isn't that correct? Who is the father, then, if I may ask?' She proceeded to tell him, trembling with fear: 'Antonis, there is nothing that I wish to hide from you. The wrong that I have done is very great indeed, and I also know that your revenge is going to be just as great. Both the child and I do not have the strength to stand up to you – see how I'm trembling with fear, just looking at you. Do whatever you wish with me, but take pity on this poor child who has no one to protect him.'

While the woman was talking to him his expression was growing more and

more sullen with anger, but he didn't interrupt her speech. He remained silent
for a few minutes and then said to her: 'You shameless woman! I am not interested in your advice, nor do I have any sympathy for you. The only thing I want
to know is the name of the man. You, I will spare. If you won't tell me his name,
I will find out myself: the whole village knows who the man you've been living
with is. When I do, then I will kill all three of you and regain that honour that
you despicable creatures have trampled upon.'

She confessed the man's name, and as soon as she did so, Koukouliotis left
the house. When he came back much later, he found his wife where he had left
her, sitting motionless with her child asleep in her arms. She had stayed up, waiting for him. However, he went and lay down on the floor and, as one would
after a feast, fell immediately into a heavy sleep until dawn.

In the morning, as soon as they were all awake, he said to her: 'We're going
to our fields; I would like to see if anybody has done me wrong there, too, so
that I may take care of him the way I did the other one.'

'You mean you've killed him?'

That morning the sun couldn't be seen rising on the horizon; the sky was
covered with clouds and so there was hardly any light. Balancing a hoe and shovel
upon his shoulder, Koukouliotis told his wife to take the child and follow him,
and so the three of them left the house to go to the fields.

As soon as they reached the fields, which were still damp from the last rain,
the former bandit began to dig a ditch.

He remained silent and pale all the while. The sweat streaming down the sides
of his face was cold. The grey light shed by the overcast sky, which gave a lurid
aspect to the surrounding landscape, expressed the man's misery. The woman
was looking upon all this, puzzled and anxious, while the child played about the
mound of soil and small stones that the man kept digging out of the earth.
Suddenly, the sun came out, and its rays caught the gold in the child's hair. He
was smiling like a happy cherub.

Then, when he was finally finished with digging his ditch, Koukouliotis leaned
on his shovel and said to his wife: 'Throw him in, face down.'

Translated by Theodore P. Sampson and Dorothy Trollope

Angelos Sikelianos (1884–1951)

Prolific, vatic, uneven, yet a master of many complex forms, no twentieth-century Greek poet is more deserving of serious attention than Sikelianos (both Cavafy and Seferis admired this poet so different from themselves: see the latter's poems 'Memory I' and 'Memory II', q.v.), yet no poet is so the despair of the translator. No writer is done more of an injustice by such an anthology as this. To look no further, Sikelianos' *Mater Dei* (1917) is one of the greatest and most subtle of religious poems; yet, where each abolished caesura in the Greek is an act of consummate creativity, the translator's powers grow faint. The result is that a poet of Rilke's stature comes to be read, when he is read at all, for his hazy – indeed, often dotty – ideas and is cut down to the stature of an H.D. without the glamour of femininity. The following selection resignedly confines itself to four poems, ranging from Sikelianos' creative high point in the second decade of the twentieth century to the terrible years of the Occupation, which still hold an interest even for the reader who has no idea of the forms which none of these versions do much to capture.

In 'Yannis Keats' (1915) Sikelianos pays tribute to the English poet whose work he could at best stumble through, memorably Hellenizing the English poet's name and bringing him into a retelling of Telemachus' journey in the *Odyssey*, with echoes of the odes to the Nightingale and to the Grecian Urn. An entirely darker vision is seen in 'Agraphon', whose 'unwritten', apocryphal story derives from the Persian poet Nizami (via Goethe). The force it takes is in part from its being written in 1942, the most terrible year of starvation in Occupied Greece.

The First Rain

> We leaned from the open window.
> All was one with our mood.
> Sulphur-pale, the clouds
> made field and vineyard dark,
> with secret turbulence
> the wind moaned in the trees,
> and the quick swallow went
> breasting across the grass.
> Then suddenly the thunder
> broke, and tore the sky,
> and dancing came the rain.
> The dust leapt in the air.

We, as our nostrils felt
the teeming earth-smell, held
our lips open, to let it
water deep in the breast.
Then side by side, our faces
as mullain and as olive
already wet with rain:
'What smell', we asked, 'is this,
that bee-like pricks the air?
From balsam, pine, acanthus,
osier, or the thyme?'
So was it that, as I breathed,
sweetness filled my mouth,
I stood, a lyre caressed
by its profusion, till,
meeting again your gaze,
blood clamoured in every vein.
I bent above the vine,
leaf-shuddering, to drink
its honey and its flower;
nor could I – my mind a dense
grape-cluster, bramble-caught the breath –
single those smells, but reaped
and gathered all, and all
drank as one does from fate
sorrow or sudden joy.
I drank them down, and when
I touched your waist, my blood
like the nightingale sang out
and ran like all the waters.

Translated by Philip Sherrard and Edmund Keeley

Yannis Keats

A bough Apollo's hand;
a plane-tree's smooth, full bough,
spread above you, may it bring
the ambrosial calm of the universe . . .

I thought how you would arrive at Pylos' broad, bright shore
    along with me,
with Mentor's tall ship gently moored
    in the sand's embrace;

how we, bound in the winged friendship of those youths
    who make that flight with the gods,
would go to the stone seats which time
    and the folk had smoothened

to meet that man who even in the third generation
    governed still in peace;
whose discourse of travels and whose holy judgements ripened
    in his mind as he grew older . . .

How we would attend the sacrifice to the gods, at dawn,
    of the three-year-old heifer,
and hear the single cry uttered by his three daughters
    when the axe roared

and suddenly plunged in darkness
    the slow-rolling, dark-lashed eye,
the dull gilt half-moon
    of its horns now useless . . .

My love, as a sister a brother,
    imagined your virginal bath,
how Polycaste would bathe you naked
    and clothe you in a beautiful tunic.

I thought how I would wake you at dawn
    with a nudge of my foot,
lest we delay while the bright chariot
    yoked awaited us;

and how all day long, in silence or with the simple talk
    that comes and goes,
we would steer the horses which are always tugging the yoke
    to one side or the other . . .

But most of all I thought how
    your two doe eyes
would lose themselves in the bronze and the bright gold
    in Menelaus' palace,

and would gaze unswervingly, burying them in depths
    inaccessible to memory,
at the heavy amber, the gilded and the white ivory,
    the carved silver . . .

I thought how, bending to your ear, I would tell you
    in hushed tones:
'Watch out, my friend, because soon Helen will appear
    before our eyes;

before us will appear the Swan's only daughter,
    soon, here before us;
and with that we will sink our eyelids
    in the river of Oblivion.'

*

So brightly you appeared before me; but what grass-covered roads
    have brought me to you!
The fiery roses with which I have strewn your tomb
    so that Rome flowers for you

point out to me your pure gold songs – just like
    the mighty, armed bodies
which you see intact in a newly opened ancient tomb, and which vanish
    even as you look at them . . . –

and all the worthy treasury of Mycenae which I thought
    to lay before you –
the cups and swords and broad diadems;
    and on your dead beauty

a mask like that which covered
    the king of the Achaeans,
pure gold, pure craft, all hammered out
    on the trace of death!

Translated by David Ricks

The Sacred Road

Through the new wound that fate had opened in me
I felt the setting sun flood my heart
with a force like that of water when it rushes in
through a gash in a sinking ship.
                                        Because again,
like one long sick when he first ventures forth
to milk life from the outside world, I walked
alone at dusk along the road that starts
at Athens and for its destination has
the sanctuary at Eleusis – the road
that for me was always the Soul's road. It bore,
like a huge river, carts slowly drawn by oxen,
loaded with sheaves or wood, and other carts
that quickly passed me by, the people in them
shadowlike.

                    But farther on, as if the world
had disappeared and nature alone was left,
unbroken stillness reigned. And the rock I found
rooted at the roadside seemed like a throne
long predestined for me. And as I sat
I folded my hands over my knees, forgetting if
it was today that I'd set out or if
I'd taken this same road centuries before.

But then, rounding the nearest bend, three shadows
entered this stillness: a gypsy and, after him,
dragged by their chains, two heavy-footed bears.

And then, as they drew near to me, the gypsy,
before I'd really noticed him, saw me,
took his tambourine down from his shoulder,
struck it with one hand, and with the other tugged
fiercely at the two chains. And the two bears
rose on their hind legs heavily.
                                        One of them,
the larger – clearly she was the mother –
her head adorned with tassels of blue beads
crowned by a white amulet, towered up

suddenly enormous, as if she were
the primordial image of the Great Goddess,
the Eternal Mother, sacred in her affliction,
who, in human form, was called Demeter
here at Eleusis, where she mourned her daughter,
and elsewhere, where she mourned her son,
was called Alcmene or the Holy Virgin.
And the small bear at her side, like a big toy,
like an innocent child, also rose up, submissive,
not sensing yet the years of pain ahead
or the bitterness of slavery mirrored
in the burning eyes his mother turned on him.

But because she, dead tired, was slow to dance,
the gypsy, with a single dextrous jerk
of the chain hanging from the young bear's nostril –
bloody still from the ring that pierced it
perhaps a few days before – made the mother,
groaning with pain, abruptly straighten up
and then, her head turning toward her child,
dance vigorously.
        And I, as I watched, was drawn
outside and far from time, free from forms
closed within time, from statues and images.
I was outside, I was beyond time.

And in front of me I saw nothing except
the large bear, with the blue beads on her head,
raised by the ring's wrench and her ill-fated tenderness,
huge testifying symbol
of all the world, the present and the past,
huge testifying symbol
of all primaeval suffering for which
throughout the human centuries, the soul's
tax has still not been paid. Because the soul
has been and still is in Hades.
        And I,
who am also slave to this world,
kept my head lowered as I threw a coin
into the tambourine.
        Then, as the gypsy

at last went on his way, again dragging
the slow-footed bears behind him, and vanished
in the dusk, my heart prompted me once more
to take the road that terminates among
the ruins of the Soul's temple, at Eleusis.
And as I walked my heart asked in anguish:
'Will the time, the moment ever come when the bear's soul
and the gypsy's and my own, that I call initiated,
will feast together?'
                              And as I moved on, night fell,
and again through the wound that fate had opened in me
I felt the darkness flood my heart as water
rushes in through a gash in a sinking ship.
Yet when – as though it had been thirsting for that flood –
my heart sank down completely into the darkness,
sank completely as though to drown in the darkness,
a murmur spread through all the air above me,
a murmur,
                    and it seemed to say:
                                        'It will come.'

Agraphon

Once at sunset Jesus and his disciples
were on their way outside the walls of Zion
when suddenly they came to where the town
for years had dumped its garbage: burnt mattresses
from sickbeds, broken pots, filth.

And there, crowning the highest pile, bloated,
its legs pointing at the sky, lay a dog's carcass;
and as the crows that covered it flew off
when they heard the approaching footsteps, such a stench
rose up from it that all the disciples, hands
cupped over their nostrils, drew back as one man.

But Jesus calmly walked on by Himself
toward the pile, stood there, and then gazed
so closely at the carcass that one disciple,
not able to stop himself, called out from a distance,

'Rabbi, don't you smell that terrible stench?
How can you go on standing there?'

Jesus, His eyes fixed on the carcass,
answered: 'If your breath is pure, you'll smell
the same stench in the town behind us.
But now my soul marvels at something else,
marvels at what comes out of this corruption.
Look how that dog's teeth glitter in the sun:
like hailstones, like a lily, beyond decay,
a great pledge, mirror of the Eternal One, but also
the Just One's harsh lightning-flash and hope.'

So He spoke; and whether or not the disciples
understood His words, they followed Him
as He moved on, silent.

         And now I,
certainly the last of them, ponder Your words, O Lord,
and, filled with one thought, I stand before You:
grant me, as now I walk outside my Zion,
and the world from end to end is all ruins, garbage,
all unburied corpses choking the sacred
springs of breath, inside and outside the city:
grant me, Lord, as I walk through this terrible stench,
one single moment of Your holy calm,
so that I, dispassionate, may also pause
among this carrion and with my own eyes
somewhere see a token, white as hailstones,
as the lily – something glittering suddenly
deep inside me, above the putrefaction,
beyond the world's decay, like the dog's teeth
at which You gazed that sunset, Lord, in wonder:
a great pledge, mirror of the Eternal One, but also
the Just One's harsh lightning-flash and hope.

Translated by Edmund Keeley and Philip Sherrard

Nikos Kazantzakis (1884–1957)

Kazantzakis was for some years a great friend of Angelos Sikelianos (q.v.), and the visit they made together to Mount Athos in 1914 was formative for them both. In Greece, reading Kazantzakis is often seen as something you do in adolescence and then grow out of, and the worldwide fraternity of his readers includes its fair share of those suffering from arrested development; but the opening part of the main narrative of *The Life and Times of Alexis Zorbas* (written 1941–3 and translated as *Zorba the Greek*), quietly echoing the opening of Plato's *Republic*, has certainly exerted its spell over the years. The most autobiographical of Kazantzakis' novels, it is also disarming – at times, alarming – in its autobiographical frankness about the sexual motive for writing. You don't get much of that from Cacoyannis' film version; any more than you can see the central role in the book of the narrator's dead friend who had gone to the Caucasus to fight for the imperilled Greeks there. Again and again with Kazantzakis' diverse contemporaries (such as Pantelis Prevelakis and Kosmas Politis, qq.v.), we shall find them turning their attention back to the years before the Asia Minor Disaster of 1922.

The Life and Times of Alexis Zorbas (*extract*)

I first met him in Piraeus. I wanted to take the boat for Crete and I had gone down to the port. It was almost daybreak and raining. A strong *sirocco* was blowing the spray from the waves as far as the little café, whose glass doors were shut. The café reeked of brewing sage and human beings whose breath steamed the windows because of the cold outside. Five or six seamen, who had spent the night there, muffled in their brown goatskin reefer-jackets, were drinking coffee or sage and gazing out of the misty windows at the sea. The fish, dazed by the blows of the raging waters, had taken refuge in the depths, where they were waiting till calm was restored above. The fishermen crowding in the cafés were also waiting for the end of the storm, when the fish, reassured, would rise to the surface after the bait. Soles, hog-fish and skate were returning from their nocturnal expeditions. Day was now breaking.

The glass door opened and there entered a thick-set, mud-bespattered, weather-beaten dock labourer with bare head and bare feet.

'Hi! Kostandi!' called out an old sailor in a sky-blue cloak. 'How are things with you?'

Kostandi spat. 'What d'you think?' he replied testily. 'Good morning – the bar! Good night – my lodgings! That's the sort of life I'm leading. No work at all!'

Some started laughing, others shook their heads and swore.

'This world's a life sentence,' said a man with a moustache who had picked up his philosophy from the Karagiozis theatre. 'Yes, a life sentence. Be damned to it.'

A pale bluish-green light penetrated the dirty window-panes of the café and caught hands, noses and foreheads. It leapt on to the counter and lit the bottles. The electric light faded, and the proprietor, half-asleep after his night up, stretched out his hand and switched off.

There was a moment's silence. All eyes were on the dirty-looking sky outside. The roar of the waves could be heard and, in the café, the gurgling of a few hookahs.

The old sailor sighed: 'I wonder what has happened to Captain Lemoni? May God help him!' He looked angrily at the sea, and growled: 'God damn you for a destroyer of homes!' He bit his grey moustache.

I was sitting in a corner. I was cold and I ordered a second glass of sage. I wanted to go to sleep, but I struggled against the desire to sleep, and against my fatigue and the desolation of the early hours of dawn. I looked through the steamy windows at the awakening port resounding with the ships' sirens and the cries of carters and boatmen. And, as I looked, an invisible net, woven from sea, air and my departure, wound its tight meshes round my heart.

My eyes were glued to the black bows of a large vessel. The whole of the hull was still engulfed in darkness. It was raining and I could see the shafts of rain link sky and mud.

I looked at the black ship, the shadows and the rain, and my sadness took shape. Memories arose. The rain and my spleen took on, in the humid atmosphere, the features of my great friend. Was it last year? In another life? Yesterday? When was it I came down to this same port to say goodbye to him? I remembered how it rained that morning, too, and the cold, and the early light. At that time also, my heart was heavy.

How bitter it is to be slowly separated from great friends! Far better to make a clean break and remain in solitude – the natural climate for man. And yet, in that rainy dawn, I could not leave my friend. (I understood why later, but, alas, too late.) I had gone on board with him and was seated in his cabin amid scattered suitcases. I gazed at him intently for a long time, when his attention was fixed elsewhere, as if I wished to make mental note of his features, one by one – his bluish-green luminous eyes, his rounded, youthful face, his intelligent and disdainful expression, and above all, his aristocratic hands with their long, slender fingers.

Once he caught me gazing lingeringly and eagerly at him. He turned round with that mocking air he assumed when he wanted to hide his feelings. He looked at me and he understood. And to avoid the sadness of separation, he asked with an ironical smile:

'How long?'

'What d'you mean, how long?'

'How long are you going on chewing paper and covering yourself with ink? Why don't you come with me? Away there in the Caucasus there are thousands of our people in danger. Let's go and save them.' He began to laugh as if in mockery of his noble plan. 'Maybe we shan't save them. Don't you preach: "The only way to save yourself is to endeavour to save others?" . . . Well, forward, master. You're good at preaching. Why don't you come with me!'

I did not answer. I thought of this sacred land of the east, the old mother of the gods, the loud clamouring of Prometheus nailed to the rock. Nailed to these same rocks, our own race was crying out. Again it was in peril. It was calling to its sons for help. And I was listening, passively, as if pain was a dream and life some absorbing tragedy, in which nobody but a boor or a simpleton would rush on to the stage and take part in the action.

Without waiting for an answer, my friend rose. The boat sounded its siren for the third time. He gave me his hand and again hid his emotion in raillery.

'*Au revoir,* bookworm!'

His voice trembled. He knew it was shameful not to be able to control one's feelings. Tears, tender words, unruly gestures, common familiarities, all seemed to him weaknesses unworthy of man. We, who were so fond of each other, never exchanged an affectionate word. We played and scratched at each other like wild beasts. He, the intelligent, ironical, civilized man; I, the barbarian. He exercised self-control and suavely expressed all his feelings in a smile. I would suddenly utter a misplaced and barbarous laugh.

I also tried to camouflage my emotions with a hard word. But I felt ashamed. No, not exactly ashamed, but I didn't manage it. I grasped his hand. I held it and wouldn't let it go. He looked at me, astonished.

'Are you so moved?' he said, trying to smile.

'Yes,' I replied, with calm.

'Why? Now, what did we say? Hadn't we agreed on this point years ago? What do your beloved Japs say? "Fudoshin!" *Ataraxia,* Olympian calm, the face a smiling, unmoving mask. As for what happens behind the mask, that is our business.'

'Yes,' I replied again, trying not to compromise myself by embarking on a long sentence. I was not sure of being able to control my voice.

The ship's gong sounded, driving the visitors from the cabins. It was raining gently. The air was filled with pathetic words of farewell, promises, prolonged kisses and hurried, breathless injunctions. Mothers rushed to sons, wives to husbands, friends to friends. As if they were leaving them for ever. As if this little separation recalled the other – the Great Separation. And suddenly, in the humid air, the sound of the gong echoed softly from stem to stern, like a funeral bell. I shuddered.

My friend leaned over.

'Listen,' he said in a low voice. 'Have you some foreboding?'

'Yes,' I replied once more.

'Do you believe in such humbug?'

'No,' I answered with assurance.

'Well, then?'

There was no 'well'. I did not believe in it, but I was afraid.

My friend lightly touched my knee with his left hand, as he was wont to do in moments of abandon. I would urge him to take a decision, he would oppose this, stopping his ears, and refuse; finally he would accept, and then he would touch my knee, as if to say: 'All right, I'll do what you say, for friendship's sake . . .'

He blinked two or three times, then stared at me again. He understood I was distressed and hesitated to use our usual weapons: laughter, smiles and chaff.

'Very well,' he said. 'Give me your hand. If ever one of us finds himself in danger of death . . .'

He stopped, as if ashamed. We who had, for so many years, made fun of metaphysical 'flights' and lumped together vegetarians, spiritualists, theosophists and ectoplasm . . .

'Well?' I asked, trying to guess.

'Let's think of it as a game,' he said suddenly, to get out of the perilous sentence he had embarked upon. 'If ever one of us finds himself in danger of death, let him think of the other so intensely that he warns him wherever he may be . . . Right?' He tried to laugh, but his lips remained motionless, as if frozen.

'Right,' I said.

Fearing that he had displayed his feelings too clearly, my friend hastened to add:

'Mind you, I haven't the slightest belief in telepathy and all that . . .'

'Never mind,' I murmured. 'Let it be so . . .'

'Very well, then, let's leave it at that. Agreed?'

'Agreed,' I answered.

They were our last words. We clasped each other's hands in silence, our fingers joined fervently, and suddenly unclasped. I walked away rapidly without looking back, as if I were being followed. I felt a sudden impulse to give one last look at my friend, but I repressed it. 'Don't look back!' I bade myself. 'Forward!'

The human soul is heavy, clumsy, held in the mud of the flesh. Its perceptions are still coarse and brutish. It can divine nothing clearly, nothing with certainty. If it could have guessed, how different this separation would have been.

It was growing lighter and lighter. The two mornings mingled. The loved countenance of my friend, which I could see more clearly now, remained immobile and desolate in the rain and the atmosphere of the port. The door of the café opened, the sea roared, a thickset sailor entered with legs apart and drooping moustaches. Voices rang out in pleasure:

'Welcome, Captain Lemoni!'

I retreated into the corner, trying to concentrate my thoughts afresh. But my friend's face was already dissolving in the rain.

It was becoming still lighter. Captain Lemoni, austere and taciturn, took out his amber rosary and began to tell his beads. I struggled not to see, not to hear, and to hold on a little longer to the vision which was melting away. If only I could live again the moment of that anger which surged up in me when my friend called me a bookworm! I recalled then that all my disgust at the life I had been leading was personified in those words. How could I, who loved life so intensely, have let myself be entangled for so long in that balderdash of books and paper blackened with ink! In that day of separation, my friend had helped me to see clearly. I was relieved. As I now knew the name of my affliction, I could perhaps conquer it more easily. It was no longer elusive and incorporeal; it had assumed a name and a shape, and it would be easier for me to combat it.

His expression must have made silent progress in me. I sought a pretext for abandoning my papers and flinging myself into a life of action. I resented bearing this miserable creature upon my escutcheon. A month earlier, the desired opportunity had presented itself. I had rented on the coast of Crete, facing Libya, a disused lignite mine, and I was going now to live with simple men, workmen and peasants, far from the race of bookworms!

I prepared excitedly for my departure, as if this journey had a mysterious significance. I had decided to change my mode of life. 'Till now,' I told myself, 'you have only seen the shadow, and been well content with it; now, I am going to lead you to the substance.'

At last I was ready. On the eve of departure, while rummaging in my papers, I came across an unfinished manuscript. I took it and looked at it, hesitating. For two years, in the innermost depths of my being, a great desire, a seed had been quickening. I could feel it all the time in my bowels, feeding on me and ripening. It was growing, moving and beginning to kick against the wall of my body to come forth. I no longer had the courage to destroy it. I could not. It was too late to commit such spiritual abortion.

Suddenly, as I hesitatingly held the manuscript, I became conscious of my friend's smile in the air, a smile composed of irony and tenderness. 'I *shall* take it!' I said, stung to the quick. 'I shall take it. You needn't smile!' I wrapped it up with care, as if swaddling a baby, and took it with me.

Captain Lemoni's deep, raucous voice could be heard. I pricked up my ears. He was talking about the water-spirits who, during the storm, had climbed up the masts of his caique and licked them.

'They are soft and sticky,' he said. 'When you take lots of them, your hands catch fire. I stroked my moustache and so, in the dark, I gleamed like a devil. Well, the seas washed into my caique and soaked my cargo of coal. It was water-logged. The caique began to heel over; but, at that moment, God took a hand in things; he sent a thunderbolt. The hatch covers were burst open and the sea filled with coal. The caique was lightened, righted itself, and we were saved. No more of that!'

Out of my pocket I drew an edition of Dante – my travelling companion. I lit a pipe, leaned against the wall and made myself comfortable. I hesitated for a moment. Into which verses should I dip? Into the burning pitch of the Inferno, or the cleansing flames of Purgatory? Or should I make straight for the most elevated plane of human hope? I had the choice. Holding my pocket Dante in my hand, I rejoiced in my freedom. The verses I was going to choose so early in the morning would impart their rhythm to the whole of the day.

I bowed over this intense vision in order to decide, but I did not have the time. Suddenly, disturbed, I raised my head. Somehow, I felt as if two eyes were boring into the top of my skull; I quickly looked behind me in the direction of the glass door. A mad hope flashed through my brain: 'I'm going to see my friend again.' I was prepared for the miracle, but the miracle did not happen. A stranger of about sixty, very tall and lean, with staring eyes, had pressed his nose against the pane and was looking at me. He was holding a little flattened bundle under his arm.

The thing which impressed me most was his eager gaze, his eyes, ironical and full of fire. At any rate, that is how they appeared to me.

As soon as our eyes had met – he seemed to be making sure I was really the person he was looking for – the stranger opened the door with a determined thrust of his arm. He passed between the tables with a rapid, springy step, and stopped in front of me.

'Travelling?' he asked. 'Where to? Trusting to providence?'

'I'm making for Crete. Why do you ask?'

'Taking me with you?'

I looked at him carefully. He had hollow cheeks, a strong jaw, prominent cheek bones, curly grey hair, bright piercing eyes.

'Why? What could I do with you?'

He shrugged his shoulders.

'Why! Why!' he exclaimed with disdain. 'Can't a man do anything without a why? Just like that, because he wants to? Well, take me, shall we say, as cook. I can make soups you've never heard or thought of . . .'

I started to laugh. His bluff ways and trenchant words pleased me. Soups pleased me, too. It would not be a bad thing, I thought, to take this loose-knit fellow with me to that distant, lonely coast. Soups and stories . . . He looked as if he had knocked about the world quite a lot, a sort of Sinbad the Sailor . . . I liked him.

'What are you thinking about?' he asked me familiarly, shaking his great head. 'You keep a pair of scales, too, do you? You weigh everything to the nearest gram, don't you? Come on, friend, make up your mind. Take the plunge!'

This great lanky lubber was standing over me, and it tired me to have to look up at him. I closed my Dante. 'Sit down,' I said to him. 'Have a glass of sage?'

'Sage?' he exclaimed with contempt. 'Here! waiter! a rum!'

He drank his rum in little sips, keeping it a long time in his mouth to get the taste, then letting it slip slowly down and warm his insides. 'A sensualist,' I thought. 'A connoisseur . . .'

'What kind of work do you do?' I asked.

'All kinds. With feet, hands or head – all of them. It'd be the limit if we chose what we did!'

'Where were you working last?'

'In a mine. I'm a good miner. I know a thing or two about metals, I know how to find the veins and open up galleries. I go down pits; I'm not afraid. I was working well. I was foreman, and had nothing to complain about. But then the devil took a hand in things. Last Saturday night, simply because I felt like it, I went off all of a sudden, got hold of the boss, who had come that day to inspect the place, and just beat him up . . .'

'But what for? What had he done to you?'

'To me? Nothing at all, I tell you! It was the first time I saw him. The poor devil had even handed out cigarettes.'

'Well?'

'Oh, you just sit there and ask questions! It just came over me, that's all. You know the tale of the miller's wife, don't you? Well, you can't expect to learn spelling from her backside, do you? The backside of the miller's wife, that's human reason.'

I had read many definitions of human reason. This one seemed to me the most astounding of all, and I liked it. I looked at my new companion with keen interest. His face was furrowed, weather-beaten, like worm-eaten wood. A few years later another face gave me the same impression of worn and tortured wood: that of Panait Istrati.

'And what have you got in your bundle? Food? Clothes? Or tools?'

My companion shrugged his shoulders and laughed.

'You seem a very sensible sort,' he said, 'begging your pardon.'

He stroked his bundle with his long, hard fingers.

'No,' he added, 'it's a *santuri*.'

'A *santuri*? Do you play the *santuri*?'

'When I'm hard-up, I go round the inns playing the *santuri*. I sing old klephtic tunes from Macedonia. Then I take my hat round – this beret here! – and it fills up with money.'

'What's your name?'

'Alexis Zorba. Sometimes they call me Baker's-Shovel, because I'm so lanky and my head is flattened like a griddle-cake. Or else I'm called Passa Tempo because there was a time when I hawked roast pumpkin seeds. They call me Mildew, too, because wherever I go, they say, I get up to my tricks. Everything goes to the dogs. I have other nicknames as well, but we'll leave them for another time . . .'

'And how did you learn to play the *santuri*?'

'I was twenty. I heard the *santuri* for the first time at one of my village fêtes, over there at the foot of Olympus. It took my breath away. I couldn't eat anything for three days. "What's wrong with you?" my father asked. May his soul rest in peace. "I want to learn the *santuri*!" "Aren't you ashamed of yourself? Are you a gipsy? D'you mean to say you'd turn into a strummer?" "I want to learn the *santuri*!" I had a little money put away for my marriage. It was a kid's idea, but I was still half-baked then, my blood was hot. I wanted to get married, the poor idiot! Anyway, I spent everything I had and more besides, and bought a *santuri*. The one you're looking at. I vanished with it to Salonica and got hold of a Turk, Retsep Effendi, who taught everybody the *santuri*. I threw myself at his feet. "What do you want, little infidel?" he said. "I want to learn the *santuri*." "All right, but why throw yourself at my feet?" "Because I've no money to pay you!" "And you're really crazy about the *santuri*, are you?" "Yes." "Well, you can stay, my boy. I don't need paying!" I stayed a year and studied with him. May God sanctify his remains! He must be dead now. If God lets dogs enter his paradise, let him open his gate to Retsep Effendi. Since I learnt to play the *santuri*, I've been a different man. When I'm feeling down, or when I'm broke, I play the *santuri* and it cheers me up. When I'm playing, you can talk to me, I hear nothing, and even if I hear, I can't speak. It's no good my trying. I can't!'

'But why, Zorba?'

'Oh, don't you see? A passion, that's what it is!'

The door opened. The sound of the sea once more penetrated the café. Our hands and feet were frozen. I snuggled further into my corner and wrapped myself in my overcoat. I savoured the bliss of the moment.

Where shall I go? I thought. I'm all right here. May this minute last for years.

I looked at the strange man in front of me. His eyes were riveted on mine. They were little, round eyes with very dark pupils and red veinlets on the whites. I felt them penetrating, searching me insatiably.

'Well?' I said. 'Go on.'

Zorba shrugged his bony shoulders again.

'Let's drop it,' he said. 'Will you give me a cigarette?'

I gave him one. He took a lighter flint out of his pocket and a wick which he lit. He half closed his eyes with contentment.

'Married?'

'Aren't I a man?' he said angrily. 'Aren't I a man? I mean blind. Like everyone else before me, I fell headlong into the ditch. I married. I took the road downhill. I became head of a family, I built a house, I had children – trouble. But thank God for the *santuri*!'

'You played to forget your cares, did you?'

'Look, I can see you don't play any instruments. Whatever are you talking about? In the house there are all your worries. The wife. The children. What are we going to eat? How shall we manage for clothes? What will become of us? Hell! No, for the *santuri* you must be in good form, you must be pure. If my wife says one word too many, how could I possibly be in the mood to play the *santuri*? If your children are hungry and screaming at you, you just try to play! To play the *santuri* you have to give everything up to it, d'you understand?'

Yes, I understood. Zorba was the man I had sought so long in vain. A living heart, a large voracious mouth, a great brute soul, not yet severed from mother earth.

The meaning of the words, art, love, beauty, purity, passion, all this was made clear to me by the simplest of human words uttered by this workman.

I looked at his hands, which could handle the pick and the *santuri*. They were horny, cracked, deformed and sinewy. With great care and tenderness, as if undressing a woman, they opened the sack and took out an old *santuri*, polished by the years. It had many strings, it was adorned with brass and ivory and a red silk tassel. Those big fingers caressed it, slowly, passionately, all over, as if caressing a woman. Then they wrapped it up again, as if clothing the body of the beloved lest it should catch cold.

'That's my *santuri*!' he murmured, as he laid it carefully on a chair.

The seamen were now clinking their glasses and bursting with laughter. The old salt gave Captain Lemoni some friendly slaps on the back.

'You had a hell of a scare, now didn't you, captain? God knows how many candles you've promised to St Nicholas!'

The captain knit his bushy eyebrows.

'No, I can swear to you, when I saw the archangel of death before me, I didn't think of the Holy Virgin, nor of St Nicholas! I just turned towards Salamis. I thought of my wife, and I cried out: "Ah, Katherina, if only I were in bed with you this minute!"'

Once more the seamen burst out laughing, and Captain Lemoni joined in with them.

'What an animal man is,' he said. 'The Archangel is right over his head with a sword, but his mind is fixed there, just there and nowhere else! The devil take the old goat!'

He clapped his hands.

'A round for the company!' he cried.

Zorba was listening intently with his big ears. He turned round, looked at the seamen, then at me.

'Where's *there*?' he asked. 'What's that fellow talking about?'

But he suddenly understood and started.

'Bravo, my friend!' he cried in admiration. 'Those seamen know the secret. Most likely because day and night they're at grips with death.'

He waved his big fist in the air.

'Right!' he said. 'That's another matter. Let's come back to our business. Do I stay, or do I go? Decide.'

'Zorba,' I said, and I had to restrain myself forcibly from throwing myself into his arms, 'it's agreed! You come with me. I have some lignite in Crete. You can superintend the workmen. In the evening we'll stretch out on the sand – in this world, I have neither wife, nor children nor dogs – we'll eat and drink together. Then you'll play the *santuri*.'

'If I'm in the mood, d'you hear? If I'm in the mood. I'll work for you as much as you like. I'm your man there. But the *santuri,* that's different. It's a wild animal, it needs freedom. If I'm in the mood, I'll play. I'll even sing. And I'll dance the Zeimbekiko, the Hassapiko, the Pentozali – but, I tell you plainly from the start, I must be in the mood. Let's have that quite clear. If you force me to, it'll be finished. As regards those things, you must realize, I'm a man.'

'A man? What d'you mean?'

'Well, free!'

I called for another rum.

'Make it two!' Zorba cried. 'You're going to have one, so that we can drink to it. Sage and rum don't go very well together. You're going to drink a rum, too, so that our agreement holds good.'

We clinked our glasses. Now it was really daylight. The ship was blowing its siren. The lighterman who had taken my cases on board signalled to me.

'May God be with us,' I said as I rose. 'Let's go!'

'God and the devil!' Zorba added calmly.

He leaned over, put the *santuri* under his arm, opened the door, and went out first.

Translated by Carl Wildman

Stratis Myrivilis (1892–1969)

Myrivilis (the pseudonym of Efstratios Stamatopoulos) wrote many novels, but no other has had the impact of *Life in the Tomb* (first version of the book, 1924). Based closely on his experiences in the trenches in the Balkans in 1917–18, which he had initially reported to a newspaper in his native Lesbos, the work is episodic in character and is narrated by a thinly disguised and now dead Sergeant Kostoulas. Although Myrivilis considerably expanded and tinkered with his book over the years, generally not to its advantage, it deserves to be read by any student of the First World War, not least for presenting a Greek perspective on the events in question – as Stratis Tsirkas (q.v.) does for the desert campaign in the Second World War.

Life in the Tomb (*extract*)

ARTILLERY DUEL

One gets used to anything sooner or later. I have noticed that human beings possess an inexhaustible inner reserve of adaptive capability which rescues them from great misfortunes and especially from madness. Here, for example, our way of life has already become a stable condition. Sometimes it occurs to me that if the stories about eternal torments in hell were accurate, each of the damned would have all the time in the world to grow used to his tortures through and through, and consequently could puff his cigarette to his heart's content inside the cauldron of brimstone, lighting it from the very flames that were harrowing him.

We either sleep during the day, lying on our backs in the darkness, or talk and play cards, our candles burning. The latter we do less and less frequently, however, because no one has the slightest appetite for idle prating. When we open our mouths it is only to pronounce the barest minimum of words necessary for our duties, or to indulge in smut, or to hurl curses at each other. Soon enough, in any case, we are overcome by sleep as though by some disease, a sleep full of exhaustion, nightmares and wet dreams. The men awake soaked in sweat and semen.

But as soon as darkness falls, this whole world comes to life and emerges from its caverns in order to fight: to wage war. Under the cover of darkness, hordes of implement-laden soldiers peek over the rim of the trench and leap across the top in successive ranks, then proceed slouchingly, and with sluggish movements, toward no-man's land. Deprived of cigarettes, with an absolute minimum of noise, they advance in this robot-like manner in order to dig, or set up entanglements, or keep their ears cocked at a listening post, or lie in ambush. Sometimes they return depleted, in which case the Order of the Day strikes certain names off the company rolls and Balafaras obtains certain home addresses so that he may dispatch his 'lovely letters', neatly typewritten.

The pyramidal ridge of Peristeri – the 'Dove' – looms blacker and fiercer in the darkness. It is swaddled in mystery, and its tip touches the sky. The oppressive silence which this fortified mountain exudes is more frightening than a thousand-mouthed cannonade.

Suddenly a slender red line burgeons from one of the flanks and ascends. The men fall flat on their faces then, no matter where they happen to be, because the top of this luminous, fading stem will blossom into a brilliant flower of light, a miniature sun. A flare like this ignites high above us in the atmosphere and hovers there, swaying in balance, as it shines down upon us with unbearable brilliance. Then it flounders in mid-air and sails off attentively into the void. It is the Dove's lightly sleeping eye, an eye whose lid lifts suspiciously in the night so that this powerful lantern may search gruffly to see where we are and what we are doing. An area of many square kilometres is illuminated as though in daylight. The lantern advances with such slow-moving deliberation that you would think some invisible giant were holding it in his enormous hand as he strolled from place to place, urgently looking for something on the ground. Eventually it descends ever so slowly and goes out, or else disappears behind some hill. No one budges during this interval; no one breathes. Soon another flare ignites, and then another and another; they follow each other in close succession, coming from both sides now. If a person ignorant of the war observed all this outpouring of light as it bathed the mountains, he would mistake it for a celebration of joy and kindness. The other evening an illuminating rocket like this fell on Magarevo, a deserted hamlet which sits between the Bulgarians and us. It landed on a rooftop and started a conflagration which destroyed three houses, after which the fire subsided of its own accord. (No one went to extinguish it!) The empty village was illuminated funereally all the while, its casements swinging open, the house interiors filled with darkness. Ignited flares have also fallen into patches of dry grass or amidst the wheat which ripened in vain for the absent reapers who will never again come with their scythes and merry songs. The fields burn and burn, until they grow tired of burning. Occasionally an attack, reconnoitring mission, or *coup de main* occurs in a nearby sector. At such times the spectacle is unimaginably grand. Igniting beside the white flares are chromatic ones – green, red, yellow, maroon – which promenade across the sky like multi-coloured caterpillars or drag their bodies laboriously between the stars as though they were fiery but wounded dragons all coiled in upon themselves. A cherry-dark stalk germinates with a whistle and explodes at its tip, whereupon varicoloured stars gush upward in a veritable geyser above our heads, then drip down in clusters, fading as they descend. All this is an agreed-upon signal for artillery barrages and other types of fire.

The cannonade begins close on the rockets' heels. It comes from the Dove, or from us, or sometimes from both at once. The batteries seek mutual annihilation. This is known as an 'artillery duel'. What happens at such times is terrible but also beautiful. Alas, I cannot escape calling it 'beautiful' since it is the most majestic spectacle a man can ever hope to experience. When the action falls outside our sector I creep into the trench, glue my chin to the soil of the parapet and become nothing but two eyes and a pair of ears diffused into this strange universe, a being who throbs with pride as well as wretchedness.

Diamond necklaces string themselves along the base of the mountains; the gems sparkle each in turn in the darkness, then fade. These are the salvos, discharged in regular succession. Next, the valleys start to roar. They weep, reverberate with imploring moans, shriek, howl protractedly and bellow. Absolute silence metamorphoses instantaneously into pandemonium. The atmosphere smacks its lips; it whistles fervidly with its fingers inserted into a thousand mouths. Whole masses of air shift position with violent movements; the sky rips from end to end like muslin. Invisible arrows pass across the void. Angry vipers lunge this way and that. On all sides are lashes incising the air and pitilessly thrashing the weeping hills, which huddle and curl into balls as though wishing to be swallowed into the bowels of the earth, in order to escape. The caves moan and sob in woeful groans. A thousand titans yawp in consternation, chew their fingers with obstinate despair and holler. The atmosphere vibrates then like a bow-string and men's hearts quake like aspen leaves in a storm.

The passing shells cannot be seen; you sense them, however, with your entire body – their location at every instant, how fast they are travelling, where they will land. Some of them remind you of an object breaking the surface of a lake; they make a refreshing noise, a kind of lapping, as though they were speeding along on peaceful waters. Others create a fearful racket. Imagine colossal iron bridges erected in the darkness between the Dove and us, and rickety wagons passing over them with full loads of clattering metal tools. That is how they sound. Still others whistle along gleefully at a standard pitch. These have been christened 'nightingales' by the men, and in truth they actually do resemble birds that have flown the coop and soared unrestrainedly into the empyrean, whistling the song of freedom.

Audible amid all these frenzied night-cries, amid this entire chaos of sound, are the amazing wails of exploding shells. A shell, when it bursts, howls with vengeful wrath. It is a blind monster, all snout and nothing else, which charges the earth and rips it to shreds with its iron fangs. Millions of men have packed their hatreds into the ample belly of this mechanized brute, have stamped their enmity tightly in, and sent the beast out to bite. When a shell explodes, all of

these hatreds lurking there by the thousands, all of these satanic embryos imprisoned in the steel womb, are released like a pack of rabid dogs which then race
to the attack yelping their own disparate cries that are so mournful and strange.

When I find myself near a bursting shell I invariably have this feeling that
human voices are inside it, voices which shriek with unappeasable passion. Inside
a shell, I insist, are howling people foaming at the mouth and grinding their jaws
together. You can hear the hysterical screech of the murderer as he nails his dagger
into warm flesh; you can recognize the victory-cry of the man who drives his
weapon into the breast of a hated foe, then, clutching the hilt in his palm, twists
the knife in the wound, voluptuously bellowing his satiated passion and drinking down in a daze the agony of the other, who writhes beneath his powerful
knee and thrashes about on the ground, spewing his life out through his throat,
along with the blood.

Whenever the shells begin to rake our own trench along with the others, we
worm into our dugouts and await orders. No one remains in the trench itself
except the sentries, and they are relieved more frequently at such times.

A bombardment is the most supremely powerful sensation that a man can
experience. You lie flat on your face at the bottom of the trench or in an underground shelter. Your mouth tastes like plaster of Paris; your soul is held in thrall
by profound grief and pulsating terror, by a preoccupation which shrinks you,
makes you roll up into yourself and take refuge in the kernel of your existence
– a kernel which you desire to be tiny as a cherry-pit and hard and impenetrable
as a diamond. Your soul is on its knees. Filled with wonder and sacred awe, it
prays fervidly of its own accord. You neither understand nor recognize the words
it uses (this is the first time in your life you have heard them), and it directs its
supplications to a God whose existence you had never even suspected. Your soul
is a tiny lamp-flame, a sickly wavering flicker which totters this way and that in
an effort to separate from its wick and be sucked gently upward by the famished
void.

A bombardment is extraordinarily cruel and inhuman. It is horrible, but also
divinely majestic. Man becomes a Titan who makes Earth howl beneath his blows.
He becomes Enceladus and Typhon, raises up mountains, juggles lightning bolts
playfully in his hands and causes indomitable natural forces to mewl like whipped
cats.

Is it not man 'who looketh on the earth, and it trembleth; who toucheth the
mountains, and they smoke'?

Translated by Peter Bien

Stratis Doukas (1895–1983)

Doukas was born in Ayvalik in Turkey. In a long career he never again reached the heights of his slim but weighty first book. Like Myrivilis (q.v.), Doukas testified to the painful historical experience of the Greeks: *A Prisoner of War's Story* (first published in 1929 but considerably revised over the years) represents a reworking of an oral testimony by a Greek refugee from Asia Minor in 1922, who had escaped only by the subterfuge of pretending to be a Turk. With the utmost concision, plainness and restraint, Doukas has pruned and shaped this oral narrative. As the unfinished business of the Ottoman Empire continues even into our own day, a book so nobly and unflinchingly unpartisan – and so short – deserves to be read by everyone. Here we print the first of its four sections.

A Prisoner of War's Story (*extract*)

At the Smyrna disaster I was with my parents on the harbour front at Punta. I was dragged from their arms. And I was left behind in Turkey, a prisoner.

It was midday when I was taken away with the others. Night fell and the patrols were still bringing men to the barracks. Near midnight the guards came in. We were crammed up against one another and they started hitting us right and left with sticks, kicking those of us who were sitting on the ground, our knees drawn up. Then they picked out as many as they wanted and led them away, cursing as they went.

We were scared they'd do away with us all.

One of the clerks, who had his office beside the door, heard our pitiful words and beckoned us to come to him

'The next time they come and start calling out, stay at the back,' he said. 'But not a word to anyone!'

From that night on, they took people from the barrack rooms very night. When we heard gunfire from Kadife Kalesi we said to each other, 'It's firing practice.'

After days spent in fear, an officer came with forty soldiers and took charge of us. They took us out into the yard and separated us from the civilians. That's when I saw my brother. They put us in lines of four and ordered us to kneel so they could count us.

The officer, who was mounted on his horse looked us over and said, 'I'll see to it that your seed is wiped out!'

Then he gave the order to march.

There must have been about two thousand men in our column.

They marched us straight to the marketplace. A Turkish mob was waiting there and, like a horde, fell on us. From all sides they threw tables, chairs, glasses – whatever they could lay their hands on. There were European sailors with them in the coffee houses and they were looking on for a bit of fun.

When we reached Basmahane a *hafiz*, a reciter of the Koran, came out and stood in front of us. He looked at us:

'Allah! Allah! What's going on?' he called out to the *asker aga,* the officer in command. The officer stopped.

'Captain, over here!' he called again.

Clip clop, the captain's horse went over. The captain saluted him.

'Is this what our Book says?' the *hafiz* asked him.

The captain saluted him again.

And we passed before them in lines.

At midday we reached Halkapinar. There they fenced us around with wire. When night fell, an *efe*, a rebel fighter from our village, came. He called to us by name, pretending he was going to save us, but his aim was to do us in. And we fell to the ground so as not to be recognized.

At dawn another officer came from Magnesia and we were ordered to our feet. We walked for hours. We didn't even know where they were taking us. But we could tell from the lie of the land that we were heading for Magnesia.

Instead of taking us along the main road they forced us up through the mountains. And as we weren't on the flat, we began to scatter. We couldn't keep to our lines of four and the soldiers kept shouting orders:

'Lines of four! Lines of four!'

We tried, but they kept on breaking up. Those who were weak and fell behind were dragged into the forest by civilians and done away with.

After a hard slog we met up with the main road. Again here were mobs waiting for us: old men, sixty to eighty years of age, carrying ancient daggers, and as we approached they ran towards us shouting at the captain:

'Let us do what we want with them!'

'No,' the captain told them, laughing.

We cried out to him, 'Captain, our lives are in your hands!'

And we moved on.

The roads all about were strewn with stinking corpses. At the springs there were guards stationed by the fountains where the water ran. At the sight of it we thirsted even more.

Many had died of thirst on the road. I was walking with my brother who was carrying a haversack belonging to one of our guards.

We've got money, I thought. Why not pay for some water?

'I'm thirsty, I'll die,' I said to my brother.

'Don't lose heart,' he said to me. 'If they see we have money they'll do us in.'

'I can't stand it any more. Give them some money for a drink.'

He gave me some money and I ran straight to the Turk.

'Some water, I'm dying,' I said to him.

'What's that, you dog? You won't get a drop out of me!'

'*Asker aga,* it will be an act of charity. Here, take this money, too.'

'Hand it over,' he said to me. 'And don't let anyone see you.'

I drank and gave some to my brother.

This was in the month of August.

Finally, one night, we reached the outskirts of Magnesia. People were waiting for us with clubs in hand.

'The prisoners are coming!' they shouted and ran towards us.

'Keep back!' the captain said to them. 'When we were doing the fighting you were all having a good time.'

They scattered, shouting that one day the *Yunanlilar,* the Greeks, would try to do away with them again.

The captain, annoyed, rounded us up like sheep in a fold and set sentries around us. No water, bread – nothing!

Those who had money gave it to the guards for water. My companions gave money to a darky and he brought us a full bucket.

'Be quick,' he said. 'The captain won't allow it.'

I drank and drank . . . My brother pulled me away so he could drink. Then the others rushed to get at the bucket and the water spilt.

The next morning, it was still dark, when the captain shouted, 'Get ready!'

We got into lines of four and moved off. He marched us into Magnesia. There he put us in some hospital grounds set amongst pine trees, enclosed with railings. He handed us over to a corporal. We were so tired we didn't feel hungry. But we were dying of thirst. We lay like the sick under the trees chewing on the green pine needles. When a few clouds showed in the sky we prayed for rain. The clouds thickened and grew darker. They hung low in the sky, then slowly disappeared again. The sun burned hotter now.

'Water! Water!' we shouted in desperation.

But no-one listened.

Five hours later, a fair-headed, well-dressed *hodja* came and with one voice we begged him:

'*Hodja, Allah askina!* For the love of Allah! We're thirsty! Water!'

He seemed to take pleasure in seeing us in our sorry state:

'That's how I want to see you till the end, creeping and crawling like snakes.'
And off he went.

Then another *hodja* came in a buggy. Once again we called out:

'*Allah askina,* some water! We're thirsty. We can't bear it!'

After having a good look at us, he said, 'I've had my bit of fun.'

And he ordered his driver to drive away.

Seven days went by like this. Those of us who had money drank water. The others drank their own piss.

Many died of hunger and thirst. The guards told us to form a fatigue party to get rid of the bodies. We fought over who would go because the fatigue party would get to drink water. About twenty men took them in carts and threw them away, far from town.

In the hospital grounds there were some prisoners of war from Magnesia who told us that the fountain in the yard held water. We didn't believe them.

That night we were woken by shouting and learnt that the Magnesians had broken the pipe and found water. We got up and scrambled to get to it. The sentries heard the noise and began to fire on us. After quite a few bodies had fallen they encircled us in barbed wire. In there, we took handfuls of mud and sucked on it.

After seven days the *hodja* returned. We cried out, begging him.

'Quiet or I'll leave!' he said. 'I've come to save you.'

As he spoke they brought us rations of dry bread in baskets. They put us in single file and gave half a loaf to every two men. Then they let each of us drink in turn at the fountain.

The soldiers told us that an important man had come that very day from Ahmetli: 'From now on you'll be treated well.'

In the evening they stripped us bare! They took whatever we had: rings, watches. Even our gold teeth.

They roused us in the morning. As we were getting ready, a group of Zeybeks with their reed pipes and drums gathered outside. They set to beating us with their rifles as we left. Another officer came. He took charge of us and we moved off.

About three hours' march from Magnesia there was a large vineyard surrounded by a fence. The officer placed us inside until daybreak, with sentries guarding us.

We scattered amongst the harvested vines and ate the leaves with our bread.

When night fell, two men tried to escape. The sentries caught them and shot them in front of us.

In the morning, the captain said to us, 'Infidel dogs! I try to help you and you run off?'

He ordered his men to get us to our feet.

We marched for hours. At a railway station where we stopped, some Turkish civilians came and asked the officer to let them search amongst us. If they found the man they were looking for they wanted to take him.

'Yes,' he said. 'Look and if you find him, take him.'

'*Aferim! Aferim!* Bravo! Bravo!' they shouted and entered the throng. They did find him. He was an Armenian, the station gardener.

'Hey, you Armenian bastard! You're the one we're looking for.'

'What do you want from me?' he said. 'I only have one life to lose.'

And he passed amongst us, head held high, as though wanting everyone to see him.

'Take him away!' the captain shouted.

When the Armenian heard this he threw himself at the man who had first laid hands on him and in a frenzy bit his throat.

The others did away with the Armenian on the spot; all he had time to say was, 'Do what you want with me, I've taken my blood.'

Leaving behind the warm corpse, which they were still kicking about, we set off for Kasaba. There everything was burnt to the ground. They put us in a stock-yard. From there we could see other prisoners being marched away, and hearing their tormented cries from afar we thanked the Lord.

In the morning they marched us towards Ahmetli. When we arrived, the captain was waiting for us at the railway station and he told us we'd be staying there.

He took us to a bare spot and left us in the sun. We begged him to put us on the other side where there were trees.

'No. In the sun,' he said and left.

In the afternoon it rained; we were glad. We drank water in cupped hands, washed and felt refreshed.

When night fell, the captain came and put us under a shelter. Dawn found us still on our feet. It had rained all night.

The captain came back in the morning. He had a clerk with him. The captain divided us up into companies and picked out the tradesmen: about ten bakers and dough kneaders, about twenty carpenters and blacksmiths and the same number of masons and plasterers. As he sorted them, he said, 'You destroyed everything, now build it again.'

And he handed them over to the soldiers.

The clerk called out, 'Isn't there a miller amongst you? We have grain to grind. Doesn't anyone of you know a miller's work?'

My brother and two others stepped forward.

The kneaders went to the bakery and baked some loaves out of unsifted barley. From that day on we were each issued a quarter of a loaf. One night two kneaders stole some dough. They'd planned to escape. The sentry caught them in the act. In the morning he took them to the captain who was lodged in a hut nearby.

'These men stole dough last night so they could escape,' the sentries told him. The captain took out his pistol.

'Whoever does such things will die like a dog,' he said and shot them in front of us. Then he put us on fatigue to clean up the station. Our eyes stung from the filth.

A sergeant called Turan, who was guarding us, set to shouting and beating us so that the women in the train passing by would admire him. If anyone's eyes were hurting badly he'd say he was taking them to the hospital for treatment but instead he'd drag them into a ditch and do away with them.

One night the captain ordered the guards to tell the neighbouring villages that whoever wanted farmhands could come and get them.

'Tell them we've got everything: shepherds, masons, blacksmiths, whatever they want.'

In the morning the village headmen came and began to choose, first fifty, then eighty, as many as they wanted, as though we were beasts.

We decided – twelve of us from my village – to wait till we heard of a good village, and when they came and asked for more men we'd all go together.

A few days later, a corporal, who liked us because we'd given him a belt he'd taken a fancy to when we were first captured, said to us, 'Be ready to go. There's a good village close by, Pinarbasi near Mount Boz. You'll be treated well.'

We asked him if he'd be coming with us.

'No,' he said. 'The captain won't let me. I'll hand you over to the headman.' He handed us over and we left.

As we walked along the road we saw a wild pear tree and fell upon the unripe pears.

'Hey, come on,' the headman called to us. 'It'll be night soon.'

We walked on again eating as we went.

We reached the village at night. We were separated, four of us in three different places.

We worked twenty days in that place and from the day we got there we set our minds on escaping. We began secretly putting aside bread for the road and whatever else from our food that would keep.

Finally we settled on the day. We'd set off on Friday, at midnight. When the time came I woke my companion and everyone in turn woke each other. But the others had second thoughts.

'We've made our minds up,' we said to them. 'We're leaving.'

And we left.

*

After we'd walked for an hour or so from the village we came to a cliff over-hanging a stream. The stream was so far down we couldn't hear its roar. We came to a stop.

There was a village close by. The dogs scented us and started barking.

'We'll be discovered,' I said to my companion. 'We'll have to cross tonight.'

'Yes,' he said.

Hugging the rocks and crawling along we started down. But we couldn't go on. Halfway down we stopped at a cave. We waited there till dawn.

When day broke we heard voices on the cliff top. The whole village was at our heels, hunting us with their dogs.

Their voices slowly faded into the distance. We stayed for a while, hidden, then began to climb down the cliff again.

It was almost midday by the sun when we reached the bottom of the hollow.

'Lord!' we said when we saw the side we had to climb up. We walked for a while, upright, alongside the seething waters. Then we entered them, treading carefully on the slippery pebbles. The water came up to our knees.

As we waded on we heard a rattling sound close by. We were frightened; we draw close together and looked about. Above us, some ravens were flying low, in circles. We bent down and drank some water, though we weren't thirsty. Then we left the stream, dripping wet and began to climb.

The sun was going down as we scaled the cliff, hanging on to clumps of weeds. With great difficulty we made it to the top. The dark had overtaken us.

When we got to even ground we looked about. In front of us, a little distance away, were some shepherds' huts. They belonged to Yuruks. Their dogs started barking. The shepherds called to each other:

'The dogs are barking. There are people about.' And they fired their rifles into the air.

We turned towards the cliff and walked along the edge, bending low, until we came to an abandoned village. As we walked through the ruins we heard a whimper a few feet ahead of us. We drew nearer.

A dog was lying on a mattress whose straw had spilled out.

When the dog saw us it tried to stand up but couldn't. It wagged its tail on the ground, blinked its eyes which shone in the moonlight and whimpered once again. We sat down next to it, leaning against a low wall in the crumbling yard. Featherless hens, dried up with thirst, roosted on piles of broken things. We thought of making off with one but were afraid to light a fire. We looked at the dog again, then set off. We walked all night in the moonlight, startled by our own shadows.

Towards dawn we reached the Mount Boz pastures where goats were graz-ing. A woman was tending them. We hurried to get past but didn't make it. The herd surrounded us. The woman was stooped over, knitting. She didn't notice us. We passed by.

On the fourth day we reached Odemis. On our way we came upon a mill.

'Hey,' I said to my companion. 'We can't just keep walking on and on.' And I motioned towards the mill.

'What?' he said. 'Break in?'

We both agreed but then changed our minds.

Afterwards we came to a main road and we went into the forest to hide. Around midday we saw a hunter on the opposite ridge. His dog was barking, we were afraid. We crawled along about ten metres and lay low behind a tree trunk waiting for the hunter to go. We got tired from waiting. He stayed till late at night. Then, crossing ourselves, we started out.

Before dawn we reached the outskirts of the town of Banos. Its olive groves stretched almost as far as Bayindir. We were so hungry we set to eating the green olives which left a bitter taste in our mouths.

After we'd allayed our hunger a little, we stood there looking at the town. Opposite us was the railway line. The train came and went two or three times. The people who got off scattered on to the roads; we couldn't get through. It was getting dark and the roads were still full of people. We left late in the night.

We passed Bayindir quickly and reached the Meander river. The water came up to our waists. We crossed over.

As we stepped out, we saw sheep. We couldn't turn back, we stumbled into the flock. The dogs rushed at us and we kept them at bay with our staffs. They kept at us. We calmed them down and, bending low, slowly withdrew.

After we'd left the flock a good way behind, we sat down. We couldn't take another step. Even a small child could have caught us.

Translated by Petro Alexiou

K.G. Karyotakis (1896–1928)

Karyotakis died by his own hand in a small provincial town, Preveza, which has achieved undeserved notoriety as a result: the whole of his last collection, *Elegies and Satires*, is in effect a suicide note; it may be seen as a bitter and ingenious expansion of Nero's last words: 'qualis artifex pereo' ('what an artist dies in me'). Karyotakis has been almost as central as Cavafy in the formation of a modern poetry in Greece (crucially in his influence on Seferis; for contemporary tributes, see Lefteris Poulios' 'To Karyotakis' and Michalis Ganas' 'In Memory of K.G. Karyotakis', q.v.) but is sorely under-represented in English – ironically, given that he was himself a translator of genius. The third of the versions below aims at close fidelity to the original's forms, at the cost of certain evident anachronisms.

I Am the Garden

I am the garden many a fragrant bloom
filled once, and cheerful twitterings of birds,
where strolling friends could whisper secret words
here in the shadows, where love was at home.

I am the garden still in that same spot.
In vain I wait for someone to return.
Instead of roses now I put forth thorns
that stifle nightingales, where vipers knot.

Posthumous Fame

Limitless nature needs for us to die.
Flower mouths open like a purple cry.
Spring may return – to disappear again;
we shall be less than shades of shadows then.

The brilliant sun is waiting for our death.
One more triumphal sunset we shall see,
and after that from April evenings flee
toward the dark domains that lie beneath.

[If in our lives we suffer the same pain,
 or age, frail children in a reverie,
we flee from here without the slightest gain,
not even memories of a wasted day.]

After us nothing but our verse will stay,
a mere ten lines of poetry, the way,
when shipwrecked voyagers fling out doves to fate,
the message they deliver comes too late.

Translated by Rachel Hadas

Marche Funèbre et Perpendiculaire

I gaze at the plaster ceiling.
The meander's dance starts to attract.
Happiness, I reflect,
Must be somehow uplifting.

Artifice of eternity,
Roses without end,
Thorns in a white garland,
A great horn of plenty.

(Art degree zero,
How late I come round to your point!)
Dream relief, I shall make your ascent
Like some alpinist hero.

Horizons of expectations
Would only close in on me later:
Life's stale bread and butter,
The affairs, the frustrations.

Yes, that nice plaster crown –
Time for its unveiling.
Framed by the ceiling,
How well I'll go down!

David Ricks, after K.G. Karyotakis

George Seferis (1900–1971)

Poet and diplomat, essayist and translator, Seferis (the pseudonym of George Seferiadis) was awarded the Nobel Prize for Literature in 1963, the first Greek to be so honoured (Elytis was the second), and no Greek poet other than Cavafy enjoys a higher reputation world-wide. Seferis has been well served by translators in his plain and morally authoritative idiom, which has not been without influence on foreign poets of note (Louis MacNeice and Derek Mahon, for example) – though some of his lighter or more intimate pieces can sound wooden in English. As Seferis' poetry is readily available in the standard translation by Edmund Keeley and Philip Sherrard – and as, indeed, the force of his work is cumulative, growing with the reader's familiarity with the whole – the following brief selection restricts itself to a number of central poems, and it does not set out to annotate their manifold allusions. Some connections are worth pointing out, however. 'Upon a Foreign Verse' alludes to many poems but not least to the Cretan romance *Erotokritos*, the model of Solomos' 'The Cretan' (q.v.). On a quite different note, the closing phrase of the opening poem of *Mythistorema* evidently but enigmatically echoes Karyotakis' 'Marche Funèbre et Perpendiculaire'. 'The King of Asine' ingeniously blends material from Cavafy's 'Caesarion' and Sikelianos' 'Yannis Keats' (qq.v.), while Sikelianos, perhaps Seferis' deepest though only belatedly acknowledged influence, is the subject of two fine posthumous tributes in 'Memory I' and 'Memory II'.

Upon a Foreign Verse

To Elli, Christmas 1931

> Happy is he who has made Odysseus' journey
> Happy if at the setting out he has felt sturdy a love's rigging
>   spread through his body like the veins in which the blood hums.
>
> Of a love with an indissoluble rhythm, unconquerable as music
>   and eternal
> because it was born when we were born, and as for whether it
>   dies when we die, we know not, and nor does anyone else.
>
> I ask God to help me to say, in a moment of great bliss, what
>   that love is;
> I sit sometimes, surrounded by foreign parts, and hear its
>   distant hum like the sound of sea that has mingled with an

inexplicable squall.
And there appears before me time and again the apparition of
    Odysseus, eyes red with the wave's salt
and the maturing desire to see once more the smoke emerging
    from the warmth of his house and his dog that has grown old
    waiting at the door.

He stands tall, whispering through his white beard words of our
    tongue as it was spoken three thousand years ago.
He extends a palm knotted by rope and tiller, with a skin
    worked by a dry north wind, burning heat and snow.

You would say he was wanting to banish from our midst the
    superhuman Cyclops who sees with a single eye, the Sirens
    that you hear and become forgetful, Scylla and Charybdis –
so many complicated monsters that prevent us from reflecting
    that he too was a man who struggled in the world, body and soul.

He is the great Odysseus, he who ordered the Wooden Horse to
    be built, and so the Achaeans won Troy.
I imagine that he is on his way to instruct me how to make a
    Wooden Horse so that I can win my own Troy.

For he speaks with humility and calmly, effortlessly, as if he
    knew me as a father,
or like some old seamen who, leaning on their nets at the time
    of storm and the wind's anger,

would tell me, in my childhood years, the song of Erotókritos,
    with tears in their eyes;
in those days when I used to be scared in my sleep on learning
    of the unjust fate of Areti descending the marble staircase.

He tells me of the difficulty and pain of feeling the sails of your
    ship swollen with memory and your soul's becoming the tiller.
And of your being alone, dark in the night and ungoverned like
    chaff on the threshing-floor.

Of the bitterness of seeing your companions sunk among the
    elements, scattered one by one.
And of how strangely you take courage from speaking with the

dead when the living left to you are no longer enough.
He speaks – I still see his hands, that knew how to test whether
    the mermaid was well fitted to the prow,
granting me the waveless blue sea in the heart of winter.

Translated by David Ricks

from Mythistorema

[1]

The angel –
three years we waited for him, attention riveted,
closely scanning
the pines the shore the stars.
One with the blade of the plough or the ship's keel
we were searching to find once more the first seed
so that the age-old drama could begin again.

We returned to our homes broken,
limbs incapable, mouths cracked
by the taste of rust and brine.
When we woke we travelled towards the north, strangers
plunged into mist by the immaculate wings of swans that wounded us.
On winter nights the strong wind from the east maddened us,
in the summers we were lost in the agony of days that couldn't die.

We brought back
these carved reliefs of a humble art.

[4]
Argonauts

And a soul
if it is to know itself
must look
into its own soul:
the stranger and enemy, we've seen him in the mirror.

They were good, the companions, they didn't complain

about the work or the thirst or the frost,
they had the bearing of trees and waves
that accept the wind and the rain
accept the night and the sun
without changing in the midst of change.
They were fine, whole days
they sweated at the oars with lowered eyes
breathing in rhythm
and their blood reddened a submissive skin.
Sometimes they sang, with lowered eyes
as we were passing the deserted island with the Barbary figs
to the west, beyond the cape of the dogs
that bark.
If it is to know itself, they said
it must look into its own soul, they said
and the oars struck the sea's gold
in the sunset.
We went past many capes many islands the sea
leading to another sea, gulls and seals.
Sometimes disconsolate women wept
lamenting their lost children
and others frantic sought Alexander the Great
and glories buried in the depths of Asia.
We moored on shores full of night-scents,
the birds singing, with waters that left on the hands
the memory of a great happiness.
But the voyages did not end.
Their souls became one with the oars and the oarlocks
with the solemn face of the prow
with the rudder's wake
with the water that shattered their image.
The companions died one by one,
with lowered eyes. Their oars
mark the place where they sleep on the shore.

No one remembers them. Justice.

[7]
South wind

Westward the sea merges with a mountain range.
From our left the south wind blows and drives us mad,
the kind of wind that strips bones of their flesh.
Our house among pines and carobs.
Large windows. Large tables
for writing you the letters we've been writing
so many months now, dropping them
into the space between is in order to fill it up.

Star of dawn, when you lowered your eyes
our hours were sweeter than oil
on a wound, more joyful than cold water
to the palate, more peaceful than a swan's wings.
You held our life in the palm of your hand.
After the bitter bread of exile,
at night if we remain in front of the white wall
your voice approaches us like the hope of fire;
and again this wind hones
a razor against our nerves.

Each of us writes you the same thing
and each falls silent in the other's presence,
watching, each of us, the same world separately
the light and the darkness on the mountain range
and you.
Who will lift this sorrow from our hearts?
Yesterday evening a heavy rain and again today
the covered sky burdens us. Our thoughts –
like the pine needles of yesterday's downpour
bunched up and useless in front of our doorway –
would build a collapsing tower.

Among these decimated villages
on this promontory, open to the south wind
with the mountain range in front of us hiding you,
who will appraise for us the sentence to oblivion?
Who will accept our offering, at this close of autumn?

[16]
The name is Orestes

On the track, once more on the track, on the track,
how many times around, how many blood-stained laps, how many black
rows; the people who watch me,
who watched me when, in the chariot,
I raised my hand glorious, and they roared triumphantly.
The froth of the horses strikes me, when will the horses tire?
The axle creaks, the axle burns, when will the axle burst into flame?
When will the reins break, when will the hooves tread flush on the ground
on the soft grass, among the poppies
where, in the spring, you picked a daisy.
They were lovely, your eyes, but you didn't know where to look
nor did I know where to look, I, without a country,
I who go on struggling here, how many times around?
and I feel my knees give way over the axle
over the wheels, over the wild track
knees buckle easily when the gods so will it,
no one can escape, what use is strength, you can't
escape the sea that cradled you and that you search for
at this time of trial, with the horses panting,
with the reeds that used to sing in autumn to the Lydian mode
the sea you cannot find no matter how you run
no matter how you circle past the black, bored Eumenides,
unforgiven.

[17]
Astyanax

Now that you are leaving, take the boy with you as well,
the boy who saw the light under that plane tree,
one day when trumpets resounded and weapons shone
and the sweating horses
bent to the trough to touch with wet nostrils
the green surface of the water.

The olive trees with the wrinkles of our fathers
the rocks with the wisdom of our fathers
and our brother's blood alive on the earth
were a vital joy, a rich pattern

for the souls who knew their prayer.

Now that you are leaving, now that the day of payment
dawns, now that no one knows
whom he will kill and how he will die,
take with you the boy who saw the light
under the leaves of that plane tree
and teach him to study the trees.

[20]

In my breast the wound opens again
when the stars descend and become kin to my body
when silence falls under the footsteps of men.

These stones sinking into time, how far will they drag me with them?
The sea, the sea, who will be able to drain it dry?
I see the hands beckon each dawn to the vulture and the hawk
bound as I am to the rock that suffering has made mine,
I see the trees breathing the black serenity of the dead
and then the smiles, so static, of the statues.

[21]

We who set out on this pilgrimage
looked at the broken statues
became distracted and said that life is not so easily lost
that death has unexplored paths
and its own particular justice;

that while we, still upright on our feet, are dying,
affiliated in stone
united in hardness and weakness,
the ancient dead have escaped their circle and risen again
and smile in a strange silence.

[24]

Here end the works of the sea, the works of love.
Those who will some day live here where we end –
should the blood happen to darken in their memory and overflow –

let them not forget us, the weak souls among the asphodels,
let them turn the heads of the victims towards Erebus:

We who had nothing will school them in serenity.

December 1933–December 1934

Translated by Edmund Keeley and Philip Sherrard

The King of Asine

and Asine, Iliad

We looked round the fortress all morning,
starting from the shady side, where the sea
green and without reflection, a killed peacock's breast,
received us like time without an interval.
The veins of rock came down from high above,
twisted shoots naked with many tendrils quickening
at the water's touch, as the eye following them
struggled to escape the tiring rocking,
ever losing strength.

On the sunny side a long open shore
and the light boring diamond shapes on the great walls.
Not a living creature, the wild doves fled
and the king of Asine for whom we have been searching two years now
unknown, forgotten by all even by Homer,
only one word in the *Iliad* and that uncertain,
thrown down here like a gold funeral mask.
You touched it, remember its sound? Hollow in the light
like a dry jar in dug earth;
and in the sea the same sound as our oars.
The king of Asine a void beneath the mask,
everywhere with us everywhere with us, beneath a name:
'and Asine . . . and Asine . . .'

                                 and his children statues
and his desires bird's flutterings and the wind
in the interstices of his thoughts and his ships
moored in an invisible harbour;
beneath the mask a void.

Behind the big eyes, the curving lips, the curls,
in relief on the golden cover of our existence,
a dark point seen travelling like a fish
in the dawn calm of the deep sea:
a void everywhere with us.
And the bird that took flight last winter
with broken wing,
life's tabernacle,
and the young woman who went off to play
with the dog's-teeth of summer,
and the soul which twittering sought the underworld,
and the country like the great plane-leaf carried along by the flood of the sun,
with the ancient monuments and the present affliction.
And the poet lingers looking at the rocks and asks himself,
do they exist then,
among these broken lines the points the projections the hollows
and the curves,
do they exist then,
here at the meeting-place of the passing of rain wind and corruption,
do they exist, the movement of the face, the shape of the affection
of those who have so strangely dwindled in our lives,
of those who are left as shadows of waves and thoughts with the
boundlessness of the deep sea,
or perhaps no nothing remains but only the weight,
the nostalgia for the weight of a living existing thing,
there where we now wait insubstantial, swaying
like the boughs of the horrible willow piled in the duration of despair
while the yellow flood slowly brings down reeds uprooted from the mud,
image of a form which has turned to marble at the decision of an
eternal bitterness.
The poet a void.

Shield-bearing the sun continued to rise in battle,
and from the depths of the cave a startled bat
struck the light like an arrow on a shield:
'and Asine and Asine . . .' Perhaps that might have been the king of Asine
for whom we have been searching so carefully on this acropolis,
sometimes feeling with our fingers his touch on the rocks.

Asine, summer '38 – Athens, January '40

Translated by David Ricks

An Old Man on the River Bank

To Nani Panayiotopoulo

And yet we should consider how we go forward.
To feel is not enough, nor to think, nor to move
nor to put your body in danger in front of an old loophole
when scalding oil and molten lead furrow the walls.

And yet we should consider towards what we go forward,
not as our pain would have it, and our hungry children
and the chasm between us and the companions calling from the opposite shore;
nor as the bluish light whispers it in an improvised hospital,
the pharmaceutic glimmer on the pillow of the youth operated on at noon;
but it should be in some other way, I would say like
the long river that emerges from the great lakes enclosed deep in Africa,
that was once a god and then became a road and a benefactor, a judge and a
    delta;
that is never the same, as the ancient wise men taught,
and yet always remains the same body, the same bed, and the same Sign,
the same orientation.

I want nothing more than to speak simply, to be granted that grace.
Because we've loaded even our song with so much music that it's slowly sinking
and we've decorated our art so much that its features have been eaten away by
    gold
and it's time to say our few words because tomorrow our soul sets sail.

If pain is human we are not human beings merely to suffer pain;
that's why I think so much these days about the great river,
this meaning that moves forward among herbs and greenery
and beasts that graze and drink, men who sow and harvest,
great tombs even and small habitations of the dead.
This current that goes its way and that is not so different from the blood of
    men,
from the eyes of men when they look straight ahead without fear in their hearts,
without the daily tremor for trivialities or even for important things;
when they look straight ahead like the traveller who is used to gauging his way
    by the stars,
not like us, the other day, gazing at the enclosed garden of a sleepy Arab house,
behind the lattices the cool garden changing shape, growing larger and smaller,

we too changing, as we gazed, the shape of our desire and our hearts,
at noon's precipitation, we the patient dough of a world that throws us out and
    kneads us,
caught in the embroidered nets of a life that was as it should be and then became
    dust and sank into the sands
leaving behind it only that vague dizzying sway of a tall palm tree.

Cairo, 20 June '42

Last Stop

Few are the moonlit nights that I've cared for.
You can read the abecedary of the stars more clearly,
spelling it out
so far as your fatigue at the day's end allows,
extracting new meanings and new hopes.
Now that I sit here, idle, and think about it,
few are the moons that remain in my memory:
islands, colour of a grieving Virgin, late in the waning
or moonlight in northern cities sometimes casting
over turbulent streets, rivers and limbs of men
a heavy torpor.
Yet here last evening, in this our final port
where we wait for the hour of our return home to dawn
like an old debt, like money lying for years
in a miser's safe, and at last
the time for payment comes
and you hear the coins falling on to the table;
in this Etruscan village, behind the sea of Salerno
behind the harbours of our return, on the edge
of an autumn squall, the moon
outstripped the clouds, and houses
on the slope opposite became enamel.
Friendly silences of the moon.

This is a train of thought, a way
to begin to speak of things you confess
uneasily, at times when you can't hold back, to a friend
who escaped secretly and who brings
word from home and from the companions,

and you hurry to open your heart
before exile forestalls you and alters him.
We come from Arabia, Egypt, Palestine, Syria;
the little state
of Kommagene, which flickered out like a small lamp,
often comes to mind,
and great cities that lived for thousands of years
and then became pastures for cattle,
fields for sugar-cane and corn.
We come from the sands of the desert, from the seas of Proteus,
souls shrivelled by public sins,
each holding office like a bird in its cage.
The rainy autumn in this gorge
festers the wound of each of us
or what you might term otherwise: nemesis, fate,
or, more simply, bad habits, fraud and deceit,
or even the selfish urge to reap reward from the blood of others.
Man frays easily in wars;
man is soft, a sheaf of grass,
lips and fingers that hunger for a white breast
eyes that half-close in the radiance of day
and feet that would run, no matter how tired,
at the slightest call of profit.
Man is soft and thirsty like grass,
insatiable like grass, his nerves roots that spread;
when the harvest comes
he would rather have the scythes whistle in some other field;
when the harvest comes
some call out to exorcize the demon
some become entangled in their riches, others deliver speeches.
But what good are exorcisms, riches, speeches
when the living are not there?
Is not man perhaps something else?
Is he not that which transmits life?
A time to plant, a time to harvest.

'The same thing over and over again,' you'll tell me, friend.
But the thinking of a refugee, the thinking of a prisoner, the thinking
of a person when he too has become a commodity –
try to change it; you can't.
Maybe he would have liked to stay king of the cannibals

wasting strength that nobody buys,
to promenade in fields of agapanthi
to hear the drums with bamboo overhead,
as courtiers dance with prodigious masks.
But the country they're chopping up and burning like a pine tree – you see it
either in the dark train, without water, the windows broken, night after night
or in the burning ship that according to the statistics is bound to sink –
this is rooted in the mind and doesn't change
this has planted images like those trees
that cast their branches in virgin forests
so that they rivet themselves in the earth and sprout again;
they cast their branches that sprout again, striding mile after mile;
our mind's a virgin forest of murdered friends.
And if I talk to you in fables and parables
it's because it's more gentle for you that way; and horror
really can't be talked about because it's alive,
because it's mute and goes on growing:
memory-wounding pain
drips by day drips in sleep.

To speak of heroes to speak of heroes: Michael
who left the hospital with his wounds still open,
perhaps he was speaking of heroes – the night
he dragged his foot through the darkened city –
when he howled, groping over our pain: 'We advance in the dark,
we move forward in the dark . . .'
Heroes move forward in the dark.

Few are the moonlit nights that I care for.

Cava dei Tirreni, 5 October '44

'Thrush' (*extract*)
The Light

>   As the years go by
>   the judges who condemn you grow in number;
>   as the years go by and you converse with fewer voices,
>   you see the sun with different eyes:
>   you know that those who stayed behind were deceiving you

the delirium of flesh, the lovely dance
that ends in nakedness.
It's as though, turning at night into an empty highway,
you suddenly see the eyes of an animal shine,
eyes already gone; so you feel your own eyes:
you gaze at the sun, then you're lost in darkness.
The Doric chiton
that swayed like the mountains when your fingers touched it
is a marble figure in the light, but its head is in darkness.
And those who abandoned the stadium to take up arms
struck the obstinate marathon runner
and he saw the track sail in blood,
the world empty like the moon,
the gardens of victory wither:
you see them in the sun, behind the sun.
And the boys who dived from the bowsprits
go like spindles twisting still,
naked bodies plunging into black light
with a coin between the teeth, swimming still,
while the sun with golden needles sews
sails and wet wood and colours of the sea;
even now they're going down obliquely
toward the pebbles on the sea floor,
white oil-flasks.

Light, angelic and black,
laughter of waves on the sea's highways,
tear-stained laughter,
the old suppliant sees you
as he moves to cross the invisible fields –
light mirrored in his blood,
the blood that gave birth to Eteocles and Polynices.
Day, angelic and black;
the brackish taste of woman that poisons the prisoner
emerges from the wave a cool branch adorned with drops.
Sing little Antigone, sing, O sing . . .
I'm not speaking to you about things past, I'm speaking about love;
adorn your hair with the sun's thorns,
dark girl;
the heart of the Scorpion has set,
the tyrant in man has fled,

and all the daughters of the sea, Nereids, Graeae,
hurry toward the shimmering of the rising goddess:
whoever has never loved will love,
in the light;
          and you find yourself
in a large house with many windows open
running from room to room, not knowing from where to look out first,
because the pine trees will vanish, and the mirrored mountains, and the chirping
    of birds
the sea will empty, shattered glass, from north and south
your eyes will empty of the light of day
the way the cicadas all together suddenly fall silent.

Poros, 'Galini', 31 October 1946

Memory I

And there was no more sea

And I with only a reed in my hands.
The night was deserted, the moon waning,
earth smelled of the last rain.
I whispered: memory hurts whenever you touch it,
there's only a little sky, there's no more sea,
what they kill by day they carry away in carts and dump behind the ridge.

My fingers were running idly over this flute
that an old shepherd have to me because I said good evening to him.
The others have abolished every kind of greeting:
they wake, shave, and start the day's work of slaughter
as one prunes or operates, methodically, without passion;
sorrow's dead like Patroclus, and no one makes a mistake.

I thought of playing a tune and then I felt ashamed in front of the other world
the one that watches me from beyond the night from within my light
woven of living bodies, naked hearts
and love that belongs to the Furies
as it belongs to man and to stone and to water and to grass
and to the animal that looks straight into the eye of its approaching death.

So I continued along the dark path
and turned into my garden and dug and buried the reed
and again I whispered: some morning the resurrection will come,
dawn's light will glow red as trees blossom in spring,
the sea will be born again, and the wave will again fling forth Aphrodite.
We are the seed that dies. And I entered my empty house.

Translated by Edmund Keeley and Philip Sherrard

Memory II

Ephesus

As he spoke he was sitting on a piece of marble
That appeared to be some part of an ancient gateway;
To the right stretched out the endless empty plain,
To the left came down from the mountain the final shadows.
'The poem is everywhere. Your voice sometimes
Rises, emerges at its side, like the dolphin
That for a while accompanies the journey
Of some swift golden schooner in the sun
And then is lost again. The poem is everywhere
Like those wings of the wind within the wind
That touched just for one moment the seagull's wings.
Our life itself, yet different, just as when
Woman's nakedness is revealed and her face changes
And yet is the same face. Those who have loved
Know this. The world, in the light of other people,
Withers away. But this you must remember:
Hades and Dionysus are the same.'
He spoke these words and then he took the highway
That leads to the ancient harbour over there,
All overgrown with rushes. The twilight
Was, you might say, for the death of an animal,
So naked was it.
                        I can still remember;
He was on his way to the Ionian headlands,
To empty shells of theatres where now
Only the lizard crawls on the dry stones,
And I asked him 'Will they ever be full again?'

And he replied 'Perhaps, at the hour of death.'
And he rushed into the orchestra, yelling out,
'O let me listen to my brother's voice!'
And the silence stood around us hard as rock,
Making no trace upon the glass of blue.

Translated by Rex Warner

On Stage IV

The sea; how could the sea turn out like this?
I was detained for long years in the hills;
blinded by glow-worms.
Now on this shore I await
the landfall of a man
a relic, a raft.

But can the sea turn purulent?
Just once, a dolphin tore it
and so, just once,

did the edge of a gull's wing.
And yet it was sweet the wave
into which I would drop as a child and swim
or again when I was a young man
looking for shapes among the pebbles,
in search of rhythms,
and the Old Man of the Sea spoke to me:
'I am your country;
perhaps I am no-one
but I can be just what you want.'

Translated by David Ricks

Pantelis Prevelakis (1909–1986)

Prevelakis had a different experience of the Asia Minor Disaster from Seferis. Though he was in some ways a nationalist, and went on to write several novels and chronicles about the Cretan struggle for union with Greece, he also felt keenly, in the turbulent 1930s, that something had gone for ever when the old multi-cultural Ottoman order of his home town disappeared in 1923, and with it the Greek-speaking Muslims, and he set down his recollections of old Rethymno (Rethemnos) as an act of remembrance. *The Tale of a Town* (1938) is a deceptively modest book, not without affinities to Stratis Doukas' presentation of the equally multi-cultural world of Asia Minor from which the Greeks were driven out – in strong contrast to his friend Kazantzakis' *Freedom or Death*. The book paved the way for similar explorations by Dimitris Hatzis (q.v.) and others of the pre-modern world they had known and lost.

The Tale of a Town (*extract*)

As I write all this, I feel inside me the fear lest the man of today may not know about such things, that he will look down on them and find it a waste of his trouble to read about them. But the man who forgets the arts and customs of the life of the past forgets life itself, which is made up of the struggles and passions of men. The history written in books to be read in schools is a nothing compared to the daily sweat which men shed over the tools and materials of their work, to fill the world with richness and beauty. Within the limits of his power each man – this one at the carpenter's bench, that one at his anvil or his wheel, that other with his hammer, his shuttle or his needle – has increased the heritage of man and has done more good to himself and other men than any champion swordsman who destroys rather than creates and devours the labour of others. And so, when I speak only of the arts and the tools of the men of other days, I seem to myself to be turning back in time, penetrating into their lives and entering into their souls by a way no warlike history could lead me. That is why I should like to draw my reader along with me and let him not resist me, because my purpose is a good one.

Of the guilds which flourished at Rethemnos, I should mention the metal-workers, the carpenters, the tailors, the shoemakers and the printers. The most important of the metal-workers was the bell-founder, Stergios, who made the chandelier in the Church of the Presentation and worked at it for three years. The most famous of the workers in wood was the sculptor Portalis, who carved the screen in the same church and the story of the Annunciation on its mahogany doors. Among the printers the name of Yannakos Vlastos, nicknamed Gutenberg, was renowned as far as Venice. Vlastos had the oldest printing-press I have ever encountered, dating as far back as 1550 and cast in Paris, as an inscription on the machine records. It was on this press that I myself printed my first poems and shed the first drops of sweat I was destined to spill over the machines and ink of the printing-house.

The odd thing was that, in spite of all the skill which the guildsmen of Rethemnos had shown in the work of their hands, in my time each of them regarded his trade a trifle impatiently. You had the impression that all each of them required of his particular profession was that it should afford him imme-diate security from poverty by some miracle. Let me help you to understand more clearly what I am saying by referring by name to Moundrinos, who from being a carpenter longed to become the captain of a ship which would be unsink-able in any weather; or again Kosti Kavros who launched from the beach a sort of raft furnished with pulleys which he claimed would outride all the motions of the sea and would work twenty-four hours a day for his satisfaction. Or there was Pikromanolis who flew like a bird from the roof of his house long before the West invented aeroplanes. Besides these men a whole crowd of others thought up their own inventions and wanted to catch birds in the sea and fish on dry land. I nearly forgot my own uncle, Ioannis Voulgaris, who from being a public pros-ecutor dropped his work and went to dig with a team of thirty navvies to find the treasure which a Turkish soldier had told him of. This treasure, he said, consisted of a gallery built deep down in the earth, full of marble statues of princes, shrines and columns – a complete town of them which the soldier had come upon by chance when climbing down a well. Later they were unable to find the mouth of the well; they moved a whole mountain of earth and the whole enterprise went with the wind. Poverty is a wretched thing; it soaks whatever it touches. You may have enough to live on, you may be making your way in life, but poverty will wrap itself round you from all sides and bring you as low as it does anyone who is naturally poor. Well, look at Ioannis Voulgaris. What need had he to go fortune-hunting? The end of the month came: he drew his pay. But there was so much poverty around him, such a general desire to be free of it once and for all that he left the public prosecutor's office and set about digging the earth with a spade till he found the bottom of it.

All these guilds, some of which on the one hand adorned and supplied the town with their work and on the other produced feather-brained fellows who would have sifted the sea through a sieve, were to be seen ranked behind their banners at every parade and procession. Those were the times to ponder who it was that by their blood and sweat make history and how much injustice they receive from the historians and literary gents who do not deign to write about them. First of all you saw the boatmen and sailors with their oars over their shoul-ders and St Nicholas painted on their gold-embroidered banner, then the bakers with the Lord Christ breaking the bread with His hands, the gunsmiths with an armed St Barbara, the blacksmiths and metalworkers with St George in his coat of mail. All these portraits of the saints had been painted on velvet with wax and they hung in one piece stretched along the crosspieces of the banner-pole. Wind or no wind, they stayed outspread in their full width and caught the sun on their gold. All around them fluttered silk tassels tangled with pearls, silken fringes sparkled and silver threads, spangles and embroidered ribbons darted points of light. All this made a glory which was fully deserved by the working-folk who had honoured their guild with such a superb ensign.

I don't ask you to admire anything else about the Rethemnos procession, but do just turn around and take a look at the way the men march. Have you ever seen the like? These men have not come out to the square to show off nor have they prepared such a noble spectacle out of vanity. Time has worked for them, an aristocratic tradition has refined them, thousands of years of humane civilization have given them that suppleness and that bearing. What royal prince, bred in a palace, holds up his head with such dignity? What choreographer could have taught them a lightness of step which the ballet might envy? Turn again and look at that banner-bearer, tough and resilient as the bough of a tree, and tell me what you think. He darts forward, his body cuts through the air, a bend of the knee and his other foot shoots forward. A simple matter, you say, but he walks as if he were dancing and the ground seems to send him bounding upward as if he were a rubber ball. He marches, not to cover the ground but as a sort of sport. The shadows which the clouds cast over him between one step and another and the sunlight sifted down upon him by the leaves above, all seem to be playing this same game with him. His marching strikes you at once as something with no set purpose, having no other satisfaction in view but its own beauty. He draws everyone else after him; he is like the dancer who takes the lead in a chain-dance. They all follow his step and hold their heads up as if someone were calling out to them from somewhere above them. And the sun smiles on them from above and gilds the dust and surrounds those lordly figures with a haze of gold. Just turn your eyes and admire Rethemnos going by!

You will see it do so when it accompanies on his way one of its own folk who has paid the common debt to Nature and has gone to his rest absolved from all his sins. The funeral takes the road out of town, bordered with poplars and mulberries. Perfuming the air with incense, it arrives at the cemetery by the sea. Here again one finds in all the grace and dignity of the town something to be proud of and in the subdued and sorrowful townsfolk in this long cortège who know each other like brothers and mourn for the one who is gone and part from him at this inevitable moment with stricken hearts. No one is missing from the procession even if the one who is being buried is the humblest in the place: toil and business have not hardened any man's heart and there is no greater or more insistent duty than to bid farewell to some offshoot of the town who has withered before their eyes. You could say, perhaps, that this seemly procession of citizens, walking in silence behind the standards topped with the figures of the Seraphim, took on, as the years went by, a hidden significance for the Rethemniots which said much in brief, and that everyone secretly thought of it as a common ritual, the only one which really fitted the town. As in other places they greet the sunrise or celebrate the return of spring, here this procession of mourning was acknowledged by all as a communal celebration without anybody's explicitly saying so.

Rethemnos became used to regarding its fate with patient stoicism. That difficult achievement which wise men attain at the end of their lives, the ability to look death in the eyes and smile at it, this declining town could also achieve. Its knees never gave before the terror of death but its lips took on a smile at its irreversible fate. Within itself it mourned daily, as one by one it took its children and committed them to the earth, in the hope, you feel, of meeting them again in a place of light and in the fullness of joy. There was no complaint on its lips, it allowed no useless lamentation. It only smiled wryly at times, behaved itself with dignity even in its dreams and had its hand always ready to wave its own farewell to the world.

This bitter, voiceless sorrow has gently opened up in people's hearts a love for everything that is beautiful, simple, humble and transitory in the world. The townsman of Rethemnos has learnt to recognize and appraise such things since he will have to say goodbye to all of them one by one, each by its own name, when the remorseless moment comes. He has deeply loved his own folk, the animals around his home, the trees and the flowers. All that he has raised and given life to with love he finds near him at the last, at the moment of parting. He has wanted to see even the gate to the World Below set about with flowers and he has wreathed it in flowers with patience and affection. The cemetery at Rethemnos in spring is the most delightful garden your eyes could see. You could see marguerites in great clusters, vines intertwined with honeysuckle, camomile and mallow spread low along the paths of grass and gravel. And near all these, roses which have flourished above the breasts of the dead, pinks and carnations that are redder than blood, begonias, rosemary. And round about, from the open fields which spread right up to the gravestones, come the yellow flowers of the broom, the blue amaranths, a thousand kinds of anemone. Behind the graves is the shimmering light of the calm sea and the white crosses stand up against a pure, silky background as the heads of saints do against their golden haloes. All this you must imagine in a yet deeper silence, with only buzzing of the bees, those bust harvesters of the dead who themselves bud and bloom like all things sown.

This pleasant transformation which turns the cadaver into honey inside the furry belly of the bee moved the enterprising mayor of the town to have a public garden made out of the Turkish cemeteries when the Turks left Rethemnos. He overturned the Turkish tombstones, took their marble for building material and ploughed up the ground with its dead. The bones came to the surface and whitened under the rains, and the gardener came every so often to dig over the soil. They sowed it with seed, planted shrubs, laid out flower beds and trenched about the pines and pine-shoots which were there from the Turkish time. In short, within two or three years the cemetery had turned into a garden, every root of which had heartlessly found a skull to nourish it. The trees grew up and put forth buds and flowers; their leaves rustled in the wind. The birds heard that and hurried to take possession, they nested and burst into song. There were here clematis and all kinds of climbing plants, oleanders, cedars, cypresses, lemon-trees, almond-trees and anything else you can think of. There was absolutely no special selection of trees or flowers. On the contrary, the planting was entirely haphazard and you might see lilacs growing side by side with olives and poplars; everything simply grew where it grew and that was that. This was what encouraged the birds, who believed that the garden had been planted for their enjoyment and came there quite casually to sing themselves hoarse. And which of them failed to come? You heard finches warbling, orioles trilling, the goldfinches twittering, and then, the nightingales in those spring nights! They hid in the creepers, tangled in the bushes, and there set about weaving their patterns of sound. In their song you heard what you chose to hear, your longings, your joys, your griefs, all turned to song. Whatever you yourself wove into the song, the song carried it. The music soothed every passion of the soul: it was enough for you to possess the soul to hear it. The barriers of Paradise were suddenly thrown down and all its scent and its music were spilt abroad. The dead were forgotten and the years passed and their bones turned into leaves, flowers and branches, where the birds were hiding, and it seemed as though the trees were singing. Life had overcome death, the moon silvered the blackness of the night, the highways of the sky were filled with song.

On a spring night like this, scented with fruitful growth, Rethemnos comes to my mind and I feel myself near it. I have taken this chronicle from its sufferings. It may be sad but it has comforted my heart in exile, and to Rethemnos I offer it. I hold it like a thank-offering over my heart and I do not know how I can ever part from it or offer it. I would like it, too, to be wreathed in flowers and perfumed with the best I have in me, I would like it to triumph over time. I would like it to live today and tomorrow and for ever and never to lose its freshness. I would like it to be indestructible and imperishable, so that its destiny should be the opposite of my town's or that of any town built of wood and stone. I would like Rethemnos to live on here, to live on through this part of me, who am a shoot of its stock. And may this work of mine, well compacted and sturdily built like a living body, bear the memory of Rethemnos through the seas of time as St Christopher bore the Holy Babe through the swirling waters.

Translated by Kenneth Johnstone

Kosmas Politis (1888–1975)

Born Paris Tavoularis, Kosmas Politis, as his pseudonym punning on 'cosmopolitan' suggests, took a quite different approach to the lost world of the years before 1922 than that of Prevelakis or indeed of Stratis Doukas (qq.v.). In what remains his most beguiling, and perhaps most difficult, novel, *Eroica* (1938), Politis sets the action in a never-named town which seems much like his native Smyrna, probably just before the Great War; but the dreamy and unreliable narrator is separated from the events not just by the lapse of time that has brought him to a regretful middle age, but also by a filter of literary and other culture that occludes as much as it illuminates the vanished world of Smyrna. The cosmopolitan bourgeois teenagers whose doings make up the book's plot are veiled in a dense web of allusions, not least to music, with the shades of Symbolism stalking the scene – Politis self-consciously but unslavishly follows the path of the early Joyce. The scene extracted here subtly draws both on the *Iliad* (with its associations for the irredentist Great Idea) and on Chapter 5 of Jens Peter Jacobsen's *Niels Lyhne* (1880).

Eroica (*extract*)

That afternoon, soon after lunch – about two o'clock – we started for Psomalonos. Apart from Stavro, the rest of us were meeting Louis for the first time after . . . after all those days. As the two of us arrived with Laios we found Louis among the others, talking in his usual way. Only Louis was more sunburned, and there was a serious smile at the corner of his lips.

'Who's the one walking with him?'

'Who?' said Laios with a start. 'Oh, what am I thinking of . . . it's Petrovik. Wasn't there someone else?'

'Oh, for God's sake! Don't drive me mad!'

Behind the station some gypsies had pitched their camp. We went further away, towards the sea. It seems that Louis and Stavro had come beforehand and arranged everything. We found the course already marked out and the posts set.

'That pile of wood will be in our way,' said someone.

'No,' said Stavro. 'The course goes the other way. There's the starting point.'

It was a pile of thick timbers coated with tar – ties for the railroad – stacked loosely crosswise. The pile went higher than our heads, far higher.

The boys got ready. Under their clothes they already had on their sports things – shorts, thin shirts – and then they took off their boots to put on the proper shoes. No one asked why the sports were taking place today, or what was the meaning of the sudden summons. We all felt a bodily desire for immortality, a desire to show our strength as a challenge, as a revenge for what happened.

Waiting for the sports to begin, one boy practised throwing and another did trial exercises for running or jumping. The elastic bodies were stretched and muscles played. It was a liberation, under the steady sunlight. At that minute everything changeable, ideas and such shifting phenomena, were of no account. The lines, the tension of the bodies, signified something static and eternal: the statuesque harmony of the gods who triumphed untroubled above human misfortunes.

'You, what do you want here?' called Cleobulos to two barefooted young gypsies.

'I told them to come,' said Louis.

The other gypsies and the small fry remained apart, round the tents, sitting cross-legged on the ground. They smiled a bitter, somewhat ironical smile at all that they did not understand. In their dark faces, their white teeth shone out. The women in holiday dress blossomed in the sunlight like many-coloured flowers, startling by their absence of green leaves.

You would have said the sea and land were first divided on that day. The summer was sending messages of its coming. On the ridge of Akorphos, towards the north, the snow was cut askew where the sun struck the mountain, and was almost transparent on the rock. Further down the flanks were green, and as they went lower they were soft as the soil on the low foothills. And the foliage grew thickly – silk, velvet, cotton, silver . . . in some places darker, in others as light as a first coat of paint. Behind the railroad some trees with white blossoms were precociously in flower. And there beside us in the broad ditch under the embankment arum lilies dominated the thistles and nettles. They had freshly unfolded all their new green leaves. They crowded and intermingled; they were jostling one another, and the place seemed too small for the great spring that was coming. The thistles were still in bud. One or two little flowers, ever so small, stood in surprise on their stems in front of the sage bushes.

Louis was looking quietly at a stately ship that was sailing out to sea. Then he went slowly to the shore where the waves spread out against it, and dipped his hands in the water. The winter greenness of the sea had now turned to blue. The water retreated with the coquetry of springtime, and left millions of drops behind, on shells and pebbles. The foam smelled of oranges and rosemary. Who knows how long Louis would have gone on standing there. But Stavro put an arm round his waist and brought him back to us.

*

Standing by the pile of timbers, the two gypsy children began a tune, the boy with a pipe, the girl with a drum. The games started.

They lasted till the evening, till the hour when the wind fell – and the day, hiding behind the mountains on the other side of the gulf, turned, reddening, to look at us for the last time. Then a thick band of mist spread over the foot of the mountains and only their summits showed, reflected vaguely in the quiet waters of an inland sea or a shoreless lake.

Louis took no part in the games. So two first places were won by visitors – Laios and Petrovik – and there were two others that Louis would certainly have won. But now everything was over. Only nothing and emptiness were left here below.

'Bravo!' said Stavro to Aleko. 'If you paid more attention to the position of your left foot . . .' and he began giving him technical explanations.

Louis sat on a stone and looked on. At the half-mile – someone ought to have been there – he stood up to follow the course better. He always kept the same calm. Only he could not contain himself when Michael burst into tears over nothing. The discus had hit him lightly on the wrist on a throw of Antony's.

'Fool!' he said. 'What are you crying for? People far better than you are dead!' And if Cleobulos hadn't stopped him in time he'd have twisted Michael's hand so that he would have been maimed for the rest of his life.

It was getting dark when a train whistled as it went by. It didn't stop at the freight station, but went straight on into town. The last daylight shone on the roads and the low foreshore.

First of all the stars, Venus shone out from behind a dark cloud. In the green twilight horsemen were galloping after some mythical beast with twisted tail and spread wings engraved in crimson. The trees, which all day long tell the pure and simple truth, at this hour were mocking, as if playing some fantastic role.

Louis sat on his stone, apart, silent, looking at the shadow which lengthened on the ground. He would not raise his eyes off the earth – nor his mind.

It was already nightfall. It was just as well that the gypsies had lit fires and we could see something. As we passed in front of the tents we saw them sitting in the same position, gazing somewhere into the void with the flame of the fire on their faces. They seemed to be looking far away, into the future – a long journey without an end. That's how Laios explained it. And then he said: 'Let's go near them again.'

We went by them once again, right beside them. We looked down from above. But this evening the gypsy women had their necks weighted with chains of coins, and we could not make out their breasts.

Aleko walked silently.

'How is it they didn't go into the town today as it's Carnival Thursday?' Laios wondered. Then he added: 'I dare say Louis paid them to stay.'

The outskirts round the station were quiet and empty, as always in the evening. The madness of the Carnival would begin by the fish market. The first sign of it was a dirty clown at the corner holding a hard balloon made out of a cow's bladder, with which he hit the street boys on the head.

'Lights, lights!' The street sellers were crying their wares, and from time to time they lit a flare and hurled it up into the air – either those red ones or the kind that break into stars and smell of sulphur. And when one of them fell on the paper festoons that decorated the butcher's there was an uproar; everyone ran up and it all ended in a row.

Aloe Street with the cafés – to the right of the shopping street – was quieter. It was rather chilly, in spite of the lovely evening, and the clients preferred to stay inside. Some families had brought even their small children with them, most of them in fancy dress as *Evzones* or country girls. The little things sat quietly, holding small muslin bags of confetti. They amused themselves by watching their elders eating various sweet things, and commenting on the company near them. All this could be seen from the street, amid the cloud of smoke behind the heavy glass doors.

At one moment there was an uproar in the street. Some tattered ragamuffins with blackened faces stood in front of the Grand Café, playing drums and moving their bodies like bears. Behind them shouted the street urchins. Everyone left the tables to watch. Mothers picked up their babies, and they flattened their noses against the windows. One of the ragamuffins passed round the plate for five- or ten-lepton pieces. Then the crowd round them became sparser. Someone called: 'Here come the police!' . . . and the street boys took to their heels, pulling up their skirts to run better.

Three urchins went up to a bigger one and said, pointing to a brightness shining above the houses: 'What's that over there? Fireworks? Let's go see.'

Fireworks? Why should there be fireworks at this carnival? It's only on Good Friday evening that people amuse themselves by lighting squibs and throwing rockets. The fact is that the sky was red down towards the station. It couldn't be the gypsies' fires, just a few sticks!

On the following days there were a lot of rumours about that evening. Some people said the gypsies wanted to set fire to the station and had set a light to the tarred railroad ties; others said some boys were to blame – it appeared some rich young man had followed a whim and had been drinking till dawn with the gypsies – and that sort of thing. It was further said that they had stolen a cow and roasted it alive.

But the few who were present, either at the end or from the beginning – none of them confessed to it – witnessed a most solemn ceremony.

*

It is true that something living escaped half roasted from the pyre. It wasn't a cow nor a donkey, nor a dog. It rolled on the ground and then took to its heels, mewing like a cat. And there were picked up among the ashes a tin helmet half melted by the fire and other iron objects – hooks and the blade of an axe.

The fire only burned the ties and went no further – and indeed it could not have happened otherwise, as they stood apart in the middle of the field. They caught like a torch, and the fire soared straight up in the still air. The crackle of the flames made the gypsies' horses neigh. As for the gypsy women, they collected together and started a lament, tearing their hair and weeping, each of them, with some sorrow of her own, calling to mind secret and forbidden memories. They beat their breasts and sang words that shook the heart – even though no one understood their language – and their storm-tossed bodies rocked backwards and forwards with the tune of the song as they swayed from the waist.

The two gypsy children were wearing out the pipe and drum. And their elder sister, the gypsy madonna, began a slow dance of half movements – and so the sorrow was held in control – and coin clinked faintly against coin, and bracelet against bracelet. Bare-breasted, burned golden by the fire, as sure of herself as pleasure, she danced – and beyond this loveliness reigned the obscurity of the night.

And from the bare stone walls the lizards poked out their heads, deceived by the fire, and stood watching on the rocks.

All who saw with their eyes can bear witness that this and nothing else is what really happened.

Translated by Robert Liddell and Andreas Cambas

Nikos Gabriel Pentzikis (1908–1993)

We have seen Kosmas Politis building on the techniques of early Joyce (unaware how many snatches of – often obscene – modern Greek were shortly to find their way into *Finnegans Wake*, 1939). Pentzikis, who translated part of *Ulysses*, is, like Joyce, indelibly associated with a particular city – in his case, Thessaloniki – which he mapped out on his work, artistic and literary. Taking the Byzantinizing mysticism of Papadiamantis a step further, with recourse especially to the Hesychast spirit that had flooded his native Thessaloniki in the fourteenth century, Pentzikis wrote many baffling yet often deliciously comic texts. The following is an extract from *Mother Thessaloniki* (1970), a relatively late and – despite its unruly flood of allusions – lucid work. It opens up for the reader a whole world of consciously and ripely Orthodox writing which can find itself as much at home in the second city of the Byzantine empire and of the modern Greek state as in Papadiamantis' Skiathos (q.v.).

Mother Thessaloniki (*extract*)

Where Thessaloniki is concerned, people should make their entry to it from the sea. The sea forms the subject matter of the paintings by Chadzis, of *The Thermaic Gulf and Olympus* by the painter Maleas, of the tales of the sea by Karkavitsas.

Sailing on a caique to Thessaloniki is described by Papadiamantis in 'The Poor Saint', by Moraïtidis in 'On the North Wind's Waves'.

The voyage to the city should have a religious character. As an image let it recall the 'Voyage of Dionysus' by Rangavis. Thus, in its description, nature, the sea and the sky, everything, should be filled with the memory of the handsome ancient gods. As on Hiero's vase, Amphitrite should be shown gazing at Poseidon. In their hands both of them should be holding a dolphin. The innocent creature of the deep that saved the poet and the Saint. Escorts or advance guards to ships sailing over the ocean, their tails break the surface at times, when, changing places as they swim, they pass one over another like acrobats; their breath, when they rise from the sea floor's depths, shoots high into the sky in a stupendous spout. The traditions of our people reveal an extraordinarily intimate relationship between animals that swim and man. They always appear to be innocent, man is often shown behaving towards them badly. Only the other day, when the fishermen caught one on our beach, they slit its gut open with a knife. The waves turned red with the blood. Did the shore, perhaps, do the same with the kiss, at the mouth of the river where the kerchief was washed? In any case, the sea never loses its colour. If you imagine it a young maiden, fair as can be, then after all its unions it remains a virgin. A mystery that the Christian so marvellously cele-brates, making of it the simple daughter of the soil, Mother of God, seat of the one king who rules over all.

And of the bleeding corpuscles in the sky, which from their Purple gave birth to beautiful Aphrodite, who rises inflamed by desire, no trace is preserved in the foam, which, like a white-fleeced flock of sheep, grazes its carefree laughter on the surface of the sea.

Eternal aspect, full of consolation, saintly countenance, virgin, the sea has something in common with Artemis who, as mistress of the beasts, is shown with a salt-water fish seated on her stomach.

If this unsophisticated representation dates from before Christ, it should inspire in us no less reverence on that account, like the marks scored on prehis-toric pots in the hallowed shape of the Cross. Man has always in his dreams divined something of the world's sense, the Mother Sea, Virgin, with the Sacred Fish in the immaculate womb, Jesus Christ Son of God Saviour.

Before Thessaloniki was built in honour of Alexander's sister by Cassander, with the name of the girl whose noble mother died giving birth to her, when, at the back of the gulf, which had a different shape, there were twenty six settle-ments, sited where, near water, on ancient river beds, the tumuli have preserved their traces, from the south, where the way of the Gods is, ships brought deco-rated pots, which the local workshops gladly copied, reproducing the geometric designs, or the manifold soft undulations of the sea bed, from which they haul up alive, and smash, as many as the days of fasting, forty times on the ground, before by man it is eaten, the dangerous creature of the sea, the octopus with its terrible tentacles.

Indicative of man's struggle with this creature, the statue by Zigias, the whole of Hugo's romantic text in *Workers of the Sea*.

When we live its substance, outside theory, the bitter-billowing sea is a painful element, as well as all the rivers it drinks up all the tears. It is kept sated by history with shipwrecks.

Historical fact Kameniatis' narrative, in which, in the apostate pirates' holds, sailing in the direction of Crete, the one-time Minoa, in the opposite direction to the Gods, coming down to die from the north or to be sold as slaves, the captive populace arrives at one point in the Northern Sporades.

The islands on which Mount Athos had estates. The Skiathos of naturalism; Piperi, where the publisher of St Simeon the New Theologian, of the poet of 'Divine Loves', wrote; Skyros with the poetic modern ephebic statue; antique Alonnisos with the Chamois: the picturesque Christian islands, a point on our road at which terrestrial sufferings seem to coincide with theory, stand as our starting point, as we head out towards the mother city. Before, however, we trace on the map our course from the point above, and without being afraid of geography, in the belief it may kill poetry, we must imagine the voyages, on the sea into which Aegeus fell, of all who head up towards the Mother. The route known, of course, right from the outset, of the journey of the victorious lover of the labyrinth, who sails away from Crete, unlike Kouvouklesios' fellow-citizens, who meet their end there. Points of contact exist between the former route and that from Egypt, along which, as we know, the King and God, Dectenavos, followed Alexander to spawn like a snake.

The songs of today, though, are different. They bring Rhodes to people's lips, where a hag forces her daughter into a mixed marriage. There, where the fruit of the bride-like lemon tree comes from, it is usual for those who marry to go somewhere pleasant. Left halfway, frozen in romantic balladry, that is usually how people see the free Southern Sporades. But this sea route extends, in reality, all the way to the Holy Land, a pilgrimage to the Holy Sepulchre. The devout who go on till the end meet a prophet in Rhodes, a hermit who, high on the mountain, precisely predicts what will happen in the Imperial Capital. He and St Porphyrios, the Thessalonian bishop of Gaza, converse together. And his acolyte Markos, while he is returning to the Mother city, to assist the old man's release from the things of this world – an act which will wonderfully restore Porphyrios' ailing body – stops on his way at the island of Rhodes, and the route thus is made glorious.

The other routes that come from the east, from the Imperial Capital to the present, lead the exiled footsteps of truth to the second city. Kept there in exile by his father, until, by a mimetic bird, the dark suspicions are dispelled, Leo composes the marvellous 'Matins', far away from the Court. Expelled from his monastery in Constantinople, St Theodore the Studite, defender of the icons, arrives by ship. Some of those who flee the persecution settle, before they even reach the Mother of the Poor, as monks on Athos. Others, captivated by Pindar, who speaks of the pious, untroubled happiness of the Hyperboreans, proceed deeper into the interior.

In the maternal gulf, whatever the circumstances, everyone finds welcome. Full ships from Smyrna. The fugitives of the catastrophe cast anchor for a new life.

We have reached the open sea, we have passed through the channel. We are leaving behind us the reef whose existence has been known since antiquity. Of the shipwrecked, all those who stayed on the surface were saved by an opulent liner with every comfort and luxury. The survivors, unlike the writer of short stories, think that in this case they were the ones delivered. He, though, by the intervention of the Reef, by which they were delivered, refers to those who sank on the 'Deliverance'. We had better not, for the moment, venture a judgement, optimistic or pessimistic, on what will assuredly continue and will under no circumstances change.

For the shape of the ship on which we are sailing: the plans of ships in Vasileiou; the historical exhibits relating to the navy in 1821 in the Benaki Museum, the Ethnological Museum, the Louvre; the stamps with the *Averoff* on them; the old lottery tickets showing the fleet; the popular panoramic scenes with our own large ships or foreign ones, ocean-going liners and battleships; images in sentimental films or the news at cinemas; pictures in history textbooks at secondary school; small sailing ships; triremes in the Encyclopaedia; postcards in boys' albums, so unlike those of their sisters; the scale models of ships, in bottles or mounted in public rooms – sources for the definition of our own, which is all the ships of all the ages, friend or stranger, which have entered the bay inside the gulf of the living Mother, the bride of Christ's representative, blissful, graced in every way, beautified by all things, land of the Blessed, New Helicon, as it has been proudly adjudged, in contrast to the ordinary everyday mud, which prevents all who cast a material eye on her seeing her as she is in the sight of God, securely built, all-surpassing, resplendent.

As the wind carries us there, our ship becomes more like a toy. A truth children know how to hold, somewhat like St Nicholas in Church, who holds in his hand the vessel he saved with all hands.

Rather as Homer presents it, when Hermes leaps down from Pieria, from the Heavens above to the sea, must be how St Nicholas comes. For eyes that can only see nature, the poet likens the Saint to a gull. Truly, on the unharvested sea, there is much the bird can deliver the soul from, when even awake we do not see. If, however, the eyes of sleep open, as happens with monks who pray, without their tears ever drying, with their minds far from handsome long-haired girls, then in the air consolatory, without need of material cause, clay filled with divine ambrosia, the Hope of the world and the worship of Angels, appears.

In her renowned temple, our ship is an offering, a silver lampion full of oil, which with its flame lights the faithful, who accept the miracles the Virgin Mother of God performs.

As to how this ship is built, don't just listen to the goldsmith. Ask all the tradesmen, learn the tricks of all the trades of men. Visit all the shipyards on the sea-sprayed margins. Each and every humble story in the yard, like 'The Orphan', like 'On Watch Over the Quarantine Ships' or like the Caulker Michael who in Byzantium became king, contribute to the completion of the skeleton – with its crossbeams from the forest – of the age-old animal of memory, the arc which saves the world, the body in which God inheres.

Do not, as a logical consequence of the above, form a lifeless, one-sided picture of the ship's crew. Don't be in too great a hurry to banish Evil. The crew and the passengers are alive. Some of their more apt expressions are to be found in *Tales from the Prow*. Insults mostly and banter. The things that lead to quarrels, to one man killing another with an axe.

There is also about the immortal water the characteristic tradition that blood that is spilt is lost.

But for it to be appreciated on a scale appropriate to the dimensions of human misery, the book forms the basis from which all the material must be extracted. Essential additions should be made on the basis of other texts. Much has been and is being written about life at sea, about sea voyages. Interesting descriptions in the newspapers, about the queasiness of passengers on deck. Look at 'Three Days on Tinos'. The sketches by Demetriades in the *Vima* describing those going to the religious festival. For the romantic adventures usually met with on board, 'The Medusas' in the *Heroic Adventure* by Alkiviadis Yannopoulos. Also a story by Vizyenos. Remember too Politis and Karagatsis. For all the talk on board ship of fairly general social interest, what Pallis says in *Brousos*. A ship's description is given by Papatzonis. For a romantic view of the sailor, *Marabou*. Conrad speaks with greater seriousness. A play from abroad about the stoker.

In general, as regards nautical adventure, to sentimental interpretations, the actual accounts of seafarers are to be preferred. A help in understanding the line we are taking is to be found in Defoe, in the dialogue between Panurge and the drover in Rabelais, however little these may seem to be religious. Modern and classical men of the sea agree fundamentally with the Byzantine, that the whole world is no more than a trunk – adorned with the presence of the Man God.

If in the pitching and swaying of the soul the trunk or its contents is lost in the infinite, the sea rises up to take us, wheat grains on the threshing floors of Death.

On the other hand, the captain who is wise saves the whole of the cargo of grain.

He was near Chios, the story goes, ready to take cash for grain, which multiplies miraculously, decomposing in the fertile ground. But he was advised to do otherwise by Mother Thessaloniki's Guardian son, on whose name her children swear. Before him, in his own person, most virtuous and vigorous, the Great Martyr appeared. He who makes the city grow and saves her from her adversaries' assaults, her marshal against the enemy's hordes, the living reservoir from which cures for every ill gush forth. He is to take the grain to the City, says the Great Saint Demetrios.

Thus the City is delivered from famine, and our ship on the limitless oceans finds the straight path.

II

After the entrance from the sea, the chart open at the sea between the Sporades and Kassandra. Consult the nautical pilot. Observe with what computational skills the Captain sets his course.

In the Sound, in between Magnesia and Skiathos, where the ships passed before the war, on the reef whose existence has been known since ancient times, we remarked a shipwreck. Warships have foundered and merchantmen, in the waters of the Thermaic Gulf. They run aground in the shallows round the headlands, on the silt deposits from the rivers. The soil of Thessaloniki, maternal placenta, is liberally irrigated. Over the whole of the wonderful gulf, a venerable bishop presides.

So that Votsis should not miscarry, rushing in to drive out the enemy, Faith guided him all alone. Thus, armour and barricades into the air are thrown, flames sky-high. Magnificent spectacle the vessels set on fire, in the grip of fortune. Lighters and three-masters, iron-clad ships, lose their existence in the depths. Times are when the cargo survives of horses. Times are when a part of the load is offered as salvage for sale.

Descending below the surface, the divers haul up corpses, a good soldier and an untimely death: a spongy mass of flesh. On the rotted clothes epaulettes. He was a general, they say. Eyes eaten by fish. In his armpits squid, marine organisms, had deposited their eggs. A drowned man was found with his head deep in the sand. In the inner waters also, the weather, a wild southerly, a turbulent northerly, engulfs all that is human, ships, life rafts, lifeboats. In a sudden summer storm, a fisherman rushes into the sea fully dressed, to save his boat. The gusts of wind, cries over the waves, 'Help', carry as far as the closed shutters. Before jumping into the sea, the despondent woman let out a cry. In the night everybody heard it. Doors opened, people ran. Lifeless, the body they pulled out. In her mouth, when we bent over her with the lantern, we saw pathetic froth. A shipwreck on the breakers of the mind. With that other tragic creature, abandoned by the husband she loved, they could not, for all that the ship stopped, find the corpse. She had leapt from the bridge, leaving behind her all the new clothes she had had made.

For the wind, bird of the sea, set fair, to fill the white sails they wait, at sea on the maternal gulf, the young who are favoured. In the storm that tosses the boat, they see the swart waters above, the ancestral essence itself walking.

To honour and save the gods of his household and his parents, Aeneas, on his way to found the world dominatrix, built on the Great Headland, on the impregnable cape with the lighthouse, a city named after him. To lay the body to rest of his father, he anchored, I believe, further round, where the land drops down to the fish farm, by the low, flat area, where, like machines, birds lie to. Between the two prehistoric settlements with the pitchers. With his father, he must have walked, in his arms. Between the lofty poplars, where on the trees Eros carved hearts and names. And near there, in point of fact, with bracelets and crowns of gold, they have found funeral gifts, traces of human remains, the graves of venerated ancestors. Confirmation too may be found in the curative waters, which but from the sacred remains of ancestors spring.

Mother city most reverent, be not downcast in misfortune, being possessed in faith of roses, that you may in sacrifice lay, riot of spring, on the graves. Myrrh did your protector from his monument pour forth. If it did in thraldom run dry, a medicine too, powerful and marvellous, is the earth of the grave. When science all hope has lost, with the Saint and Father's earth under his pillow, will the sick child be cured.

Desecration of the graves is forbidden, then, of those who have left us behind, here in the ephemeral world. Inscriptions on the marble sepulchres expressly proscribe it. With roofs and gables the sepulchres, like houses, are completely enclosed. Houses in the name of memory. The dead often rest seated on top, in the round, with the folds in their robes, with the shoulder of the wife close, tucked under her husband's arm.

Believing in physical forces, we must not, just because the years go by, treat the sites of memory as lifeless marble. Do not think, in times of danger or urgent need, of using the sepulchres as stone, as lifeless matter.

The Thessalonians did so once, imagining they could prevent the enemy invasion. To no avail they threw ancient tombs into the sea, that the enemy ships might not come in. They came, however, and they plundered.

In its weakness the flesh that recognizes beyond itself no other life suffers destruction. The land is blessed when it is filled with statues, creatures of another life in which man advances towards God. Below Olympus with the peaks, with the springs and the gods, at the foot of Pieria with the Muses, from the place that, grieving over the heedless prey gripped in his talons, the eagle looks down on from a height, from Dion of the kings, they took, when we became subject to the Romans, a thousand and more gold statues.

Be not faint-hearted in the face of calamity.

Survival has in worlds gone by been the rule. On the opposite shore of the Thermaic Gulf (in the direction that depending on the time of year, the beehives take in the sailing caiques, from one side of the gulf to the other) where recently the isthmus was cut, on the site of what used to be Phlegras, Pallene was built and Eurydikeia flourished, with Kassandreia, Pinakas and Portes, and today, named after the ancient town, the village of Nea Potidaia has been established. There, where for the sake of freedom invasions were ever resisted, where were heard tremendous cries charged with the memory of what the Archangel said to the Mother of God, who shed a tear, that in time it would be ours again, that he would rise again, the king who had been turned to stone, whose head, there being no Christian to take it, the angels had saved, and it had not fallen into the infidels' hands, there, from Argyropouli, sailing in the waters of Kassandra, Nikotsaras and Stathas, their sails black as the sorrows we bear, their hope-bearing flag the sky, fell fearlessly upon the infidels, and routed and sank the enemy fleet. The ocean turned red. The blood ran from the scuppers. Thus is man born, new from his mother into memory.

Sailing for Thessaloniki, in the maternal gulf, believe in the Resurrection. After the burial, Christ was resurrected.

On the sea, which, when we open the window of our cramped room, dazzles us like a pretty girl, radiant in its beauty, is where, even though we might never marry the girl we love and might have to dispatch her to a nunnery to be rid of her, we must live the ancestral inheritance of the fathers, must avenge the ghosts that the surf deposits on the shore, advancing constantly and receding.

Further round from the lighthouse, on the low tongue of the saltpan where they toil, the lovely beach of Metamorphosis. A broad expanse of vineyards, of fields of sesame, cotton and wheat, and a stretch of fruit trees, separate the principal village from the coast. From there a procession of women dressed in black files down the road, a pallid prayer, to light candles in the Chapel of the Saviour, oil lamps to brighten the house. The children spill on to the beach after shells, a wave off the land. They relieve the ugliness of the defunct boat, which displays the gaunt wooden bones of an animal washed up by the sea, the belly open, and intestines, entrails, spilling out.

Inhabitants of the city of Thessaloniki, where we are now arriving, with Paul's Epistle, *But I would not have you to be ignorant, brethren, concerning them which are asleep, that ye sorrow not, even as others*, we were the first Christians to learn from the Apostle to the Gentiles, who visited us, of the hope we must have.

Of Paul's journey to Thessaloniki, which was fraught with adventure, the *Acts of the Apostles* tell. Writing of the same subject, Renan describes the place. He has an eloquent pen, but, too sure of his own good name, he has no understanding of the Hope that was built by Christ. More instructive the society of fishermen, who, in their humble village almost opposite the site of Pydna, which differs from other comparable, crowded ones not at all, with the precious relics of faith, put up, where there had been nothing, a church where the Mother of God works miracles.

Going past Mikhaniona, after Angelokhori on Karabournou, the wide, open part of the gulf narrows, it turns left, with the shallow, brackish waters of Kavoura and the fish farms of Paliomana, and the opposite shore grows closer, with the flat beach of Roumlouki, where the freedom-fighters came ashore at night, through the reeds in secret.

Between two rows of light-buoys, the ship avoids the shallows. To keep the things inside secure, there was a barrier across the strait.

The moment that we double the cape, we admire the city's panoramic scape. The smoke of the ships departing cannot be seen from inside. On a baking-hot day in July, by the blue cape on the horizon, the Saracens' sails appeared, in the bay at the back of the gulf, which looks like a lake.

It calls to mind the lake of Geneva, birthplace of the nature-loving romantic, Rousseau. He describes it often in the *Confessions* and in *La Nouvelle Héloïse*. A landscape frequently depicted since then, by Byron and in novels. In engravings too. Every trick of the colourist has been deployed by artists on the sailing boats that cross it at sunset. Truly, sunsets are wonderful things, especially in Thessaloniki in autumn. However, for the sails on Thessaloniki's boats more appropriate are the lines of *After Rain* – the lines of the sonnets by Mavilis, who from his beach gazed in wonder on the twilight. The image, more popular in style, of Krystallis is appropriate when you look from the fields of Pylaia.

The back of the bay of Aeneas, with the Farm School's trees, brings to mind the Italian Primitives. At a different time, with more orange on the horizon, looking from Sedes, the same haunt of desired love recalls the artist of 'Soyez amoureuses vous serez hereuses'. Secret love becomes romantic, when we notice the hues on Khortiatis. Around October, a pink on the smaller peak of the range, or below the refuge towards Platanakia and on the spurs of the peak of Christ, comes from wild heather in bloom.

The green beautiful, in summer, of the dense kermes oaks in Peristera with the abundant waters. However, their location is usually concealed from the observer by the pyramid of Lanari. Skirting Thermovouni, on which the snow rarely settles, we enter a triangular valley that runs, between Ouvranos and Kalavros, through the heart of Chalkidice as far as Vavdos. When the air on the slopes of the trapezoid mountain is clear, one can make out the houses on it, and Aï Nikolas.

These distances are important – for the gradations of blue in our landscape, for us to appreciate the extent of its serenity, the repose it gives to the soul.

Sown throughout the countryside in Thessaloniki's vicinity, where the bitter Vardar blows, making the dry thistles whirl, where the crop is destroyed if the Livas catches it ripening, were rooms welcoming callers on the renunciation of the world.

On Khortiatis, which soars up like a Gothic cathedral, to the east of the city, there was the renowned Monastery of Khortaïtos. Along with the purest of Greek traditions, traces of mosaic have been preserved in it, there where the writing excelled of religious scholars and geometers.

Demetrios Kydonis, an excellent writer, who lamented the catastrophes in the double uprising of the Zealots in our city, renewed Thessaloniki's ties with Italy and Crete. At the time when Byzantium was being destroyed, when everyone was hesitating over which of the conquerors to choose, and when, so that the Faith should be preserved untainted, the Tsaous monastery was actively promoting the change of overlord in Thessaloniki, still, at that stage, in Venetian hands, his letters show how he felt, steeped as he was in the spirit of the Renaissance in Italy, where so many fugitives achieved distinction.

It has been said that even the Macedonian school of the painter Panselenos

bears some traces of contact with the West. But the land here is altogether different, however much the passes through the hills to the woods around Seïkh-Sou
may recall the female forms of Botticelli.

If, looking at Thessaloniki, one is able to rebut the poetry of *The Waste Land*,
in which all cities are reduced to non-existence, it is because here in the ruins,
in what all things new will eventually become, one senses that everything exists,
not for what it was but for something other than that, which never entered our
minds when we were building. This unlooked-for other makes it possible for
you to live in Thessaloniki, so that however dismal your starting point, you are
always when you set out optimistic about the Resurrection.

From the peak of Sivris in the David range, the wilderness riven by torrents
below, down beneath Aghiasma, Oraiokastro and Niokhorouda, looks like a
wretched corpse. The threshing floor of death, Kharmankioi has been called.
Yet, for all that, the marshland lying lower almost than the sea, where fifty were
executed, the shoreline which reminds one of the Flemish masters, is a new land
taking shape, with fine vegetable plots that grace it. Thickly wooded too is the
area round the extensive cemeteries of Zeitenlik.

Once you have come to know this place in detail, enduring in the sun all the
unhappiness, to appreciate it wait for the rains, when the clouds pile up on the
ramparts, recalling the prospect of Toledo by Theotokopoulos. Go out in the
night when the moon is full. Love of Hecate lets us see the beauty of the beloved
and that of the mother who suckled us combined. As happened to the Poet's
man, fighter bereft of hope on Crete.

That is a more accessible, sentimental face of the unique brilliance, which,
the city's second Protector, Gregory the Great, speaking of the light of the Holy
Transfiguration, which each as much he might saw, teaches man may see, by
means of painstaking exercise in the contemplation of death.

The Relic of the Saint and Father is preserved in the Cathedral, its treasure.
Into the homes of Christians, the Priest, reading the Prayer Book to himself out
loud, 'by the assaults of sorrows is the soul tormented', brings, in a richly decorated silver casket, the Hallowed Head for them to kiss, the faithful on their
knees like children.

III

Dear friend,
Here I am at last in Thessaloniki. It's about time. I was beginning to think
that I would never make it, that the difficulties would again, and perhaps for
ever, keep me away. How long, after all, can one keep on finding the strength to
begin again?

And yet there is, for all that, I am certain of it, a fullness in things. The fullness of time, the satiation with material things . . . call it what you will. And I am living that fullness now. Once that has come, our souls can open the door, or rather, can see the gate open of itself, give way.

I agree with what I imagine you will want to say: that is, that contained in every adventure, even this voyage on the Thermaic Gulf, is Desire. So it is.

That was why, precisely because I knew this to be so, I failed to make any mention of the yachts, the light skiffs, and the craft of other kinds, whose courses, after we doubled the cape, crossed our own as we sailed across the inner waters. Nor did I mention the people who go and bathe in the summertime on the beaches. All these encounters strongly reminded me of the pages of D'Annunzio's novel *The Fire*. I find truly marvellous in it the description he gives of the hands of his companion in the boat and of her movements. It is sensuality like his that gives the Italians their charm. I discern, running through the whole of the boat trip he describes, a symbolist thread. They meet the Queen first, who has gone out on another launch. Then they find themselves in front of a barge fully laden with rich produce. But such a meaning, we know, however sumptuously we may dress it up, is incapable of standing face to face with decay. I had no desire, then, to be described as decadent or as perhaps furthering the cause of decadence.

I feel incredibly young and renewed, as if I am really alive for the first time. That is the meaning of my arrival in the city.

If we did not have as our pilot our inherited Orthodox faith, I do not know whether in the end we would have been able to avoid the reef I have hinted at above.

Even before the 'excavated harbour', I was ready, perhaps in reaction to the impression made on me by the shipwrecks, the sunken ships' skeletons, to succumb once again to dreams.

On countless occasions, while I was there, on the soil where I was born, has the imagination lured me away to other worlds, so that my helplessness and smallness should not be exposed.

How I did not get lost, God alone knows.

Perhaps I have unhappiness to thank for that, whose blows, cruel to the point of despair, have given me no ease.

Thus, even though, to supplement and enrich my imagination, I ran from library to library, I never managed, at least not for any sufficient stretch of our ephemeral life, not for one long enough to allow in a positive sense some rest, to weave anything from beginning to end, not, that is, a single complete piece of cloth which might allow me to clothe myself, so I should not see my terrible mortal nakedness.

The cloth would tear each time, under the burden of wretched things. Things that have no mind or speech. A packet of cigarettes, my glasses that got broken, an unwashed foot, would, with the wretchedness of their silence, make holes in the weaving.

By this I do not mean to say that I accepted defeat and became resigned, deciding to accept the nakedness of the flesh.

Each time, putting into it all my strength, I would make a new start. Even as we were entering the harbour, I had, as I told you, started to make plans in my imagination. I was basing them on the Byzantine chronicles. I had read once in Pachymeres about the arrival of one of the Palaeologues in Thessaloniki. Fusing this event with the familiar photographs of the entry of King George and the heir to the throne into our town, during the liberation, on the festive day of the Feast of the City's Protector, my imagination found a rich meaning in which I could clothe myself. Rich delight was also afforded me by the text 'On Order in the Kingdom' by the never to be forgotten emperor Constantine Porphyrogennetos.

I thought that with an enthusiastic, triumphant, and magnificent welcome, I would be able to connect the somewhat more recent 'White Tower', previously the 'Tower of Blood', in the square in front of which the pictures show today's Sovereign, to the gateway decorated with fine reliefs in Vardar Square, through which we must most probably suppose the Palaeologue entered. The opportunity afforded by a picture of the Greco-Roman structure, the so-called 'Golden Gate', not even the ruins of which survive today, was enough for my imagination to incorporate all of those statues too, in the Endymion and Aphrodite groups, which had later been removed to the Louvre, from the place which was known as 'The Idols', which at one time they had richly adorned.

In that way, clothed in the whole of antecedent time, I thought that I would disembark as an important person of particular significance in the maternal city. Just as, when going for a walk along the walls or walking by the sea on the quay, which with the waves of the heavy swell, with the winter gales, is awash over all of its narrow width (something which is such a blot on the comfort and charm of the city) I used, in the old days, at the time when I took delight in the Norwegian expounders of individualism, to see myself dressed in the medal-laden frock coat of the great social reformer, moving beyond time and space.

But the fact that I am here today in this city of ours has nothing to do with any of that.

It is a pilgrimage.

Perhaps, if you like, you can blame my luggage. It is true that the trunk I had with me was both heavy and old. In the struggle to get it out I fell. I fell flat on my face.

I didn't set foot on land like a man, but like a child that trips and falls.

Or perhaps again, bearing in mind the old saw, the fall had to do with learning. Don't people say that he who knows it all is heading for a fall? Such is the way of the Lord with man, his child.

A fall brought me back to the present. The reality of the Mother.

The immeasurable Mother takes, from the triple-natured, consubstantial and indivisible number of the Whole, the child up in her arms.

She holds it to her breast like a slice cut from a watermelon with the deep and burning intensity, the glory of the lovely scarlet colour. The colour that is like blood. The blood from the fecund undefiled loins. The loins, Life-giving Source from which healing flows. Waters of health, youth and joy.

Our Lady the People's Leader has the holy church of Lagoudiani in our city. It was built by a lad who fell into a deep sewer without his soul going out of him. In the dark, subterranean depths, the Virgin Mother took him to her breast. In exchange the lad gave all things beautiful and precious to the Mother.

He himself put on rags. The raiment of his new joyous existence. The rags of the relics of time gone by, the past.

Truly these few material relics, small in number, constitute a raiment of imperishability.

Dearest friend, I have been thinking about your son Luke. About his future and his prospects. It is good to teach him to have on him, as his only raiment, a rag from a precious and glorious relic. In Thessaloniki these days, they change the shroud on the hallowed remains of St Theodora every year. From her old raiment, they distribute among the needy faithful a piece of threadbare weft, so that in the misfortunes of life they may be clothed as human beings. That little is enough for one to feel happy and healthy, which I wish for you always, you and your family. I prayed especially for your son, in front of the image, an old, plaster-covered fresco, which was brought to light again only recently in the Protector's Holy Church, now being restored, of your compatriot, St Luke, whose name your son bears.

This so you should know you are not forgotten. I shall be writing again.

With love

IV

We are subject to checks in the real world. Every traveller is required to make a declaration: give his place of origin, his name. To put on display whatever he has brought with him. After the great ocean of desire, being crowded into a confined space is disappointing. In the vastness inside ordinary discourse, our destination, the journey's end, is, we understand, no more than a mark, an almost indiscernible black speck on the map. Of course one knows that, like everywhere else, there will be shops, houses. You'll find yourself a job of some sort. You'll soon have a roof over your head. For all that, many worry and wonder. They are afraid that they will find themselves alone. That they won't know how to fill the empty hours.

Later, with the bitter ironic coloration of the commonplace, their affairs move on through phases roughly analogous to the stories of Maupassant, the Frenchman, or Chekhov. An unimaginable crowd of caricatures, confusion. It has been said that confusion reaches its zenith, when, for example, you do not know where the head is, or you mistake it for the shoes.

Of course, as with everything, the problem is not so acute for those who have money or a specially printed guide. In the space which is other than the self, they move around effortlessly by car. They know that the city was built in the past. How though can they relate to Cassander or anyone else before Christ, when Christ himself already lies so far in the past? The reality of the things of the past in the present they value only as a diversion from their boredom.

Should the terrible quotidian sun, which reduces the phenomenon to horror, to sharp dust, the fruit of drought, hide behind clement clouds, by following the perimeter of the walls, they may find in the west, in the varied placing of the bricks, a decorative design to put on a bag.

It is not generally given to them to see the real. Not because over the years the guardian, miracle-working icons built into the walls have gone from their places. Nor because the crosses constructed in the walls are not clearly visible, or because demolition has turned whole sections of the ramparts into a skeleton, scattered bones, heaps of dead stone. It makes no difference either that there is only half the marble relief over the segment of the ramparts with the broken-toothed battlements, which swells lower down like a woman in the family way. Nor either as regards the perception of the real is it of any great relevance to those strolling about to know who exactly Hormisdas was, who compassed the city about with impenetrable walls. It is of no account that the name of Duke Apokaukos is scarcely legible on the lichen-blackened tower wall, which was erected with the support of the mighty Despot Manuel. Nor if the letters in brick on some other tower are no longer legible. A gateway once open has now been filled in. It is not just that all of the picturesque walls of the fortifications belong for them in the past. A similar incomprehension fills them in the face of the modern: balconies with elaborate railings, the overhead cables running down the streets from post to post, the lines on roofs of multi-coloured drying clothes, which obscure the doors and window frames, in conjunction with the branches of consumptive vegetation, which suddenly disclose large bare surfaces painted ochre, green slates and red bricks, shadowy doorways. One's soul must become the plaything of the wind, if one is to see the glory of the real, the consonance of shapes and colours, which manifest themselves in a way altogether comparable to the frescoes of the Greek Orthodox Church.

Orthodox houses of worship, moreover, do not seek to impress with their exteriors. Often without even the slightest ostentation, they are lost in the throng of similar roofs on the houses. When they are discovered with the help of the tourist guide, they manifest at first sight a depressing monotony. Only with difficulty does the eye come to discern the survival in the present. One is never sure whether the representations have preserved their original form authentic and intact.

Those who walk around Thessaloniki meet with no specious attractions, like those that entertain people in the name of the futile and the ephemeral. If anything manifests itself as a spectacle capable of making an impression, it is the impressive progress of the funerals through the streets. Death is also sensed filling the frequent unbuilt and empty spaces between the houses. A limitless expanse of cemeteries bisects the fire and quake prone city. Anyone who sets out with no metaphysical inclination prefers to abandon all his luggage, and go on to what, where deceptive immediate gratifications are concerned, are richer pastures.

The beauty of the real is only revealed to those who can endure it. Beauty is not desire for the individual who is naturally blest; it is perseverance next to, close to that which you are not.

Serving ordinary needs buses are a lesson to us. I do not mean the usually misspelt ordinances: Do not speak to . . . Pull the cord . . . No entry . . . No exit . . . the phrases one usually reads inside the vehicles. The buses also go where the trams do not, carrying people in large numbers, each with his worries and thoughts.

The importance of transport is well-known. Long-distance buses and railways connect the outside world and the periphery to Thessaloniki. Their proper functioning inspires confidence in the existence of something larger, where the individual, dutiful, obedient, fits into some organized structure of phenomena. His mind on his own affairs, only when his arteries become diseased does anyone feel distress breathing within the totality. It really is hard, going from the Depot, down the road to the market, on foot in the cold and the mud. It is moving to see the spectacle, presented along the whole of its length, of scattered individuals walking. Poor people and casual workers, coming down from the upper districts, cross the Via Egnatia every day. Women as much as men. One person comes up with, overtakes another. You yearn for a familiar face. They talk, so that the distance they traverse each day shouldn't seem so great. From the scattered individuals, the voices carry such despair, that on hearing it the mind boggles. To such a boggling of the mind must we attribute the madness of Caligula. In response to the problem of the voices, he sought to restore wholeness by slaughtering the whole of humanity, as if it only had a single head. To this Roman thought, the sequel was Theodosius' notorious massacre of the Thessalonians in the Hippodrome. His imperial person, however, as he dragged himself repentant to the church, was taught that nothing good is gained by violence. The truth, in which there is room for us all, and to which no-one has the monopoly, is reflected in the phenomenon like a picture, in existence as the likeness of God. Our lives it is impossible for us to narrate, the image of the city impossible for us to see, if we rely exclusively on what we are, if we do not remember that we were baptized, with an iconic death, receiving life in our flesh in the name of an ancestor and Saint, of one who had journeyed before. Time, space, our movements, stood in my memory like myth, when after a funeral, leaving the graveyard behind, I headed for where today, in the hollow of an old quarry, stand the closely packed houses of a suburb. It is reported that going there to wash their cloth once, in the waters under the plane trees, they found buried treasure and got rich. As I was going across the uneven ground between, where, left from blasting with sticks of dynamite, there was an amphitheatre of sorts, which still had isolated rocks standing at its centre, like others that were on the hillside further up, an escort, as in what they call the street of Titans, of people who have turned to stone, I named every thing, giving them the names of ancestors. Ours the land that memory has named. The sky above it, God. All of the twenty-four letters may be read, indited in every style. His memory, whose bones lie scattered in an unknown place, gives life. Full of life the registry office and the space belonging to the other life, with Alpha inscribed, and Omega, in the compositions on its iron door. In experiencing the breath of memory, we inhabit the reality of Thessaloniki.

V

At a distance the city is seen, in the haze where the earthly is vaporizing into garlands of the spirit, under the sway of the aerial motions of the sky, on the baked brick of the mountains, an expanse of winking eyes, of dark eyelids and eyebrows. Characteristic the way, with the coming out or going in of the Sun, the shadow of the clouds is cast on the face of each house unequally. Behind the cubes and polyhedrons – the white apartment blocks on the sea – everything plunged in deep violet. A slanting white line rising towards the ramparts – the whitewashed huts on the rocks. High up on the crest, a white mark in front of the Kara-Tepe – the prison. The small grey houses inside the citadel wall cannot be made out. The picturesque descents – towards the Sykeon ravine with the poplars, from the gardens of Eskintelik to Rodokhori with the vineyards – make up the rear and are likewise hidden from view. From the ward of Neapolis, one can see only what lies on the shoulder. An earring on the ear, the building above the Mevleane, where at one time Dervishes danced, close to the church of the Martyrs: of Irene, of Chionia, of Agape. In the distance a section of bare hillside has been reafforested, for the enjoyment of those who live nearby. All the gardens on the view's comely breast are green, up as far as the embowered monastery. The green of the cypresses dull at the Evangelistria, as too in Aghia Paraskevi's enclosure, in the place where a Neomartyr met his end, near the swarming crowds of Xirokrini. Pines around the Hospital, on the hills of Axekizla, above the firing range, in Aspri Petra. Behind the Eptapyrghion some plane trees. Today 'The Thousand Trees' is what people call Seïkh-Sou with the café and the spring which wells up from a grave.

In the ravines further down, more country houses, near walnut trees. Pines surround almost every house. On the front with the fringes, between the White Tower and Allatini, are the electricity company's installations, in the first of the little harbours in the filigree of bays. Then come the houses of Arigoni. A villa reminiscent of Morocco. The wharf of the tile factory, in front of where the torrent, the Trelou Dere, which floods in front of the Palace when it rains, discharges, next to the ruined mansion of the Bey, ruined not so much by ghosts as poverty. Ghosts appear further on, in the picturesque old villas of the rich. An old man who hanged himself. A mother dressed in black for her offspring who sank into imbecility and died. The whole of that stretch that served for a time as a dockyard, after they demolished the Levantine family's house, lies empty now but for some fish stalls. Destruction of the big old houses the rule, it continues to where the traffic starts, out on the trunk road. The strangest uses and shapes replace the former glory. All that is left is the crest on the iron railings. In one garden they felled sixty-six huge elms. Naked new houses fill the area once occupied by ancient vegetation. Where the Sultan was imprisoned and the treaty of surrender signed, a magnificent canopy of pines still survives; for it has not yet been turned into a night club or a villa.

The image of the real is not exhausted in a single period, no matter what vantage point we adopt. The city is spreading today, with new villas appearing in the direction of dew-drenched Arsakli. Land has been bought up there by the American College foundation. In Venizelos' time, over towards Karabournaki, a row of houses was built, on this side of the Franco-Greek company, over whose ruins the stench of the tannery hangs, on the spot where at one time there used to be a winch, where, near the shore once, an island of sand appeared. On the tip of the small cape, beyond the picturesque cafés, beyond the big buildings of the cavalry regiment, by the masts of the old telegraph, was where, so it has been maintained, the market town used to be, during the Neolithic period, for all the populous villages of the area marked by the Toumbes, the tumuli. Ano and Kato Toumba, two villages near the foot of the mountains, grew up there after the exchange of populations with Turkey.

In the colour of the view overall, the influence of red is strongly felt – in the plethora of roofs which contrasts with green. Behind the roofs of Kalamaria, the grove green in the British military cemetery. Trees, too, on the Switzerland Hill, in front of the houses of Pylaia. Corrugated iron roofs and acacia fronds harmonize in Triandria. Red dominates in the buildings in the harbour, in the street-blocks full of oil shops, in the industrial section of the town. The bricks red of the factories, as, too, of the chimneys, which can clearly be seen, high against the backdrop of hills, where Niokhorouda is and Oraiokastro, from beyond Bekhtsinari, where the vegetable plots, the trees and reeds begin, and from as far away as Kalokhori.

Wanting to compose a symphony of the place, a composer who in his youth had known triumph in the West, submerged himself in the contradictions of phenomena. The vivid Mediterranean colour, together with something Arabian that Spain brought to music, allowed him to take delight in the vision of diversity. He could see the Minarets and the Souk, the Turkish baths with the domes, the display of carpets in the covered ways, the merchandise, the produce in the Kampani, the luxurious Europeanized Yeni Tzami. Seeking the harmonious purity of these features, he would wander in the upper town, where a road crosses it that is like a balcony, with a clear view over the houses. He was trying to find in the oldness of the buildings, which, painted over with indigo and ochre, is palpable in the houses with the enclosed balconies, the lost heritage of the glorious Byzantine era. He even turned to the people, going out to the fields of Pylaia, down the roads that consciousness follows in all who try to connect the present and the past, seeking to find the genuine in the villagers' lives, pitiful in the eyes of the city.

Someone proclaiming that they would never take the sacred land of the Macedonians caught an infection, quenching his thirst at a river. We were still battling with enemies then, we were not tearing at our own flesh, looking for the reality of life through educational dogmas which pursue happiness and end in pessimism, unlike the Hope of Christ.

Below the Aghiasma, the Holy Water of the Apostle to the Nations, it had not yet become built up, new houses had not been built at the cemeteries, around Khoratzides. Looking from below at the road that ran uphill, with the leaning columns on it, the future skeleton of the University could not be seen, and all they could see were the labours of 'Hercules' free of charge. The University was then a Pandidactorio, a Turkish school. The churches, mosques rendered in stucco, inaccessible. Entry was not permitted to the glorious temple of the city's Protector, but only to his tomb. Regular services were being held only at the churches of 'The Purification', of 'St Thanasis', of 'Dexa', which continues to receive the old biddies every Monday. In the surviving remnant of the church of Monydrios, a Saint with the same name as a Prophet, the representation of a vision of Christ as a youth was confounded with the Virgin Platytera. The defiled site of the Church of the Coppersmiths was not recognizable as one dedicated to a celebrated church. Below the gateway of the Most Godly Empress the church of the three Archangels was languishing. Airy as a courtyard, St Catherine's was being desecrated, as was Holy Apostles, which the bricks' varied placement graces. It was impossible to raise your head up high, towards the Angels drawing the Lord of Heavenly Powers on his chariot, who overturns the natural order with his light, confounding even his Disciples on the dome of the Wisdom of God.

You could not gaze on your supports, the first Bishops, ecstatic before the palaces of eternity, in the building planted amongst antiquities, on the same axis as the Hippodrome, which beyond the Arch that marks the triumph over the Parthians is soaked in the blood of massacre.

Losing the person you loved, running in tears behind the hearse that was taking your life from you, it was impossible for you to breathe the whole of the memory inscribed on the windows, as certain evidence of the transcendence of death. In the Dungeons and the numbers of the night, explaining a flower-pot walled up in darkness, it was not possible for the years of childhood to be projected as life, years which contain, within a range of a hundred paces, in and around the family garden, out as far as the well, the whole of the world. Shut inside himself, the sinner could not hear the voice of his mother, or the greetings of the flowers, which the Lord picks. The senses could not bear to feel the raw and untempered loneliness without the flowers that belong to the other hand.

The multitude though of efforts today, renewing with ever verdant growth the forgotten face of the monuments, allow us to perceive the clear shape of the Cross – in the Sanctuary, there where the diverse arcs intersect of the world's Glory, in the enclosure enlarged by Faith – with the riven slabs of might, with the thousand-year-old vessel of clay, the symbols reviving, of eternity, wondrous wings of common feeling, caress that allows us to see, rising on the night of the Resurrection, through the real Sky of the Mother, doves made of mortal hands.

Within the generality of the real, the scale which allows every detail to exist organically is, in Homer's *Odyssey*, precisely gauged. In our own time as in that of Alexandria, the imitators of the epic are many, of the novelists or Nonnus and of the various commentators relatively few. While the perfection of the ancients was being mourned by Akominatos of Athens, Eustathios, having been wedded to Thessaloniki's cathedral church, indited into a most Christian text, in parallel with the Patriarch's *Myriobiblos*, everything written concerning Homer. With his help we can, I think, at the Zero point, where we become enmired, losing the world today with our thought, place the floating island of Aeolia. After this adventure comes the visit to the realm of Hades by the wandering man. The pleasant slumber of the imagination outside the real in Calypso's caves, which is not merely desire, but like desire symbolizes the world, leads in its symbolism, if we do not stop there, after a seven year interval, to the final shipwreck near the shore, on which a rare maiden is dreaming of her nuptials.

The Belgian symbolist poets, Verhaeren who hymns his wife, Rodenbach who describes Bruges, locate the symbols of love on the same erroneous plane of the terrestrial. They are not suspicious of sleep's symbols, they have not understood that the imagination sends them to sleep. They condemn, with bitter complaints, the intrusion of the real which wakes one up. With greater experience of this, Mallarmé confesses to weariness after each disclosure, trapped in a blind alley. Thus, neither is the return accomplished, with the prodigious feat against the Suitors, nor is the chastity of Nausicaa rendered credible. Conversely, by locating the symbols elsewhere, in love for God, the faithful resurrect the ancient Hope.

'Myself', says Psellos, 'I mistrust, the Mother of the Word with all things I entrust.'

On the breast of the Mother of God the reality of Thessaloniki is to be found in its entirety.

Thus the paltry doings of an insignificant couple in Dublin, of Mr and Mrs Bloom, a vanished day of our century and all the delirious ravings of the night, need only the 'plus' sign of the Cross, instead of the abstraction of all of life's affairs, for them to change from being the acts of ghosts into the acts of real people, for city and characters to exist. For them not just to be the indices of pain, of fruitless searches in time past, where every vision, we know, is a wall in our stifling room, with all the undulations in the memory, of time that has been engulfed by the waves.

When we turn our backs to the wall, we understand the meaning of the *Odyssey*.

Having once grieved for seven years feeling homesick for our starting point in desire, we do not fear our own destruction, on the raft's humble frame, of tree trunks hewn from the vegetation, in Hades' sea with the Demons' horrid trident.

The daughter of Cadmus, who by way of the Greeks taught the alphabet, when once we admit we have lost our identity, with her veil, Leucothea, brings from the depths of the sea our salvation, the sky above our Mother City, to which all the phases of the flesh, from the yards where the hens are grubbing in the dust, ascend, columns of smoke, from humans in the Almighty's hands, the essence.

All honour and reverence to him, who saves city and mankind alike.

Translated by Leo Marshall

Nicolas Calas (1907–1988)

Calas, who also wrote under the names Nikos Kalamaris, Nikitas Rantos and M. Spieros (this last an echo of Robespierre), made an early appearance as poetic and critical *enfant terrible* of both Surrealist and Marxist affiliations, with salutary praise for Cavafy (below) and critical dispraise for the Establishment figure of Palamas (q.v.). It wasn't long (1938) before he left the Greece of the Metaxas dictatorship to pursue a career as an art critic in France and later the United States, writing in French and English – though in his last years he made a limited further contribution to the Greek literary scene. The compression of his early work shows that in Greek poetry Calas was something of a lost leader.

Cavafy

His azure stare tints the verse with the sea's horizon.
Anointed words weave a song on Aeolian harp-strings,
the melody runs on the wind with Ionian currents
and arrives at Byzantium, in the port of Nicomedia,
where the crews of wealthy traders row to Syria's shores,
but raging waves overwhelm the merchant galleys,
and hysterical gulls relay the barbarous echoes
of shattered oars to darkening Alexandria.
There the poet hears them and drinks down
the insubordinate sea with scented oil.

Santorini VII

Gone are the long summer nights,
the dappled shadows of fall now blaze on other beauties
and joys, dulled from the flood of memory's downpours,
now stifle recollection with their waters.
They've passed, the flames, the desires that reared them,
even the waves that fondled such joys have dried up;
conches and pebbles have stopped their wordy game
on the strand of expectation.
The callous shoreline watches the wind hauling the clouds
toward the heaven that I loved for the sweet song of its collapse.

The long nights of summer have passed
and the deep-toned shades of autumn cause the sun to blink,
dazzling my foreign life, warming it with their mute, impoverished rays;
craters without breath, feeble craters.

The Dream

The night is heavy with dreams,
the icons of well-tilled desires grow cold in the silence
and the uproar impels us to full and deeper sleep,
but waking to the bright sun of evening is hard
and heavy are the chains that curb the soul's release.
Night consumes the body, famishes it,
weighs down upon us in life's remote pastures.
Night supplicates us in dreams,
draws us to the ground that evening uplifts,
hurls us from charted stars to weary heavens,
fire-ships on the sea dotted with black masts,
wooden beams securing our ragged hopes,
tattered sails that swell the sprawling dark,
its mesmerizing vault over the vine-spawning sea.
The larger the waves, the brighter the vision,
forcing out figures and thoughts that cloud the darkness,
the warmest anchorage of our lives,
where we set down pitchers on thirsty tombs,
hidden in the shade of the cypresses
that cast our lives into a form of prayer.

Translated by Avi Sharon

Andreas Embiricos (1901–1975)

Embiricos is increasingly being recognized as one of the finest Greek poets of the twentieth century, but this isn't easy to explain to the English reader: the immaculate rhythms and diction of his finest work, especially in the 1946 collection *Hinterland*, allow of no lesser comparison than Wallace Stevens, whom Embiricos had probably read, but resist translation. In any case, it takes a little clearing away of Embiricos' reputation to get at the best poetry: his fame was founded on the *succès de scandale* of a polished but ultimately not terribly interesting orthodox Surrealist collection, *Blast Furnace* (1935), and he has recently been best known for a tumescent pornographic novel, *The Great Eastern*, posthumously published in ten volumes. The poems and prose texts printed below were published in book form between 1946 and (posthumously) 1980. *Sui generis*, Embiricos' poems are a reminder that there could be a Greek Modernist verse which was, unlike that of Seferis, free of Eliot's somewhat uncomfortable shadow.

Orion

To Odysseus Elytis

> The indeterminate season with its storks
> Floats on the ice-floes and sails westwards
> Naked icicles naked swallows in the sun
> Sing of the crossing on the downward voyage
> Earth's impetus
> Quivers of spring
> The ice does not roam the seas without some hope
> The warmth of each voice contains all its meaning
> The leap of the keel
> With the mighty storks on the downward voyage
> Polar iridescence is reborn in the clouds
> And from yesterday's shadows the nets draw fish
> The sky yawns and insects take wing
> This is the gift of hallucination
> There is no need for the seagulls to hide
> Sailors stand and search for the horizon
> An ark appears on Ararat
> A nereid brings the olive branch

She holds a ring in her teeth
Her fingers are eloquent
Her message is clear at a distance
Thirty years we waited on the ice-floes to meet the siren
Then the ship's siren was heard
And she appeared in her smile
Certainly she had waited for us since morning
When words hurry the voice arrives
And the storks fly about in her light
Sunrise sunrise
The sun's keel in the dawn
Downward voyage of the ice-floes
Each of our domes fills with rosy feathers
Many of us smoke pipes of black coral
Others pipes of meerschaum
And the splash as we reach the shore
Brings to mind the name of an ancient city
We all run to see if she has appeared
Since the horizon glows
Since it resembles her so much.

Insight of Morning Hours

To Yves Tanguy

Natural inclination
The dove of our heartbeat spreads it around
The tears of rivers flow always
They are tears of unconcealable happiness
They are lakes where snow-white storks lived long ago
No south-westerly settles in the sugar-canes
And even if at a gunshot the clouds lift
And rise into thinner layers
Where the corvettes spread their sails
Down on the earth a shadow searches for its lost body
The weather in the valley which stole it from her
Thickens the mists that hide it
The lake's treasures are restless, their fur rises
Seaweed and elemental matter stir in its depths
A jellyfish weeps for yesterday's transparency

Which will return with the first fishing-light
Before winter sets in
Before anyone thinks of lighting the beacon
Under which a blonde woman considers her future
The lighthouse-keeper bends to her lips and kisses them
As mariners kiss their Symplegades.

Translated by Paul Merchant

The Texts

To Nikos Gatsos

Behind the walls.
    In the anxiety of a beleaguered city.
    In the houses, mistresses and maids, after the curfew, sparingly fed the fires with the last stored chopped wood, adding old shelves, boxes, all sorts of rubbish and even frames of paintings. Groceries, markets and bakeries were all completely closed down, their place taken by a few state distributors guarded by army detachments with machine guns. The little food available was given to the hungry population on ration books and in very small quantities. With the exception of a few military vehicles and still fewer trams, there circulated in the streets only some buses, a few emaciated pedestrians and one cyclist.
    This man was middle-aged and wore ordinary civilian clothes. Although completely unknown before the siege he became well known to all by the end of the first month. Although the sight of him frightened the inhabitants, although he did not become popular even for a moment, he succeeded, in spite of this, in becoming necessary not only to the eyes of the people but to the conscience of the authorities as well. All considered him in some way or another as the animator of the hopeless defence.
    Sitting on his saddle, he went coolly round the city cycling day and night, even during the heaviest moments of bombardment. Nobody knew where he came from. Nobody knew who he was. Nobody could boast that he had pushed aside even one fold of the mystery that surrounded and followed him everywhere. He alone seemed to know everything. Casually making his way into all quarters of the city (much as the hand of a skilful pickpocket slips into the purse) he frightened the inhabitants. At the same time he inspired them with new strength, giving them faith in the happy outcome of the war. This he did, not with words, but through his modest, unconcerned expression, the steady revolution of his bicycle-chain, the powerful repetitiveness of his innumerable passings. There was no exhi-

bitionism, no acrobatic showings off or rabble rousing, nothing of this kind to account for the extraordinary and deep impression he produced on the inhabitants.

Once, on the first day of his rounds, which later became legendary, a green-grocer slung a basket at his head. At the same second the largest credit establishment in the city crashed to the ground. A few days later, an old woman attempted to stab him with her umbrella. The same moment, a fire broke out in the cathedral and burned it down.

Since then, no one ever thought of attacking the cyclist or preventing his passing. The truth is that he was never loved by the inhabitants. But while they all considered him an evil omen at first, little by little, and without anyone knowing the reason why, each one of them, without exception, began to think of him as a symbol of victory and therefore as good luck. During the last week the population completely identified its destiny with the destiny of the cyclist. Some offered him flowers, others a little food and others still tubes or other accessories for his decrepit bicycle. He, however, refused to accept anything and continued on his way day and night, resting for about two hours each day on a bench in a quiet corner of the public garden.

During the third month of the siege, however, this man expressed a wish that was in the nature of a demand. The mayor had invited him one morning to offer him, on behalf of the inhabitants, a new bicycle. The cyclist did not accept the present but asked to receive the young and beautiful wife of the mayor in marriage.

The mayor, insulted, hit the man. The cyclist fell and in falling was seriously wounded. After a while, the city was informed that, in spite of the doctors' treatment, he was at the hospital and dying.

That same day the mayor was assassinated. The inhabitants, terrified, prayed in their houses, in the churches, and in front of the hospital, begging that the dying man be saved.

But there seemed no hope. On the contrary, heavy clouds gathered over the city and on the evening of the same day, the enemy, breaking through the walls, entered the suburbs and advanced into the main squares.

On the following day, the cyclist died. Few escaped. The men were slaughtered, the women and the children taken slaves, the city was burned, and on its ruins the conquerors established the bicycle-racing stadium where the greatest and most glorious bicycle races take place today.

Aphrodite

That night, I had been looking at the stars, the constellations; I thought, however, of the day. You looked at me in its light, beloved, rosy, lightly dressed, and every now and then you dreamed, increasingly the bright flood of light in me.

And still, outside, was night. But what a night! A night loaded with miracles, a night pregnant with spells.

I had been looking at the stars, the constellations, but I was seeing You at the same time. Behold! there's Sagittarius, I was saying, and Capricorn, Sirius and Orion. But I was seeing You all the time.

Beloved, rosy, lightly dressed, you stood in me in a luxurious flood of light. Sometimes you leaned your head to the right and sometimes to the left, with Orion and Sirius in your hair and Sagittarius in your heart.

I had been looking at the stars, the constellations. Behold! there's Sagittarius, I was saying, Capricorn, Sirius and Orion. But all the time I was seeing You.

Beloved, rosy, lightly dressed, you had been sitting on a chair within my heart, in an incredibly bright flood of light, your shadow sometimes on the right, sometimes on the left. But you yourself were motionless, simple, sweet, most beautiful, sitting on your chair in such a manner that I was tempted to take you on my knees, one hand upon your breasts, the other underneath your dress, between your thighs.

And I was saying over and again: Behold! there's Sagittarius, look at Capricorn, Sirius and Orion; and I was always looking both at the constellations and at You.

This time, though, you were lying down – completely lying – hair spilling in the air. My hand caressed you. Your eyes talked to me. And I kept saying over and again: 'Behold! there's Sagittarius, look at Capricorn, Sirius and Orion,' but I could only see You now.

A wonderful miracle happened then. All the stars were extinguished and You alone remained in the sky, with me, in an eternal day and by my side. I looked at you in exaltation and I repeated your name endlessly.

And You?

You, sweet one, my Virgin full of grace, were holding in your hands, my heart.

Translated by Alan Ross and Nanos Valaoritis

In Philhellenes Street

To Conrad Russell Rooks

One day as I was walking along Philhellenes Street, the asphalt was turning soft under my feet and in the trees in the square cicadas could be heard, deep in the heart of Athens, deep in the heart of summer.

Despite the high temperature, there was a lively bustle. Suddenly a hearse passed by. Behind it followed half a dozen cars with crapes, and as my ears caught the bursts of stifled lamentation, for just a moment the bustle came to a halt. Then some of us (total strangers in the throng) looked right at one another in anxiety, each trying to divine the other's thoughts. And then, in a trice, like a surge of tight-packed waves, the bustle resumed.

It was July. Along the street the buses made their way, jam-packed with sweating folk – with men of every kind, slim youths and heavy men, moustachioed, with housewives fat or skeletal, and with numbers of young women and schoolgirls, against whose firm buttocks and ripening breasts many of the jostling men were, as was only natural, trying with might and main (each of them aflame, each of them erect like Heracles with his club) to bring about, with open mouth and dreamy eyes, the contacts customary in such places, in all their significance and ceremonial, each one of them pretending it was by accident, from the crush supposedly, that there would come about against the receptive schoolgirls' and young women's rounded charms those purposeful, ecstatic contacts so familiar in such conveyances – the touchings, bumpings-against and rubbings-up.

Yes, it was July; and not Philhellenes Street alone, but Missolonghi Castle and Marathon and the Phalloi of Delos were brandishing their ripeness in the light, just as in Mexico the desert cacti straight and tall brandish their sharp lengths, in the mysterious silence which surrounds the Aztecs' pyramids.

The temperature was rising steadily. This was not warmth but heat – the heat which high noon generates. And yet, for all the heatwave and the swift inhalations of the short of breath, despite the passing of the funeral cortège a little while before, no passer-by felt any heaviness, and nor did I, although the street burned so with heat. Something like a cicada full of life was in my soul, forcing me on, with light and frequent step. Everything all around me now seemed clear, tangible even to the sight, and yet, at the same time, everything was turning all but immaterial in the heatwave – the people and the buildings – so much so that even the grief of some few sorrowful ones all but evaporated under the direct light.

Then, with a mighty beating of the heart, I stopped for a moment, motionless in the throng, like a man graced with a vision in the twinkling of an eye, or like one who has seen a miracle before his very eyes, and drenched in sweat I cried out thus:

'Great God! This heatwave is needful to bring about this light! This light is needful to bring about some day a glory shared, a glory common to all men, the glory of the Hellenes, who were the first, I hold, here in this world below, to make the fear of death a lust for life!'

Translated by David Ricks

King Kong

For Yorgos Makris

Sleep would not come and I had gone out into the streets of Paris, where I was living in those years (between 1920 and 1930). It was the time when, after midnight, began the reign in Europe of the music of the negroes.

Sleep would not come and I had gone out into the streets. It was the time when I would thrill to the joy of Picasso, bathed – no, baptized in the shimmering radiance of the spirit of André Breton.

Sleep would not come and I had gone out into the streets, filled that night with ennui, because I had not found the company I craved.

The sounds of day had long faded away and I trod the macadam, reluctant to turn home, because my flat smelt musty and it was hot indoors, stiflingly hot and dusty.

Inhaling deeply, I took no notice of where I was going and went forward, saying over and over again like a charm, the words of André Breton: *'Lâchez tout, partez sur les routes . . .'* with the hope in my heart that, perhaps, at long last, with the aid of chance, I would happen upon something pleasant, and all the while my mind was ablaze with the (to me) astonishing figure of André Breton.

Borne thus from Montparnasse and led almost mechanically by my footsteps I arrived finally in the streets of Montmartre (there, in the rue Fontaine, lived Breton), filled with the ennui I mentioned before, and continued to walk idly among the alleys that surround the Place Blanche, as well as that square with the multi-coloured neon lights, whose name is Place Pigalle.

Above me the stars panted in the sky and the night was magic, filled with stars, filled with the joy of the Cosmos.

Around me rose the houses – remnants from the age of Haussmann and other periods, and among them many buildings from the time of Baudelaire, of Paul Verlaine, of Jules Laforgue and of Rimbaud, and in their midst, by God, the souls of these poets can often still be seen to wander today, crowned with haloes and clearly visible, utterly alive.

'Lâchez tout, partez sur les routes . . .' I kept saying over and over again and went forward, lightening the burden of my ennui and anguish.

'Lâchez tout, partez sur les routes . . .' and from the corners of the alleys and the doorways of old buildings came whispers of feigned desire: *'Venez faire l'amour, chéri . . . Pour une moment . . . Pour toute la nuit . . . Pour une branlette . . . Pour une sucette . . . Laissez-moi faire et vous verrez les anges . . . Venez, monsieur . . . Venez! . . .'*

'Lâchez tout, partez sur les routes . . .' I kept saying to myself, and went forward, while further off, here and there, with their short capes folded and

thrown carefully over their shoulders, policemen slowly paced, and now and then, their bicycle chains humming in a quiet free-wheel and always in twos, always paired, slowly passed in the night, astride their machines, the law enforcers of Paris, the *agents-cyclistes*. And each time, I thought I would hear burst out from chests dressed in dark shirts, or in tight vests, I thought I would hear burst out, projected passionately upon the night, a sudden cry, blazing like a knife-slash:

'Mort, mort aux vaches!'

All of a sudden, the small street that was dimly lit, everywhere else, by sparse streetlights and, at the point that I had reached, vividly by the sign for some base-ment cabaret with a first-rate negro band, and while I was passing in front of a cinema that had closed its doors some hours before, I hear issuing from the cabaret the long-drawn-out, yearning notes of saxophones and a man's voice – which from its accent must belong to a negro singer – crooning:

> I'm just singing the blues of the world
> just singing a song
> just singing a song.

It was a marvellous voice – a little hoarse – a voice that issued from the soul of the universe. At once I stopped and listened, at the same time staring with astonishment at the placard outside the adjacent cinema.

The coloured advertising poster depicted a giant gorilla, much taller than the big trees that were shown surrounding it. In its left hand, the beast was holding, and looking tenderly upon, a small, tiny, terrified woman, who fitted easily into the span of its hand. Struck diagonally across the placard was the inscription, in red letters: 'Coming next week' and next to it, in the middle of the picture, in huge black letters on the upper half of the placard, had been printed the title of the film:

KING KONG

The nostalgic song continued. Finally applause and shouts were heard in the basement. Then, abruptly, like a tempest breaking out and in an instant swelling to its climax, there broke upon the night a burning music, vividly alive, hotter than the desert khamsin, with words that sounded like inarticulate cries mingled with the bellowing, the heavy breathing of wild beasts furiously in rut.

The negroes were now playing a dance tune, with drums, cymbals and rattles, a dance that could easily be heard outside in the street, a dance that swept every-thing before it, and brought to the place where I was standing the corybantic surge of deepest Africa, with fast throbbing pulses and frenetic, orgiastic leaping.

Then something incredible happened and continued for some time. From the outside world began to pour within me, like a great river, the almighty lord, he of the basement cabaret, he of the caves of Creation, ruler of absolute 'being', king of life's instincts; from the outside world began to pour within me, swelling, gushing and yelling, the full rhythm of the 'id'.

All at once, every trace of ennui, of melancholy within me was dispersed and I felt a boundless happiness, as though I were not a single individual, but a whole Edenic people. It was as though a great earthquake shook me to the foundations and all of a sudden it seemed to me that there, before me, the asphalt of the street burst open, and in my presence spouted forth, like a giant geyser, warm, from the depths of the earth, from the depths of creation, viscous and white, the spermatic fluid of the panting world.

The music, the song and the frenetic dance continued. The street, where I was standing, became with every moment endless, wide open, a temple filled with the sound *tam-tam*. All I remember is the pitch of the voices, the timbre and the fervour, with which the negroes vented their passion, a passion that made the entire surrounding space shake and tremble, like a place of mysteries, like a sacred place. But the sense and the tune of that song remained indelible in my memory, in the same way as, even when we no longer remember the words, the sense remains of the pronouncement of an oracle, or a special poem, or an initiation, especially when one or other of them encapsulates the flash of archangels' wings, or, like the clash of heavenly arms, the crash of thunderbolts.

Yes, the music, the song and the dance continued. The emotion that held me in its grip was such that, although I wanted to run to that cabaret and take part myself in the frenzy of the dancers, for a space I was incapable of movement. In my throat I felt a great lump, as though a sob were rising from my inmost being and I stood rooted to the spot, facing the entrance to the basement dive on the side of the cinema, staring in amazement at the giant gorilla of the placard, staring (O Kenya! Ruanda-Urundi! Uganda! Zululand!) staring at the black king.

Then something happened once again. From the entrance to the cinema and while the voices from the cabaret could still be heard, easily demolishing the building, as though in response to the voices of the negroes, like a great brother to them, or like a Messiah coming forth from the groves of Eden, with terrifying grunts burst forth the great gorilla ape, King Kong, with his sexual organ at the ready, quivering fully erect and twitching in the air, its crimson head indescribably pulsating.

The gorilla was fantastically large – like a seven-storey building. The head was a massive cliff; the legs the colossal trunks of baobab-trees and the hairy, broad chest a thick Sargasso sea. With his right hand, which every so often brushed the street, leaving only the negroes' cabaret untouched, he threw down or just lightly swept aside (but with the deafening crashes of wholesale destruction) stone, concrete and wooden beams, as though the time had come and Armageddon had broken out, and all the while (miracle of miracles) in his left hand, setting her free from the plot of the film and the bonds of daily servitude, in his fist he held a white, blonde woman of ravishing beauty, who was life-size, but appeared in the gigantic palm quite small, tiny, like a plaything of a woman, a toy for very small children. The teeth and face of the giant gorilla bore an expression of ferocity out of this world, but his eyes were full of tenderness and the great ape, emitting grunts highly charged with desire, took especial care, as he traversed the wreckage, not to let the tiny woman fall from his grasp and in falling break her ribs.

It was a staggering sight. No sooner did Kong appear than the few pedestrians in the street scattered in panic, emitting farts and exuding in great profusion the shit of their holy terror, here and there, far from the triumphant gorilla, and among them five whores, two pimps, various characters of the night and there even went, pedalling with all the strength of their legs, fleeing at top speed on their gleaming bicycles, their hearts in their mouths, went fleeing helter-skelter, paired even in flight, two *agents-cyclistes*.

But I stood my ground, shaken and vibrating like a chord stretched to the limit, with the certainty that at last a great good had come upon the world. The place of the boredom and ennui in my soul was taken by a great enthusiasm. A holy tremor shook me and my soul was in ecstasy. Finally, the lump in my throat dissolved and what had been on the way to becoming a sob became a howl of triumph, and, as I saw the black giant going forward, his footstep slow, hieratic on the macadam in front of me, as I watched the white woman in his fist, as I saw him go forward in triumph and desire, I shook all inertia from me and running after the passionately grunting king, as he receded at the far end of the street, and while from the basement dive came sounds and speech of the jungle, mingled with the sounds and speech of heaven (Tam-tam! . . . Hallel-u-jah! . . . Tam-tam! . . . Hallel-u-jah! . . . Gong-gong! . . .) I ran after the beast blazing like a forest, I ran after him with joy, crying out, shouting aloud with all the strength of my lungs, as though in my soul a great gong were beating, I ran after the gorilla, shouting at the top of my voice:

'Hail, Messiah (Hallel-u-jah! . . . Hallel-u-jah! . . .) Hail, Adam risen from the dead! (Tam-tam! . . . Tam-tam! . . .) Hail, Phallus and Navel of the Earth! (Tam-tam! . . . Gong-gong! . . .) Hail, O great genius of the Universe! Hail, O hail the deliverer – Hallel-u-jah! – King Kong!'

Glyfada, August 1964

Translated by Roderick Beaton

Odysseus Elytis (1911–1996)

Elytis (the pseudonym of Odysseus Alepoudelis) followed Seferis in winning the Nobel Prize for Literature in 1979. Some of his work has great delicacy and beauty, even if – like Palamas – he was not the best judge of what was his best work: *The Axion Esti* (1959), his *magnum opus*, gives a hieratic role for the poet that verges on blasphemy and which has browbeaten many readers into a respect for Elytis' poetry when some of his shorter, quieter pieces might have won them over. The following selection takes poems ranging from Elytis' first collection, *Orientations* (1939), to his penultimate book, *The Oxopetra Elegies* (1994). Elytis' range is wide. In *Heroic and Elegiac Song for the Lost Second Lieutenant of Albania*, first published in 1945 and unsurpassed by the poet in later years, Elytis, who had fought the Italians on the Albanian front in the heroic winter of 1940–1, commemorates an Everyman not unlike the narrator of Myrivilis' *Life in the Tomb* (whose Christian language Elytis' poem to some extent shares, q.v.), though behind the young male figure also lies the poet's dead companion, the poet George Sarantaris. In his late poems, Elytis becomes increasingly (and sometimes irritatingly) preoccupied with the poetic pantheon in which he seeks enshrinement. Note, for example, the title of 'With Light and Death', which comes from Andreas Kalvos' (q.v.) ode 'To Death', or the very late poem, 'Solomos: Submission and Awe', ·in which Elytis voices more openly than before his reverence for Solomos (q.v.), whose portrait, hand on heart in Masonic fashion, is evoked here.

Helen

Summer was killed with the first drop of rain
Words that had given birth to starlight were drenched
All those words whose single goal was You.
Where will we stretch our hands now the weather no longer takes us into
    account?
On what will we rest our eyes now the distant horizons have been shipwrecked
    by the clouds
Now your eyelashes have closed over our landscapes
And – as though the fog passed through us –
We are left alone, utterly alone, encircled by your dead images?

Forehead to windowpane we keep watch for the new sorrow
Death will not lay us low so long as You exist
So long as there exists a wind elsewhere to enjoy you fully

To clothe you from close by as our hope clothes you from far away
So long as there exists anywhere
A green plain reaching beyond your laughter to the sun
Telling the sun secretly how we will meet again
No, it isn't death we will confront
But the tiniest autumnal raindrop
An obscure feeling
The smell of wet earth in our souls that grow continually farther apart.

And if your hand is not in our hand
If our blood is not in the veins of your dreams,
The light in the immaculate sky
And the unseen music inside us
Still bind us, sad wayfarer, to the world
It is the damp wind, the autumnal hour, the separation,
The elbow's bitter prop on the memory
That awakens when night starts to cut us off from the light
Behind the square window facing toward grief
Revealing nothing
Because it has already become unseen music, flame in the fireplace, chime of
    the huge clock on the wall
Because it has already become
A poem, line succeeding line, sound keeping pace with the rain, tears and words –
Words not like others but these too with a single goal: You.

Form of Boeotia

Here where the lonely glance blows over stone and aloe
Here where time's steps sound deeply
Where huge clouds unfurl their golden banners
Above the sky's metope,
Tell me from what source eternity sprung
Tell me which is the sign you care for
And what is the helminth's fate

O land of Boeotia made shining by the wind

What became of the chorus of naked hands under the palaces
Of mercy that rose like sacred smoke
Where are the gateways with the ancient singing birds

And the uproar waking the people's terror
When the sun entered as though triumphant
When fate writhed on the heart's spear
And fratricidal twittering caught fire
What became of the deathless libations of March
Of the Greek lines in the waters of greenery

Foreheads and elbows have been wounded
Time, in an abundance of sky, has rolled vermilion
Men have forged ahead
Full of pain and dreaming

Acrid form! Ennobled by the wind
Of a summer storm that leaves its white-hot tracks
In the lines of hills and eagles
In the lines of destiny on your palm

What can you confront, what can you wear
Dressed in the music of grass, and how do you move on
Through the heather or sage
To the arrow's final point

On this red Boeotian soil
In the rocks' desolate march
You will light the golden sheaves of fire,
Uproot memory's evil fruitfulness,
Leave a bitter soul to the wild mint.

Translated by Edmund Keeley and Philip Sherrard

Heroic and Elegiac Song for the Lost Second Lieutenant of Albania (*extracts*)

I

There where the sun first made its home
Where Spring opened with the eyes of a girl
Just as the wind made snow of the almond blossom
And the cavalry charged over the crests of the grass

There where the vigorous plane-tree clapped its branches
And a signal rang out high over earth and water
Where the rifle sat so lightly on the shoulder
While the whole labour of the sky
The whole world shone like a dewdrop
In the morning at the foot of the mountain

Now, as if through God's sighing a shadow lengthens.

Now stooping agony with skinny hands
Touches and withers one by one the flowers upon her
In the famine of joy the songs
Lie in the ravines where water has collected;
Hermit crags with frozen hair
Silently cut the bread of desolation.

Winter goes to the brain. There is some evil
Smouldering. The mane of the mountain horse grows wild

High in the air the vultures divide the crumbs of heaven.

VII

The trees are of coal which the night does not kindle.
The wind runs wild beating its breast, the wind still beating its breast
Nothing happens. Forced to their knees the mountains roost
Beneath the frost. And roaring out of the ravines,
Out of the heads of the corpses rises the abyss . . .
Not even Sorrow weeps any longer. Like the mad orphan girl
She roams about, wearing on her breast a small cross of twigs
But does not weep. Surrounded only by pitch-black Acroceraunia
She climbs to the peak and sets the moon's disk there
Perhaps the planets will turn and see their shadows
And hide their rays
And stand poised
Breathless with amazement at the chaos . . .

The wind runs wild beating its breast, the wind still beating its breast
The wilderness is muffled in its black shawl
Crouching behind months of cloud it listens
What is there to listen for, so many cloud-months away?

With a tangle of hair on her shoulders – ah, leave her alone –
Half a candle half a flame a mother weeps – leave her alone –
In the empty frozen rooms where she roams leave her alone!
For fate is never a widow
And mothers are here to weep, husbands to fight
Orchards for the breasts of girls to blossom
Blood to be spent, waves to break into foam
And freedom to be born always in the lightning flash!

XIII

In the distance crystal bells are ringing –

They speak of him who was burnt by life
Like the bee in the fountain of wild thyme;
Of the dawn strangled between the breasts of the mountains
Just as it was announcing a radiant day;
Of the snowflake which flashed across the mind and was lost
When the whistle of the bullet was heard far away
And the Albanian partridge flew high in the air wailing!

They speak of him who had no time to weep
For the deep heartache of his love of life
Which he felt as the wind gathered strength in the distance
And the birds croaked on the mill's broken rafters
Of the women who absorbed the outlandish music
Standing at the window clutching their handkerchiefs
Of the women who disillusioned despair
Expecting a black speck at the edge of the plain
Then the thunder of hooves at the threshold
They speak of his warm, uncaressed head
Of his huge eyes brimming with life
So deep that it could no longer escape from them!

Translated by Paul Merchant

The Genesis (*extract from* The Axion Esti)

IN THE BEGINNING the light And the first hour
>> when lips still in clay
>> try out the things of the world

> Green blood and bulbs golden in the earth
> And the sea, so exquisite in her sleep, spread
> unbleached gauze of sky
> under the carob trees and the great upright palms
>> There alone I faced
>> the world
>> wailing loudly

My soul called out for a Signalman and Herald
>> I remember seeing then
>> the three Black Women

> raising their arms toward the East
> Their backs gilded, and the cloud they were leaving behind
> slowly fading
>> to the right And plants of other shapes

> It was the sun, its axis in me
> many-rayed, whole, that was calling And

the One I really was, the One of many centuries ago
the One still verdant in the midst of fire, the One still tied to heaven
>> I could feel coming to bend
>> over my cradle

And his voice, like memory become the present,
assumed the voice of the trees, of the waves:
>> 'Your commandment,' he said, 'is this

world
>> and it is written in your entrails
>> Read and strive
>> and fight' he said

'Each to his own weapons' he said
And he spread his hands as would
a young novice God creating pain and mirth together
> First the Seven Axes, wrenched with force,
> pried loose from high up in the battlements,
> fell to the ground
>> as in the great Storm
>> at its zero point
>> where a bird gives forth its fragrance

from the beginning again
the blood was homing clean
and the monsters were taking on a human shape
So very manifest, the Incomprehensible
Then all the winds of my family arrived too
the boys with puffed-out cheeks
and tails green and broad, mermaidlike
and others, old men: familiar, ancient
shell skinned, bearded
And they parted the cloud in two, and these again into four
and what little remained they blew away, chasing it off to the North
With broad foot and proudly, the great Tower trod the waters
The line of the horizon flashed
so visible, so dense and impenetrable
THIS the first hymn.

BUT BEFORE hearing the wind or music
as I was setting out to find a vista
(climbing a boundless red sand dune
erasing History with my heel)
I wrestled with my bed sheets What I was looking for was this,
innocent and tremulous like a vineyard
deep and unscarred like the sky's other face,
A drop of soul amidst the clay
Then he spoke and the sea was born
And I gazed upon it and marvelled
In its centre he sowed little worlds in my image and likeness:
Horses of stone with manes erect
and tranquil amphorae
and slanting backs of dolphins
Ios, Sikinos, Serifos, Milos
'Each word a swallow
to bring you spring in the midst of summer' he said
And ample the olive trees
to sift the light through their fingers
that it may spread gently over your sleep
and ample the cicadas
which you will feel no more
than you feel the pulse inside your wrist
but scarce the water

so that you hold it a God and understand the meaning of its voice
    and the tree alone
        no flock beneath it
        so that you take it for a friend
        and know its precious name
    sparse the earth beneath your feet
        so that you have no room to spread your roots
        and keep reaching down in depth
    and broad the sky above
        so that you read the infinite on your own

THIS WORLD
this small world the great!

Translated Edmund Keeley and George Savidis

The Monogram

I

Destiny will shift the lines in your palm
like a switchman at the tracks,
and time, briefly, will consent.

How else, since we love each other.

The sky will perform our passions
and innocence will lash the world
with the sharpness of death's black.

II

I mourn the sun and the years
that arrive without us, and I sing
of the years that have passed, if they are true.

Bodies in concord and boats that sweetly collide,
the guitar that strums under water,
the 'believe me' and 'don't',
one in the wind, one in the music.

These two small creatures, our hands,
that yearn to mount secretly, one on the other,
the pot of basil in the open courtyard,
patches of sea that came together
above the dry stone wall, beyond the hedges,
the windflower that perched on your hand
and quivered its mauve three times, three days above the waterfall.

If these are true, I'll sing
of the wooden beam and the square cloth on the wall,
of the mermaid with the loose flowing hair,
of the cat that glared at us in the darkness.

The boy with frankincense and a crimson cross,
the hour when night falls over the distant rocks,
I mourn the dress I touched and all the world came to me.

III

In this way I speak of you and of me.
Because I love you and in love I know
always to approach like the full moon
toward your tiny feet under the endless covers.
I know to pluck the jasmine
and to take you asleep and show you
moondrenched paths and the sea's hidden caves
and enchanted trees, silvered by spiders.

The waves know you,
how you caress, how you kiss,
how you whisper your 'what' and your 'oh?'
around the neck of the bay,
we are forever the light and the shadow.

You ever the little star and I ever the dark ship,
you ever the harbour and I the strong-side lantern,
the damp sea wall and the glimmer above the oars,
high up in the house, the climbing vine,
the bound roses and the water growing cold,
you the marble statue and I its lengthening shadow,
you the tilting shutter, I the air that forces it open,

because I love you and I love you,
you ever the coin and I the worship that cashes it in:

So much is night, the cry in the wind,
so much the dewdrop in the air, the stillness,
the tyrannous sea all round,
the starry vaults of sky,
so much your last breath

that I have nothing to call
in these four walls, the ceiling, the floor,
but you, and my voice strikes me,
I catch your scent and men begin to rage
because mankind cannot stand the untested
or the foreign, and it's early, do you hear me,
it's still early in this world my love

It's early to speak to you and of me.

IV

It is still early in this world, do you hear me
the terrors have not yet been tamed, do you hear me
my blood astray, the jagged knife,
do you hear
it runs like a ram in the heavens
and snaps the branches of the stars, do you hear
It is I, do you hear me
I love you, do you hear me
I hold you and take you and dress you
in Ophelia's bridal gown, do you hear me
where are you leaving me, where are you going, and who is it, do you hear

who is holding your hand above the flood?

The day will come, do you hear me
when gigantic trees and the volcano's waves
will bury us, and years later, do you hear
will turn us into gleaming fossils,
do you hear
so that man's cruelty may glitter above them, do you hear

and scatter us in a thousand shards, do you hear me

In the water, one by one, do you hear me
I count my bitter stones, do you hear
and time is a great cathedral, do you hear
where the eyes
of the saints, do you hear
flow with real tears, do you hear
and the bells high up, do you hear
open a steep way for me to pass
and the angels await me with candles and hymns
but I'll not go alone, do you hear
neither one goes, or both of us together, do you hear me

This flower from the storm and, do you hear
from love,
we have plucked once for all time, do you hear
and never may it blossom again, do you hear
in another land, another star, do you hear me
the land, the air, they don't exist
once we've touched, do you hear me

And no gardener was ever so lucky before.

After such a winter and so much wind, do you hear me
to make one flower bloom, just us, do you hear
in the middle of the sea,
out of love's yearning alone, do you hear
have we raised an entire island, do you hear
with grottoes and headlands and flowering crags,
listen, listen,
who speaks with the water, who cries out, do you hear
who seeks the other, who shouts, do you hear
It is I am talking, it is I am weeping, do you hear me
I love you, I love you, do you hear me

V

Of you I spoke in ancient days
with wise nurses and veteran rebels
about how you found that feral grief,

the brightness of your face like trembling water,
and why I'm bound to approach you,
I who want not love, but wind,
the bareback bounding gallop of the sea.

No one had heard of you,
not the dittany, not the mushroom
on the high mountains of Crete, nothing –
God chose to guide my shaping hand for you alone.

Here and there, around every inch
of the shore of your face, around the bays and the hair
streaming out to the hill's left

Your body in the pose of the solitary pine,
eyes rich with pride and the transparent deep,
and in the house with the ancient wardrobe,
its yellow lace and cypress wood,
alone I await your epiphany,
high up in the house or by the courtyard tiles,
with the horse of St George and the Easter egg

like a crumbling fresco,
as large as little life wanted you,
you fit the volcano's stentorian blaze inside the candle's flame.

For you, whom no one's seen or heard
in the ruined houses of the wilderness,
not the ancestor buried by the courtyard's far wall,
not the old witch with her magic herbs

for you, perhaps, just me, and the music
I chase away returns louder,
for you the unformed breast of a twelve-year-old girl,
eyeing the future with its crimson crater,
the bitter perfume, like a pin,
pierces the body and pricks the memory
and here the soil, the pigeons, our ancient earth.

VI

I've seen so much, and in my eyes the earth seems more beautiful,
more beautiful than the golden mists
the jagged stones more beautiful,
the deep blue of the Isthmus and the waves' frothy crown,
the sun's rays through which you pass without walking,
invincible over the sea's mountains, like the Lady of Samothrace

I've seen you so that it's enough
that all time be found innocent
in the wake you leave behind;
like a virgin dolphin following

playing in the white and blue my soul

victory, victory by which I am conquered
before love and now with love, go,
seek the passion flower and the mimosa,
go, though I'm lost,

alone, though the sun you hold is a newborn child,
though I am the homeland that laments,
though the word I sent holds a bay leaf to you,
alone the strong wind, alone the rounded
pebble in the winking eye of the sea's dark,
the fisherman hooked into paradise and cast it back again at time.

VII

I've seen an island in paradise,
your twin, and a house in the sea

with a great bed and a tiny door;
I cast an echo into the sea's depths
to see myself each morning as I rise,

half to watch you passing into the water,
and half to weep for you in paradise.

Translated by Avi Sharon

The Fresco

Having loved and lived for centuries within the sea I learned to read and write

So that now I can see   backwards to a great depth   the generations one above the other   much as one mountain rises up before the other's finished

And the same again in front:

The dark bottle   with the new Helen on the arm   her side against the quicklime

Pouring the Holy Virgin's wine   half her body already fled to Asia across the water

And the entire embroidery   displaced in the sky   with the swallow-tailed birds the yellow flowers   and the suns.

Death and Resurrection of Constantine Palaiologos

I

As he stood there   erect before the Gate and armoured in his sorrow

Far from the world which his soul strove to reckon by the span of Paradise   And much harder than stone for he'd never been looked at tenderly – sometimes his crooked teeth gleamed strangely white

And he passed with eyes focused a little above people's stature   and picked out One of them   who smiled at him   the True One   whom death could never touch

He was careful to pronounce the word *sea* so that all the dolphins within it gleamed   And the wilderness vast enough for God   and each and every drop rising steadily to the sun

As a child he had seen the gold braid on adult shoulders blaze and vanish   And one night   he remembers how during a great storm the ocean's maw groaned and it clouded   and yet did not consent to wait

To live this life is hard, yet worth it for a little pride.

II

What now my God   Now that he had to strive with thousands as well as his
own loneliness   he   he who with just one word could slake the whole world's
thirst

What if they'd taken all from him   His cross-gartered sandals and his sharp
trident and the castle wall which he bestrode each day holding the reins against
the wind like a fractious and playful sailboat

And a sprig of verbena   rubbed on a girl's cheek   at midnight   to kiss her
(how the moon's waters rippled over the stone steps three flights above the
sea . . .)

Noontide of night   And not a soul alongside him   Only his faithful words
running their colours all together to place a spear of white light in his hand

And opposite   along the whole length of the walls   heads set like ants in plaster as far as the eye could see

'Noontide of night – life's but a flash!'   he cried and rushed into the fray   dragging an endless golden line behind him

And felt at once   from a great distance   the deadly pallor taking him.

III

Now   as the sun's shuttlecock spun ever faster   the courts dipped into winter
and emerged again dyed red by the geraniums

And the little cool domes like blue medusas reached ever higher each time
towards the silver which the wind filigraned for the depiction of other times
more distant

Maidens their embrace lighting a summer daybreak   brought him fresh laurel
leaves and from the deeps myrtle branches still dripping iodine

While underneath his feet he heard   engulfed in the great sewer   prows of
black ships   the ancient blackened wood   from whence   wild-eyed Virgins
still standing called reproachfully

Horses sprawled upon the earth banks   the ruined buildings great and small
turmoil and dust swirling in the air

With one unyielding word always between his teeth   fallen

                            He
                  last of the Greeks!

Translated by John Stathatos

The Little Mariner (*extracts*)

With Light and Death

16

Where shall I speak it, night, in the wind
Among the loquat stars, in the blackness reeking
Of sea, where speak the Greek of bitterness
In capital trees, where write it so
The wise will know to decipher
Between the second and the third wave
Such heavy burning mood of stones that didn't sink
You, St Salvador, who dress in storms
Raise the sea's eye and let me travel
Miles in its green transparence
To where the masons excavate the sky
And find again that moment before birth
When violets filled the air and I knew not
That thunder knows nothing of its flash
But strikes you thrice – all light!

17

As in the sky in spring
Grey-green you appeared
Winnowing a rain of myriad rays
And walking toward a slippery slope
Of stars with a flask of sleep you
Evaporated having trampled

The idle-tongued.
he mountains were veiled by armies
Of crystalline frankincense
And not to be outdone night's
Poppies bloomed until
Thousand-winged
Words from your lips
Restored now wholly
The once grasped dreams
Of mariners.
Like a goatherd's solitary lantern you
Lit our soul in the abyss, Kore.

Translated by Olga Broumas

Solomos: Submission and Awe

The town half-emerging from sleep. Belfry spires
Flag poles and some first rosy hues
On the marble sill of your tiny – still lighted – window
                              Ah that there I might
Leave you a branch with laurel berries to bid you good morning
After your night of sleeplessness. For I can see it
On white paper more treacherous even than Missolonghi's
    stone slabs

Yes. Because he once had need of you God gilded your lips

And how mysterious to speak and your cupped palms to open
So too the stone to long to be the new church's quoin
And the coral to sprout sleek clusters to imitate your breast
Fair face! Bronzed in the glare of the tongue you first heard
    and inexplicably now
Become a second soul inside me. While the first
In a violet-blue land with tempests' wild manes
Engaged in shining shells and other finds of sun
As though your mind's casts had not forged already
A nature passed through all the flashes of the Gods' fury
Or within me for a while because of you
The Unviewable had not remained half-visible!

But the lion passes like a sun. Men go on horseback
And others on foot; till they vanish in the nights. Like

The things I sought to save hunched over my desk but
In vain. What else. When your thought alone long ago become sky
Your thought alone consumed all my writings
And the delight that my second soul
Took in killing the first went away with the waves
Unknown as I was again unknown to become
Dreadfully the winds reproaching
While on the scrubbed floor where I lay writhing
The sun's spear
                  finished me.

Translated by David Connolly

Nikos Engonopoulos (1908–1987)

Like his fellow Surrealist Andreas Embiricos (q.v.), Engonopoulos outraged literary opinion with his first book, *No Talking to the Driver* (1938). But, though his career as poet and painter was a long one, he owes his prominence above all to the long poem *Bolivar*, which he read to Resistance gatherings during the Occupation and which was published in 1945. It is a very different work from Elytis' *Heroic and Elegiac Song* (q.v.): Engonopoulos deliberately refracts his material through the South American continent (Bolivar's revolution was, like the Greek one, in 1821) and chooses as the exemplar of Greek heroism not a pure, Christ-like figure but the controversial Odysseus Androutsos (on whom Makriyannis, q.v., had expressed himself in no kindly terms). The poem is an odd one, which calls out for annotation – and the poet did give a hostage to fortune by providing some – but it is best to swallow it whole to begin with.

Bolivar
A Greek Poem

> ΦΑΣΜΑ ΘΗΣΕΩΣ ΕΝ ΟΠΛΟΙΣ ΚΑΘΟΡΑΝ, ΠΡΟ
> ΑΥΤΩΝ ΕΠΙ ΤΟΥΣ ΒΑΡΒΑΡΟΥΣ ΦΕΡΟΜΕΝΟΝ

> Le cuer d'un home vaut tout l'or d'un païs

For the great, for the free, for the brave, the strong,
The fitting words are great and free and brave and strong,
For them, the total subjection of every element, silence, for them tears, for
    them beacons, and olive branches, and the lanterns
That bob up and down with the swaying of the ships and scrawl on the
    harbours' dark horizons,
For them are the empty barrels piled up in the narrowest lane, again of the
    harbour,
For them the coils of white rope, the chains, the anchors, the other manometers,
Amidst the irritating smell of petroleum,
That they might fit out a ship, put to sea and depart,
Like a tram setting off, empty and ablaze with light, in the nocturnal serenity
    of the gardens,
With one purpose behind the voyage: *ad astra*.

For them I'll speak fine words, dictated to me by Inspiration's Muse.

As she nestled deep in my mind full of emotion
For the figures, austere and magnificent, of Odysseus Androutsos and Simon
    Bolivar.
But for now I'll sing only of Simon, leaving the other for an appropriate time,
Leaving him that I might dedicate, when the time comes, perhaps the finest
    song that I've ever sung,
Perhaps the finest song that's ever been sung in the whole world.
And this not for what they both were for their countries, their nations, their
    people, and other such like that fail to inspire,
But because they remained throughout the ages, both of them, alone always,
    and free, great, brave and strong.

And shall I now despair that to this very day no one has understood, has
    wanted, has been able to understand what I say?
Shall the fate then be the same for what I say now of Bolivar, that I'll say
    tomorrow of Androutsos?
Besides, it's no easy thing for figures of the importance of Androutsos and
    Bolivar to be so quickly understood,
Symbols of a like.
But let's move on quickly: for Heaven's sake, no emotion, exaggeration or
    despair,
Of no concern, my voice was destined for the ages alone.
(In the future, the near, the distant, in years to come, a few, many, perhaps
    from the day after tomorrow or the day after that,
Until the time that, empty and useless and dead, the Earth begins to drift in
    the firmament,
The young, with mathematical precision, will awake in their beds on wild
    nights,
Moistening their pillows with tears, wondering at who I was, reflecting
That once I existed, what words I said, what songs I sang.
And the gigantic waves that every evening break on Hydra's seven shores,
And the savage rocks, and the high mountain that brings down the blizzards,
    will eternally and untiringly thunder my name.)
But let's get back to Simon Bolivar.

Bolivar! A name of metal and wood, you were a flower in the gardens of
    South America.
You had all the gentleness of flowers in your heart, in your hair, in your gaze.
Your hand was huge like your heart, and scattered both good and evil.
You swept through the mountains and the stars trembled, you came down to
    the plains, with your gold finery, your epaulettes, all the insignia of your rank,

With a rifle hanging on your shoulder, with chest bared, with your body
    covered in wounds,
And stark naked you sat on a low rock, at the sea's edge,
And they came and painted you in the ways of Indian braves,
With wash, half white, half blue, so you'd appear like a lonely chapel on one
    of Attica's shores,
Like a church in the districts of Tatavla, like a palace in a deserted
    Macedonian town.

Bolivar! You were reality, and you are, even now, you are no dream.
When the wild hunters nail down the wild eagles, and the other wild birds
    and animals
Go from their wooden doors into the wild forests,
You live again, and shout, and grieve,
And you are yourself the hammer, nail and eagle.

If on the isles of coral, winds blow and the empty fishing boats overturn,
And the parrots are a riot of voices when the day ends and the gardens grow
    quiet drowned in humidity,
And in the tall trees the crows perch,
Consider, beside the waves, the iron tables of the cafeneion,
How the damp eats at them in the gloom, and far off the light that flashes on,
    off, on again, turning back and forth.
And day breaks – what frightful anguish – after a night without sleep,
And the water reveals nothing of its secrets. Such is life.
And the sun comes, and the houses on the wharf, with their island-style arches,
Painted pink and green, with white sills (Naxos, Chios),
How they live! How they shine like translucent fairies! Such is **Bolivar!**

Bolivar! I cry out your name, reclining on the peak of Mount Ere,
The highest peak on the isle of Hydra.
From here the view, enchanting, extends as far as the Saronic isles, Thebes,
Beyond, Monemvasia, far below, to august Egypt,
And as far as Panama, Guatemala, Nicaragua, Honduras, Haiti, San Domingo,
    Bolivia, Colombia, Peru, Venezuela, Chile, Argentina, Brazil, Uruguay,
    Paraguay, Ecuador,
As far even as Mexico.
With hard stone I carve your name in rock, that afterwards men may come in
    pilgrimage.
As I carve sparks fly – such, they say, was Bolivar – and I watch my hand as it
    writes, gleaming in the sun.

You saw the light for the first time in Caracas. Your light,
Bolivar, for before you came the whole of South America was plunged in
  bitter darkness.
Now your name is a blazing torch, lighting America, North and South, and
  all the world!
The Amazon and Orinoco Rivers spring from your eyes.
The high mountains are rooted in your breast,
The Andes range is your backbone.
On the crown of your head, brave palikar, run unbroken stallions and wild cattle,
The wealth of Argentina.
On your belly sprawl vast coffee plantations.

When you speak, terrible earthquakes spread devastation,
From Patagonia's formidable deserts as far as the colourful islands,
Volcanoes erupt in Peru and vomit their wrath in the heavens,
Everywhere the earth trembles and the icons creak in Kastoria,
The silent town beside the lake.
Bolivar, you have the beauty of a Greek.

I first encountered you, as a child, in one of Phanar's steep cobbled streets,
A lighted lamp in Mouchlio illumined your noble face.
Are you, I wonder, one of the myriad forms assumed, and successively
  discarded by Constantine Palaeologus?

Boyaca, Ayacucho. Ideas both illustrious and eternal. I was there.
We'd already left the old frontiers far behind:
Back in the distance, fires were burning in Leskovik.
And in the night, the army moved up towards the battle, its familiar sounds
  could already be heard.
Opposite, a grim Convoy of endless trucks returned with the wounded.

Don't anyone be alarmed. Down there, see, the lake.
This is the way they'll come, beyond the rushes.
The roads have been mined: the work and repute of that Hormovitis man,
  renowned, unrivalled in such matters. Everyone to their stations. The
  whistle's sounding!
Come on, come on. Get the cannons uncoupled and set up, clean the barrels
  with the swabs, fuses lit and held ready,
Cannon-balls to the right. Vrass!
Vrass, Albanian for fire: **Bolivar!**
Every pineapple that was hurled and exploded,

Was a rose to the glory of the great general,
As he stood, stern and unshaken, amid the dust and tumult,
Gazing on high, his forehead in the clouds,
And the sight of him caused dread: fount of awe, path of justice, gate of salvation.

Yet, how many conspired against you, **Bolivar**,
How many traps did they not set for you to fall into and vanish,
One man, above all, a rogue, a snake, a native of Philippoupolis.
But what was that to you, like a tower you stood firm, upright, before
    Acongagua's terror,
Holding a mighty cudgel and wielding it above your head.
The bald-headed condors, unafraid of the carnage and smoke of battle, took
    fright and flew up in terrified flocks,
And the llamas hurled themselves down the mountain slopes, dragging as
    they fell, a cloud of earth and rocks.
And into the dark of Tartarus your enemies disappeared, lay low.
(When the marble arrives, the best from Alabanda, I'll sprinkle my brow with
    Blachernae's holy water,
I'll use all my craft to hew your stance, to erect the statue of a new Kouros in
    Sikyon's mountains,
Not forgetting, of course, to engrave on its base that famous 'Hail, passer-by.')

And here it should above all be stressed that Bolivar was never afraid, never,
    as they say, 'lost his nerve',
Not even at the most murderous hour of battle, nor in the bitter gloom of
    unavoidable treachery.
They say he knew beforehand, with unimaginable precision, the day, the
    hour, even the second: the moment,
Of the Great Battle that was for him alone,
In which he himself would be army and enemy, both vanquished and victor,
    triumphant hero and sacrificial victim.
(And the lofty spirit of such as Cyril Loukaris reared within him,
How he calmly eluded the despicable plots of the Jesuits and that wretched
    man from Philippoupolis!)

And if he was lost, if ever lost is such a one as Bolivar! who like Apollonius
    vanished into the heavens,
Resplendent like the sun he disappeared, in unimaginable glory, behind the
    gentle mountains of Attica and the Morea.

invocation

Bolivar! You are a son of Rigas Ferraios,
Of Antonios Economou – so unjustly slain – and brother to Pasvantzoglou,
The dream of the great Maximilien de Robespierre lives again on your brow,
You are the liberator of South America.
I don't know how you were related, if one of your descendants was that
other great American, the one from Montevideo,
One thing alone is sure, that I am your son.

CHORUS

strophe

(entrée des guitares)

If the night, slow in passing,
Sends moons of old to console us,
If in the wide plain phantom shades
Burden flowing-haired maidens with chains,
The hour of victory, of triumph has come.
On hollow skeletons of field marshal generals
Cocked hats soaked in blood will be placed,
And the red that was theirs before the sacrifice
Will cover with rays the flag's lustre.

antistrophe

(the love of liberty brought us here)

the ploughs at the palmtrees' roots
and the sun
that rises resplendent
amid trophies
and birds
and spears
will announce as far as a tear rolls
carried by the breeze to
the sea's
depths
the most terrible oath

the more terrible darkness
the terrible tale:

Libertad

epode

(freemasons' dance)

Away with you curses, come near us no more, corazón,
From the cradle to the stars, from the womb to the eyes, corazón,
Where precipitous rocks, where volcanoes and seals, corazón,
Where swarthy faces, thick lips and gleaming white teeth, corazón,
Let the phallus be raised, the revels begin, with human sacrifice, dance, corazón,
In a carnival of flesh, to our ancestors' glory, corazón,
That the seed of the new generation be sown, corazón.

CONCLUSION

Following the success of the South American revolution, a bronze statue
of Bolivar was erected in Nauplion and Monemvasia, on a deserted hill
overlooking the town. However, the fierce wind that blew at night caused
the hero's frock-coat to flap furiously, creating a noise so great, so deafening,
that it was impossible for anyone to get a moment's rest, sleep was now out
of the question. So the inhabitants complained, and through the appropriate
steps, succeeded in having the monument torn down.

SONG OF FAREWELL TO BOLIVAR

(Here distant music is heard playing, with incomparable melancholy, popular
nostalgic songs and dances from South America, preferably in sardane time.)

general
what were you doing in Larissa
you
from
Hydra?

Translated by David Connolly

Yannis Ritsos (1909–1990)

In the politically polarized world of post-war Greece, Ritsos, a winner of the Lenin Prize, was sometimes regarded as the Seferis of the Left – and the poems 'Non-Hero' and 'Trivial Details' (1965, q.v.), contain swipes at the recent en-Nobelled poet. Ritsos' gigantic *œuvre* contains, it is true, much orthodox Stalinist material. But Ritsos was always a bigger poet than that, and his poem *Romiosini* (written 1945–7, published 1954) is one indication that, however bound up Ritsos was with the century's misfortunes and crimes, he always maintained a vision of Greekness as a big tent. After this poem Ritsos continued to work on a large canvas much of the time, but he also cultivated the short poem, a move which a long-overdue reassessment of Cavafy for the latter's centenary had helped to bring about. In the bulk of material, there is much chaff – Ritsos seems to have been reluctant to employ the waste-paper basket – but also many understated gems. 'Penelope's Despair', for example, is deservedly celebrated and may fruitfully be read in conjunction with Wallace Stevens' 'The World as Meditation' (1954). As with many of Ritsos' poems of this type, the date at the foot of the poem is a reminder of the menacing presence of the Colonels' Junta and its tawdry myth-making. Ritsos was still producing some of his best work in his last and posthumous collection, *Late into the Night* (1990). The present selection can only scratch the surface of Ritsos' work, but this fine poet is generously represented in English elsewhere.

Romiosini

I

These trees are not content under any less sky,
these stones are not content under any stranger's step,
these faces are not content without their sun,
these hearts are not content without justice.

Here the land is hard, like silence,
it hugs the scorched boulders to itself,
clutches in the light its orphaned olive-trees, its vines,
grinds its teeth. There's no water. Only sunlight.
The path loses itself in the sunlight and the shade from the sheepfold is iron.

The trees, the rivers and the voices turn to stone in the whitewash of the sun.
The root collides with the marble. The dust-covered cord.

The mule and the rock. They're painting. There's no water.
Everyone thirsts. For years now everyone chews on a mouthful of sky to
    chase the bitterness.

Their eyes are red now from the watch;
a deep grove is wedged between their brows,
like a cypress between two hills at sunset.

Their hands are welded to their rifles,
their rifles have become part of their arms,
their arms have become part of their souls –
they have anger on their lips,
and a yearning, deep down in their eyes,
like a star in a pit of salt.

When they clasp hands the sun comes up cocksure of the world,
when they smile a tiny swallow flies from their bristled beards,
when they sleep twelve stars tumble from their empty pockets,
when they are killed life tramps uphill with drums and banners.

So many years everyone hungers, everyone thirsts, everyone is killed,
besieged by land and sea;
drought gnawed their fields, brine drenched their homes,
wind lashed their doors and the few lilacs still left in the square,
death comes and goes through the holes in their coats.
Their tongues are as acrid as cypress cones.
Their dogs have died, curled up in their shadows,
the rain drums down on their bones.

Turned to stone, high in their outposts,
they smoke horse dung, they smoke the night,
they scan the reeling sea,
where the broken mast of the moon has sunk.

Out of bread, out of bullets,
they load their guns with their hearts only.

So many years, besieged by land and sea.
Everyone hungers, everyone is killed, but not one died –
Their eyes flash out from their posts,
a great flag, a great fire, deep red,

and every dawn a thousand doves soar out of their palms toward the four
   doors of the horizon.

II

In the evenings when the thyme sizzles in the stone's embrace,
a drop of water burrows down into the silence, to the marrow,
and a bell dangling from the old plane tree cries out the years.

Sparks drowse in the embers of the desert
and rooftops ponder the golden down on July's upper lip –
yellow fur, like the plume on the corncob,
smoked in the longing of sunset.

The Virgin lay among the myrtle with her wide skirts stained from the grapes,
in the street a child cries out and from the fields the ewe who lost her lamb replies.

There is shade by the spring. Frost on the barrel.
The blacksmith's daughter, her soaking feet.
Bread and olives on the table,
the light of the evening star woven into the climbing vine,
and high above, revolving on its spit, the galaxy,
fragrant with garlic, pepper and burnt fat.

What silken thread of stars is needed for the pine-needles to embroider 'this
   too shall pass' over the charred sheepfold of summer?
How long still must the mother wring her heart for her seven slaughtered
   sons before the light can find its way up the steep slope of her soul?

This bone rising from the earth measures out the land,
step by step, and the echoes from the lute,
the lute and the violin, from sundown to sunup,
they speak their yearning to the rosemary and the pines,
and the rigging on the schooner quivers like a lyre's strings,
and the sailor drinks the bitter sea in the wine-cup of Odysseus.

Oh, who will barricade the pass, and what sword will slice through courage,
and what key will lock fast your heart when its two doors open wide,
and it gazes up at the starry orchard of God.
The hour is huge like Saturday nights in May by the sailor's tavern,
the night is huge like an oven-dish on the blacksmith's wall,

the song is huge like the bread on a sponge-diver's table.
And there the Cretan moon ranges over the rooftiles,
clack, clack, with twenty rows of cleats in its high boots.
There the men climb up and down the steps of Nafplion,
stuffing their pipes with thick-cut leaves of darkness,
their thick moustaches, like the star-splashed thyme of Roumeli,
and their teeth, sunk deep as pine-root in the rock and salt of the Aegean.

They have passed through fire and steel, they have conversed with stones,
they have toasted death with raki served in their grandfathers' skulls,
they have danced on the same threshing-floors with Digenis
and sat themselves down to feast there,
breaking their sorrow in two, the way they break their barley loaves across
    their knees.

Come, lady, with your eyelashes flaked with sea-salt
and your hand bronzed by a beggar's cares and the many years –
love waits for you among the rigging,
the seagull hangs for your blackened icon in his cavern,
and the bitter sea urchin sweetly kisses your toenail.

In the black nipple of the grape the must boils deep red,
the holly shoot seethes on the burnt-out ilex,
the dead man's root seeks water underground to hurl the fir tree,
and the mother clutches tight the blade in her furrowed brow.

Come, lady, you who hatch the thunder's golden eggs –
On a sea-blue day you will toss your scarf and take up arms again,
and the hail in May will fall upon your brow,
and the sun will break open like a pomegranate in the lap of your apron,
and you will share it out, seed by seed, to your twelve orphans,
and the sea will shimmer round like the blade of a sword, or the snow in April,
and the crab will emerge on to the shingle to sun himself and cross his claws.

III

Here the sky will never thin our eyes' essential oil,
here the sun shoulders half the weight of the stones on our backs,
and without a moan the rooftops splinter on the knee of the midday sun.
The men advance before their shadows, like dolphins before the caiques of
    Skiathos;

later their shadows turn into eagles, tinting their wings in the sunset,
and then, perching on the men's skulls, they contemplate the stars,
while the men recline on the veranda beside the blackened raisins.

Here each door is graven with a name over three thousand years old,
a holy man is etched on every stone, he has wild eyes and rope for hair,
on every man's arm is sewn, stitch by stitch, a scarlet mermaid,
each girl claims a handful of salted light beneath her skirt,
while the children have five or six bitter crosses on their hearts,
like the tracks of seagulls in the evening sand.

No need to recall it. This we know.
Every path leads to the Upper Threshing Floors.
There the air is sharper.

When the Minoan fresco of the setting sun unravels in the distance,
and the blaze on the haystack by the sea is quenched,
the old women clamber up the rockcut steps
and gather round the Great Stone, spinning the sea with their eyes.
They sit and count the stars as though they were counting their family silver,
then, late in the day, they descend to feed their brood on gunpowder from
    Messolongi.

The Bound One in the icon has two sorrowful hands pinioned in the ropes,
but the brow above his bitter gaze stirs like a boulder verging on a fall.
From the swelling depths surges the wave that heals no appeal,
from high above the wind streams down with vein of resin and breath of sage,

Ach, let it blow once to sweep clean the orange trees of memory,
let it blow twice to choke out a spark from the iron rock like a percussion cap,
let it blow three times to madden the cedar woods of Liakoura and pummel
    tyranny to the ground,
and to tug on the bear's star-notched collar until she dances us a tsamiko on
    the ramparts,
and to thump on the tambourine moon until the island balconies swell with
    raw awakened kids and Souliot mothers.

A messenger arrives from the Great Valley each morning,
the sweating sun glistens on his face;
Under his arms he hugs Romiosini tightly to himself,
the way a labourer holds his cap in church.

'The time has come,' he says. 'Be ready,
every moment is ours.'

IV

They marched through the dawn with a hungry man's disdain,
a star seeded in their steady eyes,
they hauled the wounded summer on their shoulders.

Right here the army passed, the banners clinging to their flesh,
the men grinding their stubbornness in their teeth, like a sour pear,
the moon sand slogging in their thick boots,
the night's coal dust pasted in their ears and nostrils.

Tree after tree, stone after stone they crossed the earth,
and passed some sleep on a pillow of briars;
they lugged their life between their two parched hands, like a river.

With every step they won a fathom of sky – in order to give it away.
They turned to stone at their outposts, like burnt trees,
and when they danced in the square, the ceilings shook
and the glass-ware clattered on the shelves.

Ah, what a song rocked the mountain-tops –
They held the platter of the moon between their knees and dined
and crushed the 'Ach' in their hearts,
like a tick between their coarse fingernails.

Now who will bring you the warm loaf at night to feed your dreams?
Who will loiter among the cicadas in the olive's shade lest the cicada fall silent?
Who, now that the whitewash of the midday sun glazes the wall of the horizon,
erasing their grand heroic names?

This earth that smelled so sweet at dawn,
this earth that was theirs and ours –
their blood – the earth – so fragrant –
And how is it that our vines have suddenly bolted shut their doors?
How diminished is the light on the rooftops, on the trees –
Who could bear to tell it,
how half of them are beneath the earth
and the other half in chains?

The sun nods 'good morning' with so many leaves,
the sky shimmers with so many banners,
while half are in chains and half beneath the earth.

Keep quiet. The bells could toll at any moment.
This earth is theirs and ours.
Beneath the earth, in their crossed hands,
they hold the bell-rope – they wait for the hour,
sleepless, deathless,
they wait to ring in the resurrection. This earth
is theirs and ours – no one can take it from us.

V

They sat beneath the olive trees round noon,
sifting the ashen light with their thick fingers.
They undid their packs and gauged how much toil
was crammed into the night's march,
how much bitterness in the knot of wild marrow,
how much courage in the eyes of the barefoot youth who held the flag.

The last swallow lingered in the field,
yoked to the wind like a black ribbon on the sleeve of autumn.
Nothing else remained, just the gutted homes, smouldering still.

The others under the stones left us long ago
with their tattered shirts and their oaths carved on the fallen door.
No one cried. We had no time. The quiet just spread,
and the light along the beach was as tidy as the slain girl's kitchen.

What will happen to them now when the rain seeps through the earth with
    the rotten leaves of the plane-tree?
What will happen when the sun dries out on its blanket of cloud, like a
    crushed bug on a peasant's bed?
When the snow, like an embalmed stork, perches on the evening's chimney?

The old women cast salt into the fire, dirt in their hair.
They've uprooted the vines of Monemvasia lest even a single black grape
    sweeten the enemy's mouth.
They stuff their grandfather's bones in a sack along with the family silver and
wander outside the walls of their homeland,

looking for a place to take root in the night.

It will be difficult now to find a more cherry-blossom tongue,
less loud, less stony –
those hands that were left in the fields
or up on the mountains or under the sea,
they do not forget, they will never forget –
It will be hard for us to forget their hands,
it will be hard for hands that grew callused on a trigger
to ask love of a daisy,
to say 'thanks' resting on their knees, on a book,
or on the lap of starlight.

It will take time and we must speak
until they find their bread and vindication.

Two oars fixed in the sand at dawn, a storm brewing – where's the boat?

A plough sunk in the earth and the wind blowing hard.
The charred earth. Where's the ploughman?

The olive, the vine and the house, all ashes.
Miserly night, hoarding her stars in a sock.
Dried oregano and laurel in the cupboard on the wall.
The fire didn't reach them.

A blackened kettle on the hearth – the water boiling
all alone in the bolted house. There was no time to eat.

The forest's veins upon their singed doorposts –
blood flows in the veins.
And the step is known. Who is it?
The familiar hobnailed step on the hill.
The edging of the root through stone. Someone comes.
The password, the response. Brother. Good evening.

So the light will find its trees, and the tree will find its fruit.
The dead man's canteen still has water and light.
Good evening my brother. Good evening.

The old woman from the west sells thread and spice by her wooden shack.

No one buys. They have risen too high.
Hard now for them to descend.
Hard for them to account for their stature.

On the threshing floor where one night the young men dined,
there are olive pits and the moon's dried blood
and the fifteen-syllable folk song echoing from their guns.
All around the cypress and the laurel groves remain.

The next day sparrows ate the crumbs of their bread rations,
and the children built toys with the matches
they'd used to light their cigarettes and the stars' thorns.

And the rock where they sat at noon under the olive trees by the sea,

tomorrow it will whiten in the kiln,
and the day after we will whitewash our homes and the rock of St Saviour,
and later still we will plant seed where they slept,
and a pomegranate bud will burst open,
the infant's first laugh on the bosom of sunshine.

And afterward we will sit on the ground and read their hearts
as though we were reading the history of the world from the very beginning.

VI

With the sun smack against the sea
whitewashing the opposite shore of day,
two and three times you suffer the agony of thirst and confinement,
you suffer the old wound again from the very beginning,
while your heart is roasted dry in the sun,
like onions scattered on the doorstep.

Every day their hands look more like the earth,
every day their eyes look more like the sky.

The jar is emptied of oil. Some silt remains, and a dead mouse.
The mother is emptied of endurance, along with the clay pitcher and the cistern.
The gums of the wilderness are acrid from the gunpowder.

Where will you find more oil for the oil-lamp of St Barbara?

Where will you find more mint to burn for the golden icon of the afternoon?
Where will you find one more mouthful of bread for panhandler night to
    play you a Cretan star-couplet on her lyra?

In the island's upper fortress the prickly pears and asphodels have turned to
    phantoms.
The earth is gouged by cannonfire and graves.
The plundered headquarters, patched with sky, gapes all round.
There is no room for any more dead;

there is no room for grief herself to pause and braid her hair.

Burnt-out houses scan the marble sea with their empty eyes;
the bullets are driven deep into the walls,
like knives in the belly of the saint they bound to a cypress tree.

All day long the dead bask face-up in the sun,
and at evening the soldiers slither by, their bellies dragging on the burnt rocks.
They grope with their nostrils for some air not touched by death,
they search the moon's shoes, chewing a tag of bootleather,
they pound the rock with their fists, maybe the knot of water will flow?
But from the other side you can see it's empty,
and they hear, once again, the bombardment, the whirling of the shell
    dropping in the sea,
and they hear, once again, the howl of the wounded before the gate.

Where can you go? Your brother is calling you.
The night walls you in with the shadows of foreign ships,
the roads are all closed off by rubble.

The only other path leads uphill,
so they curse the ships and bite their tongues,
and listen to their pain, which hasn't yet hardened into bone.

Up in the towers, the dead commanders stand and guard the fortress,
while their flesh decays beneath their clothing.
Hey, brother, aren't you tired yet?
That bullet in your heart has budded now,
five hyacinths have sprouted in the armpit of the dry rock,
breath by breath the fragrance tells the story – don't you remember?
Stitch by stitch your wound reports on life,

the camomile planted in the grime of your big toenail
declares to you the world's beauty.

You grasp a hand. It is your own, wet with brine.
The sea too is yours. You uproot a hair from the scalp of silence
and the fig dribbles its bitter milk.
Wherever you may be, the sky will look after you.

The evening star twists your soul between his fingers, like a cigarette.
In this way, lying on your back, you could smoke your soul,
splashing your left hand in the starry night,
clutching in your right hand your rifle, your betrothed.
Remember that the sky has not forgotten you
as you pull his old letter from deep within your pocket,
and unfolding the moon with your burnt fingers
you read of men and glory.

Later you will climb to the island's highest crag,
and with the star as a percussion cap you will shoot once in the air,
above the walls and the masts,
above the hills that stoop like a wounded foot-soldier,
one shot just to startle the ghosts, chasing them into the vast blanket of shadow.

You will fire once directly at the bosom of heaven, searching for the sky-blue
    target there,
as if you were seeking through her blouse the nipple of the woman who
    tomorrow will suckle your child,
as if you were groping, after many years, for the handle on the gate of your
    father's house.

VII

The house, the path, the cactus, and the chickens pecking at the rinds of
    sunlight in the yard,
These things we know, and they know us.
Among the brambles the tree snake has shed her yellow blouse.

Here is the ant's hut and the hornet's castle, thick with soldiers,
on the same olive tree the shell of last year's and the voice of this year's cicada,
over the cord your shadow trails, following behind like a dog, noiseless,
    long-suffering, a faithful dog.

At noon he sits by your rocky sleep, sniffing the oleander,
at night he curls up by your feet, peeping at a star.

There is a silence from the pear that nestles between the thighs of summer,
a sleepiness from water that loiters among the carob roots.
Spring has seven orphans asleep on her apron,
an eagle dying in her eyes
and high up, beyond the forest of pine,
the chapel of St John the Eremite parching in the sun,
like the sparrow's white dung drying in the heat on a mulberry leaf.

The shepherd wrapped in sheepskin,
a dried-up river in every hair,
a forest of oak trees in each hole of his flute,
and on his wooden staff the same knots as on the oars that first lashed the
    deep blue of the Hellespont.

No need to recall it. Your blood flows in the plane-tree's vein,
in the island asphodel and caper.

From deep down the silent well sends up to midday a rounded voice of
    black glass and white wind.
A voice as round as the old wine-jars – the same primeval voice,
and the sky rinses the stones and our eyes with indigo.

Each night in the fields the moon overturns the magnificent dead,
she searches their faces with rough, frozen fingers,
she will know her son by the scar on his chin and by his stony brow.
She searches their pockets. She always finds something.
We always find something:
a wooden cross, a crushed cigarette,
a house-key, a letter, a watch stalled at seven.
We wind the watch again. The time passes.

Tomorrow their clothes will rot away
and they will lie there, naked among their army buttons,
like strips of sky among the summer stars,
like a river amid the oleander,
like a path through the lemon trees of early spring,
and then perhaps we'll find their names and then perhaps we'll shout: I Love.
Then. But these things seem a bit far off, they seem a bit too close,

as when you shake someone's hand in the dark and say 'good evening'
with the sour understanding of the exile who returns home
and isn't recognized, not even by his own kin,
because he has known death,
because he has known the life before life and beyond death.
But he recognizes them; he isn't bitter. 'Tomorrow,' he says, certain that the
    longest road is the shortest way to the heart of God.

And now as the moon kisses him sadly by the ear,
the seaweed, the flower pot, the footstool and the rockcut stairs say 'good
    evening.'
The mountains and the seas and the cities and the sky say 'good evening.'
And then, flicking his ashes through the balcony railing,
he may weep in his assurance,
he may weep with the assurance of the trees and the stars and his brothers.

Athens, 1945–7

Translated by Avi Sharon

The Meaning of Simplicity

I hide behind simple things so you'll find me;
if you don't find me, you'll find the things,
you'll touch what my hand has touched.
our hand-prints will merge.

The August moon glitters in the kitchen
like a tin-plated pot (it gets that way because of what I'm saying to you),
it lights up the empty house and the house's kneeling silence –
always the silence remains kneeling.

Every word is a doorway
to a meeting, one often cancelled,
and that's when a word is true: when it insists on the meeting.

Translated by Edmund Keeley

Misunderstandings

His ambiguities infuriating: they force us into enquiries;
and the man answers the enquiries in the same way, blatantly betrayed
by his obscurity, his hesitancy, his ignorance, timidity,
and his lack of solid principles. Surely he is going to involve us
in his own perplexities. And he gazed somewhere beyond us
as if he had been generous somehow, or indulgent (like those who have to be
     indulgent)
in his snow-white shirt, his impeccable slate-grey suit
and a chrysanthemum in his button-hole. Nevertheless,
when he left, in the place where he had been we could see on the floor
a small, bright-red pool, finely outlined
almost like a map of Greece, like a miniature atlas,
somewhat abstracted and with great inaccuracies of frontier,
the frontiers almost lost in the uniformity of the colouring,
an atlas in a closed, white school in the month of July,
when all the students have left, on a dazzling excursion by the sea.

Translated by Paul Merchant

Non-Hero

He who, hearing his comrades' departing
tread on the pebbles, in his drunkenness,
instead of coming down the ladder he had climbed up, jumped
straight down,
breaking his neck, arrived first
at the black opening. And he had no need
of those prophecies of Tiresias. And he did not so much as touch
the black ram's blood. The one thing he asked for
was a yard of ground on the shore of Aeaea
and for them to set his oar there – the one which he used to row
next to his comrades. Honour, then, and glory
to the handsome lad. They said he was light in the head. And yet
didn't he too help to the best of his ability
in their great journey? It is for this, indeed, that the Poet
picks him out for special mention, albeit with a certain superiority,
but perhaps for that very reason with the more love.

Translated by David Ricks

Trivial Details

When Eumaeus, the swineherd, stood up to go out to the stranger
his dogs were barking at over by the sty,
the fine, well-tooled cowhide he was shaping
for his sandals fell off his knees. Later,
when he moved off to slaughter the two pigs
as a gesture of hospitality toward the old man, he tightened his belt.
These things – the hide, his sandals, the tightening of his belt – their secret
    meaning (beyond gods and myths,
beyond symbols and ideas), only poets perceive.

Niobe

This statue, the artistry first-rate, made of unusual stone,
was not carved by a sculptor: we see a disdainful, unsubmissive woman
bending over her seven slaughtered sons, the arrows still in their chests,
and her seven dead daughters. Here, after having exhausted
her last appeal, her last curse against gods and men,
climbing, step by step, the ladder of silence and immobility,
she finally turned into the statue of her very own self – a jet-black rock
with two limpid springs gushing under her huge forehead,
water for the young shepherds on the slopes of barren Sipylus during
    summer afternoons,
for the sheep, despondent musicians and lost travellers. Today, of course,
many people contend that the springs of her eyes are nothing other than
the water from the neighbourhood well carried to her eyes by thin secret pipes,
and there are others who insistently propose
that we knock down this wonderful statue – the pride of our poor region –
simply for the pleasure of discovering the clever mechanism of the thing.

10 April 1968

The Tombs of Our Ancestors

We ought to protect our dead and their power in case someday
our adversaries disinter them and carry them off. Then,
without our protection, our danger would double. How could we go on living
without our houses, our furniture, our fields, especially without

the tombs of our ancestral warriors and wise men? Let's not forget
how the Spartans stole the bones of Orestes from Tegea. Our enemies
should never know where we've buried our dead. But
how are we ever to know who our enemies are
or when and from where they might show up? So no grand monuments,
no gaudy decorations – things like that draw attention, stir envy. Our dead
have no need of that; satisfied with little, unassuming and silent now,
they're indifferent to honey-liquor, votive offerings, futile glory. Better
a plain stone and a pot of geraniums, a secret sign,
or even nothing at all. For safety's sake, we might do well to hold them
    inside us if we can,
or better still, not even know where they lie.
The way things have turned out in our time, who knows,
we ourselves might dig them up, throw them out someday.

20 March 1968

Penelope's Despair

It wasn't that she didn't recognize him in the light from the hearth: it wasn't
the beggar's rags, the disguise – no. The signs were clear:
the scar on his knee, the pluck, the cunning in his eye. Frightened,
her back against the wall, she searched for an excuse,
a little time, so she wouldn't have to answer,
give herself away. Was it for him, then, that she'd used up twenty years,
twenty years of waiting and dreaming, for this miserable
blood-soaked, white-bearded man? She collapsed voiceless into a chair,
slowly studied the slaughtered suitors on the floor as though seeing
her own desires dead there. And she said 'Welcome,'
hearing her voice sound foreign, distant. In the corner, her loom
covered the ceiling with a trellis of shadows; and all the birds she'd woven
with bright red thread in green foliage, now,
on this night of the return, suddenly turned ashen and black,
flying low on the flat sky of her final enduring.

21 September 1968

The Usual

In time, houses collapse, the doors fade. In the garden
a rusted stove comes apart, crumbles, falls
like the leaves of a quince tree. In the afternoon it rains.
    The potholes
in the road fill up with water. Three old street lamps
light up beside the soccer field. The evening star
hovers over the mountain, very high up. A blue glow
comes out of the grocery-store doorway. The bicycle's
    shadow
grows longer on the wet road. With that shadow, that
minimal light, you might accomplish something deeper
    inside.
But poets are glorified for their worst poems.

11 February 1969

Afternoon in the Old Neighbourhood

They set the café tables out on the sidewalk.
The old men come to sit there in the afternoon. The sunshine
stretches over their newspapers, wipes away the news.
They can't read any longer. Maybe they're angry about it too,
maybe they even forget, because death always
takes over the back pages of the newspaper
as it does the courtyards with the closed wells.
And it's quiet of an afternoon in the old neighbourhood
as though all the pregnant women have moved to a new place.

Athens, 20 March 1971

Sources

There were still – beyond denial – certain places and events:
the gardener's footsteps beside the wall, the morning train
in the deserted station under fog, a dried-up lemon tree,
when they left the large wooden boxes on the stairs,
and the faces of the young were so distant, unreconciled, lovely,

changing the future almost into the present, approaching the windowpanes,
holding an apple in two fingers only, not knowing
whether to bite into it or use it to break the mirror –
and later a certain word, every now and then, late at night, the moon out,
the word that is most ours, summer, between two strokes with the oars.

Athens, 28 February 1972

The Same Course

A piece of red cloth against the dark blue.
Olive trees, poles, plastic bags, bathers kissing,
faces, hands, bodies spoiled by time;
bitterly, bitterly sustained interests. The crickets –
voices abandoned in space; you didn't notice them – foreign voices.
You hear them or you don't, see them or don't – nothing, nothing, he said.
A forgotten astringent odour from cut grass.
So sit down here on the ground, on the warmed earth.
Undo the knots in the napkin one by one, eat your bread,
biting deeply, farther in than death. And then,
with dusk, the eggshells – so white and fragile –
creaking under the feet of the great blind man heading calmly
toward the altar of Colonus, guided by a small tortoise.

Kalamos, 25 June 1972

Translated by Edmund Keeley

Tokens

One by one the sleek bathers will leave.
The fiery autumn sunsets will linger on the sea,
with one sad skiff – and still
we put off the rain, the rampaging winds,
still we put off the inevitable (for how long?).
Already yellow leaves pile up on the garden benches.
Perhaps, uncelebrated on its hill, the chapel to the Holy
Trinity remembers us. Meanwhile, here in the house,
the floor is littered with summer sandals
and little Persephone's blue towel.

Karlovasi, 16–7–87

Pilgrimage

They journeyed for days on end. Their faith in the miracle never faltered.
It would come, at any moment it would come: around a bend in the road,
over this hill, or the next. They would see it with their own eyes,
proclaim it with their tongues, perhaps even hold in their hands
a piece of his golden tunic. At the start of the second month,
weariness overtook them. All then lay on the ground
and instantly fell asleep. The moon rose above them –
detached, absorbed in its own sorrow. Then the great boulders
tumbled soundlessly into the great void. And they woke up.
All about them – absolute, blinding brightness. And no moon.

Karlovasi, 21–7–87

Two in the Afternoon

In the yellow field, a straw hat and a red cow.
A white horse switching greenflies with its tail.
I remembered the dead poet's cornfield, and sunflowers.
I checked my watch: two o'clock. Some skin divers
were coming back from the water, still in their wetsuits.
One of them, carrying his blue fins and a large octopus,
looked at me expectantly, as if he knew me. 'Hello,' he said.
'Hello,' I said back, and felt like I should have said more.
Then a breeze came down off the mountain, the olive trees
shivered, the cicadas stopped. With a feeling of peace,
I stepped forward to stroke the white horse's mane.

Karlovasi, 29–7–87

On Silence

It is precisely the things you never said
that pumped blood into the words you did say, that hung
suspended in air, equivocal, opaque – notes
from some dark music out of the future. Now,
you have nothing to say because you have nothing to hide. Silence
muscles you out of things – so you eavesdrop

on the mating cry of motorcycles out on the coast road,
you hear the whistles of the *Samena*, the *Ikaros*, the *Aegean*
as they depart, night and day, in rough seas and calm,
their final destination that vast, unlighted anchorage.

Karlovasi, 7–8–87

Ticks of the Clock, 13

The stones you painted
– pretty faces and bodies –
leave you cold.
Smoke rising from a cigarette
left burning in an ashtray
is smoke from a hearth
on some lost Ithaca – with Penelope
sitting at her loom,
dead.

Translated by Martin McKinsey

Nikos Gatsos (1915–1992)

Elytis' *Heroic and Elegiac Song*, Ritsos' *Romiosini*, and – in a slippery and self-ironizing fashion, Engonopoulos' *Bolivar* (qq.v) – constructed ideal Greeces of the mind in the face of the appalling suffering of the 1940s. Gatsos had in fact got there first with his poem *Amorgos* (1943), a more mysterious poem. Its obscurities were not just to protect the author from the consequences of writing such a poem under the Occupation but were the result of a natural verve issuing in a poem written, as legend has it, by 'automatic writing'. After this, along with just two short poems which are essentially pendants to it, Gatsos abandoned poetry in the normal sense for ever, confining himself to translations and to the delicate popular songs from which he made a living.

Amorgos

To a Green Star

'The eyes and ears are bad witnesses
for men with barbarian souls'
Heraclitus
(Diels, *Die Fragm. der Vorsokr.*, B. 109)

I

With their country bound to the sails and their oars hung on the wind
The shipwrecked voyagers slept tamely like dead beasts in sheets of sponge
But the seaweed's eyes are turned to the sea In case the South Wind brings
    them back with their lateen rigs freshly dyed,
For a single lost elephant is always worth more than the two moving breasts
    of a girl,
Only in the mountains let the roofs of deserted chapels light up at the whim
    of the evening star,
Let the birds flutter in the masts of the lemon tree
With the steady white beat of a new tempo;
And then the winds will come, bodies of swans that remained spotless,
    tender, motionless
Among the steam-rollers of the shops, cyclones of the vegetable gardens,
When women's eyes turned into coal and the hearts of the chestnut vendors
    broke,

When the harvesting stopped and the hopes of the cricket began,

And that is why, my brave lads, with wine, kisses and leaves on your lips,
That is why I would have you enter the rivers naked
And sing of the Barbary Coast as the woodman seeks out the mastic tree,
As the viper slithers through fields of barley,
Her proud eyes all anger,
As lightning threshes youth.

And don't laugh and don't weep and don't rejoice
Don't tighten your boots uselessly as though planting plane trees
Don't become FATED
Because the golden eagle is not a closed drawer,
Nor a plum-tree's tear, nor a water-lily's smile,
Nor a dove's vest, nor a sultan's mandolin,
Nor a silk kerchief for the head of a whale.
It is a marine saw carving gulls,
It is the carpenter's pillow, the beggar's watch,
It is fire in a smithy mocking the priest's wives and lulling the lilies to sleep,
It is the Turks' in-laws, the Australians' feast,
The Hungarians' mountain refuge
Where the hazel trees meet secretly in autumn:
They see the wise storks dying their eggs black
And then they too weep
They burn their nightgowns and wear the duck's petticoat
They spread stars on the ground for kings to tread on
With their silver amulets, the crown, the purple,
They scatter rosemary on garden beds
So the mice can cross to another cellar
And enter other churches to devour the sacred altars,
And the owls, my lads,
The owls are hooting
And dead nuns are rising to dance
And tambourines, drums and violins, with bagpipes and lutes,
With banners and censers, with herbs and magic veils,
With the bear's breeches in the frozen valley,
They eat the martens' mushrooms
They play heads and tails for St John's ring and the Black Man's florins
They ridicule the witches
They cut off a priest's beard with the cutlass of Kolokotroni
They wash themselves in the smoke of incense,

And then, chanting slowly, they enter the earth again and are silent
As waves are silent, as the cuckoo at daybreak, as the lamplight at evening.

So in a deep jar the grape withers, and in the bell-tower of a fig tree the apple
    turns yellow
So, wearing a gaudy tie,
Summer breathes in the tent of a vine arbour
So, naked among the white cherry trees, sleeps my young love,
A girl unfading as an almond branch,
Her head resting on her elbow, her palm on her golden florin,
On its morning warmth, when, silent as a thief,
Through the window of spring the dawn star enters to wake her.

II

They say the mountains tremble and the fir trees rage
When night gnaws the tile-pins to let in the Kallikantzari
When hell gulps down the torrents' foaming toil
Or when the groomed hair of the pepper tree becomes the North Wind's plaything.

Only Achaean cattle graze vigorous and strong
On abundant fields in Thessaly beneath an ageless, watching sun
They eat green grass and celery, leaves of the poplar tree, they drink clear
    water in the troughs
They smell the sweat of the earth and then fall heavily to sleep in the shade of
    the willow tree.

Cast out the dead said Heraclitus, yet he saw the sky turn pale,
Saw two small cyclamens kissing in the mud
And as the wolf comes down from the forests to see the dog's carcass and
    weep
He too fell to kiss his own dead body on the hospitable soil.
What good to me the bead that glistens on your forehead?
I know the lightning wrote its name upon your lips
I know an eagle built its nest within your eyes
But here on this damp bank there is one way only
One deceptive way and you must take it
You must plunge into blood before time forestalls you
Cross over opposite to find your companions again
Flowers birds deer
To find another sea, another tenderness,

To take Achilles' horses by the reins
Instead of sitting dumb scolding the river
Stoning the river like the mother of Kitso
Because you too will be lost and your beauty will have aged.
I see your childhood shirt drying on the branches of a willow
Take it, this flag of life, to shroud your death
And may your heart not fail you
And may your tear not fall upon this pitiless earth
As a penguin's tear once fell in the frozen wilderness
Complaint achieves nothing
Life everywhere will be the same
With the serpent's flute in the land of phantoms
With the song of brigands in aromatic groves
With the knife of some sorrow in the cheek of hope
With the pain of some spring in the screech owl's heart –
Enough if a sharp sickle and plough are found in a joyful hand
Enough if there flower only
A little wheat for festivals, a little wine for remembrance, a little
    water for the dust . . .

III

In the griever's courtyard no sun rises
Only worms appear to mock the stars
Only horses sprout upon the ant hills
And bats eat birds and piss out sperm.

In the griever's courtyard night never sets
Only the foliage vomits forth a river of tears
When the devil passes by to mount the dogs
And the crows swim in a well of blood.

In the griever's courtyard the eye has gone dry
The brain has frozen and the heart turned to stone
Frog-flesh hangs from the spider's teeth
Hungry locusts scream at the vampires' feet.

In the griever's courtyard black grass grows
Only one night in May did a breeze pass through
A step light as a tremor on the meadow
A kiss of the foam-trimmed sea.

And should you thirst for water, we will wring a cloud
And should you hunger for bread, we will slaughter a nightingale
Only wait a moment for the wild rue to open
For the black sky to flash, the mullein to flower.

But it was a breeze that vanished, a lark that disappeared
It was the face of May, the moon's whiteness
A step light as a tremor on the meadow
A kiss of the foam-trimmed sea.

IV

Wake up limpid water from the root of the pine tree so that you can find the
sparrows' eyes and give them new life, watering the earth with scent of basil
and the lizard's whistling. I know you are a naked vein under the menacing gaze
of the wind, a voiceless spark in the luminous multitude of the stars. No one
notices you, no one stops to listen to your breathing, but you, your pace heavy
in the arrogant ranks of nature, will one day reach the leaves of the apricot tree,
will one day climb the slender bodies of young broom shrubs, will fall from the
eyes of the beloved like an adolescent moon. There is a deathless stone on which
a passing human angel once inscribed his name and a song that no one yet knows,
not even the craziest children or the wisest nightingales. It is now locked up in
a cave of Mount Devi, in the gorges and ravines of my fatherland, but someday
when it breaks out and thrusts itself against destruction and time, this angelic
song, the rain will suddenly stop and the mud dry up, the snows will melt in the
mountains, the wind will sing like a bird, the swallows will come to life, the
willows will shiver, and the men of cold eyes and pallid faces – when they hear
the bells tolling of their own accord in the cracked bell-towers – will find festive
hats to wear and gaudy bows to decorate their shoes. Because then no one will
joke any longer, the blood of the brooks will overflow, the animals will break
their bridles in the mangers, the hay will turn green in the stables, between the
roof-tiles fresh poppies will sprout, and May flowers, and at all crossroads red
fires will rise at midnight. Then slowly the frightened young girls will come to
cast their last clothing into the fire and dance all naked around it, just as in our
day, when we too were young, and a window would open at dawn to show a
flaming carnation growing on their breasts. Lads, maybe the memory of ancestors is deeper consolation and more precious company than a handful of rose
water, and the intoxication of beauty no different from the sleeping rose bush
of the Eurotas. So now goodnight; I see a galaxy of falling stars rocking your
dreams, but I hold in my fingers music for a better day. Travellers from India
have more to tell you than the Byzantine chroniclers.

V

Man, during the course of his mysterious life,
Bequeathed his descendants tokens varied and worthy of his immortal origin,
As he bequeathed also traces of the ruins of twilight, snowdrifts of celestial
    reptiles, diamonds, kites, and the glances of hyacinths.
In the midst of sighs, tears, hunger, wailing, and the ashes of subterranean wells.

VI

How very much I loved you only I know
I who once touched you with the eyes of the Pleiades,
Embraced you with the moon's mane, and we danced on the meadows of
    summer
On the harvest's stubble, and together ate cut clover,
Great dark sea with so many pebbles round your neck, so many coloured jewels
    in your hair.

A ship nears shore, a rusted water-wheel groans.
A tuft of blue smoke in the rose of the horizon
Is like a crane's wing palpitating.
Armies of swallows are waiting to offer the brave their welcome
Arms rise naked, anchors engraved on the armpits
Children's cries mingle with the song of the West Wind
Bees come and go in the cows' nostrils
Kalamata kerchiefs flutter
And a distant bell painting the sky with bluing
Is like the sound of a gong travelling among the stars –
A gong that escaped so many years ago
From the souls of the Goths and the domes of Baltimore
And from lost St Sophia, the great cathedral.
But up in the high mountains who are they who now gaze down, eyes calm,
    faces serene?
Of what conflagration is this cloud of dust the echo?
Is Kalyvas fighting now, or is it Leventoyannis?
Nor have the Germans begun to battle the noble men of Mani.
Silent towers guard a ghostly princess
The tips of cypress trees consort with a dead anemone
Shepherds unperturbed pipe their morning song on a linden reed
A stupid hunter fires a shot at the turtledoves
And an old windmill, forgotten by all,

Mends by itself its rotten sails with a needle of dolphin bone
And descends the slopes with a brisk north-west leading it
As Adonis descended the paths of Mount Chelmos to bid the lovesick
    shepherdess good evening.

For years and years, O my tormented heart, have I struggled with ink and
    hammer,
With gold and fire, to fashion an embroidery for you,
The hyacinth of an orange tree,
A flowering quince tree to comfort you –
I who once touched you with the eyes of the Pleiades,
Embraced you with the moon's mane and we danced on the meadows of
    summer
On the harvest's stubble, and together ate cut clover,
Great dark loneliness with so many pebbles round your neck, so many
    coloured jewels in your hair.

Translated by Edmund Keeley and Philip Sherrard

Dimitris Hatzis (1913–1981)

Hatzis was born in Yannina in Epirus shortly after its annexation by the Greek state. He began his career as a writer as a militantly engaged veteran of the Resistance, with his novel *Fire* (1946). Forced to flee into exile after the defeat of the Left in the Civil War (1946–9), Hatzis eked out an existence in various places on the other side of the Iron Curtain before settling for a longer period in Budapest. From there he published his first important book of short stories, *The End of Our Small Town* (1952; an extensively revised edition appeared in 1963). In later works Hatzis would go on to explore with great sensitivity the predicament of marginalized people, such as Greek 'guest-workers' in Germany. In this extract he explores, with reference to a never-named town – though one with many features of Yannina – the various transformations it underwent between the inter-war slump and the Civil War. In some ways, the feeling is close to that of Pantelis Prevelakis' *The Tale of a Town* (q.v.), and a Marxist strand of belief that changes were inevitable and that individuals are pawns in the hands of history never blunts Hatzis' stories' recognition of the consequences for individuals, as the author tackles subjects as painful as the virtual extirpation of Greek Jewry. The following story's presentation of the fate of the tanners' dying trade resonates beyond its intensely local setting, idiom and concerns.

Sioulas the Tanner

Deep and blue-green, the lake spreads out beside the small town. In its waters are reflected the high walls of the old medieval castle, which some say goes even further back.

Just outside the eastern wall of the castle, right on the edge of the lake, were the tanneries. The tanners who lived in this quarter were known as *tabaki*, a similar name being used at Serres, Volos, and, I believe, on Syra.

The animal hides used to be stretched tightly on wooden frames in the lake water along the whole length of the quarter. When quite soaked the hides would be taken and tanned in the workshops.

In all, there were some fifteen to twenty of these workshops or tanneries, in a row beneath the castle wall. Each one was two-storeyed, built of stone and had a large arched doorway. The ground floor had small windows like loopholes and consisted solely of a broad stone-paved entrance-hall, wooden wash-tubs lying about here and there. In these halls, either barefooted or shod in a kind of large boot, stripped to the waist and trouserless, the tanners worked on the hides. The upper floor jutted out half a metre above the road and had large Venetian-style windows. Here were the living quarters, reached by a small wooden staircase from within the workshop. The whole district stank with the pungent reek of animal skins.

The tanners descended from the town's earliest inhabitants, as well as from the leading families who had lived within the castle until ejected by the Turks after the Skylosophos uprising in 1612. And indeed, they spoke the town dialect in a purer form than anyone else, keeping it intact both in vocabulary and pronunciation.

They scarcely ever went up into the town except on special business and, in fact, had very little to do with it. They were disdainful of newcomers and it's highly likely that they had no idea even of the neighbourhoods where the refugees from Asia Minor had made their homes. The tanners lived in their own isolated, self-sufficient world, beyond the castle walls.

At no distance at all from their workshops stood the woodyards where Vlachs from Metsovo and the Zagoria worked. The tanners had absolutely nothing to do with them. And a couple of roads further up were the coopers – Metsovite Vlachs, too, with others from the villages of Vovousa and Dobrinovo. For years these men had pounded away with their wooden mallets at the wild pine and beech they used for their barrels. Yet here again the tanners kept to themselves, for though they knew these men well enough to bid them good morning and had no quarrel with them, this was as far as it went. After all, such people were mere carrot-crunchers, *datskanaraii* – uncouth villagers.

At the front the workshops looked towards the *Skala,* or Steps, as the landing stage was called. It was here that the large lake-going caiques, slow-moving skiffs, unloaded goods such as firewood, slaughtered livestock, cheeses and butter from the villages opposite. But the tanners only bought things there when it was necessary; otherwise they kept to themselves, for, once again, what had they in common with villagers? In the evenings they went to their own wineshops where no villager ever set foot except for the boatmen from the small island in the lake. These would sometimes have a drink or two with the tanners before going back home for the night. It was only because the two groups shared a passion for hunting that the tanners let them join them.

During the winter, braziers would be placed in special holes in the low tables in these drinking dens and the tanners would sit round on stools that were low, too, warming their wine in copper pots before drinking it. The conversation always revolved upon past episodes, hunting and the like. Hard and proud men, they rarely brought work or such matters into the talk – they thought it beneath them to do so. Nor did they discuss politics, for all were of one mind, being staunch Venizelists: the greater 'Greece of the Five Seas', as befitted the descendants of castle notables. They always voted for the Venizelist mayor and the

Venizelist councillors of the Cathedral of St Athanasios. And here the matter
ended, for they were totally self-sufficient in their moral, social and political
outlook.

And in professional matters, too, for their trade guild, according to those
qualified in such knowledge, was one of the oldest in the town, and had remained
unchanged over the passage of time. Tanners neither left the guild nor did
newcomers enter it. The only difference was that during the years I'm writing
about, since the remaining tanners were all interrelated, they reorganized their
workshops into partnerships. There was now no distinction between head workman and apprentice – everyone was a head workman and a steady respectable
citizen at the same time. But it was only in this instance that the guild tradition
had altered. In every other way it continued to function as it had always done
since its inception in those distant days when the tanneries were first established.
The tanners took no interest in how their trade was carried on elsewhere. They
came by their dyestuffs from local natural sources, and used them in ways traditionally imparted to them. Even their glue – *toukali,* as it was known – was
obtained from the fish in the lake. Indeed, everything they used was acquired in
a similar manner and employed according to practices handed down from generation to generation.

And it was by family tradition that Sioulas had become a tanner, for he was the
son of a tanner and his wife was the daughter of one. He'd grown up amongst
the tanneries and played the games of childhood there: knuckle-bones and
sklentza, as they called tip-cat, and quoits, leap-frog and prisoner's base. He'd
taken part in the stone-throwing fights with the children from the nearby neighbourhoods. There too, he'd learned to read and write, and had first attended
church and gone hunting on the lake. Then eventually he'd entered the tanning
trade, married, and founded his own family. And all the time he was possessed
of an ingrown pride. Steadfastly moderate in everything, he saw any kind of
innovation as blatant showing-off.

A relative of his had gone to live abroad for a while: an extremely rare occur-
rence. And then suddenly he was back again, complete with gold watch-chain
on his waistcoat and flaunting his money. Blood being thicker than water, he
kept to his own kind and roamed around the tanneries by day and sat in the
tanners' wineshops by night. All quite natural, yet what irked his companions
was the way he would all at once hold forth about his experiences abroad, never
able to suppress the desire to regale them with tales of the wonderful things he
had seen. At first they looked at him angrily; then they spoke sharply to him a
few times. But it was of no avail.

One midday in the summertime the tanners, as usual nearly naked when they'd
been working, came out of their workshops for a break and to give the food

they'd just eaten a chance to settle. Our traveller was there and on the point of launching into one of his stories.

'I wonder if you could tell us,' began Sioulas suddenly, slowly rising and going over to him, 'did you learn anything of those foreign languages whilst you were away there in Europe?'

'Yes, sure, a bit,' answered our unsuspecting friend.

'Right, then, perhaps you'd like to tell us what it says here.' So saying, Sioulas turned his back on him and slapped the label on his underpants.

The tanners roared with laughter, as did their wives at their windows.

Sioulas kept angrily slapping his backside:

'Come on, mate, read it out!'

From that day the man was never again seen wearing his watch-chain or speaking of his travels or money – certainly not in the presence of the tanners. There was no more trifling with them.

Meanwhile time passed, everyone gradually aged, and year by year the castle walls slowly crumbled. But people were too preoccupied to notice the changes going on around them. Sioulas' hair began to turn white without his realizing it. The evening would often find him with his legs stiff from the long years they'd been immersed in water when he was working. Every year Sioulaina, just like a rabbit, would produce a new little Siouling, and a tribe of children has to be fed, clothed, shod and sent to school. When you're in that situation, ground down by daily worries, there's no time to look around and take stock of things.

All the tanners, in fact, were too harassed to take much account of what was happening around them, of how and when the changes in their trade – now steadily worsening – had started. Materials and goods, cheaper and better produced, had begun to be brought in from elsewhere: kid-leather, patent-leather, shoes, raincoats, even calf-hide and the leather for soles. A few of the older leather businesses in the town's bazaar now found it more profitable to obtain their raw hides and send them directly to Italy, Marseilles and even Syra for machine-processing, rather than troubling with the tanners.

An atmosphere of gloom began to settle over the oppressed tanners every evening in their wineshops. A number of them only worked two or three days a week now. There were those burdened with the knowledge that there was no food in their homes for the evening meal. And everyone knew that their women-folk begged from one another, sharing their misfortune among themselves, though they would not admit this to their husbands and each sought to conceal the tanner's plight within his own household when he had no work.

The men themselves never complained about their poverty, nor revealed signs of it. They would certainly have been ashamed to do so before one another. Nor would they have dreamed of finding other work outside the tanneries – it would have seemed an act of treachery. They all rallied to the defence of their besieged profession. And in the town every Sunday morning during the winter their double-barrelled shotguns could be heard resounding from the lake, like a mighty witness to their noble and manly passion for hunting.

At the great shoots on the lake when the birds would be steadily enclosed – a big event in which everyone took part along with the regular hunters – the tanners excelled themselves. It had been established as a sort of right that they would start out from the farthest end of the lake before dawn, rowing softly, driving the frightened flocks of waterfowl towards the centre of the lake by firing their guns. There were *yesia* and *kanaves* – as the male and female wild duck were called – and black coots with white bills. And sometimes there were the large beautiful wild-geese whose soft fleecy underwing, below their breasts, and known as *balsamo,* is kept by the womenfolk as ideal for treating wounds.

With their shotguns ready, the other hunters from the town and island would be standing in their small boats which were lined up in the middle of the lake. Since the birds would fall upon them in their hundreds, all that was required was one pair of hands to keep firing a gun and another to load it – a job usually done by the boatman, who would also ease his boat over the water to gather the birds in. Each bird was accounted as belonging to the boat it had fallen nearest, regardless of who had actually shot it.

On these great lake shoots, or on his own solitary Sunday hunting expeditions, Sioulas would relive the sorrows and longings of his proud soul from the days of his youth to the beginnings of old age, when life had taken such a turn for the worse, reducing him to poverty. Now in the evenings he would return home in a state of exhaustion, his legs stiff from sitting all day in the narrow boat and his clothes sodden. He would back into the doorway, shoulder the door open and drop his catch in the middle of the room, and then stretch out face downwards beside the hearth, on the place called the *bassi* that all houses had in their winter room. He would get his children to tread up and down his aching back, which they would do with yells and shouts of laughter, giving him delighted kicks. He would shout out with them, whilst the dog went wild, not knowing who to bark at first. It was the one moment of happiness amidst the general cloud of darkness that had engulfed the tanneries.

But at the same time Sioulaina would be kneeling on the floor counting and recounting the birds: four for themselves, a pair for her sister, a pair for her mother-in-law. And the rest? What if they sold the rest? This was a thought she dare not reveal to him even by the look in her eyes. The boatmen, the islanders and the other poor men of the town would go hunting and enjoy themselves, eat what they wanted of their catch and then sell the rest in the bazaar – they on their own or their women and children. But a tanner – never. Not for the whole world.

There came a time when Sioulas' workshop stood idle all week. Nor was there any proper work at the other workshops. His wife only managed to cope by scouring the house for what scraps of food there were, seeking help from the other women, and, in fact, by secretly selling things to the Jewish rag-and-bone man who had got wind of what was happening in the tanneries. Sioulaina didn't speak to her husband all that week; she asked for nothing from him, she didn't even look him in the eyes. But now she could take no more. She sat crying with her head in her arms, waiting for the others to come in for their midday meal – only to find she had nothing for them.

He made his way up, entered the room, saw her sitting in a corner and felt his children's eyes fixed upon him.

'What do you mean by letting the children go hungry like this?'

She didn't speak. She sat on in the corner with head bowed.

'Didn't you try to get anything from the grocer's?'

She raised her eyes and looked at him, without sorrow, complaint or anger, just an unspoken plea to him not to go on. But he grew more angry.

'Why don't you say something for goodness' sake? What's the matter with you?'

She lowered her face again.

'He won't let us have anything more.' She said it humbly, as if she were to blame.

'And what about bread? How come you didn't get any?'

'The baker won't let us have anything either.'

She got up and hurried out to hide the choking tears – tears at his unfairness rather than the misfortune that had befallen them.

The children fled, she followed, going to her sister to seek mutual solace. He stayed in the room, alone in the empty house all afternoon, not thinking about their plight nor of his wounded pride and his shame before his children but about his wife, about his injustice to her. He kept catching back a sob – this was the first time in their twenty married years that he had ever seriously thought about her.

It was beginning to get dark when he rose. None of the others had returned home yet. He took down the shotgun and looked at it carefully several times before putting it under his arm and going down out of the house.

'What's the problem?' asked the gypsy, about to take the gun.

He had no appetite for small talk. The fellow was in every way a gypsy, a back-street gunsmith who repaired poor men's guns for next to nothing in a mean hole in the *bizestenia* next to the bell-makers' workshops. Sioulas kept hold of the gun, staring at the other keenly.

'I'm selling it,' he said briefly, finally handing him the gun. 'I'm getting another one.'

It was a fine Belgian double-barrelled shotgun, twelve-bore, without hammers.

The gypsy knew it of old and left it in the tanner's hands, without even looking at it. He regarded him, the dark mischievous eyes playing in the swarthy face.

'No, don't do that, Sioulas, old pal.'

'What, you'll not take it?'

'Sure, I'd take it all right, and make a fair bit on it.'

'Come on, no gypsy tricks, I'm not going to haggle. What'll you pay?'

'I know you won't get another one,' said the other calmly, used to being called 'gypsy' and not troubled by it. 'You've got problems. No work. There's your kids. But don't sell the gun, old pal, you'll never see it again.'

The gypsy wasn't bargaining.

'I know what it's like. There's been other tanners here, things are rough. But when they've only had the one gun I've not taken it. For years I've made my living from poor blokes like you, so give it to someone else. I'm not dirtying my hands doing a thing like that.'

Sioulas stared at the ground. A gypsy had called him a poor bloke, and wouldn't dirty his hands with his – Sioulas' – gun. But it was not because of these things – he was not even thinking about them. It was something else: for the second time the same day he found himself thinking about his unjust behaviour. 'Why didn't you get some bread from the baker's?' 'No gypsy tricks with me!' If the gypsy hadn't at that moment taken out his tobacco for them both to roll cigarettes he would have left quickly, quite ashamed.

'Yes, you're right,' he said, after a moment or two, without raising his eyes. And then he did raise them, and looked at him. 'You're a good man.' He said it smiling, as if it were the gypsy's just due. He made to go.

The gypsy stopped him.

'I know what it's like,' he repeated. 'You've difficulties, no work, the children. But don't let the gun go; you're a tanner, you'll not get over it.'

He took out a hundred-drachma note and gave it to him.

'Pay us back when you can.'

Sioulas took it: took it and felt no shame. He clutched it in his fist and as he did so began to feel a tender euphoria seep right through him, body and soul, like a new warmth. And it wasn't because he'd have some money to take home. It was because for the first time in his life he had felt close to other people, to poor people, as he himself had been called by the gypsy; because he felt an understanding of himself: you aren't an unjust man, Sioulas. As he made his way through the streets back down to the tanneries he felt this new warm living thing astir within him, glowing there. Something almost like joy at the heart of the black despair, something that could never die.

Night had fallen by the time he walked past the woodmen's and coopers' yards. He heard someone calling him. It was a round, ruddy-faced cooper from Metsovo with a back misshapen from perpetual bending over work.

'Good evening.'

'Where are you going with your gun at this time of day?'

'Oh, it needed straightening a bit, I've just taken it to the gypsy. He's a good man,' he said unexpectedly, without meaning to.

'Don't know him,' said the cooper. 'Still, he hasn't done anything to us, has he? Come and have a raki.'

He had never been in this wineshop before – it was a khan and wineshop combined where wood-yard men, coopers, respectable family men, poor men of the neighbourhood and villagers staying the night in town went. The cooper brought him a raki and started talking about the lack of work and great difficulties.

'You people aren't in too good a shape, either,' he said at one point.

'No,' replied Sioulas. He didn't feel at all ashamed at saying this. 'We're certainly not.'

'So what will you do?'

'No idea. No one has.'

'It's a lousy business,' added the cooper.

He wasn't listening to him any more. At that moment he was aware of something overflowing within him, prompting him to do nothing but get up and buy everyone in there a drink: Vlachs, gypsies, villagers, poor men, every single one of them. But it remained an impulse, and after treating the cooper to a return raki he bade him a cheerful goodnight.

'He's a good man, too' he thought and kept repeating it to himself to get the full flavour and meaning of it. 'But where the hell have they all been hiding?'

Entering the street where the tanneries stood he came upon one of his own youngsters. He called him and surreptitiously slipped him some money to give to his mother, and handed over the gun as well. He felt too self-conscious to go up himself at that moment and only came back late at night when he could be sure she would be in bed asleep. He lay beside her on the mattress and neither of them spoke or stirred all night.

Before dawn he rose and tiptoed down with his gun, his wife still not stirring. He got in the little boat and headed for the open lake, to the part known as the Great Deep. He thrust his oars deep into the water, hurriedly rowing through the reed-beds.

By the time he returned home a cold bright winter's day had already fully dawned. He stood outside the door of his workshop and shouted. His children came down and stared awe-struck at the rich game. He unslung the gun from his shoulder and handed it to them, along with three ducks.

'Give them to your mother,' was all he said.

He set off again, taking about ten of the birds with him, without glancing back at the house where he knew, behind the window-pane, her eyes were full of tears. He made his way right through the tanneries, past the workshops, to the bazaar, his head high and his steps ringing out.

And that's how the first tanner took his game to sell in the bazaar. The others followed. The trumpets announcing a new dawn that day toppled the tanners' Jericho to its very foundations amidst the deafening roar of machinery. Spring was drawing near and flocks of wild geese began flying ever higher above the lake. It was as if they, too, had taken fright.

Translated by David Vere

Takis Sinopoulos (1917–1981)

Sinopoulos presents in his poems a world with a family resemblance to that of Hatzis' stories: a provincial setting with all the scars of the Occupation and the Civil War. This remains a constant through a long career characterized by nagging ambition (an intensely competitive attitude towards Seferis is apparent in many poems) and constant formal experimentation: recollections of the internecine slaughter of the 1940s – Sinopoulos served as a doctor in the National Army – are never dispelled but are struggled with in a painful but artistically fruitful variety of ways. In this steadfastness, this rootedness in a landscape and this attempt to find a meaning of, in some way, a Christian kind, Sinopoulos deserves comparison with his more widely read contemporary, the German poet Johannes Bobrowski (1917–65). Fortunately, there is a generous range of Sinopoulos' work available in English – which makes it the more surprising that his name is not often conjured with when we speak of modern Greece's major poets. The pinnacle of his achievement is *Nekrodeipnos* (here translated as *Deathfeast*), a work which germinated until its eventual publication in 1971 and which, like a powerful magnet, draws into its pattern all the fragments of the Civil War experience. Christian symbolism, Homeric catalogue and, in the cinematic sense, documentary elements all cohere within a distinctive form to make a Greek poem that everyone should know.

Philip

Philip will not return. I tell myself,
to this motionless valley.
We had promised him much by way of plunder and sirens,
but he turned towards to other visions.
He dreamt of an unbounded homeland. Where are your faces,
he cried to me, your real faces?
He left me, weeping, to scale the shining mountains.
Then the sea was choked up with ships.
The land turned black, marked by an evil winter.
The mind turned black. A long river of blood.
Philip will not be back. The wind is high tonight.
Midnight in Larissa, the deserted café.
A waiter's rheumy face, and the night
harrowed by fires and gunshots.
A city fantastic and unmoving.

Trees fallen in the building yards.
What is the warrior's justice,
one struggle leading on to another?
Philip will not be back. He always, unrepentantly, grew stubborn.
The dark days and the ruined faces irked him.
Hearing, his blood scaled the high mountains.
And I remained alone
walking and whistling in hollow Larissa. And then,
as far deep as Macedonia, moving half-closed
under the wide winter moon,
speaking only of the body, the widowed
Madame Pandora. Her husband
died of consumption in the days of '44.

Doanna

You snap this branch you snap the other branch
but the waters you searched for are not here.
Though you cross stones and earthen banks
you'll not find the white river.
Nothing but reefs and sand and desolation
red bushes in the sun
red rocks and logs
and wood and iron fragments further on. Call out.
They'll hear your voice and answer
with that same voice. But they no longer recall
when they came what they sought
at this dark crossing.
                                        Do not go on.
The dust will ravage you the dust will cover you
and you must not call out.
So in this boundless light the white river
will not come wait
it will never come
the white river
the white river.

The Mother Interprets the Land

1

Dreams and omens brought us here. We took root.
Though wise men look for signs,
dreams alone will not tame the land.
These forests shifting in the water's mirror
sometimes catch fire at night.
Primordial trees extend the vegetation to the sea.
Fields and roads wind among them,
distant plains little more than stone and sky.
Morning.
Out of greyness the mountains bring the sun
wrapped in the cloak of legend. The wind comes ringing down.
Noon smells of antique drums.
The light falls between the fig-tree and the vine,
slanting and motionless. At night you hear again
the rasp of wind on reeds. Other sounds can be heard,
of loneliness and need. Of the tenants
some sleep some explicate the stars
while others under a dim light
sharpen their knives across some awkward stone.

2

The deep river lies further back,
darkens at sunset full of images.
Brings coolness from the mountain. At night
a long dugout loaded with animals and fruit
slides luminous across the water, wrinkles the river's husk.
Voices look for an answering hail
as lamps move slowly through the reeds. Then suddenly
you fling the sharpened punt pole down
to shiver in the sand. The mountain sends its coolness.

3

The need to stay here, to possess your own life
must, I have dreamt, be rooted in the blood.
Wrinkles come hand in hand with toil

and death is fitting.
Because there is both drought and thirst.
Because the land suddenly shrinks at night.
Because there are pitfalls and traps.
And the neighbour,
spawned under the wolf's sign
rapacious, vilely restless
follows his quarry bush by bush
into the aged silence of the valley.

A black flight of wild geese
winging into the crimson sun
explains the sudden and merciless murder.

The Window

We bricked the window up, the window blew from the rubbish dumps, what did we gain? What did we lose?

Walking speechless in these hard, these incoherent years.

There was a room, so desolate. A lamp hung from the wall and the light swung face to falsehood.

We turned it round towards the time of memory.

Just a small river, its name lost in the silence of the sands.

We closed the window. The soil outside was restless and the tree raved at the waxing moon.

Heavy with menace, the real moon emerged out of the dream.

Above the Seasons

Night had already covered half of me and I said I shall discover stones and springs, other deposits to enrich your laughter – you were laughing

and I could hear my years wasting on the sands.

The day grew darker, I was not alone. Above the seasons came the unseen flash which carried me up high to the echoing intervals.

The scales lay shattered down below.

the sound of bugles on the twilit frontier.

Translated by John Stathatos

Sophia Etc

Inscrutable, at her zenith, among the thirsty trees of July, Sophia undulated night after night, her father died in a terrible

accident, six months ago, black dress, and her body persistently browned at noon on the beaches of Athens, her bosom as she bent down

really beautiful, proud those two breasts of hers, and Lefteris knew, he alone: shut up tight, that Sophia, even if she would flirt a little, and her legs restless under her chair while

we would sit our evenings on the sidewalk to cool ourselves, she gossiping with Fani, giggling, and on our way back that beauteous body would sway at the rear,

Lefteris close behind, I questioned him whispering, he laughed, his moustache blonde above his lip, good-looking boy that,

I took fire then, wrote poems madly, been looking through them today over a cup of coffee, can't face it, absorbed by the writing anyway,

There's a knock on the door, my brother John, wanted a loan and got it, see that you get married, he says, it's high time,

John, I says, Johnnie boy, what did you get out of it? Lola deserted you, left you stuck with that problem kid, always whining,

he'd brought the kid over some time ago to have me look at his throat, tonsils as big as walnuts, you have those out, I says to him, those buggers mean trouble, full of pus, so who should I go to? he whines, and I says to the devil, giving him the address of Pastras' clinic,

your worthy brother failed to appear, Pastras tells me, pompous words to hide
his inner emptiness, behind him Magda looking on,

a pure cypress tree that Magda, window and light on her left, and those eyes
of hers, rivers, birds ascended,

come on, Magda, but she just looked on, smiling vaguely,

wholly absent, nothing doing there I gathered, Pastras must be really in,

punk by the wine-dark sea, a mirror at the far end so I studied myself, not bad
looking despite the years, and I said to myself

Christ what a girl, then Magda left, on the back of her hair an orphan glow,
and it was sunset, flooded by green I wandered alone among vegetable gardens,
someone called out 'Helen!' from the far side of the fence,

Helen came dragging along, she made me sick, stumpy, unbearable, nice getup
you got there she says admiringly, and my tailor looked sour, I couldn't pay
him, and his father silent on the bench,

he was a sexton at Ayandreas, Demetro old man you've got it made, but what
kind of job is that really with candles and incense in the middle of summer not
to mention the heat rash from the frock, and I was

down there on the dry river bed, flat on my face, damned wind from the slanting ravine, vertical mountains above,

the machine guns threshing, echoes, thousands of stones bursting into myriads,
a motionless sun high above giving birth to other suns and no

grass, no water, thirst only, sadistic flies, and son of a bitch I forgot to call Litsa,
we had

Poros in mind for Sunday, Litsa and Marika, and Antonis from Larissa, as I
touched the heel of her hand she shivered, slipping away, a boat and water,

further on the sand burning, body on the sand, memory, a huge light, clay higher
up if you turn around, bridges, straight ahead,

to the eye Litsa on her back a golden Epsilon, the toenail red, the toe stirring, the foot slowly, lazily, toying with the water,

seaweed, slate, seashells,

great sea, sparking, diamonds and

great black light.

Magda

Great black light.

All night long the light and Magda's eyes, the birds crossing Magda's eyes, the ceaseless memories of Magda's body, her birds on the night's every branch, then the dark head divided by the light, the darkness on her lips, a new love rising.

And the corridor beyond, someone outside whistled waiting for an answer, and the night full of trees, and as the light turned it caught the kiss in the distance and clouds of breath concealed the sky.

The failing darkness flooded with riches. Everything

becoming a dark net, so large, and mirrors motionless throughout the house, on every wall, in every corner, mirrors enigmas deepening to infinity, you couldn't tell which, where your face was.

Then Magda got up, a glimpse of her naked body, and without a word Magda went through to the inner room, was transformed, came back, was now Artemis, Mina, Demetra, was now distant Nana in the darkness of Larissa, behind the station, alone, bleeding, running distraught.

And as Nana approached Paul arrived too, sick, crippled by war, and he gazed at the sky speechless, and as Nana approached, the wild kiss darkened, higher up the dim ridge of the shoulder steamed and a slanting path ascended.

And beyond, the shops of Pyrgos and the great forest of Kapeli, and beyond, the afternoon and the bay of Ayandreas and the myriad pebbles and the sand and the water blood only.

And as knees buckled all bloody, the gunshots threshed the shore and we crawled off with the departing day, scurried through that iron doorway, and suddenly the burst above our heads, and then

the next burst, and the next, and the next, and I trembled listening.

Footsteps approached and faded, approached again, faded, Magda, and her hand a bird inside the shirt, I gazed then at the mark on the neck growing dusky, turning red, below her nape the hair exploded like a city blasted.

So beautiful, and the darkness reaching the thighs, I held her and she had an odour of burnt sea, then John and Jerry arrived, and many others, but I couldn't recognize them even.

So many years had passed since they were born and grew up and took to the rifle, the knife, the axe, whatever each could manage, and then got lost on the black road,

strewn with splinters of iron and glass from the veranda shattered by the blast, the whole house seeming naked, deserted to its inmost room.

And then footsteps again, and more footsteps.

And then,

at the window, the moon in her hands: Magda, and behind her, soundlessly: Nana and Artemis and Demetra and Mina, on the right and the left: darkness, between the black and the green: their eyes.

Night eyes, eyes that kept moving towards love, eyes fixed, divining love, eyes made suddenly wide by beauty, strange-coloured, as in a station when a train arrives and raises a steamcloud and then they reappear, those eyes.

And the train passed, crossing the room, and I drew back my leg in fear – the other I lost fighting in Albania – and as I found myself with paper and pencil in hand, beginning with the phrase 'Great black light'

my hand was writing this poem, the light was turning away from the paper, the paper was growing dark, I realized Magda was leaving, the moon was leaving, slowly descending the steps, into the garden, into the trees, moving away.

I suffered hearing her sound.

I suffered hearing her body.

Huge gagged words inflated my chest.

Translated by Edmund Keeley and George Savidis

Deathfeast

Tears scorched me as I wrote alone, what was I, speaking like this with

year upon year quickening the lost faces, and from the windows came

glory, dull golden light, benches and tables all about

the windows mirroring the underworld. And they came
dismounting one after the other,
Porporas, and Kontaxis, and Markos, and Gerasimos, dark
hoarfrost on the horses and the day slanting
through quiescent air, Bilias came and Gournas
gypsies imprinted on the dusk, and Fakalos, carrying
mandolins, flutes, guitars,
the soul leapt at the sound, the house smelt everywhere
of rain and wood, and when,
only when they'd lit a great blaze to warm themselves, then only
did I call them.

There came Sarris, and Tsakonas,
Farmakis, Toregas, and

Face pox-scarred, bitter, clawed the ground with his nails by the castle at Akova,
he bled, spoke of pain and debauchery, so dark was he that I became afraid, ran
stumbling off down the hill.

We took the low road, ashes everywhere, iron, burnt earth, a black X painted
on the doors told death had passed that way, days and nights and the machine
guns reaping

and you would hear oh! and nothing more. And many

came. Before them came Tzannis, Eleminoglou, Papparizos, followed by

Lazarithis, and Flaskis, and Constantopoulos – no one can say in which church they were sung, in what ground buried.

Then I helped him climb out, he'd fallen backward in the ditch, and as I held him he died n my arms, and the next month his wife smelling of grass, at noon deep in the garden telling her of his death, the full dark body whimpered on my chest, at night the forests and the roots would glow, for years the voice persisted and.

Moon, moonlight, close days, winter building itself a tower of stone, sunless and hard, I heard the first knock and the second knock, at dawn they smashed down the door and dragged us out breathless, 'wait here', and so much light was dawning.

There came old men and children.

How could they survive in such ragged clothes,
how could the children grow up in such horror?
The old ones creaking, taller than their bodies.
And the children,
clutching the axe, the knife, the hatchet
contempt and menace in their eyes, nor did they speak.

Ditches, wastelands, mothers in black wailing, whom did you kill, whom did you kill, how many have we killed?

So much blood and then we came across Louka's hands in the gully, and others severed at the wrist, we'd find them in the gully after months on the move,

here today, tonight elsewhere

murderers, narks, thieves and fornicators, soldiers, policemen, householders and shopkeepers

and many others riding on time's back and from among them

ruin's daughters stepped out, hunger and fever, set up against the wall, an ill wind blew. And there came

Fani and Litsa sweet-apple trees, Dona came and Nana, slim as the wheat, Eleni's maidenhair still green,

laurels, myrtles, wild vines
small lost rivers.

And one morning

that morning when I woke the tree had turned all green, I loved it so much that
it rose to the sky.

And birds arrived, birds of sunlight and joy, filling the place with colours and
feathers, perwits and felderels and other such fantastic species, skimmers and
calicocks and morrowdims, and gifts of the Lord, merry birds, constant slashes
in the blue sky. And among them came

Yannis Makris, Petros Kallinikos, Yannis the lame.

We sat on the embankment, Rouskas took out his pocket-knife and cut down
the young grass.

And mist over the plain. And you could hear spring coming, a door whose wood
smelt of the sky.

Then came the days of forty-four
and the days of forty-eight.
And from the Morea up to Larissa
deeper yet into Kastoria,
a black pestilence on the map,
Greece's breath rasping –
we held a count that Easter in deserted Kozani,
how many stayed on high, how many travelled on
stone, branch and hill,
down the dark river.

Prosoras came holding his broken rifle,
Alafouzos, and Bakrisioris, and Zervos
approached the gathering. Look, I shouted, and we looked:
a flood of light, the fruitful sun a monument
to the obscure dead. The years have passed, I told them,
our hair's turned grey.
Tzepetis came, and Zafoglou and Markoutsas
they settled themselves on the bench
and Constantinos nursed his foot at the end.

The voices gradually grew calm.

Gradually, as they had come, they disappeared,
took to the valley, scattering the wind.

For the last time I watched them, called to them.
The fire sank to the ground and from the windows came –

How just a single star can make night navigable.

How in the empty church is the unknown dead anointed
his body laid to rest among the flowers.

The Train

Sleep kept evading him, hot as Hades, blazing noon, the room an inferno, flung himself down again, Fani across from him,

her eye motionless in the frame, dead these seventeen years, and beyond the room the railway station, ramshackle engines sinking into rust.

A train at twelve, a train at three, a train at four-fifteen, then the train jerked forward lazily, you could hear couplings and bones, wheels and bones, and the wide sky behind the houses, and the black sky behind the trees, the train

rolling downhill, parched wastelands, he leaned out of the window, that nameless woman did not come to the level crossing, her face like dust and ashes, to drag the heavy chain across, the asphalt road stayed open, nor did the dog budge, hidden in the carnations, the train

went down the other hill, dead ahead, and to the right a pine tree sucked up the light, the sea thirty feet further down, glittering like a mirror in the sun, the salt smell of the sea, the meagre sand, the water in imagined continuity, the meagre sand burning his body, burning beneath the sun.

So naked and supine, thrust into summer, his head rang, swelling full of cypress trees and cicadas.

Within him darkness and echo and numberless sparks, and outside on the sand a great light, a wide unmown field of light, and he swollen like that and naked, supine, in this incredible obliteration, his vacant eye recording the sky's incidents, the motionless cypress trees and a flight of black birds, banking,

stooping down on his corpse, ravening at the entrails, shoving each other, they feasted greedily and the terrible wings could be heard beating in the light.

Silence descended all about.

God came down with his harrow.

He sat down all in white, enormous, sat down beside the stool, his clothes obscuring the sand, and his broad hand dug down, his white fingers sifted the sand, and God

said, slowly raising his hand, let the birds be gone, and they fled, startled, flying between the cypress trees, fled, covering the horizon.

And God said.

And Fani came, walked dark and speechless down to the stones of the beach.
And the caretaker came, limping,
Nikos from the kiosk and the wide
river beyond Larissa, and then the bridge, and the road outside Kozani, and the machine guns, and the company commander's cry from the dark ravine, Fani came,

to the endless hospital, passages and light, and higher still red hills, the hills red, impossibly red, then black as night came down and they strode with lamps through the timber, Zafoglou cursing and swearing and there came

thousands of documents and rubber stamps and seals and signatures, the committee at work and the dark wall behind them with the annotated map, fly shit, fag ends, the stooped voices stooping.

And then from the sand dunes, walking placidly, the woman came to the level crossing, slowly took up the chain, passed it over the hook, and her hand severed at the wrist, dry as a stick, her hand a cinder.

And five trucks pulled up one behind the other on the tarmac, then the dog struggled up, flew like a rocket at the train, as the train picked up speed, and

the bones started up, wheels and bones, iron-bones, and then the dog howled.
And he heard, in the depths, he heard.

And made to stand, stood up, fell again of a sudden.

The sea took him, lowering darkness darkening and freezing from the window,
the sea took him, rock stones and water vanished,

the chain, the asphalt, the five trucks,

the red rocks, stone gravel and sand and sky,

only the hollow sky.

Translated by John Stathatos

Yorgis Pavlopoulos (1924–)

Born in Pyrgos, Pavlopoulos comes from the same West Peloponnesian milieu and circle as Sinopoulos, with whom he remained in constant touch, but his much smaller body of work over the years has its own distinctive colour and contribution. A late developer, whose first book appeared only in 1971, under the Colonels' dictatorship, Pavlopoulos combines a devotion to the moral seriousness of Seferis and, behind that, of Makriyannis (qq.v) – honoured in 'Written on a Wall', a quietly eloquent protest against the dictatorship – with his own laconic and obsessive reflections. These poems have accumulated into a quiet *oeuvre* with a solidity which will outlast the flashiness and publicity of many others.

Written on a Wall

They put out our eyes
they ripped away our speech
and of that murdered voice
remain the root and blood
that split rock for water
and come back in blossom.

The Cellar

(Memory of Makryiannis) for George Seferis

We had shut ourselves with the poet in an old house.
I began fumbling for the papers of one like us
who looked for Justice,
I heard his voice always diminishing with no sense
that his voice sounds as this world is and even
when there is no-one any more.

And it was dark, turning up the lamp
I saw a chest and opened it with a shiver of hope,
found nothing, only the dust from destroyed
things that had rotted away, time consumed them;
at the bottom a pistol; I think I handled it.

The wind from the castle blew demonic through the rooms
and in the cellar you would have said someone unnailed the dead,
the earth, bones. Then quit. And again the wind
like a horse clattering by the garden wall –
it went, came back, and suddenly leaping the chasm of my dream
entered the yard, you could hear its hooves clear on the cobbles,
loud on the veranda, galloping upstairs.
It pushed the door and stood there among us
unhaltered, unbridled, panting, sweating, grey horse.
Looked into our eyes, grieved, lifted a foot,
stamped hard with one hoof and smashed the floorboard.
Stoop and what do you see? the poet said,
and kneeling over the black opening
I saw and recognized a mass of chained men –
the cellar filled with wasted bodies
groaning, and looking for Justice.

And so weeping took hold of me as day dawned,
and I went out, leant on the garden wall.
No one was near me. No poet, no grey horse.
Day broke darkly. Only behind the cypresses
a sword's light hanging in the wind.

Translated by Peter Levi

It Could Nowhere Be Found

We turned the world upside down searching
in humble huts and palaces
inside the fern in springtime
amid sands and snows
and we went down into wells
even into graves
but it could nowhere be found.

And wherever we asked, no one spoke
and wherever we knocked, no one opened
the courageous laughed
the cowardly were frightened
all who heard our names.

We turned the world upside down searching
and the years turned
and men vanished
and it could nowhere be found.

Details from a Poem

I found a stone with the marks of a very ancient script.
I meditated on the faces. Then his face came to the fore. On a noon black
   with too much light.
I was afraid to give him my hand. He was as yellow as a corpse.
I preferred walking beside him without looking at him.
For years now trapped in a room he nailed his eyes on the wall where spiders
   descended.
I don't know from where his voice emerged. As though he was speaking to
   someone whom he had not arrived in time to see in the past.
Many times in my dream I heard him burning and ran to save him from the
   flames. Nevertheless he kept on burning.
Afterwards he was found frozen. The landlady on the floor below howled.
That night I kept beating on the wall of this room that he might hear me as I
   shouted loudly to him in the underworld.

Translated by Kimon Friar

A Child's Drawing

It's snowing in Athens and in Warsaw
it's snowing in the whole earth
down here is the earth and the wagon
with the dead children
here the men that make war
the circus is empty
the horse keeps turning all alone
here is the weeping clown
he wipes his tears with newspapers
then lights them to get warm
it's cold we are hungry
it's snowing in Athens and in Warsaw
it's snowing on the whole earth.

Translated by George Thaniel

The Heifer

For Vangeli and Maria

> One night in spring
> she cut away from the herd
> and jumped into the sea with flowers on her horns.
> All night she swam
> and shivering at daybreak
> she came out to the sands and the pine trees
> and made love with a bull.
> They say that her desire opened ditches in the moon
> and the bull saw the woman naked
> in the bronze of the moon
> and waited for her by the waves
> with his nostrils dripping.
> And they say it was a crazy lady
> a nun from the convent on the Strophades
> who was transfigured into a heifer.
> If you pass by those parts
> among the sands and the pine trees
> there is a rift
> and that place is always damp
> and that, they will say,
> is the Nun's ditch.

Translated by Peter Levi

Miltos Sachtouris (1919–)

Sachtouris has, like Yorgis Pavlopoulos (q.v.), an intensely disturbing imagination; as with Pavlopoulos, the roots lie in the nightmare of the 1940s, which – though he is not a political poet – Sachtouris has constantly been trying to exorcize. Over the years he has established a somewhat unvarying but undeniably powerful climate of dark Surrealism. Sometimes this has affinities with a poet to whom Sachtouris has more than once paid tribute, Dylan Thomas (think, for example, of 'The Hunchback in the Dark'); sometimes it draws on the rich tradition of Greek folk poetry and above all the atmosphere of 'The Night Journey' ('The Ballad of the Dead Brother'), with which this anthology begins.

The Dead Man in Our Life, John Benjamin d'Arkozi

To Nikos Engonopoulos

John Benjamin d'Arkozi who died – 'in life' – and was resurrected as soon as night fell slaughters his herds every evening – goats cows and many sheep – drowns all his birds empties his rivers and on the pitch-black cross he has erected in the middle of his room crucifies his beloved. Afterwards he sits before his open window smoking his pipe poor and tearful and thinks if only he too had herds of cows goats many sheep if only he had rivers with swift pellucid waters if he too could marvel at the fluttering of birds if only he too could take joy in a woman's warm breath.

He Is Not Oedipus

A huge sky filled with swallows
enormous hall doric columns
the hungry ghosts
sitting in chairs in corners
weeping
the rooms with dead birds
Aegisthus the fishing net Kostas
Kostas the fisherman the afflicted
a room filled with tulles of many colours fluttering
in the wind

bitter-oranges break the windowpanes
and enter
Kostas killed
Orestes killed
Alexis killed
break the chains on the window
and enter
Kostas Orestes Alexis
others return to the streets from the fiesta
with lights with flags with trees
they call on Maria to come down
they call on Maria to come down from Heaven
the bones of Achilles fly in the heavens
rockets attend their flight
the sun rolls down from hill to hill
and the moon is a green lantern
filled with alcohol
then silence falls like night on the streets
and the blind man comes out with his cane
children follow him on tiptoe
he is not Oedipus
he is Elias from the vegetable market
he plays an exhausting and fatal flute
he is dead Elias from the vegetable market

The Scene

On the table they had set
a head of clay
they had decorated their walls
with flowers
on the bed they had cut out of paper
two erotic bodies
on the floor snakes slithered
and butterflies
a huge dog kept guard
in the corner

Strings stretched across the room
from all sides

it would be imprudent for anyone
to pull them
one of the strings tugged at the bodies
to make love

The unhappiness outside
clawed the doors

Nostalgia Returns

The woman undressed and lay on the bed
a kiss opened and closed on the floor
savage shapes with knives began to appear on the ceiling
hung on a wall, a bird choked and vanished
a candle leant and fell from its holder
weeping was heard outside and the clatter of feet

The windows opened a hand entered
afterward the moon entered
embraced the woman and they slept together
All night long a voice was heard:

*The days pass
the snow remains*

Translated by Kimon Friar

The Dove

The dove would soon be passing by
the people had lit torches in the streets
still others waited by the trees
children clutched little flags
the hours went by and it began to rain
later still the whole sky went dark
a bolt of lightning muttered terribly
and the cry broke out from man's throat
then did the white dove with the feral teeth
howl like a dog at night

Translated by John Stathatos

My Brothers

My brothers who disappeared down here on earth
are the stars that now light up one by one in the sky

and there's the eldest
with a black spring tie
who got lost in blindback caves
as he rolled playing
on red anemones
he slipped
into the blood-stained mouth of the wild beast

and then my other brother who was burned
would sell yellow fireworks
he would sell and set yellow fireworks ablaze
– When we light – he would say – a fire
we shall chase the ghosts from the gardens
the ghosts shall cease polluting the gardens
– When we set – he would say – yellow fireworks ablaze
one day the sky will flame up in blue

and then the third and youngest
who would say he was a bat
this is why he loved the moons
and the moons one night encircled him
stuck around him and closed him in
stuck around him and choked him
the moons around him dissolved him

my brothers who disappeared down here on earth
are the stars that now light up one by one in the sky

Translated by Kimon Friar

The Inspector

The sky
is a garden full of blood
and a little snow
I tightened my straps
I must once more inspect
the stars
I
the heir of birds
must
though with broken wings
take flight

The Watch

The sun was black
in my mother's garden
my father
in a tall green hat
charmed the birds
while I
with a deaf
and dubious watch
count the years
and wait for them

Translated by John Stathatos

The Visit

That afternoon I woke up with a strong desire to go to Piraeus and visit the K
family. With this family in the old days we were very close. However, as often
happens in these cases, with time these encounters thinned out, until finally
we didn't see each other at all. It must have been five to six years since the
last encounter.

These thoughts I had when I woke up that afternoon with the tyrannical, strong,
persistent desire to go on that same afternoon and visit the Ks. When I went
out in the street, I realized that something unusual was happening to me; an

unimagined calmness, an odd joy had flooded me. With this mood I entered the first taxi I found and said:

'Piraeus.'

It was a cloudy afternoon in March. From the cab's windows, as we drove, I was looking at the clouds which had taken something from the charm, something from the lightness I felt.

As we arrived at Piraeus the cab went to the port.

I took off in front of a huge white ship which was whistling, smoking, full of people.

I went up and asked for the captain.

'It's OK,' he said, smiling, 'you are leaving finally; all your expenses are taken care of forever wherever you are. You are finally leaving,' he repeated. And really, as I looked out from the cabin window we were already out of the port of Piraeus.

Translated by Dino Siotis

Manolis Anagnostakis (1925–)

Anagnostakis represents a remarkable case in poetic history, quite apart from the merits of his highly consistent and complex poetic *œuvre* with its unflinching comment on the state of Greece in the 1940s and after. He made an astonishingly precocious poetic début as a student in his native Thessaloniki, but the shape of his career was always to be affected by the death sentence – later commuted to a prison term – which was imposed upon him in a counter-insurgency trial of 1948: with characteristic defiance and probity, Anagnostakis refused to acquaint the military court with the extenuating fact that he had already been expelled from the Communist Party. A radiologist by profession, Anagnostakis commented on the Greece of the post-Civil War years with a physician's dispassion only just conceal-ing the intensity of his grief. By way of resistance to the Colonels' régime (and in collaboration with several other notable writers who feature in this volume, Seferis at their head), Anagnostakis produced one last collection, *The Target*, in which his sarcasm is taken to its limit – and then shut up poetic shop. Since then, he has published an anthology, some tren-chant personal and artistic jottings and, most oddly and enjoyably, a spoof biography of a fictional *alter ego* who wrote formally witty and *fantaisiste* verse of the kind which Anagnostakis wishes circumstances had allowed him to write *in propria persona*. But this element of engagement with other voices is evident right through his work: with Kipling in 'If'; with Cavafy (and Seferis, under the double-edged appellation of 'the Poet') in 'Thessaloniki, Days of AD 1969'; and finally with his contemporary, Titos Patrikios (q.v.), in his very last poem (the second by that name), 'Epilogue'.

Haris 1944

We'd all be together tirelessly unfolding the time
Singing softly of the days which would come laden with colourful visions
He'd sing, we'd fall silent, his voice would awake little fires
Thousands of little fires igniting our youth
Day and night he played hide-and-seek with death on every corner and in every
    alley
Would get out of breath oblivious of his own body that he might give others a
    Spring
We'd all be together but you'd think he was everyone.
One day someone whispered in our ear 'Haris is dead'
'He's been killed', or something like that. Words we hear daily.
No-one saw him. It was dusk. He'd have had his fists clenched as usual

Indelibly engraved in his eyes was the joy of our new life
But all this was simple and time is short. No-one's in time.
. . . We're not all together. Two or three went into exile
A third went off far away with a vague air to him and Haris was killed
Others left too, and came back to us new, the streets are packed
The crowd pours out unrestrained, flags once again flutter
The wind lashes the banners. In the chaos songs flapping.
If among the voices which of an evening pitilessly pierce the fortifications
You pick one out – it is his. It lights little fires
Thousands of little fires igniting our unbridled youth
It is his voice buzzing round in the crowd like a sun
Embracing the world like a sun slashing through grief like a sun
Showing us like a bright sun the golden cities
Spreading before us bathed in Truth and the clear light.

The New Song

N.M.

Nearer still; and your bonds will never be broken if they don't break now
We shan't be able to ask our thirsty expectancy:
Why do they never die now, the days which have ransacked us so?
Or in the year we started to love like men and girls would tug away a hand
    without knowing why
And yet, perhaps, it might have been fine, like an open book, had the hours
    passed noiselessly surrounded by security
And if we could forget death, we who envied the butterflies of our summer
    memories.

One day I shall write the history of my times
A garden with unready roses pointlessly picked
A sea on which ships sail with no destination
People squandered just when they had succeeded in lightly touching a
    carefully hidden side of us
People whose love was a wound in us; I'll write this down for you.
Meanwhile on the banks of the noonday rivers pale Narcissi are no longer
    sleeping, they and their sensitive souls
On the park pond children are no longer sailing their fresh daydreams on
    their little paper boats
I remember our secret expectancy: the tightening-up at the sight of the first

yellow leaf leaving an unrelievedly bitter taste in the mouth.

That's enough of the days that tired us so
(Painful bodyings-forth of immaterial visions)
That's enough of the azure Aegean sky with poems sailing to insignificant
islands to awaken our sensitivity
Of girls falling in love with their own form in the mirror and waiting to
dandle their delicate dreams
In big cities people love impulsively and die
They run, their words grow prematurely heavy, their hearts hammer away
like metal
In the noisy harbours I went and breathed a chest-full of mist at the docks
which are unwilling to grow old
I came down to bring you the love I sought so intensely from you and I
search for it breathlessly
On the dark ships dropping anchor, laden with maritime images and coal
In the low-ceilinged rooms of the great tall buildings which hold fire and
mystery
And the clocks beat rhythmically. I haven't time.
Sole vision of my expectancy.

On the thresholds of demolished houses defeated soldiers await their home-
coming without hope
In their empty skulls war-cries wander
The horror of senseless battle kills their nightmarish time
Pale words compose wounded elegies
And I am dreaming of one day trampling on my dead verses in order to
make emphatic in red letters (victorious trumpets) my new song.

Instead of Clamouring

Instead of clamouring and jostling
With the soapbox orators and mountebanks –
Prophets of doom and visionaries –
When my house was demolished
And dug deep under with all my possessions
(And I'm not talking about money and that sort of thing)
I took to the streets alone whistling.
It was of course a great reversal
But the city was so beautifully in flames

Inconceivable fireworks ascended
To the mild sky advertising
Sudden deaths and apostasies.
Soon the news arrived that
All official archives and libraries had burned down
The new clothes in the shop windows, the museums
All the registry's details of births
And deaths – so that now no one
Knew if he was dead or still alive –
All the agents' transactions
The girls' records in the houses of ill repute
The presses and the newspaper offices.
Extraordinary night, decisive and unique
Definitive (not at all like the dénouements
Of thrillers at the cinema).
Nothing was now for sale.
Light now and superfluous, I took to the streets
I found Claire coming out
Of the Synagogue and arm in arm
Under the arches of the cries
We crossed the other bank with pockets
Now emptied of earth, of photographs and so on.

Nothing was now for sale.

There . . .

There you will find them.

A certain key
Which you'll take
Only you will take
And you'll push open the door
Open up the room
Open the windows on the light
The dazzled mice will hide
The light bulbs will be woken by the wind
There you will find them
Somewhere – among the suitcases and old hardware
Among the snapped nails, fissured teeth,

Pins in pillows, frames with gaps in,
Half-burnt bits of wood, ships' wheels.
You will be left alone a little in the light
Then you will shut the windows
And curtains carefully
Growing bold the mice will start to lick you
The mirrors will grow dark
The light bulbs fall still
And you'll take the key
And with sure movements without remorse
You'll let it drop in the sewer
Deep, deep in the thick waters.

Then you'll know.

(For poetry is not a way to speak,
But the best wall to hide our face behind.)

You Came When I . . .

You came when I was not expecting you. As every night
Burning the memory of grievous deaths
Feebleness of old age, terror of birth
In dark caverns, in the loop of pleasure
Beyond the empty plains of fragments
You came when I was not expecting you. Oh how you would have lived
You and I in times like those
Rotten fruit in the hold of a
Drunken ship on which everyone is dead
Sinking, thousands of holes in our bodies
Dim eyes insulting the light
Stray mouths on the rind of life
Burning the recollection – Dead men
In a period of irrevocable death
You came when I was not expecting you. And not a gesture
A word, like a bullet in the mark on the throat
Not a human voice because no
Voice had yet been born
The wild river had not yet been born
Which flows to the fingers' ends and then falls silent.

Recollection of a life – when will you start
So that I unscrupulous and mild of manner may hold forth
May at the cenotaphs utter lamentations
Worn by the obsolescence of the vocables
And you locking away tiny pleasures
Not trampling on your dead verses
Because if there are bones, love-affairs, and one-storey houses
With the blanket hung in the front doorway dividing the world
In two, hiding the spasm and the despair
And, outside, passers-by chanting in defiance of the faithful
In defiance of the sick child and the winter
Oh how you would have lived in times. And he unscrupulous,
Time, shattering thought
Fixed plans and violent decisions
Hovering whys, damp smiles
You came when I was not expecting you. Do not deceive me
These are not the thresholds I have knelt at
These crypts in which the rodents shiver
Have nothing of the taste of mud
Or of the soft touch of the dead in our dreams
Because something is left – if it is left –
Beyond death, perishability, words and action.
Imperishable in this ash I burn
As every night the memory of deaths
Of grievous and inexplicable deaths
Writing poems without sounds or words.

Epilogue [I]

It may be that these verses are the last
The last among the last that will be written
Because the future poets are no longer living
They who'd have spoken all died young
Their forlorn songs turned into birds
In some sky elsewhere with a foreign sun
Became wild rivers coursing to the sea
Whose waters you can never separate
In their forlorn songs there took root a lotus
That in its juice we might be born more young.

Poetics

— There you go betraying Poetry again, you'll say,
The most sacred manifestation of Man
There you are using it once again as a means, an instrument
Of your dark purposes
In full knowledge of the damage your example
Is doing to the younger generation.
— *You* tell me what you have *not* betrayed
You and your kind, year in year out,
Selling off your possessions one by one
In the international markets and the neighbourhood bazaars
And you are left without eyes to see, without ears
To hear, with sealed mouths, saying nothing.
In the name of what that is sacred to man do you imprecate us?

I know: more preaching and rhetoric, you'll say.
Well, all right then! Preaching and rhetoric.

Words need to be nailed down like *tacks*

Not to be gone with the wind.

Thessaloniki, Days of AD 1969

In Egypt Street – first side-street to the right –
There now rises the headquarters of the Bank of Exchange
Travel agents and emigration offices
And the small children can't play there any more for all the traffic
In any case the children are grown up, those times you people knew are over
They don't laugh any more, don't whisper secretively, don't trust each other,
Those children who've survived, that is, for since then grave sicknesses came on
Floods, drownings, earthquakes, armoured soldiers;
They remember father's words: you will know better days
It's not to the point whether in the end they did know them, they repeat the
    lesson to their own children
Always hoping that at some point the chain will stop
Perhaps with their children's children or their children's children's children.
For the moment, in the old street we were talking about, there now rises the
    Bank of Exchange

– I exchange, you exchange, he exchanges –
Travel agents and emigration offices
– We are emigrating, you are emigrating, they are emigrating –
Wherever I travel Greece wounds me, the Poet said
Greece with the lovely islands, lovely offices, lovely churches.

Greece of the Greeks.

If

If – I say if . . .
If everything had not happened so early on
Your expulsion from High School class five
Then Haïdari, Aï-Stratis, Itzedin,
If at 42 you weren't suffering from arthritis
After twenty years in jail
With two expulsions from the Party on your back, one recantation
When they got you on your own in the Psychiatric Clinic
If – today a clerk in a food business –
Useless now to anyone, a squeezed lemon,
A burnt-out case, with ideas long obsolete,
If, as I say if . . .
With a little good will things had turned out differently
Or through some chance incident, as with so many, many
Classmates, friends, colleagues – I'm not saying with a clean nose
Anyway . . .

(That'll do. Poems can't be written out of that sort of stuff. Don't keep on.
They need another air to them in order to please, another sort of
    'transfiguration'.

We've really gone overboard writing about subjects.)

Epilogue [II]

And above all no self-deception.

At the most conceive of them as a pair of dim searchlights in the fog
As a card to absent friends with the single phrase: I'm alive.
Because, as my friend Titos once so rightly said,
'Not one verse today sets in motion the masses
Not one verse today overturns regimes.'

So be it.
Cripple, show your hands. Judge that you be judged.

Translated by David Ricks

Aris Alexandrou (1922–1978)

Alexandrou (the pseudonym of Aristotelis Vasileiadis) is represented here, as few of the selected writers are, by work in both verse and prose. If in his case the influence of the latter has proved more pervasive – it is hard to imagine that Yorgi Yatromanolakis or Rhea Galanaki (qq.v.), among contemporary experimenters in prose fiction, could have gone about things in quite the way they have without Alexandrou's example – Alexandrou's poetic contribution (essentially completed by 1959) has its own colour and value. Perhaps best described as a humanist anarchist, Alexandrou, a native of Leningrad who moved to Greece as a child, suffered all the personal consequences of Left engagement, with long periods of internment in the 1940s and 1950s, without any of the consolations of allegiance to the Party; his poems anthologized here dramatize his predicament, some-times in terms recognizably adapted from Cavafy. In 1975, shortly after the fall of the Colonels, Alexandrou published *The Strongbox*, a complex novel about the Civil War (but 'about' in the way that Kafka's *The Trial* may be said to be 'about'), in which an increasingly self-entangled and unreliable narrator preparing a lengthy confession to whom he knows not unveils on a larger canvas the moral ramifications of Greece since the 1940s which have in various ways coloured the writing of all of Alexandrou's worthiest contemporaries.

Promotion

> Everything was so superb last night
> that the sea crystallized on the rocks
> and became salt
> the clouds crystallized up in the sky
> and became stars
> our silence crystallized down here
> and became a kiss.
> Everything was so superb last night
> except that it all came rather late
> just as one who's died in battle receives
> notification of his promotion to lance-corporal.

Translated by Peter Mackridge

No Man's Land

Be very careful with your words
just as you are with a badly wounded man
you carry on your shoulder.
Where you press on in the night
you may slip in shell-craters
you may get tangled in barbed wire.
Fumble your way in the dark barefoot
and stoop as little as possible
lest his hands drag along the ground.
Go forward ever firmly
as if in the belief that you will get there before his heart
    stops.
Exploit
every gleam of machine-gun fire
to keep your direction
always parallel to the lines of the two fronts.
Breathless go forward
as if in the belief that you will reach the water's edge
there in the morning shade of a great tree.
For the moment be very careful
just as you are with a dying man you carry on your shoulder.

Translated by David Ricks

The First Anatomist

Nikandros, the first anatomist of Corinth
silently, by lamplight, plunges the scalpel
between the jutting breasts of the Egyptian slave-woman
who was found
    raped
       murdered
          among the reeds.
Upstairs in the hall, on the couch
still lies the papyrus from his friend Danae.
Nikandros perceives clearly, he knows
all this 'you've gone far in this town
ruled by Christians who revere the corpse as the soul's repository

367

while pagans worship only the living flesh.
You've gone far, what will your brothers say,
Christians who apostasized and now observe the forms of the liturgy,
you've gone far and don't belong anywhere
how will you live and how will I live
cast out from the town
                outcast among outcasts?'
Let her talk.
Now his task is to cut open this breast
he has to do this first
here in this cellar by lamplight
hidden from everyone
                as though committing a crime.
As for the papyrus
the first anatomist of Corinth – after Galen –
isn't pressed at all.
Let the unopened papyrus
                lie on the couch.

Translated by Peter Mackridge

In Camp

Gnathon, former gladiator, now poet
watches the stars the camp sentries
and generally his spirit is a reed-bed beaten by a south wind.
How could he not be upset now that the deeds of the general of the Goths are known?
Not that Gnathon is responsible for the flight of the German.
He had simply fitted to prosody and metre
epithets used by Spartacus in his speeches
words of praise that figured in every gladiator's conversation as long as the Goth
    was their ally.
Of course he wasn't responsible.
And yet he would much prefer that he had settled
for lampoons on the Roman Senate.
Enough and more than enough the fame the jet-black mare and the golden
    mounting-block won already.
What had he been after with his hymn in honour of the German?
He wasn't responsible, of course; but then on the other hand why were people
    looking askance at him?

Why the turned backs and covert conversations?
This doubt must end.
Muse, bring rhythms to the aid of tired Gnathon.
Supply him with the form of a new lampoon.

Meditations of Flavius Marcus

Of course you may translate verses of Homer.
This is an occupation legitimate, sometimes profitable;
at any rate it helps you to pass in the eyes of some
as a man of letters and – with a certain note of condescension – a connoisseur
    of poetry, *grosso modo* a poet.
Translate with zeal, albeit with care.
One thing alone is to be avoided.
Take care lest you translate into your life
the demeanour and the passions of the heroes
however much they seem to be your own
however certain you may be that you could have fallen
before the walls of Troy.
Remember your belief your knowledge your conviction
that ultimately
        on entering the city
you
    would have found
            smoke and ash.

Chaerephon to Pindar

            Engraving your verses
            involuntarily you press on the wax
            your gold ring.
            Your far-shining odes
                            gilded
            will be preserved
                will be copied
                    with abundant notes
            with resolutions of ambiguous words
            with a detailed record of all the talents
            that you demanded and received for fee.

All those used to buying
positions medals glory
will announce you as a poet of talent.
What I write will soon decay
                              like flesh
but if by chance a few lines are preserved
as a jaw is preserved in the dust of a skull
palaeontologists will be able to reconstruct
my human form.

Translated by David Ricks

I Confess (*extract from The Strongbox*)

SUNDAY 13 OCTOBER 1949

Comrade investigator, I am beginning to wonder whether you are really a comrade after all. Or I might as well say that I'm definitely beginning to believe that you are no such thing. I'm telling you this quite bluntly and I don't care if it makes you angry. Just this once, try to put yourself in my place, try and look at the situation through my eyes, and then tell me if I'm wrong in saying that the whole business has taken a most unnatural turn. I've noted down a whole series of events, I've mentioned specific data, names, dates, etc., I've gone back on my account to include details that might elucidate some obscure points, I've even confessed that in certain instances I didn't tell the whole truth, yet you insist on remaining silent, you simply will not act your part properly, you refuse to question me, you let me flounder about wondering which points may possibly be of interest to you – but how on earth am I supposed to know?

And so, one supposition leading to another, it has eventually occurred to me that I am not really dealing with a comrade – yes, I confess there were days when I even suspected that the town of K had fallen again into the hands of the government forces, which explains why I wanted a table in my cell, I thought I would stand it in my bunk so as to take a look at the flag flying from the topmost loophole of the Venetian fortress, I wanted to find out if it is still our flag, because if it isn't our flag, the deposition I am writing will go straight into the hands of the enemy. Now do you realize in what a difficult position you are placing me?

Yes, of course there were times when the things I said were inexact, but concealing the truth wasn't the only reason, I also had another purpose in mind. The inexactitudes, I may say, were meant to act as bait, they were my way of trying to give you a chance to stop me and say: 'Ah no, I cannot accept that, in this particular instance I am in a position to know you are lying,' that is the sort of reaction I was expecting and aiming at, just so as to establish some sort of contact with you. I expected you to summon me to your office and subject me to a regular interrogation, night and day if need be, depriving me of sleep, even forcing me to remain standing for hours on end, under a blinding lamp or projector, the light falling straight down on my face, while you or your deputy sat back in the darkened room, nice and comfortable, yes, I would even accept that, I wouldn't mind standing there without bread or water, for hours on end, day and night, while you ate and drank in my presence, striking me across my face, even that, subjecting me to the *phalanga*, anything as long as I could be sure nothing has changed since the day you submitted me to the preliminary interrogation and decided I should be detained pending trial; whereas now, I repeat, your silence raises all kinds of suspicions in my mind, justified suspicions, you've got to admit, because if you do belong to the government forces, it would be only natural that you should have qualms about meeting me face to face, as you would have every reason to suspect, or rather to be convinced, that I am personally acquainted with the investigator of the anti-government forces. Of course you could easily have found a way out, a sufficiently plausible solution such as sending me a note via the warder, who has remained at this post ever since my arrival here, as far as I am able to ascertain, though how can you possibly expect me to be sure he is the same man, seeing that he flings open the iron door of my cell every morning, pauses on the threshold, gun in hand, orders me to get up and stand face to the wall, hands raised (to tell the truth, he actually ordered me to do that the first morning only, now he simply points to the wall with his gun and I obey), and only then, when my back is turned to him, he steps in and removes the used slop-pail and brings an empty one, so that by the time I finally hear the door clanging shut and lower my hands, he's already left, having placed in the corner of the cell a loaf of bread, a jug of water and a sheaf of writing paper, each page stamped with your seal. No matter how hard I try, I never manage to see his face clearly. All I can discern in the dark is a vague silhouette (for he always comes at sunrise, when the beams of light, creeping horizontally through the window, hit the opposite wall, a few inches below the ceiling), while I stand waiting – after he has left the cell – for the moment when the bright square of light will slide down the wall, at which point I go and press my back against the peeling wall, standing on tiptoe, so that the square of sunlight, glowing bright crimson, steeps through my eyelids, and I have the impression that the shadows of the two vertical bars in the window frame my face, their shadows running exactly along the line of my ears – I know this is only an impression of mine, the shadows of the bars have already become diffused by the time they reach the wall, but if it weren't for this natural law of diffusion, I am certain the shadows would coincide exactly with my ears – to resume them, it is only natural that at such a moment the light streaming into my cell should make the corridor appear so dark in contrast that I am unable to distinguish the warder's face, particularly as I keep my eyes focused on his gun.

Yet even if the warder brought me a note from you, even if he brought it in bright daylight and appeared before me without any attempt at concealment (so that I might at least have a chance to make sure he is indeed wearing the honoured uniform of the People's prison warders), even then a note from you would not be sufficient to persuade me that the town of K has not been recaptured by the government forces, for the simple reason that one can't exclude the possibility of disguise; we disguised ourselves as peasants when the need arose, didn't we? So why shouldn't you have a warder of the government forces put on the disguise of an anti-government warder? And to tell you my whole truth, so that you may realize what hideous suspicions cross my mind on account of your inadmissible, your preposterous, your totally unprofessional behaviour, I want to tell you that I've even begun to have doubts about the preliminary inquiry, in the sense that I wouldn't be at all surprised if even then, a few hours after my arrival in the town of K, you were quite simply a government agent disguised as an investigator of the People's Army, and consequently the reception I was given there was no more than a put-on job, a farce, in which a large number of townsfolk participated as extras. Or perhaps it was exactly the other way round, the townspeople took no part in the farce at all, but merely carried on as if nothing had happened, and they kept it up even when I drove past the church in the cart, reached the main square, and finally stopped outside the café to ask the way to Military Command from a group of corporals and soldiers who were watching two men playing backgammon, upon which one of the corporals asked me: 'What do you want Military Command for, pal?' and nettled at his tone I replied loudly so that everybody could hear me: 'I've come from N, I've brought the strongbox,' yet even then nobody in the café paid any attention, the backgammon players went on casting the dice in passionate concentration, while the others looked on with undiminished interest, except for the corporal, who told me in a tone that clearly implied it was high time I left him in peace: 'Drive straight on, turn left at the third corner, and a few yards farther on, you'll come to the high school. That's where it is.' Well of course, it was only natural that they shouldn't know what it was all about, since this was supposed to be a military secret, but let's not fool ourselves, our military secrets are never all that secret, there's always bound to be a leak, so in this particular case what may have seemed theoretically normal, natural, took on a thoroughly unnatural aspect, which fully justifies me in suspecting that the whole 'natural' atmosphere of the scene in the café was a put-on affair.

You see then what a state I've been driven to: here I am suspecting the entire town of K just because you refuse to show some sort of reaction, even in the case of events that are undoubtedly known to you – supposing, of course, that you are indeed the comrade investigator – such as the incident with the sleeping guard, for instance. At first I concealed the fact that the guard was asleep (or rather I simply omitted to mention it), because my sole concern was to prove that I have always remained loyal to the Leninist faction, and I considered that the guard was, in a manner of speaking, irrelevant, since he had no connection with any of the factions. On the second occasion, when I realized that the main point, the essential point, was not my personal attitude regarding the inter-party conflict, but my activity as a conscientious Party member, in other words the nature of my services to the Party as an entity, irrespective of personal disagreements, or rather – if you like, I will even go as far as confessing that, too – when I began to suspect that the Party leadership might have changed once again and that the historic decisions of the General Assembly of 29 August might have been reversed by another equally historic General Assembly, this thought naturally leading to the suspicion that perhaps I was not addressing myself to a Leninist investigator but to someone else who would use different criteria in judging me (doctrinaire criteria, why shouldn't I say so, I'm not afraid of words, I've run down the doctrinaire often enough), but on the other hand, just try and put yourself in my place, don't you think it is natural for the accused (supposing I do indeed stand accused), isn't it natural for the accused to plan his defence in conformity with the investigator's criteria, or I might as well say, with his individual inclinations, provided of course that the accused is fortunate enough to know what these inclinations may be, but anyway, the main point I wish to stress, allow me to insist on this, is that my change of tactics may appear at first glance like a kind of opportunistic manoeuvre, deserving to be characterized in the most censorious terms, but at bottom it was the only correct stand, and I should have adopted it from the start, because factions are only temporary, ephemeral phenomena, whereas the Party endures and will go on enduring, and consequently I was mistaken in carrying on about the trees while ignoring the forest, and now I make bold to place before you the view that in manoeuvring as I did and changing, or rather correcting, my standpoint, I not only dealt correctly with the problem in question, but also elevated you to a higher and therefore more honourable position (because in continuing my deposition in a true party spirit I was proving that I considered you fully capable of deserving this high position, appealing to your nobler, your more enlightened nature, meaning by this your nature as a loyal Party member, regardless of the faction to which you might happen to belong), and it was only natural that in correcting my standpoint I should find myself faced with the necessity to refuse certain parts of my deposition, not so much on account of the half-truths and lies I had told you previously, but mainly because this change in my standpoint allowed me to see things under a different light, which was the natural, the required thing to do, in consequence of which, having so to speak adopted the Party standpoint, I recounted the incident of the sleeping guard in much greater detail and made my self-criticism as a dutiful Party member, rising above all factional considerations, in other words I confessed that I had failed to report the guard, that is to say I had failed to perform my duty as a soldier and Party member.

On the second occasion, then (but I have to insist on this point once more: in retracting my former statement and therefore actually, or indirectly if you prefer, confessing that I had been lying, I truly believed that I was offering you a chance to step in and make an appearance at long last, showing your true face as my investigator, so as to put an end to the innumerable suspicions that keep tormenting me, as I have described above, admittedly with a touch of exaggeration – not that I deliberately overstated my suspicions in my deposition as an afterthought, no, they really did cross my mind during those long sleepless nights when I tossed and turned on my straw mattress – all I mean to say, quite simply, is that the suspicions I have put before you in all frankness did admittedly contain a certain amount of exaggeration,) on the second occasion then, as I was saying, I had the impression that the incident with the sleeping guard could not possibly fail to elicit some sort of reaction from you. While I was reporting the incident in writing, I kept telling myself 'Now he's bound to lose his temper, he'll give me hell, it's a sure thing, because Leninist or doctrinaire, no matter, you should have realized straight away that I was telling a brazen lie when I insisted that I hadn't reported the guard, affecting to offer my self-criticism in the process, so as to make my deposition more convincing. If you are really an anti-government investigator (Leninist or doctrinaire, that is irrelevant), you ought to have known that the guard (his name was Lysimachus) was executed at dawn on 7 July 1949, exactly five days and five nights after I arrived in the town of N, he was executed for that very reason, for 'having been caught sleeping while on guard duty', in other words he was executed precisely because I reported him. (The execution order was posted all over the centre of the town of N, because it was meant as a warning, an exemplary measure, and had to be brought to the attention of all and sundry, although my personal opinion was, and still is, that it was unnecessary to post the order since the guard was shot against the wall of the Zoodochos Piyi, this being the site where all public [so to say] executions take place.) And don't you try telling me: 'How was I to know all that occurred in the town of N at that time? I am under no obligation to know which guard was executed or which soldier was confined to quarters, nor do I care,' don't you try giving me that sort of talk because Lysimachus' execution is closely related – in fact, very closely related – to the whole business of Operation Strongbox, and I am in a position to prove it any time you should ask me to do so. In fact I challenge you to ask me. If you don't, I will have every reason to believe, better still, I will be absolutely convinced, that you are no comrade, in which case I must be deemed either a madman or a traitor if I carry on with my deposition under these circumstances – for who else would knowingly address his deposition to the enemy? I am challenging you once again. If you still refuse to demand an explanation from me on this point (in a manner that will persuade me that you are fully familiar with the case, in brief, that you are indeed the comrade investigator inquiring into the particulars of Operation Strongbox), you may be sure I will refuse to add another word.

Translated by Kay Cicellis

Titos Patrikios (1928–)

Patrikios is a poet whose name is often included with those of his fellow poets of the Civil War generation, Anagnostakis and Alexandrou (qq.v.), as part of a triumvirate which, forth from the Civil War emerging (to adapt a phrase of Whitman's which resonated in the ear of Nikos Engonopoulos, q.v.), devoted their powers to a memorializing of the dead and to intense moral self-examination and poetic self-questioning. (As we have seen, Patrikios' poem 'Verses 2' is actually quoted in Anagnostakis' last collected poem.) Like these other two poets, Patrikios paid for his Left allegiances with periods of internment and exile. More directly involved with the Party, however, Patrikios comments on the political atmosphere of 1950s and early 1960s in an equally mordant but much more direct and approachable way than does Anagnostakis – so direct that Takis Sinopoulos (q.v.) felt, unfairly but revealingly, that there was little enough of poetic substance. The poem recalling the show trial of the Hungarian Communist leader Laszlo Rajk in 1948, and its haunting of the poet's conscience, is a good example of this. Patrikios has laconically contributed, as his contemporaries Alexandros Kotzias and Thanasis Valtinos (qq.v.) have done in their novels, to documenting the low dishonest decades that followed the Second World War. In recent years this steady-minded poet has moved away from political poetry altogether, as demonstrated in the last two poems here.

Memories of Villages on the Spercheios

> The smell of stables, of damp grass,
> the smell of smoke from wet firewood
> the steam from our clothes drying
> the blistered feet, the lice.
> Sleep in the hay
> would come to us hungry as we were and full of optimism
> after a poem
> or a discussion about the distinction
> between *kolkhoz* and *sovchoz*.

Athenian Summer in 1956

> This year we had so many events . . .
> Nonetheless, the summer was the same as ever,

the same ice-creams in the confectioners
and the same concert programmes.
Lots of people were also discussing change
which they located principally
in the restoration of ancient monuments
or in the hairstyles of ladies
some of whom had actually
once been active in the Resistance.

At the Cinema

Politely we relax side by side
laugh or are moved
pursuer and hunted
tortured and torturer
lover and husband.
For just two hours in the dark
calm, anonymous and well-disposed.

Idyll

She was drinking an orangeade
in the background hair salons and travel agents
while the fellow next to her
was entrancing her with idiotic verses.
And yet
her name was Antigone.

Rehabilitation of Laszlo Rajk

However much I'd like to I cannot mourn you, Laszlo
since I too was visiting your cell back then
in the fearful guise of Peter Gabor,
since I was there when they interrogated you
when they tortured you, when you confessed,
since I continued to condemn you even at the very time
I was starting to hear inside me the cracks opening up.

May '56

Like Grave-Robbers

And if poets in our time smell too much for your taste of corpses
it is because at night they hang around the cemeteries like grave-robbers
searching the dead in the hope of finding even a scraping of truth.

Verses 2

Verses which make an outcry,
verses which supposedly stand tall like bayonets
verses which threaten the established order
and with their few feet
make or break the revolution,
useless, fake, boastful,
because no verse today breaks regimes
no verse mobilizes the masses.
(What masses? Between ourselves, now –
who thinks of the masses?
At the most it's a personal release, if not a way of getting a reputation.)
That's why I no longer write
in order to provide paper rifles
weapons out of verbose, hollow words.
It's just to lift up an edge of the truth
to shed a little light on our forged life.
As long as I can, and as long as I hold out.

August '57

Indebtedness

Out of all the death that has come down and is still coming down,
wars, executions, trials, death and more death,
sickness, hunger, random accidents,
murders of enemies and friends by paid assassins,
systematic undermining and prepared obituaries,
it is as if the life I live has been granted by act of clemency.
A gift of chance, if not theft from the lives of others,
for the bullet I escaped did not vanish
but hit the next body which found itself in my place.

So as a gift I was not deserving of life has been given me
and such time as I have left
is as if granted to me by the dead
to limn them.

November '57

Words

'Mother,' I said to her through the bars of the holding cell,
'I've talked so little with you . . . Once I get out . . .'
The gendarme was standing right there.
I was facing the possibility
of never seeing her again.
When years later I went home
she fell into my arms and started to cry,
but the words once again came out inadequate.
And I took my shaving things
to go and have a bath and shave.

Eight Years

He was away eight years.
Prison, Makronisos, exile.
When he returned
his friends set about embracing him and asking him questions.
But what he had to say seemed so simple
so ordinary . . .
And he shut his eyes for a moment
in order to see once more the frozen isolation cell,
the nights in the ravine,
to re-live just a little the agonies of each day
which now, in the well-fed town,
were turning into oft-repeated clichés.

Half-Forgotten Poem

We are the children of the rain and of the wild lightning
the liberating earthquake of a storm to change the world . . .
Big words, you'll say, bad poetry,
and I can't even remember who wrote it,
yet in those days that's exactly how we felt.

Epitaph

Were I a better poet
I would fit your bare names
into one unending sequence going forth to meet the future
with nothing but their own intrinsic music.

Translated by David Ricks

A Town in Southern Greece

This town has crippled me, just as long ago
a town might have crippled me,
with its barracks its empty factories
its black walls topped by broken glass
its narrow streets, treeless, dry
its swarthy, salty women
mobile, fluid, with coal-black eyes
olive skins lightly perspiring
just enough for transient, fleeting love
on shadowy, half-deserted sea-shores
with their stones, tar, rust and thorns.
This town cures me with its nights
the nights of my country that never change.

Loves

A love is born within love
grows larger in its belly
spreads into its space, inhabits it
desires permanence, lays claim to time
prevails, enjoys its superiority
and as soon as it is satisfied with its gains
another love is born in its belly
grows larger, spreads into its space
threatens to tear it to pieces.
But sometimes loves stop
feeding on their adversaries' flesh
and exchange stone likenesses
that remain unaltered within the surrounding decay
and coexist without pointless hostilities
more or less amicably, like the busts
of rival leaders in cemeteries.

My Language

It wasn't easy to preserve my language
amid languages that tried to devour it
but I went on counting in my language
I reduced time to the dimensions of the body of my language
I multiplied pleasure to infinity with my language
with it I brought back to mind a child
with a white scar on his cropped head where a stone had hit it.
I strove not to lose even a word of it
for in this language the dead spoke to me.

Translated by Peter Mackridge

Stratis Tsirkas (1911–1980)

Where many Greek writers seeking to express their response to the 1940s sought to do so in a highly condensed, oblique and personal manner, this novelist of ambition waited almost two decades after the end of the Second World War to set out on a large canvas the political vagaries of the wartime Middle East (and to generate, by extension, a sweeping critique of the post-war years). Tsirkas (the pseudonym of Yannis Hatziandreas) took his trilogy's title, *Ungoverned Cities* (1960–65), from a poem by a much respected friend, Seferis (q.v.), and in one sense the trilogy, set in the cities of Alexandria, Jerusalem and Cairo (the author's native city), is a vast extrapolation of Seferis' preoccupations in his *Log Book II* (1944; see especially the poem 'Last Stop' above) and, behind that, of Cavafy's historical irony. (It may also be seen as a strongly Greek and Left-wing counter to Lawrence Durrell's *Alexandria Quartet* (1956–60).) The following extract comes from the start of the second and perhaps most immediately engaging of the three novels, narrated by the protagonist, Manos Simonides. (The Little Man is an orthodox Stalinist who dogs his steps just as much as the imperialists.)

Drifting Cities (*extract*)
Book II: Ariagne

> ... *the baffling and intricate passages from*
> *room to room and from court to court were an*
> *endless wonder to me, as we passed from a*
> *courtyard into rooms, from rooms into*
> *galleries, from galleries into more rooms,*
> *and thence into yet more courtyards.*
>
> Herodotus, *Book II, 148*

> *And yet we ought to consider where we are going;*
> *Not as our pain would have it and our starving children*
> *And the gulf of calling from friends across the sea.*
> George Seferis, 'An Old Man on the Riverbank', Cairo, 20 June 1942

Hundreds of miles in the rear of the Eighth Army, on that fatal Sunday 13 December 1942, Sergeant Michalis Saridis and I were 'hastening' to catch up with the First Greek Brigade before it began to move up the west coast of the Gulf of Sidra. Rommel was retreating steadily. Wishing to avoid a confrontation with Montgomery, he conducted a series of elusive manoeuvres; these flank movements, traced on an army map, emphasized how right the Bedouins were when they named him, six months ago, the Desert Fox. But our progress was very slow; I used the word 'hastened' only as a manner of speaking. Neither Michalis' knowledge of mechanics nor my relentlessness could make our vehicle do more than a hundred miles a day. It was quite unbelievable, the amount of water that old tin coffin could consume. An ancient truck, it had the shape and colour of a frog and the pace of a turtle. Michalis said, 'If the big industrialists of Milan have saddled Mussolini with jalopies like this to tow his anti-tank guns, then I must say the anti-Fascist workers of the Fiat factories are not alone in deserving a medal for passive resistance.'

On our right was the Mediterranean – at its very best. Since the day before yesterday, we had a spell of halcyon weather, though the Allied communiqués kept deploring 'highly unfavourable weather conditions' in Tunis as an excuse for the fact that our advance had come to a halt. On one occasion, I took a bucket to fetch sea water from the foot of the cliff. But Michalis stopped me: 'Salt water won't do, Simonidis, try to understand! In half an hour, the radiator will only be good for the garbage dump.' The old Fiat truck was Michalis' own personal war booty; he had got it at El Alamein. He had changed its pistons, patched up its tyres, repaired the holes in its tank, and then managed to get a regular transit permit to join the Brigade, it was thanks to all this that I now found myself rolling along through Allied outposts, only just controlling my impatience to reach the front and find my real self at last. The exasperating procrastination of our people in Jerusalem had deprived me of a chance to fight at El Alamein. Luckily, moving from one liaison to another, I had finally come upon Michalis Saridis. 'No problem at all!' he said. 'That's where I'm heading. And that's why I'm getting the old jalopy back into shape.' This conversation took place in Mersa Matruh, under the casuarina trees edging the road that led to the salt flats. 'But you'd better wear your epaulettes and your cap. The Allies are not like our people; they respect officers. A little bluffing won't do any harm. I'll pretend I'm your driver, and they'll think this fine limousine left the garage for the express purpose of taking the uniformed gentleman to the front.'

At first he refused outright to let me take the steering wheel. 'You'll wreck it, you're so jumpy. This jalopy needs a gentle, coaxing hand – you're in such a state one would think a pack of hounds were after you. If you're in such a hurry, get yourself a lift with one of those Allied drivers who keep waving at us.' It was true: Poles, British, Australians, Free French, in sedans, in trucks, in every conceivable sort of vehicle, would stop and offer a lift when they saw us tinkering over the steaming engine of the old Fiat. But Michalis knew very well that I couldn't accept their offer. It would take time to get friendly with them and talk them into driving me where I wanted to go. Getting into the first car or truck that happened to come along, on the chance that everything would work out, would be sheer foolhardiness. Michalis finally admitted that we'd never catch up with the Brigade if we didn't drive by night as well; so he relented about letting me drive but not without imposing certain conditions. I promised him anything he wanted. He allowed me a trial drive for about an hour, and then he leaned back in his seat and went off to sleep.

It was a moonless night, but the stars were very bright. The surrounding sands were white as chalk, and the road cut across them like an endless black ribbon. As soon as I caught sight of another vehicle on the road, I switched on our dim blue lights to stop if from colliding with us; in the rear of the truck, a tiny red light, no bigger than a cigarette but, shone constantly as a warning to anybody in a hurry. I suffered from the cold, and soon I was seized by an irresistible desire to sleep. I'm not sure, but I think that after a while I did fall asleep, with my eyes wide open, clutching the wheel. A tall, thickset Crusader, dragging his armour and breastplate, strode along with us. He fixed his eyes on me and lifted his great sword with his left hand, in a sort of protective gesture. I had seen that armour before, hanging above a large fireplace in the castle built by an eccentric Frenchman from Alexandria in the middle of the desert, about forty miles from El Alamein. That was where I had been put in touch with my liaison, another Frenchman, badly wounded at Bir Hakim; he was supposed to help me get as near the border as possible. I had found him sitting in an ancient armchair in the banqueting hall of the castle, obviously enjoying every minute of the days, or even hours, that he had left to live. He raised his bright eyes to the armour hanging on the wall, and then lowered them to the cross of Lorraine that adorned the marble mantelpiece: 'Well, comrade, what do you think? We're all crusaders! Only this time the purpose of the struggle is truly holy.' I told him I had come from Jerusalem. 'What a long way . . .' he said dreamily. 'Not very many years ago I was a royalist, one of Charles Maurras' followers . . . Fortunately, "Guernica" – no, not the massacre itself, I mean Picasso's painting in the Spanish Pavilion.' I nodded approvingly so as not to interrupt him. He smiled at me; he was pleased I understood. 'That's the way we intellectuals function. Sometimes we need a strong, living experience, a sudden flash of intuition to make us understand the essence of things. Your statue of "Victory" at the Louvre . . . Do you remember her clipped wings? Right here, in this very armchair, I heard those mighty wings flap over our heads and shake the foundations of the world. It was nine-forty, on the night of 23 October, when the eight hundred field guns of El Alamein –' He broke off. Then: 'Why am I telling you all this? I've got a high temperature today. It is better simply to be grateful for the present moment, as it slips through the narrow neck of the hourglass . . .' He lifted an orange to his nose and inhaled deeply, reverently.

I must have been trying to remember his name when the lower layers of my subconscious were disturbed and I was jolted out of my half-sleep. From then on, as soon as I heard the armour clanking along the road, I'd shout angrily at myself, 'Manolis, you're sleeping again!' and I'd be wide awake instantly.

All this happened on Friday night going on Saturday. At dawn on Sunday, we found ourselves somewhere in Cyrenaica, between Derna and Apollonia. We were driving along a wide asphalt road on the brink of a sheer cliff; to our left rose the green slopes of Gebel-el-Akhdar. Suddenly the front part of the truck filled with smoke and there came a smell of burnt oil. It was a good thing Michalis was in the driver's seat. He parked on the left side of the road, near a little cottage in ruins, under a wild mimosa tree. The engine petered out. We climbed down in a hurry and lifted the hood. 'Just what I feared,' said Michalis. And he shouted at the little Bedouin boys who had gathered out of nowhere: '*Yalla, roukh!*' The children came to a standstill on a little mound of sand nearby, and stared at us silently.

'I'll tell you what we're going to do,' he said. 'You go and find a sheltered corner among those ruins and light a fire so we can make tea. We haven't had a thing to eat or drink since yesterday. Then you can go and have a nap or you can go down to the sea and bathe, if you like. I'm going to be busy for five or six hours, but I won't be needing your help. You'd only get on my nerves.'

'Five or six hours?' I cried in despair. 'Then all is lost.'

'What are you talking about? I promised a friend of mine who got stranded in the desert to help him tow his field gun out. And I'm going to keep my promise if I have to beat the devil to do it! As long as we get to Benghazi – we're bound to find some spare parts there.'

There was no arguing with him. I made tea and brought him a steaming cup. He crawled out from under the Fiat, scowling and filthy, and he grabbed the biscuit I offered him with his oil-smeared hands and dipped it into the tea. I left him at his task and climbed carefully down to the seashore. Halfway down, I sat on a rock and lit a cigarette. The sea sighed gently below, emerald green under the golden sun. I thought I heard larks singing high up in the sky; but could it possibly have been larks? Farther along the coast, the rocks formed a kind of amphitheatre. I saw a couple of sea gulls suspended in the air; then they took a sudden plunge toward the open sea, which turned a deeper, indigo blue in the distance.

The winter sea sighed at my feet, foaming thinly around the large smooth pebbles on the beach. 'Why, Manos, why?' Who had spoken? Who could it be uttering this bitter complaint? And what was I doing, what was I hunting along these shores, littered with the marble fragments of another world? Would I really find myself again once I had caught up with the Brigade? Was this lost self ahead of me, or had I left it behind? Was I secretly running away from it? That old passion of mine, those promises I had made to myself about writing one or two books someday, books that would live on after me – how had I managed to betray them? Here I was, carrying high my scimitar among the brigades of the new Crusade – belated, divided, useless! But why useless? Was the Little Man right, after all: was my place at the Remington, turning out endless articles and editorials? *The Fighter* . . . Back in Cairo, they'd given me the last issue, which Michalis now carried hidden away in the inner pocket of his greasy great-coat. 'Well, what do you think of it?' asked the short, freckled-faced man whom everyone called Phanis, as he handed it over to me. He was the Secretary of our group. The new issue contained an evaluation of the role played by the First Brigade at the battle of El Alamein; it commemorated our dead and reported the heroic deeds of our soldiers and officers. The editorial was brief and simple, and it ended with a set of propositions that had a clear, immediate impact, because they were balanced and enlightened. But then on the back page somebody from Palestine had written a report concerning the Second Brigade. It was a long and confused piece of writing, half reportage, half editorial, rather in the style of 'the order of the day', full of phrases like 'uncontrollable enthusiasm', and so on. I immediately recognized the grandiloquent noises usually emitted by the Little Man. Sitting opposite me, Phanis waited, breathing in that special, wheezing way of people who have a collapsed lung. I glanced at his hands, which were crossed on the little marble table of the café in which we sat. They, too, betrayed the flabbiness of an overfed tubercular. I answered his question, giving him my honest opinion about the positive and negative points of the new issue; I added that as the news-sheet was no longer published in Jerusalem, one could hope that pieces like the one on the back page would eventually grow scarcer. Phanis laughed out loud; his shiny face puckered into the tiny wrinkles of a man who has toiled much in life; he must have been a fisherman or farmer back home, on his island. 'I see you just can't stand the man,' he said, and his eyes suddenly grew serious. Yet I hadn't mentioned any names. Only Garelas had ever heard me discussing my difficulties with the Little Man. It was quite clear that Phanis was in the know, or else he wouldn't have got my meaning so quickly. 'I beg your pardon,' I said; 'I only see what's there to be seen. Here is an article that is simply out of place; it jars on your ears after the simple, humble sacrifices described on the other pages. It gives me the impression of a man who has climbed to some high spot and is trying his damnedest to squeeze some big talk out of himself, just to make others feel small. He gabs away like a "talking head" but he doesn't really believe a word he says.' 'Now, hold on a minute,' said Phanis. 'Maybe he believes what he says, only he doesn't know how to express himself. We don't all necessarily have the kind of education you've had.' 'No need to go that far for an explanation,' I said. 'Your words reflect what you *are* – whether spoken or written. There are no excuses. The way you express yourself is the surest indication of how you stand in relation to other people, to mankind in general; how much you care for people, how much you respect them – that's where it all shows. Now, take Makriyannis –' 'I know,' Phanis interrupted. 'We used to read him in prison.' In the end, he admitted half-heartedly, rather unhappily, that it was true, yes, the Little Man did sometimes try to appear taller than he actually was: 'Those are the times when he walks on tiptoe, and of course it only makes him limp.'

We were supposed to spend the whole evening together, but he had to meet some refugee politician, so we parted. I was sorry to leave him, even though he wasn't much of a talker. He was much more a listener; he asked questions, he hesitated, he wondered, he cogitated, he asked some more questions, and in this way, before you knew where you were, he led you (and himself) on to the right course. All very quietly – no gnashing of teeth, no swearing. Later on, as I walked along on my own, I caught myself whistling in the cold of the night. I had circled round the statue of Ibrahim Pasha, and was now gazing at the grey façade of the Opera House. I remembered my father, who had lived in this city as a young man and had seen Eleonora Duse perform here. How he had despised D'Annunzio for preening himself in the Khedive's box so shamelessly, with the air of a Calabrian beau! And after the performance, there had been the collective delirium of the Italians, Levantines and Greeks as they unharnessed the horses from the Diva's landau and drove her in triumph to Shepheard's Hotel – which wasn't that far, to tell the truth. The ululations of the crowd, the streets full of trampled roses mingled with horse dung – nothing has changed much since those days. There's the Pasha, the ravager of the Morea, on horseback, turning his back to the Opera House; there are the stone troughs used by the horses of hired carriages, there's the sound of their hoofs on the cobbles, a rhythmical staccato, like a string of worry beads meting out the long hours of waiting: and the sweetish smell of clover, and water stagnating in the fountain, and farther away, that other smell, treacherous and exotic, from the lebbek trees and sycamores of Ezbekieh . . . I managed to get rid of two drunken English soldiers who wanted to borrow money from me, and was about to go back to bed, at the house of an old couple from the island of Icaria, when I suddenly came to a halt. Had it been Phanis, perhaps – had he been the one who persuaded my comrades in Palestine that my views concerning the officers were correct, after all? But had he been in Cairo at the time? I had submitted my views in February, and the reply had only come through in June, when the Little Man informed me that the others had adopted my stand and the decision against me had been cancelled. Four whole months for my report to go from Kfariona to Cairo and back? Except if the Little Man had held it up. 'It is not impossible,' I said to myself. The memory of his silhouette – his voice, his smell – was enough to fill me with gloom instantly.

I met Phanis again, several times; and one day I put my own dilemma before him: the Remington, or the front? He started talking slowly, in a low voice, enumerating the requirements of each sector, information and military, folding down a finger at each point he made. Finally he said, 'Well, now it's your turn, try and see what you can do.' I thought hard for a moment and I gave him my answer. Without losing any time, he told me whom to contact in Alexandria. 'Just stick around a week with them,' he said. 'You know, our comrades in the navy want to start a newsletter of their own. Teach them everything you know, and then you can go off to the front, since you want to so badly.' We said good-bye, almost casually, as if we were going to meet again next day. But just as I was about to turn the corner of the street, he called me back. 'About those disagreements you've had with our friend – have you ever discussed them, in his presence, with some of the other boys?' 'No,' I said. 'That was a mistake,' he said. 'I know,' I answered. 'It would have been more honest of me to do that, although it still wouldn't have made any difference.' He couldn't understand why I said that, so I had to give him the whole story in detail. As we couldn't very well go on talking in the middle of the street, we went into a little café. Phanis sipped his sage tea with a loud slurping noise and looked me straight in the eye. 'Some of the things you've just told me are quite serious,' he said. 'But they lose a measure of their validity because they come from you, and I know you are biased; you hate his guts. We'll need some more evidence.' What was I to say to that? 'All right, then, why don't you investigate the matter, and if it turns out I have been biased, then you'll just have to take the necessary measures against me.' He shut his eyes and fell into deep thought. 'We've got other work to do, friend,' he said. 'There isn't time for that sort of thing. And we'd have to hold a meeting to decide whether there should be an investigation or not. And *he* would have to be notified, too. However, the matter will have to be cleared up sooner or later, in the presence of those concerned – if we live long enough.' I was silent. 'Off you go, now,' he said. 'You'll miss your train.'

The week I was supposed to spend in Alexandria dragged on to a full month. A number of minor problems concerning the new publication cropped up in quick succession and demanded attention. 'Stay till Christmas,' they told me. Meanwhile the Brigade was still in hot pursuit of Rommel. One day I really lost my temper and started shouting at them. So they agreed to put me on an LST that was about to sail for Tobruk. But there was a hitch when I reached the control officer at the gangway; he happened to be a Fascist. 'Hey,' he said, 'where's this guy going? Come here a minute!' We nearly got into trouble. In the end they put me in contact with the French officer at Bir Hakim, who was called . . .

Stretched out on the rock, I had become oblivious of time and place. I flexed my muscles because I had gone quite numb. The sun seemed to have mellowed my bones. How was Michalis getting on with the old truck? I was wearing yellow suede boots with crêpe soles; climbing back over the sharp rocks was easy. I was soon back on the main road, under the wild mimosa tree: Michalis was nowhere to be seen. I gave a shout. 'Over here,' he replied, somewhere among the ruins. 'I'm shaving.'

'What's come over you – going to a wedding or something?' I said, but I was sorry the moment I said it; until now I had been the one to nag at him about the necessity of shaving daily.

'Bad news,' he said. 'Seems I have to go to Benghazi. The ball bearings need changing. I'll get a lift on an Allied truck and when I've finished, I'll manage to squeeze into one of the ambulances.'

'Benghazi is two hundred miles from here,' I said to him. 'You'll be late coming back. You might even get held up there – and it'll be goodbye to all our fine plans.'

'Don't worry,' he said, 'I'll manage. I'll be back before dark, you'll see. What are you going to do?'

I considered for a moment or two. 'I'll wait for you here,' I said finally.

'Fine,' he said. 'I think that's the wisest course.'

'Why don't we ask one of those guys to tow us along?'

'You must be crazy,' he said. 'The moment they find out the sorry state this old truck is in, they'll just pitch her on to that heap of scrap iron.'

A number of Allied Bren carriers were rusting away in the small amphitheatre down by the seashore.

Michalis scrambled down to the sea and scrubbed away at his grease stains with a piece of pumice stone. Then he got dressed, put on his army coat, planted his helmet under his arm, and waited for an Allied vehicle to go by. But first he made sure I was carrying my identity card.

'You old bastard, you,' I said. 'I can just see you sleeping in the arms of some lovely girl tonight, while I sit freezing here all alone.'

'Now, remember, don't light a fire after sunset,' he said, 'you might get into big trouble. The airports of Crete lie due north from this spot.'

'Yessir,' I said.

'And that's an order,' he said.

An Australian truck came along, loaded with barrels. Michalis shouted, 'Greek, Benghazi,' and they picked him up at once. He was about to jump on to the back of the truck when he paused and looked at me. I understood. I had the same thought. The Australian truck could easily accommodate me as well; we'd manage somehow, once we got to Benghazi. But who would look after the Fiat? Michalis was the one to decide. If he gave me the signal to climb on the truck, I would obey without a word. But as the truck drove away, I saw him giving me a military salute and pointing to the ground, meaning, 'Meet you here tonight.'

The Bedouin children who had brought Michalis water for shaving were shouting at me: *'Maya, maya.'* I gave them the bucket. They ran away in a bunch through the trees on the slope, on the other side of the main road. In a little while, they came back with the bucket full of water. They tried to convey, gesturing, that it was drinking water. I took a mouthful and felt a pair of pincers gripping my teeth; it was ice cold. I went over to the corner where I had brewed tea, collected some twigs, piled them up between two bricks, and then sprinkled them with some gasoline from the Fiat. I set fire to them. 'Chaï, chaï,' shouted the children, clapping their hands. 'Just be patient,' I said to them, in Greek. While the water was getting hot, I brought over my shaving kit, a small mirror, a mess tin, cans of sugar and tea. The children hung around, watching the proceedings. When I puffed out my cheeks to get a closer shave, they puffed out theirs. Then they poured out some water for me to wash, and finally, at a sign from me, they sat down cross-legged and waited. I put lots of sugar in the mess tin. I knew the Bedouins like their tea black and thick with sugar. Each little Bedouin took two loud sips from the mess tin, passed it on to his neighbour, and rubbed his stomach to show me how good it was. I went and got them some biscuits, too. We became great friends.

As time went on, though, they became a bit of a nuisance. They wanted cigarettes from me, they kept shouting things I couldn't understand, they lifted their gallabiyehs and pissed all over the place, giggling loudly. In the end, when they started climbing over the old Fiat, I got into a hell of a temper. 'Yalla, roukh!' I shouted. They paused wonderingly, as if to make sure I really meant it. I pretended to pick up a stone. They turned their backs on me, disappointed, and departed with great dignity. A while later, I heard them bickering down by the seashore, running after each other. Then I heard them no more. And suddenly I was engulfed by boredom. I didn't want to stay on the main road, in case the military police came along and began asking questions. So I sat in the Fiat, which was hidden from the road by the ruined hovel. I remembered we had brought along an Alexandrian newspaper, several days old. I hunted for it in the pocket of the door, intending to read the editorial which I hadn't had time to look through. But instead of the newspaper I found a bundle of letters. As soon as my eyes fell on the opening sentences, I turned the page and examined the signature. It was Michalis' mother, writing to her son. Ariagne Saridis. I folded the letter immediately and put it back in its place.

'Ariadne,' I had corrected him, the first time he mentioned her name to me.

'No, this is the right way to say it: Ariagne, from Naxos. That's where she comes from, you know. An English classical scholar who lived in our neighbourhood assured me that my mother pronounces her name much more correctly than most educated people."

'And what's your father's name? Theseus?'

'No, Dionysis. Why are you laughing?'

How was I to explain? I could just imagine the Englishman sinking into profound meditation at all these coincidences, and it suddenly seemed intensely funny to me. I tried to convey my amusement by telling him I had once known somebody called Dionysis whose nose was always very red because he drank too much wine.

'Well, my father likes a drop of wine now and then, but he prefers ouzo. We can tell when he's had too much, because he gets nasty and picks a quarrel with everyone.'

His father was a waiter, an old trade-unionist; he had got wounded in the thigh in a strike long ago. The family lived in a working-class neighbourhood in Cairo, not far from the Palace. There were four boys and twin girls. Michalis' mother had married very young, barely sixteen years old.

'By Jesus, Simonidis, it's not because she's my mother, but she's still a fine-looking woman, even though she'll never see forty-five again. And she's got guts. When she was only twenty years old, and pregnant, she saved an Egyptian demonstrator right under the noses of the British and their Tommy guns; a big hunk of man he was, and he still hasn't forgotten it.'

There was still a little water left in the bucket. The children were nowhere to be seen. I supposed they lived in some little farm beyond the woods. After a while, I opened a can of meat and had my lunch. I soaked my biscuit in the water at the bottom of the bucket. The air was warmer now; I could see it quivering over the ground and the rocks. I felt sleepy. Using my kit bag for a pillow, I curled up on the double seat of the Fiat. Before going off to sleep, I did my bit of self-criticism: 'Manolis, you didn't present your problem to Phanis in the right perspective. You should have asked him: action or art? But you didn't dare; you knew what his reply would've been. Nor can there be any other reply at the moment. And yet this crusade of the common folk needs writers and poets to express it, to help people grow aware of its greatness – otherwise it will all be in vain. But that can be done later, you may say; right now other things take first place; there are priorities. Yet why should one thing exclude the other – can't both be done at the same time? Certainly. Only one single individual can't do both jobs well. He's got to choose. I remembered the French leftist writer Jean-Richard Bloch telling me in Paris, at the time of the Spanish Civil War: 'It's an almost insoluble problem. Which is preferable? To live your life, or to record your life? To throw yourself headlong into any experience that comes your way, or stand aside and describe it? It is much more exciting to hunt after events and live them fully; but then they simply stream past, you retain nothing. Capture them on paper – that is the only way to save them from the universal shipwreck of time; but then life slips you by, you don't really participate in it . . .'

When I woke up, the sun had set, leaving only a pink brushstroke at the far end of the horizon. A buzzing sound, like a green fly's raced over the leaden-grey sea. It came and went, and started again. 'A Dornier plane,' said a voice in me. I thought I recognized the drone of a German transport aircraft – or was I wrong? Suddenly a flame leaped out of the tumble-down walls of the hovel. There was a burst of clapping and laughter. The little Bedouins had stolen my mess tin and other implements and were busy making tea. Hell, the Dornier, I thought. I jumped out of the Fiat shouting at them. The aeroplane was coming along fast over the amphitheatre, making a terrible racket. It dropped a whole string of bombs. They were quite small, the kind we used to call turtledove eggs. I ran over to the broken-down hovel; I would be more sheltered there. Opening my arms wide, I fell to the ground and landed on top of the children. There was a green flash, a horrible noise, and the air . . . The same air that blew out the lamp in Picasso's painting. I knew I was wounded, or sick. The blood, and the screaming and the confusion. Whenever I fell ill, I always had this nightmare of the lamp: I would feel it scorching my temples, pressing against my tongue, and then overturning on my chest, the hot glass against my skin . . . It had been like this at Premeti in the Albanian war. And now at Apollonia. And farther inland lay ancient Cyrene. The whole world is our grave.

Translated by Kay Cicellis

Alexandros Kotzias (1926–1992)

Kotzias grew up not only in a time of civil war but in a family divided by it: he fought for the right-wing EDES resistance, while his brother Kostas, also a well-known novelist, was a Communist. In his writings Alexandros Kotzias got closer to the heart of the darkness of his time than perhaps anyone else and almost certainly earlier: his first novel, *Siege*, narrated by a brutal right-wing paramilitary, was published as early as 1952. Kotzias never attempted to dispel the shadow of what he saw as a Thirty Years War (1944–74), and he created over the years a harrowing succession of anti-heroes, the richest of which is the informer under the Colonels in *Usurpation of Authority* (1979) – which would defy any translator. The Dostoevskian lineage of these heroes is not obtrusive, nor is the tentatively Christian analysis of the moral problems – again of Dostoevskian inspiration. In the late novella excerpted here (1987) we return once again to that traumatic period: in 1958 an embittered Communist schoolmistress meets at Athens airport her ex-sister-in-law over from America, who is not only involved in the classic situation of an inheritance dispute but is also suspected of having betrayed her late husband to his political opponents. The journey that follows is one that traverses an Attic tragedy, ancient and modern.

Jaguar (*extract*)

I won't cry, no. I'm not the crying sort. My eyes have gone slightly moist, but that's weariness, because I *never* cry. Neither at Security where they tortured me, nor in solitary confinement did I break down and cry, nor at the court-martial when the monarchofascists gave me a life sentence and their hirelings roared, Death to the Reds! Of the Sixty-Four I was the pluckiest, in full control, poor Elias at the very back of the dock as white as a sheet, but he never broke down, poor fellow. Me, even if they'd stood me up against the wall I'd have faced the firing squad with contempt . . . me during the Occupation . . . even the most dreadful betrayal, the most disgraceful betrayal wouldn't bring me to my knees. I'm a hard nut to crack, a Kallimanopoulos. – Lord, what's the time, where's this brainless creature taking me? Without glasses I can't read my watch in the dark. Normally I'm home by ten o'clock at the latest. – Of course I'm tired, I've been up since the crack of dawn. – All right,, let's say that after her father's death she sold the shop and the house, that she was not to be seen on the terrace . . . I'm irritated, I loathe lonely places and the dark more than the worst treachery . . . Now, I don't quite remember when her father died . . . more than the worst treachery; I feel a physical loathing like an allergy – why should I have to keep running around here aimlessly, since I'm shaking with apprehension? Ultimately I feel an ideological repulsion for . . . for criminals, for the underworld, as they call it, Stalin himself said the same thing somewhere. – My feet are hurting, my back is killing me, I'm dead beat. So why should I err through these dangerous streets in the dead of night like one accursed? – Where is this callous creature leading me through this obscure maze? She looks right and left, stops short, walks back, walks forward again, what's she looking for?

'Philio!'

'No, no, that's not . . .'

'There's lightning again.' Did I whisper it or think it, because she's turned impetuously into a devil's alley, Kathemeia Street, it says. We're going further and further away from Lenorman Street, she's making me go into that pitch-black tunnel between doors shut tight, unlit windows, just one bleary light bulb hanging from a wire overhead, it's dark as hell. What can the time be? And if that air force man, or that man in the dark windbreaker loitering by the bell tower is still following us? For all my determination I don't dare look back, me, who defied the Gestapo during the Occupation! And what if here in this dark corner I'm attacked by some ruffian with a knife? Tears come to my eyes despite myself. I feel betrayed. It is as if, while swimming off Acrata beach and out of your depth, a shark attacks you. Or if here on this corner a leopard or a tiger suddenly jumps out at you. Is that what they call panic? I who defied the Chief of Security though he pulled out my fingernails, and then you have this irresponsible female with her American manicure – she's smoking again like a streetwalker, but I don't hold it against her; let her call me names, I feel for her . . . poor thing, so much horror! Yet I can't fathom her. Since she arrived exhausted from the journey, how can she go on walking intrepid like the Wandering Jew; she's swallowed sedatives, barbiturates, of course, two days without sleep, all the way from Boston without a wink . . . What sort of work does she do in Boston, she hasn't told us. Why doesn't she mention her husband? I noticed it at the airport café, where I bought her a brandy, there's no wedding ring and some Mister seems to be sponsoring her in Boston . . . and where does she use this vulgar language of the underworld? And the fact that she didn't appear on the terrace in *those* days, is that good enough reason to shout balls! at that air force man? And now the vulgar hussy's telling me to my face, you don't remember, Dimitra, she says, you only remember what suits you, only what suits me indeed – her unfair sharp tongue, the vulgarity of it! – We were in Antiphanous Street just now and I said to her, Philio my dear, let's go back home, I said, what are you looking for in Antiphanous Street in the dead of night, you're dead beat without sleep, I said. I'm not holding it against her that she insulted my mother, calling her an old hag just now, in front of the church, under the cross. I don't take offence, I'm a Kallimanopoulos, daughter of gentlefolk, and I have understanding, but this horror I cannot endure. I understand what she was referring to covertly just now when we were looking at their old shop on the square and she said betrayals! It's just occurred to me what she meant, though she's accused me of not remembering anything. I don't blame her or hold it against her, poor thing, I pity her running through the night like a maniac, my heart bleeds for her . . . it's awful, poisoning your life, believing that . . . That's why she didn't attend his funeral, neither did she go into mourning nor did she want him at her wedding, she demanded that Phanis marry her secretly in a remote chapel, nobody attending the ceremony except the couple itself and the best man, arriving at our house as a surprise, with just the clothes on her back. – I remember everything as if it were yesterday . . . It's awful for her, poor thing, to believe such a horror, that he who fathered her went to the Gestapo, to the Germans and their Greek collaborators, because the other one was dragging him to court over the inheritance from his mother . . . No, I refuse to have anything to do with such common gossip disseminated by eager informers, petty women's talk pretending to sympathize with Thanos who was executed . . . Her father was one of us, there's ample proof . . . I'm startled in the dark, there's suddenly a threatening rustle.

'The air force man, Philio!'

But it's not the air force man – not a soul, we've come across two or three other nightwalkers only in our mad roaming of the streets; none other than the air force man has taken any notice of us, they crossed our path and vanished. With my heart beating in my throat I whisper in her ear:

'Someone's groaning!'

On Miller Street only a black cat slipped past me – yet here there's something rustling and groaning, wheezing, Philio, I'm weak with fright inside. We stop at the corner. Colonus hill rises before us like a giant awakening. The pines on the hill rustle and the clouds, so low those clouds, they're about to settle on our heads, and still no rain. I don't suppose that lunatic intends to drag me up there? I shudder. Beyond the first trees the shadows coagulate into impenetrable darkness, at night the hill becomes a den of iniquity. – And us lingering here on the edge of total darkness is dangerous; what if some junkie, some human beast, should suddenly appear before us? A small light shines down the road. Please let it rain! I'd run home like mad, I'd run though I'm dead tired. By ten the latest I . . . by now it must be past midnight, whereas on all other nights . . . Elias sits in front of his open books, his 'papers' spread out on the table under the beaded fringe of the crystal light fixture, the little ones are asleep – where's this lunatic going?

'Philio!'

'This isn't the place,' she retraces her steps to Miller Street.

'What have you been looking for all this time?'

'The streets have changed, they look alike.'

'It's the dark. We'd better come back tomorrow.'

'It's not here.'

We cross Jocasta and Cappadocia Streets, we turn a corner, she's managed to drag me into that maze again, we're lost in the desolate night. I've no idea where I'm going, my feet won't carry me any more, Clytia and Scamander Streets . . . Xanthippe Street, Dodona Street, Ascra and Harax Streets . . . and back to where you've already been, Jocasta Street, Xanthippe Street, Ismene Street, Anchialos Street – my aching back, my feet won't carry me any further, I'm about to collapse – Dodona Street, Phoenicia Street, Pagasae Street, Nemea Street – what glorious names for these miserable alleys, I've never in my life been here, though we live nearby . . . except perhaps during the Occupation . . . we wrote slogans on the walls in nearby neighbourhoods and even farther afield like St Constantine's, or Sepolia, the nights were pitch-black, you couldn't see your own nose much less read street signs – Antigone Street . . . Dryos Street . . . Dodona Street – The most resolute amongst us went out as a group just before daybreak, barefoot so the enemy beasts wouldn't hear and massacre us, two carrying the can of paint, me and . . . three with guns keeping watch on street corners, we were risking our necks, a fifty-fifty chance we had. Was the hornets' nest hereabouts? We're a stone's throw from my own house, but I'm not sure where I am exactly. Throughout the area, all the way from St Meletios to the stream, to the railway line, not a soul dared come out into the streets during the last year of the Occupation, the fascists reigned supreme, terrorizing, beasts of the Apocalypse. It was our sacred duty to write slogans on the walls, even if we were mowed down by machine guns for it, we slid barefoot through the dead of night, covered the walls all the way to the hornets' nest: DEATH TO THE TRAITOR – what was his name? Papa-something, or Pana-something, in any case, no one accused Petrides directly, only mumbled threats, half-statements . . . Besides, I recall people saying that Old Stavro went to stand outside the prison at all hours of the day and night in the cold, hoping to smuggle an orange in to Thanos. When he learned they'd shot him he fell ill, I remember – so why has this wretch poisoned herself with such a horror story? Well, perhaps Old Stavro wasn't an active fighter, he certainly wasn't! Perhaps one could, in private, describe him as a toothless meany, because he certainly was! Yet Stavro Petrides did his duty like a class-conscious proletarian, he has earned the crown of eternal glory . . . We young girls in the area worshipped him secretly, a legendary comrade, a monument for Red Square. – Hey, the bricked-in window in this wall reminds me of something, why has Philio stopped? The hornets' nest was hereabouts, the fascists barricaded in two houses, in that alley we just walked through perhaps. Just think, if that was the den of . . . I wrote DEATH in big red letters on this wall here . . . the new block of flats on the corner is confusing me. Philio too is glancing all about her in the night – has she been searching for the fascists' den all this time?

'They've pulled down so much, you can't make out . . .'

'I've got trouble recognizing the place myself, Philio. Let's go home, it's late.'

'The blocks of flats all look alike.'

'Lots of new housing going up,' I agree with bitter sympathy. – Why should she believe such a thing, he was her father after all.

'In that alley,' she points resolutely, I don't know whether for my or for her memory's sake, points to the dark alley that I've recognized too. '. . . no longer here.'

'What are you looking for, Philio?'

'It was here . . . it's been pulled down,' and she walks off with weary steps, deflated. – Thank God our house is only a stone's throw away – but she's still looking around. 'Somewhere here an enormous tree . . . there, right there at the crossroads. This side of the street was not built then.'

'I don't recall,' I stammer in front of the three-storey house. She's panting, exhausted by this vain quest. Something is holding me back, preventing me from . . . Silence! it commands, do not disturb the peace of the dead . . . I don't remember a tree, I'm thinking, I'm annoyed by her laboured breathing. And if there had been a tree, I say to myself, they'll have felled it to build this three-storey house. Meanwhile, weary, Philio walks on with heavy but steady step, turning this way and that without the slightest hesitation now she's got her bearings. I follow her relieved, she's not searching any more, we're going home.

'It was an enormous poplar, casting its shadow . . .'

'Where?'

'In that vacant lot . . . it was a poplar, a black poplar, spreading rather like an oak.'

'I don't recall, my dear . . . honestly, I have no idea where we are, I'm all mixed up.'

Are her teeth rattling? I ask myself. We keep walking – are we on our way back? – she turns another corner. A young girl is closing a garden gate and disappears behind it. Not even flashes of lightning any more, the clouds are covering us like a quilt, an old man is walking slowly past leaning on his stick, we overtake him. The city's hum of car engines is swelling – is Lenorman Street so near? Suddenly Philio takes hold of my arm for support, first time in fourteen years, since she came into the family.

'You're a teacher, Dimitra.'

I'm moved, and quite rightly too. We march on in the night, just the two of us, Philio leaning wearily on my arm. I'm listening.

'What does expiate mean? . . . I sort of know . . . expiate . . . but . . .'

My heart bleeds for her, it's awful! In the dark I can sense her internal torment.

Ever since the years of the Occupation she has silently carried the burden of an unjust accusation and suffered . . . Thanos was her brother, Petrides her father – dreadful! She's gone to pieces, she's hovering on the brink of . . . With my left hand I squeeze her shoulder. 'But why, my dear Philio, what makes you believe it?'

'Believe what?' Dismayed, she drops my arm.

'He's gone to his rest, Philio. No prosecution, no evidence. Forget the neighbourhood gossip.'

She stops short in the dark, and I feel her hesitating. Now she'll ask me what I mean, who wasn't prosecuted and for what. And I'll abandon all reserve and give it to her straight, remove from her mind and heart the burden of the curse that, for no good reason, she's been dragging around with her all her life.

'I believe nothing, mind your own business!' she snaps and moves on in the night.

Oh, my dear Philio, I'm thinking tenderly, nostalgically even, in the hornets' nest of capitalism where you've chosen to live, the majority are madmen, drug addicts, alcoholics, they're driven insane by greed and rapacity; without realizing it you've gone round the bend too, my poor Philio. Once we're safely back home I'll give you a piece of my mind, because you know these things of course, but you're constantly suppressing them or pretending that . . . When that Venizelos, double-crosser that he was, I'll tell you, sent the army, the sons of the People, to the Ukraine with the Anglo-French imperialists to crush . . . well then, I'll tell you, your father – lucky man, your father, Philio; history reserved a place of honour for him, I'll tell you – your father went bravely into battle at the crucial hour and fought for the October Revolution, the most historic event since Man has walked the earth. Philio dear, I'll tell you, your father fought at Lenin's side, though a recruit in the imperialist army, I'll tell you, he fought virtually at the side of comrade Lenin, of comrade Stalin, comrade Bulganin, alongside those giants . . . and with our boys at the front fighting like one man. I've been told by comrades who heard him talking about it, before the Metaxas regime, heard him tell his story in the basement tavern; they said his features were transfigured, grew almost saintly as he talked of marching in the depths of Russia, the snows of winter, they said, and Kondylis almost court-martialled them in time of war to have them shot on the frozen steppe – and are we to ignore such a glorious record, Philio? . . . And what if he was a bit mean and devious, I'll tell you. What he was like later, when he'd grown old, doesn't count; what counts is his contribution to the Revolution, I'll tell you, objectively Petrides is an immortal hero of the internationalist Soviet Union, he fought as a Bolshevik, a proletarian pioneer, honour and glory are his due, Philio, I'll tell you. – We're approaching home, I think, and I feel the need, an ardent desire to unburden my heart in the night, my heart's that gnawed by profound grief. Ah, Philio dearest, I want to tell her, and Elias, my Elias, Philio . . .

'. . . four years my junior, what's to become of me?'

Horrified, I hear my moan escaping me and rising to the clouds. I'm foundering!

'The Primary School!' Philio groans hoarsely, turning the corner in a terrible state, then stops dead.

I'm startled. Which primary school, and so what? I guess she's too distracted to have realized that I . . . bright illumination from an arc light all over the open area – a small square with stunted oleanders and acacias, I'll collapse on this bench, my legs are no longer holding me up . . . exhaustion, shame. Stiff as a pole Philio stands beside the lamp post bathed in cold light. I make an effort.

'Is this the school you went to, Philio? But why, since in our neighbourhood we have . . .'

She's not listening, I'm sure – let's hope she didn't hear the loud moan I sent up to the clouds either. Her pale face is stony with an inexplicable savagery – murderous, a voice tells me inside all Americans are killers, gangsters, bloodthirstiness is contagious . . . she looks into space.

'It was dark . . .'

When, I wonder.

'Very dark, but a starlit sky . . .'

'When, Philio, during the Occupation?'

Stiff as a sleepwalker she approached the corner of the school building. A huge two-storey ruin opposite must have been a factory before the war. A long narrow alley like a drainpipe, dimly lit at the far corner separates it from the wall of the schoolyard. I trust this abnormal creature won't drag me in there. No way will I go in . . .

The windows of the ruined factory, deprived of their frames, gape black like infected wounds. As we keep walking I feel squashed between that dead monster of a building and the high school-yard wall. – I feel trapped, I feel, let's go, Philio! Asthmatically she's whistling close to my ear; the whistled fragments of an old signal escaping from her lips take me back vaguely to my youth; they're like a long drawn-out tune, but I can't make out what they're trying to reassemble, it's as if she's cast her line far out and deep into the past, and it's caught in the rocks, and she's pulling at it in vain. Somewhere halfway she stops, her hoarse voice nightmarish. 'There's no crunching now . . . It was very dark.'

What should be crunching, I ask myself, as she peers up and down anxiously as though expecting someone to appear suddenly, and us here at his mercy between two walls, no way of escape all the way to the end of the alley – what is this addled brain recalling behind those hard black eyes? Though those eyes are staring at me intensely, they don't see me, I'm sure. I'm seized by terror – what if she has a fit right here in this solitude, in this black night?

'They've asphalted it . . . the crunching gravel is gone.'

'Let's go, Philio, I'm scared, I'm getting panicky.'

'It was very dark.'

'It's past midnight.'

She goes up to the shallow recess in the wall, where the corner of the factory joins the yard wall. She passes her hands over the stones, not caressingly but expertly investigating, retracing something. She again attempts to summon that long-drawn whistle out of the dark, but it chokes her. She lets out a small cry and, hiding her face in her hands, breaks into sobs.

'For goodness sake, my dear!'

She jumps when I touch her shoulder, her dark gaze cavernous.

'Damn you, Dimitra, that killer, that bastard . . .' she screeches. 'Damn you!'

Translated by H.E. Criton

Kostas Tachtsis (1927–1988)

Tachtsis published just one novel, *The Third Wedding* (1963), arguably the most brilliant and certainly one of the most widely read post-war Greek novels. Through the first-person narrative of an engagingly feisty middle-aged woman, Nina, and through the recollections of her ex-mother-in-law, Hecuba, it seems that every tribulation and every vagary of a Greek middle-class family from the early years of the century through its especially troubled middle years is traced – sparing no social phenomenon, however repressed (the homosexual escapades of married Greek men are just one example). All this broad canvas is painted with unmatched brio, a cunningly hidden formal ingenuity and (a feature found too little in the present volume: translators take note!) knockabout humour. Tachtsis launches us right in from the start.

The Third Wedding (*extract*)

No, really I can't, I can't stand her another moment! Dear God, why did you send me such a burden to bear? What have I done to deserve such punishment? How long must I put up with her, see her horrid face, hear her voice, how long, Oh Lord, how long? Surely there must be some misguided Christian who'd want to take her? Somebody to take this monstrous freak of nature off my hands, this souvenir her father left to avenge himself? The devil take those who stopped me having the abortion!

But why am I cursing them? They're all dead now. Anyway, it's not their fault. I shouldn't have paid any attention to them. On things like that you have to make up your own mind. When she was little I used to comfort myself thinking she would change as she grew up. 'She'll change,' I said to myself, 'she'll improve. Anyway, sooner or later, she'll get married. She'll be on somebody else's back.' Well, there you are. It just shows how wrong I was. The way things are going, it looks as though she'll stay an old maid for life. And no wonder, either, with her the way she is. I hope she's satisfied, that monster Erasmia, the way she's ruined her with all that sermonizing of hers. I'd like to know what man would turn round in the street to give her a second glance, the way she dresses, the way she behaves, the way she talks. Would any normal decent man want her for the mother of his children, with those ridiculous ideas of hers, all those neurotic habits, the way she's always scratching the pimples on her face and never letting them dry up? No, she's booked to stay on the shelf, that's for sure. And, God pity me, I don't know who to be more sorry for, her or myself. Because, no matter what I say, blood is thicker than water, let's face it. I'm her mother, and I feel for her.

But I feel for myself, too. Every time she upsets my ulcer drives me mad with pain. 'God made you ugly,' I tell her, 'but at least you could dress up a bit more. You never know, you might fool somebody!' But I'm afraid she's not like me, even in that. Not that I'm beautiful or anything. But I have a way with me. I always knew how to dress. At her age I was as bright as a button. When I walked down the street you could see the men's heads turn like sunflowers following the sun. I wasn't like this ugly little lizard. Who on earth does she take after, I'd like to know? Not me, not her grandmother. She's nothing like her grandmother, and even less like her father. He may have been a rogue, or anything else you like to call him, but he was a real man. He was handsome – more handsome than was good for him . . .

No, I'm no beauty. But I know how to live. There aren't many women my age as well preserved as I am. All my friends and all the girls who were at school with me have grown old. I see them in the street and I shudder. They've become grandmothers. Not because they have grandchildren – Julia hasn't any – but they've just let themselves go to seed. They've neglected themselves and grown old. The body doesn't grow old unless the heart grows old first. 'Let my daughters have the gay life,' they say. 'Let my children enjoy themselves at balls and parties. I've had my day.' But they say it because their children are worth any kind of sacrifice. They don't have Maria! They don't know what it's like to have a daughter like Maria. That's why I don't blame them for when they criticize me for getting married again, instead of trying to get her married off. They don't know how I weighed up all the pros and cons before I took the plunge and married Theodore. Maria, I said to myself, is like somebody drowning in the sea. If I go to save her, she'll drag me down to the bottom with her. The best thing is to save myself, at least. Give her time to grow up a bit, become more of a woman. 'Marry her off', they all used to tell me, 'and you'll see she'll change out of all recognition.' Marry her off? Why me? Can't she find a husband for herself? Does she have to have him served up on a plate? At her age I had ten men courting me at the same time. They fussed round my skirts wherever I went. All I had to do was to lift my little finger at any one of them, and he'd have come crawling on all fours to take me. I suppose you'll say: if that's how it was, how could you be so daft as to pick on Fotis. But that's another story. I'd rather not think about it. It only upsets me more than ever. Maybe, I sometimes tell myself, it was fate that I should marry him. Maybe it was God's will that I should suffer everything I suffered. Maybe I was fated to give birth to this Medusa! . . . But then again, I sometimes think it has nothing to do with God or with fate. It's my own fault and nobody else's. I was pig-headed and I insisted on having my own way. I said 'I'll marry him' and marry him I did. Out of sheer cussedness. Just because nobody in the family would hear of him. Not even my poor old father, who was always so careful about expressing an opinion. I had no intention of letting them interfere again in my affairs, poking their noses into my life like they did before. They did enough damage sticking their fingers into the pie with Aryiris. I wasn't eighteen years old any more. I was twenty-seven. I was independent and determined to do exactly as I pleased. I did. And cut my own throat!

But that's neither here nor there. Everyone is entitled to make one mistake in his life. But is that any reason why I have to pay for that one stupid mistake for ever? How long have I got to live? Ten more years? Twenty? Who knows? I might go out today and get flattened by one of those cars that race about like mad things. But even if I've only got one hour left to live, I mean to live it the way I like! There's no hope of old Galatia producing another Nina. She's deep under the ground. God, just to live without her constant nagging, to concentrate a bit, to put my mind on something more serious than the everlasting subject of Maria! Dear God, won't you ever do me that little favour! . . .

It's two or three days now since she's been fed up with Theodore. She gets her rages at intervals. She slams the door in his face. She refuses to eat with us at the same table. And when I'm alone with her, she lets loose a non-stop stream of insults against him and his. And the poor man hasn't done the slightest thing to deserve it. She's jealous of me, damn her squinty eyes! How else can you explain it? 'If you must have a man,' I said to her today, 'go to the park and find yourself some strapping brute or other! The park's just down the road. Go and find yourself some sailor or a soldier to cool your hot pants! Do I have to find him for you? When I was your age I'd not only had you, but I was getting ready to marry for the second time!' 'Go on,' I told her, 'get dressed and go out. And I swear on the bones of my father, the man I loved better than anything in this world, bring anybody you like back home with you, I don't care who or what he is, and if you tell me "this man here is my friend, my fiancé, my husband", I won't raise the slightest objection, I won't express any kind of opinion! I'll even bow to him, ten times over if need be. It's not me who's going to marry him. It won't be me in his bed. It's you who'll have to sleep with him. Just so long as he doesn't make a fool of you – and it's usually the snivelling little virgins like you who get caught – and run off after he's eaten up your dowry, leaving me with you on my back again, and this time with some little bastard child as well! Go on, get dressed', I told her, 'and get out of my sight! And if you don't want a man – and God knows, you're so crazy you don't know yourself what you want out of life – then go and shut yourself up in a nunnery. There are still some left. Go and join St Miriam at Keratea! Go and be a nun like Erasmia, the one you take after so much! Do you suppose your father left you behind deliberately to make my life a purgatory? Go on. Get dressed. And do what you damn well like. But I'm giving you one last warning: if you aggravate me again like you did today, and especially in front of Theodore, there'll be murder done in this house. I'll chop you into little pieces like mincemeat! And don't you ever dare take those photos of my father and old Hecuba off the sitting-room wall again! I don't care if the frames are ugly. And I don't care if it's no longer done to hang photos on the wall. As long as I'm alive, this is *my* house. I run things here, and I'll hang any damn thing on the walls I want to, do you hear? When you get married, God willing, and set up your own house, or when I peg out, as you say, and you get my money – and the way you upset me you won't have very long to wait – you can hang cowbells on your walls, for all I care. But as long as I live, as long as my eyes are open, I want to see the photos of the people who loved me and who died, more's the pity, and me with a shrew like you to eat me alive!' I told her and went to hang the photos of papa and old Hecuba back where they belong.

When she saw what I'd done, she literally frothed at the mouth. 'Oh yes,' she said, 'we mustn't insult your old washerwoman of a mother-in-law, must we?' And I answered back: 'It's you who's the washerwoman, and you act like one.' That's how our row started today. 'It's you who's the washerwoman,' I said. And, with one thing leading to another, it wasn't long before we were almost hitting each other. I was furious. She insults Hecuba on purpose to get me wild. You can imagine what'll happen if Theodore ever hears her call his mother a washer-woman. He'll grab her by the hair and shake her till she rattles. And who'll get upset? Theodore and me, of course. Not Maria, not on your life. She just dotes on a good bust-up, she just can't live without constant rows.

But even if it wasn't for Theodore, as long as I live I mean to see Hecuba's photo in its proper place. Not because she's my mother-in-law. What woman likes her mother-in-law? If she were alive, she wouldn't dream of letting me marry Theodore, that's certain. She may have been the best friend a woman ever had, but she'd have been no good as a mother-in-law. And I ought to know. The way her mind had become during those last years, she wasn't fit to have anything to do with other people. She wasn't the Hecuba of the old times, with her jokes, her faith in life and in people – for all that she always seemed so pessimistic. She wasn't the Hecuba you came to with all your troubles, and she'd give you the kind of advice you never got from anyone else. No, if she'd been alive at the time Theodore came back from the Middle East, it would never have crossed my mind to marry him and become her daughter-in-law. It would have been absurd. Impossible to imagine. We'd have quarrelled. To say nothing of what people would have said. How they'd have laughed at us! Even now I sometimes meet women I used to be friendly with at the time, women I haven't met for years, and they say: 'Just fancy, Nina, did you ever imagine that one day you'd become her daughter-in-law.' And they say it so sarcastically! But I pretend not to notice. If I didn't I'd be constantly squabbling with everyone. When all's said and done, I tell myself, they're not altogether wrong. It is funny, the way things worked out. But not the way other people see it. Which of those tittle-tattle females really knew old Hecuba, or knew what a heart she had? Sometimes I wonder if I really knew her myself, in spite of everything we went through together . . . Some women found her amusing. Some turned up their noses at her, like that snob Julia. She couldn't understand how I could be so friendly with her. She never said so straight out, but in all kinds of roundabout ways. 'You're so good-hearted, Nina dear,' she used to say, 'you make anybody welcome in your house. I always say so to my Lily. Lily, I say, Nina has the kindest heart in the world.' She simply couldn't understand how I could possibly prefer Hecuba's company to hers or Mrs Carouso's.

To Martha, Hecuba was like some kind of clown. I remember her telling me once: 'You're like those Emperors with their court jesters.' In spite of all her so-called book learning, even she couldn't understand the reasons why Hecuba sometimes acted like a clown – because she was so modest and humble. Hecuba loved to dramatize her life. But the more she dramatized it, the more jokes she made, always at her own expense, never at the expense of others.

As for Aunt Katie with her prudish ideas and her absurd moral principles, she regarded Hecuba as the very incarnation of the devil. And from one point of view she was right. Hecuba was a devil. But on the other hand she was also a saint, and nobody can possibly know it better than I do, I who followed her story to the very end, and knew what was in her heart, better even than her own children! . . .

Her children. Pfff! With the daughter I've got, I'm in a position to know that, of all God's creatures, there's probably none in the whole wide world who understands us less than the one which comes out of our belly. And if all that is not good reason enough why I should want to see her photo, let's say it's because we went through some unforgettable times together. For I opened my heart to Hecuba, as I never did even to my own mother. When all's said and done, she'd suffered from her own daughter and all her other children (after all, Polyxene behaved no better to her in the end than Eleni did). She was the only one of all my friends and relatives who sympathized with me from the bottom of her heart, the only one who understood and shared my sadness, the bitterness I felt at my wretched luck in giving birth to a child-monster! . . .

I first met her in 1937. Or rather no, it wasn't '37. It was the summer of '36, August. I remember it because it was just before the Feast of the Virgin Mary. That was the name-day of Her Highness the Grand Duchess herself, and I had to give the house a thorough cleaning, polish the parquet floors and so on. I was on the roof with Marietta. We were both in our bare feet, shaking out the velvet curtains from the parlour. It was the last job we did that day. That's enough for now, I was thinking. Tomorrow's another day. 'We'll just finish shaking these curtains out and then take a bath to cool off,' I was saying to Marietta, when we heard the little bell that tinkles every time the front gate opens. 'Go and see who it is,' I said. 'Give me the corner of the curtain and see who it is. I hope it isn't a visitor, with my hair all over the place. If it's somebody who doesn't know me he'll think I'm a gipsy or something.'

Poor Marietta! She gave me the corner of the curtain and jumped like a deer down on to the little balcony in front of the wash-house. From there you can see the whole way along the path from the gate to the front door. She half closed her eyes with a suspicious look, the way she did every time she saw somebody new. I watched her and smiled. It must be some stranger, I said to myself. When Marietta screws up her face like that, it's always some stranger. That's how she was. Like a growling bulldog. She came back to the terrace and took hold of her corner of the curtain again to get on with the shaking.

I could see she had no intention of being the first to speak. I knew her ways. 'Who is it?' I said. 'Nobody.' – 'What do you mean, nobody. I heard the bell.' – 'Ooof! It's nobody, I tell you.' That's how she used to speak to me. 'It's Erasmia,' she finally condescended to tell me, 'with some shrew or other.'

For Marietta, Erasmia was 'nobody', just as Odysseus was for Polyphemus. So it is some stranger, I said to myself. I was right. But I had no idea who it might be. One of those queer characters Erasmia has met at holy Ephemia's place, I thought to myself, otherwise Marietta wouldn't have called her a shrew. Shrew was the name she used for any woman she didn't take a fancy to, whether she was a friend or a stranger.

The trouble was she had the habit of calling Antoni's mother 'the shrew'. It was 'the shrew' here and 'the shrew' there. It just came naturally – she was the shrew with a capital s. We'd caught the habit and called her the shrew, too, when Antoni wasn't at home. I used to tremble at the thought that it might slip out accidentally one day when he was there. I knew he wouldn't say a word, but it would upset him very much, and he had enough troubles already, poor man, from my daughter, what with the lashing she used to give him with her tongue every now and again. Boros had told me a hundred times: 'Nina, try to stop him getting upset. His heart's in a terrible state. Look after him.' But everything I did with my care and patience my daughter undid with her tongue. If he tried to scold her, she'd say: 'Leave me alone. I don't give you the right to speak to me. You're not my father.' And that's when she was only twelve years old. She made the poor man tremble like a fish.

We had brought Marietta from the island of Andros, one summer when we'd gone to spend our holidays with Aunt Bolena, a cousin of papa's who had a house there. Marietta was from the village of Pisomeria. And the Pisomerians, ask anyone from Andros and he'll tell you, are notorious for their lack of hospitality and their sharp tongues. Marietta was a Pisomerian and no mistake. She loved me like a faithful dog. And she respected Antoni, even if she did play him up no end. Deep down, she knew he was the master, and she was a little bit scared of him. But she had no mercy on all the others. Relatives or strangers, she led them all a merry dance. She had a nickname for everybody. Aunt Katie she called 'missus bishop.' For my Grand Duchess, it was 'the booby'. I pretended it made me angry when she said it. I didn't want to let her get above herself. But I couldn't help thinking what a good nickname it was. She's always been a booby and a booby she'll stay for the rest of her life.

But it was Erasmia she liked least of all. She just couldn't stand the sight of her. Every time she came it would turn Marietta's stomach over. And when she toted her friends along with her to show off our house to them, it was all I could do to stop Marietta turning her out. Quite often she'd tell people I was ill and couldn't see anybody. 'Go and make us some coffee,' I used to tell her. My poor mother had taught me to be hospitable to everybody, and papa always told me not to be a snob and never to condemn people before I'd got to know them a bit. And how can you get to know a person if you don't have a chat over a cup of coffee? 'Go and make us some coffee. And bring a little cherry jam,' I'd say to her. And, on her way to the kitchen, she would stand where only I could see her and make faces which meant: 'You don't catch me making coffee for that lot. Who do they think they are? And jam, indeed! Not likely!' Sometimes it was quite embarrassing.

But I let her get away with it. After all, most of the time she was only saying out loud what I was thinking to myself. And then she was honest, hard-working and devoted. And there was another thing: in those years, before the war, what with unemployment and Antoni being ill all the time, we owed her ten months' salary, and yet she never uttered a word of complaint. So, with all her faults, she stayed on with us. And I'd just give the visitors a wink. They all knew her, anyway, and didn't take offence. There's no harm in it, I used to tell myself. Let her think she's a member of the family and entitled to express her opinions.

'Come on, let's finish shaking out these curtains,' I said. 'I'm fed up. To hell with name-days and all the rest of the nonsense. One of these days I'm really going to put my foot down and refuse to let people through the door! ... What's she like, this shrew of Erasmia's?' I said. I knew she wouldn't open her mouth unless I asked her a direct question. But, even then, she wasn't the type to give way easily. 'Ooof! ... just a shrew, I tell you!' ... She wasn't one for long speeches. To me she'd got used to speaking familiarly with the 'you' in the singular. She only used the less familiar plural 'you' to poor papa. If anybody had heard us who didn't know us, they'd have thought she was the mistress and I was the servant.

This time, probably for the first time ever, Marietta was wrong. Hecuba was not a shrew. She was quite unlike the ogres Erasmia insisted on dragging along with her when she came to the house, in spite of my telling her straight out not to bring strangers. (She took no notice of what I said, she had Antoni on her side.) No, old Hecuba was no shrew. My eye took her in at once. And I didn't change my mind about her, even when I discovered that I had guessed right that she'd met Erasmia at holy Ephemia's place. What I had only gone through, and was still going through, on account of that old fraud! . . .

Holy Ephemia was a so-called 'nun.' When she was young, she used to go round the houses selling candles, incense, bits of holy wood from the cross and books with the lives of the saints. She must have read the books and realized that it wasn't difficult to make yourself out to be a saint. So when she got old and couldn't walk any more she rented a little room near the church of St Lefteri and set herself up as a holy woman. She lived on the voluntary gifts left by the faithful (a hundred grams of sugar, fifty grams of coffee, and so on). It was her daughter-in-law – she had two sons – who, as I found out later, sold these offerings for ready cash. Her reputation rested on two things: first, she had not eaten meat for forty years; and second, she could prophesy the future.

Well, I set off to see her one day. Not to get my fortune told, mind you. I knew my fortune better than anybody – a clear dawn brings a fine day. I went to humour Antoni. Poor man, God rest his soul, he'd suddenly taken to religion in those days. When we got married he was more atheist than the devil himself. I'd never seen such a blaspheming godless man in all my born days. I don't mean to say he was godless just because he swore. There are lots of religious people who trot out an endless stream of Christ Almightys and God-damns with the greatest of ease: and there are those who set no store by religion and yet never a swear word passes their lips, like my poor father. It's a question of how you're brought up, you see. Now Antoni was neither the one nor the other. When he swore, he swore with passion, meaning every word he said. He made fun of everything to do with God and the Church. He even taunted me when I used to light the little oil-lamp – to have my sins forgiven, he used to say. He had a nerve, talking about *my* sins. Anyway, I only used to light it out of respect for the memory of my poor mother. It wasn't right, I thought, just because she was dead, to stop something we'd always done at home ever since I could remember. And, to tell the honest truth, I never really liked sleeping in the pitch darkness. I'm talking of the time before Antoni got ill.

When he had his stroke and his left leg was paralysed, he turned over his business to a cousin of his (who ended up by robbing him right and left), and we went to spend the summer at Koroni. It was the first time he went back to his village after all those years in Athens. It was I who persuaded him to go. We could have gone to Andros like we used to. But I thought the climate at Koroni might do him good. In Andros it's a bit damp. At the same time I thought it might do him good psychologically to go back, after all those years, to his old haunts where he spent his days as a child and as a young man. It'll buck him up, I thought, make him feel stronger in himself. And, as things turned out, I wasn't wrong. Except that it didn't happen quite as I expected.

Boros, his doctor in Athens, had told him to take a walk every morning to get his muscles moving. Usually, he walked up to the castle. If you've never been to Koroni, you just don't know what a beautiful landscape means. When I was a girl we used to go ever so often on excursions to Aigina, Methana, Sounion, Andros and suchlike places. But I've never seen a place to touch Koroni for sheer beauty. I hope, now that this filthy business has ended, now that we've stopped slaughtering each other, that, God willing, I'll go back there, even if it's only just once, before I close my eyes for good. We used to have a book by Athina Tarsouli with pictures from different places in the Peloponnese, and Koroni was in it. But I've no idea what happened to that book. I haven't set eyes on it for years.

The castle is Venetian. Next to one of the ruined walls there was a path going down to the sea. There was a cave there, and centuries back they'd found in the cave an ikon of the Holy Virgin painted, they said, by the Apostle Luke himself. The ikon was supposed to work miracles, like the Virgin of Tinos, and every year, on Presentation of the Virgin day, people from the nearby villages used to come to the cave to kiss the ikon. Many incurable people had become well. I found out about all this afterwards. For one thing, I liked the view from the castle. And usually I went with him because I didn't like the idea of him going alone. (I was afraid he might slip and knock himself unconscious on a rock.) I used to take along a basket with hard-boiled eggs, cheese, tomatoes and home-baked bread, and when we reached the top we'd sit on the grass and have a picnic. Or I'd send my slob of a daughter with him, if I could dig her out of bed – she was always sleepy. 'Get up you lazy slut,' I'd tell her. 'Have you been bitten again by the tsetse fly?' But on the day I'm talking about he didn't want her with him. 'Don't wake her up,' he said, 'I'll go by myself.' I knew what a stubborn mule he was. Once he said something he'd hardly ever change his mind. And even if he'd told me to go with him, I couldn't that day because we'd arranged with his cousin Artemis to make some home-made noodles to take back to Athens with us. We were planning to go back home after ten days or so. We'd been in Koroni more than three months, and I'd begun to be homesick for Athens. We couldn't stay on any longer. And he, too, was beginning to get fidgety. His mind was on the business. Staying on in the country was beginning to do him more harm than good.

I knew he usually got back by about eleven. 'Eleven o'clock,' I said to Artemis when I heard the clock strike. 'Why not go and put on the coffee pot. He'll be back soon . . .' But half-past eleven went by, and twelve o'clock and half-past twelve, and there was still no sign of Antoni. 'Run and see if he's at his cousin's place,' I said to the Grand Duchess. 'And if you don't find him there, dash round

to the coffee shop in the square. He may have gone straight there!' But the little
bitch began to dress up and primp herself as if she were going to a wedding.
Instead of being worried like I was, she stood there in front of the mirror combing her hair as though she had all day to spare. When she got one straggly wisp
of hair in place she had to go back to another and start all over again. It made
me mad to see it. 'You unfeeling slut,' I screamed, 'you miserable bitch. You'll be
the end of me! Haven't you got an ounce of shame in you, a little snot like you
standing there for hours in front of the mirror combing your hair when I've asked
you just a little favour? . . . Don't worry, my girl, I'll settle your hash when I get
back!' And I just left the noodles half-done and dashed out of the house. I rushed
over to his cousin's place, then to the coffee shop, then like a mad thing all over
the place asking if anyone had seen him. Nobody had. He must have slipped and
fallen down, I thought. He's slipped and fallen and I'll find him dead! As I hurried
up towards the castle I imagined every kind of disaster, except the one that had
actually happened.

I had almost reached the top, with my heart in my mouth, when I saw him
coming down the hill holding his walking-stick over his head so that I could see
from the distance that he was walking without a stick. 'Aren't you ashamed of
yourself?' I said when he came up to me, and I burst out crying after the fright
I'd had. 'Aren't you ashamed of yourself, scaring me out of my wits like that?
Didn't you stop to think? I might have gone crazy worrying about you!' And I
cried like a baby. He put his arm around my waist and we went on down the hill
holding on to each other.

He didn't tell us how the 'miracle' had happened. How the Tripolis and
Kalamata newspapers managed to publish so many details was a second miracle.
The villagers came crowding into the house to see with their own eyes the man
the Virgin had picked out. They touched him and stroked him to see if he was
real. 'Good old mister Antoni,' I remember one of the villagers saying, 'you'll
be a marathon runner yet,' and he gave him a really good kick on the knee.
Artemis' front yard was suddenly full of blind men, lame men, syphilitics. It was
impossible to believe that all that sickness and misery had existed in the village
all the time, hidden unsuspected inside all those clean-looking freshly whitewashed houses. And when the word spread that mister Antoni was handing out
money to the poor, I decided it was time to put my foot down. I took him almost
by force and we packed off home to Athens. And it wasn't a week after we got
back before his leg became paralysed again, worse than it was before! . . .

Translated by Leslie Finer

Yorgos Ioannou (1928–1984)

Ioannou began as a poet of talent but devoted his writing life to deceptively modest genres of short prose in an *œuvre* largely devoted to his native Thessaloniki. His preferred form is not so much the classic short story as a kind of text more evidently, yet teasingly, auto-biographical. (The story selected here is typical of Ioannou's earlier and perhaps richer vein – he possibly overdid the slyness towards the end.) Ioannou's style is unobtrusive, creeping up on the reader through telling detail and lightly worn allusion, and bridging the gap between the author's peasant forebears in Eastern Thrace and his own position as an educated homosexual in a state of emotional exile. In a manner quite different from the Joycean Modernism of Nikos Gabriel Pentzikis (q.v.) or the Faulknerian enterprise of Nikos Bakolas (q.v) – and different, too, despite its humour, from the large canvas of Kostas Tachtsis' *The Third Wedding*, Ioannou cumulatively creates a richly prismatic and humanly telling picture of Thessaloniki in woe and weal, and his body of work contributes to that troubled city's particular good fortune in its modern memorialists.

'Voungari'

No sooner had we learned that the Germans had hanged her husband than she arrived herself from Florina dressed in black, with the child in her arms. All at once the house was filled with weeping and gruesome tales. She was a Vlach and talked on and on, without pausing for breath, the way all Romano-Vlach women do. She told us first the bare facts and then the details of how they'd taken him, put him at once through a court martial, and hanged him in front of the main barrack block early next morning, along with ten others.

At dawn there had come a knock at the door and he got up to answer it. He was slightly flustered, not surprisingly, but didn't bother to get dressed, thinking it would only be his assistant from the power plant, where some mysterious break-down had occurred the day before. But in a few seconds he was back in the room, deathly pale, groping for his jacket and trousers. A German soldier stood in the doorway, helmeted, with the badge of the military police on his front. With him was some bastard of our own, an interpreter. She had no time even to get up out of bed, half-naked as she was. He gave her a frozen kiss and went with them.

Next morning, when she heard the dreadful news she went running in a frenzy to the German commandant, a cold-blooded major, and insulted him grossly. The interpreter, scarlet in the face, could not translate fast enough. Finally the commandant said only, 'According to regulations I ought to hang you too, but you have a young child and I don't want to.' And he left the office scowling with rage.

They wouldn't let her near, so she went instead to the house of the three girls, which was opposite the main barracks. The house was a single-storey affair of mud brick, and gave a poor view of the gallows. As darkness fell she and the girls climbed into the tall plum tree and from there she could see him dimly in the moonlight. Tall and blond, he seemed even taller up there on the gallows, standing out among all the others. They'd put him second in line – his assistant was first. She stayed there, alone, until morning. Her hands and face were bruised with clinging on. Sentries with fixed bayonets came and went. They wouldn't let her near that day either. His straight blond hair blew in the wind for three days and three nights. In the end he was buried almost secretly. Only the girls risked it and went.

We felt a heavy responsibility for all this and, to tell the truth, a degree of weariness. It was we who had brought them together, and apart from its tragic end, the relationship had already passed through many other difficult phases. The girl was exceptionally unlucky. The last summer before the war we had spent the summer in Florina as usual, and we'd invited her to spend a few days with us. Of course we had thought of match-making between them, since we knew the girl, who was in danger of turning into an old maid, as well as the poor soul, who lived across the road from us and worked as an engineer at the power plant. He was a sensible character, and melancholy. He had just separated from his first wife, who had proved an insatiable whore, although he'd dried himself out trying to satisfy her. I heard him one day enumerating his efforts to my father and hid for shame. Their child, a boy big for his age, she had taken with her to the capital, where she had placed him in a Christian institution and paid steeply after regularizing her profession. They said she was very beautiful. All these, and other things, made us look kindly on the poor soul; neither were we at all disturbed by the supposedly secret liaison he kept up with the youngest of three sisters in the neighbourhood, since it was perfectly plain he harboured no serious designs on that featherbrain. Weighing up the situation my parents, a young couple themselves, decided to talk to him. And when, after some hesitation, he accepted the proposition, this was followed by the invitation to the as yet unsuspecting girl. As soon as he saw her, a tall dark woman, getting off the train, he whispered to my father, 'This makes a difference,' from which we realized that until then he had not taken the business too much to heart.

Two or three days after her arrival, once they had become acquainted and the ice was broken, we organized a big outing to a festival of All Saints, up in the mountains near the Serbian border. From my first impression of the place I remember only lots of trees and the morning cool that hung round the mountain. Most of the women, who had come down from the surrounding upland villages, wore local costume, with embroidered aprons and coloured kerchiefs. As earrings they wore a kind of curved goose feather, from the middle layer of the breast of the goose, which I heard them call *poufkes*. The men wore their wedding best, of dark wool. Even now, whenever I see paintings by good folk artists of central Europe, it is mostly of that festival that I am reminded.

We didn't stay long at the chapel: in any case it was full of people. We quickly spread ourselves under the trees and began to prepare for a small celebration, which never came off in the end because everyone scattered in different directions. As well as the couple in whose interest we were acting, we had a number of people with us, to camouflage the fact a little and to establish the right kind of atmosphere, as well as serving other needs. First of all we had an extremely ugly spinster, a schoolteacher who came to Florina every year to undergo, so she said, tomato therapy with the celebrated tomatoes of the region. She was especially disgusting during the therapy itself, when she endeavoured with bloodless lips and fangs to gouge out the inner part of the fleshy tomatoes rejecting the indigestible skin. Needless to say, she consumed whole hampers of them. Each year, moreover, she became more horrific of countenance, but admittedly kinder of heart. Perhaps in time she would be blessed with wisdom and a clearer conviction that tomatoes, even those from Florina, sadly do not hold the key to health and beauty in this world. Still, that day she was our most faithful and obedient follower. All the others had ideas of their own. But with only the schoolteacher, of all people, there was no chance of a celebration. The other person with us was the daughter of our landlady, a beautiful woman and madly in love with a barber in the central square. Her mother, a Vlach shrew who was forever grumbling, was rabidly against it and harassed them constantly, so the two had no chance to have enough of one another. They had thought up all the devices in the world to be able to exchange a few words now and again, although some well-wisher would invariably see through them. When he passed her with his handkerchief to his nose that meant, 'I must talk to you.' She had then to find a way of getting to the agreed place. And she would do the same, when she had anything of importance to tell him. She would pass casually by the barber's shop, in front of the hanging of coloured beads that filled the doorway and holding her handkerchief ostentatiously to her nose, slacken her pace a little. He would then make some excuse to abandon his customer and run to a shop some two or three doors along, where they made Turkish delight and where he knew he would find her. The amount of Turkish delight they must have gone through at home was nobody's business. He had persuaded everyone that he had a craze on the confection. And all these tribulations only to be able, most often, to exchange greetings and a tender handclasp! These encounters were so fleeting that very often the beads were still moving and jostling from the violence with which he had thrust them aside on leaving, when the barber returned. When we went in the summer, the

Turkish delight was in less demand. I carried notes for them myself and took their orders. The previous afternoon, as soon as we had snatched the consent of the wily old lady, I ran to the barber's to tell him that the next day we would be going to the festival. We had hardly finished spreading out our things when the svelte barber turned up. He had been there before us apparently, since the crack of dawn.

Despite the morning cool the heat began to rise quickly and the men made a start on the dark red wine and pickled chilli peppers. The cicadas had gone mad and the wasps came round in clouds as we threw down skins of watermelon and other sweet things. The expedition, like all expeditions, was good only until lunchtime, and had already passed its peak. At one moment a great hullabaloo was heard behind the church. A couple of drunken gypsies had fallen to with knives. We ran in that direction but couldn't make out what was going on. There was a great crowd of gypsies, all shouting at once. It seemed that the knifing had occurred over some affair of the heart. They had come to blows over a slut who now stood moaning on one side. She was terribly ugly, although we read in the newspapers a few days later that the case concerned a rare beauty. Despite this unhappy example, our own pairs of lovers were quite undaunted. One by one, they found an opportunity to slip away. The engineer and our guest went for a walk, which lasted however a very long time, and the barber lay down with his beloved a short way off behind an evergreen oak, with a newspaper folded over their heads like a tent. Constantly from beneath the newspaper came sounds of stifled laughter, sighs and kisses exactly like the loud popping of corks from bottles of old wine. The schoolteacher was placed in a quandary. For a moment we were afraid she would make trouble. What could we do with her? We had taken pains with her too, but no one had wanted her. In the end, exhausted, she covered herself in the same manner with a newspaper and feigned sleep. But that didn't last long. She suddenly let out a screech and jumped up. A wasp had stung her on the right cheek. The lovers interrupted their kissing to offer first aid. Ammonia, naturally enough, was not among our provisions. I was then required to piss, and with my piss which, she said, was still pure, we had to make a mud paste and apply it to her swollen face. This was the barber's medicine lore. To cheer her up we told her in comforting tones that wasps are attracted to sweet things, not sour; which she then believed and began to put on airs like a spoiled brat. We could hardly restrain our laughter. The truth, however, was that the wasps left everyone else alone. Still, I don't believe the hysterical schoolteacher did it on purpose. But she certainly doused our spirits. A little later I was chased by a ram, but fell down before it could butt me, and the ram charged triumphantly over me. In addition, it was given out that a spy had been caught.

Finally we were only just in time for the bus, since the newly matched couple took so long, they put us quite out of humour. God only knows where they had been and what they had been up to in all that time. Anyhow, I'd seen them link arms before they were properly inside the wood. 'To the bride and groom' my father had said, raising his winecup, and the toast proved prophetic. All the way back she murmured sentimental songs and gave him languishing looks, while he burst out laughing at the slightest thing as if someone was tickling him. That was when we began to be a little uneasy.

The worthy barber didn't come back with us, so as not to reveal his relations with the girl. For all his delicacy, however, this tête-à-tête was to be their last, because in a few days an unforeseen event turned everything upside down.

Early in the morning there came a knock at the outside door of the house where we were staying. The landlady's daughter went down in her night-dress to see who it was. It was a middle-aged expatriate, a Greek from America, who was looking for some women in the neighbourhood. The girl excused herself for a moment, threw on some clothes and politely took the 'American' and pointed out the house he wanted. It turned out later that he was supposed to marry someone there. However, as soon as he set eyes on the girl they had arranged for him, eyelids swollen with sleep and rather ungainly, he thought to himself, 'Oh no!' and the wind dropped out of his sails. On the contrary our landlady's daughter stuck in his mind. She was the one for him! She had struck him as very beautiful and fresh, although she had just woken from sleep. Had it been the schoolteacher who answered the door, it would have been a different matter. In fact, the aspiring bride was particularly unfortunate – the comparison was crushing. The 'American' had been instructed by his mother, who was nobody's fool, to visit the bride unexpectedly, early in the morning, because then, she said, it shows whether a woman is really young and beautiful. He spared no effort to find out about our own, and since she by this time had despaired of her unbending relatives, and the barber too, she finally accepted his offers and before long they were engaged. The poor barber now held his handkerchief only to his eyes and not, alas, with any hidden meaning. When he left, the day of the wedding was not far off. The 'American' was in a terrible hurry, his restaurant was being looked after by others. Besides, he saw no point in staying on here with his task accomplished.

The married couple left for America some time in September and the first news of them arrived shortly before war broke out. The girl was leading a life of bliss. The letter was full of things unheard of in Florina. She never drank water from the tap but only out of bottles, she never had to wash socks, combinations or underwear but threw them away as soon as they got dirty. With handkerchiefs it was the same. These she could not have washed in any case, had she wished to, because they were paper. We could hardly believe her good fortune. We thought of her a good deal during the Occupation and still more after the liberation, when the relief parcels began to arrive from over there. But we had lost their address and she never wrote to us. Now that I think of it, their silence doesn't seem at all a good sign.

Two or three days after the festival our house-guest left Florina, declaring with a boldness that took us by surprise, that she wanted to marry the engineer and that it was now up to us to talk to her parents and make them agree. We heard more or less the same from the engineer – apparently there was an understanding between them.

All the same, he was a single man and his visits next door to the three sisters continued, they being compassionate and in reality only two. The third, and eldest, he had himself managed to marry off, by forcing a dandified NCO, who had left her pregnant, to come back and take her. What the girl had been through, however, during that time, is another story. They had shut her up in a sunless room and insulted and beaten her constantly. She had no mother, but she had a terrible grandmother who didn't speak a word of Greek. Even now, although bedridden, she still sorely oppressed the other two girls, to such lengths that they went and lit candles in the church, praying that she would die as soon as possible. They told her this, too, as a piece of news to shut her up. They were not like their elder sister, who had paid dearly. As the house was situated opposite the main barracks the girls, whether they wished it or not, every now and then made the acquaintance of some soldier. Let's be honest, wherever you find a barracks, defence is not easy. Young men are headstrong, and when they want something badly nothing stands in their way. All day at exercises they would gaze tirelessly at the low house. Every time they took their bayonets and ran through the straw dummies hanging in a line, they would let out comic cries and look over their shoulders at the girls. For their part, once they'd begun their day with a hot iron curling their long hair into pigtails like sausages – a practice which earned them the nickname, the 'Saucies' – the girls would climb into the plum tree and watch the boys exercising, and at the same time escape from the crone and their old father, who after the experience of the eldest, wouldn't let them stand around too much at the door. There was a well just by the foot of the spreading plum-tree, and when we brought down melons and cucumber to be chilled, you often saw, even at midday, the moon reflected in diverse phases. Still, it wasn't true what they said in the neighbourhood, that they wore nothing underneath. The truth was merely that the Saucies had misconstrued the words of a song then current, and instead of

> Baby, you've nothing, but by God you've got 'em
> With what you've got, you're a great kid at bottom,

they said, 'you're great in the bottom'. What could you do with them? How good was their Greek?

In the evenings the enkindled youth of the barracks came out to walk up and down in front of the hovel, although the road was a handspan deep in dust that was mined with broad ridges from the hooves of the cows. But the sweet desire that loosened their limbs and the inadequate municipal lighting made it seem like a fairy tale. The boys shouted up taunts or riddles, and they answered with one voice. They were socially very cultivated. From time to time a group of boys would climb up to discuss the answer in greater depth.

This is how the NCO had seduced the eldest. He had asked for a plum and the conversation had started from there. So far only plain soldiers had taken any interest in her and she was especially touched by the braid. Even the old woman stopped grumbling and was eager enough to make a fuss of the captain. Their home was humble and very poor, but he was not to be put off. He let it be known, of course, that he was a rich man in his village – which was no more than the truth. The worst thing of all about the house where the girls lived was the toilet. In fact, there was no toilet. At night they went out to the field opposite that flanked the barracks. The sentries behind the wire whispered randily in the darkness. Occasionally they made a mistake and a furious row would break out. By day they went to the stable, where they kept an age-old pig and a stall for the cow. Once, when I was put in there for a shit, I got the fright of my life when I felt a warm breath on my behind. It was the pig, rooting about in the half-darkness. Later, when they'd pressed the youth into marrying the girl he had seduced, their toilet was one of several matters he took in hand. Perhaps the pig had terrified him too – with luck it might even have bitten him. But this kind of thing was more than the poor soul would put up with. He no sooner found out where the captain came from than he went straight to his village and told the whole story to the good lad's father, a landlord of the old school who was quite aghast at the exploits of his prize cock and threatened the latter with disinheritance if he didn't marry her without delay. No matter now, if from the moment she entered their house they treated her worse than a slave and all laid into her together. But this fact had a decisive effect on the poor soul's future. Without realizing it, he had signed his marriage contract.

Back in Salonica we went ahead with the match. The girl seemed particularly ill at ease and kept pushing us. We supposed she must be severely smitten. I was sent on fairly frequent errands at night to fetch some full bottles from an old magician woman, which I had to pass in to her by the window, so that her mother, a terrible hunchback, wouldn't see. Later I learned that she too had got pregnant and wanted at all costs to get rid of it.

At the beginning of October, soon after the letter from America, on a cool evening with thunder and rain, the betrothal took place; we were there in a body. The rain was considered a sign of fruitfulness, and everyone foretold them a happy life and plenty of offspring. Her dear brothers turned up too, six in number, although without the least concern for their sister. They seemed sensible enough, but their wives were a choice bunch. The wedding was fixed for November, but with the declaration of war the groom was drafted into the army and the girl fell into despair.

Our neighbourhood, which consisted entirely of old Turkish-style houses, was practically flattened. Some people thought of their villages, others moved into districts where the houses had a lot of concrete. We found refuge in Athens, with my fat grandmother, in a tumbledown house in Plaka. Needless to say, we had lost touch with our protégée. But as I was taking the Easter lamb to the oven during an air raid and the flak was bursting over my head, while the potatoes thundered on the tray, I saw the girl from Salonica looking up at the numbers of another street. She was crying, as I led her back to the house. She had the baby in her arms already, a little girl. She had given birth secretly in Athens a short while before, and none of her relatives knew about the child. We made a mental count of the months – beyond doubt it was the product of that now remote outing. Black despair enveloped her – and us too. Some of us were here, others there and we weren't even sure who was alive.

When the Germans finally came, the disbanded army began to arrive back in droves. Many of the women who had had husbands or sons in the war went down to Rendi station every day and waited while the methodical enemy permitted the goods trains to offload the soldiers. The women took bundles of civilian clothes with them – shirts and trousers. The rumour had gone round that the Germans were particularly sensitive to the sight of soldiers in Greek uniform in the centre of Athens and had threatened to herd them into camps. These trains had no fixed timetable, obviously, but usually arrived in Athens in the late afternoon. The goods wagons, all of them that the Occupation authorities would allow, went up as far as Thebes or Levadia – further on the viaducts were down – and loaded up with soldiers who had had to make it so far on foot, to take them all gradually back to Athens. Every afternoon a gaggle of women would set out from the neighbourhood, headed by my grandmother, with shirts and trousers thrown over one arm, and water flasks or shopping bags with food and provisions on the other hand. They went to welcome the naked and hungry men, to reach them just as soon as they put a foot off the train. The girl went with them, although there was practically no hope. She left the baby with us and went. Understandably, the clothes, and food in particular, seldom came back. Someone they knew would always turn up, or some haggard young boy would collapse on the platform and they would give them to him. This afforded relief for the women too, a hope of recognition from God, who these days was lower in the sky and saw everything that went on. But there was no sign of anyone from the neighbourhood, and the women went to Gorgoepikoos and chanted prayers in unison, with tears and a catch in their voices.

The very next day, at sunset, someone from the neighbourhood showed up. He was a known queer and it was certain that none of the women had prayed to the Virgin for *him* – he lived all alone and shunned his relatives. Still, the Virgin had found a way of sending a sign. He had stolen a horse, he explained simply, and so was the first to arrive. Most of the army was on the road and coming on without hindrance. The women crossed themselves and relaxed a little. But late in the evening two grim-faced boys brought the news to the blind man's house opposite that his son-in-law had been killed during the withdrawal. You would have thought from the shrieking that it was the end of the world – the whole neighbourhood fell into a panic. He had been killed at the very last minute, at a time when everyone thought the killing, at least, was over. No one slept a wink that night.

Next morning there was a stampede of women down to Rendi station. The girl was among them. Soon however, the younger son of Thodoroula turned up, as bland as anything, exactly as she had been expecting. Thodoroula had a private icon stand in her courtyard, a relic of the old Church of Our Lady, and for days now she had been saying that the Virgin had told her to expect the younger son first and then the elder. Truth to tell, the younger son was a good deal brighter and sharper than her firstborn, who had made a living selling vestments to priests. Told of the news in advance by her younger children, Thodoroula opened the outside door and went down on her knees before her son. Praise be to God, the one was safe. A short while later voices were raised in Polyxeni's house – her husband was ponderously climbing the steps. But the neighbours who scuttled round to see found the door locked fast. Polyxeni's husband was a brusque sort and took no notice of courtesies. 'Lucky Polyxeni,' the more charitable of them commented. 'It'll be better than a wedding night in there tonight.' By evening, at least half the men of the neighbourhood were back, and late at night came the first beating, heard by the neighbourhood with silent enjoyment. Dimitroula's husband was beating her savagely because in her confusion she had been one of the first to go and hand in his pistol to the Germans, who as soon as they arrived had issued stern decrees about arms.

Kyr-Manthos, the protector of lone women while the war had lasted, had gathered a number of the new arrivals together on his courtyard parapet and held forth about the terrible lack of supplies which had already become evident in the market. From the lighted cigarettes which glowed brightly at every draw, you could see that the new arrivals were in the throes of grave anxiety. Kyr-Manthos told them that at the restaurant where he worked, they no longer cleaned the vegetables but tossed them into the pot with the skins and rotten stuff, so as not to lose any weight. In any case there was no risk of losing customers; every lunchtime you had to fight to sit down. Kyr-Manthos watched all these people piling into so much garbage as he served and took orders. Every now and again he would shout, 'Eat up, pigs, eat up!' No one was offended, but nobody laughed either. Kyr-Manthos spoke nothing but the truth. And at the same time he lightened the hearts of the new arrivals. But when the restaurant closed and Kyr-Manthos died of starvation, many of these newly arrived warriors had turned into inveterate blackmarketeers. 'You die – I live,' one of them hurled in Kyr-Manthos' teeth a little later, as he was starving to death.

Listening in her small dark room to Kyr-Manthos' vivid narration, the girl hugged the child to her breast and broke down in silent weeping. It was not just loneliness that threatened her, but starvation as well. Next day she didn't go to the station, nor the next. It was pointless to deceive herself any longer.

By the end of the week all the boys from the neighbourhood had returned. The only casualty was the blind man's son-in-law. They held a memorial service for him at Gorgoepikoos, but deep down it was a thanksgiving for negligible losses. The next evening the queers of the neighbourhood gave their first party, having spent the day plucking out their beards, hair by hair, with tweezers. 'Oh, you've no idea of the agony, the *agony*,' they said, with much fluttering of the wrists. As soon as twilight fell, a glorious martial host began to collect. 'With glory did he seek after pleasure,' the ancients said, and would certainly have blessed this gathering from down below, even though, as excavations have since shown, the fun took place right above one of their cemeteries. Listening in the darkness to the cheerful commotion, we thought for a moment the pre-war years had returned and we felt grateful to the victims of our persecution. But the almost tiresome grief of the girl, huddled up in a corner, kept us from cheering up.

At some point there came a message that the engineer was well and in Florina. Next day she snatched up the baby and left via Halkis, on a northbound caique. The railway had been blown up and the sea was bristling with loose mines. But she couldn't wait any longer – she had to be married before her relatives found out everything. A considerable time elapsed before we learned that her courage had been rewarded. But what could you expect? The poor soul turned active and soon got himself involved in organizations, and the enemy, finding them isolated in that desolate province, busted them in an exemplary fashion. Instead of rejoicing in her married state, we had her back with us, decked out in black crêpe.

I was young, but I used to suffer then over almost everything. The widow's descriptions of the gallows brought a lump to my throat. I picked up the little girl in my arms and went out on to the terrace. I wanted to take the deep inhalations that, according to the well-meaning authorities, were each equivalent to a pork chop. If things had turned out differently they would have brought us real chops from Florina, but now no one mentioned the omission. Between two inhalations I said to the baby, pointing up at the moon, 'What's that, little urchin, what's that then?' She stretched out her tiny hand with a smile and lisped

'Voungari.' I asked again, and again she emphatically said the same thing. After that, to her mother's distress, the child was baptized 'Voungari' – as we still call her. We changed the well-known rime, of course, and sang a tune of our own:

> Helios and fengari
> at the wedding of Voungari . . .

A few days later she took the child and returned to Florina. True, the terrible shadow of the gallows remained there, but there was bread as well. She would go back to her old trade, as a seamstress.

She had a hard time of it and was much despised, sewing for coarse west Macedonian women who never had a kind word for her. Only the Saucies stood by her and, although Slav-speaking, they turned out to have hearts as pure as any Greek, and better than most. They had been well-trained by our soldiers. Every time they came down, Voungari was more beautiful and rounded out. In the end she burst forth as a full-fledged blond beauty to turn a man's wits. Even her uncles began to be touched and ceased to regard her existence as a disgrace to their precious family. Beauty commands respect everywhere, it must be admitted.

Last year we had Voungari's wedding. It was in St Demetrios, our long-suffering church. There was a great turn-out, and unusual enthusiasm for the wedding. You had the impression some victorious event was being celebrated. The groom, a bold village boy, had an astonishing resemblance to her father. The eminent, unbending uncles were all present, as they had been at her mother's betrothal. They stared haughtily at the fresh, simple faces of the groom's family, exchanging quiet whispers now and again. Her mother, a white kerchief over her shoulder to relieve the black of her widowhood, wiped her eyes behind a pillar. As the crowns were exchanged, we were all of us moved, remembering the past. Voungari shone with beauty and innocence. I was thinking that when her husband brought her to maturity I would have to tell her, in a light-hearted way, all that had happened on that outing, so that she would know. Looking up at the brass chandeliers, I was suddenly reminded of her father and the ten others. The biggest chandelier of all, which hung above our heads, swayed very gently as if in blessing.

And in fact, when the nine months after the wedding were up, and not at all before, Voungari gave birth, not once but to twins, a boy and a girl. Two blond, lively children, full of health.

Her father's blessings had really come true.

Translated by Roderick Beaton

Nikos Bakolas (1927–1999)

Bakalos was a slow-burning novelist who produced much of his best work relatively late in his career. With high ambition, amply vindicated in the event, he set out to chronicle the life and losses of his native Thessaloniki from the time of its annexation to the Greek state in 1912. Unlike more triumphalist accounts of the Macedonian Struggle, Bakolas' does not neglect the multi-ethnic Thessaloniki, which survived until the deportation and extermination of the great majority of the city's Jewry in the Second World War. As the following extract shows, dealing as it does with some notorious anti-Semitic riots of 1931, Bakolas extends a keen and sympathetic eye towards all classes, conditions and peoples. He does so in a technically complex but always humanly engaging manner, evidently in Faulkner's footsteps – and none the worse for that. Collective ghosts of the kind elaborately exorcized in *Absalom! Absalom!* are powerfully evoked in Bakolas' most celebrated novel, *Crossroads* (1987), from which this extract is taken. The sweep and technical range are impressive, as impressive in their way as Stratis Tsirkas' Middle East trilogy or Kostas Tachtsis' more lightly handled chronicle of Greece from the start of the twentieth century to the 1960s (qq.v.).

Crossroads (*extract*)

It all must have begun that night, when Christos returned from work as dawn was nearing, he was oppressed by a feeling of despondence that was painful and longed 'just to lie down and rest', for it had been an evening full of tension, piles of paper mounting up beside him, the telephone kept ringing but he couldn't hear what the people at the other end were trying to say to him, a writer protesting and shouting (you've ruined my article) and the teacher complaining, about his creditors, the workers, his nephew who was leading him a merry dance. But now it was all over, for a few hours anyway, and he arrived back in his neighbourhood and at his own house thinking, 'I'm like a dog taken out for a walk at midnight,' except that he had neither the strength nor the inclination to run. And in the midst of his weariness he saw a light glowing somewhere to the south, maybe in Kalamaria, among the shanties, it seemed as if trees and houses were lit up and after a moment the air thickened and was full of smoke and soot, shadows and the whole city dancing wildly. And Christos said, 'I'd better run,' but the effort seemed too much for him, maybe he was worrying about nothing; what could it be, he wondered, and he meant 'what evil?' but then he saw the glow seem to spread, he stood where there was an opening between the buildings, saw a mulberry tree, leant against it thinking how he was always robbed of sleep; he closed his eyes to trick himself for a moment and remembered his mother who'd scolded him when he slept outside, telling him that he might perhaps lose himself in melancholy dreams that would pin him to the ground. And at that point he began to walk quite unconsciously, mesmerized by the glow, it was certainly a fire, something was burning somewhere and the sky was full of the smell, not like the straw they used to set fire to in the days when he was a child in the village.

Then he heard a vehicle approaching fast, it was like one of the lorries in the war, laden with crouching men, and in a moment it passed him, metal and wood creaking and groaning, then turned the corner and came to a halt, the exhausted engine was boiling and he heard it stop, then his ear seemed to catch the sound of talking, as if the people who'd got out of the lorry were saying something hurried, maybe agreeing, maybe not, and after a little while they stopped speaking and he heard the growl of the engine once more, iron and wood once again jolting together, then everything was lost in the darkness as if sucked down by a well or into chaos. It was still night, yet the glow was everywhere, it had become stronger now and Christos thought, something stinks, and he didn't only mean the breeze which was bringing a stench to his nostrils like that of burning rags and fouled wood, or so he thought. He was still alone, standing now on the ledge in front of a garden fence, which refreshed him, and behind it lay a humble house, he thought of hurrying and felt that he was dallying inexplicably, then heard footsteps and saw someone coming towards him. It was a man who was fat and tired, after a minute he came up with Christos, his head bent and silent, passed him rapidly, as if annoyed by his presence, and then was swallowed up by the darkness – and Christos thought to himself, 'what's he doing out and about at this time of night?' for he recognized him. Then he set off in the opposite direction, reflecting, I don't like these goings on, and he meant the lorry and then also this neighbour, and he said to himself once more, 'something really stinks'. And in a little while he was out in the main street with the tramlines, the pine trees shadowing him overhead, but it was dark and in the distance the light glowed: perhaps it was at the very end of the road, past the depot and the gardens and the cursed, haunted house. And he found himself walking in that direction, his steps increasingly rapid.

And in a little while he saw someone else, then another person, then a car which passed them at speed, so that he thought, I'm not alone and it really was something serious, and finally he came upon five or six gendarmes, all of them apparently hurrying, who said, 'something terrible has happened, they've set fire to the Jews in the Campbell quarter,' and Christos' heart turned over, he thought he'd been expecting it, there'd been whispers, it had been brewing. And he remembered the EEE, it all kept weaving in and out of his mind like a well-known film, so that he started running himself, breathless, he thought he heard voices, people had come hurrying out into the street by now, but the houses were becoming fewer and more and more lowly – refugee houses – and the trees were becoming more and more numerous, trees and open spaces, gardens, neglected allotments, and all the while the stink was becoming thicker, the wind hotter. Then finally he saw the rows of shanties but most of all the flames, a world of flames and a world of shadows struggling in despair or frenzied or as if possessed, and voices, weeping, curses; he approached nearer, feeling that he was becoming one with the smoke, almost fainting with the stench, something seemed to be gripping his skull as if threatening I'm going to suffocate you. He thought, who can tell which are the victims and which the perpetrators? whereupon, without knowing how, he found himself among the former, running with a tin can of water, jumping in among the hovels and battling with the flames and the smoke. But everything had been perfectly planned, because there was only one tap and this gave nothing but a mere trickle, so that the men grabbed their old blankets and flung them on to the fire, as if they wanted to catch it, lest the evil should get away from them and grow, and the women were ululating and Christos prayed for it to rain, but it was a dry and starry night, and his own voice and his breath turned to vapour, like in bad dreams where you scream for help but no one can hear you, and he ran back to the tap, who forced me to do it, he was to wonder – but this was later, at midday when they'd fallen exhausted to the ground, choking on ashes and outrage, watching the fire brigade run to and fro who'd only arrived once the sun was up, the women and children gathered on one side and struggling to overcome their terror.*

But the woman who was really almost out of her mind was Amalia. When she saw him coming back pale and exhausted she said, 'I might have known you'd go running off to help them'; word had got about that the cause of it all was a Christian child who had been found dead near there, and some people whispered that it was in the depot, in the pit, while others said he'd been discovered among the shanties where they always hid the barrel and the nails and the blood. Christos made no reply and only murmured, 'poor people' as he remembered how they'd been screaming and running, how they weren't given any water with which to put out fires or to wash, 'poor people', he said once more. And Amalia muttered, she heated water in the copper and undressed him and shoved him

---

* The burning of the Campbell quarter took place one night in 1931 and Salonica was shocked. Everyone said that it was the work of the EEE, who used to copy the exploits of the Hitler Youth. The dreadful thing is that the whole business had received support, and some fanatic journalists, anti-Semites and other trouble-making elements, had said that Jews are reds and had reminded their readers of Benaroya and other socialists.

naked into the bathtub and gave him a row, and she boiled his clothes, boiled them again, she seemed to have entered into a sort of battle as she hung them out, dried them, made them smell sweet, and when it was almost dusk she watched Christos put on his other clothes and leave in a hurry: all she got time to yell at him was 'don't let the fact they've got rich relatives bother you,' and what she meant was the large villas of the merchants on the wide avenue, where they had five servants, a gardener and a coachman – all these villas belonged to Jews, none of whom was starving.

But he had a good think about it, he got things into some kind of order in his mind, and he told the editor with great heat, 'it was the lorry and the fat man in the night,' he'd seen them, the EEE, and the other man said, 'be a bit more careful with what you write,' always the same old refrain, as his pen ran on he'd feel a sharp stab in the lower part of his back – 'it's because you're killing yourself,' Amalia said who ached for all his trouble and effort, she told him fondly one night, 'you're too honest, that's why people rob you,' and she meant they exploited him, for the children were growing older and needed things, they never had enough money for shoes, hardly even enough for bread and sugar. But Christos insisted, 'they set fire to the poor people,' the godforsaken Campbell quarter where the children showed their little arses through the holes in their ragged breeches, and the villas were just fine and unattainable, and the coachmen in the carriages were just fine – 'don't make a melodrama out of it,' said the teacher, and at that point Mr Aristos came up behind him and Christos thought, he's reading the lines I've written and he felt that he was being robbed, that Amalia was right. But things turned out to be even worse, for they took what he'd written and read it and got in a huddle over it, they said, 'this matter requires great care' and Christos recalled the affair of the banker and all of a sudden he had a flash of memory, 'wait,' he said, 'I've just remembered the people at Michalis,' the young man and Angela, 'I've just thought of the Bulgarian' whom he'd seen in that loft where the EEE met, on a day when they had put on their short trousers and paraded and the whole neighbourhood had laughed, and as quick as a cat he grabbed his notes, 'I'm not letting you have them,' he said to Aristos, but they looked at him as if thunderstruck, and in his anger this sight remained in his mind as he went and ran down the stairs in a fury and then stood in Egnatia Street, it was completely dark by now and he saw a group of people laughing and joking with each other and singing, they were wearing their best clothes, handkerchiefs in their breast pockets, trilbies, for certain they were on their way to a party, and Christos hurried by, thinking of how he'd flabbergasted them at the newspaper, 'there's no going back now,' he said to himself and someone turned to look at him, I must be talking to myself aloud, and without noticing it he'd reached the Fountain and he could smell grilled meat and ouzo, 'perhaps I should go in and have a good time,' but he continued walking, slipping along, because such things were not for him.

And at home when his family saw him they said, 'he's ill,' for he'd got back before midnight, but he reassured them, 'I came to get a bit of rest,' he told them and smiled. And they supposed that he'd been given time off, for he'd worked himself to the bone the previous night; but Amalia muttered that 'I don't like all this,' the fact that they'd eaten their meal and hadn't exchanged a single word, Christos plunged deep in thought. In the end he said, 'make up the bed and I'll go and get some sleep' and he went to bed, he had a sharp pain like a knife in the right side of his back, and Amalia came in, she too lay down, worried, 'I heard you groaning' in his sleep or in his perturbation, and thus they spent the night, she was scolding, 'you're not cut out for getting into the hurly-burly' and only when the day was dawning did he apparently fall asleep; at one point he seemed to shake in a sudden spasm as if someone had prodded him in his sleep, and then there came a little sound like whispering, rather as if the trees were speaking, and it was a shower which after a while turned into heavier drops of rain splashing down, 'why couldn't it have happened yesterday?' he asked her and Amalia replied, 'don't think about it,' for she could sense his pain, his anguish, and she laid the palm of her hand upon his burning brow, 'don't go on fighting any more, my brave lad,' she begged as the rain came drumming down bringing them the scent of the earth, just like it had been in his father's fields, one May Day when he had spoilt everything . . .

'How can I help it hurting?' he answered her, for the wreckage had been smoking and smelling, and he just standing there as if under a spell, watching as wretchedness gathered its rags together in the drizzle, searching maybe for something that the flames hadn't reached, while all around stood the gendarmes, silent and uncomfortable, 'in a single night they were transformed into tattered bundles of rags,' Christos sobbed, before him he kept seeing people bowed and stooped as if condemned, as if wounded, and then he could take no more and set off walking along the street, and after a bit he heard behind him the creaking of a cart and horseshoes rapid on the paved road, 'come on, mate, I'm going as far as the depot,' someone called to him, it was a carter aged about fifty, smiling at him, inviting him, maybe feeling sorry for him as he walked along as if struck by death, but Christos said, 'leave me to walk and get some air' and the other man replied, 'as you like,' and he heard the whip cracked and the horse's hoofs quickening once more as the cart was borne off leaving behind it the smell of vegetables, and Christos remembered their own vegetable garden, his father in his straw hat working the rich earth, sometimes its master but also its slave, and he longed to find a water fountain so that he could drink a bit and maybe refresh his face, he could feel that the skin on it was roughened, taut, and his cheeks hurt.

Some time I'll have to speak out, he thought, about what he'd seen and suspected, so that the teacher wouldn't complain and accuse him, 'you're secretive,' just as he might have said you're one-armed or hard of hearing. And he heard the sound of running water, it was a large public fountain in the middle of the road, quite deserted, and he bent down and drank, then refreshed himself, put his head under the flowing water, let it run down over his eyes his throat, he felt his ears buzzing and a slim cold blade running down his breast, to his navel maybe or further, and then he stepped back, 'I'm still a village boy at heart,' he reflected and said to himself, 'I suddenly feel like going barefoot,' but all the same he got out his handkerchief and dried his face. And the teacher says, 'that's not enough' but Christos disagrees and grabs him by the collar, 'there,' he hears the man say, 'you've turned into a revolutionary,' he lets go of him and returns to his desk, 'I'm not letting them get away with anything,' he mutters; 'what got into the poor boy?' the others later said. A few sheets of paper with writing on them, an envelope of photographs, a set of blurred images: soldiers waiting in a queue for their rations, Christos and Kostoulas in a tent, the hut, the wireless, Christos, Euripides seated, a single star on his uniform, Christos with Amalia beneath the White Tower, the Salikourtzides gang before the firing squad, their caps flying off as they fell, a group of friends dressed as Romans and knights, with '25 February' written at the bottom, the opening of the Fair with everyone wearing panama hats, Dimitris standing at a tree with his legs apart and in front of him the mark where he'd pissed, a woman lying on the cobbles, and beyond her the workers in their best clothes with their banner, a circle marked in pencil, Christos just a felt trilby, Polychronis wearing a panama hat and gaiters sitting in a cane chair with his long cane beside him, May Day by the young plane trees, everyone lying on the grass and the tablecloth white in the middle, plates and empty bottles, three photographs attached together with a paper clip, a body lying on the carpet, two gypsies and a gendarme, a house in the upper town with its iron gate closed, and at the bottom the yellowed conduct report 'excellent', five ten out of tens and the rest nines, a girl's head with curly hair and earrings, Michalis' shack with its signs and Manos in the middle talking, at Kamara with Euripides in civilian dress, postcards from Athens, Brigitta Helm in passionate mode, and Valentino with Wilma Banky, a row of girls all dressed in white, the display at the Schina school, then press cuttings, two poems and a proclamation, the autograph of Delios and a card of his, and finally an invitation to an evening party, a postcard of roses; and Christos wondered, 'what are all these things doing here?'

When he got home he stayed out in the garden, humble low-growing plants at his feet, mallow and pansies, the rose whose flowers wouldn't open, and he sighed, 'my blood hurts inside me,' no matter if people told him that there wasn't any such malady. It was past noon when he finally went inside, smiling, but Amalia looked at his eyes and asked, 'why have you been crying?' and he wondered if he really had been crying, but was sure that he hadn't, and Dimitris and Alcmene and Antigone came home, all three of them were tall and slender, 'when did they grow so good looking?' thought Christos – but now things were going to be difficult.

And the next day he started going the rounds, to the doors of newspapers, offices, then shops, to find a job he could do and which would feed them. But he couldn't find anything then and there, he had to wait, they had to know hunger, Amalia had to tell him, 'if only you didn't strain at a gnat . . .' and she meant he was fine in other respects. And at the beginning they managed all right, the pot was boiling on the stove and there was bread, but for how long? And lucky it was that two friends came to his help and recommended him at the market, he went to work for a shopkeeper who sold salt fish in Egypt Street, he sat in a little room like a nest and kept the accounts and the books and on Saturdays he paid the wages – it was a tragicomedy, for one day they were short of hands and Vassilis the boss said, 'please, just so that we can unload,' for the cart was waiting and blocking the road and curses were making themselves heard, and that's how Christos found himself with a can of fish on his shoulder, then another, and then another, and he learnt what it is to be a porter. And in the evening Amalia complained, 'the stink has got right into your skin,' and it really was in his hair, on his shoes, right into his vest, his armpits, even if he did say 'there's no shame in work' and thus found consolation. But in the night-time both of them cried and begged, 'just let this end,' if they could only escape from the fish stink and the humiliation. And sixteen days later their prayers were heard, Christos suddenly found himself dressed in khaki once more, there had been a coup and he was sent off to a military camp. It was Kondylis again, perhaps Euripides, ambitions, discord, one night they closed down the *Independent*, people said that they smashed its windows. But Christos had already gone to Kavalla, who knows whether he was glad when he heard this news, letters were not getting through; Amalia was weeping and scurrying around, 'things couldn't be worse,' she wailed, she was at her wits' end, wrote to her father-in-law telling him of their dire straits. She received a cheque for three hundred drachmas and the next day a letter written in spidery writing, 'we can't manage anything more, bring the children and come to the village' but she didn't pay any attention, they'd be starting school any day now. One night the doorbell rang, it was a strange man, swimming in his light-coloured suit, his face waxen, 'I wanted Christos,' he said, they were looking for him at *Esperini* and he was sorry not to find him, 'he'll be back though,' he assured her, the coup was over and they were discharging all the people who'd been called up. He came in and sat for a while and smoked, then told her again, 'don't worry, we'll help him' and pressed her hand and left. And Amalia lay awake at night, feeling at her side the warmth of Dimitris who had fallen asleep all curled up, from time to time he kicked her in his deep sleep. For a moment the flame of the little lamp in front of the icon flickered and shadows danced and in the end it all turned into a dream, while outside the cock departed from his normal timetable and crowed.

Translated by Caroline Harbouri

Thanasis Valtinos (1932–)

Valtinos has devoted an entire career as a writer to the exploration of rents in the Greek social fabric, from *The Descent of the Nine* (1963), an episode from the end of the Civil War narrated in the laconic oral manner of Stratis Doukas' *A Prisoner of War's Story* (q.v.), and proceeding through manifold experiments. In *Data from the Decade of the Sixties* (1989) this extends to a cut-up technique whereby demotic and *katharevousa* passages appear *en face*, semi-literate letters jostling with pompous journalese, to create a rounded picture of the decade and its divisions. The short text by which Valtinos is represented here gives an insight into his earlier manner and an idea of the power that this single-minded writer has devoted to probing the scars of the Civil War in the five decades since its military conclusion. Where Alexandros Kotzias (q.v.) emphasizes an urban bourgeois setting, Valtinos has been persistently drawn to his rural Peloponnesian roots; but his whole enterprise has, as this story shows, been carried out with remarkable dispassion.

Panayotis: A Biographical Note

He was born in Kynouria, in the village of Karatoula. He was drafted into the Army in the class of 1919. In the autumn of 1920, after the delay of one year, he was called up for basic training.

Immediately after the November elections – in which Venizelos was defeated – he reported to the 8th Infantry Battalion in Nafplion. They kept him for three months, made a machine gunner out of him and then sent him, via Piraeus, to fight in Asia Minor.

There, from March to July 1921, he took part in all the operations towards Eskishehir and distinguished himself in battle. The field marshal himself, King Constantine, 'The Eagle's Son' as he was called, had stood before him in ancient Dorylaeum and pinned the medal to his chest.

Two weeks later, now twenty-three years old, he crossed the Salty Desert on the Army's large-scale manoeuvres leading up to the decisive attack. They marched all day and all night in the stench and the sweat, without water but with robust convictions, to Gordium. They were heading for Kokkini Milia.

When, in 1922, the front was broken at Ali Veran, several kilometres west of the Sakarya River, he was taken prisoner with General Trikoupis and what remained of the 3rd Army Corps.

It was their last battle.

He survived the Ushak Prisoner of War Camp – only one of every three men did – and after working the rock pile for eighteen months ended up in Cilicia.

In the totally unexpected exchange of 1924 he was sent down to Smyrna with some three hundred other prisoners.

A delegation from the Red Cross was waiting for them at the Basma Hané Station; they herded them together quickly and transported them to the Marika Toghia steamer, docked at the Iron Pier of the Pounta Harbour. As the boat was pulling out, Panayotis, standing on the highest deck, watched the land diminishing behind him.

Despite the debasements he had suffered, despite the rags in which he was clothed, his face retained something angelical about it.

His illness appeared much later, towards the end of 1927. His right hand began to tremble; it was a sort of Parkinson's disease. He also began to stutter. The doctors who examined him concluded that it was caused by the hardships of captivity.

A local influence peddler, an old Army buddy of his, urged him to request retirement benefits from the government. He helped him; they got his papers in order; he sent them to the Ministry and waited. Nine months later the Ministry turned down his request.

In the meantime his mother died, as well as the older brother who had been supporting them both.

Some time later, trying to eke out a living, Panayotis ran errands. Eventually he had to start begging. But his was a strange sort of begging: he would go out and pick various herbs like sage and oregano and sell them in small quantities. It kept up appearances for whatever pride remained.

A neighbour of his, a seamstress, a woman now married but who once had been his childhood sweetheart, took pity on him and sewed up several little bags out of jute, all the same size, and with pleats at the top. He would patiently fill them, then go from town to town peddling them.

Half the Peloponnese knew him as 'Panayotis'.

Sometimes on the highways, in the scorching summer heat, roguish truck drivers would stop to give him a lift, then amuse themselves over the long haul by badgering him.

In the small towns where he would pass the night, even the bums would give him a rough time. Sometimes they would tie tin cans to him, sometimes scraps of paper and set him on fire.

He took everything in his stride, not as if it were his fate, but cheerfully. Perhaps deep down inside it amused him as well.

In 1957, when I was a soldier on leave, down from Macedonia, I ran into him at a whorehouse in Argos. He was selling the girls aphrodisiacs. We were relatives by marriage and when he saw me he blushed. He was nearing sixty by then.

In 1973 he retired for good, returning to his old village. He had aged considerably and begun to lose his sight; on his route, his legs would no longer support him like they used to. Some niece or nephew of his took him in. They would give him a plate of food to eat and every two weeks one of the girls in the house would boil his only change of underwear. In return, he would graze the two or three goats they kept on the ground floor.

That same year he died in the month of August. He had gone outside with the animals, gotten thirsty and, bending down to drink out of a tiny pool, he slipped and drowned in four inches of water.

Translated by John Taylor

Yorgos Heimonas (1938–2000)

Heimonas was a forbiddingly experimental writer who, in a series of short *nouvels romans* written after 1960 extended the range of prose expression in Greece. A neuropsychologist by profession, he was expert in evoking derangement – or perhaps, to prefer Rimbaud's word, a universal *dérèglement* – against which writing alone might maintain some resistance. Many confess to finding Heimonas' opacity frustrating, but undeniably he left a small but consistent legacy of cool experimentation. This extract from a later work, *The Builder* (1979), may serve as a sample of his apocalyptic mode.

The Builders (*extract*)

It will come about that the bodies of humankind will combine. The one will fasten on to the other and whatever is of man will be stabilized. A huge common body will be created. A new skin will appear and a broad new robe of skin. An ocean of skin will cover the united bodies of humanity. It will cover the hideous lines of connection. THE MEETINGS. The beauty of the body will disappear. But before the enlargement of the bodies comes about a long time will intervene. It is then that the meetings of mankind will take place. Awesome meetings in vast settings. There they shall gather. They shall stand in silence beside one another. Motionless and unspeaking thus this epoch shall be named the meetings. They shall meet on smooth sides of mountains in low damp meadows. On vast stretches of sand the people will stand. A huge throng of women will appear. These women stand in a misty seaside place. They are wearing white robes of cheap material such as those worn in asylums. They are like field hands. But strange and silent as if in convalescence. They are barefooted and hold grey umbrellas like the priestesses of summer. But the umbrellas are closed. Even though the sun is burning over their heads. Rather like instruments they use for an unknown purpose. The women hold them like the tools of a trade. The women stand motionless covering that whole stretch of sand. The sand is arranged somehow in echelons. They are not waiting and are not in exile. Nor are they prisoners. By their own will they have gathered. Side by side and the groups of women climb up and stand there like a measureless flock of motionless birds. A slight breeze comes from the sea and lightly ripples their wide white gowns. They stand thus for a long time. Upright till they drop in heaps and then stand up again and again drop. But they do not aid one another. These meetings appear to contain some order. As if the categories of people had separated and were meeting separately. There will be a meeting of people's families. Young families with babes held in arms or on shoulders. Motionless these newly born families side by side but not in a prison camp. And the meetings of mankind do not appear to be an army. Meetings of old men on treeless slopes. They do not appear to be expectant or to be awaiting their natural death. Always the vast place beside the sea or still water and always the light of the sun. You would believe it is not a place. It is a vast day. A deep day in the domain of the sun. These people are not disturbed these meetings appear to presage nothing. Drenched in an impenetrable calm as if they are standing and listening. That the silence may confide in them

When the epoch of meetings is ended it will be so named. Then the union of mankind will take place. The categories of humanity were dissolved. The world was excavated. Substances will become independent. Then the essence of man will be isolated and stabilized. At random the bodies will unite and form an irregular mass. In the beginning the union will be imperfect. People were left to follow the united. As of old the stunned families of warriors followed war wherever it went. Isolated people will follow the difficult and slow rolling of the ball of bodies. Then you will see a man following one of the united. He cleans his face and the other shrieks his face becomes a scale and that mouth of man which conducts to the sea

THE BUILDERS. A people arose like the Dorians. The last nation of humanity crossed the horizon and came forward. They are builders from Xanthi. Nights which stretch through ages attentive to earthquakes and worshipping the design of homes. By age-old tradition families of fine craftsmen. Nomads who never settle and are forever on the move. To places where they are called and by fame made known and asked to build highly paid. This country has been ravaged and they have called the builders to rebuild. The builders have arrived and are notified. They listen and accept orders. They agree upon a structure and commence. They labour day and night and together all the builders' families labour in haste. Whoever dies at work is buried at a distance and children born here are put to death. They leave for distant funerals and return in the evening and resume work. Thus on all sides rise great residences with carved façades and upper rooms as if multiplying on their own for many clans of men and domes of crystal. Now the builders have finished and are celebrating with bonfires. They dance on live coals and moan and sob. They depart and disappear. Empty and stupendous houses and a breeze of the cold sun presses on the great windows opening and shutting them. The domes creak to keep out the light. That it not pour in and overflow and a heavy breath from the ploughed soil. Wide open and empty those houses stand empty now and only the echo of a Thracian song

How much time has passed after the water? the herald calmly asks. He leans over and falls asleep.

Translated by Robert L. Crist

Katerina Anghelaki-Rooke (1939–)

Anghelaki-Rooke is a poet who has received wide recognition in Greece and further afield. Absorbing many influences, including some subtle uses of ancient mythology, she has always concentrated on personal themes, often with a type of feminine introspection which has roots in Emily Dickinson. Such concerns are explored with patience, understatement and concision in her recent work, which has a retrospective air.

In This House Settling Time's Account

A

I came back home
From Barbara's mansion.
The dazzling marble
Had entombed my mind,
But when I saw the red
Walls of a whole lifetime
I breathed again, though time
Lies heavy here with conscience.

B

They're both up here now,
The two old men in the photograph.
Or perhaps they're still strolling
In the garden on their slender walking-sticks.
Indomitable shadows cross the threshold
And find me taking the air
On the balcony
Passing an invisible thread
Through the eye of the needle
That once had stitched me.

C ´

'The moon, the moon!'
We stopped talking
About old days – fresh-faced girls then
On our shining bicycles,
Untamed, entangling in our wheels
Our mothers' voices –
And parted the branches
To reveal the moon entire,
Like a yellow lid
On a transparent jar.

D

One was a widow, the other childless.
Through the night they unfolded their lives
Laughing loudly at the sexual episodes.
Behind their chairs rose the moon
That had so often melted
Like luminous butter on their bodies.
By the time it set, one had reached
The funeral, the other the haemorrhage.
At the door: 'Let's not lose touch
Now we've found each other again.'

E

The house sucks at memories
And grows.
And like bricks indiscernible
Beneath the plaster
The moving bodies
Of the past support
In equal measure the weight
Of the roof.

F

Last night I dreamt of a gigantic
Nest of rats
Beneath the stairs.
I smashed it and the house
Deflated and collapsed
Parachute-like on the ground.
The rats surrounded me
In alarm, for they too
Had failed to see the elevated purpose
They had served.

G

There was a time when the two-storey house
Dominated here.
Now from their concrete terraces
The neighbours observe me
As, exposed, I water the plants,
Feed the cats and the dog,
Hobbling moonstruck,
Untortured in the future.

H

The power suppliers
Came with new appliances
To increase the light
So I'd be abundantly illuminated
As I went down.
But in the dark I reckoned up
Their charges and
Thanks all the same I said but
I'm not interested.

I

Stones that never fall sick,
Branches that always come back into bloom,
This is the scene that keeps

Advancing towards the centre.
Its views carry weight and
Surreptitiously it takes the leading role.
I ask: what will the house think
When it sees me crawling
On the flagstones, begging
A few hours more in its shade?

J

Outside my window the rampant
Mastic tree keeps eating up the sky.
Once its leaves barely
Rested their eyes
On the window-sill, edging the view around.
My end will drip resin, I thought,
As I hang exhausted
From a thin blue cord.

Translated by Katerina Anghelaki-Rooke and Jackie Willcox

Kyriakos Charalambides (1940–)

Along with his senior contemporary, Kostas Montis (well worthy of attention, but whose work is not represented here), Charalambides is a poetic voice from the Republic of Cyprus, often treated by mainland Greeks as a provincial backwater, whose work has been hailed in Greece. And this not because he eschews Cypriot history or indeed on occasion Cypriot dialect. (He must also be the only poet to have written a sustained diatribe, *ira et studio*, against the Tory 'Wet' Sir Ian Gilmour.) Charalambides has in fact been engaged throughout his career in a sustained and ambitious engagement with the legacy of Seferis (q.v.), a poet who visited Cyprus in middle life and found there something he and indeed Greece had forgotten about themselves. In his recent, highly allusive, work, Charalambides has attempted to wrest Cypriot themes from his great predecessor and to turn increasingly to the very different manner of Cavafy. The poems printed here are cases of a simpler manner and matter – dealing directly and concisely with the tragedy of invaded and occupied Cyprus after 1974 – which transfer more readily into English than the dense allusiveness of the more recent work ever could.

At His Daughter's Wedding

She had four hundred acres under occupation
and her father in the depths of the East.

Fortunately, she was to marry a good man.

During the ceremony
no one paid attention to her father.
He entered secretly through the church vestibule and stood
behind a column and took pride.
Afterwards, he wiped off with his sleeve
the torn and poor tear.
They thought he was the village idiot
and left him alone.

The ceremony ends, congratulations and all.
They take a piece of cake, loukoumia and go
to their cars, they are lost.

> The loving father goes back
> to the Green line, he kneels
> takes his place again in the earth.

The Apple

> Taking an apple from the basket
> she saw the cheek bone of her child
> who now rots
> in jail, over there.
> Poor boy, he wasn't
> seventeen yet, no high school diploma,
> didn't serve in the army, didn't kill a fly;
> polite and shy, timid and innocent.
>
> She put back the apple in the basket
> because it seemed she saw
> other mothers like her during the Ottoman Yoke.
>
> No one talks about them
> but for her, for a thousand, two thousand women,
> *Doxa Soi o Theos*, she has no complaint.
>
> Memorandums and official announcements,
> committees and UN missions
> of states and governments, of organizations and individuals,
> of observers, resolutions, congresses,
> solidarity, statements, funds.
>
> Everything finely tuned, all perfectly organized,
> with archives, self-confidence, with special rooms –
> the state, like a mother, takes care.
>
> But the apple, apple in the basket.

Translated by Dino Siotis

Missing Person

The old man tied his leg to the chair,
intending to sleep deep down in Hades,
when suddenly he heard his son saying
'Don't die, father, hang on, I'm coming.'

His son spoke from behind the mountain,
hedged round with iron pitchforks,
he had a curved waist, his hands were tributaries.

'Father, I'm alive I tell you, I'm well.
My strength has become a plate of broth.
I'm hungry, I'm shivering, but it's nothing.
Or if I die, it's only raining – it must be an illness.
In my murderer's hand I count a thousand drops of blood.
I brush off the fly of life, weep in secret, and send you
my being to keep – no tears, father.'

The old man sat up straight in his black breeches
and filled his surroundings with a wild lament.
And he managed, for his child's sake,
to turn his grief into white, into saffron stones.
Through the deep arch and the window he struggles
to grasp the Morning Star, his son's leg.

Translated by Kimon Friar

Lefteris Poulios (1944–)

Poulios was a great talent who burnt out early and has written little for decades; but his meteoric fall left some sharp illuminations. A visionary poet consciously indebted to the American Beats, and to Whitman and Blake before them, but also to the nightmare visions of Miltos Sachtouris, K.G. Karyotakis and even Dionysios Solomos (qq.v) in his own tradition, Poulios has, with a deranged but often acute sensibility – a mixture of acid-head, street protester and Orthodox holy fool – evoked the darker aspects of his native Athens, especially under the Colonels: his *œuvre*, though steadily attenuated, gives an insight all his own. The odd blend of Ginsberg's tribute to Whitman, on the one hand, and an unruly homage to Kostis Palamas' (q.v.) fiery – and, alas, untranslated – *Satirical Exercises* is to be found in the second poem appearing here.

Roads

Roads – gleaming dark octopuses of this land of mine
on which shapeless and weightless
the future makes its way. Limousines, coaches, tankers,
the odd bicycle or the occasional sparrow
trundling its invisible wheels along the asphalt.
Below, underground roads. Above,
tunnels of air playing jazz.
Roads by glittering shopfronts, by
statues or among shops and
factories. You, road by the university.
By Parliament. You, national road.
Neighbourhood roads. Roads lashed
with pitch and blood. Made with shouting
and gravel. Under the weight
of steamrollers and thousands of demonstrations.
You, road, shroud of Grigoris, Sotiris, Tasos.
Paean-roads. Festival roads.
Agony-roads. Murderer-roads.
What curse is on you?

Each of us waiting at his stop,
all of us together waiting under the tin shelter.

Translated by David Ricks

American Bar in Athens

Among the wandering, hurried, idiotic faces
on the street, I see you tonight Kosti Palama
promenading back and forth through my
drunken disillusionment
looking for a whore, a friend, a resurrection
while I hold your book in my hand.
What shop windows, what a moon!
People of all kinds are strolling in the night
as are iron curs; cats are in trash cans
and you, Verne, old story teller,
what are you hanging round
the entrance to the apartments for?
I understand your thoughts, Kosti Palama, mindless
old *bon vivant*, as you enter the bar
making eyes at the whores and sipping
a double whiskey.
I follow you through fogs of cigarette smoke
and giggles about my long hair.
I slump down on a rough wooden bench
next to sitting statues
and let you buy me a drink.
– We're the most lively ones in here tonight –
the stool pigeons look at us suspiciously
and the lights will go out in an hour.
Who is going to carry us home?
Kosti Palama, old wind bag, prodigal root,
what was the 'Greekness' you were
preaching about with fire and brimstone
on the summit of hope
when night suddenly flashed out
like a knife from its sheath?
And you were left paralysed on a chair
faced with a small, smoky dawn.
I feel like a schoolboy who had
an old fogy for a teacher. I kept trying
to figure out how to get along with you.
Hideous old boy, let's go and throw up
this evening's booze on the steps
of the closed bookstores.

Let's go and piss on all the statues
of Athens, paying our respects only
to Rigas. And then part. You go your way
and I mine like a grandfather and
grandson who have had a fight.
Watch out for my madness, old man,
if the fancy takes me I'll kill you.

Translated by Philip Ramp and Katerina Anghelaki-Rooke

To Karyotakis

Costas, I know what it is that put the pistol
into your hand. Humanity takes so long to proffer
the least crumb of courtesy. There are times
when Preveza approaches me, too, dangerously.
You drank your coffee in the café of the hopeless
with your silence and your grief.
You hung your verses on the crepe of night,
hurriedly took your cap
and went to meet your old friend,
death, for the final journey
'to the dark kingdoms over there'
where Daphne crowned your phallus
in the gulfs of Lethe.

Translated by Chris Williams

Jenny Mastoraki (1949–)

Mastoraki burst on to the poetic scene in 1972 during the Colonels' dictatorship, with a weighty and astonishingly mature short collection, *Tolls*. Since that date, she has produced only three further slim collections, each eagerly awaited, each extending her range of allusion in poetry and history – well beyond the Greek world in each case. This is poetry marked by firmness of expression and a careful, meditative ambition to lodge her words in the canon. Work of this order, in which every word, every rhythm, is so carefully weighed, and every allusion both indispensable and pared to the bone, is remarkably hard to reproduce in English, and this is especially true of Mastoraki's later work. That said, it is to be hoped that even from this small selection the finest poet of her kind will be seen to be what her very name suggests – a master.

[The Wooden Horse . . .]

> The Wooden Horse at that point said
> no, I refuse to see the press,
> and why, they said, and he said
> that he didn't know a thing about the murder.
> What's more he always
> ate very lightly in the evening
> and in his younger days
> had earned his living once
> as a toy horse at the fun-fair.

Translated by Roderick Beaton

The Battle Fought and Won

> The battle fought and won.
> And yet no sign of victory
> on the corpse-strewn field.
> We asked for the casualty list
> and they handed us a sealed envelope
> with a name folded over twice.
> Tonight I must put pen to paper.

In this country news gets about
slowly, but surely.

Translated by John Stathatos

The Death of a Warrior

The death of a warrior
should be slow and studied
like the distilled
lunacy of an adolescent
who becomes a man when he first makes love.
On his tomb place
two large question marks
for life and for death
and a traffic sign
that forbids
the passing of parades.

Translated by Kimon Friar

They Sang a Song All Their Own

They sang a song all their own.
Then
from their open shirts
the soil of their homeland spilled
mountain and olive groves
in shovelfuls.
And sorrow evaporated at their temples
like steam escaping
from the lid of a cooking pot
taking with it
something of the pulse's longing
and the wild dandelion's bitterness.

Translated by John Stathatos

Note

My family always had a high regard for foreign-sounding names, so at ten I was naturalized as Jenny, perhaps in the secret hope that once I lost weight I would become a film star.

The truth is I've often tried to go back to Iphigeneia, from when I first discovered the virtues of uncommon names, but it was no longer a practical proposition. Today, as soon as you're introduced as Iphigeneia, they're making mincemeat of you, the other women with their two-syllable names.

The Match

Then everything sparkles like Greek films, the wedding-feast of my sweetheart and the good girl, and I'm waiting outside, I was always afraid of blood and music, especially when they're playing very loud and all of them opening and shutting their mouths inaudibly. You see, at times like that it's best not to talk in a loud voice, because you can wake to find yourself out on the steps at the height of summer, wearing white trousers under the statue. Tonight I'm thinking of being the rubber girl who hurls herself from the rock, I'll tell them a cock and bull story to pull the wool over their eyes, but you'll know everything's fine and dandy and just why I did it, and when all's said and done each person goes after his own bullet, in the soft parts or in there deep.

Translated by David Ricks

The Underground

In secret arcades, full of hanging bodies, weeds, a hum like running water. So much water.

Behind the walls there's something creeping, thick and huge, something already scorched by hideous flames, perhaps a well, an underground passage that explodes, contracting, sucking in. Without a sound.

That is where tender men will wait in tears, their long hair floating in the dark. The hair of men who've drowned.

Of the Underworld

Beautiful ladies of the Underworld, with long hems and eyes sore from crying. 'My fair ones!' they would call them as they cornered them. Later they turned them into songs. Exemplary ladies. With bruised necks. Crumpled petticoats. And on their linen pantalets, a stain of blood, a dark leaf, spreading.

Let that be what is left of ancient longings. And of ancient loves.

Of the Sufferings of Love

Let there be water, as in Flemish landscapes, so that no fish or light passes through, and from the depths, songs of besiegers, voices, cracks, medieval wounds, the gilded faces of barbarians – in pain.

Always a lute across the chest, a nail straight through the eye – the noble-men, the maiden, legions all around them raging.

A beautiful painting, so green, I shall call it 'The Sufferings of Love'.

Translated by Karen Van Dyck

Nasos Vayenas (1945–)

Vayenas established himself in the 1970s as the leading poet-critic of his generation, with a subtle and seminal study of Seferis and several short collections of allusive, ironical short poems. (The hint at Stevens in 'Flyer's Fall' is characteristic; equally so, the poem about Andreas Kalvos, q.v.) Minute attention and much learning is devoted to poetic self-examination in Vayenas' work, from the years of the Colonels' dictatorship to the more insidious pressures of an affluent Greek present. It would be a mistake, though, to read this *œuvre*, in verse and criticism, as ludically self-reflexive and nothing more. And what is particularly refreshing is to find a poet (here one recalls the late Donald Davie) whose critical mind knows what it is to make a poem and whose verse is, in the best sense, always critical.

Death in Exarchia

They told me you had died and now I find you once again
playing backgammon in the café with the living
you're even winning and you wear a tie
you who had never worn a tie before
or ever even come down to the square
you always locked yourself up in that house
and watched the people passing by in silence.

They told me you had died whom am I to believe
you disappeared suddenly without saying a word
without even leaving a message
your shutters closed the bell not working
the dog sulking and all the lights switched off.

Is it you or is it not whom can I believe
how your voice has changed
the others do not speak but watch you playing
they watch you smiling as you throw the dice
and you win you win constantly.

But you'd never won in your life
you always were the loser.

Translated by John Stathatos

448

A Game of Chess

How can I beat you.
You play with me as you like and take
my soldiers one by one, surrounding
my towers and frightening my horses
that mill about here and there in confusion.
But how can I beat you when
even this my queen sneaks out
and betrays me shamelessly on the grass
with your soldiers and your officers.

Translated by Kimon Friar

National Garden

As if it were a scene arranged by
a great European director in a moment of inspiration

and not by the light passing over the trees
slowly shifting the shadows towards the avenue.

The whole image had something of the atmosphere
of certain Renaissance pictures.

And if it weren't for that man on the bench
head in hand

and the woman vomiting two steps further on
it would be perfect: a picture-postcard

that you send from a country in which you've just arrived
with a few words about the weather, the people – generally
   the first impressions

from a journey that you've planned for years
and everything's found as you'd imagined.

Beautiful Summer Morning

– an unfinished painting

Beautiful morning. Full of light.
A gentle breeze is blowing.

The superb sun of Attica.
Deep blue. White birds.

Beneath, warm
chairs on the sand.
And, naturally, the sea.

Nonetheless, it could use a few trees.
And one or two boats on the sea. To show

that one's able
to depart.

Calvos in Geneva

An old settee. A creaking chair.
Curtains closed. The table narrow.

Tragedies by Alfieri on the shelf
And the enraged letters of Foscolo.

Winter. Cold air. The river.
On the other bank Count Capo d'Istria

posts letters to Petroupolis.
And he waits. He waits. He waits.

At night, in a heavy coat, he walks
through existent and non-existent streets:

Grand Rue. Place St Germain. Rue Beauregard.
Freedom. Rue du Soleil-Levant. Arete.

Or he writes something in broken Greek
on paper borrowed from the Société de Lecture.

Translated by Chris Williams

Jorge Luis Borges on Panepistimiou Street

Surviving your own death
feeling out a deflated Attic sun
you walk slowly up Panepistimiou Street with the
    thin, dusty cane of Chesterton.

Blinded Borges.
Polyphemus.
Your voice refreshes my bones.
Deeper in, you are a Greek.
Light sits upon your shoulders.
                              Behind
your dark eyelids you discern
the intoxicated shadow of Solomos.
Homer follows you in a black taxi.
Up late.
Dishevelled.
Chain-smoking.
He picks up the coin
which periodically falls
from your shining teeth.

Translated by E.S. Phinney

Barbarous Odes

XVI

I've never understood the thirst for heaven.
Nor has my forehead touched the stars.
And azaleas (and what kind of a word is that?) for me hold few
attractions.

Passing, a cloud from 1978.
A strong wind is blowing from the future.
Night, once mother of the universe,
has turned into

a grey cloth hung out in some grubby
corner of Attica. Mirrors
keep giving me a rough-and-ready
translation of myself.

A dream: blue lekythoi are softly sinking
into my chest. A fine figure of a blonde sitting
on time's knee, half-undressed, pulls the petals off
a black daisy.

Flyer's Fall

You tried out those great wings in flight.
But you were held to earth by a golden chain.
All your efforts appeared to be the height
of heroism. But weren't. (How could they be?) The sustain-

ing hope that one day you'd escape, be whirled
up to the azure, was but a cuirass,
thin, brazen, tossed away on some battlefield
of olden times. A compass

without a needle in a soldier's palm
as he succumbs, weak-kneed, to the sand
or to the steppe in a snow-storm;

a man found first and skinned
by the vultures, suffering as his warm
blood grows cold; aground.

Après le Déluge

The immortal lips unwiped.
The sun transparent, a cognac bottle dropped

as soon as drained by an abandoned
god. The doves valiantly defend

what of the high places has survived disaster.
Here and there bits of plaster

come down on the heads of the mortals who'd let
raw nature overwhelm old habit.

A peacock walking through the water-spill,
opening wide a shit-bespattered tail.

At the taxi windows a line of whores
chewing gum, tooting the horns.

Jewels gleaming on the fingers of the dark.
The winds returning to their sack.

Dialectic

The epic of change is not the sudden
violent overturn of the immutable.

It is the simple moves made by the immutable:
heaven's chessboard, or rather backgammon-table.

Translated by David Ricks

Yorgi Yatromanolakis (1940–)

Yatromanolakis has long been established as, among other things, a leading experimental novelist. The extract here is the beginning of his second novel, *History of a Vendetta* (1982). Set in his native Crete, and ostensibly telling the story of a vendetta that took place in 1928, this novel, called simply *Istoria* in Greek, explores with great subtlety the inseparable meanings of the word: 'history', 'story' and, as the epigraph from Herodotus has it (Yatromanolakis is a distinguished professor of Classics), 'inquiry'. What, then, might once have been narrated – perhaps powerfully, it is true – in the folkloristic manner of, say, Pantelis Prevelakis (q.v.) becomes instead a much more elaborate enterprise for which a label like 'magical realism' seems grossly inadequate. Once again (and Yatromanolakis' fellow Cretan Rhea Galanaki supplies in this a parallel, q.v.) we see that a deep acquaintance with the riches of Greek tradition, including Solomos' *The Woman of Zakythos* (q.v.), lies behind this subtle craftsman's narrative.

History of a Vendetta (*extract*)

When Emmanuel Zervos, son of George, aged fifty-two, was shot low in the stomach at dawn on Wednesday 8 August 1928, there was no witness other than the murderer. The murderer observed that Zervos felt great surprise as his cummerbund suddenly came undone and he lost all physical contact with the ground. The law of gravity which, as they say, holds in place all objects, animals and men, was overturned so that a vacuum was formed between the earth and the victim's knees, one that must have been two metres high, perhaps more. Although Zervos was in the prime of his life, he didn't think to stretch his arms to the ground and protect himself from the fall. On the contrary, after hovering for some time at a great height, he crashed on to the dirt-track in the vineyard with his head hanging on the vines. For two or three hours he lay there motionless, bleeding, and it was in this position that he was finally found. So not only did he fail to recover the money he was owed, but he also lost among the thick dust all the coins he was carrying in his belt. These were one English gold sovereign with the king's head facing left, a silver twenty-drachma piece of the Greek Republic depicting a woman among ears of grain, two nickel talira with the picture of an owl, seven drachma pieces and three or more little twenty-lepta coins which were worn round the edges.

On the following Tuesday, 14 August, the eve of the Dormition, at eight o'clock in the morning, Grigoris Dikeakis, son of the murderer Pavlos, stood over the spot where Zervos had fallen, holding the harvest basket. He kicked at the dried blood with his boot and this brought to light the gold sovereign, the silver twenty-drachma, the two nickel talira and four drachmas. The rest of the coins were lost for ever. Grigoris, who had found Zervos lying face down in their vineyard seven days ago, was impressed by this fresh discovery; even more so, because for the first time in the twenty-seven years of his life he held such a large sum in his hands. He calculated that this money more than covered the damage done by the dead man as he fell on top of the vines, as well as anything else destroyed in their vineyard by the people who, moved by necessity or curiosity, had gathered round Zervos as soon as the crime became known.

It so happened, however, that the murderer's son experienced something that has been observed many times: certain people, although they themselves have never committed any crime or injustice, still feel that their kinship with the perpetrator of a crime puts them in a difficult and, at times, annoying position. It is said, moreover, that if they find themselves at the place where the crime was committed, their annoyance and disquiet is even greater, because a given place may not only contribute to a criminal act but it can repeatedly recall that crime to one's memory. So given that the damage to the vineyard was not great, what had to be done now was to pick the grapes – beginning with the one hundred and forty-three vines of sultanas on the right side of the track. To the left, the seventy-nine vines of currants did not yet need picking; but because the weather in August is known for its instability and can bring heavy and destructive rains, Grigoris thought it wiser to make haste and do what had to be done on his own, as his father was a fugitive from justice.

The little house at the end of the dirt-track where the vineyard ends was completely intact, although Zervos had been shot from there, as the murderer himself asserted ten days after the crime. In fact, during the reconstruction of the murder, on Saturday 18 August, the murderer insisted that when he saw a shadow approach the house from the road, he had pushed the gun out of the little barred window beside the door and fired. Dikeakis, who was often called Dikeos – 'Righteous' – both as an abbreviation of his real name and also because he often spoke up for his rights, was not believed at the time. But during the trial it was finally accepted that he had fired straight ahead from the window – not from a nearby fence after lying in wait, as was claimed in the initial police report.

Grigoris asked himself once more where his father might be and he had no doubt that, even if a murder does not change a place, it does change, and radically so, the people involved in it: the murderer, the victim, and almost all their relatives. Therefore, by having to flee from justice, the murderer creates trouble for his own people as well as for the victim's relatives, as they all search for him, each for their own reasons. In turn, the murderer himself not only loses his regular home, but his diet changes, he goes to bed in one place and in the morning he gets up in another, unties his belt and relieves himself. In the case of Dikeos, who was accustomed to wandering round the vineyard from dawn to dusk, slept there and relieved himself there, the change was enormous, as he was to say time and time again.

Zervos naturally underwent a greater change. The bullet from the Mannlicher that killed him, however well polished and oiled by Dikeos, and however small a hole it made initially, nevertheless pierced the skin with force, entered the stomach and ruptured those vital organs which help with digestion and defecation, and finally came out making a bigger hole low in his back and breaking two vertebrae in the process. After continuous and prolonged bleeding and loss of acids, the man's body was drained and his soul (which is said to resemble the silk moth and live a little higher up in the diaphragm) fell and drowned in the still liquids, the thick blood and the bile. The only living things that Grigoris found circling round Zervos' body were several flies, the sort which are born when a man dies. But inside the murdered man's nostril was a dead fly: black, small, with big wings – the fly that lives and moves inside the blood of the living, but when their blood pours out, it too dries up and comes to an end.

Grigoris was stabbed much later, three years and three months, to be precise, in November 1931, sometime between the feasts of St Minas and the Beheading of St Catherine. He saw his own entrails pour out into the river, having been stabbed by the son of the victim, Markos Zervos, son of Emmanuel. It was then that he called to mind once more the killing of Zervos, although the place was different. Then he examined life and passed judgement on it with the speed that characterizes only those about to die and especially those who have been stabbed. His final judgement is of no interest. What is important is that Grigoris cut and compressed time so that its pace quickened and its span was shortened. From the month of November, when severe cold descends from the mountain and the constellations of Winter are in the ascent, Dikeos' son withdrew to the hot month of August, three whole years earlier. Lying half in the river and half on the bank, he heard again the flies which are born when a man dies and felt in his nostrils the fluttering of the black fly which has wings of gold and of iron, which takes a man up and lifts him two or three metres high, sometimes more, and then drops him crashing to the ground, dead.

By making time contract and expand in this manner, Grigoris found himself alive again in their vineyard on Tuesday, eve of the Dormition. He picked the grapes off four vines, began on the fifth but stopped, exhausted, with the adequate excuse that the change which sometimes comes after a killing had taken place in himself as well. The fact that it was he who first saw Zervos, heard the flies and smelled the air around the corpse, carried him home and held the wake in his house, all contributed to this change. He had heard that the terrible act of murder has an evil influence on the living for the same number of years that they have lived up to the moment of the deed. The murderer's son calculated that for him it would last another twenty-seven years, and this thought rather depressed him. He did not think it serious that his father might suffer for fifty-one years in the future, because a murderer is probably subject to different rules. He decided then to stop picking grapes for the moment and, because he felt heavy after many days' lack of sleep, he hoped to have a rest in the coolness of the little house.

Once inside, he first looked over and counted all their tools, as his grandfather had taught him, without pointing to them or speaking aloud, but silently in his mind: the big hoe, the small hoe, the crowbar, the pick, the rake, the billhook, the sickle, the spray, the four baskets, the big bucket for diluting the potassium, the eight sacks for the dry raisins and the coil of wire for catching the hare, the fox and the badger. He then thought that, if all tools have some power because they contain within them the fire and metal of the earth, then his father's rifle, the family Mannlicher, must possess even more power and more heat. Other tools may be made from fire, but a rifle can produce fire. Its metal is heated to a very high temperature, it hardens, dries out and becomes light. This is why when someone uses a Mannlicher, having previously polished and cleaned the tip of the bullet, that bullet not only finds its target but is automatically attracted by the heat of the human body and pierces the skin, the flesh and the bones in a manner described as 'humane'.

On the morning of 18 August, on the eve of the general elections, after the feast of the Dormition was over, Dikeos was caught with his cummerbund undone, relieving himself among the carob trees. When they asked him why he had polished and cleaned the five bullets they found on him, he gave a whole series of answers which began chronologically from the basic processing of metals as they come out of the earth in crude form, and ended in the Spring of 1916 when he was still serving in Venizelos' police force in Free Thessaloniki together with Zervos. Dikeos explained that a clean bullet is better than a rusty one and that in order for a rifle to be effective it has to be humane, and he repeated his whole theory. As for the sixth bullet in the Mannlicher's chamber, he said it must have dissolved inside Zervos' body; and as for the spent cartridge, it must have shot out of the little window and got lost in the vineyard.

The cartridge, however, was found among the bed clothes by Grigoris on Thursday 9 August, the day of Zervos' funeral. After it was established from other sources that Dikeos was the murderer, Grigoris walked to the vineyard, opened the little house and discovered the cartridge. He noticed that it was slightly black at the rim, but the cap had been struck by the bolt exactly at the centre, because this rifle of theirs was perfect, always well oiled and clean and it never jammed. Grigoris took the empty cartridge, smelled it, as he did with all cartridges, and put it in the inside pocket of his waistcoat. It was there that he also put Zervos' money: the sovereign, the twenty-drachma piece, the talira and the drachmas.

In November 1931, while they were preparing Grigoris' dead, blood-stained body for burial (as such things must be done and as the church teaches and custom dictates), they found in the inside pocket of his waistcoat the clean and polished cartridge, together with one sovereign and nine drachmas. Zervos' relatives did not claim this money, not so much because Markos was Grigoris' murderer, as because they did not know that it came from a member of their family. After all, the same thing would have happened even before Grigoris' death, considering that Zervos' family had filed many lawsuits against Dikeos and his son, on the initiative and advice of their lawyer. Those who dressed Grigoris handed the money to the treasurer of the church council, as there was no immediate claimant, and it covered the expenses for the funeral and for the murdered man's memorial service in three month's time.

Grigoris sat on his father's bed and looked at the world through the open window. He saw the dirt-track that divided their vineyard in two, the neighbour's harvested field, the fence with the wild roses, and the slope leading to the main road. It was this road which took him straight to his village.

The village was situated between two cemeteries: an old Turkish one and a new Christian one. For it is said that while the two peoples, Greeks and Turks, are alive, they can sit, eat and drink together, but when they die they must not be buried together, because no one knows the precise limits or the jurisdictions of the Christian or Turkish saints. It is known that the site of a graveyard corresponds with another place hidden inside the earth, two or three hundred metres deep; so it is sensible to have separated the places of burial already on the surface. The Turkish graveyard was now abandoned, as their people had long since gone. During the first Exchange of Populations in 1913, when Grigoris was twelve and his grandfather was still alive, the Turks took away in clean white sacks the bones of those who had died long before and whose flesh had completely decayed. Those who had died recently were left in the village cemetery, and no one paid them the customary rites or looked after them or visited them; but then no one disturbed them in any way either. The Greek cemetery, where Grigoris stopped, had more graves; they were built above ground, sometimes lined with marble, like Zervos' grave, with a little cubicle in front for the oil lamp and an icon of the saint who helps the dead man avenge his wrongs and intercedes for his sins.

Zervos' protector was St Eleftherios – 'the Liberator' – who, according to legend, delivered his people from evil and injustice; also, according to the followers of Eleftherios Venizelos, the saint had played a role in the liberation of the island itself. In that same graveyard was buried Grigoris' grandfather, who was killed by a fall in 1916. But his saint was a different one. In their house they kept the icon of St Michael the Leader of Armies, the sword-bearer, the measurer of justice, holding the scales in his hand. Michael is no mere saint but an archangel, fierce and implacable, so he did no favours, nor did he intercede for anyone. This was clearly shown to be true not only by the death of old Dikeakis but also by his first visit to their house in November 1901 when he found Grigoris' mother Maria in the last stages of labour.

Now during Grigoris' birth, as he learned later, a great battle was fought between Maria (who was called 'the Quiet One' because she spoke and walked quietly) and the Leader of Armies: they pulled the baby out by his right leg and this is why it was two fingers longer than the other when he walked. But when Grigoris walked inside his mind, stepping a whole metre above the earth without falling or stumbling anywhere, his legs were of the same length and well balanced. He could go from their vineyard to the village and back fifty or sixty times and his legs never missed their footing nor did he limp, even though he was a cripple. He used to stop, however, by the side of the road, so he wouldn't get too tired, and watch people pass him either on foot or on donkeys; he watched the domestic animals, the dogs (who were at once both wild and tame), sometimes a badger, a fox or a hare. And neither man nor beast ever saw him, not even the farm dog who races through the valley sniffing everywhere and creating turmoil. But if the dog of the mind happens to pass the spot where Grigoris is sitting, it sees him; and if it races a hare or chases a fox into the open, jumping over fences and ditches and dashing from one corner of the mind to the other, then the head gets heavy; this was why Grigoris would sometimes fall asleep as he was eating or working in the fields. Then Dikeos would shout loudly and Grigoris would wake up in alarm.

Although his father worked hard, slept little and deliberated endlessly about justice and injustice, he never amassed any capital like Zervos. Indeed they had both served as volunteer soldiers and later in Venizelos' civil guard in mainland Greece, but this was no reason for them both to make a fortune. Because capital may grow by itself, like a silkworm that feeds in its sleep spreading itself on its frame as it eats and digests the mulberry leaf; but first it has to be born. That is to say when someone, for example Zervos, acquires by some means or other a certain amount of olive oil, soap, silk or wax then sells the product and makes a profit, he must then lend the money to earn interest; this is the only way that profit can make more profit. And this is how it comes about that one coin attracts another, the money is nurtured in the dark and grows like the silkworm. The money-lender is always left with a profit, never a loss, unless of course he happens to be killed while carrying cash and the money falls in the dust and disappears. Even then the loss is minimal compared with the profit that comes to the household at the end of each week or month from the money that passes through the hands of strangers, the money that is loaned on interest and multiplies perpetually.

Grigoris left the graveyard because it was hot and the place smelled like honey and like a dead dog decaying in the sun after it has been poisoned or shot. He walked slowly through the village streets but did not go past either their own house or Zervos'. At the edge of the village he urged his mind to go faster along the main road and he reached the slope of the vineyard a little before noon. His head became warmer then and into his mind crawled three lizards and a field hedgehog who hurt him, because even a hedgehog of the mind has spines that can cut into a man's flesh. After that he shortened greatly the distance between the steep track and the harvested field in front of the vineyard, and in no time at all he was standing over the spot where Zervos had fallen. Had he shortened the road a little more and brought the days closer together, he would have found Zervos still alive. But as usual in such cases, Zervos was impatient to get his money back and hurried before daybreak to find Dikeos at home.

So Grigoris missed seeing either Zervos alive or his father after the murder. This was because, as the facts proved and as Dikeos himself confessed during the reconstruction ten days later, as soon as he fired and saw Zervos hovering over the vines, he had opened the door, holding the Mannlicher in one hand and a bag with some bread rusks and olives in the other, and took off in a north-easterly direction with the intention of hiding. He did however stop to lock the door and put the key under the stone as was his custom. This detail made the defendant's position somewhat worse. As the head of the detachment who arrested him observed shrewdly, instead of taking steps to protect his house by locking it and hiding the key, Dikeos should have tried to give assistance to his victim. Grigoris remembered afterwards that Dikeos gave a very vague reply and seemed somewhat reluctant to justify his action. But during the trial, months later, the public prosecutor referred to this detail again, and tried to support a charge of premeditated murder – which was of course what the prosecution was aiming at. The jury, however, did not give this point serious consideration when returning their verdict. They obviously interpreted it as a natural reaction, because after the deed a murderer wished only to protect himself and his possessions. This wish, after all, is the cause of most murders.

As he sat on his father's bed, Grigoris flew once more out of the little window, like the bullet from the Mannlicher. The difference was that this time he did not go straight ahead or upwards, but down to the time when his grandfather old Grigoris was alive, and his father was away in mainland Greece; this was between January 1914 and March 1916. It was a time when the harvest, the grape gathering, the carob-picking and all field work was still done by hand, though it felt as if it was done in the mind. And because his grandfather was able to make the day or the night either longer or shorter, there was always time left over for Grigoris to sleep, not only in his bed but also while he was eating and working. But when the old man fell off their big carob tree far up at the second waterfall of the river, the daily fluctuations of time stopped. Sometimes though, when the days grew very long and the nights short or vice versa, when a man's body grew tired and could not bear the long duration of time, Grigoris would climb as far as the waterfall by the carob tree and sit at its roots on the black rock where his grandfather had fallen and got stuck. From there he would follow the water's flow sometimes on foot but mostly inside his mind, and he would descend the waterfalls one by one as far down as the little valley behind the village.

This river, which started off with a great quantity of cold water but lost it on the way, was peculiar in that if you walked in it on foot you saw five waterfalls: two large ones and three small ones. Starting from the foot of the mountain, the second and fourth were the large ones. But if you followed the stream inside your mind, you discovered that the waterfalls were twice as many; and if you took your time, they were three times as many, though the second and fourth were always the largest.

When Grigoris, who loved the river, found Zervos on the morning of the murder lying on the ground in front of the little house in the vineyard, he was completely taken by surprise. Before running back to the village and notifying the family, he quickly took refuge for a few minutes in the river, not only because he could think calmly in its coolness, but mainly because the sight of a bloody and dusty corpse brings to mind clear and abundant waters. So he asked himself silently but specifically, what would happen now to Zervos and to all that mud and blood. And as if the river were his grandfather, Grigoris addressed himself to all categories of waters, just and unjust, sacred and profane, mineral, sulphurous and purifying: How will Zervos be cleaned and washed, Zervos the Soap-maker, who manufactures and sells soap, Zervos the Silk-winder who owns the wheel for making silken thread, Zervos the Candle-maker, who collects honeycombs and makes wax? The answer came back, again silent and specific: Let us wash him with his soap, dress him in his silk and make the sign of the cross on his feet, hands and mouth with his candles. At that point Grigoris set off limping towards the village.

Seven days after the murder, exhausted and having had no sleep for four or five days and nights, Grigoris found himself again between the big waterfall with the carob tree and the house in the vineyard. He suddenly realized that he couldn't tell what day or hour it was as he was walking aimlessly in the heat. Then, in order to avoid falling into the great chasm that has no beginning or middle, where the wind blows neither from east nor west but rushed downwards and where, as old Grigoris used to say, heavenly and earthly things mingle, Grigoris achieved with his mind as well as with his hands what is known as the technical welding-together of time. That is to say, when a man is upset by some event and the flow of his blood is altered (being that which measures and regulates time), he has a duty to himself to abandon the present, confused and unreliable as it is, and grasp a new lead, either in the past or in the future. From there he can eventually weld together the two parts of time and return safe and sound to the present. This welding occurs mostly in the mind, of course, but there are cases when one can weld time together with one's hands. So it happened that, when Grigoris put his hand in the inside pocket of his waistcoat and felt the empty cartridge from the Mannlicher and Zervos' money, time was restored to normality and at once he found himself sitting at a familiar spot, protected both from the midday heat and from the bottomless chasm of time.

Now Grigoris realized that cartridges and coins feel different to the touch not because of their shape but because of the heat of the metals. A cartridge is warm, while coins are cold. It begins as a simple piece of brass, but when it goes through the casting and charging process, that common metal acquires properties that make it unique. According to those who have worked in such factories, the bronze is first washed and cleaned thoroughly of any foreign impurities. Then it is heated to a high temperature so that it becomes dense yet at the same time light. At this stage it is as soft and pliable as dough. Then it is pressed into various moulds and shapes and, through the skill of men as well as the steady repetition of machines, the baskets fill up in no time with the finished cartridges. This is the reason why, no matter how much the cartridge cools, it always retains a temperature of its own, which affects all its parts. The lead bullet is coated with many layers of pure and tested steel (as is the case with Mannlicher bullets), so that it pierces the human body easily and disappears without trace. If one polishes and lightly oils the bullet, as Dikeos always did, the original heat of the cartridge remains undiminished and the success of a shot is guaranteed. It is also said that if the bullet kills a human being, then the cartridge takes on a reddish colour, but Grigoris had never chanced to see this phenomenon in all the years he had been collecting cartridges.

By contrast the metal of coins, whether gold, silver or copper, remains cold from the time of their making. This is probably due largely to the various devices on them, since these are almost always the severed heads of various deities, kings, governors or animals. It may be that the reputation of these decapitated creatures creates the coldness; or perhaps it is certain techniques that are used in minting and subsequently in the circulation of money. Still, Grigoris looked carefully at the king with his twirled moustache and half-closed eyes, the ancient goddess of cereals and the night owl (which is said to have peculiar sleeping habits), but he could not reach any explanation for this phenomenon.

On the contrary, as he was engrossed inside the charging and cartridge-making factories, he lost the sense of direct time, the time which runs horizontally and brings the hours and seasons, and his welding broke. Grigoris realized once again the shattering effect of the murder upon him. He was unable to chase the events away, make them go far behind the house and over the mountain, and he couldn't go to sleep. So he took the cartridge from the Mannlicher in his hands again, together with Zervos' coins, and some time between Wednesday 8th August and the following Tuesday, eve of the Dormition, he set off, walking both on foot and inside his mind, to inform the dead man's family. In his attempt not to lose sight of the dying man, Grigoris did not walk in the normal way facing forwards but moved stepping backwards. That was why he tripped over the tall wild-rose bushes and when he reached the slope of the main road he very nearly stepped on three flying lizards, those strange, aged lizards, which, they say, are born old and die young. He did not meet a hedgehog, but seeing Zervos' head on the vines may have confused him.

On the main road he halted, unsure where to go. For a moment he thought of turning not left towards the village but right towards Chora, as he had all that money in his hands. He would cross two mountains and the big valley with the vines and the harvested grain, and the four rivers that are murky and have no waterfalls or carob trees. He would see the hill with the Church of the Crucified Christ and the little chapel of Doubting Thomas where Thomas is shown placing his fingers on the stigmata in order to believe. Then he would cross the hill with the cypress trees and enter the town. But this would require at least six hours, the vines would remain unpicked and Zervos would still be on the ground. So he turned left on the familiar road to the village and after rounding the seven bands and crossing the bridges over the three torrent beds, he reached the dead man's house out of breath. The time was eleven in the morning and Grigoris saw Markos, Zervos' elder son, sitting on the doorstep eating watermelon and spitting the pips on the ground.

Flushed though he was from running and agitated by the news he was carrying, Grigoris noticed with surprise the house flies buzzing all around Markos. The strange thing was that Grigoris was able to recall this scene much later, precisely three years and as many months later, when he saw Markos holding the blood-stained knife and disappearing down the river. He probably made this connection because he received the first stab of the knife whilst sitting on the black rock under the carob tree where his grandfather had been killed. He had been trying to pick out among the tree branches that little black fly which had taken the old man up in its legs, raised him high and then let him drop and crash on the rock. He was intrigued and wondered what it was that prompted this powerful fly to lift old Grigoris to the top of the tree, push him over head-first, and then allow itself to die shortly afterwards. For Grigoris remembered well how, when they brought his grandfather to the village on the back of the donkey and placed him in the big room of the house, they found a dead black fly inside his hairy nostrils: lifeless, small, with strong golden wings like the wine fly.

Translated by Helen Cavanagh

Rhea Galanaki (1947–)

Galanaki began as a poet, with a dense and thoughtful first collection in 1975, but is now established as a novelist whose work represents an unusual combination of deep historical research and narrative intricacy. The extract that appears here comes from her first novel, *The Life of Ismail Ferik Pasha* (1989), which takes historical fact as its point of departure. The novel narrates, from more than one perspective, the life of a young Cretan who was captured during the uprising of 1822, was taken to Egypt and went into the service of the Ottoman Empire. His final mission as a general, during which he died in obscure circumstances, was to suppress the great rising in Crete in 1866 – a rising for which his brother, now prosperous and in Athens, was supplying arms. Galanaki's novel has been incautiously read by friend and foe as a nationalist tale of an estranged Greek who rediscovers his identity. But, though in a different idiom, it is best seen in the tradition of Stratis Doukas' *A Prisoner of War's Story* (q.v.) in exploring the often precarious and multiple identities of communities during the rise of nationalism. This salutary book first appeared shortly before the break-up of Yugoslavia.

The Life of Ismail Ferik Pasha: Spina nel Cuore (*extract*)

I proceeded to the eastern provinces in the wake of the Ottoman forces, who burnt and pillaged everything they found on their way. During our march, we received the news that the ship *Arkadi,* which the Ottomans had nicknamed *Seitan* – Satan – owing to its velocity and mobility, had reached the small port of Sissi, bringing many volunteers, provisions, money, medicines and ammunition. The islanders hastened to meet the new arrivals and guide them to the rebels' hideouts; they carried the entire cargo on their own mules and donkeys, and when necessary on their own shoulders. The chieftains in the region closely followed our advance and adopted harassing tactics whenever they found a chance to do so. Korakas had already sped ahead to the plateau in anticipation of the Imperial army's arrival, for he had been warned that the target of our present campaign was none other than the plateau. It had always been a well-known fact – well known to me, at least – that the plateau was a place traditionally infested with rebels; they seemed to sprout like weeds among the corn-stalks; it was even said that they had been found hiding under sheep's bellies. The civilians, we were told, willingly provided for all their needs. And indeed a considerable number of rebels and reservists assembled on the plateau.

I entered Herakleion in early March. The Greek traders who had settled in this remote corner of the Ottoman Empire had changed its name from Candia to Herakleion, in commemoration of an ancient coastal colony that had been known to flourish on that site. This new name was not the only reason for the difference I sensed in the city, or to be precise in the harbour, since that was the only part of the city I had known in the past. Many years ago, the harbour had been the place where land, language and pity come to an end. I now knew that this childish belief had been both true and untrue; still, I wondered what flight of fantasy had led history to place the fortress practically in the middle of the dark sea, with the waves gnawing at the great boulders of the outer walls like a human disease. The marble standard of the lion of St Mark endured through the centuries, though mutilated by time and almost unrecognizable, while the silk flag of the Sublime Porte still fluttered in the breeze of the present day. As it happened, it was a northerly breeze, and I welcomed its coolness on my feverish brow.

I told myself that for many centuries the conquerors and the conquered had been setting the scene for the last act of my life in a manner reminiscent of the operatic stage sets I had seen in Europe long ago. The memory of the two captive boys, forever separated in this harbour, sundered to the very marrow by their different paths, suddenly transformed both past and present into the flimsy décor of a theatrical episode. The factitious impression was so intense that I wondered whether the completed episode had ever actually taken place in real life. What could be the meaning of a brother in the role of stranger and adversary? Yet he had played his role beautifully, as if dealing with a genuine brother. But if there was one person who could prove that he had truly existed in this whole story, if there was some real, living creature still ravaged by that parting long ago, that could only be me. That was all I could vouch for. I could only acknowledge the fact of my own existence, here, in the same setting as then – experienced as reality, not as mimesis. Anything beyond that fact I could only face with doubt.

I saw the wooden fortress pasted over with painted cardboard simulating large boulders corroded by the sea. There was also the painted, open Gospel and the lion of the Most Serene Republic next to the fluttering flag of the Sultan. A small cobbled alley had been laid out in front of the fortress, lined with small fake pillars of stone. It was there, on one of those pillars, that I had touched my brother's hand for the last time.

I stepped forward, trembling, and placed my hand on the pillar. Once again I heard the background rumble of the sea, softly raving to itself as it is wont to do in a port. The pillar felt cold, as if made of real stone, but I did not care to make sure. Tenderly, I wiped away the salt moisture on it, as if wiping away his perspiration – or was it a hallucination brought on by my feverish state? If this was his brow I was touching, it was too cold to belong to a living being. Like all beings who are irrevocably lost, he made no reply years later, when I asked him his name, at that very same spot, imploring him like a beggar for the mercy of his voice. He did not speak. It was all consummated, like a murder that cannot be reconstructed. It was over, irretrievably over. Only the desire for that other body remained floating on the water, an old piece of wood discarded by the builders.

Those who were conquered, and those who conquered.

On recovering my senses, I found myself lying in my tent, surrounded by my physicians and officers. The physicians were much concerned at my sudden bout of fever and my fainting spell. My personal doctor advised me – almost implored me – to entrust my duties to one of my officers for a day or two. As he said this, I noticed a brief flash in the eyes of a Turkish officer standing close by my side. I knew he had been appointed to spy on me, but I did not fear him, precisely because I was aware of his assignment. My sudden ailment naturally favoured Omer Pasha's scheme; he had already begun to spread rumours of my secret Christian and philhellene loyalties. Despite my exhausted condition, I refused to delegate my command and announced that I felt almost fully recovered; in fact, I asked all of those present to withdraw – having first thanked them – except for my aide, with whom I wished to discuss certain matters. It was probably something I ate, I said; or else, the long march and the shifting weather had taken their toll on me.

In the next few days I was notified by the Viceroy that it would be in Egypt's interest to delay operations in the eastern provinces, for in view of Egypt's wish to obtain the sovereignty of the island, it was not desirable for our troops to engage in further clashes. He promised that he was prepared to grant the islanders numerous privileges. He also wrote that Noupar Pasha, who was now negotiating with the Porte on Egypt's behalf, had been instructed to use my ailment as a pretext to recommend that the Egyptian army should not move further eastward unless its commander had fully recovered. The Viceroy urged me to feign a graver condition than was actually the case.

It was not necessary for me to put on any kind of pretence, for the grief of my homecoming had wholly taken over my spirit. My condition could no longer be kept secret. I had begun to sense a slight change of attitude even in my closest associates.

I was informed that Omer Pasha was actively preparing for his campaign. I still had not stirred from our camp. On no account did I wish to set eyes again on the harbour. The rest of Herakleion was unknown to me; but I was afraid to step into it, just as I had feared, in childhood, entering the graveyard at night, when the whispering breeze in the cypress-trees threatened to blow out the oil-lamps flickering here and there on the graves. From various sources I heard that Omer Pasha had sent a town-crier to all the villages calling for more recruits.

The dervishes summoned the faithful to join the holy war. The main streets in the towns swarmed with agas, beys, sheikhs and horses, while anxious Turkish women flocked into the narrow backstreets. The story went round that the mother of Ali Bey, the young and handsome son of Bratzeris, had rushed out into the street without her veil to meet her son at the Three Arches. She told him their dog back home had been barking for two days without pause, and his favourite wife had dreamt an ominous dream. Her son, it was said, dismounted and kissed her hand, swearing revenge. Then he rode out of the town to join forces with Reschid Pasha, the Turkish commander in the region, who had already marched ahead and camped at Kastelli, a large village at the foot of the mountain-range that encircled the plateau.

During the time I remained in camp at Spilia, on the outskirts of Herakleion, waiting to recover from my illness and preparing as best I could for the campaign that inevitably loomed ahead, I recalled a certain piece of information Ioannis had passed on to me in Egypt. I had had no contact with him since I had arrived in Crete as commander of the Egyptian army, for fear of arousing suspicion. I knew the Viceroy's men were keeping a close watch on me. I had already taken a considerable risk in lavishing favours on him to a scandalous extent during his stay in Egypt. I had sensed at the time – and was able to confirm this impression later on – that apart from his genuine feelings for a long-lost cousin, he was also governed by a secret craving for financial gain; and this had caused him to tread lightly on what he believed to be the deep-seated guilt of my conversion. I allowed him to grow rich and to believe whatever he wished about me. I had no intention of discussing with him my precarious balance between guilt and innocence; besides, temperamentally we were two very different persons. Yet I remained under the spell of our encounter. I owed him the glad tidings that my brother was alive, and I also owed him the commencement of my ending. Not for the first time I found cause to wonder at the baffling law that conjoins good and evil along a single path, or in a single person.

To return to the information I had received from Ioannis in Egypt: when talking about our relatives, Ioannis, for some strange reason, had seemed to know them all; this would have been natural had he been the parish priest; but he was not, though he did belong to a secret society of patriots. On one such occasion he had mentioned that two of our relatives lived in a village near Herakleion, not far from the place where we had set up camp. I asked a Turk who lived in the region to go and fetch them for me. Greek subjects often came to our camp to carry out various tasks, so my summons would not necessarily appear suspect. It could only be given a suspicious slant if Omer Pasha deliberately set out to use it against me; but I ignored that possibility, since the last month of my life was already on the wane, and our mutual aversion was now an established fact.

The Turkish emissary failed to deliver my message. Once again I asked him to fetch the two villagers, adding that I was still unwell and unable to ride to the village myself. This time he did as he was told and duly located them. But it appeared that they feared I would accuse them of subversive action against the Empire, and at the very least retain them as hostages; because, they said, it was hard to believe that the commander of the Egyptian army was unable to ride over and fetch them in person. Their social status would have easily justified a visit from me, for they were among the village notables; in fact, one of them was a priest. On the other hand, they feared that to disobey my summons would cause them to be punished even more severely. Finally, the priest came to see me just as the army was about to set forth on our campaign. He bowed before me, visibly dismayed, and begged me to excuse his brother's absence; he had been taken ill, but would come to see me as soon as he recovered. I noticed him trembling as he offered this lame excuse, which, however, I did not question for a minute, just as I had not questioned the legitimate qualms that had led him to rely on his habit as a kind of protection. I asked to be left alone in my tent with my visitor. After a few minutes, having made sure we were indeed alone, I disclosed my true identity to him, mentioning my family and my thorough knowledge of the plateau as evidence. He did not believe me, but was manifestly afraid to show his disbelief; all he said was that my whole family had died a great many years ago. I was not disheartened. I told him about my meeting Ioannis and helping him establish business contacts in Egypt. I also mentioned two occasions on which he and Ioannis had met in the old days; Ioannis had described these meetings to me in some detail: how they had offered each other hospitality, acted as godparents or best men at family ceremonies, engaged in various transactions, and so forth. Finally, I spoke about the birthmark on my neck, which ran in the family, pulling my shirt open to reveal it, and adding that I never needed to show it to anyone before this day – meaning not even to Ioannis.

This was the moment of recognition. I was on the verge of confessing my fears at the portents of my approaching end, and my misgivings concerning the Commander-in-Chief; I also wanted to say that returning to the plateau in this manner caused me much distress, though I refrained from defining what I meant by that. He must not look upon this return as a sinful act. Yet perhaps, in a certain sense, it was not entirely free of sin. But most of all, the return had fallen short of what I had imagined; I hoped he would understand my meaning. I observed that he refused to be moved by my confession, not because of the distance a confessor has to maintain while listening to a true confession, but because he could not bring himself to sympathize all of a sudden with a renegade, a pasha, a conqueror. Despite his aloofness, and because I fully understood his reservations, I begged him to make arrangements for one of my blood relations to escort me during the campaign as a bodyguard, since the recent rumours spread by Omer

Pasha were likely to influence even my most loyal officers, affording them a good enough excuse to turn against me should the need arise. I voiced this request in the warmest tone, perfectly aware that in asking for this minor succour, I was letting him see the man who was a general in a humiliating light. He replied, not without a measure of sympathy, that his habit forbade him from escorting me, but he suggested his brother for this role and promised he would persuade him to accept it. He would come and meet me on my way to the camp at Kastelli, the Ottoman army's last stop before reaching the plateau.

I took the same road I had walked along as a prisoner; only this time I was on horseback, riding with a mighty army, and I was about to take other men into captivity. Before we set forth, I had made sure that the old rusty blade was in its place, tucked in my waistband. As I rode along, I pressed the blade against my body, since it was not possible for me to remove my shoes and walk barefoot on the ground. It was my only way of being in touch with the ground. I looked around, missing the company of the boy; he had not shown himself during the past few days; he was probably staying on with this people after the Easter holiday. Anyway, he only appeared when he felt like it, indifferent to my wishes. The priest's brother did not turn up either. His reluctance to escort me was only to be expected. I was astonished that I had ever believed they would be willing to accept me and stand by me.

I was completely alone. I let myself be carried away by the drift of my thoughts, unwinding like a thread out of the selfsame road taken half a century ago; a thread that on both occasions led to my exit from reality as the only possible relief. The season was different this time, and I was careful not to ask the absent ones about the labours of autumn, which related to the time of captivity, but about the labours of spring, which related to the time of homecoming: whether they had weeded the fields and orchards, spread manure over the tilled land and at the foot of the fruit-trees; whether the apple-trees were yet in bloom. At this time of the year the square expanse of the plateau would be speckled with the vivid green of new leaves, gradually darkening as the season advanced. I questioned them again, and heard all the names of the village families, the place-names marking the sculptured landscape, across the plain and mountains. They had remained unchanged. I was glad to think it would not be long before I would merge into the realness of those names, because the sound of them, inalterable through the years, seemed to be saying they were expecting me. Persons, I thought, persons – except that they lack motion and turn into enigmas.

The leave-taking and the homecoming had become confused in my mind, the one affecting the other. I wanted to make them distinct, to compare them. I soon realized that since I had made the mistake of compounding them, they could no longer be separated. If that road had not once been assigned to captivity, it would not have been assigned now to the homecoming. My return was nothing more than a variation on my departure. I was seized with terror at the thought that I would never be free of my prisoner's shackles. Why then was I seeking to return? Perhaps, I thought, I was seeking the freedom of death – of a death. But had I not also died in a sense at the time of my capture? How could I be sure that my second death would set me free?

I should have resisted playing with these thoughts, which led my imagination so far astray. Yet even as I experienced the kind of pleasure that is to be found in games most dangerous, I suddenly turned in a surge of hatred against whatever significance could be ascribed to my childhood; not the plain fact of childhood, but its soul-shaping force. I wished I had not lived in that land, not been taken prisoner. Which of the two after all had imprisoned me most, the lost homeland, or Egypt? I wondered whether the pleasure of the dangerous game I was playing with myself derived from the challenge posed by my return; but then again at no moment could I have a clear view of what were to me the known and unknown aspects of my predicament. At that particular moment, my hatred was unalloyed, but I knew that on the following day it could be frittered away and turned into the sands of the remotest desert. But if it could be said I was about to take the field against someone or something, it was against my first life. I would inflict on that land the same trials that had poisoned my life over the years. Among the raped women, the slaughtered men, the shackled, abducted children of this war, I would re-enact my family history, I would punish my own family history. I exulted to think I would be able to kill the child who tormented the man I had become. And my head swam with voluptuous delight at the anticipated bloodshed, which until then had always filled me with revulsion.

I asked to be allowed a few moments of rest. There was no need to worry, I said, all I wanted was to sit in the shade of an olive-tree and smoke. I rode into an olive-grove and dismounted. At last, here I was touching the ground. I asked my men to place my cushions on the very edge of the rug; while I smoked I rubbed a clod of earth between my fingers. My physician was watching me closely, but he made no comment. He knew my body had grown strong again and my leg was almost healed. If I had wished to confide in him, this would have been the right moment. Soon enough the fighting would begin, and there would be no other opportunity for confessions of this kind. But I did not speak, even though we both felt ready. At this point I could only talk about myself in Greek. My physician would be unable to understand me. I became convinced that every single event in our lives entails its own language, just as I had instinctively sensed, upon my arrival in Egypt, that every landscape makes a similar demand. Perhaps it was because my Egyptian life had not really been marked by any events yet. Or perhaps because the landscape of the island was eclipsed for the duration of the campaign; the colours of spring had raised false hopes in me a few days ago. I averted my eyes abruptly from my doctor's expectant face and fixed them on the immemorial river: the river of soldiers, beasts and war material streaming past us further away. There was the sound of voices and clanging metal. I did not wish to re-enter that river. But there was no other way for me, I would have to flow along with it; in a moment I would be fully recovered. The men brought me cool drinks and sweetmeats. It was a beautiful morning.

Beautiful – at the cost of whose blood?

I found myself riding my favourite horse again among the ranks of soldiers. We were nearing our last stop before reaching the mountains of the plateau: our camp at Kastelli. I set eyes on the mountains just as it began to grow dark. And as they took on the softer shade of receding light, it occurred to me that perhaps, what really goaded me on was no more than curiosity. Except that it was of the most powerful kind, almost demoniacal. The kind that leads the most foolhardy among mortals to visit the deep blue kingdom of Hades.

As soon as I had arrived at the camp at Kastelli, I received orders from Omer Pasha to lead my army up to the plateau; a local man had shown the Ottomans an unguarded passage. After a briefing session with my senior officers, I remained alone in my tent to take a rest. Ibrahim, knowing we were on the eve of a battle, came and kept me company, guided by the urgency of the occasion. He was disfigured, as before, reminding me that it was vain, not to say cheap, to place the blame on the events of my youth. He smiled, for he had mothered my second life, and he had proclaimed as much by wearing the splendid silk clothes in which he always visited me, in order to remind me of my Greek feasts. I was indeed at his mercy.

He had grown so old that I thought this must be the last time I would see him. It turned out to be a difficult meeting; he too was at a loss for words, as if sensing we would not meet like this again. Was he foreseeing his own death or some misfortune lying in wait for me? We both avoided what we knew to be inevitable. But inwardly I could not help wishing that he would soon find release from old age in a natural death, such as he had not been granted in Egypt. With a surge of emotion I began to tell him about the land I was about to behold, believing that now at last my description was something that could be shared with him. I could not tell to what extent he paid attention to my words. His eyes shone with the brightness I had known during our past years together. I suspected that he was recalling our long ramblings, our journeys along the Nile, in an attempt to keep my Greek memories at bay to the very end. Yet I persevered in my description. I was relieved to find he did not once interrupt the flow of memories that welled up in me irresistibly. He never questioned my references to any person, blood bond, rural task, song, fairy tale evoked in my description. He had mothered me in my second life, and reminded me of the fact by displaying a total indifference for my first life. I tried to break through his impervious gaze, telling him that the land I was describing would be the dispenser of my death, and I was apprehensive for I did not know in what manner this would come about. Had he any knowledge of it? Again he offered no reply, whether out of wisdom, arrogance or a final lack of concern for human affairs. I reflected that there are moments when friends, even though alive, cease to answer questions. We had reached the end, then. I drew close to the radiance emitted by the bright silks standing out against the dark recesses of the tent, and I begged him in tender terms to wait for me here till I returned from the plateau. He seemed far too old for mountain-climbing and for fighting. He nodded, or so it seemed to me, signalling that he agreed to wait.

And only then, as we fell silent, did I realize that all this time I had been speaking to him in Greek. I had never before addressed him in my long-lost language.

6

Reschid Pasha, commanding our forces in Herakleion, led many thousand regular and irregular troops in the wake of the traitor who had indicated the unguarded passage of the plateau. This passage was the gorge of Yerakiani; having marched through it, he occupied the hill named Stavroos. The rebels already positioned on the plateau had been unable to guard the numerous points of access to their positions. To be precise, the gorge of Yerakiani was not left completely unguarded; about a hundred men had been sent to defend it, but they were forced to disperse before the Turkish advance. The Imperial army seized the highest peaks of the mountains surrounding the plateau. The chieftains and their men soon found themselves practically encircled and retreated to the few mountains left unoccupied in order to regroup their forces. The plain spread out a soft green banner of budding corn-stalks, soon to be trampled by the horses of both armies. Three villages had already been set on fire on the southern side of the plateau; one of them was the village where I was born and raised. Korakas' cavalry and some of the more fleet-footed local fighters charged forth in pursuit of the enemy, disregarding the storm that had just broken out. We retreated in considerable numbers to a mountain-top called Afendis, where we found ourselves encircled by the local rebels. The battle raged for seventeen hours, till impenetrable darkness descended upon us. We were unable to effect a sortie, despite the arrival of reinforcements: a few thousand regulars succeeded in joining us after several violent clashes with the enemy. But by that time the night was far advanced and the reinforcements were no longer of any use to us. The rebels withdrew to the villages on the plateau, racked with hunger and thirst after the long day's fighting, their cartridges all spent.

The Revolutionary Committee of the eastern provinces was entrenched in the monastery of Kroustallenia, on a small hill situated on the edge of the plateau.

From our mountain eminence, we could see the local men entangled in close combat in the cornfields, the green expanse turning to brown mud. We heard Korakas urging on the volunteers, Greek or foreign, in defiance of their leaders, who were reluctant to launch them into battle. The volunteers, on their own initiative, pitched into the bright, befouled circle of the plateau to take part in the fighting. The women and children were evacuating the plateau, and their loud lament mingled with the lowing of the animals plodding ahead with their loads.

The church in the monastery still flew the flag of the Revolutionary Committee, displaying in its four corners representations of the flags of England, France, Russia and Greece, and a cross surmounting a crescent in the middle. Twenty Turkish horsemen appeared to fall under the spell of the undulating flag. The Committee members and several other men lay in wait for them, hidden behind the outer walls, among the rocks and oak-trees that were part of the monastery's property. The horsemen came within firing range. The first shots soon brought them to their senses; they turned and took flight.

Korakas dispatched part of his cavalry and infantry to reinforce the monastery. But a great many of its occupants had already abandoned it. From the tenth hour in the morning according to the Turks, which corresponded to the fifth postmeridian hour according to the Greeks, the rebels began to descend from Mount Afendis, exhausted by the unusually warm May weather. By midnight they had all come down to their villages on the plateau. From the top of Mount Afendis we fired at them throughout the night, for we suspected what was going on. The fighters in the monastery answered our shots with loud derisive taunts. But they were disheartened on discovering that the large quantities of barley they expected to find in the monastery had been stolen by the local peasants. The abbot and one or two remaining Committee members then decided to confiscate several sacks of flour in the baggage of a rebel chieftain, in the broader interest of feeding all the people sheltering in the monastery.

A second battle took place two days later. Both armies regrouped themselves, took up new positions and planned their next moves. Both received fresh reinforcements. Omer Pasha decided we should occupy all the mountains on the southern side of the plateau, thus cutting off the rebels' communications, and then attack them as they retreated to the northern villages, following which we would deploy our forces in the area between the south and north sides of the plateau. In accordance with this plan, we set out before daybreak in three different directions. The third section of the army, consisting of one of Reschid Pasha's battalions and one of mine, plus forty Albanians, advanced towards the hill of Aghia Photini. The rebels similarly split, in their case in two sections. Korakas and several chieftains proceeded south, while Petropoulakis and a number of other chieftains set off in a different direction. Korakas joined battle with the Turks and drove them back to the village where many years ago I was born and raised. At a place named Pinakianó, we applied considerable pressure against the rebels, but were unable to dislodge them. Turkish mortar-shells whizzed through the air and landed in the Christians' trenches; one of them killed three men all at once. Eventually, as May slowly distilled darkness upon us, the rifle-shots grew more infrequent and the two adversaries returned to camp. Later on we discovered two gullies near the battlefield filled with our men's bodies.

On the following day, the decimated Turco-Cretan troops rose against Omer Pasha, refusing to strike further at the local rebels; a large number of Omer Pasha's recruits from other provinces set out to return to their home base. The Commander-in-Chief sent word to Rethymnon requesting three more battalions; while waiting for their arrival, he forced all the deserters he was able to apprehend to return to the plateau; there were about three thousands of them. But it must be said that a considerable number of men from the auxiliary Christian forces also returned to their provinces.

For the next six days, both armies withdrew to their respective camps. At one point the two camps were in such close proximity that the men on guard duty could be heard exchanging insults. During this time, the Circassian horsemen belonging to the Imperial army engaged in a series of skirmishes in the plain and suffered heavy losses. A few villages were burnt down.

On the day of the third battle, Ottoman regulars set forth under cover of the morning mist. We crossed the plain and came upon the rebels' positions, while three battalions closed in on them from the rear. In this critical situation the rebels were forced to retreat to various other positions, while some of the chieftains attempted to harass the Ottomans occupying the plain. We gained hold of the entire south side of the plateau and set fire to four villages and the monastery of Kroustallenia, which housed an ammunition depot and a workshop manufacturing cartridges, no longer of any use to the rebels, since their weapons were a disparate assortment of models from different periods and of different calibres. Towards noon a fierce battle took place outside the village of Germiado, forcing us to start a retreat. At this point the rebels emerged from their dug-outs and poured into the plain with loud cheers for George I, the Greek king. They chased us all the way back to our tents. Several villagers who had been sheltering in caves witnessed this scene and came down to the plain in the evening to join the rebels.

Omer Pasha started the fourth and last battle on the following day, before the rebels had time to regroup themselves. Faced with the full strength of our army, part of the rebel forces under Korakas returned to Messa Lasithi, as they were short of ammunition. Omer Pasha then proceeded to split our army into two sections; mine went in pursuit of Korakas, while the other section attacked the chieftains who had remained at Germiado. This was to be the site of a major battle.

The rebels who had retreated to Messa Lasithi split up again into three sections. It came about that I was in command on the day of the last battle. I went in pursuit of one section of the rebel forces. Turco-Cretan irregulars in the vanguard of the regular troops burnt down a country chapel and a windmill. Then they set fire to a village and chased the women and children as they attempted to escape.

I followed their movements from the top of Mount Psaros. I gave orders to sound the retreat. Some of the irregulars disregarded the signal and continued the chase.

This was the moment when I – the Egyptian Minister of War, the general commanding the Egyptian army in this campaign, a Cretan by birth, reared as a Turk, reportedly a brother of citizen Papadakis of Athens, a speaker of vernacular Greek, and the man in charge of operations in this last battle – this was when I ordered the regular Ottoman army to fire at the Ottoman irregulars.

And the order was carried out.

7

On the day the fighting began, I caught sight in the distance of the house where I was born. We set fire to the village, and I was seized with a great anguish, though I bore no responsibility for the fire, at the thought that the house might be turned to ashes. But it remained unscathed, because a May shower, intervening in my favour, checked the flames that had attacked the adjacent houses. I was filled with awe at this demonstration of benevolence from the elements. As I sat astride my horse, wrapped in a piece of oilcloth reaching down to my horse's hoofs, welcoming the rain, which sounded as if nature were softly weeping, I told myself that this was the way it had to be: not because I had returned home, although even an iniquitous homecoming such as mine may still have been honoured with nature's weeping, but because the moment I saw the house, I remembered suddenly that I had a home.

Ioannis had told me in Egypt that according to one report, my mother had returned to the village after the massacre and met her end in the house; but its image had never tormented my spirit in the way that the memory of the plateau as a whole had done. While the rain lasted, the sight of the house pierced me unexpectedly with the sharpness of iron nails. I heard the nails being implanted in me one by one as the raindrops hit the oilcloth that covered my body. It occurred to me that during all these years I had perhaps dismissed the memory of the house in order to protect myself from the harrowing interdiction against crossing its threshold again, or from the fear that it might have fallen into ruin; the land itself, in contrast, was not subject to such dangers. The vigilance and speedy action which the imminent battle demanded of me would not leave much time to look into the matter further. All I had time for, as I listened blissfully to the rain of long ago, was to reflect that for many years I had, unawares, substituted in my memory the outer for the inner world; which meant that I had no real knowledge of all that my soul enclosed. The memory of the cave, for a number of reasons, had never become identified with the memory of the house; it had rather become a part of nature, or of my subsequent tribulations. Now I waited for the rain to stop so that I could take a second look at the house, fearing that I might have been the victim of an optical illusion.

I could have visited it in the days that followed; I longed to do so. But I kept finding excuses: the demands of the campaign, the human lives that depended on my decisions. I took part in the fighting as if drugged, and tried to keep my mind clear as best I could, with a great effort of will. Much as I longed to visit the house, I needed to prepare myself first. I still found it incredible that the house had survived, that it stood there waiting for me to return – but then, was it really waiting for me? Incredible, indeed, that I should have acquiesced to the bloodshed of this war simply in order to remember the house's existence, to receive this very quintessence of memory. I felt it held the promise of an ominous yet voluptuous catharsis; that I was somehow betrothed to it. I kept turning round to gaze at it, reintegrating it into its natural landscape, persistently probing its stone walls for some hint of their intentions. They seemed to allow me a glimpse of the interior. The house received light either from the wide open front door or from a flickering oil-lamp carried from room to room, as I began to recall in a swift rush of memory. Was it really waiting for me then, I asked again.

I decided to visit the house on the first evening after the fighting ended. I was pressed for time, because we had completed our operations on the plateau, and for my part, I could not bear to stay on and watch the looting. I found the key under the stone where we always used to hide it. I was pleased to note my spontaneous use of the pronoun in the first-person plural; it meant that the house was indeed waiting for me. I wondered whether the gentle metallic sound of the key in the lock could still imply that life – whatever kind of life – retained its continuity. The sound of the key in the lock reverberated like a gunshot, filling me with terror. I considered the possibilities: the Ottomans' weapons were probably loaded, since they had been licensed to loot the village for three days running; the Christians, on the other hand, had taken their weapons with them up on the mountains, but a straggler or two may well have been lingering in the evacuated village. I had to make haste.

The door creaked open. I stepped inside, closing it behind me. Then I leaned back against its thick boards, trying to feel the grain of the wood, its knots, the nails that delineated the door's skeleton. Sudden tears forced me to shut my eyes. Blindly I began to suck in the familiar air. Some moments went by before I could open my eyes again, having had my fill of milk. I discovered that the door I leaned against had grown taller, while I had shrunk to the size of a child. I pulled myself away from the door and attempted to walk; I felt frail, perishable. With the same childish hand I held on to the wall as I wandered round the house. I came to the fireplace, and I removed a brick from the wall; but my sling was no longer there. I told myself it did not matter; when I grew up I would go shooting birds with a gun. I placed the rusty blade from the cave and Antonis' last letter in the hole in the wall, where I used to keep my sling, returning them where they rightfully belonged; if, that is, an object can be said to belong to a particular place. I put back the brick, sealing up the hiding-place; burial, I added to myself, that might be one form of such a belonging. Besides, I did not wish to have inquisitive onlookers jump to conclusions, should these objects be found on my corpse.

I had no way of knowing whether anybody had lived in this house after my mother, since I had accepted the version according to which she had lived here and died here alone. I was unable to find any evidence of a stranger's presence, for the house was completely bare. I remembered every single object that had been in it with an extraordinary clarity: the simple appurtenances of a rural household, the few things needed to bring comfort to toil-worn bodies. But despite my memories, the house remained bare, indicating that it had not been lived in for many years. As if the horizontal and vertical lines, the curving arch, were trying to convey, in a scarcely perceptible manner, that all feeling was absent from this place; a message diffused in things like the dust, the spiders' webs in the corner of the rooms. The same childish hand would be needed to part those gossamer veils.

I stepped forward and stood exactly under the arch at the house's centre. I dug a small hole in the floor of beaten earth. But I lacked all that was required; nor could I offer any other blood but my own. I slashed the frail wrist with my *yataghan* and let a few drops of blood trickle into the hole. Then I sat back waiting, uttering the words. I waited a long time, as if the shades were resisting my entreaties. I feared they would not heed me, because I lacked what they needed, or for other reasons which would spell my undoing in this house. Finally, late in the day, a subtle change occurred, like the fortuitous flutter of an eyelid, and the horizontal and vertical lines, the curve of the central arch, began to quiver, losing their precision, spilling on to the floor, their vacant interstices quickening into vibrant space. Familiar human voices reached me, the sound of domestic animals, the sound of the weather, of singing, toiling, mourning, feasting. Then along came the smells: bodies, trees, cloth, winter fire in the hearth, harvested fields, ripe apples – that last smell invaded the house, dyeing it crimson. In the red-apple light I saw her hand, no longer in arrested motion on the spindle, twitching its fingers at last; and my father's hand, which had been frozen in the act of gripping the reins, flexing at last at the wrist.

The hands were the forerunners; the full-size figures soon followed. She was the first to approach me, to welcome her long-lost son, the fey one, tormented by a love without issue. How had he found the courage to reach down to her, undaunted by any religious restraint, she wondered? He was so handsome, though, coupling manhood in its prime with a child's innocence, as tenderly as the outline of the mountain merged into the heavenly vault before fading with it into the night. Let him draw a little closer to her, let him behold in her eyes the weariness of work in the fields, soothed by a dish of hot food and easeful sleep; so that he might also behold the weariness of his Egyptian life, soothed by the forgotten touch of her hand stroking his hair. But let him not draw close enough to witness her ordeals, let her remain forever as he had known her. He knew of course, her beloved one knew that they would soon be together and rejoice, bodiless and sinless. Therefore he need not fear the gardens and sweet flowing waters that might visit him in his dreams.

I ran to her. She disappeared instantly. I sank exhausted to the ground. After a moment I heard a voice chanting a hymn. I looked up and saw my father coming towards me, dressed in gold-embroidered vestments, chanting 'Thy birth, Jesus Christ our Lord,' for he always remembered I had been christened Emmanuel. He had registered me, in his own hand, as Emmanuel Kambanis Papadakis, son of Franghios. He no longer knew how to address me, by my Christian or my Muslim name; which was the reason he chose to chant that hymn, continuing to call me inwardly by my Christian name. Some things can never change, he said, and that is why I accept you, though I had great trouble arriving at that decision. Some things never change, even in the kingdom of the shades, only it sometimes happens that the shades, too, are maddened by the south wind and appear in a different, unfamiliar guise. I want you to know that I would rather be slaughtered again than dishonoured. However, the kind of life that has been your lot is another matter. You prospered, and that is a fine thing; only you lost the connection, the continuity; you broke off, and I was broken off with you. What may redeem you is that you never wished, or were never able, to obliterate us. I am a man who has felt the thorns and barbs of progressing along a single course, so I can recognize the difficulties of a dual course. I mean to say, I can comprehend your striving for atonement. I will pray for you. No, I do not know in what manner you will meet your death. I can only tell you that it is fated to be hard. You must be brave; you must not fear. We will meet again soon.

The sound of the Christmas hymn grew fainter; I realized he was moving away from me. I sobbed my heart out, my eyes blinded with tears. So that was why he never visited me in Egypt. He had promised to accept me; and I knew he would never break his promise. The torment of taking that decision and not going back on it was to darken the heavenly joys my mother used to herald, never letting me see that those joys were no more than splashes of bright paint on the plaster ceiling of the firmament; no, not even paint, but then I did not wish to put her faith in doubt. Her hand – if only I could touch her hand, I would swear I had never touched any other hand in the land of palm-trees and desert sands. But my father was also stretching out his hand to me in a symbolic gesture. I had not expected it, accustomed as I was to the austerity he had always felt bound to maintain, even in his most emblematic manifestations; an austerity that was finally embedded like a stone in his soul. If that stone had survived on earth, it could have served to tell his story, in the manner of a bust portraying some illustrious Roman; but a bust not completed, or fashioned in some remote province of the empire. If I were to feel some kind of guilt in his regard, it was not for having tried to look behind the stone mask – not as a child, when I had no trouble accepting it – but later on, when I was in a position, as I believed, to know better. In our relationship, I had remained the unresponsive, uncompromising boy who liked to team up with his brother. He had not wished to know me as an Ottoman in Egypt, but had waited for me to turn into a child again, to step into the old house, before he could envisage me as a person, even if it had to be as a person who had failed to embrace and forward his guiding choices. He had been waiting to see those tears in my eyes.

I did not forget for a minute that he had been slaughtered. And my mother? Perhaps slaughtered too, but dishonoured as well. Yet that had not stopped her from coming to me whenever I called her, or even of her own free will. She was able to grow old in my imagination; or simply to exchange the soiled dress of the cave for the silk robes I offered her. I was convinced that her portrait, painted in earthy colours, well preserved by the dry heat of the desert, could easily be placed among the gardens and sweet waters of her paradise; enveloped in them as she had been enveloped long ago by her tender concern for her young children and for her lord and master; never questioning, never betraying discontent.

I was filled with wonder at the reciprocity of my feelings towards each parent; at finding that whereas my feelings for my mother followed the same trend as hers, my feelings for my father, like his, were conflicting ones, not to say at war with each other. But I told myself I had been fortunate to reach this knowledge, even belatedly, not daring to go as far as to admit that I may have reached it in vain.

And finally Antonis came to me; though his being still among the living should not have permitted it. At first he appeared to me as a near-adolescent, wearing homespun clothes that barely managed to contain the vivacity of his movements. His hand was extended over a heap of apples. After a moment's hesitation he picked up an apple and handed it to me. As he did so his remembered image dissolved, only to condense again into his final aspect, as it was to be forever recorded for posterity by an Athenian photographer. The picture would show my present adversary, General Korakas, seated between two standing figures: one of them his son, Aristotle, newly arrived in Athens and about to enter the university thanks to the financial assistance of Antonis. By the time the photograph was taken the revolt in Crete would have ended, not with the island's union with Greece, but at least with a new form of administration. The time had come for a new way of life, for studies, for a measure of repose. My brother, the second figure standing next to Korakas, would have been the one to bring the veteran fighter and his son to the photographer's studio; on some previous morning he would have probably taken them sightseeing on the Acropolis. The general would be wearing his Cretan costume of dark felt and his white boots to pose for the photograph; he would be resting his clenched fists on his knees, in a manner denoting a certain awkwardness; his right foot would be flexed inwards, while the left one would be extended forward a little, in readiness to mount his horse and ride off to battle. Antonis, standing beside him, would be leaning his left elbow on the back of my adversary's chair, stooping slightly, in an elegant posture that seemed to come naturally to him, leaning towards the centre of the photograph as if he had grown tired of standing up conversing as he was wont to do in the foyer of the theatre, his elbow propped on a marble ledge, glass in hand, while carrying on his conversation. He was wearing a linen suit and a narrow cravat. His eyes were fixed in the distance in order to avoid meeting his reflection in the tilted mirror hanging above the ledge. He knew that the face of the patriot and national benefactor would reveal its resemblance to the face of the renegade and conqueror of Crete. He gazed beyond the scene in an effort to evade acknowledging the resemblance, due not only to kinship, but to a shared solitude. He had sought a new family for himself among the patriots, but I knew that he lived, and would die, utterly alone, like me.

He was fortunate enough never to set eyes on me again.

It seemed that I fell asleep as I crouched there on the floor. I loved the house, and it loved me, otherwise how could I have beheld the shades ambling across the bright green meadows, among sweet flowing waters, pausing to talk to me, and then resuming their wandering? I was awakened by the pinpricks of the morning dew. Besides, I felt the urge to rise early and look at the rising sun through the small eastern window. The image of the landscape that I had hoarded in my memory was lit up by the first sunbeams. But it appeared becalmed, untouched by the slightest quiver. I had not anticipated such a silence: it seemed to convey nature's irrevocable decision. I clutched the iron bars of the window in an effort to get a closer look. The eastern sky remained a picture painted on paper. I watched the rose-coloured reflections dissolving in the waxing light, and I suddenly found comfort in the thought that since I had set eyes at last on my paternal home, and what was more, since I had slept a whole night in its embrace and heard it speaking to me, nature – which had stood in the house's stead all these years – must now withhold its sibylline utterances, and no longer permitted me to question it.

I rode off to Kastelli at full speed to stop the soldiers from completing the village's devastation. I reached the plain and rode through the trampled crops and the uprooted trees as if entering a furnace. Though at some distance away from me, the houses that had been set on fire at dawn now blazed all around me.

In those years long past as the present time, war had been raging on the plateau; the crops had been trampled and the trees uprooted, then as now; and the same flames devoured the houses on the circumference of the same plain. In my mind the identical scene fused my two escapes from the plateau into a single indivisible event. I was no conqueror. Besides, if I had the power to conquer, perhaps I would have gained my freedom at this point. Except that my first life was not something to be subjugated, but to reflect upon. How could I subjugate my own reflections? I wished at least that the time of obsessive nostalgia would now be at an end; but how could there be an end to the sense of irremediable loss, the sense of otherness? I foresaw it would be a bitter end; bitter in the extreme.

On the banks of the sacred river, I had joined an entire nation in seeking an outlet, be it only minimal, from its frozen sanctity; some way of becoming attuned to the rush of new ideas animating the nations of Europe. I was right to do so. But I was forced to admit that the last lap of my journey had been that headlong race across the trampled green shoots, as I hastened to move out of the circle of the plateau to avoid witnessing its destruction. However dear my wish to live a little longer, I sensed that time would not grace my puny self with a respite. Not because I was merely a humble creature among a million others; but because I had allowed myself to be caught in the snare of an imaginary life. Whether the prongs of this snare were curved or straight was of no particular significance; the fact remained that the trap of the imaginary life had gripped me in its iron jaws, and it had annihilated me.

I thanked nature for its neutral silence. I stroked my horse's neck; I wanted to keep him close to me. Especially at this moment, when I knew that on returning to camp at Kastelli, I would find Ibrahim, crumpled under the weight of extreme old age.

Translated by Kay Cicellis

Michalis Ganas (1944–)

Ganas is widely held to have no superior among Greek poets today: though he is far from prolific, the steady accumulation of his four volumes of verse exercises unusual authority. He has also, like Nikos Gatsos (q.v.) before him, written some masterly popular song lyrics. Ganas combines a high degree of allusiveness with a plain yet plangent music that recalls the folk songs of his native Epirus: the central concern of his work, from the early 1970s to the present, has been the impossibility of recovering the war-scarred yet beautiful land of his childhood from behind the veil of chaotic and deracinated appearances that is modern Athens. Acute in his satires, sharp in his dirges, and always craftily ready to combine the two, Ganas has worked in a wide variety of forms, some impossible to reproduce in English, without ever surrendering to the tricksy. Ganas goes back obsessively but not bitterly to the tradition, notably to the song of the Dead Brother with which this anthology began. The late G.P. Savidis, whose critical backing of horses was without equal, and who did so much to bring the Greek writers he loved to the attention of the English-speaking world, wrote of how he suddenly and overwhelmingly felt Ganas to have attained classic status. I believe that posterity will endorse this judgement.

My Homeland Brimming

My homeland brimming with ivy,
    mountains which turn their back on you.
If you say you're leaving for foreign parts,
    if you cast a stone behind you,
        it hits you on the head.
Grigoris, Petros, Nikiforos,
    elementary schoolmasters of Thesprotia,
your classes are steadily dwindling,
    our cereal output falling,
        we shall be calling bread bee-ar-ee-ay-dee.

Translated by David Ricks

Shipwreck

The house is old, plaster drifts down
you can see the laths in the wall.
Mother sits inside;
God's finger waits outside,
ready to crush her.
Whichever room you walk through,
things turn and stare
like unwatered cattle.
Behind the kitchen cupboards
are more cupboards
and still more behind these
till you reach the depths of the wall
and the old icebox.
Here old Maria and old Leni
cradle rheumatic hands . . .
The old, much-travelled house
suddenly floods with memories and sinks.

Translated by John Stathatos

Period

The cranes at work without cease.
Something heavy and suspect
piling up in our time.
Masonic earthquakes,
bits of sleep coming down,
the blackness looking you right in the eye.
Dark iced coffee and discussions.
In the distance bald mountains
galloping. Headlong towards us.

Translated by David Ricks

George M., Florina 1949

You've been sleeping on the same side
for years, and my bones ache.
The birds stab at your sleep
pecking grain after grain
and you wake in the cornfields.
Fat raindrops fall
they work into the ground like screws
whips flail over the foliage.
That transient cloud passes
with a clatter of grappling irons.
Poor George
if only you could shift around
and look at the world's other half.

Persistence

Their pillboxes
of hollow air and limestone
still survive.
Turning white in the forest
like the bones shepherds find
but never speak of.
Though washed by water
time and again
the white endures.

Concerning the Ascension

Tracks in the snow
like a small child's and yet
they were no known beast's, were
nobody's, we searched all day all
through the night with torches, lost
two men in the deep ravines, dragged one
another along with ropes and still nothing
to show for it, till the fir trees
ended and only the mountain

rose on, the snow suddenly trackless and
no signs of blood or struggle.
We waited for the dawn eating
raisins and drinking all the brandy, till
one another's faces in the daylight
frightened us, we set off
flares, they came with helicopters
from below, lifted us off, the snow all round
trackless and with no signs of blood
or struggle.

Translated by John Stathatos

I Want to Be Buried in Chafteia

Posters are tugging me by the sleeve,
Athens my town with all your beauty contests.
I want to be buried in Chafteia;
twenty years I've been paying you rent, I have.

In my sleep, mountains and forests pass,
fairies swaddled up in mourning black.
The mulish grudge that I once had against you,
I've come to lose it – but on what bus?

What madness, tell me, beats me at the heel
and off I go, rolling like a ball,
the mute football grounds and the *tavérnes*

deep in my bowels? The people and the places –
strangers who look just like the photographs
we used to take of our younger faces.

Drowned All These Years

To Theophilos Sotiriou

Drowned all these years, and you are still
the spine of a sea-urchin in your sky.
Yesterday in your very own canoe
the brass band of Filiátes soundlessly passed by.

In the sea or in the ground your bones
would be as white, your flesh as rotted to bits.
Everything dumb and everything now said,
my words sad household pets.

If I could only lop it with a scythe,
the hand that tossed you like that to the weed,
so that the world would creak like a millstone,

the monk's proverbial fish leap from his pan,
the two of us together now, and I
never having to shut a door between.

In Memory of K.G. Karyotakis

Windows that have grown tired of the view
Of Nikaia, of Metz, of Kallithea,
And cannot ever have a change of air.

They get built one by one, pathetic little
Things, into the ribs of wall and metal
By people who are are much like me or you.

And finally the glaziers fix them up,
Scrawling on them their favourite football teams.
The pain they're in is all too evident

To us the manic tribe of peeping toms.

The tenants are putting up the curtains,
To hide what and who from it hardly matters.
They all undress alike and sit and eat
And vanish in the whirlpools of the mattress.

Why does it have to have such a sad ending,
A poem with such a growing population?
Who can have laid on me the obligation
Of knowing that behind my back they're laughing,
Tenants, contractors, caretakers . . . ?

Translated by David Ricks